Brendan
and the
Great Omission
(the second Brendan Priest journey)

Stuart Earl

Published 2011 by arima publishing

www.arimapublishing.com

ISBN 978 1 84549 491 9

© Stuart Earl 2011

arima publishing
ASK House, Northgate Avenue
Bury St Edmunds, Suffolk IP32 6BB
t: (+44) 01284 700321

www.arimapublishing.com

"Go to all nations, therefore, discipling them..."
(Matthew 28: 19)

This book is dedicated to my two daughters: Ami and Naomi, who have, in very different ways, helped me to write this book and provided inspiration.

Throughout the book, all geographical and historical descriptions have been researched as extensively as possible, and are intended to be accurate, so I apologise for any errors.

Jact remains a fictional place, Jact Methodist Church a fictional church, the North Tyneside Circuit doesn't exist, and its characters are entirely fictional – yet similar churches, Circuits and characters are all around us. This is a work of fiction, and all the characters in it are unconnected to any real individuals, except for a few real people who are mentioned in the "author's footnotes".

But, having made that clear, it is also important to me that this book contains stories about a crucial Gospel truth: that when we take the call to engage in God's mission seriously, in whatever nation or "-nation" we happen to find ourselves, amazing things can happen.

Chapter 1: Germination

At that moment Brendan Priest was a Methodist Minister "Without Appointment". This meant that he didn't have any work to do but also that he wasn't getting paid – not that he was too worried about that. Six weeks ago he'd returned, utterly exhausted, from an amazing journey which catapulted him into news headlines around the world, and also made him ridiculously wealthy.

To be even more precise, at that moment Brendan was in the bath – a location usually considered safe, but one which for Brendan was fraught with dangerous and exciting possibilities, because it was in the bath that his Big Adventure[1] had started. So bathtime was for Brendan a bit like the walk to work for the cartoon character Mr. Benn, whom Brendan's two daughters, when they wore pyjamas with feet, had loved so much. Mr. Benn left his house every day on the seemingly straightforward trip to work but then kept getting drawn into the same fancy-dress shop to have extraordinary adventures. Brendan similarly kept having baths, despite the danger.

And here, nearly three years after his first "bathtime moment", was where his second Big Adventure was about to begin too. A different adventure, a different bath – but as before the idea would germinate and start to develop like the growth of a tiny mustard seed, a simile which someone else had used two millennia previously. Brendan, of course, knew nothing of it yet, but that tiny seed was about to issue its first shoot...

Unlike last time, Brendan didn't fall asleep and have a dream – that would come later. Instead he was listening to an old cassette recording of Tom Lehrer[2], the Harvard mathematician who had made his name and fortune by writing and performing off-the-wall satirical songs in the 1960s. He found himself humming along to "I hold your hand in mine" – which sounded like a love song but concluded by revealing itself as the necrophiliac ramblings of a crazed murderer holding the severed hand of his ex-lover victim. Some people found Lehrer's humour weird, but Brendan thought it was a hoot.

The last song on that side of the tape was the "Elements Song", in which Lehrer had set a mixed-up list of all the chemical elements to the tune of Gilbert and

---

[1] For the earlier adventures of Brendan Priest, please read "Thule for Christ's Sake", Arima, 2010 (available from the author at s.earl@hotmail.co.uk, or from Arima or Amazon)

[2] The songs by Tom Lehrer are exactly as described and quoted. The lyrics quoted later in the chapter were downloaded from www.stlyrics.com/songs/t/tomlehrer3903/thevaticanrag185506.html.

Sullivan's "Major-General's Song". Brendan smiled as he tried to remember his own Lehrer-inspired "Nations Song", arranging the names of countries of the world to the same tune. He'd produced it on various church weekends away when everyone had to "do a turn" in a "talent show". Talent was usually singularly lacking – especially his own singing – but the actual song itself, he reckoned, was quite clever[3]. When the tape clicked off, he sang the start of it:

> There's Ghana, Guinea, Guatemala, Greenland, Greece and Gambia,
> Chad, Cameroon, Korea, Zaire and Zimbabwe and Zambia
> And Netherlands, Nepal, New Guinea, Niger and Namibia,
> Burundi, Burma, Brunei, Brazil, Borneo, Bolivia
>
> And Liechtenstein, Laos, Luxembourg, Lesotho, and Liberia,
> New Zealand, Poland, Iceland, Finland, Norway and Nigeria,
> Iran, Iraq, Colombia and Qatar, Cuba, Ecuador,
> Haiti, Hungary, Hong Kong, Ethiopia, El Salvador...

But, frustratingly, that was as far as he could get; he couldn't remember how the third verse started. So he went over the first two verses again. He was bemused that some of the "nations" in those first two verses had never existed. Greenland had always been part of Denmark, as far as he knew – so he wondered why he'd included it at all. In addition, Korea hadn't been one nation since 1948 and New Guinea technically was the name of the island not a country – so those two were wrong as well. And he was pretty sure that Borneo was not a nation but an island divided amongst various nations. Also, some others had ceased to exist since he wrote the song: Zaire was now the Democratic Republic of the Congo; Burma was Myanmar; Hong Kong had been incorporated back into China. The song was too out-of-date to use again now – and there were far too many inaccuracies anyway. He must have included them because they rhymed, fitted the scansion or were good for the alliteration upon which the song depended. He wondered whether the same was true for the rest of it.

Of course some of the countries listed meant quite a lot to him now after his amazing adventure, which had started at the northernmost tip of Canada and taken him down the Americas to Cape Horn, journeying either on foot, on a bike or in a converted Inuit kayak. So Guatemala, Colombia, Ecuador and El Salvador were now much more than just names on a list.

---

[3] I wrote The "Nations Song" during my own student days, and it has indeed been produced at various church "talent shows".

This in turn led him to reminisce about other parts of his Big Journey. Whilst kayaking back in foggy conditions from Cape Horn to Tierra del Fuego, he'd been rammed by another ship and ended up drifting across the Southern Atlantic Ocean until he managed to manoeuvre himself onto the southernmost of the South Sandwich Islands. He'd already shot to fame as a result of his monthly appearances on the American "See Esther" TV programme, with its (sounds-like) "siesta" set and intros, amassing a small fortune through television appearance fees and the generosity of thousands of supporters. The idea for it all had come from a dream, through which he felt God asking him to go "to the ends of the earth" to spread the Good News about Jesus. After the news of his disappearance and subsequent rescue, he'd become even more of a celebrity through further TV appearances – on Esther Blanchett's chat-show, in a BBC documentary, and various interviews and features on other channels in America and Britain. He still had a few TV slots lined up in other countries too, including one in Iceland in a fortnight's time.

He'd just returned from a trip to the Vatican, and a special audience with the Pope. The Roman Catholic Church was very helpful to him on his travels, especially in Central America where he'd been appointed "Archbishops' Envoy" to ease his passage between countries. Similar support was given in South America too. When he went missing, the Catholic Church set up prayer chains and special masses, and the Pope himself called on all Catholics to pray for Brendan's safety. Consequently, Brendan had been delighted to be invited to the Vatican, so that he could express his gratitude in person for all the help he'd received.

Last week's trip, though, had started with a brief moment of anxiety when a rather pompous customs official at Rome's Ciampino Airport noticed that his passport had only five months before expiry and declared that they weren't allowed to admit anyone who had less than six months left on their passport. Thankfully, a Vatican official appeared from nowhere, and, after a quiet word with the customs official, whisked Brendan off in a limo to the Vatican. He was accommodated in a lavish apartment inside the Apostolic Palace, and that evening had dinner with the Pope himself. Brendan had even been asked to share his reflections and story at a special meeting of high-ranking Vatican officials held in the Sistine Chapel, which was temporarily closed to tourists due to some restoration work being done on one of the Botticelli frescoes.

The Chapel was always kept deliberately dark to protect the famous artwork, and the floor-to-ceiling "Last Judgement" by Michelangelo on the front wall added to the rather sombre setting. But the Pope himself was light and cheery, commending Brendan's journey in a world increasingly hostile to the Christian faith and presenting Brendan with a Bene Merenti ("Well-Deserved") medal – the first Protestant to be awarded this papal honour, which usually recognised acts of service within Roman

Catholicism[4]. Brendan looked up at Michelangelo's amazing ceiling, and felt a tingle pass up and down his spine as he saw his favourite scene, where God extends his hand to Adam and they almost touch. Brendan felt very close to God too at that moment.

With these memories uppermost in his mind, Brendan leaned over the side of the bath and, dripping water everywhere, turned the tape over. He chuckled at the very next Lehrer song: "The Vatican Rag":

> "First you get down on your knees
> Fiddle with your rosaries
> Bow your head with great respect
> And genuflect, genuflect, genuflect.
> Do whatever steps you want if
> You have cleared them with the Pontiff
> Everybody say his own Kyrie Eleison
> Doin' the Vatican Rag."

Magical stuff, even though he couldn't somehow see the Pope and his underlings approving of his or Lehrer's sense of humour. He got out of the bath and promised himself that he would look up his own "Nations Song" and see how the rest of it went.

***

Brendan had been divorced for some years from Jenna, after their enjoyment of life with each other gradually dribbled away. He was living at the moment with his younger daughter Louisa in a house in Cullercoats which the two of them had jointly purchased a few weeks ago. Cullercoats was a beautiful place on the North Sea coast – originally an old fishing village centred round a small harbour, but nowadays expanding inland into the great North Tyneside housing sprawl extending seamlessly all the way into Newcastle. Louisa was a nurse in her first proper job, working at the Freeman Hospital, and was beginning to find her adult feet. She'd been hoping to get onto the property ladder at some point, and after Brendan rashly promised her 20% of any donations from well-wishers after his first Esther Blanchett TV appearance, she'd found herself with a lot of banking to be done but a lot of cash coming her way too. After the bumper harvest after her Dad's disappearance and rescue – and after Brendan had confirmed that she really *would* get 20% – she found herself with over

---

[4] The Bene Merenti medal, instituted in 1832, is awarded specifically to those who have given "long and exceptional service" to the Catholic Church.

£135,000 in her account, and Brendan had over £700,000 in his, once the TV appearance fees had been added in too. He'd never had £7,000 before, let alone a hundred times that amount.

Brendan had misgivings about what to do with the money he'd received during his journey. On the one hand he was very aware that he'd never previously had *any* money, property or assets of any kind, so the idea of wealth was unfamiliar. He was both excited and frightened by being rich, for his modest Ministerial stipend meant that he would ordinarily never have had the chance of either owning his own house or having the responsibility of investing or spending money wisely. It was a new thing. He was also aware that some people might criticise him for taking money for himself – even though it had been given by people wanting to show their support of him and what he was doing. He felt particularly embarrassed by the sympathy/admiration money given after he'd announced on TV that he would have to miss his older daughter Ruth's wedding in Uganda – especially as he ended up going to the wedding after all, due to Esther's generosity. So a few weeks ago he'd calculated how much money had been given after that particular interview and donated it to Watoto[5], the Christian charity in Uganda which employed Ruth.

He felt much happier afterwards about using the rest of the money to make a property investment which would give security to him and his family. His new-found wealth was not a sign of God's favouritism – he wasn't into all that "prosperity gospel" claptrap – but he did believe that it was evidence that, whenever Christians dared to live out their calling, all kinds of unexpected consequences could occur, including surprise blessings. The all-important difference for Brendan was that he was not defining or predicting the way in which God's blessing worked. He recognised that some people would see this as a compromise to worldliness, and maybe he partly agreed with them. He was also aware that his financial security as a Methodist Minister, especially one without appointment or stipend, was precarious, to say the least – and it was this which convinced him that it was OK to buy the house. He took the knowledge that he felt "unattached" to his new house and didn't feel any satisfaction about owning it as confirmation that he'd not sold his soul – well, not entirely anyway. Maybe this wealth issue hadn't altogether been resolved.

---

[5] Watoto is a wonderful organisation, transforming the lives of thousands of children, principally orphans as a result of war or HIV/AIDS. The activities and projects of Watoto are fully described in "Thule for Christ's Sake", in which Ruth begins her employment as an assistant house-mother in Suubi. I visited Suubi, one of three Watoto villages around Kampala, in July 2008, along with my two daughters and 20 other people from Cullercoats Methodist Church, who helped to build a classroom there.

And maybe the misgivings his conscience still prompted, especially with his first-hand experience of the poverty that dominated people's lives elsewhere in the world, was a further sign that the matter was not closed.

Brendan and Louisa had a quick look around various properties earlier that month, and plumped in the end for a big three-storey house on Beverley Terrace, a row of prestigious Victorian houses overlooking the sea between Cullercoats Bay and Tynemouth Longsands. It had set them back £440,000 but, since the credit crunch was beginning to even itself out and property prices were just reverting upwards again, Brendan reckoned that it was a good investment for both of them. Louisa had put in a quarter and Brendan three-quarters of the asking price, so if ever it got sold to someone else each of them would retain their proportion of the accrued value. It could even be converted fairly easily into flats, as much of Beverley Terrace had been, so Louisa could stay there living on one storey even if Brendan needed to sell his share.

In order to undertake his Big Adventure last year, Brendan had taken time out from his Circuit responsibilities as a Methodist Minister. He'd been stationed in the large village of Jact, just a few miles up the road from where he now lay in his new bath. He'd eventually been allowed to be "Without Appointment" for two years – though (to be fair) he hadn't really given the Methodist Church much choice – so he now had six months to go before he was expected to take up a Circuit appointment again somewhere else. His old North Tyneside Circuit – in which this new house was situated – was losing its Cuban Minister in August, and so far no replacement Minister had been found through the Methodist Stationing System[6]. Stationing was an annual carnival of trying to fit 120 or so Ministers needing a Circuit into 160 or so Circuits needing a Minister. There were inevitably going to be some Circuits missing out, and so far the North Tyneside Circuit looked like it would be one of them.

Brendan didn't know where he would be stationed, but he was apprehensive about "going back into Circuit" after all that had happened. He assumed that he would be very much in demand, now that he'd achieved celebrity status for a short while, but was unsure whether he wanted that old familiar pattern back in his life or now needed something completely different. Whatever happened, he wanted to serve God and be true to his calling. His journey had helped to confirm a specific vocation: to wake up the church about its responsibilities to engage with God's mission. He didn't know what form that would take, and no inkling at all about the new adventure just unfolding, which was beyond even his fertile imagination.

---

[6] I have tried not to misrepresent the Stationing System of Methodism, which changes at irregular intervals. It is a very complicated process, the rules for which in 2010 (when I last underwent the process) ran to 30 A4 pages.

***

The Nations Song was eventually found lurking in an obscure folder in his filing cabinet. The other verses were:

Tunisia, Tahiti, Togo, Tonga, Trinidad, Taiwan
And Austria, Australia, Jamaica, Jordan, and Japan
And Mali, Chile, China, Yemen, Yugoslavia, Ceylon
And San Marino, Syria and Libya and Lebanon,

Sudan, Saudi Arabia, Somalia and Surinam
And Venezuela, Upper Volta, Vatican and Vietnam,
Gibraltar, Malta, Mozambique, Malawi, Turkey and Thailand
And Italy and Ivory Coast and India and Ireland,

UAR, USSR, USA, UK, Uganda,
Uruguay and Paraguay, Romania and Rwanda,
Costa Rica, Kuwait, Kenya, Canada and Corsica,
Singapore, Sardinia, Spain, Switzerland, South Africa,

Afghanistan, Albania, Andorra and Algeria,
Angola, Aden, Bahrain, Belize, Belgium and Bulgaria,
Pakistan and Portugal and Panama and Papua,
France, Philippines, Dahomey, Denmark, Sweden, Nicaragua.

These are the only ones of which the news has come to Harvard;
There may be many others but they haven't been discarvard.

The last couplet had been nicked straight from Lehrer's "Elements Song", but it rounded off Brendan's own song rather well too. It was an amazing list of countries. He counted 123 in all, but many of them were now defunct – if they'd ever existed: Tahiti and Corsica were French; Taiwan was still a matter of contention because China still claimed it as its own; since the writing of the song Yugoslavia had been split painfully into various bits; Ceylon had been Sri Lanka since long before the song was written, but presumably its newer name didn't fit the verse so well; Upper Volta was now Burkina Faso; Gibraltar was British; Ivory Coast was now francophone Côte d'Ivoire; USSR had split into various -stans which nobody in Britain had ever heard of and definitely couldn't spell; Sardinia was Italian; Aden had once been a Crown colony but was only now a city in Yemen; Papua was part of Papua New Guinea; Dahomey was Benin... Brendan shook his head at all the errors.

He wondered briefly about rewriting the song, but couldn't be bothered. Instead, he sat in his armchair and looked through the list of countries to see where else he'd visited. Chile brought back memories of his long, cycle ride down the thin, never-ending strip of land between sea and mountains. The USA was where he'd first encountered mega-churches, the almost-a-girlfriend fellow-cyclist Carol, and, unforgettably, Esther Blanchett. Uganda was where Ruth got married to Paul, for which Esther whisked Brendan off in her private jet all the way from Chile. Costa Rica reminded Brendan of getting dreadfully wet one day in the mountains. Canada had provided many adventures, with a whiteout storm and polar bears amongst the most hazardous. Panama was where he'd briefly sampled a luxurious lifestyle on an island paradise and Nicaragua stayed in his memory as a beautiful country bedevilled with great poverty, where Brendan had spoken in front of hundreds of Esther-fan Catholic priests at the archdiocesan council. The Vatican too, he thought, ought to be added to the list of where he'd "witnessed". He'd visited other nations not in the song: Mexico, Honduras, Peru, Argentina. He wondered just how many countries there were in the world.

Then he fell asleep. And the tiny shoot grew...

Chapter 2: Explanation

When Brendan awoke, it was with a clear sense of déjà vu. He'd been caught up in a dream in which he was flying above the earth but couldn't remember too much else about it, except for The Number. Usually he was useless at remembering long numbers, but this one was indelibly printed in his dream-memory: 212819220. It meant nothing to him.

The last time Brendan had a dream of this sort was three years ago, when he'd woken up remembering another cryptic message, "Acts 1881", which had led him into his amazing journey. Surely God wasn't saying something again by this same method? Brendan was under the distinct impression that God didn't act the same way twice. He remembered explaining this to the congregation at Jact in the old days – preaching on the difference between Exodus 17 and Numbers 20. Moses had been told by God the first time round to strike a rock in the wilderness from which water would gush, and 37 years on from the first episode, he assumed that he knew what God wanted him to do when the Israelites were thirsty again. So he failed to hear God's slightly different instruction – that he was only to *speak at* the rock this time, not strike it. Brendan thought it harsh that God punished Moses for this lapse, but it did underline the need to listen carefully when God was trying to tell you something. So was God repeating Himself – or not? What was He trying to say?

Brendan googled The Number but there were only three things that came up[7]. One was a plastic button made by the Yiwu Xiaoyi Jewellery Accessory Firm in China, the order number for which on www.alibaba.com happened to be 212819220. Similarly there was a mini USB 2.0 TF/MicroSD Card Reader being sold at "only $4.90" on www.trademe.co.nz by someone called goodman6, the listing number for which was 212819220. Brendan didn't see anything particularly significant in either of these items. He didn't even know what the second item was and he'd no obvious need for a Chinese button. The third was a listing on myspace for a 22-year-old Texan called Jennifer, but Brendan didn't think that she was part of his spiritual journey either. So what was it all about?

He felt drawn to do more research into his Nations Song, and particularly into the number of countries. He discovered that his song-total of 123 countries was not only woefully inaccurate in detail, but also woefully short of the mark. Every reference book or website had a different answer, and "correct" answers ranged between 189 and 195. He found one website which claimed that the world was made up of 872 countries, territories, autonomous regions, enclaves, geographically separated island groups, and major states and provinces. But that wasn't what he was trying to

---

[7] These three references really did come up when I googled the number.

establish – it was nations he was after, not other bits and bobs like Rockall or Antarctica.

Incredibly the same website told him that there was an American called Tom. U. McHooney who was currently in the lead as MTP (Most Travelled Person) on 822 out of the 872, and seven ahead of Alf Getie (another American). Third place went to a Spaniard on 764, who presumably didn't have as much cash to burn[8]. It described the first two as "amongst the 20 people alive today who have been to all 192 nations". Aha, thought Brendan, so is that how many there are?

The United Nations' list agreed with this MTP website in having 192 members, including Montenegro and Serbia – the two newest nations. But the UN number included neither the Vatican nor Kosovo. Not all countries accepted Kosovo's declaration of independence in 2008 and the UN Security Council was split. Then there was the question about England, Scotland, Wales and Northern Ireland. Though all were widely considered individual countries and had their own football teams in the World Cup – or, rather, usually *not* in the World Cup – they were usually recognised as sub-sections of the nation called the United Kingdom.

The US State Department recognized 194 countries around the world, but their list reflected their own political agenda. So, for example, it included Kosovo but not Taiwan, because America didn't want to upset the leadership in Beijing. Most of the current World Almanacs listed 193 countries, but what about Kosovo which wasn't included in any of them? And what about Palestine? Greenland? Western Sahara?

Palestine was considered separately from Israel, for obvious political reasons, but it had never had the chance to declare independence and be recognised as a separate country for the same reasons. Gaza might be considered part of Palestine, or not, or part of Israel, or not. It was all very confusing. Brendan discovered that Greenland had voted in favour of increased self-rule in 2008 and acquired complete responsibility for internal affairs in 2009. Denmark, however, continued to exercise control of Greenland's foreign affairs, security, and financial policy so most authorities reckoned that it was still a part of Denmark, so Brendan kept it off his list. Western Sahara was a former Spanish colony, now a non-self-governing territory in the eyes of the UN, had its Sahrawi Arab Democratic Republic government in defiance of the Moroccan government who controlled and claimed this sparse bit of desert – but he still didn't know whether it should count or not. Probably not.

He decided that he needed to make a definitive list and it took him the rest of that day. He added which continent each nation was in, because he'd never heard of some

---

[8] The MTP website really does exist, at www.mosttraveledpeople.com, but I have changed the names of those at the top of its leaderboard for Most Travelled Person (but not their nationalities or "scores").

of them. He also put an asterisk against those in which he'd "witnessed" on his last big adventure, though he wasn't really sure why.

Brendan's final total was 194 nations – but he didn't know why it was so important for him to get it right. Many of the countries listed were new to him. He'd spent most of the day pouring over the atlas trying to work out where some places were. Again, he wondered why. What was he supposed to do with all this information?

He went to bed, and had exactly the same dream.

***

When he awoke this time, he remembered some more details. He'd been flying, soaring like some kind of humanoid eagle over a world that looked like an atlas rather than proper terrain. It had contour lines, national boundaries marked by a black line, and the countries were coloured either pink, or yellow, or blue, or green, or orange, or light brown – just like in the atlas with which he'd just spent so much time. And above it all, like a banner hanging in space, stretched that same mystery number: 212819220.

Brendan was sweating. It was the middle of the night still, and he was hot even though the foghorn on the other side of Tynemouth Priory was booming away in the chill February air. Something was happening – but Brendan couldn't discern yet what it was all about. He got up and made himself a coffee, and revisited the alphabetical list he'd made the previous day, to see if it would give him a clue. He listed numbers 2, 12, 81, 92 and 20 but couldn't work out a pattern – what did Albania, the Bahamas, Iraq, South Korea and Bhutan have in common?

He was still puzzling over it hours later when the doorbell rang. It was the postman with a Special Delivery. Louisa staggered downstairs in her dressing-gown while Brendan was signing for the package, and had the kettle on as Brendan came back into the kitchen.

"What you got?" she asked in a guttural, first-conversation-of-the-day monotone – different from those TV adverts where adults leap out of bed for their favourite cereal with a smile and a song. But that was TV, and this was reality. Louisa didn't do mornings. She sounded like Mr. T. off the A-Team.

"My new passport," said Brendan, having a look to see whether his photo still made him look like a corpse. And then he caught sight of The Number. It leapt out at him: 212819220. It was his new passport number. He couldn't believe it. But then it puzzled him. Why would God tell him what his new passport number was, when God surely had many more important things to do than play magic tricks? Yet, despite his doubts, it was still with some excitement that he pointed out to Louisa that the number was already significant to him, and he explained to her about his recurring dreams and his previous day's research.

Louisa wasn't particularly impressed. "Sounds to me like a Bible reference," she said, as she turned back to put some bread in the toaster.

"What do you mean?" asked Brendan.

"Well, look at the end of it. It can be read aloud as 28:19-20. Sounds like a Bible reading to me." And she went back to watch the toaster. But Brendan's mouth fell open. Everything fell into place. The Number was a code for the Great Commission at the end of Matthew's Gospel – in the second of the two Testaments of the Bible (2), the first book (1), chapter 28, verses 19 to (sounds like 2) 20: "Go to all nations, therefore – discipling them as you go: baptising them in the name of the Father and of the Son and of the Holy Spirit, and teaching them to obey everything I have commanded you. And be assured: I will be with you always, to the end of the age[9]." God was telling him to go journeying again, and this time to all nations. *That* was why he'd been nudged towards discovering how many nations there were – because he was being told to "witness" to people in all of them. Everything suddenly fitted into place.

But how on earth could he visit every nation? There were 194 of them. It would take him years, even though on his first Big Adventure he'd already "witnessed" in 16 of them. Only 178 to go, then, but how long would that take? He was due to go back to work in September - how did this new calling fit into that? But in his heart of hearts he already knew that he wasn't meant to go back into Circuit ministry. Not immediately, anyway. After everything that he'd experienced, Brendan knew that such a move would be restricting his energy and enthusiasm – and his potential impact. He was a global name now, whether he liked it or not, and this gave him a unique opportunity to influence things on a scale that no-one else could. Surely this now confirmed God's call – he was to pursue a wider calling than any one Circuit in British Methodism could offer.

Once he'd explained all this to Louisa, who looked bleary-eyed but also shocked, he began to assess whether he was up to this new challenge. There was nothing in this new Word from God about him having to refuse conventional means of transport, which meant that he wouldn't be restricted to slow means of getting from A to B – or from A to Z, come to that. But he rather liked the idea of doing some of it by bike or kayak, because it was that which had appealed to the TV audiences last time, and they just might be hooks to draw the public's attention a second time... He had a lot of research to do, but he also had to go and see his District Chair, to tell him that he wouldn't be available after all for Stationing that year, and probably not for quite a few years to come. It hadn't gone down too well last time, so the prospect

---

[9] The translation used here and at the start of the book is my own, from the Greek.

was as exciting to Brendan as Christmas was to a turkey. The difference, of course, was that he *knew* that he was going to be stuffed.

He also knew that he had to tell Ruth. Last time she'd been royally cheesed off because he hadn't told her his plans directly and she'd found out from her sister. He wouldn't make the same mistake again. Ruth would undoubtedly put up some resistance to this new idea, because she was the most sensible one in the family. She could foresee difficulties but also think laterally how to get round them, so she would be an asset, as long as Brendan broached the matter quickly and sensitively.

Ruth was back on the road. She and her new Ugandan husband, Paul, had both been re-employed by Watoto for a few months now, specifically to co-ordinate the fundraising and ongoing financial support for a Bulrushes home/hospital in Gulu – to help the very youngest children. A Bulrushes home had been operating in Kampala for several years now, but Gulu had been considered too dangerous for aid to be directed there. It was the centre of conflict for several years in the 1990s and many children had been orphaned, displaced, or abducted and recruited as boy-soldiers. Only now were agencies getting involved and there was much to be done.

Brendan was very proud of the work that his daughter and son-in-law were doing, travelling around with the Watoto Children's Choirs, which consisted of children from the various Watoto villages, who toured various parts of the world to publicise Watoto and raise funds for the work. Ruth and Paul spoke at the choir concerts, showed a DVD they'd produced themselves whilst in Uganda, and handed out leaflets appealing for special help. They were raising vast sums of money, especially in America and Canada – and were presently on tour with a choir in Canada, so it was some days before Brendan was able to get in contact.

Ruth was delighted to receive the phone call from him, but was wary when, after the initial greetings and catching-up, he announced that he'd something to tell her. "You're not ill, are you?"

"No, nothing like that."

"You're not getting married to that Carol lady, are you?"

"No!" Brendan laughed, though he was surprised by Ruth's nervousness now to the brief friendship he'd enjoyed with a fellow-cyclist during his journey south through America.

"You're not going to live abroad, are you?"

"Weeeeeell... Not exactly." He carefully explained his plans, such as they were.

Ruth was silent on the other end of the phone. Then, to Brendan's huge relief, she laughed. "Why can't you just have a normal midlife crisis like every other bloke in his fifties? But, seriously, Dad, are you sure you're up to it? I'm pleased that you've found this next chapter in your life, because I wondered what you'd do next, but are you sure that this is where God is calling you? It's all very well moving on to the next chapter but the last chapter was almost your *very last* and the book was off to the printers!"

Brendan laughed. "Yes, it was a bit hairy, wasn't it? I certainly don't want to put you or Louisa through that worry again, so I promise that I'll back off and become my usual boring self if it doesn't look right."

"Fair enough, Dad. I don't think you could ever be boring, even though I used to fall asleep in your sermons. But will you promise to keep me posted on all your plans before you commit yourself to anything?"

Brendan promised. He'd at least been given the thumbs-up to start planning in earnest. The way seemed suddenly much clearer – or was he just deluding himself?

Chapter 3: Insubordination

Jack Turner[10] felt that he was very patient – and that people, and especially Methodist Ministers, often took advantage of that. He himself was a Minister, of course, but he'd always been very dutiful and obedient within the Methodist system: playing by the rules; doing what he was told; fulfilling his congregations' expectations even when they were hopelessly unrealistic or unfair; and (most importantly of all) keeping his nose clean with the Powers That Be.

He'd been one of the youngest Ministerial candidates Methodism had had in years when he'd thrown himself into the various processes 25 years ago now and came through them all unscathed, having given the right answers even when he wasn't sure whether he actually believed what he was saying. College for him had been a cloistered and relaxed breeze through a Manchester BA in Theology and a few add-on courses on practical stuff like CPD[11] (the Methodist rule-book) and how to fill in marriage registers. He'd been stationed for five years to serve ten chapels in a rural Circuit in Norfolk, even though he'd said that he wanted to stay in the North where his family and most of his friends lived. In his fourth year in Norfolk, after the Superintendent Minister had a heart attack, Jack found himself looking after the Super's seven churches as well as his own for nearly a year as he was the only other Minister in the Circuit. Fortunately no-one expected him to do anything except try to keep things ticking over, which is what he achieved – without committing any unforgivable sins like dropping a baby at a baptism, saying the wrong name at a wedding or forgetting to turn up to a funeral.

Methodism had an unwritten rule that Ministers moved on from their first appointment after five years. Circuits usually shrugged off the various faux-pas of Probationer Ministers fresh from College, putting them down to inexperience – for a few years at least. So the usual wisdom was that, having been given almost enough rope to hang themselves, they should move to pastures new before they completed

---

[10] All references to Methodist Ministers, including Jack Turner, are products of my imagination. The personalities, gifts, experiences or ministries of me, my colleagues, the present Newcastle District Chair (Revd. Leo Osborn), or any other Minister are not reflected in any way by anything in this book. I have great respect and admiration for all my colleagues, including Leo. Any resemblances are products of your imagination. The processes and procedures of the Methodist Church, however, are described accurately, I hope.

[11] CPD is the Constitutional Practice and Discipline of the Methodist Church, in two volumes, running to nearly 1,000 pages.

their own execution. The young Jack had dutifully agreed to move, and, because of his recent experience as emergency Super, he was given the Superintendency of a large town Circuit in the Midlands and care of just one large traditional church in the town centre. He loved it from the start because he inherited a choir which sang anthems and plenty of newly-retired people who knew what to do and got on with it. He was free to visit people and organise things, and preach in the high central pulpit from which the great Methodist preachers of the Victorian era had rallied the troops and converted the ignorant. Even though he was still only in his early thirties, he'd been well-received as Minister and Super, and was blessed with good and hard-working colleagues.

He'd stayed there five years before moving to a larger Circuit in Yorkshire as Super, where he'd been involved in some District restructuring and been given the role of Synod Secretary, which not only gave him a bit more stipend but also got him noticed by people throughout the District. He'd been along to Methodist Conference every year and even spoke a few times and got his face known "connexionally" (Methodist-speak for "nationally").

He'd found himself in 1993 embroiled in the biggest debate the Methodist Church had had in living memory. The annual Conference was at Derby and it was the year of the Human Sexuality Report. Everyone had been apprehensive about the outcome – it could have led to a massive split and untold disaster. On the day of the debate, Jack found himself sitting next to someone wearing a big badge with "GLC" on it. Jack discovered that this didn't stand for the Greater London Council but the Gay and Lesbian Caucus. He and his neighbour chatted away while the endless speakers sent off repeated salvoes from their fortified positions on either side of the no-man's-land – and the two of them decided to put forward a compromise notice of motion which ended up saving the day and leaving everyone a bit bewildered but rather relieved[12].

---

[12] The Methodist Conference in 1993, held at Derby, debated the Human Sexuality Report, and six declarations were agreed which subsequently formed the "Derby Resolutions" as they became known. Representatives (of which I was one) discovered at the end of the debate that they'd ended up, by the grace of God, at a position which meant that the Methodist Church could retain its unity whilst recognising that its members had strongly-held but different viewpoints on such potentially-divisive topics. That day, through both the manner of its debate and the resulting Resolutions, has proved to be a historic, unifying and reaffirming stepping-stone for the whole denomination.

He shot to fame as the co-author of this "pilgrimage of faith" resolution[13] and acquired a reputation as a holy pragmatist, even though it had been a bit of an accident.

On the strength of various pre-prepared and carefully-scripted visits to the microphone at subsequent Conferences, he became known as a "safe pair of hands" and two years ago had been appointed Chair of the Newcastle District whilst still only in his early forties. It had been a steep learning curve but he now felt that he'd begun to find the balance between his natural instinct to come down hard on any imperfections and the pastoral need for him to apply a gentler touch. Because of his natural respect for authority, though, he still found it hard when Ministers whom he expected to defer to his suggestions seemed not only to ignore them but even to flaunt their insubordination. And there was very little that he could do about it unless they breached one of the serious rules – and even then there was a complicated discipline procedure in which everybody lost. He sometimes wished that he was a bishop and could chuck his weight around, but Methodism wasn't into hierarchy like that.

His patience was particularly tried last year when the Minister from Jact in the North Tyneside Circuit had defied him and gone off gallivanting down the Americas. Part of Jack was rather envious, because he knew that he'd never dare take risks either with his life or his career. Brendan Priest, on the other hand, had been prepared to chuck in the towel because he wasn't getting much out of his appointment, leaving them all in the lurch. Jack had to step in and sort out the mess, suggesting various possibilities, and in the end managed to find them a really good Minister from Cuba who'd shown what could be done if you put your mind to it and were prepared to put in a lot of hard graft. The appointment of Caridad Diego had been a real feather in Jack's cap.

To make matters worse, Brendan Priest kept sending Jack emails from various God-forsaken places describing hi adventures, expecting Jack to pass these messages on (as if he didn't have better things to do). To cap it all, the silly man had gone missing which meant that Jack had the newspapers to deal with and even BBC News coming round and forcing him to say nice things about a Minister he didn't really like

---

[13] Resolution 6 states: "The Conference recognises, affirms and celebrates the participation and ministry of lesbians and gay men in the Church. The Conference calls on the Methodist people to begin a pilgrimage of faith to combat repression and discrimination, to work for justice and human rights and to give dignity and worth to people whatever their sexuality." This Resolution stands in a creative tension alongside Resolution 4, which begins: "The Conference reaffirms the traditional teaching of the Church on human sexuality, namely chastity for all outside marriage and fidelity within it..."

or respect. What is more, Brendan Priest had then turned up and become some kind of instant global mega-star and everyone thought that he was great even though he'd run away from his calling as a Methodist Minister. When Ministers were short on the ground, the Church could do without the likes of Brendan Priest.

Jack would have to go round to see him soon about Stationing. Most people had been allocated their new appointments by now but until Brendan arrived back in Britain and confirmed his availability for Stationing, nothing could be initiated. Jack was adamant that Brendan Priest's next appointment would be outside his District – someone else could have him. Then, lo and behold, he got a phone call from Brendan Priest himself saying that he wanted to come round and talk about Stationing. At last the great globetrotting super-hero might have acquired some sense of responsibility...

So here Jack was, in his study, having just opened the door and ushered Brendan in. He was a great believer that hospitality was making your guests feel at home, even if you wished they were. Over the customary cup of coffee, he began the process of assembling the paperwork. He needed to get Brendan to write a profile of himself so that even at this late stage the most suitable appointment could be found. Frankly there were only a few dodgy places left which had been turned down by a succession of Ministers sent to "have a look at a possible match". But there were always a few extra places cropping up as Ministers died or had to move unexpectedly, so the profile was a necessary part of the process.

"Actually," said Brendan, interrupting Jack's chain of thought as he juggled papers, "I've come to say that I'm not going to be applying for another appointment this year."

Jack had just taken a mouthful of coffee and sprayed most of it over the papers on his knee as he took in what Brendan was saying. "What do you mean?" he spluttered. "You can't do that! You've just had a year off, swanning around doing what you wanted, while the rest of us have been working hard to keep the show on the road. You can't just... just... not come back." He finished rather lamely because Brendan was smiling at him. How *dare* he!

"I'm sorry," said Brendan, not looking sorry at all. "I believe that God's calling me to another journey which will build on what I did last year, and hopefully have an even bigger impact. So I can't go into Stationing this year and need to ask for an extension to my "Without Appointment" status."

"I don't believe it!" said Jack, conscious that he sounded just like Victor Meldrew. "We're umpteen Ministers short, churches closing down left, right, and centre because they don't have sufficient resources either in money, people or leadership to carry on, and you think that you can just go off when you want, do what you want and expect the Church to pat you on the back and say "Well done!" Well, you're wrong!"

Brendan put down his coffee cup and stood up.

"Where do you think you're going?" yelled Jack, in outraged-headmaster mode.

"I don't think there's much point continuing this discussion, is there?" said Brendan. "Can you please take what I've said to the next meeting of the Stationing Committee, and let me know what they say? I think you're meeting next week, aren't you, when I'm off to Iceland."

Jack instantly thought of the shop where he bought his pizzas, but then realised that that wasn't what Brendan meant. He looked up and saw him smiling, sneering at the comparatively small map on which Jack lived. And with that, the insolent fellow stood up and walked out.

***

Two weeks later, Brendan made another appointment and Jack found himself having to face him again. And Jack wasn't looking forward to the meeting at all, because at Stationing Committee, things had not gone as he would have wished. He'd pressed hard for Brendan to be put on a list of "Ministers Unstationable[14]", which was the Methodist equivalent of a shamed samurai receiving in the post a sword along with a book called "A Beginner's Guide to an Honourable Death". But within the Committee he'd sensed a sort of hero-worship for Brendan, from Ministers who should have known better. He'd been up against it for another reason too.

When Brendan came into the study and sat down, he annoyed Jack straightaway by not apologising for his rudeness on the previous visit. There was no polite chit-chat either, because Brendan refused Jack's offer of a cup of coffee and immediately asked how Stationing Committee had gone.

"Well," said Jack, with the oiliest smile he could manage, "We decided to give you another example of how caring the Methodist Church is. Some people were after your blood, but the majority view was that you should be allowed to go off on this trip of yours. We'll have to do without you again, unfortunately – but hopefully you'll come back refreshed and reinvigorated and ready to return to your calling."

Jack was seething inside, but tried hard not to let it show. The final straw in the Committee had been that, while Brendan was away in Iceland, the procedures of Methodism had been shown on the BBC to be really uncaring towards one of its Ministers, and the Stationing Committee knee-jerked over-generously towards Brendan to prevent Methodism getting even more vilified, especially as Brendan was still in the public spotlight.

---

[14] I don't think that such a list exists on paper, but there will always be individuals whom it would be best not to station, for everybody's sake.

The Methodist Church had been proud to feature in BBC's "The Island Parish[15]". Set on the Scilly Isles, the programme sought to capture what island life was like, including the Methodist Circuit on the islands, cared for by a hard-working and well-loved Minister called David. The filming coincidentally happened just when an extension to David's appointment was being considered. Surprisingly, some people voted in the secret ballot against his re-appointment and the necessary majority didn't happen. The programme showed the shock on the faces of David and his District Chair, neither of whom (because of the secret ballot) would ever know who had voted against or why. Questions were raised in the national press as well as across the Connexion about how uncaring and unsatisfactory the re-invitation process seemed, and the Stationing Committee debated at length how they should change the Church's procedures in order to avoid more bad publicity. So Brendan was given license to go off around the world – well, to be "Without Appointment" anyway.

Brendan smiled, stood up, thanked Jack, and walked out. At least Jack didn't have to talk to him any more. He was glad to see the back of him.

---

[15] The "Island Parish" coverage of the re-invitation of the Methodist Minister in the Scilly Isles occurred as described and was broadcast on 5th December 2008, so I have been "creative" with the time-sequence. The Minister is called David in real life. Procedures regarding re-invitations were changed the following year to prevent a "surprise" no-vote, and implemented for the first time in the summer of 2010.

Chapter 4: Examination

It was now a few weeks on from The Dream, and the revelation of what The Number signified.

Brendan's trip to Iceland had turned out to be an all-expenses-paid luxurious short break in Reykjavik. It was a hard life being a celebrity.... The invitation was to speak at the Hallgrimskirkja, a modern Lutheran church whose tower rose high above the other buildings in the capital. Brendan particularly liked the statue outside of the Viking sea-captain Leif Erikson, reputedly the first European to have landed in North America. They must have a soft spot for travellers here, he thought. And indeed they did, for his evening talk went down very well. He was taken the following day to the magnificent Gullfoss waterfall and Geysir geothermal area, and enjoyed a surprisingly warm dip in the mineral-rich waters of the Blue Lagoon.

Brendan had recovered from both visits to see "Tina" Turner, the young-blooded but old-cracked-record Chair, who was nicknamed Tina not because he resembled the "Queen of Rock & Roll", but because some Ministers whom he'd told off likened him to Margaret "**T**here **I**s **N**o **A**lternative" Thatcher. The first visit was not as bad as he'd feared — it was worse, and he'd gone to Iceland thinking that his days as a Methodist Minister were numbered. Driving again to the Chair's manse after his return, he'd felt like a fish swimming into a stretch of river hosting an angling competition. Surprisingly his visit ended not with Brendan being landed, filleted and served up on a platter, but with him being allowed to slip off the hook and escape downriver.

Pleasantly surprised, and even, he admitted to himself, feeling a bit smug at the sour look on the Chair's face, Brendan applied himself wholeheartedly to his journey-preparation, trying to work out what the possibilities and difficulties would be. He spent several days pouring over maps, drawing lines on his old atlas, and ticking countries off his Big List. He spent many hours on the Internet researching transport links, air routes, war zones, dangerous territory for bandits, pirates, corrupt border guards and countries which didn't like Christians and especially didn't like clergy.

In the end, he came up with a draft itinerary. He needed to tick off 178 countries to complete his mission, and felt that he could only justify ticking a country off the list if he'd done his best to speak about his faith there. If he was in a country which prohibited any proselytising, he would at least wear his cross overtly in public, and do his best to hand out at least one copy of the New Testament in the language used in that country.

First of all he split the 178 countries into groups, chosen by their proximity to each other. He quickly discovered that there were two countries which didn't fit into any grouping. The first was Palau, which he'd never heard of, but discovered that it was a tiny island nation located about 370 miles east of the Philippines, well-known apparently amongst scuba-divers. No wonder he hadn't heard of it, then. More importantly, 370 miles was too far across the ocean for him to kayak, there were no ferry services, so it would have to be a flight. But the only flight to Palau was from the Philippines, so Brendan had to build in a return flight to fit Palau in at all.

The second country nowhere near anywhere else was Sri Lanka. It was very close to India, of course, but Brendan was hoping not to have to trail down the whole of the Indian sub-continent just for Sri Lanka. He solved this by discovering that he could stop off at Colombo on one of his long-haul flights – from Georgia to Australia. The other isolated nation was Iceland, but he'd already been there. And Greenland and Antarctica didn't count, thankfully.

He couldn't do it all by bike and kayak, with an occasional flight across vast tracts of ocean. So he explored other options: hire-cars, trains, cruise-ships and aeroplanes – and ended up with an itinerary involving the following "legs":

1. By car from Cullercoats to Lisbon (Portugal)
2. By plane to Rimini (Italy)
3. By car to Thessaloniki (Greece)
4. By train to Istanbul (Turkey)
5. By plane to Larnaca (Cyprus)
6. By kayak to Haifa (Israel)
7. By bike to Eilat (Israel) – the only bit of cycling, because he didn't want to "rush" Israel
8. By kayak to Sharm-El-Sheik (Egypt)
9. By plane to Tripoli (Libya)
10. By kayak to Tangiers (Morocco)
11. By plane to Dakar (Senegal) and Cape Verde and back
12. By car to Bissau (Guinea)
13. By kayak to Lomé (Togo)
14. By car to Acalayong (Equatorial Guinea)
15. By kayak to Luanda (Angola)
16. By plane to Maseru (Lesotho)
17. By car to Mombasa (Kenya)
18. By cruise ship around the Indian Ocean and back to Mombasa
19. By plane to Djibouti
20. By kayak to Basra (Iraq)
21. By RAF plane (he hoped) to Kabul (Afghanistan)
22. By car to Singapore
23. By plane to East Timor and Brunei
24. By ferry to the Philippines
25. By plane to Palau and back
26. By ferry to Japan and South Korea

27. By bus to North Korea and back
28. By ferry to Beijing (China)
29. By train to St. Petersburg (Russia)
30. By kayak to Amsterdam (Netherlands)
31. By car to Tbilisi (Georgia)
32. By plane to Sydney (Australia), Auckland (New Zealand) and Nadi (Fiji)
33. By sailing boat around various Pacific islands and back to Fiji
34. By plane to Los Angeles (USA) and Montevideo (Uruguay)
35. By kayak via the Parana, Paraguay, Tapajós and Amazon rivers, then the Atlantic Ocean to Belize
36. By plane to London and Cullercoats
37. By car and ferry to Brandon Bay in Ireland for a symbolic finish.

It looked quite achievable when it was written down like that, but quite daunting too – especially the very long kayak trips. It was both exciting and scary. Some of the journeys, like number 27, were easy and quick, whereas others, like number 35, would take months and lots of careful planning and physical energy. It would mean virtually going round the world twice, crossing the Equator 17 times by car, plane, cruise ship, sailing boat or kayak, and going to some places where Christians were not made welcome and sometimes were persecuted, arrested or even worse. He would have to employ different styles of "witnessing": big speaking events in Europe; village gatherings in Asia; surreptitious entries into Saudi Arabia and Somalia with, at best, a conversation with a villager in each; and, even more dangerously, the attempted handing of a copy of the New Testament to a North Korean guard round the unfriendly side of the table at Panmunjom.

Brendan then made another list of things to sort out:

- Visas
- Insurance
- Contacts in each country, wherever possible, for accommodation and speaking opportunities
- Consultation with the Bible Society about them providing one copy of the New Testament for each country
- Detailed timetables for public transport, especially flights and the Trans-Siberian trains
- Car hire (sponsorship?) and its availability in specific towns
- Esther (to see if she was interested)
- BBC (to see if they were interested)
- Kayak purchases in the appropriate towns
- Sailing boat hire in Fiji

- Cruise possibilities around the Indian Ocean from Mombasa
- Background reading about all countries, plus the major faiths he would encounter en-route
- Research into the Persecuted Church around the world
- RAF (about a flight from Basra to Kabul)
- A rough timetable for the whole trip

There would be much more, no doubt – but this was enough to be going on with. Brendan reckoned that it would take him a good six months to do all this preparatory work, so he extended that to allow for unforeseen difficulties and set himself a starting date of January 1ˢᵗ 2012. It was by now nearly the end of February 2011, so that gave him ten months to sort everything out. The clock was ticking...

Chapter 5: Elimination

Some of the items on Brendan's list were relatively easy to "solve". Others proved rather more difficult.

Insurance was straightforward. He still had his account at the Halifax, which gave him unlimited travel insurance for only £12.50 a month, for which he got lots of other good deals as well. The small print didn't exclude going into war-zones or piracy hot-spots[16].

Brendan then did some research on visas[17] and discovered that 96 of the countries he would have to visit required no visas from British citizens, whilst a further 36 required a visa but issued them at the point of entry, usually for about £30 but sometimes more. The problem was going to be the other 46. For 43 of these, he needed to apply for a visa from their embassies in London, but each needed to stamp their visa into his passport – and he only had one passport, which he needed to take with him. With most visas only valid for a short period after issue, it was a nightmare. It was going to be pricey as well, because whilst some were free, most were at least £30 and some like Nigeria and Libya were £100. Russia's was £115.

That left only three countries – and they could be the biggest problem of all. It would be impossible to get a visa for Saudi Arabia, because they were only issued for specific business appointments or to visit relatives. Likewise visas for Somalia were only issued "for humanitarian purposes". Brendan's only option appeared to be to try and sneak his way across the borders and hope that he didn't get caught in either place. To qualify for a visa to Tajikistan he would have to supply a letter of invitation from someone living there, which could be tricky because Brendan had never heard of Tajikistan before, and his list of contacts was unsurprisingly non-existent.

He made enquiries, through an RAF Chaplain with whom he'd done his Ministerial training at Manchester, about catching an RAF flight from Basra to Kabul. A few days later he was told that even if it were possible, it would be impossible to arrange anything in advance. Such uncertainty was no good, so Brendan had to look elsewhere. The trouble was, though, that neither Iraq nor Afghanistan were exactly tourist destinations, and there was no airline flying directly between these two countries, so extra mileage to another country would be necessary.

---

[16] I haven't read the small print as carefully as I would if I were accessing this for myself, but unlimited multi-trip travel insurance is what Halifax offer their Ultimate Reward account-holders. Please check carefully – I accept no responsibility for your insurance cover!

[17] The details of visa requirements and fees were correct at the time of writing.

He had a very encouraging phone conversation with Arnold Joseph, the man from Oracle Productions in Detroit, who said that Esther kept referring to the "Brendan factor" so would probably be interested in covering his next adventure, but that he couldn't promise anything until he'd spoken to the Lady Herself.

The BBC producer who'd put together the documentary on Brendan, shown shortly after his rescue, was less enthusiastic, complaining to Brendan about cuts and budgets.

Brendan had a brainwave when it came to contacts in each country. He needed a pre-arranged place-to-stay for some of his visa applications, and hit on the idea of tapping into the international contacts for the Alpha Course currently operating in 163 countries[18]. He also contacted a charity called Open Doors[19] whose main focus was on those areas of the world where Christians were most at risk of persecution, and asked if it might be possible for them, with whatever safeguards they thought were appropriate, to release details of their contacts to him.

***

A fortnight later, Brendan was still trying to find his way through the maze of logistical arrangements, and was also coming up against difficulties with his proposed route.

He quickly discovered, for example, that there was no single cruise itinerary that included all the places he needed to visit in the Indian Ocean, and that such cruises were phenomenally expensive and geared to meet the needs of pampered and usually elderly passengers used to luxury and a slow pace of life, neither of which he was seeking. He would have to revise his plans for the Indian Ocean leg. But what options were available? It was easy to get a return flight from Colombo in Sri Lanka to the Maldives and back, so the Maldives could easily be fitted into the itinerary en route from Tbilisi to Sydney. For the western part of the Indian Ocean, he might have to charter a boat. The route to the Comoros, the northern tip of Madagascar, Mauritius and the Seychelles, was, apart from Mauritius, quite a sensible circular sailing route, albeit with massive distances and costs.

But then Brendan noticed on the map the tiny speck of the Agalega Islands, situated 700 miles north of Mauritius itself but, crucially, part of the *nation* of

---

[18] These details about the globally-acclaimed Alpha Course were correct at the time of writing.

[19] Open Doors is a charity specialising in raising Western churches' consciousness about the Persecuted Church, whose CEO has given his encouragement for this book, which I hope may draw attention to their vital work.

Mauritius. That would make the circular sailing route much easier and cheaper. Likewise, closer scrutiny revealed the existence of Aldabra Island, part of the Seychelles but 700 miles closer than Mahé, the main island. The round trip was looking easier and easier. When he looked again, though, the mileages were still intimidating: nearly 600 from Mombasa to Comoros, 400 from there to Antisiranana in Madagascar, 500 to Agalega, 500 to Aldabra and 300 back to Mombasa. The round trip was still 2,300 miles, and would take a long time. Maybe he would have to charter a plane – but that would be even more expensive.

It was the same, if not worse, for the South Pacific. The distances involved were even greater. The only realistic possibilities seemed to be very expensive: chartering a boat for two months or a plane for a week. These ocean trips were going to be a real problem. An additional difficulty with the Pacific Ocean was its sheer vastness, with few airports. The direct route from Tonga across to South America required a refuelling stop right where St. Helena was – but it didn't have an airport. Sea-planes didn't have the range either. The eastern Pacific required stops at Hawaii and Los Angeles then the long flight down to Uruguay. It was a lot of mileage more than the shortest route – which mattered for another reason.

Brendan had been toying with the idea of setting himself a time-limit and maximum distance. His first estimates for the itinerary (before all the complications) had been 300 days and 150,000km – an average of 500km a day. These sounded like nice round figures, so Brendan decided to make this an extra challenge for his journey. So deviations from the shortest route were not acceptable. He put the South Pacific route on one side for the moment and turned his attention back to visas.

He wondered about the possibility of acquiring several passports, and seeing if he could persuade Louisa to work out what visas he needed at which points, go down to London to get them for him from the various embassies, then get that particular passport out to him in exchange for the one he'd been using. He wouldn't get round the world anyway just on one passport because it only had 25 pages for stamps and visas. The direct.gov website, however, said that British citizens could only have one passport. But what did everyone else do who travelled a lot? When he asked a friend from Cullercoats Methodist Church who travelled all over the world, he found that having multiple passports was possible, but that it was complicated and the Passport Office required an applicant to attend an interview to argue their case, particularly if they couldn't produce full passports from the past to support their application. It was another item for Brendan to research more thoroughly.

The difficulties seemed to be stacking up, but then he got a phone call from Detroit which lifted his spirits. "Hi, Brendan," said a rather husky female voice. "My name is Fahada, and I'm Miss Blanchett's P.A. Are you doing anything next Tuesday?"

Momentarily, Brendan felt as if he'd been asked out on a date by the honey-voiced goddess on the other end of the phone, but then he realised how ridiculous such a thought was. "Let me just check..." he said. Then, "I'm free." He immediately thanked the Lord that the owner of the wonderful voice wouldn't have seen the "Are You Being Served?" character of Mr. Humphreys. As it happened, Brendan's diary was spectacularly empty. He'd found this such a wonderful change from the previous diary-packed, always-available and thus never-available days at Jact.

"Good," said Fahada. "Esther wants you to fly out to Detroit next Tuesday to have a chat with her. Then, if you can, she'd like to fly you up to that place in the Arctic where you got the kayak, and film a reunion between you and the guy who built it and whose paddle you lost at Cape Horn. Is that OK?"

Brendan was thrilled. He would love to see old Nannuraluk again. The Inuit hunter from Resolute Bay had converted a two-man sea-kayak for Brendan's use in the Arctic, but Brendan had kept the kayak for the whole of the journey, trundling it overland on a trailer – and its sturdiness had saved his life in the South Atlantic. Brendan would love to see Nannuraluk's toothy grin again, and express his gratitude in person.

"Oh, one more thing," purred Fahada. "Esther's got an interesting proposal that she wants to discuss with you about this new trip of yours. I'll look forward to seeing you at the airport."

Chapter 6: Combination

Brendan stepped off the plane at Detroit Metropolitan Airport and was immediately ushered to a VIP arrival suite, where the gorgeous Fahada was waiting for him. And gorgeous she certainly was. Beautiful dusky skin, a tall elegance, hour-glass figure, no wedding ring – all of which Brendan noticed in a split-second. Her beauty may or may not have been only skin-deep, but at that point neither Brendan nor the gawping passport official was wondering about her pancreas or her soul. Brendan shook hands with Fahada and burbled a string of inane phrases as they walked out to the limo waiting outside the main door. Ten minutes of further verbal diarrhoea from Brendan later, they arrived at Oracle Studios, and Fahada was taking him up to Esther's private office – which had the same acreage as the lobby of a five-star hotel but with better furniture.

"Hello, Brendan," said Esther, as she rose from a bright white leather sofa, came across to him and shook his hand very formally. Then she said, "Aw, what the heck!" and gave him a big hug. "Good to see you again," she murmured into the side of Brendan's head while they embraced. Fahada withdrew quietly, but Brendan couldn't help but notice a dark cloud pass over her eyes as he was being hugged by her boss.

The last time Brendan and Esther had met had been back in those very studios just a week after Brendan had returned home from the South Atlantic. Esther had flown him and his daughters over in her Learjet, even though he was too weak to enjoy it or take any of it in. He didn't really remember very much at all except the joy of having Ruth and Louisa with him as he was interviewed by Esther live on her TV show. He was glad now to meet Esther again and thank her properly for her care and support.

Esther had started reporting on his journeys after Brendan was "spotted" at the Minnesota Fringe Festival in Minneapolis. He'd been giving one of his talks in front of thousands, including Robert Wilkinson (the boss of the Festival), who knew Arnold (the executive talent-scout for "See Esther") – and the rest, as they say, was history. Esther organised monthly interviews with Brendan wherever he was in the world, and even came down to Tierra del Fuego in person to conduct the final interview in the most southerly village in the world. Her personal interest in Brendan's journey enabled him to "witness" to millions more than he could have ever hoped. And his fame as "friend of Esther", as one priest described him, helped him secure contacts throughout the Americas.

"Now," said Esther, "I want you to explain these plans of yours – then I'll tell you about an idea that *I've* had and why I want to take you back to meet that Inuit guy who built the kayak."

So Brendan sat down in the most amazing armchair he'd ever sat on – both beautifully soft and beautifully firm at the same time, and bright white leather, or was it suede? He described how the idea had come to him. He half-expected some scepticism, but then remembered how readily Esther had accepted the fact that his first adventure began with a dream. Then he outlined his proposed route, and some of the problems which he still had to solve. He also mentioned the idea of setting himself some limits on both time and distance, at which Esther's eyebrow rose marginally.

"The ocean crossings worry me most," Brendan explained, with a shrug. "I'm getting absolutely nowhere with the long distances involved for both the Indian Ocean and the South Pacific."

Esther looked curiously at him. They'd both come to identical conclusions, as if they were psychic or tuned in to one another. "Yes, I've been thinking about that too and have some suggestions. I've got a yacht that I use in the Seychelles," she said, as matter-of-fact as someone describing their allotment. "It doesn't belong to me, but I've got an arrangement with the owner and I'm sure that you could have it, if you wanted. It does about 65 knots if you need it to, but cruises at about 45. It's quite small but comes fully equipped for a nice restful cruise. I've used it a few times. I'll get Fahada to arrange for you to have it for a week if you wish." Brendan had no idea how much a boat like that would cost for a week's charter. It was a wonderful offer.

"And I've been thinking about the Pacific too. The distances are just too big for anything other than using your own plane, so how about I loan you the Learjet for a week? We should be able to fit it all in nicely. What's more, I'll have a good excuse for filming you for the show."

Brendan exhaled slowly, to try and stop his heart racing. This was more than he could ever have hoped for. But she hadn't finished yet.

"I've got another idea which links into your idea about targets and deadlines. Tell me again what your projections indicate."

Brendan could feel the pulse in his neck banging away with a surge of adrenalin. The journey had quickly changed from speculative to possible to highly probable. He laid out his calculations: 300 days and 150,000km, which he thought was feasible – especially with Esther's help.

But Esther interrupted him. "That's not going to grab people's attention. It's been done before – I've had Fahada organise some research." She told Brendan about two New Zealanders who visited 191 countries in 167 days in 2002, to raise money for the Save the Children charity[20]. "They even wrote a book about it," she said, dismissively. "So you've got to do it differently. They just hopped on planes all over the place – you've got to do better than that."

---

[20] The journey of John Bougen and James Irving was called "All Nations Quest" and is described in their book: J. BOUGEN, J. MALCOLM & J. IRVING, "An Absolutely Outrageous Adventure", Penguin Books, 2004.

Brendan was surprised that someone else had tried to do something similar. Yet in a way he wasn't. Curiosity and adventure had always been powerful incentives – Brendan himself as a boy had idolised famous explorers. But his plans *were* different. "I'll be using a bike and a kayak, as well as trains, cars, boats and planes, yet still visit 178 countries in 300 days. By using different forms of transport it will capture people's attention again – especially if I start with the bike and kayak which I used last time."

Esther nodded. "Yes, but you need a bigger challenge that will really fire people up. I want to set you some new targets. Your itinerary of 150,000km is about right, so we'll fix that, but I want to set some other rules. You can't use a plane for more than half of that, so your limit is 75,000km. To make sure that you don't get boring and stick with just one or two forms of transport, we stipulate that the distances on land and on water must both be over 35,000km, and – here's the USP..." Brendan looked blank at this point, so she explained: "Unique Selling Point, Brendan, don't you know anything about business?" He shook his head and acted the village idiot. "The USP is that 30% of all land and water transport must be under your own power, like last time. The viewers really loved that. I think that'll really fire them up again."

"But I'll never manage that in the time-limit," said Brendan, whose mind was racing through the implications of all this.

"Oh, your time's extended to a full year, 365 days. My researchers reckon that it can be done. The only sticking points for them were the two oceans, so now the whole project is achievable."

She still wasn't finished. "I want to film you again, one interview each month, but not on a contract dependent on you making contact on a set day – that nearly undid us in Colombia. This time we keep in touch continually with you, and plan where the interviews will happen – always adjusting the dates if we have to, but hoping that we won't because we won't have much leeway. For each "See Esther" programme you feature in I'll pay you $30,000. But I want to suggest another twist. Those New Zealanders were smart in selling their trip as a charity fundraiser, and that's what we have to do. So I propose that we get your lovely daughter involved and raise the money needed for her orphanage idea in Uganda. I'll publicly start it off on the programme by pledging $10,000 of my own money for every country you visit, and if you get round to all of them within the year I'll double it. We can get people around the world to sponsor you too and raise loads of money. What do you think?"

Brendan thought it was marvellous. Gulu Bulrushes still needed a big injection of capital before it could open for business – and Watoto already had plans for all kinds of other projects in need of money, as well as plans to share the principles of Watoto with start-up projects in other African countries too – so this was fantastic. He was still uncertain how he could complete the itinerary and tick every box– but he'd plenty of time to look at all the various possibilities.

Brendan agreed to it all, signed the contract (pre-prepared in anticipation of his co-operation), and asked himself whether he minded that it was now pretty much Esther's project rather than his. He decided that it didn't matter because the "witnessing" would still happen, and the benefits of Esther's support would be massive. He wasn't really worried about money because he still had plenty left in the bank even after the house purchase, though an income of $30,000 a month was not to be sniffed at. But Esther offered not only unlimited money but also the expertise and get-up-and-go of the Oracle organisation, which would be even more valuable.

Chapter 7: Coronation

When Brendan emerged from Esther's inner sanctum, Fahada escorted him to the office, or rather suite of offices, of his old friend Arnold Joseph. Then he was whisked off with Arnold back to the airport, where he climbed up the familiar boarding-steps into Esther's Learjet and met the two pilots and two film-crew. As they roared off into the sky, Brendan settled into the plush white leather and snoozed to the background hum of the engine and the quiet conversation of the film-crew with Arnold.

After 2,284 miles, one refuelling stop, and seven hours asleep, Brendan awoke as the wheels clunked down ready for landing at Resolute Bay. An array of Arctic clothing lay ready for Brendan, who'd forgotten that it was still winter up here – utterly dark and utterly cold. The others were already dressed in theirs, so as the wheels hit the runway Brendan quickly pulled on various long-johns, under-trousers and over-trousers, vests, shirts and fleeces until he was sweating profusely. Then Arnold opened the door. Immediately the heat was sucked out of the aircraft, and the pilots urged them to get out as quickly as possible. The pilots were going to refuel and taxi across to the hangar, where they would bunk down after setting up heaters inside and outside the plane, ready for the flight back tomorrow.

So four of them emerged and tried to breathe, while the door whooshed back into place, as if the plane was sighing with relief that it could get warm again. The air outside was so cold that it hurt Brendan's throat. It had never been this cold on his previous visit to the frozen North, even at the rarefied latitude of Alert. He'd started his last journey at over 82°N, just 500 miles from the North Pole, but that was in May and it had "warmed up" by then to -25°C. This felt colder than that – much colder. A few minutes later he caught sight of a thermometer on the outside of their Sno-Cat. It read -33°C. Brendan was surprised that it wasn't even lower.

They were met by the Abominable Snowman. At least, that's what it looked like. Whoever it was beckoned them quickly into the warm interior of a large Sno-Cat. When they'd all clambered in and shut the doors, the Abominable Snowman shook off his hood and introduced himself. He was a she. Her face was familiar too, wonderfully familiar. Paula Okpik was the priest at Resolute Bay and had been very welcoming towards Brendan when he'd passed through Resolute Bay on his way up to Alert, and even more helpful when he'd returned,. lending him a satellite phone to contact other settlements in the Arctic. It was great to see her again.

Esther had remembered Paula's name and got Fahada to contact her about the arrangements. And here she was to greet them, having borrowed the Sno-Cat from the Qausuittuq Inn, which used it regularly to ferry tourists – and goods for the next-door Tudjaat Co-operative store – to and from the runway. Paula explained that there was a big meeting arranged at the church for an hour's time and everyone was very eager to meet Brendan again and hear about his adventures since leaving Resolute Bay nine months before.

They rumbled their way along the snow into town. All they could see in the headlights of the Sno-Cat was whiteness, and then suddenly they arrived at the hotel. Arnold and Brendan jumped out, and the film-crew were driven off by Paula to set up their equipment at the church.

Soon afterwards, Paula returned and drove Arnold and Brendan back to the church. They had had time to find their rooms and have a hot drink, but not much more. When they arrived outside the church, they could see that a great crowd had squeezed inside. A great roar went up when he entered the church, and it took several minutes for him to make his way to the front. The film-crew were capturing it all on camera, and got a close-up of Brendan as he greeted a smiling Nannuraluk, who was carrying a tiny baby.

Brendan was thrilled to meet his old friend, but puzzled by the baby. He pointed at the newborn, and raised his eyebrows at Nannuraluk, who laughed his three-toothed grin and said, "This is Brendan, born six days ago to my wife. We named him after you because we reckon he was conceived on the day you came to our house." Another roar erupted at this, with many of the men giving Nannuraluk a thumbs-up and many of the women giggling and nudging one another. Brendan was thrilled for the old man – obviously not as old as he looked – and greatly honoured to have a child named after him.

Paula came forwards and announced that Nannuraluk wanted little Brendan baptised and big Brendan to do the baptism. Brendan was thrilled. He felt a bit out of practice, but Paula led the little service in Inuktitut, and all Brendan had to do was hold the baby, grin at the proud parents, and splash water over little Brendan's head at the appropriate point. Paula finished the liturgy off quickly, and handed over once again to Brendan.

The crowd hushed, and Brendan told them about some of his adventures. He explained how he'd paddled through Bellot Strait and all the way across to Hudson Bay. Great aaaahs went up when Brendan described the attack by the polar-bears and his navigation up the Nelson River to the great Lake Winnipeg. They were amazed when he described the trailer with which he'd pulled his kayak overland, and laughed at the thought of him pulling his sledge and his kayak behind his bike. The Inuits had seen a bicycle only once but remembered it well, when a strange man had brought one with him on the plane in the mistaken belief that Resolute Bay would have roads that were snow-free. There wasn't really much call for cycling in the Arctic.

When Brendan described his travails in the kayak in the South Atlantic, they were silently attentive once again to every detail. First they were shocked when he described losing his paddle because they knew only too well what that meant. Then they were puzzled as he described his makeshift sail and finally amazed as he described how fast he'd sailed through the sea. They patted Nannuraluk on the shoulder as Brendan described how sturdy and dependable the kayak had been, right to journey's end, and applauded as he described his successful landfall and subsequent rescue.

And then it was over, except for one last ceremony, announced by Paula. "We Inuit are very respectful of the Queen. But we also have a local custom called "King for the day", when after a particular achievement someone is crowned King. It is usually the occasion for loud rejoicing and prolonged drinking. Let the coronation begin!" A big armchair painted gold was carried in and set at the front, and Brendan was invited to sit on the "throne" and Paula placed a large plastic crown on his head, which instantly slipped down over his face. The crowd roared with laughter, clapped and shouted, and went off to the bar to get more drinks. Brendan felt rather silly sitting there on the throne, but everyone had been so hospitable and friendly that he smiled and relaxed. Nannuraluk shuffled forwards with a drink in his hand for Brendan and they shared a few more words before Nannuraluk left to walk his wife and little Brendan back home. The crowd hung around for a while as more drinks were served and cakes were passed around, but then they wrapped themselves up and went back home too. Paula drove the film-crew, Arnold and Brendan back to the hotel, and agreed to meet in the morning. The film-crew needed to re-enact their arrival and meeting with Paula for the camera, and film their farewell too.

As Brendan relaxed at the end of a 36-hour day because of time-zone differences, he considered how little control he had about what was happening, how little he worried about it, and how fruitful and productive it all was. God not only had kept him safe through his travels, but also deepened his relationship with his two daughters, clarified his understanding of God's mission, and even extended his fruitfulness to enable old Nannuraluk to become a father. Well done, God.

Chapter 8: Co-ordination

A month later, midway through April, several important developments had taken place. Brendan returned from the Arctic with a really sore throat but still recorded another interview with Esther back in Detroit before going home to continue his preparations. Fahada personally handed over the cheque for $30,000, and looked him up and down as if marking him out of ten – or were his hormones running male-menopausally haywire?

The film of the reunion in Resolute Bay had been shown on "See Esther" the following week, along with Esther's interview with Brendan which outlined the new plans. None of the British media picked up on it much, including the Whitley Bay News Guardian, which usually was anxious for any news at all. Having been headline news across the world just a few months before, Brendan realised how quickly he'd become history.

Brendan had sorted out the sponsorship plans with Watoto, through Ruth, who was very excited at the prospect of so much money coming in. It would not only guarantee the establishment of Gulu Bulrushes but also bankroll many more developmental projects which Watoto were planning. The Watoto board in Kampala had given their full approval for Ruth to co-ordinate the fundraising and had released her and Paul from their choir-tour responsibilities for the foreseeable future. Both of them would be travelling to the various interview locations, and giving monthly updates on how the sponsorship was going. Ruth was thrilled, because not only would she get to see her Dad on a regular basis, but would also get to travel with Paul to some amazing places.

Ruth and Paul were busy preparing a further DVD to send out through Watoto contacts across the world, containing edited highlights of the original fundraising footage, but also an interview with Brendan by Ruth explaining the idea of the Big Trip. The DVD was to be called the Great Omission, and highlighted the rich world's neglect of the poor and orphaned children of Uganda alongside the Christian Church's neglect of God's call to engage in mission. The two themes sat neatly together as a damning indictment of the so-called developed world.

Watoto wanted to extend the impact of its work beyond the borders of Uganda. Their dream was to see 10,000 churches across Africa take up the challenge to look after 60 million orphaned and vulnerable children. Already three projects in Kenya had been started and countries like Rwanda, South Africa, Malawi and even China were considering setting up programmes along the Watoto model[21]. Initial funding

---

[21] The Watoto website, www.watoto.com, outlines these and other projects/plans.

was often the biggest challenge, and Brendan's Big Trip would kick-start all kinds of investments and projects.

Brendan had contacted the Bible Society, who promised to provide him with a gold-covered New Testament for every nation, but were keen to discover his exact route so that they could choose the most appropriate language for each. They were delighted to support Brendan, because 2011 marked the 400th anniversary of the authorisation of the King James Version, and they needed another high-profile project to boost the campaign. Brendan was worried about how to transport the Bibles as well as his other stuff, but at least the monthly meetings with Esther and Ruth meant that he would only have to take one month's supply – as well as food, clothes, maps and a new passport full of the correct visas.

He'd also seen Eric Tate, the CEO of Open Doors[22]. Eric was a tall undertaker-looking chap who looked as if he couldn't get excited about anything, but came alive when he talked about Open Doors. The light went on and he seemed to bounce with passion for his job. Open Doors was operating in so many different countries, and Eric was thrilled at the opportunity to explain how difficult but also how rewarding his job was. He promised that he would give Brendan as much support as he could. "Their stories need to be told. It's another big omission on the Western Church's part. How can our churches sit there comfortably when our brothers and sisters are being martyred for their faith?" Brendan promised that he would highlight the plight of the Persecuted Church whenever he could. He came away with piles of literature and many contacts.

The route-planning had proved a nightmare. It had been settled, after much calculation, then altered when it was found that it would take Brendan over 150,000km, then altered again because the kayak/sailing-boat proportion was not quite up to 30%, then altered again because it would take him just over a year instead of within it. Now the itinerary looked rather different:

---

[22] Eric Tate is nothing like Eddie Lyle, the real-life CEO of Open Doors, except in his boundless energy, passion and heart for the Persecuted Church.

Original itinerary	Final itinerary
By car from Cullercoats to Lisbon (Portugal)	By bike from Cullercoats to Andorra
By plane to Rimini (Italy)	By plane to Nice, by bike to Rijeka (Croatia)
By car to Thessaloniki (Greece)	Sail down the Adriatic coast to Albania
By train to Istanbul (Turkey)	By car to Istanbul
By plane to Larnaca (Cyprus)	By plane to Larnaca
By kayak to Haifa (Israel)	By sailing boat to Haifa
By bike to Eilat (Israel)	By bike to Taba (Egypt)
By kayak to Sharm-El-Sheik (Egypt)	By plane to Cairo
By plane to Tripoli (Libya)	By plane to Tripoli
By kayak to Tangiers (Morocco), plane to Dakar (Senegal), Cape Verde and back to Dakar	By speedboat to Tunis (Tunisia), kayak to Tangiers, plane to Lisbon, Cape Verde and Dakar
By car to Bissau (Guinea)	By bike to Colicunda (Guinea-Bissau)
By kayak to Lomé (Togo)	By speedboat to Lomé
By car to Acalayong (Equatorial Guinea)	By car to Acalayong
By kayak to Luanda (Angola)	By speedboat to Luanda
By plane to Maseru (Lesotho)	By bike to Maputo (Mozambique)
By car to Mombasa (Kenya)	By car to Mombasa
By cruise ship around the Indian Ocean and back to Mombasa	By Esther's super-yacht around the Indian Ocean and back to Mombasa
By plane to Djibouti	By plane to Djibouti; car to Ethiopia and Somalia
By kayak to Basra (Iraq)	By speedboat to Basra
By RAF plane to Kabul (Afghanistan)	By Esther's plane to Kabul
By car to Singapore	By car to Mandalay (Myanmar), plane to Hue (Vietnam), car to Ho Chi Minh City, plane to Singapore
	By speedboat to Indonesia; car to Malaysia; plane to Brunei and the Philippines
By plane to East Timor and Brunei; ferry to the Philippines	
By plane to Palau and back to Philippines	By chartered plane to East Timor and Palau
By ferry to Japan and South Korea	By chartered plane to Japan, ferry to South Korea
By bus to North Korea and back	By bus to North Korea and back
By ferry to Beijing (China)	By ferry to Beijing

By train to St. Petersburg (Russia) By kayak to Amsterdam (Netherlands) By car to Tbilisi (Georgia)	By train to St. Petersburg By speedboat to Brugge (Belgium) By bike to Odessa (Ukraine); ferry to Poti (Georgia), train to Tbilisi, car to Azerbaijan and Armenia and back to Tbilisi
By plane to Sydney (Australia), Auckland (New Zealand) and Nadi (Fiji) By sailing boat around Pacific islands and back to Fiji By plane to Los Angeles (USA) and Montevideo (Uruguay) By kayak to Belize	By plane to Colombo (Sri Lanka), Male (Maldives) and back, Sydney, Auckland, and Nadi By Esther's plane to Pacific Islands By Esther's plane to Fray Bentos (Uruguay) By kayak/catamaran to Grenada with brief road trip in Brazil; speedboat to Belize
By plane to London and Cullercoats By car and ferry to Brandon Bay in Ireland for a symbolic finish.	By plane to Shannon (Ireland); chartered sea-plane to Brandon Bay and back to Shannon By plane to Newcastle, and by Metro to Cullercoats

The full itinerary was sent to Fahada, checked by the researchers, and declared to be distance-accurate. Of course it was an entirely different matter whether or not he would keep to the same distances or routes when it actually came to the journey itself. This itinerary *just* got him above the 30% for travelling under his own power by land and water, and *just* got him below the 50% for air travel. There were eight days and 1,750km to spare – but it was the percentages he would have to watch.

There were other important developments too. Fahada phoned one day and instead of purring seemed to growl. More leopardess than pussycat, Brendan thought – having, in an idle moment the previous week, looked up "Fahada" and discovered that it was Arabic for "leopardess". "Esther is pleased to announce," she hissed – or was it just his imagination? – "that she wants to conduct most of the interviews with you in person on location. This is a big sacrifice for her as it will disrupt her work in Detroit repeatedly and sometimes for long spells at a time. She also wants you to know that she is particularly keen on using her Learjet to fly herself and you from Iraq to Afghanistan."

Brendan was thrilled with this news. "That's great! It solves the RAF uncertainty, and I'll also enjoy the flight much more if I'm with Esther."

There was a silence at the other end. "What do you mean?" asked Fahada, in a suspicious monotone.

"Esther's Learjet is much better than a Hercules. I'll choose plush leather armchairs over a metal jump-seat any day."

"Yes, of course!" said Fahada with a laugh – but it sounded forced to Brendan. He wondered what was going on – but at least some of the itinerary was becoming clearer and more definite.

There were even rest days or half-days built into the itinerary so that the interviews could take place. These were spaced out at roughly one per month, but strategic places en route were chosen for their significance, so that each interview would have its own "edge". The venues were as follows:

Interview 1 (Day 4)	Canterbury – plus an interview with and commissioning from the Archbishop
Interview 2 (Day 37)	Cairo – first reflections on travelling in Islamic countries
Interview 3 (Day 73)	Conakry, Guinea – so that Esther could visit her Guinean "kinfolk"
Interview 4 (Day 102)	Luanda – the start of an epic bike ride across Africa
Interview 5 (Day 139)	Gulu – focussing on what the money is being raised for
Interview 6 (Days 175/176)	Basra and/or Kabul – war and peace issues today
Interview 7 (Day 204)	Beijing – the Persecuted Church
Interview 8 (Day 232)	Vaduz, Liechtenstein – small countries matter too
Interview 9 (Day 261)	Fray Bentos – at the end of the Pacific leg
Interview 10 (Day 289)	Diamantino, Brazil – halfway through the longest kayak journey in the world
Interview 11 (Day 321)	Grenada – transition from kayak to speedboat for the final spurt
Interview 12 (Days 356/357)	Brandon Bay and Cullercoats – celebrations, hopefully...

Esther had called her friend in the Seychelles and the luxury yacht "The World Is Not Enough" – Brendan wondered why the boat was named after a James Bond film – would be given on free charter for the Indian Ocean leg[23]. "It's usually a quarter of a million euros for a week," Esther told Brendan. "But I talked to the guy about Gulu Bulrushes and he's prepared to give it free if it isn't already booked."

---

[23] The World Is Not Enough is one of the sleekest and most expensive super-yachts ever built. The details of the yacht are taken from its makers' website: www.peterkehoe.com/The_World.htm.

Another of Esther's contacts was Micky Yehu, the CEO of Bailey, Rindic and Coulter, a private investment firm who owned most of the Hertz Corporation[24]. Hertz had been started by Alfred L. Joseph as a car-rental operation in Detroit with a dozen Model Ts. Alfred just happened to be Arnold Joseph's great-grandfather, and the Esther Blanchett empire always used Hertz when they needed to hire a car. Brendan wasn't sure whether it was out of loyalty to Arnold, or because of the charitable trust links between Esther and Micky Yehu. Whatever the reason, the result was the same: Micky promised free use of Hertz vehicles wherever Brendan needed them, and he also got tapped for $1,000 per country.

Esther had instructed Fahada to arrange and oversee the employment of a visa enabler in London, but the task was made much easier when a high-up official from the Home Office spending a weekend at Esther's estate in Antigua confirmed that Brendan could have as many passports as he needed for securing visas at the appropriate times. The official agreed that a letter from him to the foreign embassies might enable many of them to be persuaded to issue year-long visas rather than the usual monthly or quarterly visas – for the appropriate fee, of course – which Oracle Productions would cover under the visa enabler's generous expenses account[25].

Things were ticking along nicely, but then Esther dropped the bombshell.

---

[24] Micky Yehu and his company Bailey, Rindic and Coulter are entirely fictional. The Hertz Corporation is actually owned by a two-partner private equity group. Its early history is as described, except that its real-life founder was Walter L. Jacobs, not Alfred L. Joseph.

[25] All Home Office officials, I am sure, are untouchable by such mutually-beneficial but corrupt arrangements. This is pure fiction.

Chapter 9: Detonation

The bombshell came in the form of a telephone call.

"Hello Brendan," Esther said, to Brendan's great astonishment. He'd assumed that she got Fahada to make all her phone calls. Maybe there was bad news coming. "I've got some good news and some bad news," she said. "Which would you like first?" It was like chatting to Louisa 15 years ago at the primary school gate.

"The good news, I think."

"Well, the good news is that my man in the Seychelles confirms that you can have the yacht free and he will also contribute $1,000 for every country you visit."

"That's great," said Brendan, half-enthusiastically. "And the bad news?"

"It's only free for one week in the next nine months, and that's October 8 through 14."

Brendan desperately tried to remember when the Indian Ocean leg came in his revised itinerary. He flicked through his notes and said, "But that's days 148 to 154, which is five months in. We can't do that, because I'd have to set off in May and it's already April now."

"I know, dear," said Esther. "May 16 actually. But we still reckon that you can be ready. We'll do everything to help you, and we think you can do it."

Brendan was flabbergasted. It wasn't the early start or all the work he would have to cram into the next six weeks that had knocked the wind out of his sails, though it was seven months earlier than he'd expected to start this next journey, and only five months after the end of his last one. No, it wasn't that – it was the date. May 16th was the feast day of his namesake, St. Brendan, the Irish monk considered crazy by his friends for setting off in a little boat to journey to the end of the earth in obedience to God's call. God was reassuring him that all would be well, as it had been for the first mad travelling Brendan. It was a sign.

***

The pressure was well and truly on, but Brendan refused to panic. Fahada was looking after many of the arrangements, so his main job was to continue with his planning. He'd much more research to do about all the countries he would be visiting, and had contacts to establish in many of the countries so that he could apply for visas. He wrote hundreds of letters to people whose names and details he'd acquired through the Alpha Course, and, for those countries which Alpha had not yet reached, he used church contacts at Church House in Westminster and at the Vatican. It was useful to have friends in high places.

He'd been doing some more thinking about the aims of the whole trip. He'd been quite touched by the title which Ruth and Paul had given their fundraising DVD –

the Great Omission. It seemed to capture a two-pronged challenge to the Christian Church: to do something spectacular to bring justice to the poor and vulnerable in the developing world; and to do something revolutionary to turn around its neglect of mission and outreach.

Brendan knew all too well the omissions of the churches where he'd served. Some years before, Conference had approved a declaration entitled Our Calling[26]: "The calling of the Methodist Church is to respond to the gospel of God's love in Christ and to live out its discipleship in worship and mission. It does this through worship, learning and caring, service and evangelism."

Brendan had been rather proud of these four headings of "Our Calling". The declaration not only defined what should be done but by implication indicated what should *not* receive effort and resources. Fellowship, for instance, was *not* part of the church's aims. It could be a sub-section of "learning and caring", of course, but it was not an end in itself. Many churches had been challenged to do a careful re-think when they realised that what they had prided themselves on actually should be only a means to a more important end. Brendan had presented "Our Calling" to the Methodist Church at Jact with excitement and relish, but they took on board the first two headings and still refused steadfastly to engage in the third and fourth. They could cope with worship as long as it meant worship that they liked. They could cope with learning and caring as long as it meant listening to sermons and looking after each other – and as long as it didn't mean going to bible study, forming home groups or caring for anybody else. But service and evangelism got the big elbow. "We're too old," they whined. Or they told Brendan that it was *his* job.

This was too often the problem with Methodism – and probably the rest of the British Church as well. They knew the Great Commission off by heart but thought it referred to the there-and-then of the Bible rather than the here-and-now of their own lives. The Church and the Kingdom were suffering because of the Church's Great Omission. The more Brendan thought of this title, the more he liked it.

He looked up "Great Omission" on the Internet[27] and found that there were various publications with this title, ranging from one bemoaning the neglect of faith formation in children to one complaining about US seminaries not sending out Ministers capable of giving proper Biblical teaching from the pulpit.

---

[26] Our Calling was approved and adopted at the Methodist Conference of 2000.

[27] All the articles and books referred to under the "Great Omission" theme exist. I apologise if I've misrepresented them in any way, but I've done my best to describe them accurately.

There was a book called "The Great Omission: Reclaiming Jesus's Essential Teachings on Discipleship" by an American called Dallas Willard, which argued that discipleship was what the Church was paying least attention to, and that this was the reason why there was the shortage of missionaries being sent out from America. So this one was about mission, indirectly. Brendan, skimming through a review, read one quotation from the book which stuck in his mind[28]: "The last command Jesus gave the church before he ascended to heaven was the Great Commission, the call for Christians to "make disciples of all the nations". But Christians have responded by making *Christians* not *disciples*. This has been the church's Great Omission, the failure to make people wholehearted disciples." Brendan definitely agreed with Willard's general argument, because many loyal Methodists he'd come across had been believers rather than disciples – but he didn't see how Willard's perspective helped him otherwise.

There were other books with "Great Omission" in their title which referred directly to mission, but they weren't much use. One referred to the care for missionaries' health as the Great Omission, suggesting many improvements from better strategies against malaria and hepatitis to an insistence on their use of seat belts. Fascinating stuff, but not quite what Brendan was looking for.

He was, however, deeply impressed by a book by Steve Saint[29] called "The Great Omission: Fulfilling Christ's Commission Completely". Brendan was so excited by it that he read it through in one day from cover to cover. Steve was the son of a martyred missionary, who'd been amongst a group of five missionaries killed by the Waodani Indians of Ecuador in 1956. Despite this, some of the women on the missionary team stayed and successfully planted Christianity among the Waodani, and Steve spent some of his childhood among the very people who'd murdered his father. In 1994, when the last of these amazing women died, the Waodani called him from his business career in Florida to live among them again.

When he arrived in the Ecuadorian jungle, Saint was shocked by the parlous state of the Waodani churches and the fragile faith of the Christian converts. The churches were weaker and less functional than he remembered from his schooldays. Initially, the Waodani churches had been self-governing and self-supporting, but now they waited for outsiders to build their church buildings and conduct their Bible conferences. This type of dependency caused what Saint called "The Great

---

[28] The review quoted is at www.dwillard.org/books/GreatOmission.asp.

[29] S. SAINT, "The Great Omission: Fulfilling Christ's Commission Completely", YWAM Publishing, 2001. The book is as described. I was impressed by it, and hope that I've reflected this in this review.

Omission," that is, it prevented indigenous believers like the Waodani from taking their part in fulfilling the Great Commission.

Brendan was impressed by Saint's observations and conclusions, which were similar to the views of Paul, his son-in-law, to whom he'd chatted at length in the brief time they'd spent together over Christmas. Paul had seen similar things happening in Uganda – and his boyhood hero, the local poet Okot p'Bitek, eventually abandoned Christianity altogether because of the Church's unwillingness to let indigenous cultures formulate their own faith without a dependence on European influence. Brendan was enthralled by Saint's book, which argued that any missionary effort which created dependence in indigenous believers ended up sapping the strength and patience of both donors and receivers, and it was difficult to cure after it became established. The real goal of mission was to plant healthy indigenous churches that could play their own part in fulfilling the Great Commission. Yet many indigenous believers were so suffocated by the good intentions or inappropriate standards of western Christians that they felt inferior and incapable, and sat on the sidelines, waiting for "more sophisticated" Christians to minister to their needs.

Saint concluded his book with a comparison between modern missionary methods and those of the Apostle Paul. In contrast with Paul's method of turning over responsibility to his converts at an early stage, modern missionaries tended to stay too long in leadership over their converts, expecting them to attain similar or better qualifications than the missionaries themselves before they were prepared to hand over responsibility. Saint, on the other hand, believed Paul's approach minimised dependence, characterizing it as "Know-Go-Show-Blow." Missionary work should be about *knowing* God personally, *going* where God is not yet known, *showing* the people there how to follow Jesus, and *"blowing"*, that is, leaving that place sooner rather than later in order to start from scratch somewhere else. By this approach *all* converts would be brought into the ongoing work of evangelism and thus help to fulfil the Great Commission.

This was exactly what Brendan himself believed. Serving in the North-East of England made him a great fan of the Celtic missionary monks. In contrast to the missionaries who moved up to England from Europe and brought with them the Roman "package" (order; hierarchical institutionalisation; the imposition of a foreign system; disdain for indigenous culture and faith-stories), the Celtic monks wandered from place to place, shared stories and trod lightly on local ways without crushing them. It was a shame, thought Brendan, that the Romans "won" at the Synod of Whitby, and Celtic influences diminished under the subsequent Roman rule. In the last 40 years or so there had been a re-emergence of Celtic ideas. Perhaps there was hope yet...

In plain language and with concrete examples from his own experience, Saint seemed to be saying what Brendan instinctively knew to be true: that mission methods needed to revert to their earliest forms if they were to be effective. The goal of mission must once again be the formation of healthy indigenous churches in every culture, rather than imposing a foreign culture upon people as the vehicle in which the Gospel must be delivered.

Brendan decided that he would call his project the "Great Omission Journey", or "GO Journey" for short. He wanted to draw attention not just to the need to re-engage in God's mission but also *how* to engage in God's mission. If Brendan's journey merely reinforced the old stereotypical idea of patronising and imposing Westerners bringing in the right answers, he would be doing more harm than good.

"Go, Brendan, GO!" he said to himself, and it sounded so good that he decided that that would be his slogan.

Chapter 10: Denomination

Jack Turner, Chair of the Newcastle District, struggled to adjust to the Stationing Committee allowing Brendan Priest to wriggle away from his responsibilities. For him, ministry was about order, tidiness, and things fitting together. In contrast, Brendan Priest, in Jack's opinion, embodied disorder, loose threads and "doing his own thing". For Jack, Methodism's strength was its principle of connexionalism: everything serving as part of an ongoing dynamic movement, pointed in a unified direction by careful strategic steering from its leadership but aware always of its heritage. Church order had always been very important for Methodism, and thus for Jack. Liturgies were "authorised for use"; congregations were organised into Circuits and prevented from becoming independent or self-sufficient by having to share their resources with churches in a more difficult position. Jack loved that: the rich helping the poor and the strong helping the weak. That was the Methodism he loved – but he needed it to be organised and properly accountable. Brendan had upset him so much because his approach was so different and so... untidy.

As Superintendent, he'd always stipulated that everything in the Circuit was to be brought to his attention; which some criticised as over-bearing micro-management, but Jack justified as dutiful oversight. The deeper truth was that he hated surprises, especially when they created anomalies. As District Chair he'd quickly discovered that he had little power to influence Circuit decisions, but could exercise some control over personnel deployment, both for Ministers (via Stationing) and lay employees (via his influence over grant applications). Mavericks like Brendan Priest didn't fit into the tidy picture he sought for his District. He liked to be captain of a happy ship – and mutineers unsettled that.

Jack had had to go with the flow of some of the progressive ideas that were now, in his view, muddying the waters. All that post-modernism stuff had seeped into the Methodism he wanted to preserve, like an oil slick polluting a beautiful beach. People who thought they were being clever were talking about post-Christian this and post-Christendom that, calling themselves post-evangelicals – whatever that might mean. "Fresh Expressions" was the flavour of the moment, and there seemed to be a plethora of cafe-style worship and down-the-pub projects that in his opinion seemed to attract grants but not grow Christians. The trouble was that the faithful Methodists in the more traditional "inherited church" or "Stale Expressions" of church (as he'd heard them being called) were the ones funding it all.

There was a head of steam building up. "Fresh Expressions" became so common a concept that it had lost its apostrophes and become Fresh Expressions. The Blackpool Conference of 2007 encouraged Methodism to prioritise setting up fresh ways of "being Church", and since then the number of such off-shoots had grown dramatically. There were now FEASTs (Fresh Expressions Area Strategy Teams), designed to support and guide the developments of these mission initiatives, and most Ministers had been on some sort of "mission-shaped" training, or at least a Vision Day.

More recently, tricky issues had been raised and searching questions asked. The rate of establishing new Fresh Expressions had levelled off a bit, so was it a lasting and revitalising dynamic movement of the Spirit or merely the death-spasm of a terminally-ill institution? Could Fresh Expressions make the move from dependence to a fuller interdependency within the whole of Methodism, seeing that they couldn't raise their own resources? How could the Church identify leaders from within Fresh Expressions and train them appropriately? How could they be Fresh Expressions of *church* when there was still no strong sense of "church" and most of their people had walked away from the "Stale Expressions"?

The "experts" were saying that it would take a long time before the balance shifted away from the old to the new, but would there always be somewhere for people like Jack who wanted a more traditional and ecclesiastical setting? Everything might be changing, but prematurely dismantling what had been important for so many centuries seemed unnecessary and counter-productive – especially because that's where the cash was coming from to support the new ventures.

Jack still had lots of questions. How were Fresh Expressions supposed to relate to the existing structures? What made any of these Fresh Expressions identifiably Methodist, or was that the wrong question? How were they accountable and able to be challenged? Should Methodism shift its personnel across to Fresh Expressions, and, if so, when, and how? Should Fresh Expressions provide sacramental worship, and rites of passage? The current official view seemed to be "wait and see", but Jack wasn't satisfied with such woolliness.

Jack felt that his beloved Methodist denomination was at a crossroads[30]. Its leadership didn't seem sure whether they wanted Methodism to continue or whether they should pioneer a "post-denominational" future for Christianity – another of those dreadful "post-" words. In 2003, Methodism signed a Covenant with the Anglicans, but few Anglicans seemed to have heard of it, and fewer still thought it important. If they liked the idea at all, it seemed to be because they thought that Methodism was chucking in its hand and that their numbers would be boosted. A further campaign called "Embracing the Covenant" seemed more like trying to grab a wet bar of soap. Currently there were "talks about talks" with the United Reformed

---

[30] Methodism remains very loyal and respectful to its ecumenical partners, and its representatives at every level are often foremost in pushing the ecumenical agenda. So the sceptical, almost cynical views expressed in this chapter are not by any means official Methodist perspectives – and certainly not intended to describe my or anyone else's thoughts. Jack, remember, is a fictional character...

Church but that didn't fill too many people with glee, as the URC seemed to be even more impoverished than Methodism. Most Methodist Ministers seemed to favour working more closely with the livelier Free Churches, because they believed that linking up with the Anglicans was the equivalent of being towed across the Atlantic by the Titanic, and that linking up with the URC would be like having to take your little brother with you on a date.

He didn't know what the future would hold. Already he'd accepted that the Methodism he knew and loved was rapidly running out of steam, evidenced by the age-profile, the lack of bums on seats and cash in the collection plates, the shortage of Ministers, and shrinking away from "broad church" into focussed factions. He knew that change was inevitable and that structural tidiness was its first casualty. He was still keen, however, to hold onto as much "familiar Methodism" as he could. Ministers who jumped ship like Brendan Priest, or those who left Circuit ministry to pursue more specialised ministries in education, chaplaincy, ecumenical work or consultancy just accelerated the speed of decline and diminished the available resource yet further.

Chapter 11: Divination

Esther Blanchett couldn't tell what the future would hold either – but it didn't stop her trying. She hadn't got where she was today by not having an eye on what the next thing was going to be. She'd been born into a black Pentecostal family in the poorer end of Detroit, but was pushed by her ambitious mother into stage school and dancing lessons. Esther grew from a rather gawky child into a tall, leggy, curvy young lady who'd been quickly snapped up by a modelling agency, before catching an even luckier break and finding her way into movies.

Her stunning beauty catapulted her into a celebrity lifestyle which she didn't have the maturity to use to her advantage, so she'd made several bad mistakes about what films she starred in and which men (and women) she slept with. She'd cut loose from her upbringing, running headlong into hedonistic pleasures and the accumulation of experiences, not particularly caring whether they were good or bad. But then in her mid-thirties, at the height of her film career, she puzzled everyone, especially her agent, by retiring from Hollywood, returning to Detroit and going it alone into television.

She bought a house in Novi, Michigan, about 30km from the city – but it wasn't just any old house. It was number 21,000 Turnberry Boulevard[31] and included over 20 acres of landscaped grounds. She bought the estate for $14.5 million which seemed a lot for a house with only six bedrooms, and then spent a further $5 million on the landscaping. She liked but wasn't hooked by the trappings of wealth: 24-carat gold chandeliers; circular wine-tasting room; meditation room with its own flotation pool; master bedroom with its own cinema; master bathroom multi-suite with his-and-her Botticino marble baths and limestone heated floors; library with panelled walls and herringbone leather floor. What *really* appealed to Esther were the large guest-house and adjacent servant quarters (because her home was entirely hers), the woods, waterfalls, pools and fishponds (because she could wander freely in a beautiful, tranquil, and solitary setting), and the security gates, two security stations and discreet high barbed-wire alarmed fence (because she could live as a hermit after so much previous exposure). The property also boasted its own airstrip and helipad, which meant that she was saved the long drive into work.

She kept a selection of opulent private properties in various sun-drenched parts of the world, and visited them when her hectic schedule allowed – but she liked her Novi retreat best of all. She'd allowed various individuals to share Novi with her, mostly men, but latterly her favourite was a tall, reserved, beautiful woman in her late twenties, called Fahada.

---

[31] Esther's home is a real house, featured at the website www.realtor.com/ realestateandhomes-detail/21000-Turnberry-Blvd_Novi_MI_48167_M33118-53579?

Esther's skin was a deep, dark brown, but Fahada had a skin colour which was curiously both olive and honey, and highlighted the smoothness and lustre of her complexion, and Esther was intoxicated by Fahada from the moment she'd joined the administrative team at Oracle. It hadn't taken long for Esther to bring Fahada onto her own office staff, and within a year she'd been appointed as Esther's PA and introduced to Esther's private world – and her bed. Over the last three years, Fahada had established an unassailable position within Oracle. Arnold Joseph, Esther's second-in-command, had been edged out into peripheral and often foreign assignments, which is why he'd been the main contact with Brendan on his first journey. His moon waned as Fahada's waxed.

Fahada's own apartment was in River Rouge, overlooking the lake and handy for work but not in a well-regarded neighbourhood. Her meteoric rise meant that most days she commuted into work from Novi by helicopter. All that was known about her was that she had no family in the USA, and arrived in Detroit eight years ago in her early twenties from London, but was rumoured to be of Egyptian parentage. It didn't, of course, stop rumours flying around – whether about her sex life or links with Al-Qaeda or Egyptian aristocracy. She gave very little away – and never said anything about her family or her background. She spent long hours at Novi in the meditation room and kept a Muslim prayer mat there, as well as one in the office. She usually went to the mosque on Friday lunchtimes but didn't seem particularly interested in talking about what she believed. Esther enjoyed the physicality of their relationship but had no desire to commit herself to anybody, and Fahada seemed to understand that and never took anything for granted.

One Sunday afternoon, as they lounged in reclining chairs next to the swimming pool at Novi, Esther broached the subject of Brendan. "What do you think of our intrepid English explorer, then, Fahada?"

"What do you mean?" asked Fahada, rather defensively.

"He's quite dishy, isn't he?"

"Esther, are you trying to make me jealous? He's in his fifties, bald, and has nothing going for him whatsoever. Surely you can't fancy him over me?" She knew Esther was teasing her.

"But it's not just about looks. He's got something that makes him very appealing but I can't just put my finger on it – something deep and alluring."

Fahada looked sharply across at Esther to see how serious she was, but couldn't read her expression because they were both wearing sunglasses. She probed back: "What do you think of this new venture of his?

"Hmmm. I don't know, really. I think he'll complete it, but maybe not within a year. He's certainly a man with drive and he'll do everything he can to be successful. I like that in a man. I like the way he gets on with his daughters as well." Esther paused, weighing Brendan up. "He's certainly fanatical on his evangelising, which I respect but don't find particularly appealing. I think it's his zeal that I admire – and the fact that he couldn't care less about money and all the usual things people strive for."

"He doesn't *have* to care about money after you've made him so wealthy over the last year," snapped Fahada, fairly brusquely. "Maybe you're committing too much of yourself to this one project, and letting other things slide."

Esther bridled at that. Fahada may share her bed and her home but she was still her PA not her partner. "I don't think that's fair, Fahada. There's something really rather special about Brendan, and I'm very happy to help him in any way I can. It makes me feel good to use my wealth for such a good cause." Esther paused. "Actually, it's more than that. I've got a funny feeling about Brendan. There's something about him that's really got to me, and I don't know what it is or what it means. I've got a strange feeling about him. This year's going to be very exciting for us all as he starts his journey and we travel to meet him every month."

Fahada sat up sharply. "What do you mean: "*We* travel to meet him"? You don't mean *me*, do you?" She wasn't at all thrilled at the thought of trailing round after moony-eyed Esther and the sad old Minister.

"Oh yes, Fahada, I need you with me wherever I go. You'll be the one keeping me in the picture so that other things *don't* slide. Of course you're coming with me. Arnold will be there as well. He and Brendan get on so well together that I'm almost a bit jealous myself. I need Arnold for the technical stuff, and you to sort out all the arrangements – you're so good at that, dear!"

Fahada kept quiet. She hated it when Esther went all patronising on her. Fahada had a funny feeling about Brendan too, but not one that thrilled her. His infidel mission was a challenge to her call of duty and a test of her loyalty. She lay back, wondering how she could make the future pan out the way she wanted. Maybe it was a sign that the first main interview was going to be in Egypt, where, Insha'Allah, she could re-connect with those whom no-one in America knew about. Insha'Allah, the future could get quite difficult for Brendan.

Maybe she could tell the future, like her father had told her she would. Her family were descendants of a Muslim astronomer Abu'l Hasan Ali ibn Ridwan Al-Misri, the observer a millennium ago of the supernova SN 1006, the brightest stellar event in recorded history[32]. But he'd also studied the Ancient Egyptian astrologers and instructed his son in their future-telling skills, which in turn were passed from father to son for over 1,000 years. Her own father had passed the gift on to her, the first

---

[32] Abu'l Hasan Ali ibn Ridwan Al-Misri was an Egyptian astronomer of great repute, famous particularly for his observations of this supernova, or stellar explosion, which he described as "three times as large as Venus, low on the southern horizon. The sky was shining because of its light."

female allowed to know what it was all about. Maybe now she was beginning at last to realise that not only could she foresee the future, but she could alter it.

Insha'Allah.

.

Chapter 12: Incarnation

Monday May 16th 2011 dawned damp and decidedly chilly, even though it was late spring. It didn't work like that, of course, on the North Tyneside coast. A sea-fret meant that the fog-horn behind Tynemouth Priory kept booming away while Brendan enjoyed a lie-in, having packed and unpacked everything several times the night before. But by noon, he was standing on the pavement across from his house on Beverley Terrace, his new mountain bike plus "my little GO-kart" propped against the kerb. He'd had the small trailer made locally for the three main cycling episodes in his year-long journey – cleverly disassembled into a lightweight fibreglass box containing its wheels and telescopic connecting-bar, which could be packed in a car boot or sent by air-freight. It bore a brightly-painted message: "Go, Brendan, GO!" above the smaller strap-line "doing something about the Great Omission".

Brendan had yet another sore throat, but he was up for it. He was surrounded by well-wishers and journalists, and a shivering cameraman called Dwight from "See Esther". The poor guy inexplicably arrived in shorts. He'd borrowed long trousers, coat and scarf from Brendan for protection against the cold breeze but, despite this, was still red-faced and kept blowing on his fingers as he operated the big camera perched like a black parrot on his shoulder. The start had been scheduled for noon, and everyone counted down to zero and cheered as Brendan swung his leg over the crossbar and wobbled away, but then the fog-horn boomed and Dwight yelled for them to do it again. He fiddled around for a couple of minutes with sound levels, so Brendan finally pulled away from the kerb at 12.04pm, according to Louisa's watch. The fog-horn boomed its sombre farewell to Brendan just as he pedalled away, the crowd shouting and cheering till he was out of earshot. He pulled past St. George's church and headed up the gentle incline to the Aquarium. The fog-horn gave one last boom as he turned away from Longsands, under the Metro bridge and up to the Broadway roundabout.

Only 150,000km to go, he thought, as he pulled up Beach Road to Tynemouth Pool and on to the Billy Mill roundabout. Some cars tooted as they passed, and a few people waved out of their windows, but once he turned off the Coast Road at Silverlink down to the Tyne Cycle Tunnel he was on his own. It drizzled for most of this long first day all the way to York, 132km from Cullercoats. The A19 was straight and in excellent condition, so he maintained a good speed, but got very wet very quickly through spray and rain, reminding Brendan of Costa Rican downpours and the steady drizzle of Tierra del Fuego – memories which curiously kept him going.

He was surprised how well he'd adapted back into cycling again. He'd done several long journeys a few weeks ago to test out the bike and himself and had gone out every day since to recapture a bit of fitness. But it was still nearly 8pm when he arrived at York Minster, though still well in time for the special Compline service arranged for 9.30pm.

Brendan had first met the Dean when he'd helped arrange the retirement celebration of the District Chair of York and Hull and they'd held the celebratory worship in the Minster. Now Brendan had asked the Dean for a special service to "see him off", and a dozen people gathered in the vast expanse of the Minster, dark apart from the dimly-lit quire. The atmosphere was heavy with the comforting weight of centuries of spirituality, the silence as vast as the space they were in, so when the Dean began with "The Lord Almighty grant us a peaceful night and a perfect end," the murmured "Amen" seemed to echo back from all corners and all centuries.

After a good night's sleep at The Deanery, Brendan set off through the streets and out of the city. Thankfully, the weather had cleared up, and it was exhilarating to be both dry and fast as he cycled down the A19 to Selby, then on through old pit villages. The smell of the glue factory at Bentley was less pleasant, but that, and Doncaster, were soon past. He headed out for the A1, and on and on... He arrived in Leicester exhausted but glowing. It had been another good but long day.

The next day was speedy and sunny too, so Brendan was soon past Northampton and Bedford. He gave a metaphorical wave to his distant ancestors in the graveyards at Henlow, Clifton, Shefford and Arlesey when he saw signs off the A6 for those places. His family had lived in these parts, working as farm labourers or straw-plaiters for several centuries until the 1870s, when an enterprising William Absalom Priest, Brendan's great-grandfather, ran off to Derbyshire to marry the lace-mill-owner's daughter after getting her pregnant. Further back the family tree included various criminals and also kings of England – because a female ancestor in the 15th century produced a son after a fling with the Lord of the Manor. Sex outside marriage was not a new phenomenon[33]. One of Brendan's earliest memories was hearing his Grandad boast that he was descended from a "long line of bastards" but his Mum hadn't been too impressed when the pre-school Brendan showed off his new word at the Church Playgroup.

Brendan continued through Luton and St. Albans to reach his destination for the evening: All Saints Pastoral Centre at London Colney, the location for the final part of his gruelling Ministerial Candidates Selection process – a 24-hour marathon of interviews, group work, worship and conversations. The ex-convent accommodation had been a bit ropey then, and was still a bit basic – but it reminded Brendan at the

---

[33] A snapshot of my own family tree.

start of his trek of the journey he'd been on for the last 26 years. The plumbing still banged, but he felt at home[34].

After a cholesterol-packed breakfast, he set off towards London, excited not just because he'd arranged to meet up with Ruth, who was flying in for a fundraising summit, but because of his other "date" for the evening. He negotiated his way through London, passing all the famous sights,and found himself on Old Kent Road, which brought back all kinds of Monopoly memories but looked less squalid than he'd imagined for the cheapest place on the board. He was still glad to move off into the suburbs and out through Rochester, Sittingbourne and Faversham towards his evening destination of Canterbury.

The day had been deliberately planned as easier than the others, only just over 100km, so that he would be able to arrive at Canterbury ready for 6pm and his live appearance on "See Esther". He arrived with an hour to spare, and met up with Ruth by arrangement at the Cathedral's south-west entrance. Brendan gave her a big hug, wheeled his bike into the Cathedral and sat in a tea-shop just opposite, where they enjoyed a cream tea and watched Dwight set up for the "live link". He seemed to have acclimatised to English weather and was full of bounce, having found a good spot where the Cathedral provided an impressive back-drop.

When 6pm approached, the live feed from Detroit came up on the large monitor and Brendan watched the opening credits roll and Esther promenade onto the set, beginning the programme with a catch-up piece about Brendan's last journey, before introducing Brendan's new journey, and showing footage of him leaving Cullercoats. Then suddenly Brendan saw himself on the monitor and realised that millions of people around the world were looking at him. He tried his best smile which looked a bit lop-sided so he waved at the camera instead and said hello.

"Tell me about the rules of this new challenge," said Esther. So he explained them. "Tell me what it's like getting back on a bike." He described his aches and pains. "Why are you doing all this again?" asked Esther, so he talked about his renewed sense of call. But then he hauled Ruth into the picture to give the information about Watoto which needed highlighting. Then it was back to Brendan.

"Tell me," said Esther, "how can people out there help you?"

"Well, I hope that the generosity of the viewers (which was so amazing last year) will come up trumps for me again. So, please – will you consider sponsoring me, so much per country visited, with 18 already under my belt from last time? It doesn't

---

[34] I have taken some liberties with the chronology here about the location for the Ministerial Candidates Selection Committee. MCSC was held for many years at All Saints, until its move in 2011 to High Leigh, Hoddesdon. But in Brendan's time it will have been held in one of the four Methodist Ministerial training colleges which existed at the time.

matter how big the amount is, but obviously the more the merrier for those needy children in Africa." That was as gushy as Brendan was prepared to be.

It was time for the final question, which had always in the past been a bit deeper, leaving the audience with something to reflect upon. "Tell me, Brendan, why are you pulling a little trailer around with you which describes you as "doing something about the Great Omission" – what does that mean?" On cue, Dwight panned in for a full view of the GO-kart.

Brendan hadn't expected that particular question, but it was a good opportunity to explain his deeper motivation. "It's all about highlighting where the Church has gone wrong in the past by centring its focus on itself. The Great Commission at the end of Matthew's Gospel clearly tells Christians to centre on other people, on our mission to all nations. We haven't really made that a priority and that, in my opinion, is the Great Omission. But there are two other strands to it as well. I'm hoping also to highlight the plight of Christians in countries where faith costs the most, because too many Christians also ignore their brothers and sisters in the Persecuted Church. The fundraising for Watoto highlights our responsibility to people in the third world, which is the Church's *other* Great Omission. Quite a lot to do something about, really... I hope I can be a symbol of what needs to be done, and I hope you'll all join me to make things a bit better."

Esther thanked him for the interview and said, "I believe you have a special supporter there with you, Brendan..." and Brendan, now rather embarrassed, stepped back as the camera panned round to the beaming figure of none another than the Archbishop of Canterbury[35], wearing, over the top of his purple clerical shirt, incongruously, clashingly, appallingly, a red tee-shirt with "Go, Brendan, GO" printed on it.

"Hello Archbishop," said Esther, "and that's the first time I think I've ever said that."

"Hello Esther," said the Archbishop, "and this is the first time I've ever been on an American chat-show, so it's a first for both of us."

Esther laughed. "If you don't mind me saying so, you aren't dressed much like an Archbishop."

"Well, I don't usually dress like this, but I wanted you all to know how much the Church supports Brendan's project – and this seemed a good way of doing that. I

---

[35] I have taken the liberty of giving roles to both the Dean at York Minster and the Archbishop of Canterbury. I hope the present incumbents don't object to me doing this. I have carefully avoided any description of the Dean or Archbishop to avoid personalising the role – except, I suppose, that I have assumed that the incumbents are male...

accept that the Church hasn't always done much about the Great Commission, but maybe Brendan will kick-start a new enthusiasm within the Church to take our role in God's mission more seriously. That's why we're going to commission Brendan in a special service in the Cathedral tonight and pray for a safe and successful journey."

Esther smiled, thanked the Archbishop and looked appealingly to the camera. "And now it's your turn, folks. I'll be encouraging y'all to follow Brendan's progress by coming out myself every month for a whole show devoted to this. Ruth will be there each month too to update us on how the sponsoring is going. I'd love it if you could help us by raising money for such a worthwhile cause. Ask your friends too. I've asked a few people in the broadcasting industry here in the States and we've already raised pledges of over $28,000 per country. The 18 countries Brendan has already visited mean that we've already raised over half a million dollars and there's still 176 countries to go! The guys with the calculators have told me that it will already be worth $5.5 million if Brendan completes his challenge. But..." (here she leaned forward into everybody's homes) "...I *know*, I just *know* that this is only the start."

The camera zoomed out, and Esther turned to a different camera and slickly introduced the next item on the show, which was about "our boys in Afghanistan". Brendan's bit was over – and it seemed to have gone well. He'd have to wait and see whether people responded.

The Archbishop and the Dean at York Minster had trained together, apparently, and were good friends, and that was how this commissioning service had come about. Brendan was really impressed that, with everything else that was happening in the Anglican Communion, the Archbishop still found time for him – and had even agreed to wear the tee-shirt. So Brendan and Ruth found themselves at 7.30pm sat in one of the stalls up in the Trinity Chapel, looking at the candle on the floor marking the spot where Thomas Becket was martyred, a shrine to which pilgrims like those in Chaucer's "Canterbury Tales" journeyed. Now he was a pilgrim too, listening to the Archbishop lead prayers for his safety and protection around the world, for Watoto and other Christian charities working in Uganda, and for present-day and future martyrs in the Persecuted Church.

Eric Tate from Open Doors had been able to get to Canterbury from the charity's base in Oxfordshire, and he too led prayers for Brendan's journey, particularly in going to countries where Christians faced persecution. Then Brendan knelt and the Archbishop and Eric laid hands on him and commissioned him, with the Archbishop reiterating Jesus' words at the Great Commission: "Go to all nations, therefore, discipling them, baptising them in the name of the Father and of the Son and of the Holy Spirit, and teaching them to obey everything I have commanded you. And be assured that I will be with you always, to the very end of the age." It was very humbling, and very special.

Brendan and Ruth were to stay in the Cathedral's hospitality suite that evening, but they went out for a pizza with Dwight, and had a good time chatting about Esther and life in general. When Dwight discovered that Ruth was married he seemed deflated, but focussed on Brendan instead to hide his embarrassment. He was intrigued by Brendan's "madventure" as he kept calling it, and Brendan found himself doing some "witnessing" even as they chatted in Pizza Hut. He also gave Dwight one of the special 194 Golden New Testaments (GNTs, as Brendan affectionately christened them, fond as he was of an occasional gin and tonic) – the one designated for the USA – and Dwight was really honoured that he should be its recipient. He opened it and read the printed inscription, which in each one was translated into the appropriate language:

Congratulations!

You are the owner of one of only 194 Golden New Testaments, one for each country of the world visited by Brendan Priest as part of his "Go, Brendan GO" journey.

GO stands for the Great Omission, for Brendan seeks to draw the attention of the worldwide Church back to the Great Commission of Jesus, which you can read at the end of Matthew's Gospel, and which the Church has so far omitted to fulfil.

This Golden New Testament may be worth a lot of money after Brendan's journey is over – but it is worth much more than that, for it contains the Word of God, as relevant now as when it was first written down two thousand years ago. Treasure it.

Brendan would love to hear how you progress on your journey of faith. Please contact him through www.go_brendan_GO.org.

Brendan had already posted the other 17 GNTs designated for those countries he'd already visited. He'd been saving the American one for Esther herself, but reckoned on the spur of the moment that Dwight was a more fitting recipient. The Canadian one had been sent off to Nannuraluk's little son, Brendan. The others had been sent off to various clergy whom Brendan had met in the various countries, but with the instructions that they should give the GNT away to the most appropriate recipient.

The following morning, Dwight's new word "madventure" seemed very appropriate, for it was pouring down again. Ruth went to the railway station to catch the train back to London, and on from there to Newcastle to stay for a few days with Louisa. Brendan sped off in the other direction, quickly reaching the ferry terminal at Dover, and had a comfortable and relaxed breakfast on the ferry as it sped off across the Channel. The windows were all steamed up, and there was nothing to see anyway, so he stayed inside and looked over some of the arrangements for the next few days. He was about to enter the first of the 176 new countries he was to visit in the next year. He'd no idea what lay ahead, but he was up for it.

Chapter 13: Nations 19 - 20

Brendan's destination that night was Arras, which held a special fascination for him. A while ago, researching his family tree, he discovered that Arras was where William Absalom Priest's son Nathan – Brendan's great-uncle – had been killed in the First World War[36]. A Lance Corporal in the Sherwood Foresters, he had been killed on 25th March 1916, though his body was never found. His was one of 35,000 names inscribed on the Arras Memorial in Faubourg D'Amiens Cemetery. Brendan's plan was to locate Uncle Nat's name on the Memorial and say a prayer there. As far as he knew, no-one from the family had ever visited Arras, so it seemed a really good God-incidence that Arras was exactly en route for him.

He found the whole place extremely moving. Arras was close to other battlefields and on the way down from Calais Brendan saw signs for various graveyards. Faubourg D'Amiens Cemetery consisted of rows of small white tombstones in perfect line, just as he'd expected. There were other monuments too but it was the size of the Memorial itself which took his breath away. Long columned porticos divided the various bays, each of which contained thousands of names. He found Uncle Nat's name surprisingly quickly in Bay 7, and stood silently in front of the inscription. Brendan's thoughts wandered to those currently being killed for their faith in various countries, laying down their lives if necessary for what they believed. Brendan didn't imagine that Uncle Nat had much choice about what he'd done, and so "courage" and "bravery" were maybe less accurate words for him than "obedient" and "terrified" – but that was true also of many modern martyrs in the church. They too found themselves in the wrong place at the wrong time. They, like Uncle Nat, could have turned and run away – but they hadn't, and that was well worth remembering and honouring.

The following day, Brendan sped off down various quiet, straight D roads heading towards Paris. He was scheduled to stop at the little town of Luzarches, 20km short of Paris, where he was giving his first public speaking engagement at the parish church. The Roman Catholic Church had once again come up trumps, offering Brendan high-profile speaking opportunities in various cathedrals on his journey – and in several parish churches too. The Pope himself had contacted each archbishop urging them to support Brendan's journey and they were jumping over themselves to show their generosity. So Luzarches would be followed by the cathedral at Orléans and then a few smaller churches before the cathedral at Toulouse – and that was just in France. There were many more cathedrals to follow.

---

[36] Again, a snapshot from my own family tree, and exact details of my great-uncle Nat's death and memorial.

The priest, who was called Hugo, introduced Brendan to the congregation after Mass and said that he would be translating while Brendan spoke. Brendan had prepared a talk some weeks ago which he hoped would suit most places, with local variations depending on the context. This was his first try-out, and he was a bit nervous.

He began by recapping his first journey, telling the story of how God was calling him to challenge the church in every place to witness in the spirit of Acts 8:1 – firstly to people similar to themselves locally (Jerusalem), secondly to people nearby who had very different lifestyles from theirs (Judea and Samaria), and thirdly to the ends of the earth. He told the stories of his encounter with the polar bears and of being stranded in the South Atlantic and given up for dead until his dramatic rescue. He thanked them for their prayers during that last sea-journey, because every Catholic diocese had called for special prayers at the request of the Pope himself. Then he asked them to pray for him again in this second adventure.

He described Esther's challenge – and when he mentioned her name he could see people's faces light up, especially the men's. He explained that the aim was to do something about the Great Omission, with its three-pronged emphasis on mission to all nations, solidarity with the poor and solidarity with the Persecuted Church, all of which the Church historically had failed to fulfil.

Then he told them what the next part of the journey consisted of. He hoped that after a few weeks he would be able to tell people stories of what had already happened to him, but didn't think that telling them about spray on the A19 would be of interest. He mentioned the work of Open Doors and Watoto, and about Ruth's fundraising for Gulu Bulrushes. He asked them to join in the worldwide sponsoring campaign and highlighted the website where they could get more information, pledge their support and chart his progress.

He encouraged them to think who their "Jerusalem" friends were, who their equivalents of Judea and Samaria were, and how they engaged with the rest of the world, before finishing with a prayer that they would engage in mission in all three "areas". Hugo then clapped enthusiastically to start the general applause and announced a retiring collection to support Brendan's fundraising for Watoto.

The vergers had been supplied with copies of a business card to be given out to everyone as they left. He had a plentiful supply, translated into the main language of every country on the itinerary till Cairo, when he would be re-supplied by Esther's team. He'd tried to calculate how many in each language he might need, but he had to lug these cards around in his GO-kart, so he'd erred on the lighter side. The business card looked like this:

Matthew 28: Jesus said, "Go to all nations..."

*Brendan Priest is going to all 194 nations
raising funds for orphans in Uganda
and other African countries*

please see **www.go_brendan_GO.org** *for further details*

The people filed out, collected their "business cards" and gave generously into the collection plates. Brendan was very pleased with how this first speaking engagement had gone.

The following day he skirted Paris and found the D road leading out towards Orléans. Despite his first puncture, the cycling was lovely, passing through a succession of sleepy villages. As he neared Orléans, his ears caught the traffic roaring along the main road from Paris before he saw the vehicles hurtling along a few kilometres to his left. He was glad for the quieter route, even though it meant extra distance.

Earlier in May, Fahada had emailed him in Cullercoats to say that she was sending a custom-built GPS unit and satellite phone on which he had to press a button at regular intervals each day of his journey. This automatically told him and Fahada's assistant in Detroit where he was and how far he'd come since the last recorded position. What it couldn't record, however, was which form of transport he was using, so at the end of each day he was to phone such details through to the answering machine back in Detroit. At each "See Esther" interview he would be told whether he was within the predictions and "percentage limits" for each mode of transport.

Orléans appeared on the horizon – the big towers of the cathedral looming over the other buildings, looking strangely similar in design to Notre-Dame Cathedral in Paris. The city was not as influential as it had been, and its main industry seemed to be taking advantage of the Joan of Arc tourist trade, with models of her rallying the city to repel the English and even of her being burnt at the stake. There was even, bizarrely, a Joan of Arc Steakhouse where presumably (this being France) their steaks were rare or medium/rare and definitely not burnt. The evening went smoothly, and the Dean seemed quite proud that he'd stacked up lots of points, but whether with the archbishop or the Pope or God was unclear.

Over the next few days Brendan stayed and spoke in the small towns of Châteauroux, Saint Germain des Belles and Espère, before arriving in the city of Toulouse. The days passed without much incident – except when he managed to get himself evacuated out of one priest's house rather hurriedly in the middle of the night when the fire alarm went off. Fortunately it was a false alarm but a befuddled Brendan went out barefoot and didn't realise that he'd trodden in some dog muck until he'd left a trail all the way back upstairs to his bedroom. His O-Level French was insufficient for him to understand fully what the priest's housekeeper had said about it the following morning, but perhaps that was a blessing.

Toulouse was a large, bustling city with modern buildings, designer shopping malls and a lop-sided Cathedral. It looked as if two different churches had been joined together, neither of which was complete. Everything, including the audience, was unsymmetrical – with a large group on one side of the church and only a few on the other. It was all rather odd.

Brendan arranged with the Dean of the Cathedral to store his bike and GO-kart at his house while he travelled by bus to his second new country, Andorra. Toulouse nestled at the foot of the Pyrenees, and Brendan had cleverly planned *not* to bike up into the mountains. Travelling there and back by bike would have used up two full days as well as a huge amount of strength and energy, so he was pleased to catch the Novatel bus from the centre of Toulouse and arrive three relaxed hours later in Andorra la Vella, the highest capital city in Europe at just over 1,000m. It was simultaneously a picturesque little town, a ski resort and a commercial centre, with modern glass-fronted shops and centuries-old churches side by side. Brendan liked the town, not just because it was journey's end for that day but because it was very compact and throbbing with a colourful mixture of tourists and locals. As the daylight faded, there was a beautiful sunset behind the mountains, the reflection of which shimmered in the water of the Gran Valira river. The evening talk in the Church of St. Stephen was well-attended and Brendan managed to give away all the rest of his French "business cards" and over 100 in Catalan too.

His bus back down to Toulouse was due to set off at 5am. As he prepared for bed, he realised that he'd forgotten to give away his Catalan GNT, so he got up well before dawn and set off for the bus station looking for a likely recipient. The only other person around was a street-sweeper, brushing the debris outside the clubs and bars into his cart before the morning traffic began. Brendan tried to give him the book, but the man shrugged his shoulders, jabbering something that could have been "I've got no money". Brendan showed him the Catalan inscription in the front of the GNT, and he took the book and read it slowly, pointing at each word with his finger before moving on to the next. He obviously didn't read very well, but when he got to the end he beamed, shook hands with Brendan and bowed his thanks. Brendan could see tears in the man's eyes, and felt that he'd chosen Andorra's recipient well.

As the sun rose and climbed into the cloudless sky, the bus took Brendan down the winding mountain roads to Toulouse, where he picked up his bike and GO-kart from the Dean's house and cycled off to the airport to catch the 11.05 flight to Nice.

And that was the point at which things started to go wrong.

Day: Date	Itinerary (* indicates TV interview) ([18]indicates new nation)	Bike (km)	Car/ Bus (km)	Train (km)	Kayak/ Sail (km)	Boat (km)	Air (km)
(18 nations already visited: Canada; USA; Mexico; Guatemala; El Salvador; Honduras; Nicaragua; Costa Rica; Panama; Colombia; Ecuador; Peru; Chile, Uganda; Argentina; UK; Iceland; the Vatican)							
Totals brought forward		0	0	0	0	0	0
1: 16/5/11	Cullercoats to York	132					
2: 17/5/11	Leicester	149					
3: 18/5/11	London Colney	139					
4: 19/5/11	Canterbury *	104					
5: 20/5/11	Arras, France[19]	125				40	
6: 21/5/11	Luzarches	150					
7: 22/5/11	Orleans	152					
8: 23/5/11	Chateauroux	135					
9: 24/5/11	St. Germain les Belles	155					
10: 25/5/11	Espère	148					
11: 26/5/11	Toulouse	148					
12: 27/5/11	Andorra[20]		185				
Totals carried forward		1537	185	0	0	40	0

Chapter 14: Assassination

The news broke early on May 26th, but Fahada didn't catch up with it until the lunchtime bulletins. She'd just been finalising the arrangements for Brendan's use of the chartered super-yacht in the Indian Ocean when she heard a snatch of news on her assistant's radio. Jayne had been told many times not to have the radio on at work, but she claimed that she couldn't concentrate without music playing, so Fahada relented, even though the inane Western music often drove her to distraction. They'd compromised on the volume being turned down low, so that for Fahada it was just a background murmur.

Fahada's hearing picked up a mention in the opening headlines of a senior al-Qaeda figure in Afghanistan having been killed by an American missile. Her heart suddenly started beating fast, and she concentrated all her attention on the announcement by the newsreader, who was jingoistic and triumphalist in tone[37]: "United States officials have confirmed earlier reports that the senior commander of al-Qaeda operations in Afghanistan has been killed, along with members of his family, in a successful US missile strike. This is probably the most serious blow to the terrorist movement since the US campaign against al-Qaeda began. The Egyptian-born Mustafa Abu al-Yazid, also known as Sheik Saeed al-Masri, was a founding member of al-Qaeda and the group's prime channel to Osama bin Laden and Ayman al-Zawahri. He was a key figure in day-to-day control, with a hand in everything from finances to operational planning, according to our sources in the US military..."

Fahada felt both faint and heavy. She slumped back in her chair, eyes and mouth open wide. She'd always been aware that this might happen, but hadn't really expected this day to come. Her oldest brother had proved indestructible over the years, from the earliest days in Egypt when he'd formed his friendship with al-Zawahri and joined one of his radical student groups. He'd built a power-base for himself in the three years spent inside an Egyptian prison after being linked to the group responsible for Sadat's assassination in 1981. He came out of prison with quite a following, much to their father's pride, but then disappeared to Afghanistan where he became one of the founding members of al-Qaeda. Fahada grew up with the knowledge that her brother, 26 years older than her and whom she'd met only very

---

[37] The news story about the killing of Mustafa Abu al-Yazid, the Egyptian-born leader of Afghanistan's Al- Qaeda programme was broadcast on the very day I was writing this chapter: 1st June 2010. The biography of Mustafa and the account of terrorist groups in Egypt described in this chapter and chapter 22 are accurate, except, of course, for his relationship with the fictional Fahada, and the activities of their fictional father. The text and tenor of the announcements are taken from the actual news on the day.

occasionally, was a hero fighting against the "evil empire" – as her father described the United States. She had six other brothers, but Mustafa was the favoured first-born who could do no wrong in their father's eyes.

Fahada had suffered a similar shock in 2008, when her brother was falsely reported killed, but she knew that this time the reports would be true. Indeed, almost in direct answer, the newsreader continued, "...American military sources thought they assassinated him in 2008 but he escaped. This time, however, al-Qaeda has given, without any details, confirmation via its propaganda wing Al-Sabah about the death of "the martyr", as they call him. Their website has claimed that "his death will only be a severe curse upon the infidels. The response is near. That is sufficient." What a chilling threat!"

Fahada tuned the rest of the bulletin out, though the voices droned on in the background. She wasn't interested in further details. It had happened, as she'd dreaded. Her father had told her in a rare secret phone conversation in 2007 that Mustafa had now risen to number three in charge of al-Qaeda, when his predecessor, Abu Ubaida al-Masri, had died of hepatitis in Pakistan. Fahada was very proud of her brother, who was like a mythical hero to her. What would she do now? And did this change anything for her? Was she going to be asked to play a part in avenging her brother's death?

She'd arrived in America in early 2001 via various other countries to mask her journey. Courtesy of her father's contacts, she carried a British passport and papers about working for an uncle in his North London grocery business. In reality she'd been recruited and groomed in Egypt as a trainee terrorist when her beauty and intelligence became apparent as a teenager. She was given crash-courses in computers, secretarial skills and basic espionage, then sent to the US as a sleeper for the radical Muslim group in Egypt with which her father was involved. She'd been frightened and lonely, but, obeying orders from her Egyptian "handler", had secured a job in a large media company.

Ten years on, Fahada sat in her office trying to gather her thoughts and emotions together. It was important that no-one saw her distress or made any kind of link. She'd always carefully avoided any question about her childhood or early adult life, shrugging it off with her cover story about life in Britain, and how boring it had been until she'd escaped to her new life in America. She traded on Americans' smugness reflex, triggered whenever anyone chose to join the "best nation in the world" for whatever reason, and no more questions had ever been asked.

She used her beauty to charm her way up the ladder at Oracle, and because of her indifference to all things sexual she didn't mind when Esther herself had started coming on to her. She revelled in all the sudden attention and pampering, convincing herself that it was on sufferance for the sake of her assignment, whilst knowing all along that she'd instantly loved the luxury and power that wealth brought, and wanted to safeguard her position at all costs. Esther was her ticket to continuing this opulent lifestyle, so whatever Esther wanted, Esther always got. Was it going to be different now? This awful news-story snapped her back to her original assignment, and particularly her responsibility to her family and to Allah.

Then she thought of Brendan and wondered whether she could sabotage his journey. Esther had entrusted his travel arrangements to Fahada, though she'd delegated to Jayne monitoring the distances and other minor details. She would have to be clever, because sabotage would have to be disguised as mistakes and attributed to Jayne, as Fahada didn't want to jeopardise her favoured position. She definitely didn't want to help Brendan achieve his target, because she didn't like the way in which Esther had gone all lovey-dovey about him. She recognised that Esther's sexual wiring, like her own, was complicated – and that she might well have yearnings for men as well as women, even ones as ugly and old as Brendan. He was nearly as old as Mustafa, she thought, which brought the lump to her throat once again.

She looked down Brendan's itinerary for how she could throw some spanners in the works, without drawing attention to herself – and spotted a few possibilities immediately. She'd been about to confirm alternative arrangements for Brendan's flight out of Toulouse, because Air France had announced a week ago that they were cancelling the May 28th Toulouse to Nice flight because of insufficient bookings. She'd been in the process of organising a private charter flight, but maybe now she would just leave Brendan to fend for himself...

Chapter 15: Nations 21 - 24

Brendan's morning in Toulouse started badly, but turned out well. It was but a foretaste of things to come. The first hiccup came when he contacted Air France about luggage restrictions, only to discover that they weren't flying to Nice at all that day. "Didn't you know that?" asked the man on the other end of the phone. "We always contact everyone who has booked on a flight we have to cancel."

Brendan was eventually assured, after nearly 20 stressful minutes looking at various possibilities, that he could join a group of pilgrims who were flying by special charter from Toulouse back to Nice after their highly-fruitful trip to Lourdes, which was about 150km west of Toulouse. Apparently one of the passengers forced to lie across three seats on the way to Lourdes would now be able to sit upright for the flight home, so two extra seats were now available. "They are all very happy for you to join them," said the Air France man. "I'm sure the person whom the Blessed Virgin healed will want to share his story with you."

Great, thought Brendan, who usually hated people talking to him on trains or planes, but then he chided himself for being so ungrateful and uninterested in how God had transformed someone else's life. Surely the very least he, a Minister, could do was to listen to someone's testimony – especially as he really needed the seat...?

He also needed to check with Fahada that the rest of his flights weren't going to be jinxed as well, so he phoned her up on his special satellite phone and asked her to look into it. She was purringly apologetic for the mistake which her assistant must have made with the flights, and promised that she would personally double-check all remaining travel arrangements.

When he got to the airport, he met up with the organisers of the Lourdes party, thanked them for their help and asked whether they had room for his luggage in the hold. "Don't worry about that!" he was told. "We've several wheelchairs that won't be making the return journey, so there's plenty of room for your stuff." Obviously the Blessed Virgin had been very generous with her blessing.

Fortunately for Brendan's English reservedness, most of the pilgrims seemed exhausted by their experiences either of Lourdes or of the coach journey back to the airport, and were fast asleep by the time Brendan got to his seat, and the flight took off on time at 1.05pm, only two hours later than his original flight. He knew that he'd plenty of flexibility that day, though, because from Nice he only had a short bike ride along the coast to his evening destination, Monaco.

It was pretty hot still in Nice by the time Brendan managed to get through the airport and resume his journey, even though it was mid-afternoon. He smeared himself liberally with suntan cream, but could still feel the heat on his arms, neck and thighs – and his cycling helmet was like a poultice on his head, but at least it kept his bald head from burning. There was surprisingly little traffic for a major route with such spectacular views, and no other cyclists. Perhaps they are sensible, Brendan thought. Mad dogs and Englishmen are the ones who go out in the midday sun, but Brendan hadn't seen any frothing canines yet, maybe because it was well past noon and they had probably all gone back in for a rest.

Less than two hours later, he was entering Monaco, and thus – another country ticked off on his list – added at least $28,000 to the Watoto kitty. At the Cathedral Brendan discovered that his visit coincided with that of the Archbishop of Marseilles, who was on his annual official check-up to see how everything was going, and was very excited that Brendan Priest from England was going to be there too, as the Archbishop was another "See Esther" fan.

The Cathedral was the final resting-place for most of the Grimaldi family, including Grace Kelly and her husband Prince Rainier. The sepulchral feel was enhanced by the white marble, but the atmosphere inside was rich and warm, especially in the sultry heat of a Mediterranean evening. Hundreds of people packed in and the evening was a great success, though it felt a bit odd having an Archbishop sitting in the big chair while Brendan gave his talk. A retiring collection netted the richest haul yet – nearly €4,800. Presumably some of the wealth of this tiny seaside principality had found its way into the church as well as into the casinos. The "business cards", translated into French, were handed out as people left. Brendan gave the GNT, translated not into French but Monégasque – a language almost extinct but now being re-introduced into schools – to a local headteacher.

Over dinner back at the bishop's house, the Archbishop asked about the GNT. "I noticed that you are using the New Revised Standard Version, whereas the majority of Christians in Europe are Roman Catholics and use the New Jerusalem Bible. Why choose a Protestant version?"

Brendan chose his words carefully. "It wasn't an easy decision and I discussed it at length with the Bible Society[38]. You may have heard that as part of their preparation for the 400th anniversary of the 1611 King James Version, the Bible Society dared to raise the subject of getting all the denominations to authorise just one version of the Bible."

---

[38] There are serious but protracted discussions between Protestant and Roman Catholic theologians about the most appropriate biblical translation(s) for the 21st century, and about using identical materials. An International Commission for Preparing an English-language Lectionary (ICPEL), under the chairmanship of Archbishop Coleridge of Canberra, was at the time of writing working to resolve these inconsistencies.

"But if we like it best," said the Archbishop, with a wink, "Why can we Roman Catholics not keep our own Jerusalem Bible and you keep your own, like we've done since you deserted the one true Church?"

Brendan was glad that the Archbishop had given (and that he'd spotted) the wink – it wasn't a serious jibe. He decided to go for it, and dived in: "Because no-one cares today about the old arguments of whether it's the Greek or the Hebrew text which should be translated, which was what caused the different versions in the first place, as you well know. The Bible Society believes that it's far more important for the Church to show unity as it re-establishes the Bible's position of authority and prominence."

"A good answer!" the Archbishop laughed. "But why *your* version not ours?"

Brendan didn't know how provocative the Archbishop wanted him to be, so he decided to give him the "official line". "It's because many different versions have been produced over the last 60 years, but none has usurped the place and authority of the King James Version, even though it's now very dated. Significantly, the Vatican implicitly acknowledged this by setting up a Commission under Archbishop Coleridge of Canberra to work out the inconsistencies between the new version of the KJV and your own authorised texts."

"I know," said the Archbishop. "Actually, I'm a member of the Coleridge Commission. I was just testing you." And he burst into laughter. "I've always liked the King James Version. It has such wonderful phrases, even though they were written by that heretic Tyndale." He chuckled, as if he were re-living with relish how the Vatican had had Tyndale strangled and burnt at the stake in 1536. "Of course the translation doesn't matter as much as the place that the Bible has in people's lives. How sad that people across Europe don't appreciate how central the Bible has been throughout our history! We in the Roman Church have a fondness for our Jerusalem Bibles, but then we liked the Rheims-Douai version before that. If the Holy Father commends a new version, I'm sure we'll submit. We usually do what we're told – eventually." He added that last word with another wink, opened another bottle of Rioja, and changed the subject. "Now, more importantly, do you think that your Wayne Rooney is anywhere near as good as our Thierry Henry?" He was definitely a trouble-maker, thought Brendan. And Thierry Henry was *ancient*.

***

Brendan's journey east along the Mediterranean coast the next day took him swiftly back into France and then, 10km further, into Italy, Nation 22. Another one off the list, once he'd spoken that evening in the little coastal town of Varazze.

The following three days of cycling through Italy were full of quiet roads and hot sunshine. The distances weren't dreadfully exhausting, but the conditions were. At lunchtime on the second day Brendan decided to have a longer stop for something to eat, and ended up sleeping under a tree for 2½ hours. He'd tried to find cover from the sun but when he woke up he had a willow-pattern tan on his arms and legs reminiscent of his Grandma's tea-set. He followed the SP1 all the way to Pisa, before branching inland to Firenze, which Brendan had always known as Florence.

Brendan didn't have much time to spare in Pisa, so he contented himself with a quick ride through the Piazza del Duomo – the wide, walled area at the heart of the city. Brendan's attention was drawn not so much by the famous Leaning Tower as by the Duomo Cathedral's claim to have one of the water-jars from Cana in which Jesus changed the water into wine. Soon he would be visiting Cana himself, and wondered how many "authentic" water-jars the various churches there claimed to have.

At Firenze, the capital of Tuscany, Brendan had a little longer. The historic centre contained numerous elegant piazzas, Renaissance palazzi, academies, parks, gardens, churches, monasteries, museums, and galleries – but Brendan counted himself a cultural quadriplegic, and had no yearning to visit all these supposedly remarkable places. All he wanted was a nice dinner, a pleasant evening speaking at the Cathedral, and a good night's sleep before the trek over the Apennines the next day.

The Cathedral, though, took his breath away. Its enormous brick dome was mind-boggling, especially when he learnt that it was the first ever built without either buttresses on the outside or a wooden frame on the inside. Apparently they'd considered buttresses politically incorrect because that was the way their northern enemies did it, and were too tight-fisted to buy any timber for the frame. Typical church politics and corner-cutting, thought Brendan ruefully. It was an achievement anyway, but even more so against such pettiness. His talk that evening seemed to echo round the huge empty space underneath Brunelleschi's dome, but it was an amazing and humbling experience. The audience were very appreciative and the Dean was gushingly grateful. Perhaps he was an Esther fan too.

Rising early, Brendan set off for the mountains, hoping to complete most of the climb before the sun reached its height. It took him 5½ hours of hard, physical graft but he made it right to the top of the Mandrioli Pass at 1,173m before he stopped for lunch. The scenery was wonderful and the road pretty deserted because of the recently-opened E45 motorway. It had been a steady slog up the Tuscan side, but after lunch the descent was steep, down craggy slopes with narrow sharp turns and short straight sections through a broken maze of rock faces, terraces and gorges. Brendan had a hard job keeping the bike on the road, and used his brakes unsparingly the whole way down into Bagno di Romagna before branching east to the San Marino border. Tired but exhilarated that one of the physically most demanding days of the whole journey was now behind him, he free-wheeled up to the neo-classical Basilica of San Marino, whose eight Corinthian columns made it look more like an ancient temple than a modern church.

Brendan had been intrigued by the small enclave of San Marino ever since as a lad he'd been given for his stamp collection a postcard sent from there by his Uncle Bob. It was the world's oldest republic, founded by a stone-cutter called Marinus who escaped the anti-Christian persecutions of the Emperor Diocletian and set up a place of refuge there in the hills for other Christians fleeing like him. Brendan thought back to the way in which the early church had spread throughout the Mediterranean area after the persecutions recorded in Acts 8:1, and wondered why tyrannical governments never cottoned on that the Church always grew and flourished when it was persecuted. This was borne out today by Open Doors, and the testimonies of Christians in countries where persecution of the Church was still commonplace.

Brendan moved under the portico of the Basilica, out of the hot sun, and wheeled his bike and GO-kart inside to stop them getting stolen. He explained who he was to a surprised elderly attendant, who promptly ordered him to leave his bike outside as if it was an abomination. The old man rushed off to get the priest, who was not so flustered about the bike, and told Brendan to wheel it down one of the three naves through the side-door of the apse into his own quarters.

"I'm sorry about the attendant's attitude to you bringing the bike in," said the priest in surprisingly fluent English. "He's a bit over-sensitive because a German tourist brought his motorbike into the church a few weeks ago, which resulted in more strict guidelines being issued."

Brendan shook his head in amazement – a motorbike! The priest laughed. "It wouldn't have been so bad if he'd just wheeled it in, but he rode it in."

Brendan was astonished at the thoughtlessness of it all – but that still wasn't the end of the story. "And that wouldn't have been so bad," said the priest, "if I hadn't been saying Mass at the time, and several of the communicants got a bit upset."

The priest made Brendan very welcome, asked him to stay there overnight, and explained that most of the better hotels would be full anyway, as there was always a glut of tourists in San Marino – either Italians seeking the cool mountain air or foreigners buying souvenirs proving that they had been there. They would dine at a local restaurant after the talk, because the evening air was delightful and no-one ate until much later anyway. Brendan used the priest's computer to send off a few emails.

The talk went well, and Brendan was particularly pleased that the attendant was "in attendance" once again, but this time with a smile for Brendan not a scowl. He was the recipient of the San Marino GNT, which surprised and thrilled the old man. The "business cards" distributed, the retiring collection locked into the priest's safe, they went off into the darkness for dinner. The restaurant was in a narrow street just across from the Basilica, but they were led through to the back of the building, where a balcony looked out over the twinkling carpet of lights towards Rimini and the black bulk of the sea beyond. It was magical, and the Risotto Fantasia that Brendan ordered was just as good. So was the wine – all three bottles of it between the two of them.

Bizarrely, Brendan dreamt that night of Fahada wearing only a windswept veil, wielding a huge scimitar as she crossed the room towards him. He woke up in a fright, vowing to drink less in future.

***

The long, winding descent down to Rimini was followed by eight hard hours through the fertile lowlands to the small town of Corbola on the banks of the river Po. It was a long way, but over-egging the distances today meant a longer time to explore Venice tomorrow. Brendan had managed to arrange over the phone for the priest in Corbola to host an evening's meeting, at which Brendan passed the Italian GNT onto a young couple married in the church two weeks previously.

The next day started early with a leisurely pedal across the Viadotto Po, the long road-bridge high above the river, followed by more of the same as yesterday: long stretches of straight road between small towns, until six hours later, Brendan cycled along the Della Liberte into the centre of Venice, 80km from Corbola. He'd never been to Venice, and was sorry that he could only spend two hours there because he still had a further 68km to his overnight destination in Portogruaro. Cycling slowly through the narrow streets to the famous Rialto Bridge over the Grand Canal, he followed the signs to the Basilica of St. Mark, amazed at the masses of tourists – and locals keen to make a living from them. The square was heaving, and Brendan sat down by the waterside to rest and view the lagoon. He dangled his cycle helmet off the handlebars while he mopped his brow – only to discover that his helmet vanished. He saw a small boy scurrying off through the crowds but knew that it would be useless to give chase. Welcome to Venice, he thought. Or rather... you're *welcome* to Venice. He didn't bother going in the Byzantine basilica itself in case his bike and GO-kart disappeared, and looked longingly at the adjoining prison of the Doge's Palace, thinking that it ought to be re-opened for certain Venetian children.

Leaving the crowds behind, he entered a dark labyrinth of narrow passageways, alleys, canals and delicate bridges, chancing upon Campo Santa Maria Formosa, the home of another explorer, Marco Polo. Brendan would be visiting some of the Asian cities Marco reached in the course of his 24 year, 24,000km journey, but if Brendan travelled at the same pace he would be over 200 years old before he finished.

He finished his little tour back at the Rialto Bridge, and pedalled slowly across the Della Liberte, turning east onto the SS14 which took him all the way to Portogruaro. He didn't count the 20km Venice detour in his official log, but it had still been a long, long day – officially 148km, but, more tiringly, 14 hours in the saddle.

He was getting a bit saddle-sore now, and was looking forward to Rijeka, the end of this cycling "leg". But there was still a day and a half to go, so he set off resolutely, trying to ignore the chafing which was making life a little unpleasant down below.

This last stretch was not going to be dreadfully difficult, with easier distances and straightforward route-finding, but it was getting a bit tedious. The inland route via Trieste took him into Slovenia and he stopped for the night at Obrov so that he could get a "witnessing opportunity" in his eighth new nation.

It had all been arranged some weeks before, but Brendan was obviously the most exciting thing to happen in Obrov for ages. The local priest flapped around worriedly as if Brendan was the archangel Gabriel come to inspect how well he'd been doing, but he needn't have worried. The little Church of the Annunciation was only one of several in the Hrušica Parish, but the priest must have recruited folk from the other villages, because it was packed inside. For a village with officially (Brendan learnt) only 187 inhabitants, the turn-out of 250+ was astounding. There were even flags flying in the streets – though, looking at the state of them, Brendan wondered whether they were the same that had flown on Independence Day in 1991, or even when they became part of Yugoslavia in 1943.

The official language was Slovene, but thankfully the priest translated the talk and the evening was a great success. Brendan had shown the priest the Slovene GNT beforehand, and asked him who should be the recipient. So, just before the end of the evening, the priest led Brendan into the packed congregation and introduced him to a very old lady called Josepina who was the grandmother of Benka Pulko[39], whom Brendan had never heard of but was apparently one of the most famous women ever. He learnt that she held the world record for the longest solo motorbike ride ever: 180,000km in 2,000 days. Brendan saw the obvious travelling link, and was grateful for it, but the toothless old lady seemed pleased with the GNT and that was all that really mattered. The priest later told Brendan that Benka had been Slovenian Woman of the Year in 2003 and was the first motorcyclist to reach Antarctica. Brendan wondered how she could have reached Antarctica on a motorbike, but the language difficulties prevented further investigation.

The following morning, it was only 12km to the Croatian border, and only a further 32km to Rijeka itself, which Brendan reached, as planned, by 11am. There, by the waterfront, he met Borut, the key person for the next stage of his journey.

Borut was not, however, quite what Brendan had been expecting.

---

[39] Every reference to Benka Pulko is factual, except for her grandmother.

Day: Date	Itinerary (* indicates TV interview) ([18] indicates new nation)	Bike (km)	Car/ Bus (km)	Train (km)	Kayak/ Sail (km)	Boat (km)	Air (km)
Totals brought forward		1537	185	0	0	40	0
13: 28/5/11	Monaco[21]	18	185				466
14: 29/5/11	Varazze, Italy[22]	156					
15: 30/5/11	La Spezia	142					
16: 31/5/11	Firenze	146					
17: 1/6/11	San Marino[23]	145					
18: 2/6/11	Corbola, Italy	160					
19: 3/6/11	Portogruaro	148					
20: 4/6/11	Obrov, Slovenia[24]	118					
Totals carried forward		2570	370	0	0	40	466

Chapter 16: Discrimination

Back in Cullercoats, Louisa was adjusting well, she thought, to being on her own again – though the house in Beverley Terrace was huge for just one person. She enjoyed playing the Lady of the Manor, but it would help to have servants to do the work. She was sharing this thought one night with her boyfriend Ben as they dined out at Mama Rosa's, the Italian restaurant just along the road above Cullercoats Bay.

"I could be your servant," said Ben, with a smile.

Louisa giggled, light-headed after a bottle and a half of Frascati. "Ben! You naughty boy – I didn't mean anything like that!"

"Nor did I," said Ben, reddening. "What I meant was that I'm paying nearly £90 a week for my dingy flat in Whitley Bay while you're rattling around in a huge house moaning about the housework. I'm sure that we could come to a better arrangement." Just as Louisa was about to reply, he quickly added, "And I don't mean us sleeping together. Much as I love you, I'd rather wait until we're married for that."

Now it was Louisa's turn to blush. "Gosh, Ben. That almost sounded like a proposal..."

Ben reached across and took her hand. For a split-second she panicked, thinking that he might get down on one knee – but he didn't. "Well, Louisa... I really do think that you're the one for me – but I don't want to rush into anything. We've only known each other for eight months, so I don't think we should take that step till we're both absolutely sure. Let's see how we go, eh? But I'd love to rent a room while your Dad's away. What do you think?"

Louisa was thrilled. Before Ben came along she'd begun to despair a bit about blokes. She'd enjoyed a raucous social life since cutting free from parental control as a teenager, which meant that she'd made mistakes – though she hadn't been prepared to admit that to anyone until a year ago, when she started to look seriously again at Christianity and realised that she should exercise some self-control or she'd end up in a mess. She never imagined that she might end up with a Christian boyfriend – the ones she'd known had all been geeky and spotty. But then she went last August to Greenbelt and saw Ben perform as part of a beatboxing group, only to discover the next month that he was working at her Dad's old church in Jact and they'd met and clicked. And now he was moving in...

"Ben, that'd be great. I'd love that. The bottom floor, as you know, is full of boxes from our moving in, so we could clear that and you'd have it all to yourself. Unless, of course, you wanted to invite a guest sometimes..." She wasn't very good at being coy and the two of them burst out laughing.

They walked arm-in-arm down the road. Louisa wanted Ben to sleep over on the sofa but he had an early start the following morning at Whitley Bay High School, so he wobbled off on his bike to his flat, leaving Louisa to soak in a hot bath.

She really was thrilled to bits with Ben, and thought like he did that this was The Real Thing. She was coming round to the view that sleeping together should only happen after you'd made a commitment to each other, though still couldn't see why that had to be marriage. She'd been brought up with that traditional Christian teaching drummed into her, but it had been like a red rag to a bull and catapulted her into experience after experience just to assert her freedom. She regretted some of it now, but felt that maybe the way in which she was wired meant that she needed to experiment in order to find what she really wanted. And, curiously, that haphazard route had brought her back to Christianity... and to Ben. Thank you, God.

She was happy with everything except her job. In fact, worries about her job dominated her thoughts even more than Ben, which showed their seriousness. They swept over her now, as she relaxed in the bubbles. For four years she'd been working in the Cardiovascular Unit at Freeman Hospital[40], and loved it – but was starting now to feel that she should move. She knew that she was good at her job, and especially at getting alongside the patients. She herself had been in hospital a few times as a teenager, sorting out some early ovarian cysts and having her appendix out – and these experiences taught her what a difference it made when nurses were friendly rather than aloof.

In the unit she dealt mostly with transplant patients, some of whom were young and all of whom were scared. She felt that she really made a difference to them, chatting and laughing with them as she eased them through the speedy preparations and helping them adjust to the slow aftermath of the operation, explaining the anti-rejection drug therapy and being their friend through the physical recuperation. Whilst she liked chatting with older patients, she felt herself best suited and drawn to the younger ones where she felt that she had a special rapport.

But now she was getting a bit restless. Every day was different, and most of the patients were lovely, but she was always the one being told what to do. She'd always had a problem with authority, and wondered if she ought to try for a more senior post. But doing what? She didn't want another branch of adult nursing. She wasn't put off by the dirty stuff – clearing bed-pans or vomit and washing patients was care given as part of the relationship formed with them in her relatively small unit – but in a general adult ward there was never the opportunity to spend much quality time with

---

[40] The Cardiothoracic Centre at Freeman Hospital has a wonderful reputation. I have no knowledge of the staff there, but Sister Lilian is an entirely fictional character, so any possible resemblance is the product of your own imagination.

the same few people, and it didn't appeal at all. She'd done most of her placements in such wards and hated it – especially because the other staff usually hated it too and took it out on the patients and each other. She didn't want to jump from a comfortable but frustrating frying-pan into an uncomfortable but better-paid fire.

She'd enjoyed one Mental Health placement during her training – in a secure unit for schizophrenics, meeting one man who thought he was Henry the Eighth and another who'd murdered his children. She'd listened, befriended and really cared for each of them, especially the murderer who was really gentle now that medication controlled his illness, yet knew that he'd be institutionalised for the rest of his life. It made Louisa sad, and that was part of the reason why she'd concluded that Mental Health wasn't really her calling.

She wondered about working with children, but wasn't sure whether she could cope emotionally. She'd been really upset in her own unit after a teenage patient whom she'd befriended had her transplant cancelled at the last minute because the harvested organ proved incompatible. She'd wept inconsolably a few days later when the patient died, so how would she manage with little children?

She'd probably be content just to trundle on, throwing herself into her work and still getting a huge buzz out of the patients, if it wasn't for one colleague who was making her life hell. One Sister, called Lilian Hood but forbidding anyone to call her Sister Hood because "I'm not a bloody nun", hated everything religious, refused entry onto the unit to any visiting chaplains unless it was open visiting hours, refused to have the times of worship in the hospital chapel displayed on the notice-board, and had all the Gideon Bibles removed from the lockers until a member of Gideons International was admitted to the unit and threatened to sue the hospital if they weren't put back. It'd been OK till a year ago. The Sister was bossy and loved throwing her weight around, but she'd treated everyone the same, but since Louisa started wearing a fish symbol, she'd been targeted for special attention.

The NHS policy about religious jewellery and clothing had come up repeatedly in the national press. There had been a recent campaign in the Daily Mail[41], because Muslim doctors and nurses had been allowed to wear long sleeves, even though there was a strict and proven NHS dress code of "bare below the elbow" to prevent the spread of deadly superbugs such as MRSA. The no-jewellery rule had been relaxed to let Sikhs wear Kara bangles as long as they could be pushed up above the elbow when dealing with patients. A Christian nurse, however, lost her discrimination battle against a Hospital Trust which claimed that the tiny silver cross round her neck was a hazard because it might scratch patients. This contrast between a petty rigidity

---

[41] I have tried to represent the Daily Mail campaign accurately. The case of the Christian nurse is similar to the real-life case of Shirley Chaplin, who lost her case at an Employment Tribunal on 6th April 2010.

towards Christianity and questionable flexibility towards other faiths didn't end there. The Employment Tribunal rejected the Christian nurse's case on the grounds that her cross was not a *requirement* of her faith, but the Daily Mail made much of their discovery that the Koran was unclear on whether Muslim women were *required* to wear long sleeves at all times.

Most of the staff in the hospital wore discreet jewellery of one sort or another – and Louisa had seen other nurses in the canteen wearing a fish symbol so there couldn't be an official ban. Sister Lilian kept telling her to take it off, and whilst Louisa did so to keep the peace she still kept wearing it at the start of every shift just to make the point. The other staff recognised that Louisa was now getting far more than her fair share of the dirty jobs and encouraged her to speak to the Union about it.

Caridad Diego, still the Minister at Jact until the summer, had recently preached a series of sermons about outreach at work. He was a great advocate of being seen and known as a Christian wherever you were, and encouraged the folk at Jact to be much pushier about their faith at work. One particular Sunday he'd preached about not hiding your light under a bushel. Louisa didn't know what a bushel was, but got the message.

Caridad, in his usual flamboyant preaching style which involved lots of arm-waving, had gone into oratory-overload: "How come no-one bats an eyelid at Sikhs wearing turbans or Jews with those prayer-cap things (he didn't know the correct terminology, but everyone knew what he meant), and we now even have women walking around Whitley Bay in those Muslim outfits where you can only see their eyes (he obviously wasn't familiar with burqas either or the whole concept of purdah, but again everyone knew what he meant)? But if a Christian wears a cross or a fish or has a sign on the back of their car then everyone thinks they are fanatical! Be proud of your faith, my brothers and sisters! Be proud of Jesus!" He'd bought in a consignment of fish badges and given them out, explaining that this had started out as a secret sign by which Christians were able to recognise each other in times of persecution, but which had become a discreet sign to non-Christians that the person wearing it was a person of faith. Louisa had started wearing it for work the next day, and felt rather proud of herself as well as her faith, especially when Sister Lilian made her take it off.

She wondered how best to be a Christian at work. She would never assert her beliefs on any patient unless she was asked what she believed, but felt that she shouldn't just give in to the prejudices of this bolshy Sister who was making her job difficult and frustrating. Should she do a Shirley Chaplin and make a stand – or would that just alienate her from everyone else and have her branded a fanatic, even though she wasn't? Should she show the humility and deference to authority that the Bible also encouraged? Should she gently keep pushing without confrontation, building a rapport with sympathetic colleagues so that Sister Lilian became alienated – or was that cruel? Maybe she should bring the whole subject up with the Sister without being aggressive and see if they could find a way forward?

Chapter 17: Nations 25 - 28

Brendan knew that he would be sailing with a luxury catamaran charter company called Split the Difference which operated out of... Split. Oracle had paid for the Privilege 585 to sail up the day before from Split on a week's charter, skippered by Borut Belobrajdic, complete with its own chef and an extra deck-hand.

What Brendan had *not* been told was that Borut was a rather portly gentleman who wore women's clothes.

Brendan had not exactly had a sheltered upbringing, but he was a bit flummoxed at the sight he encountered in the harbourmaster's office in Rijeka. Borut was dressed in a long shiny gold dress with naval epaulettes and, extending a hand full of jewellery for him to shake, said in a deep baritone voice something that sounded horribly like "Hello, sailor. I'm going to take you away for a few days of fun."

The harbourmaster grinned insanely behind Borut's gold lamé back. Brendan on impulse shook Borut's hand with the most muscular grip he could muster. "Pleased to meet you," he growled in a deep bass voice which was as artificial as Borut's campness.

They left the office and Borut minced along the quayside to an incredibly posh-looking catamaran called Helena. They both stepped on board – well, Borut hopped on board with a little cry – and Brendan stepped down into the large saloon, furnished with two bright-white leather sofas and an armchair clustered around a coffee table, and a bar which seemed to be very well-stocked. There were bookshelves across the far wall but wide windows all around giving a panoramic view of the harbour. It was a boat for the seriously rich, and must have set Oracle back over $10,000 for the week.

His cabin was one of four, each of which had a queen-size bed and ensuite bathroom. He noted with some relief that each bedroom had a lock on the door. As Borut was showing him round, he was introduced to a young couple called Celestina and Malik, who were the chef and deck-hand and very much in love, if the naked embrace they were indulging in when Borut opened the door of the staff quarters was anything to go by. It was going to be an interesting trip.

Borut showed him the vessel's glossy brochure, and Brendan read all kinds of technical data which didn't mean much to him, except that it was powered by two 150HP Yanmar engines, which at that point fired up and Brendan shot back in his chair as they power-boated out into the harbour. He rushed out, shouting, "No engines!" Borut looked at him as if he was simple. "No engines!" he repeated, and explained that this leg of his journey had to be by sail, because he could only do so many kilometres under engine-power. Borut shrugged. "I need engine get out of harbour safe, then – no engines!" And he saluted as he gave a passable, if rather camp, impersonation of Brendan. The engines were duly cut, the sail unfurled and set with a crack as the gentle breeze filled it, and they were swept forwards more quickly than Brendan would have thought possible.

"Is good, eh?" said Borut, sidling up and putting an arm round Brendan's shoulders.

"Yes, very good, thank you," said Brendan as he moved sharply away. Borut laughed.

The cabin to which Brendan retreated had every luxury imaginable: air conditioning or heating, drinks refrigerator and ice-maker, TV, CD and DVD unit, internet satellite connection, jacuzzi, silk bed sheets. If he could keep Borut away, he'd have a good time.

They sailed out into the Adriatic. Even though this part of the Dalmatian coastline was peppered with islands, with the autopilot on and the radar sweeping round to make sure that nothing stood in their way, all the crew were sunning themselves on deck. Celestina kept nipping down into the galley and rustling up pastries, cocktails or cakes, and then returning to sunbathe topless on the cabin roof.

The catamaran whizzed silently through the water, propelled by the wind in the huge sail. Borut sat down opposite Brendan at one point and explained about the speed of any sailing boat being dependent on several factors, including, but not limited to, wind speed, water conditions, and hull drag. Brendan was not really well-versed in nautical matters and hoped that hull-drag was a reference not to nautical transvestism but how many barnacles it had. Borut's accent was so terrible that he wasn't sure that he caught it all, but it went something like this: The higher the wind-speed, the faster the boat would go, except that it then bounced because the waves were bigger, and as a result, slowed down. So you had one force trying to speed you up, and one trying to slow you down. When Borut tried to explain that hull speed (in knots) was 1.34 times the square-root of the waterline (in feet)[42], Brendan gave up. To show interest, though, he foolishly asked why catamarans were quicker than ordinary boats – and Borut got very excited.

"Ah, my friend, is all to do with weight. Catamaran is lighter because no need for keel counterweight since gap between hulls give more stability, so less displacement and drag. Wider beam mean can carry more sail than monohull without tippy-over, and also sail stay upright in strong wind, so more power than leany-over sail of monohull..." But when Borut droned on about the hydrodynamic drag coefficient being reduced in a less bulbous hull design, Brendan's eyes glazed over and he found himself watching Celestina rubbing on suntan lotion. Several minutes later he realised that Borut was still explaining about speed variations. "...so coastal waters is best for catamaran, because sheltered water mean boat reach and keep top speed easier."

---

[42] I hope that the details about catamarans in particular and sailing in general are accurate. They are the product of research not personal knowledge.

"Yes, we've done well today, haven't we?" said Brendan, trying to hide the fact that he'd been indulging in mental tourism (his mind had wandered off).

"Not well," Borut replied. "Only 15 knots average, so not finish today for dinner till 7pm."

They anchored off Vir, an idyllic setting for dinner, with the sunset resplendent, the stars twinkling, the moon reflecting on the quietly lapping water – and a fully-clothed Celestina serving them a very exotic meal of cuttlefish risotto, followed by lobster salad and savijača (a sort of apple strudel) to finish. And plenty of wine. The evening got hazier and hazier, but Brendan endured Borut's Marlene Dietrich impersonation before negotiating the passageway to his cabin, carefully locking the door behind him, collapsing on the wonderful bed and falling instantly asleep, despite Borut continuing to sing "Falling in love again" – presumably to himself.

They had been sailing for some time the next day when Brendan staggered out of his cabin, to find Borut sporting an indelicate pink outfit and struggling to hold onto his matching admiral's hat with the wind blowing hard in the wrong direction. "Not good, Brenda!" he said. Brendan wondered whether he'd deliberately given the feminine version of his name to provoke a reaction, but he didn't bite.

"What does it mean?" asked Brendan, hoping that he wouldn't get a long explanation.

"It means not quick," said Borut. "But is no problem. We still make Split by dinner. Just work harder."

Brendan realised that they were no longer sailing in a straight line, but tacking from side to side to catch as much of the wind as they could, with the sail positioned cleverly to take them diagonally forwards. There was some buffeting from the choppier waves, but nothing that seriously rocked the boat either literally or metaphorically.

It wasn't exactly sunbathing weather, so Brendan stayed in the saloon, looking over the travel itinerary and sending some emails. Malik seemed to be doing all the work, and Celestina explained that Borut always tried to have a sleep in the afternoon if he had an evening gig. When they arrived in Split in late-afternoon, Borut duly appeared with full make-up, wearing a long sequinned dress and feather boa, and waltzed off the boat singing "Just a Gigolo", which might have been a hit for Marlene Dietrich but probably wouldn't, in Brendan's opinion, sell many records for Borut.

Brendan headed off in the opposite direction for the Cathedral of St. Duje, whose tall Romanesque bell-tower could be seen from the harbour. The priest-in-charge tried to give Brendan a history lesson about it being built over Diocletian's mausoleum but not much of it went in, like Borut's hydrodynamic theories. Perhaps Brendan was getting too old for his grey cells to stretch and exercise like they used to.

Back on the boat after a successful evening, Brendan was woken in the early hours by Borut returning with more Marlene Dietrich songs. Brendan thought blearily that one was called "The Boys in the Back Room" but that may have just been his imagination running riot about what Borut had been up to.

The following morning they sailed effortlessly down the coastline, the wind at their backs, the sail full, confirming Borut's analysis that coastal waters gave a catamaran its maximum speed capabilities. They glided past various towns before reaching Neum by mid-afternoon. Bosnia and Herzogovina had proved one of the most difficult countries to get into the itinerary, and it was decided that Neum was the easiest way to access it, even though it meant a long sail round the Trpanj peninsula. There was only a 24km long strip of Bosnia and Herzogovina on the Adriatic, splitting Croatia into two, with the small port of Neum in its centre.

Brendan and a violet-catsuited Borut jumped off the catamaran into the dinghy and rowed into the harbour. Brendan went off with his Bosnian GNT and a few cards printed in Bosanski, the distinctive local dialect of Serbo-Croat. At the little Roman Catholic Church high up on the hill, he spoke to the housekeeper in the presbytery, who informed him that the priest was on holiday – presumably another communications foul-up. Brendan showed her the cards explaining his mission and, not knowing what else to do, gave her the GNT, with its inscription open. When she read it, she clasped the New Testament to her rather huge bosom and then flung her arms round Brendan and gave him the same treatment. Brendan had once been on a water-bed and it was a similar sensation, and similarly unpleasant. He beat a hasty retreat, and made his way back to the harbour through streets strewn with seedy-looking hotels. He assumed that if the country only had one coastal town, it would inevitably end up looking like Morecambe.

Back on the boat, Borut set sail back up the straits, tacking against the wind, before resuming an easier passage down to their overnight destination, 30km north of Dubrovnik, where they dropped anchor in the little bay where the Prapratno-Sobra ferry docked. Sobra was the main entry port of Otok Mljet, one of the most popular holiday islands in the Adriatic, but Prapratno was little more than a quay. Ston, 30 minutes' walk for Brendan across the peninsula, had a shop and a church, at which he was due to speak that night. But when he knocked at the house adjoining the church, the priest himself answered but looked rather bemused, even when Brendan showed him a Croatian "business card". Somehow the communications seemed to have messed up again, and no-one was expecting him, least of all the priest. He was invited inside, and said that he was expecting to speak in the church that evening, but the priest shrugged his shoulders and shook his head. It was pointless trying to press the matter, especially with the language difficulties, so Brendan trudged back to the boat, had a leisurely relaxed dinner, and enjoyed his unexpected night off with the CD collection in his cabin, played at a sufficiently high volume to drown out Marlene Dietrich next door.

The following morning, they set sail again in a following breeze, coasting down past Dubrovnik and out of the lee of the offshore islands. The sea was fairly placid, however, and they maintained a decent speed for the rest of the day. Around midday, Borut shouted, "Is Montenegro" – but it looked the same as Croatia. The afternoon dawdled by, with the blue sky giving more opportunity for sunbathing. Brendan noted that Celestina wore a bikini now that she was out of Croatian waters. They stopped at Ulcinj, the southernmost port of Montenegro, and Brendan hopped ashore and made his way to the church, only to find a similar story to the previous evening – no-one knew about him and nothing was planned. The priest seemed very apologetic, and pleased to receive the GNT printed in the Montenegran dialect of Serbo-Croat, but again there was no possibility of a greater "witnessing" so Brendan returned to dinner and the CD collection on the boat once again. His GPS told him that they had sailed 563km since Rijeka, and it had been very restful and luxurious. Something odd was happening in the arrangements, though. He tried to contact Fahada but couldn't get through, so left a message.

Over breakfast on his last day on board Helena, Brendan gave Borut the Croatian GNT. He'd been wondering about this for a time, and decided that he would be a worthy recipient. Borut looked at him a bit strangely, but then gave him a big hug, whispering, "I treasure muchly."

By 10am they'd docked at Lezhe☐ in Albania, and Brendan stepped ashore, waved goodbye, checked in at the harbour office and customs point and headed for the Hertz office to pick up his hire-car to take him all the way to Istanbul. The trouble was that there wasn't a Hertz office in Lezhe☐. In fact, there wasn't *any* car-hire place at all. He was getting a bit cheesed off with the inaccuracy of his travel arrangements, and phoned Fahada up. He immediately sensed a defensiveness in Fahada but she promised to look into these latest glitches. She put him on hold while she arranged for a 4x4 to be driven over from Tirana's Mother Teresa Airport, just half an hour away to the south-east. But when it arrived it wasn't a 4x4 but a little hatchback. The driver smiled, shrugged his shoulders and kicked the tyres, as if to say that it would be OK up in the mountains, but Brendan wasn't convinced. Albania had only recently emerged into modern times after its difficult four decades under Enver Hoxha, but was still desperately poor and finding it difficult to catch up with the rest of Europe. Brendan gave the driver $20, which made him smile even more, and the Albanian GNT, which made him cry. Brendan was deeply touched as the man reached inside his shirt and pulled out a crucifix which he kissed and put back inside his clothing.

Brendan didn't have much alternative except to get into the Opel Corsa and drive away. There was an interesting rattle somewhere in the engine which didn't bode well for the next few days.

Day: Date	Itinerary (* indicates TV interview) ([18] indicates new nation)	Bike (km)	Car/ Bus (km)	Train (km)	Kayak/ Sail (km)	Boat (km)	Air (km)
Totals brought forward		2570	370	0	0	40	466
21: 5/6/11	Vir, Croatia[25]	44			144		
22: 6/6/11	Split				158		
23: 7/6/11	Ston, via Bosnia[26]				198		
24: 8/6/11	Ulcinj, Montenegro[27]				163		
Totals carried forward		2614	370	0	663	40	466

Chapter 18: Consternation

As Jack Turner, District Chair, opened his post, his blood boiled at the way in which ministry was being squeezed to support mission. He knew that mission was important, but he'd been brought up in the belief that you had to look after the church because a strong church would attract others to join. So, whilst he knew it was both/and rather than either/or, he felt that the balance was swinging too heavily in one direction.

He had seen the point of the Methodist Conference making Districts employ Evangelism Enablers, because it saved him from having to bang the drum for mission, so he could concentrate on ministry (and Ministers in particular). He'd managed to get a DEE who was really bouncy and engaging – a good investment even though it was another good Minister unavailable for Circuit ministry. But recently Conference had told each District to employ a DDE – a District Development Enabler – to help the whole Church manage change and implement the stated priorities of the Church. It was all part of "Mapping the Way Forward: Regrouping for Mission" which was laudable but initially was getting bogged down with geography and personnel redeployment rather than projects which might make a difference. But again, it was another competent Minister, taken out of Circuit ministry, who'd become DDE. Given the shortage, Jack wondered whether the Church could afford to take out quality Ministers for a more hit-and-miss ministry across the District.

Much to his frustration he'd now received a proposal for something called the Pioneering Ministries Scheme, which claimed it was a bold and exciting initiative. Under the heading "ventureFX"[43] these "pioneers" would establish Fresh Expressions among young adults with no Christian heritage "within a culture of holy risk-taking". *More* skilled Ministers, especially those with some fire in their belly, were to be taken out to resource this trendy Fresh Expressions will-of-the-wisp. "Pah!" yelled Jack, hurling the paper into his in-tray.

He continued opening his post, only to find more of the same in the next letter from the DEE, asking for advice about a proposal from Caridad Diego at Jact, who wanted District support to establish a project called Tubestation, a Fresh Expression for surfers, at Tynemouth, based in Crusoe's Café on Longsands beach. Apparently

---

[43] I have tried to be as accurate as possible about the development of Fresh Expressions and ventureFX in the Methodist Church – my apologies if I have missed out anything important or made any mistakes.

the original Tubestation in Polzeath in Cornwall was a great success[44] and Caridad, who had lived many years in a Cuban surfing resort, wanted something similar in Tynemouth, which hosted the British Surfing Championships fairly frequently. Caridad was offering his services free as long as Methodism provided him with a manse. No chance, thought Jack. Ministry to surfers – whatever next? Specialist anorak churches at railway stations for train-spotters? Vision days for bird-watchers? Pah! Caridad had done a great job transforming the church deserted by Brendan Priest, but his two years were up in the summer and Jack suspected that Caridad wanted to stay in Britain and was grasping at any straw to achieve that. That one got thrown into the in-tray too. He couldn't just throw it in the bin, because the DEE was too enthusiastic to let it rest. He would have to explain why he thought it was a waste of money.

The next letter was about a small church in the Borders applying for permission to cease public worship. This was the mechanism by which a Methodist church went about closure – its Church Council asked permission from the Circuit Meeting to cease worship, which recommended it on to the District Policy Committee for ratification. Another one hits the dust, said Jack to himself, in resigned but sad acceptance. But what might have happened if only the Circuit or District could have put a bit more help in there? Maybe the village community would have rallied round... Everyone was tired, and they couldn't get much more help from their Minister because she was miles away and had six other churches. "If only we had more Ministers!" Jack yelled to no-one in particular.

The last letter was from the District Candidates' Secretary, reporting that as of last Thursday they had no-one wanting to candidate for the ordained ministry the following year. The deadline was not till the end of September, but by now anyone interested would have asked for details. The District only had two candidates last year, despite seven people taking the EDEV (Extending Discipleship, Exploring Vocation) course into which Jack had thrown a lot of effort, and one of those two got turned down at connexional level. This year's EDEV still had a few weeks to run, but the cohort this time was not as strong and the lack of enquiries about candidating was not altogether surprising.

The phone rang. It was one of the Circuit Superintendents telling him that one of his colleagues had been rushed into hospital with a suspected heart attack. "It doesn't look very good," said the Super. Jack asked a few questions and phoned a few people to cancel meetings, before rushing off to visit the hospital.

---

[44] Tubestation is one of the best-known Fresh Expressions, set up in 2006 and looking at the possibility of a second Tubestation a little further down the Cornish coast. But there are no links, as yet, with the North-East surfing community based at Tynemouth.

***

By mid-afternoon he was back home, after a dreadful time at the hospital. The Minister had been declared "dead on arrival", so Jack spent hours consoling the widow and then chatting to the Super. There were only two weeks to go to the Methodist Conference, so it was not impossible for another Minister to be found, even at this late stage. The trouble was that if he did find a replacement, the poor widow and her disabled grown-up son would have to vacate the manse early in August – which would be far too early and heartless. Jack had encouraged the Super to go for a year without a Minister, in the hope that Jack could find someone through next year's Stationing to start the following September, giving the widow a whole year to make decisions about what she and her son would do. But how would the Circuit cope? The Super had lost a valued colleague, a really good Minister who was not just a "safe pair of hands" but well-loved because he'd earned people's respect and trust by doing the hard graft of pastoral visiting. He was now in an awful predicament. What should he advise? How could they reorganise pastoral oversight and still keep things going? Then there was the funeral to organise, the people to contact – it was going to be a nightmare. And of course there was the poor widow and her son for him to care for. Going down suddenly from three Ministers to two was impossible if the work was to continue in any recognisable form. It was hard enough at the best of times to keep all the plates spinning on the top of the poles, but now several would have to be allowed to fall and smash.

Jack instantly resolved that he himself would have to help the Circuit out on the Preaching Plan, and he would have to see if he could persuade supernumeraries (retired Ministers) to lend a hand too. The Super would need a lot of care too so that he didn't burn out. And then there was the sensitivity required to discuss strategies for the future even as everyone was consumed with grief.

***

In the evening, when Jack was settling himself after the upheavals of the day, he opened his emails to discover one from Brendan Priest, who was in San Marino. He deleted it without bothering even to open it. That was the last thing he needed: bloody Brendan Priest, letting the side down. Pah!

Chapter 19: Nations 29 - 34

The Opel Corsa chugged steadily north-westwards, but when Brendan got within sight of Shkodër and its lakes he turned up into the hills – and the Corsa started to rumble rather than chug. Over the next few hours, he managed to maintain an average speed of about 40kph as he climbed up the switchbacks. The exhaust system leaked fumes into the interior, so when Brendan arrived in the little Albanian town of Pukë, he stopped and got some air to avert the possibility that he might puke in Pukë. The scenery was magnificent, however, and he spent half an hour in a cafe having bread and fruit for lunch and felt much better.

More hairpin bends followed along a ridiculous but spectacularly cliff-hugging road to Kukes, a small town near the Kosovan border nominated for the Nobel Peace Prize in 2000 for accepting over half a million refugees during the Kosovan conflict. Now it was a pleasant, quiet little town on a beautiful lake surrounded by rugged mountains. Brendan pressed on, crossing the border and arriving at Prezren shortly afterwards. He'd arranged to speak at 3.30pm to Kosovan civic leaders in the 19th century Cathedral, and was relieved to find that the arrangements this time hadn't been fouled up. A priest greeted him warmly with the news that this was one of the few churches left standing during the Kosovan conflict, probably spared because of its lack of heritage when more historic mosques and churches were blown up or burnt out. The majority of the Kosovan population were Albanian, but most leaders came from the Turkish community, so Brendan was a little nervous about handing over the Kosovan GNT, which had been printed in Albanian. He explained this to the priest, who laughed and told him not to worry. "We happy family now. I give to Muslim friend." Brendan nodded approvingly. Most of the civic leaders seemed to have at least a little knowledge of English, but the priest translated what Brendan said anyway. They laughed when he described Borut and nudged one another when he described Celestina, but they really got excited when he talked about Esther Blanchett. She really did have a worldwide following.

Back on the road two hours later, Brendan crossed the Macedonian border at Blace. He was running a bit late because of the afternoon talk, so he pressed on into Skopje, capital of Macedonia and his evening destination. He gave his fourth GNT of the day to a small boy playing outside the Mother Teresa Memorial House, opened in 2009 on the site of the church where she'd been baptised. Brendan was a bit put off when he read that part of her relics had been moved here, and wondered who decided which place got which bit. It was too bizarre for his Protestant tastes. He'd admired her, because she lived out her faith and made a huge difference for the Kingdom of God, and her well-known humility would have hated the fuss Skopje was making about her now.

On a hill overlooking the city stood what was claimed to be the biggest cross in the world, the 66m high Millennium Cross, commemorating two millennia of Christianity in a land proud of being mentioned in the Bible. Quite what the local Muslims thought of it wasn't so certain, though they had the Mustafa Pasha Mosque to boast about, a beautiful Ottoman building on the hill opposite. Skopje seemed to be an eclectic mixture of Christian and Islamic cultures, with each competing to make itself more prominent than the other. Brendan wondered whether this struggle, at best a friendly town rivalry and at worst threatening an apocalypse, had ever done either religion any favours. The only winners in religious wars were the Devil and the atheists.

The following day Brendan only notched up three more GNTs, but seven in two days was pretty impressive – and would net Watoto a pile of money. He wondered how the sponsoring was going, and looked forward to meeting up with Ruth when he had his next Esther interview in Cairo in 11 days' time.

From Skopje the Opel Corsa rumbled north-eastwards to Preševo in Serbia, where Brendan located the local Orthodox priest and gave him the Serbian GNT, which the Bible Society, aware that his visit was only touching this extreme south-eastern corner, had printed in Albanian. The priest smiled and nodded as he read the inscription on the inside of the GNT – they'd got the choice of language spot on once again.

Brendan backtracked across the border into Macedonia, and arrived two hours later in the tiny village of Monospitovo, the birthplace of Boris Trajkovski[45]. Boris was a likeable Methodist lawyer who became not only President of the Macedonian Evangelical Methodist Church but also President of Macedonia, until his death in an air crash in 2004 at the tragically early age of 47. Brendan had met him in Berkhamsted (of all places) in 1981, where Brendan had being staying with a friend from College, and Boris had been part of a Methodist Youth Exchange programme.

The M6 (a less-impressive road than its British counterpart) continued across the Bulgarian border, and soon Brendan reached Petrich, a small town nestling in the shadow of the Belasista mountain. The Roman Catholic priest expressed in faltering English his civic pride in their two factories (which produced water level detection equipment and spares for cranes) and the greenhouses which grew and exported peanuts. Another afternoon meeting had been planned with important figures in the local community. Everybody smiled a lot, and the GNT was handed over to a portly gentleman with an even portlier wife, who happened to be sitting in the lucky seat. Some sort of raffle, based on seat numbers, had been conducted without Brendan knowing what was happening.

---

[45] All the details about Boris are accurate, including his visit to Berkhamsted.

It wasn't until mid-afternoon that Brendan managed to extricate himself and drive through the Promachonas border-crossing into Greece. Winding through several sleepy towns, Brendan finally reached the Aegean coast at Kavala. The little Corsa was holding up well. Across the shimmering blue waters, Brendan could see Mount Athos, the secretive Halkidiki centre of Orthodox Monasticism, but he turned east towards his evening destination at Xanthi, arriving shortly after 7pm, just as the Roman Catholic Church was filling up ready for a 7.30pm kick-off for his talk. The priest was fretting and hugely relieved that he'd made it on time, and the evening went really well.

Afterwards, the priest took him out to a café in the main square, and they shared a massive dish of moussaka and a couple of bottles of wine. Brendan was so impressed with the moussaka that he gave the café owner the Greek GNT, which he'd forgotten to hand out at the talk. Brendan was also impressed with what little he saw of Xanthi, which described itself as "the city of a thousand colours" and certainly there was a fair degree of gaudiness in the square and the bars.

The following day brought a straightforward stretch of road: to the Turkish border at Kipoi, across to the Sea of Marmara at Tekirdağ and along the Thracian coast to Istanbul. Brendan was scheduled to speak at the WOW Attaturk International Airport Hotel, and wondered whether WOW referred to the reviews from customers or was an acronym for the hotel chain.

Because he'd arrived in good time he was able to drive into the city, seeing some of the famous sites but also many industrial estates, concrete buildings and shoddy housing. He hadn't really appreciated how massive a city Istanbul was, and this was only the European half – it was the only city in the world situated on two continents – but he did manage to catch sight of the Blue Mosque, Saint Sophia, the Gelata tower and the Topkapi Palace.

He checked in his valiant little Opel Corsa at the Hertz office back at the hotel, with some gratitude. He'd driven 925km in it, even though the interior smelled like he'd been trying to kill himself by carbon monoxide and the engine had retained its distinctive drum-beat throughout.

The meeting in the Airport Hotel had been organised as a high-profile black-tie affair by the local Catholic Bishop, who was high up in the city's power-networks. There was a grand dinner – after which Brendan was the guest speaker. He felt a bit conspicuous in his crumpled clothes, so he tried to make a joke of it by saying that he didn't have room for a dinner jacket – but few people smiled. It made Brendan even more nervous, for this was an entirely different setting from anything he'd been in previously. He passed the Turkish "business cards" around the tables, and decided that he'd start by explaining what the GNTs were all about. He held it aloft, read the inscription and described some of the very different individuals who had received the Testaments up to that point. Then he explained about Watoto and the fundraising, and decided on impulse to lighten the mood and hold an auction for the Turkish GNT. To his amazement, the people suddenly sparked into life, and started huddling together around their tables to discuss how to pool their resources to win it.

Brendan began the bidding at €1,000 but quickly realised that he'd set the bar ridiculously low. Within a minute it reached €40,000 before it emerged that two tables were battling against each other, one of which seemed to be led by a big, flash-looking man, and the other by a small lady with a necklace of gold and jewels which reminded Brendan of a school trip to see the Crown Jewels in 1968. There was something strange going on between the two tables, which everyone but Brendan seemed to recognise and find hilarious – but he didn't really care as long as they kept pushing the price up. Half an hour later, one table finally admitted defeat when the price had shot up to €130,000. It was the lady's table that won, and she came across with her cheque-book and wrote a cheque out with a flourish, crossed over to the man on the other table and gave him a big kiss. The Bishop leaned across to Brendan and explained, "They married. Very happy."

Brendan was a bit bewildered by the way that the evening had worked out. He talked for a few minutes more about his plans before deciding that no-one was listening. He thanked everyone for coming and sat down to a huge round of applause. As the people slowly filed out, he saw a stack of envelopes being deposited at the door. The Bishop had organised these envelopes as a discreet way of tapping everyone for a donation, and Brendan went back to his hotel room with a big box full of them. When he opened them and sorted them out, there were just under a hundred cheques, totalling over 800,000 euros, which astounded and horrified Brendan in equal measure. He phoned down to reception, and arranged for all the cheques he'd been given so far to be sent by courier to Oracle in Detroit. It had been an amazing and profitable evening, in which he'd raised nearly a million euros for Watoto but worried about a world in which certain individuals could have so much wealth to dispose of so lightly whilst others experienced only grinding poverty and hardship. Maybe that was what the point of the journey was – to experience those inequalities and even perhaps try to address the issues.

As he nestled down in his comfy bed, Brendan thanked God for such a positive ending to the first of his two journeys through Europe, and asked for God's continuing guidance and protection for the next stage of his journey – to the Middle East and then the Islamic coastline of North Africa.

Day: Date	Itinerary (* indicates TV interview) ([18]indicates new nation)	Bike (km)	Car/ Bus (km)	Train (km)	Kayak/ Sail (km)	Boat (km)	Air (km)
Totals brought forward		2614	370	0	663	40	466
25: 9/6/11	Lezhe, Albania[28]; Prizren, Kosovo[29]; Skopje, Macedonia[30]		205		34		
26: 10/6/11	via Serbia[31] to Petrich, Bulgaria[32]; Xanthi, Greece[33]		351				
27: 11/6/11	Istanbul, Turkey[34]		369				
Totals carried forward		2614	1295	0	697	40	466

Chapter 20: Impersonation

Things were getting harder at the Freeman Hospital for Louisa. The nasty Sister was upping the bullying week by week. When Louisa plucked up the courage to ask why she was being singled out for the dirtiest jobs, Sister Lilian replied, "Don't be ridiculous! Who the hell do you think you are, young lady? You need to go away and ask yourself whether you're cut out for a career in nursing because if you are, you need to pull your socks up, stop whingeing and show a bit of commitment!"

Thankfully only half of Louisa's shifts were when Sister Lilian was on duty. The other Sister was excellent and listened to Louisa's problems, but because she too was an employee of the Trust she couldn't be expected to side with a junior colleague against a more senior one. Louisa didn't particularly want Sister Lilian punished – but wanted to ensure that others didn't suffer as she was suffering, and that the unit became a happier place for both staff and patients. The best way, of course, would be to persuade the Sister that her conduct was inappropriate, unproductive and vindictive – yet the chances of that happening without Louisa digging a deeper hole for herself were about as good as England hosting the World Cup (it might happen one day, but not within the next 30 years).

She was getting really cheesed off with the Sister's patronising pettiness and downright nastiness and was beginning to think about resigning just to escape. But wasn't Christianity supposed to be about dealing with truth, because "the truth will set you free"? Others were beginning to suffer too, but Louisa was still the main target, being aggressively told off on a regular basis in front of patients and colleagues, like a schoolchild in front of a Victorian headmistress. If Sister Lilian's footsteps were heard in the unit everyone looked busy because they knew that she'd be looking for somebody to criticise.

Louisa would try to do things the way the Sister wanted them done, only to find that the boundaries had changed and that things should be done in a different way. None of the nurses could concentrate on nursing for they were too busy trying not to upset Sister Lilian. One or two registered a complaint and were told to forget it, because they couldn't *prove* that the Sister was bullying them with intent or was negligent –she was too clever and scheming to fall for that. So Louisa felt more and more isolated, and the bullying picked up. She gave Louisa more dirty looks, never bothered replying to greetings, overlooked Louisa for training opportunities and embarrassed her in public. Louisa's opinions were not welcome at meetings, and she criticised almost every action and decision Louisa made. The only reasons she stayed there and tolerated it were that she loved working with the patients, she (sort-of) needed the salary, and she still refused to give in even to the impossible expectations of this Hitleresque Sister. Louisa suspected that Sister Lilian was envious of the rapport she had with the patients, because the bullying became worse whenever this rapport was mentioned or highlighted. In a laudable Christian way, Louisa felt compassion for her – even though she was making Louisa's life increasingly intolerable.

Word went round that Sister Lilian had enrolled and registered under old training protocols which didn't require a degree, and someone drew a cartoon showing a Sister with a dunce's hat on and pinned it to the door of the staff kitchen cupboard. It was obvious at whom it was aimed because the shape was uncannily close to Sister Lilian's rather cubic profile – she was built not with an hour-glass figure so much as that of a carriage clock. Sister Lilian immediately but wrongly attributed the cartoon to Louisa, and started dropping snide comments about lah-de-dah graduates and making sure that everyone knew that *she* was in charge.

One day Louisa was singled out for criticism because there had been an infestation of ants in the staff kitchen on the ward. "I told you to clean this kitchen last week!" shouted Sister Lilian.

"Yes, and I did it. I spent two hours making sure that it was really good."

"Well, you obviously didn't do it very well at all. We've got ants – and you're going to exterminate them." She swiped a hand at the scurrying ants. "Look! They're all over the place. Exterminate them! Exterminate them!" Sounding like a Dalek, Sister Lilian harrumphed her way past Louisa and bustled off down the corridor.

Louisa couldn't help it. "Exterminate! Exterminate!" she warbled, doing her own impersonation of a Dalek but with the ant-spray held straight in front of her like the killing arm of the Daleks, at the same time turning round and round like some kind of demented dodgem. "Exterminate! Exterminate!" she repeated, spinning round and round before realising that the other nurses, previously laughing, were now silent as Sister Lilian stood, hand on hips like an angry pair of scissors, glaring at Louisa, who felt like a naughty schoolgirl caught having a fag behind the bike shed. "Sorry, Sister," she said, stifling a giggle, "I got carried away. I'll get on with it now."

"Just as well," growled Sister Lilian. "Or it'll be you next for extermination. And don't think that I'm joking."

And with that she swept off down the corridor, leaving Louisa feeling as if everything she did was doomed to failure or ridicule. "I can't win," she wailed and burst into tears.

The other nurses expressed sympathy with Louisa, but then scurried off to their own duties while Louisa set to work with the ant-spray, making everything as sterile as she could afterwards. At the end of the shift she slunk off, avoiding everyone, but then met up with one of the other nurses at the bus stop, whereupon they both started doing Dalek impersonations again, much to the amusement of others in the queue.

"I don't know how you put up with her," said Bridget. "She's so horrible to you. The rest of us feel awful for you but we know that if we say anything out of turn she'll have a go at us as well."

"I know," said Louisa. "I think that she's had it in for me since the start, but since I became a Christian she's stepped up the bullying."

"Yes, I agree," said Bridget. "Which church do you belong to? I go with my parents to the Catholic Church in Backworth, but I don't enjoy it – and I wouldn't dream of wearing a fish like you do!"

"I go to a Methodist Church in Jact, but I also go to a new church for younger people in the Life Centre. It's really good there, but I stick it out at Jact because it's where my Dad used to be the Minister and my boyfriend works there now. They've got a Cuban Minister there at the moment who's really good. He's the one who introduced me to the fish symbol."

"Isn't that the church where that Brendan came from who was on "See Esther"?" Then the penny dropped. "That's your Dad, isn't it?"

"Yes, that's my Dad!" said Louisa, and realised that she'd said it proudly rather than in embarrassment for the first time that she could remember. The two of them continued chatting about Brendan and Church on the bus to Four Lane Ends and then on the Metro till the other nurse got off at Northumberland Park. Louisa smiled to herself all the rest of the way round to Cullercoats – she was now doing the same sort of witnessing as her Dad was always banging on about.

Chapter 21: Nations 35 - 38

The following morning brought another fraught air travel experience for Brendan. A seat on the 7.25am Turkish Airlines flight to Cyprus was indeed booked in his name, but it wasn't going to Larnaca, as Brendan had expected, but to a place called Ercan, which was the main airport for Turkish-speaking Northern Cyprus – another foul-up by the team in Detroit. The taxi-driver seemed pleased to take him to the south-eastern resort of Ayia Napa, where his evening speaking engagement was to be hosted by the local Greek Orthodox priest in a hotel full of English tourists. The taxi driver, once he'd got through the border-crossing, took 30 minutes to drive the 59km, but as most of the route was on bendy local roads, it was not a particularly pleasant experience, made more nauseous by the foul cigarettes by which the driver poisoned the whole vehicle.

When a green-faced Brendan arrived at the Alion Beach Hotel, he discovered that the tourists were all from Britain, and most seemed to be leftovers from a wedding party, sticking around for a few extra days of sunbathing and relaxation while the blessed couple flew home to Manchester to check on their cats. Brendan couldn't work it out: getting married in Cyprus was much cheaper for the couple than a British wedding because of the over-inflated UK wedding industry, but it cost everyone else an arm and a leg. At least the arms and legs got well tanned. By now, however, they were getting a bit bored with the nightlife in the Square and wanted a quieter night back at the hotel. What they got, though, was an invasion of Orthodox Christians coming for a missionary meeting. The British took it all in good spirits, though. Mostly vodka.

Actually, Brendan enjoyed the chance to chat to a few of them who were still sober, and discovered that they came from various places around Manchester which he knew well from his three years spent in Rusholme during his Ministerial training. They were a bit more sociable than the Orthodox crowd, who seemed very polite but a bit stiff in comparison. Brendan gave the (Greek) GNT to a teenage Cypriot girl brought along by her father and bored-looking till that point. She brightened up when she read the inscription about it possibly being worth a lot of money one day.

The siting of the hotel was excellent for Brendan's plans, but again the plans fell through. He was supposed to link up with a yacht owner called Demetrios Papadopoulos in the hotel foyer early the following morning, but when he enquired at the desk they raised their eyebrows and told Brendan that Papadopoulos had been arrested three months earlier for drug-running. Brendan was appalled at the administrative cluelessness in Detroit. The man behind the desk at the hotel, though, was most helpful when Brendan explained what he needed. He made a few phone calls and then beckoned Brendan over. "Hokay," he said in a curiously Manuel-like accent from Fawlty Towers – how did that happen in Cyprus? – "I arrange everything for you. Not cheap, but I harrange it."

Brendan had serious doubts about this Spanish-sounding Cypriot hotel receptionist, used more to helping British tourists find the best place for fish and chips than sorting out yacht charters. But he should have had more faith, because he was to prove Brendan's unlikely saviour.

"My brother work in Ayia Napa harbour-master's office and he know what boats come and go. He say there is one boat called Isokratia which just arrive after sailing from Greece with very rich Germans who got very sick and now fly home. Boat ready for hire if you want. Discount price only €1,000, including commission." And he winked, as if to say, that is my cut and a bit for my brother too.

But Brendan wasn't that bothered because Oracle would be picking up the bill, having messed up the original arrangements so badly. So he bought €1,000 over the counter with his Barclaycard, then handed it back to Manuel to sort it all out while Brendan went off for a swim. An hour or so later, Manuel found him and said, "Mr. Priest, is time now. We go. My brother harrange it."

So Brendan rushed out to meet Manuel's brother who looked remarkably similar to Manuel but even shadier. He grabbed Brendan's GO-kart box and threw it into the back of his car before jumping in ready for the quick dash to the harbour.

Isokratia was a catamaran, like Borut's "Helena" on the Adriatic, and almost as sleek and luxurious – but the skipper didn't seem to have a thing about Marlene Dietrich or women's clothes. Brendan was amazed that somehow it was working out, despite Detroit's bungling. He explained to the skipper where he wanted to go over the next three days, that it had to be by sail-power not engines, and that the skipper would have one extra day to power back to Cyprus before sailing the yacht back to Athens as scheduled, but €800 better off without telling the owners. So by 11am, they were off, sailing past the rock bridge at Cape Grecko on the south-eastern tip of Cyprus but then hitting a strong headwind as soon as they got out into the open sea. The skipper came to Brendan immediately. "Is no good. Too strong wind in too bad direction. Must use engine or never get there."

The route was virtually due east, aiming to hit the Syrian coast just north of the Lebanese border, but it was 180km away, and would take till well after nightfall even under engine-power, but without the engines they would be tacking backwards and forwards and the crew would be exhausted as well as cheesed-off. Brendan gave the skipper the thumbs-up. He would have to make compensations for it somewhere down the line, but that was a problem for the future. Right now he needed to reach the mainland.

His mission demanded some kind of witnessing opportunity in Syria and the handing over of the Syrian GNT, so he was a bit concerned that he would have to "wing it". Instead of the large Syrian port of Tartus, the skipper was now aiming for a fishing village called Al-Hamidiyah, just 3km north of the Lebanese border. The sea passage itself was very bumpy, with the engine chugging the boat into the head-on wind. There were hardly any boats or anything else to see, so Brendan stayed in his cabin most of the time, even though he felt seasick. It was dark and late when the skipper finally dropped anchor, but Brendan was already in bed, feeling dreadful and only vaguely registering that the crossing was completed.

Brendan woke early and discovered that they were just outside a harbour, with a village beyond. He was given a cup of coffee more like bitumen than any coffee he'd encountered before, but which sorted out his acidic stomach very effectively. He then rowed ashore in a dinghy to give the GNT away, and immediately found a fisherman about to leave in the "Flower of Mecca" – an odd name for a boat because Mecca was in the middle of a desert. The fisherman had no problem reading the Arabic, grinned when Brendan showed him the inscription inside, and took the GNT gladly. Brendan shook his hand and bid him "as-salaamu alaykum", which was all the Arabic he knew. The fisherman smiled and said lots of stuff at which Brendan nodded and smiled, and they parted as if they would remain friends forever.

More importantly, the task had been completed, another country ticked off, and Brendan nipped back to the catamaran where the skipper set sail down the coast, this time under sail, and soon Syria was behind them and Lebanon was next. All that Brendan knew about Lebanon had been learnt through media coverage of the protracted civil war, so it was a surprise, as they glided along on a gorgeous sunny day, to see children playing on the beautiful sandy beaches, groups of young men playing Frisbee on the sand or drinking in the seafront bars, and ordinary seaside towns getting on with their routines. There was some pock-marked masonry still – particularly in the outskirts of Beirut, where shell-fire had damaged but not demolished the buildings and no-one had got round to doing repairs.

As the afternoon wore on, the GPS informed Brendan that his overnight destination of Saida was also Sidon, and that a city near the Israeli border, Sour, was also Tyre. The names were familiar. "Babs" Elliot had taught Brendan's Ancient History A-Level class about the Phoenician sailors who'd colonised this coast, so Brendan began to see Lebanon as a place rich in history and adventure as well as a modern war-zone. Saida/Sidon eventually appeared in the distance – a modern, cosmopolitan city with busy streets and shops below the two castles and the old city with its vaulted maze of narrow alleyways, winding streets and arched pathways.

Brendan was due to speak at the Basilica of Our Lady of Mantara that evening. Sidon had quite a substantial Catholic minority living alongside the Sunni Muslims, and their Basilica, the third largest church in the Middle East, looked suitably impressive high up above the city, its tall tower topped by a large bronze statue of the Madonna and Child overlooking the whole coastal strip. Inside, it incorporated a shrine in a cave where Mary was supposed to have stayed while Jesus went preaching in Sidon. Brendan smiled – his family never listened to him preach either... The nearby village of Magdhdouché turned out in force, as did many from down in the city, and the evening was rather splendid, with fantastic views out across the city, the Mediterranean, and the lush hills, valleys and citrus groves of Lebanon. The GNT went to the village bus-driver, who was also the Basilica caretaker.

Day 31 took Brendan down the Lebanese coast-line. Past Tyre, they crossed the Israeli border or "Blue Line" at Rosh HaNikra. The kibbutz there had once been the home of Sacha Baron Cohen, better known as Ali G, but Brendan didn't know how or why he knew that. Halfway through the afternoon, the catamaran was briefly boarded and searched by Israeli patrol boat officers, who scrutinized Brendan's passport and couldn't work out why he was undertaking such a strange journey. He explained by showing them the Israeli GNT, and the chief officer was so intrigued that Brendan gave him it.

It was only a short sail down past the tourist promenades of Nahariya and the old fortress city of Akko, before docking in Haifa's marina. Brendan shook hands with the skipper, and set off with his re-assembled GO-kart trailer to the nearest bike-hire shop, called Psychlepath, where he discovered that the cheaper and easier option was to buy a mountain bike for $100 than to hire one for $25 per day. So he set off on his smart new bike, riding then walking up the long zig-zagging ascent of Mount Carmel, past opulent houses and palm-trees in well-tended gardens, to the big church at the top where Elijah was supposed to have won his altar-burning challenge against the prophets of Baal. Brendan had always thought that this story was a bit macho, especially with its gory aftermath, but arriving at its probable site brought it out of fairy-tale into serious reflection. Why did the Old Testament revert so often to winners and losers? Why did the world today still think that that's what it was all about?

This was to be the location for his evening meeting, organised by the Carmelite Order whose Stella Maris Monastery was situated right across the street from the Old Lighthouse and the cable-car station. Brendan was cross when he realised that he could have got there by cable-car, but the magnificent view of the sea soon brought him round. The Stella Maris church itself was a beautiful structure, with Italian marble so brightly and vividly patterned that it looked as if the walls had been painted. Brendan was particularly struck by the colourful paintings on the dome, the most dramatic being the scene of Elijah swept up in a chariot of fire. The cave situated below the altar, which Brendan walked down into, was "Elijah's Cave," where the Old Testament prophet was believed to have lived.

To speak about Christian mission was one thing in such a biblical location, but to speak about the religious persecution of Christians at a place where a minority religion had been crushed by a biblical prophet was something else. The audience seemed a curious mixture of tourists and Christians from Haifa, so it was hard to assess what they took from his talk – but they did take Brendan's Israeli "business cards" as they left.

After a lovely quiet night in one of the pilgrim cells in the monastery, Brendan pedalled along the crest of Mount Carmel and reached Nazareth for an early lunch after less than three hours. He cycled up to the white Basilica of the Annunciation, locked his bike and walked down into the area where the shrine was situated, reputedly in the place where Mary had lived and received her heavenly visitor. It was very airy and serene, and rather holy, Brendan thought. Outside, the streets were full of rubbish and there was a channel cut into the middle of the alleyways down which sewage flowed into the drains at the bottom of the hill. It was definitely not a swanky setting for Jesus' childhood, but that's what incarnational stuff was all about, wasn't it? Brendan found it all rather exciting – this was where Jesus grew up and would have seen that boulder, or that stream, or the shape of that hill. It brought home to him that the story of Jesus was actually real. He already knew it intellectually, but now he *felt* it.

Of course the Basilica might not have been built in exactly the right spot (who knew?) but that didn't matter to Brendan. That was brought home as he biked down the hill to Cana and the water-jars. One church boasted it had five of them, all authentic, of course. Another boasted a further six. And then there was the one in Pisa... One church had a shrine underneath it which purported to be the site of the house where the miracle of the water into wine had taken place. And funnily enough the other church made exactly the same claim too. Was it even the right village – at least three other villages claimed to be the true Cana...?

Continuing along the road east, facing the curious Horns of Hittim, the Third Crusade battle-site where Saladin defeated the Crusaders in 1187, Brendan found himself challenging his own inherited prejudices. The Horns were the twin peaks of a saddleback mountain appropriately resembling the execution block on which Anne Boleyn got her head chopped off. Again, Brendan found the traditional romantic notion of going off to serve God in the Crusades challenged by visiting the scene of their slaughter. Winners and losers again...

Then he crested a brow and the wonderful sight of the Sea of Galilee opened up in front of him. And suddenly he was swept up in a timeless sense of following in the footsteps of Jesus. This view undoubtedly was something which Jesus regularly saw, and it wouldn't have changed much. The hazy Golan Heights in the far distance would have looked much the same 2,000 years ago. He could see little boats on the lake, just as there would have been then. He got off his bike and sat down, awe-struck at the beauty, stillness and God-nearness of it all.

He made a quick detour north of Tiberias to Tabgha (feeding of the 5,000) and Capernaum (Peter's home), passing underneath the slopes of the Mount of the Beatitudes. It was biblical overload, really, and Brendan was quite pleased to cycle back to the modern city of Tiberias to find some space to take it all in. After a wonderful dinner of St. Peter's fish (and chips) by the lakeside, he stayed overnight in a hostel, but the night was dreadfully warm and the ceiling fan didn't work, so he didn't get much sleep.

The next morning he cycled along the main lakeside road to the baptism site at the exit-point of the Jordan River, then pressed on southwards towards Jericho. It was a hard 100km, not because of the excellent road surface but because of the heat. The Sea of Galilee was over 200m below sea-level and the steep-sided Jordan valley kept the heat in. By the end of the day Brendan had dropped to 260m below sea-level at Jericho, the lowest city in the world, as well as the one continuously inhabited for the longest time. More importantly for Brendan, it had a hotel with air-conditioning and a swimming-pool. He quite enjoyed being a pilgrim, but he also liked occasional comforts. He strolled up to the archaeological site of the old city walls at Tell es-Sultan and went a little further to view the cliff-hugging Greek Orthodox Monastery of Temptation, but decided he would yield to the temptation of the air-conditioned hotel rather than try anything holier.

From Jericho the next day he cycled further south and ever lower, coming quickly to the Qu'umran site where the Dead Sea Scrolls had been discovered. He stopped for a cold drink at the café, and walked across to see the cave. But he wanted to spend time at both Ein Gedi and Masada, so he didn't stay too long. He bought himself a few more cool drinks and then continued along what was now the lowest road on earth, running alongside the Dead Sea, 422m below sea-level. It didn't *feel* any different, but a quick float in the salty water at Ein Gedi proved how different it was. Brendan enjoyed the cold shower on the beach but then turned his attention to Masada. Tourist buses rumbled past as he approached this hill-top fortress to which nearly a thousand Jewish rebels had fled from the Roman invaders, only to find themselves besieged. The Romans built a slope up to the fortress over several months, and just before they reached the top, all the Jews committed suicide rather than give the Romans any sense of victory. That was more like it, thought Brendan – who "won" that battle?

He caught the cable-car up to the top and wandered around the ruined fortress for a short while before sitting down and wondering whether he would have the courage to commit suicide for his beliefs rather than deny them or be killed for them. Yet that was a choice countless Christians had faced over the centuries and many still faced today, as Open Doors could graphically testify.

Across the valley was the nation of Jordan, Brendan's proposed destination for the night. His route lay not in the nearby yet dangerous salt-bridges or foul salt marshes but round the bottom of the Dead Sea and across the border by road near the Jordanian town of Feifa. The only problem was that when he was at the border, late in the afternoon, there was no way through. There were two barbed-wire fences,

100m apart, with an ominously bare raked strip of sand between the two which yelled "Mines!" even before he saw the skull-head signs. So much for that idea, then. Well done, Detroit – yet again. Heads would have to roll, he thought, but then he thought back to the Horns of Hittim and he thought that compulsory redundancy was probably his preferred exit strategy for whoever had made so many mistakes. Or was it sabotage?

He knocked on the door of the kibbutz at Ein Tamar which nestled up to the Israeli barbed-wire fence, and was given a meal and a bed for the night. They couldn't understand why he'd thought that there might be a border crossing here, for there never had been. There was the road to their kibbutz, and a road to a border hamlet from the Feifa road on the other side, which might *appear* to be one continuous road on a map, but researchers should have been able to discover the truth. Furthermore, they told him that they'd heard that visas couldn't be obtained at the border; they had to be arranged ahead. Brendan didn't care – he was too tired.

It left him with some phone calls to make the next morning before he set off, phoning Fahada to arrange an emergency visa from Eilat into Aqaba and an emergency speaking engagement in Aqaba – and asking her to find out what was going wrong. She said that she would do her best, and that he should proceed on the assumption that she would sort it all out before he arrived at Eilat. Another long, hot day followed through the Arabah Valley section of the Negev Desert – and Brendan's thoughts went back to the endless, barren wastelands of the Atacama Desert in Chile. It was similarly empty, lifeless, and hot. He'd stocked up with water at the kibbutz but the heat was intense. It was like cycling all day underneath a hovering patio heater. Brown rocks, dusty mountains, cracked wadis, mud craters, no life except for the poisonous clattering of army lorries and the softer whoosh of tourist buses, and Brendan just kept going, hour after hour, trying to ration his water but glad of an occasional petrol station where he could fill up his water-bottles.

Eilat eventually arrived at about 5pm, and Brendan sat in a cafe while he phoned Fahada, who explained that she'd set him up with a speaking engagement for 7.30pm in Aqaba and that he definitely wouldn't need a visa in advance. His talk would be held at the Moevenpick Resort Hotel, where he would stay the night. Everything was arranged. But unfortunately, inevitably, it didn't pan out like that.

Brendan found his way to the Israeli side of the Wadi Araba border crossing, and showed his passport to the Israeli officer. "I will need a Jordanian visa," he declared.

"It depends how far into Jordan you go," said the burly Israeli official.

"How do you mean?"

"A visa to Jordan costs $15, but if you stay in Aqaba which is a tax-free zone, the entry visa to Jordan is free."

"Oh, excellent!"

"But you will have to pay the Israeli Departure Tax, which is 99 shekels, or $25," said the official, holding out his hand for Brendan's passport.

"I'm coming back tomorrow," said Brendan with a smile. "There isn't a Jordanian Departure Tax as well, is there?"

The official didn't seem to get the joke. "Yes," he said. "But it's only $8."

Brendan fished in his pocket for his wallet, which contained his emergency dollars, and counted off the notes into the hand of the official, who folded them carefully into his back pocket and promptly arrested Brendan.

He hadn't even stepped foot into Jordan. He was ushered to an Israeli jeep, pushed in and driven off to a fortified police station at the side of the main road back into Eilat. His bike was back at the border – with all his stuff. He was allowed one phone call, in which he left a message for Fahada for emergency help.

It really was all falling apart.

Day: Date	Itinerary (* indicates TV interview) ([18]indicates new nation)	Bike (km)	Car/ Bus (km)	Train (km)	Kayak /Sail (km)	Boat (km)	Air (km)
Totals brought forward		2614	1295	0	697	40	466
28: 12/6/11	Ayia Napa, Cyprus[35]		59				767
29: 13/6/11	Al Hamidiyah, Syria[36]					180	
30: 14/6/11	Saida, Lebanon[37]				143		
31: 15/6/11	Haifa, Israel[38]				88		
32: 16/6/11	via Nazareth to Tiberias	107					
33: 17/6/11	Jericho	121					
34: 18/6/11	Ein Tamar	116					
Totals carried forward		2958	1354	0	928	220	1233

Chapter 22: Assignation

Fahada knew that she was treading a tightrope. The more she tried to sabotage Brendan, the more likely it was that she would be found out.

She was quite pleased with the ease with which some of the arrangements had been undone. The failure to set up different arrangements for the Toulouse-Nice flight after Air France cancelled was easily blamed on Jayne, as was omitting to inform Brendan later that he was due to enter Cyprus at Ercan not Larnaca. Brendan, though, had been fortunate in finding the Lourdes party at Toulouse and wasn't really inconvenienced by the change to Ercan. The earlier flight alteration could have been wonderfully disruptive to his schedule but it hadn't quite worked out right. The later one would have been a problem for Brendan if he couldn't have got across from Northern Cyprus to the rest of the island, but it proved far too easy.

The scuppering of the arrangements in Neum, Ston and Ulcinj had been pleasing but hadn't really handicapped Brendan either, except for him not *publicly* "witnessing" in two of the countries. She wasn't so bothered about him evangelising, even though her fundamentalist Muslim background should have found this an offence against Allah. Over her time in America, she'd found her upbringing often clashed with her observations, experiences and feelings. The American way of life wasn't evil at all – in fact it was quite attractive. Christianity seemed to be a harmless hobby for most Americans rather than the rallying-call to exterminate Islam, as she'd been told. She was keen to disrupt Brendan's plans in order to unsettle him and make him give up, but had no real religious motivations to thwart his journey. It was personal – she wanted Esther's full attention for herself.

She'd hoped that sending the wrong car for his trip through the Balkans would slow him down considerably, but that sabotage attempt had failed too. Having asked for the cheapest car they had in Albania, she was sure that it would be a dreadful example of scrap-car inefficiency, but the Opel Corsa had proved dogged and durable, as had Brendan. He seemed to have a charmed life.

She was particularly proud of her interventions in Israel. The border-crossing error by the Dead Sea was ironically a simple mistake, assuming that a road that went straight to the border one side and a road heading in the exact same direction on the other side would be linked to each other. No-one had thought to double-check. The researchers really were to blame for that one. Her master-stroke was getting Brendan arrested. Finally, the anonymous tip-off to the border-guards had borne fruit. Not only should that mess up his Jordanian visit, with luck it would delay him for a few days at least and mess up the Esther interview in Cairo. Fahada knew that this would annoy Esther, especially so close to the event and when Esther was already in situ. Brendan would definitely be knocked off the hero-pedestal onto which Esther had put him. It had all come good, at last.

Fahada and Esther were already in Egypt. It was a very strange experience for Fahada – the first time she'd been back to her homeland since leaving in 2001. Esther was busy with the arrangements for the programme, so Fahada could sneak away for a meeting with her "controller" and her father. In the light of the news about her eldest brother, she was worried about her father, who'd idolised him and would be devastated by his death. She'd not had a chance to make contact in the last few days, so it was with some apprehension that she arranged a visit for the following morning, when she knew Esther would be up to her eyes in meetings and rehearsals.

Fahada was brought up in the Embaba shanty-town district of Cairo in the heady days of the post-Sadat resurgence in Islamic influence. Ikwan, or the Muslim Brotherhood as it was known in the West, had been officially outlawed but still operated openly as the main opposition voice in Parliament. But in the shadowy back-alley world beyond Ikwan's blue posters, more extremist groups flourished, including her father's which was known as Holy War. It was a Holy War cell within the army which assassinated Sadat and brought about her brother's arrest – even though ironically he'd had nothing to do with it. Her father himself had taken charge of Holy War after the capture of Khaled al-Istambuli who'd masterminded the Sadat killing, and it was her father who organised the shooting of the former Interior Minister Hassan Abu Basha, who led the anti-fundamentalist purge which had netted Mustafa. But Abu Basha wasn't killed, and Fahada's father was chastised for failing.

She'd been sent upstairs to her bedroom many times while intense, bearded young men in white robes gathered downstairs in their "cell", debating obscure theological points but also working on political tracts and collecting weapons, which were then hidden in the cellar. She'd been forbidden to visit the cellar by her father, but she'd watched the weapons being stashed, from the knot-hole in the bedroom floor-boards which none of them knew about.

Most of the Islamists in Egypt were not particularly radical, and used their respectability within the community to work inside the system and through the ballot-box. Fahada's father, however, continued to seek more direct and uncomplicated methods for changing his country. He recruited straight from the hotbed of the universities and the tides of teenage immigrants into Cairo. One recruit formed a different group, Gama'a al-Islamiyya, which quickly shot to fame with the killings of a parliamentary speaker, the head of the counter-terrorism police, and dozens of European tourists.

In December 1992 the army occupied Embaba, arresting and removing over 5,000 radicals but curiously Fahada's father was overlooked, though his organisation was decimated. He tried to hit back the following year but again his attempt to assassinate Prime Minister Atef Sedky failed. Unfortunately a schoolgirl bystander was killed by the car-bomb and Fahada's father once more found himself heavily criticised.

In 1997 the "Islamic Group" under Rifai Taha killed 71 Europeans at Luxor, and Holy War became somewhat side-lined. In an attempt to make long-term plans, Fahada was trained and sent off to America, but was told that it would be years before she was called into action. In 2002, Holy War, reinvigorated by the guidance and influence of Mustafa in Afghanistan, joined the Abdullah Azzam Brigades. Fahada's father wasn't high up in the new organisation, but hoped to rise in prominence with a major strike on an American target – through Fahada, who would provide him with the kudos for which he yearned. The Abdullah Azzam Brigades in 2004 sent suicide bombers to the Taba Hilton killing 34, and killed 83 in 2005 in a triple car bomb attack in Sharm-el-Sheik. These successes thrilled Fahada's father, but also stoked his jealousy and yearning for a pre-emptive strike of his own. He kept silent about his daughter's infiltration into America in order to protect her, but also to make her eventual action that bit more spectacular and glorious.

With all this expectation hanging over her, Fahada had been happy to enjoy life in America, but now she was back in Egypt and faced an emotionally and strategically difficult but important assignation with her father and Saeed, her "controller".

She met her father in a restaurant in the centre of Cairo, because he found crowds less threatening than the quiet alley-ways of Embaba. She dressed modestly in order to please him, and he was delighted when she spoke to him from behind her head-dress and he recognised her voice. They embraced, and her father burst into tears as he spoke about Mustafa. "Now you must act on my behalf, as your dear brother has done for so long. The others are weak, but Mustafa and you are the children of my heart. Insh'Allah you will be able to continue his work against the enemy."

He asked for details of her position in the Oracle organisation, and got really excited when she described how close she was to Esther. She didn't go into details of exactly *how* close, of course, because her father would have been utterly offended by such behaviour. He made a phone call to Saeed and told Fahada that he would be joining them shortly. Meanwhile he asked about what had brought her to Egypt, so she told him about Brendan and exaggerated the anti-Christian motivations for her thwarting tactics, which fascinated her father. He'd never heard of Brendan or either of his journeys. He asked for more information, and thought hard. "So this Christian is going round the world, including Muslim countries, trying to lure true Muslims and others into his infidel religion. We must help you stop him."

At that point Saeed joined them, trying his best to look important and shady but still looking like a spotty teenager auditioning for a minor role in a James Bond spoof. He was excited too at the information about Brendan and asked for a copy of the itinerary so that he could think how best to proceed.

"Tell me more about this Esther Blanchett," ordered her father. "I am interested to know how a woman can rise to head a big organisation. It is against all Muslim laws, of course. We know that such power is for men only."

Fahada bit back a retort. This was not the time or place to argue with her father. She'd discovered that she rather liked the equality enjoyed by American women. American society was still riddled with inequalities and corruption, but at least on women's rights she approved. She described proudly the power Esther enjoyed as head of a major TV franchise organisation, the glamorous home she lived in, the wealth she'd accumulated, and the global position of influence she'd gained through the worldwide popularity of "See Esther".

"That's *very* interesting," said her father – and she realised too late what a mistake she'd made.

Chapter 23: Nations 39 – 41

Back in the Israeli police station, Brendan explained that he was expected at the Moevenpick Resort Hotel to give a talk that evening, and that if they wished to check he would be happy to wait. One officer went away and the other one went painstakingly over the circumstances of Brendan's entry into Israel from Lebanon and asked repeatedly why there was no evidence in his passport for his passage from Syria to Lebanon to Israel. Brendan explained that he was only a very temporary visitor to Syria and Lebanon but the officer became more suspicious, if anything. The minutes dragged on before the other officer came back to report that there was no arrangement with anyone at the Moevenpick Resort Hotel and that Brendan was lying.

"But Fahada promised me that she'd booked me in!" Brendan cried, and then realised that he'd really put his foot in it.

"Fahada?" the officer enquired. "Who is this "Fahada"? That sounds to me like an Arab name."

"It is," said Brendan. "It means Leopardess. She works for Oracle Productions in America – a TV company."

The officer wasn't impressed. "I suppose it's irrelevant that she's Muslim?"

Brendan gulped, but wisely said nothing. The silence grew...

"So, just to summarise where we've got to, Mister Priest. You admit to smuggling yourself illegally across the Syria-Lebanon border and entering Israel by private boat, evading customs. You claim that you met a patrol boat but there's no record of this or stamp in your passport. Since then you cycled across towards Golan then down the border with Jordan. You confess that you wanted to cross into Jordan at Ein Tamar but were put off by the minefield, so you made your way south thinking that you could smuggle yourself and your transport out of Israel without us noticing. You admit further that you are only going to Aqaba for a meeting in a hotel set up for you by a Muslim faction in America. The hotel knows nothing about you. You admit that you plan to return to Israel and then smuggle yourself over to Egypt. Frankly, the only people who border-hop like that are smugglers and terrorists. Where will you be going next? Gaza? Libya?"

"Actually, it is Libya next, after Egypt."

The officer threw up his hands in disbelief. "Do you take us for fools, Mister Priest? You say quite openly that you're smuggling Christian Bibles into these Muslim countries but we Israelis have to be extra-vigilant with people like you. We received an anonymous tip-off that somebody would be attempting to border-hop down here and that we ought to pay you special attention, and here you are. Who knows what you are really smuggling?" He turned to the other officer. "Take his bike apart, bit by bit. And I want him searched. Thoroughly."

***

Three hours later, Brendan was still in the police station. If ever there had been a meeting planned in the hotel, he'd missed it. He'd been subjected to a strip-search, which added uncomfortably to his list of never-again experiences. His bike and GO-kart had been totally dismantled, the trailer spars drilled through to check for counterfeit drugs or weapons, his belongings thrown in a puddle, including a few Arabic "business cards". He was cross because he must have been set up by somebody on Esther's staff. Then the officer returned. "What do you want now?" Brendan snarled.

"I want you to leave Israel right now – and never come back."

Brendan was manhandled out of the police station, shown the mess which had been his bike, and presented with the GO-kart, which contained nothing except its drilled-out trailer handle and the Jordanian GNT. No clothes, no cards – nothing. The officer shoved him into the jeep, drove back to the border, yanked him out and pulled him over to the border post, where Brendan was told to cross. The officer held out his passport, showing him the page which proclaimed in bright red ink that he was not permitted to enter Israel again.

By now it was dark and cold. Brendan stopped at the taxi-rank, asking the driver to take him to the nearest hotel. But when they drove into the driveway of the first hotel, Brendan saw that it was the Moevenpick Resort Hotel, so he told the driver to continue to a town-centre hotel. There he told the receptionist that he wanted to go to Taba in Egypt but not go through Israel, and the man nodded and said, "Sindbad".

"Yes, yes," said Brendan, "Sinbad the sailor. So I have to go by boat, do I?"

"Sindbad," said the man. "Next door."

Brendan went out of the hotel to find that he was, indeed, next door to the offices of Sindbad Marine Transportation[46] – and they were open! It was 10pm but they were open – he couldn't believe it. He rushed inside, to be told that the ferry only ran once a day and he'd just missed it. The receptionist was finishing off the paperwork before going home. The earliest he could travel was tomorrow night at 7.30pm, so he booked his ticket and wondered what to do till then. He decided to be a tourist, and booked a one-day tour to Petra.

***

---

[46] Sindbad Marine Transportation and Water Sports provide quality services at the northern end of the Red Sea, including the high-speed catamaran Sindbad XPRESS from Aqaba to Taba.

Exactly 24 hours later, Brendan stepped off the Sindbad XPRESS in Taba, ready (he hoped) for a quick transfer by taxi to the airport for the last flight of the day to Cairo at 9.45pm. For once, everything went smoothly. He nestled back in the plane seat, reflecting on his day. He'd somehow managed to keep to his travel schedule, but he'd also achieved one of his all-time tourism ambitions. The trip to Petra had set him back $200, but it had been awesome, especially the camel-back ride down the Siq canyon to emerge in front of the rock-hewn Treasury.

***

As he stepped into the arrivals area at Cairo International Airport, he was greeted by his daughter Ruth and her husband Paul. He broke down in tears. It had been a hard "leg", with a happy ending.

***

He woke up the following morning in the Novotel and lay there reflecting on his journey thus far. He was only about half a day later than planned, and it didn't matter because there had been a "rest day" planned for the TV interview – so he would fly out from Cairo to Tripoli as planned tomorrow, Day 38. Despite so many things going wrong, he was still right on track.

It was great to see Ruth and Paul again at the airport last night, but he'd been too tired to enjoy it. The Petra tour, catamaran to Taba, taxi to the airport and flight to Cairo had all gone wonderfully smoothly – but he'd been absolutely exhausted and went straight to bed. Now he'd woken up feeling much better. Hopefully the lack of activity today would be beneficial too, for the time difference was such that a live 2pm show in Detroit meant 9pm in Cairo – so he had all day to relax, enjoy and catch up on what was happening.

The first thing he did was to join Ruth and Paul in the garden for a late breakfast. "This is the life," he said to them as they ate beside the swimming-pool. They updated him on their journeys around Scandinavia and Canada since his May 16th departure, and on the amazing response of sponsors through the website. They already had over 30,000 "hits" on the website, and over 20,000 people from all over the world had made sponsorship pledges. Ruth projected over $25 *million* for Watoto if he managed to get round all the countries, as the current tally per country was just over $130,000 – and she already had 50 people pledged to double their sponsorship (like Esther) if he did it all in the year. It all sounded like Monopoly money to Brendan, but he knew that these amounts would enable Watoto to expand and diversify their care programmes in Uganda and in other parts of Africa. Hopefully the pledges would keep coming in as he spoke to audiences around the world and as the

"See Esther" programmes charted his progress. The next three weeks would have very few speaking engagements because he'd be travelling across the top of Islam-dominated North Africa, but hopefully this interview with Esther would keep the money coming in from the rest of the world.

It was to be filmed at the Pyramids themselves, which seemed a bit bizarre but the backdrop would obviously make the programme special. The three of them were free till 3pm when they would be whisked off by limousine for a meeting with Esther , so they stayed by the pool, relaxing.

"This is the life," said Brendan – aware that he was beginning to repeat himself.

***

The limo pulled up at the eastern Sphinx entrance area on Pyramids Road. They were swept past the crowds queuing at the ticket office, "wanded" by the guards' metal detectors, sniffed by explosives-dogs, and escorted through to the pyramid area itself. In front of them loomed the Great Pyramid of Khafre, which, according to the leaflet Brendan picked up, was the tallest building in the world for nearly 4,000 years until the spire of Lincoln Cathedral was completed in 1311. They passed close by the noseless Sphinx which was much smaller than Brendan had imagined, and joined the crowds thronging the sandy paths and open areas linking all the sites. The entrance to the Great Pyramid was cordoned off, but they were given tickets to enter the smaller pyramid of Menkaure.

The interior of the pyramid was hot, humid and somewhat claustrophobic, with the passages steep, dusty and hard to move through, but actually getting close up against the interior walls and passageways gave Brendan an even deeper appreciation of the achievement of its builders so long ago, even though the workers were slaves and hadn't any choice.

They spent an hour or so trailing round but the heat was too intense and they were glad when their guard/guide suggested that they might adjourn to the nearby Pizza Hut. As they walked in, Brendan was surprised to see Fahada and Esther talking together at one of the tables – he'd expected them to be somewhere a bit flashier than this. Esther got up and gave him a big hug, whilst Fahada looked on. Here we go again, thought Brendan, remembering the funny looks he'd got from Fahada previously. A cool handshake followed.

"This is dandy, isn't it?" asked Esther, with a chuckle. "Actually we're here because of the roof."

Brendan, as she'd intended, looked blank.

"I'll show you," said Esther, and they trooped off upstairs, through a metal door and out onto a terrace which had the most amazing view over the pyramids. The technicians were already setting up ready for the interview that night, fussing around with cables and generators.

"Quite a view, isn't it?" Esther was obviously pleased with the backdrop she'd arranged. "And it'll be even more impressive tonight because of the Sound and Light Show."

Brendan had seen signs for this Show, which happened at hourly intervals each night from 8.30 onwards. "Won't it be a bit distracting?" he asked.

"Well, I've had a productive conversation with the man in charge." Esther made the familiar gesture associated with money changing hands. "Usually they shine a spotlight right at this terrace to stop tourists seeing the show for free. But they aren't going to do that tonight. Also, they're going to re-position the speakers so that the sound is directed away from us. The technicians seem to think that it'll be just right – swirling colours in the background but no sound disrupting the interview. I'm quite excited about it. I've never been here before and it's so awesome, isn't it?"

Brendan agreed. It should make for an amazing TV experience. They went back downstairs, leaving the techies to it, and went through plans for the interview, which would be similar to his evening talks but spiced up by Esther's questions. His previous on-the-road interviews had all been shorter – just one part of a programme rather than the whole of it. But he'd also done three whole-show interviews: at the bottom of South America; immediately after his rescue; and promoting this new adventure. It was that relaxed format they were going for now, giving more time to tell stories and promote the causes at the heart of it all – and this should make it easier for Brendan because his answers could be longer and more descriptive, as in his talks.

As they went through the various topics to cover, Brendan felt more and more at ease about it, even though he was going on live television for 30 minutes without a script. Ruth was more worried, but was assured by Esther that she'd only be brought on for a few minutes near the end. Esther also wanted Paul to be with Ruth during the interview, but he was assured that he didn't have to say anything.

Brendan then told Esther about all the things that had gone wrong during this first month of the journey – stressing how fortunate he'd been to get through to Cairo, let alone to keep to the schedule. Fahada jumped in quickly to report that her investigations identified her assistant Jayne as the breakdown point. "She protests her innocence, of course, but I've now given her a final warning." Esther looked shocked both at Brendan's complaints and at the cold, detached tone of Fahada's statement, but nodded her agreement. It was clearly news to her that things hadn't been running smoothly. No mention was made of the anonymous tip-off which had caused his arrest in Israel. Brendan was sure that somebody within Oracle had it in for him – and he wondered whether it was Fahada herself rather than her assistant. He kept his counsel for now – he didn't like confronting people with stuff like that, especially as he couldn't prove anything.

***

The evening was cooler than the earlier baking heat of the day, but still warm compared to evenings on Tyneside. Brendan had never been able to understand how in all seasons, but especially winter, the scantily-clad revellers in Newcastle survived without becoming one big goose-pimple. Back home he usually wore a jacket in summer and a coat in spring and autumn. In winter he wore everything he could.

The backdrop was as spectacular as they'd hoped. The swirl of colours across the Great Pyramid was beautiful and dramatic. They could see the "See Esther" live feed on a screen placed beside the camera, which also ran autocues for Esther's questions. The interview began with Esther introducing Brendan, Ruth and Paul and asking Brendan about his adventures so far. He described the cycle ride down through France, catching a plane full of healed pilgrims from Lourdes, and having his helmet nicked by a child in Venice. He told them about Borut the Marlene Dietrich impersonator and about the lucrative auction of the GNT in Istanbul, which led on nicely to an update on the sponsoring and a brief chat with Ruth about the work of Watoto which would benefit.

As planned, Ruth mentioned that at the next interview she would be able to show them video footage of Watoto children, but today wanted to show some photos of children in the Kampala Bulrushes who were the immediate beneficiaries of their generosity. And on cue various photos of tiny children were shown as Ruth spoke: stick-limbed children in incubators; bewildered children in bundles on worker's laps holding their own bottles of milk because there were too many for the workers to be able to tend to each one; happy children playing outside with toys and balls. It was all very emotive and very powerful. The camera swung back to Brendan as they drew to a close.

"What are your thoughts now as you visit some Muslim countries with little kindness towards Christianity?" asked Esther.

"Well, some of the new Balkan countries I've already visited have worked through some of the tensions which there used to be, and received me warmly. Turkey was the first officially Muslim country I visited and, as you have heard, their welcome and support was considerable. I was arrested, but that was in Israel as a suspected smuggler. So I hope to be a sort of a peace ambassador and good advert for Christianity wherever I go."

"But some of the places you'll be visiting over the next few weeks are places where Christians are persecuted for their faith. Will you be able to do anything to help them?"

"I hope so," said Brendan. "But at the very least I can show that Christianity is not out to disrupt or threaten governments or other faiths. We in the Christian Church have worked through some difficult questions about our attitudes to other faiths, and as I meet people I won't be eager for their *conversion* so much as an ongoing *conversation* – about spirituality, and about our different journeys which reveal similar truths. I still believe that Jesus gives a unique insight into God, but I want everyone to know that God loves them and I believe people discover that in many different forms."

"But what about the Persecuted Church?" pressed Esther.

"Look behind you," said Brendan, waving an arm at the pyramids. "Amazing things are done by people who aren't free – but the achievements are even more wonderful when people are free to respond gladly to the challenges and excitements of life. It's a crime whenever people of *any* faith are persecuted for what they believe, and the work of Open Doors (which I'm proud to flag up) is dedicated to supporting Christians whose freedom is threatened or taken away. It's time for Christians to wake up to the plight of other members *of our own family* who are struggling in ways we can't begin to understand but need to recognise and do something about."

"So that's it, folks," said Esther, turning to face the camera. "You've heard what this is all about. You've heard Brendan's challenge to get involved. Now *do something about it*. On the screen you'll see details of the website and the numbers to call to pledge your support for Watoto and find out more about Open Doors and the Persecuted Church. I *want* to make a difference, don't *you*? I hope that when we meet Brendan again, we'll have lots more good news to report. Journey on, Brendan, with our prayers and love..."

And that was it. The cameras focussed on the Great Pyramid as the credits and theme-music ran. Afterwards, Esther was full of it, enthusing about how well it had gone and how pleased she was. "Can't wait for next time," she announced. "I've always wanted to visit where my folks came from, and now I'm going to get my chance."

Brendan knew that there were thousands of kilometres to journey before next time. He was excited about what lay ahead even though he felt a bit apprehensive about his encounter with Islam – and about Fahada.

***

Brendan's flight to Tripoli in Libya left on time the following lunchtime. He'd enjoyed sharing dinner, then breakfast, with Ruth and Paul. They were flying back to Kampala for some meetings about Gulu Bulrushes. One of the problems was that they needed money *now* and most of the fundraising was only going to accrue at the end of the journey, so they needed to think how they could release some of it much sooner.

Brendan's GO-kart had been filled with new clothes and nearly 1,000 Arabic "business cards" even though there were few speaking engagements planned. He also had some cards ready for Malta, Spain, Portugal and the West African countries he'd be visiting before he would see Esther again.

***

At Tripoli airport, Brendan was met by a man who introduced himself as Giovanni, which sounded interestingly Italian. Brendan thought that the Italians were expelled in the aftermath of the 1969 Revolution – and Giovanni nodded, but added that some, like him, had been allowed back. Gaddhafi's opposition to Christianity had relaxed after the Vatican refused to cut ties with Libya after the Lockerbie bombing.

The Christian cause in Libya had continued unbroken from earliest times, when Simon of Cyrene carried the cross of Jesus and St. Mark from Cyrene wrote the earliest Gospel. During the last millennium, however, the rise of Arab Islam pushed the indigenous Christians out and the Church survived only in ports such as Tripoli, and then only because of visitors and missionaries.

The Church of St. Francis in the Dahra suburb of Tripoli was an impressive white-stoned building, with a grand entrance of three high arches leading into its high-vaulted nave. Giovanni brought Brendan there via the city, showing him the sights, including the former Cathedral in Algeria Square. It had only been opened in 1928 but was requisitioned in 1970 into the Maidan al Jazair Mosque, and, over dinner, Brendan asked what had happened to the congregation.

"Most joined the small congregation at St. Francis," said Giovanni. "This new church was built when the joint congregation had grown in size and when Gaddhafi's modified views allowed the building of new churches."

"Is evangelism allowed?"

Giovanni sucked in his cheeks, steepled his fingers, and then seemed to find his answer – which he delivered slowly, anxious that he got it right. "Christian outreach in Libya is a complicated, risky and yet very rewarding challenge."

***

The evening's meeting was well-attended. Brendan sensed that the main aim was to encourage the faithful few rather than persuade them to support his journey or the causes he was championing. He found, however, further confirmation (through a retiring offering) that those who struggled were always amongst the most generous in every way.

124

The following morning he was taken by Giovanni down to the harbour, hoping to charter a boat along the coast to Tunisia. Fahada had given him the name of a boat company with whom she'd made a provisional booking, but when he found the boatshed it was all boarded up. He wandered up and down the wharfs but only met with shoulders shrugged in a gesture of hopelessness. Giovanni explained that there had recently been a clampdown on boats leaving Libya filled with Africans trying to get to Europe, and many boat owners had their boats seized and confiscated.

There used to be a ferry to Malta, but this also was curtailed due to clampdowns and travel restrictions. Similarly freight ships previously carried passengers to Malta but the likelihood was slim if it hadn't been pre-arranged.

Brendan was stuck in Libya. He could catch a bus west to Tunisia, but that would over-egg his motorised land percentage. He could catch a flight out to Malta, but that similarly would over-egg his flight percentage. But he had to do one or the other – the boat option seemed a non-starter.

Day: Date	Itinerary (* indicates TV interview) ([18]indicates new nation)	Bike (km)	Car/ Bus (km)	Train (km)	Kayak/ Sail (km)	Boat (km)	Air (km)
Totals brought forward		2958	1354	0	928	220	1233
35: 19/6/11	Aqaba, Jordan[39]	158	8				
36: 20/6/11	Cairo, Egypt[40]		42			34	346
37: 21/6/11	Cairo *						
38: 22/6/11	Tripoli, Libya[41]						1740
Totals carried forward		3116	1404	0	928	254	3319

Chapter 24: Alienation

Louisa felt stuck too. She was beginning to have anxiety attacks before going into work, though the problem wasn't going into work but the ten-hour wait to return home. Sister Lilian stepped up the harassment on all the nurses, but on Louisa most of all. She took to bringing Louisa into her office just as her shift was coming to an end, and giving her a job which would take 20 minutes at least to complete. When Louisa dared to complain, she was ignored and given still-worse duties, though others were given them sometimes too so that Louisa couldn't prove that she was being singled out. There were more compulsory meetings during *her* breaks, more criticisms of *her* work in team briefings and more snide comments about *her* commitment. Sister Lilian organised extra meetings in which the nurses were told to make suggestions — if they didn't they got criticised and if they did their suggestions got dissected and ridiculed, so it was one more clever tactic: appear democratic but reinforce the domination. The amount of time available for patient care was reduced, so caseloads mounted and patients complained.

One of the young patients died rather suddenly — of an unexpected complication in another underlying problem. Everyone on the unit was devastated, but Louisa especially as she'd had most to do with him. Sister Lilian refused to let Louisa swap shifts so that she could attend the funeral, but Louisa couldn't complain, because someone did have to work that shift, though she knew that the Sister was just being nasty.

Sometimes Louisa got told off for doing something that Sister Lilian wanted her to do yet hadn't actually *told* her to do, only to find that the next time she went to do it unbidden she got told off for doing it. Things came to a head one day when the Sister accused her in a ward-round of being incompetent and not following proper nursing procedures, when it was actually Sister Lilian herself who hadn't passed on the doctors' instructions. Things were getting dangerously out of hand. One of the other nurses, however, had the courage to back Louisa up, the complaint against her was dropped and Sister Lilian became almost human for the next few shifts, before her normal abusive behaviour resumed.

Louisa started to hate going into work — and everything else became contaminated by this issue. Ben got frustrated at not being able to help — she would sound off at him and he just had to soak it up like a sponge. He said this once, and Louisa made him a huge foam ear with the message "Thank you for listening". But he still felt useless.

She chatted with friends from her old cell group, but they weren't much help — telling her to get another job or send in an official complaint. Louisa was tempted, but she wanted to change things not just escape from them. How could she stand up for herself when the odds seemed stacked against her, and without it looking like revenge? What would Jesus do? She wore a bracelet when she wasn't at the hospital which asked that very question: "WWJD?"

Louisa found out one day that Sister Lilian had called a meeting in Louisa's lunch break for everyone except her, and when she asked Bridget about it, she blushed and pulled her to one side. "I'm not supposed to tell you this, but Sister Lilian told us to distance ourselves from you because you're on your way out. We think she's trying to pressure you into resigning. Penny said that she was disgusted and would report it to the Union but it only took one look from Sister and Penny shut up. I think it's horrible but I don't know what we can do about it!"

Louisa was shocked. She knew that the Sister had it in for her but this was totally over the top. What had she done to upset her so much? She wondered whether she ought to report what had happened, but feared that Sister Lilian would turn it around somehow and she'd be in even more trouble. What could she do?

She was surprised when the answer came to her. She'd never had any kind of inspired thought, "word of knowledge" or anything like that before. She wasn't even sure that she believed in that sort of thing. But she instantly knew that she must pray – for Sister Lilian, and the whole unit, nurses and patients alike. So that's what she did, down in the hospital chapel. She prayed long and hard for Sister Lilian, trying to picture her and Jesus side by side. It was a bit of a stretch of her imagination, and when she managed to get them both into the same "frame" she imagined that Jesus had a bit of a frown. She told herself off and tried again, trying not to project her own negativity onto her prayer, and this time she saw Jesus giving Sister Lilian a big hug, even though he couldn't get his arms all the way round because of her girth. It made her feel so much better – and she glowed as she went back to the unit.

"Are you OK?" asked a worried Bridget, as if Louisa must have snorted coke for her to be suddenly so radiant in the face of such hostility.

"I'm fine," said Louisa, over her shoulder, as she breezed along saying hello to everyone. She felt like a million dollars, and that nothing could harm her. And the feeling lasted the whole of the rest of the shift.

She met up with her friend at the bus-stop again, but there were no Dalek impersonations this time. Bridget asked, "How did you manage to put on such a brave face all afternoon?"

"I prayed!" said Louisa, confidently and brightly. "That's what I did, I prayed for you all, and I prayed for Sister Lilian too – and suddenly it all seemed different."

"Gosh. That's great... I wish I had your faith."

"There's nothing clever or special about it," said Louisa. "I'm not a super-Christian, but I do feel that God wants our unit to be different and I think that prayer's going to be part of that. Why don't you try it?"

"You know, I think I will. I'm fed up of the atmosphere on the unit and the way she treats you. I'll pray about it tonight before I go to bed."

"So will I," promised Louisa. "And tomorrow before I come into work."

"Me too," said Bridget.

Chapter 25: Nations 42 – 48

Giovanni came running along to Tripoli bus-station and just caught Brendan before he bought his ticket for the long ride to Tunisia. "Brendan! Brendan! I've found you a boat to Malta!"

Brendan didn't know whether to laugh or cry. If he left Libya by sea he would still preserve his distance quotas, but Malta would take him away from his planned route. Everything was getting mucked around – but he asked Giovanni for more details.

"Well," said Giovanni. "I phoned up the harbour-master and asked whether any container ships were leaving Tripoli which would take a British citizen either to Malta or Tunis. I said "British citizen" very loud to assure him nothing losco was going on."

Brendan looked blank. "Losco?"

"Sorry – losco, sospetto, er... I think you say panky-hanky."

Brendan understood. "Dodgy," he said.

Giovanni nodded too. "Ah, yes – *dodgy* – good! The harbour-master is Coptic Christian and I know him through the friend of my cousin, so he's happy to help. He says there is a Lebanese ship leaving tonight to Valetta."

"And are you sure that it'll be OK?"

"Oh yes," said Giovanni. "I arrange it." He smiled. No doubt a nice back-hander had found itself into the captain's pocket for him to take Brendan without it going on his official log. Brendan realised quickly the advantage of this new route – sailing across the Mediterranean rather than going round the coast-line then across to Malta would probably save 400km of powered water-travel. He'd let Jayne work out the implications, but he was going to go for it. Giovanni got the Libyan GNT – he'd earned a memento of his strange English visitor.

***

Twelve hours later, Brendan was reflecting on the most unpleasant night of his life. The entry onto the ship was completed successfully by hiding Brendan in a container full of frozen tuna which had swayed and banged and lurched and dropped. The fish were going all over the place and Brendan with them. He felt horribly sick but managed to keep it in until the container smashed down onto the floor of the hold, at which point he threw up all over the tuna lying at that moment in his lap. It didn't object, but its frozen eye looked up at him accusingly. Brendan's throat hurt and his glands seemed to be swollen. He'd been let out by the captain, who was not impressed by the sight or smell of Brendan but led him up the gantry to one of the lifeboats, which was Brendan's berth for the journey. The night had been long and freezing cold. The region may be scorching hot during the day but it was freezing at night, especially out on the Mediterranean. The ship rocked quite a bit and this together with the fact that his clothes smelled of fish and vomit didn't make for a happy or healthy voyage. He hadn't slept at all, but still had most of the day to wait before docking in Valetta. He vowed never to travel as a stowaway or eat tuna again.

***

The entry into Malta was far more pleasant than the exit from Libya. The crew didn't notice or care when Brendan shuffled down the gangplank. When he showed his passport in the harbour office, the customs official wrinkled his nose and enquired why Brendan had no exit stamp from Libya, but when Brendan shrugged his shoulders he didn't persist as the smell was making the small office increasingly muggy. Brendan exploited this by asking multiple questions: "Is there a ferry from here to Tunis? When does it leave and where from? How much will it cost? How long does it take?"

The customs officer had enough, and showed Brendan the door. "GNV – over there," he pointed, and ushered him out. Brendan walked across to the Grandi Navi Veloci office and booked himself a day-cabin for the passage to Tunis. He'd had enough of roughing it.

It was odd to be in an English-speaking country again, even though it was only for one night. The Genoa-Tunis ferry would dock in Malta the following morning at 8.30am and set off again an hour later, which suited Brendan fine. He made his way to the Methodist Church and made the acquaintance of an old College friend, Lawrence, whom he hadn't seen in years. When the door opened, Brendan said hello, then asked for a shower, which puzzled Lawrence until he breathed in and caught the intoxicating aroma of dead fish and old vomit.

The GNT for Malta was printed in Maltese, which seemed obvious to Brendan until he realised that most people spoke English. Lawrence said that most Maltese people spoke both and Maltese was taught in schools, so the Bible Society had got it right again. He agreed to give the GNT to the local school and explain in their next assembly what it was all about. After a wonderful meal with Lawrence and his wife Jill, Brendan enjoyed a good evening at the church. A large crowd turned up; there was no need for translation so the talk was uninterrupted; the audience had heard of Brendan and some had seen him on cable TV a few days before.

***

It took 12½ hours for the Malta-Tunis ferry to reach its destination, so it was dark when they docked at Halq al Wadi on arrival, so Brendan never actually made it into the city of Tunis. He booked in at the nearest hotel and went straight to sleep, but was woken by the call to prayer. He didn't feel particularly prayerful at 4.30am so he went back to sleep, hoping that God would understand. At what he felt was a more decent hour, he began his day – the first task of which was to buy a sea-going kayak. He was spoilt for choice, because kayaking was one of Tunisia's most popular sports and most Tunisian children seemed to love it, judging by the clusters of kayaks on the inland canal to the city. Sea kayaking was another matter, of course, but several shops seemed to cater for that too, and Brendan was able to buy a 5.3m Nordkapp LV sea kayak for 3,000 Tunisian dinars, which was the equivalent of about £1,300. A lot of money in a way, but he hoped to sell it later.

The new Nordkapp design reminded him of Nannuraluk's kayak which had served him so well, but this was a modern sports/touring model giving maximum cargo capacity, ease of straight-line paddling, and comfort on long journeys. It had a similar spraydeck and sufficient width for the GO-kart box to fit snugly into the cargo space, and had surprising stability despite the extra weight. Brendan was relying on it for the next 15 days and 2,000km. As he paddled out into the Gulf of Tunis past the ruins of ancient Carthage he realised that he was not the first one to dream big dreams. Babs Elliot had enchanted him and his schoolmates with tales of heroic Hannibal who'd set off from here on a roundabout route through Spain and France to occupy northern Italy and harass Rome. The Nordkapp glided smoothly through the waves, responding well to the paddle, and enabling an excellent cruising speed of 9kph. It was with some surprise that Brendan found himself already out of the Gulf of Tunis by early afternoon and paddling sedately past the gorgeous beach resort of Raf Raf round the other side of the headland. The shortie wet-suit which Ruth had given him in Cairo was exactly right for this leg of the journey, because water did splash in to cool his lower half without discomfort and the run-off from the paddle kept his hands and arms cool while a baseball cap stopped the fierce sun from burning him up. It couldn't get much better.

By late afternoon he could see the new Goga super-marina east of Bizerte coming into view. Instead, Brendan headed for the old port, "defended" from the sea by a double Byzantine kasbah containing too many nondescript houses crammed into unfeasibly narrow streets. Bizerte was built on the sea-front itself – unlike most Tunisian "coastal" towns which were up to a kilometre inland and joined to the sea by canals. But Brendan's overnight destination was 5km north – at Cap Blanc, the northernmost point in Africa. He'd already "bagged" several "continental extremities" and this was another one to add. Bizerte's beach seemed to go on and on, right up to the cape, some stretches overcrowded but others secluded. Brendan continued round the cape to a deserted beach, where he pulled the kayak well up beyond the high-tide line, and set about preparing his evening meal.

His little primus stove and freeze-dried meal reminded him of the start of his first journey up at Ellesmere Island. The chewy curried chicken now brought an instant sensory flash-back to the cardboard taste of evening meals in the high Arctic – but he wolfed it down all the same. He didn't have a tent because there should be no rain or snow to need shelter from, but he did have his old trusty sleeping-bag which had kept him warm in the ice and would now keep him snug on cold beaches. Looking up at the stars in the sky reminded him of the Atacama Desert in Chile. He felt curiously refreshed and strong. Past accomplishments brought reassurance and renewed resolve.

The long next day was made bearable because of the ever-changing coastline, mostly stunning seashores falling steeply into glistening water, and beaches adorned in cork and mimosa trees. That evening, he was befriended by a young lad in Tabarka called Hatem who even spoke a little English. Brendan shared his meal with Hatem then gave him the Tunisian (Arabic) GNT, laughing as Hatem ran off home shouting, jumping and punching the air.

Then Brendan crossed into Algeria, which meant more of the same. In fact, the next few days till Algiers were very similar to the Tunisian coastal journey: long days, mostly rocky cliffs, wooded hills, and small bays with golden stretches of sand, but occasional small towns or resorts which provided opportunities to stock up with water and bivouac on the beach.

He arrived in Algiers on schedule in the afternoon of his fifth Algerian day. He was due to speak in the Notre Dame d'Afrique Catholic Basilica, an imposing domed church on a cliff overlooking the bay. The Catholic Church was allowed to continue under governmental license, but Protestant Churches had been decimated by the imposition of Ordinance 06-03 which prohibited any Christian activity outside of a state-recognised church building[47]. The authorities made it very difficult for that re-registration to take place, so most churches had been closed within a year, with evangelicals officially declared "dangerous". The Catholic churches fared a little better and continued as long as they didn't attempt to convert anyone. Algeria was the 22nd worst nation for persecuting Christians according to Open Doors[48] and the worst part was that Christians couldn't talk openly about their faith. Brendan believed that evangelism was at the core of what Christians were called to do, so how would he cope in such an oppressive setting?

The priest, called Bernard, fended off Brendan's questions, and was very reticent about saying anything critical of the state. The atmosphere throughout the evening

---

[47] The real-life Ordinance cited, and its interpretation and implementation, is typical of the legislative ways in which churches in Islamic countries are persecuted.

[48] Open Doors publish an annual World Watch List of the "top 50 countries for persecution of Christians". The "positions" cited are from the 2011 List. Both Algeria and Morocco were higher (i.e. worse) than in 2010.

was restrained and muted, but Brendan loved the apse of the church, decorated with garish blue tiles and the inscription "Notre Dame d'Afrique priez pour nous et pour les Musulmans" which seemed to be an appropriate prayer in the circumstances: "Pray for us and the Muslims"... There were several suited, tough-looking guys with sunglasses, whom Brendan guessed were official observers. No-one spoke to them or even looked at them. At the end of the evening they stood by the exits and monitored people as they left. A few people picked up the Arabic "business cards" with the website details on, but not many. There hadn't been a collection or any questions after the talk – it was oppressive and discouraging.

Brendan wondered how on earth the Christians kept going when they were forbidden any encouragement or joy, yet he'd seen quite a few smiles in the audience, many seemed to be listening hard, a few cried and one older lady seemed to be praying all the way through. Brendan went up to one of the observers and offered him the GNT but got no response. He put it down on a table and when he looked back it had disappeared. He hoped that it had been pocketed for the observer's own unofficial reading later, but it might just have been picked up as evidence or to stop anyone else reading it.

The five days that followed were similar to the five before Algiers. He spent the nights on isolated beaches along the coast: near Gouraya, Ain Brahim and then in the city of Oran, where he had another speaking engagement in a similar church both in its imposing location and its lack of passion and expression. Our Lady of Santa Cruz Basilica was situated on the majestic Djebel Murdjadjo plateau above the city, near to the even-more-imposing fortress of Santa Cruz, standing as reminders of past conflicts and the need for peace.

After Oran, he paddled ever-westwards, spending his last Algerian night near El Ziatane before crossing into Morocco at lunchtime the following day and reaching the Spanish (yes, *Spanish*) town of Melilla that evening. Brendan too couldn't quite believe this, but Melilla was an enclave of Spain, and part of the European Union. Of course Morocco claimed sovereignty but the borders were secured by the Melilla border fence, a 6m-tall double barrier with watch-towers. Brendan was told by the priest over a pre-talk meal that refugees still frequently managed to cross illegally, so detection wires, tear gas dispensers, radar, and day/night vision cameras were soon to be installed. Brendan had been stopped by patrol boats out in the bay – the officials carefully checking his papers to make sure that he wasn't an illegal immigrant. It made for a fortress mentality, and for the jingoistic assertion of Melilla's status in Spain and Europe, but life seemed very vibrant and upbeat.

Brendan was amused to tick Spain off his list while still in Africa. He passed the Spanish GNT to an ex-Muslim convert who was thrilled to get his own (and such a special) copy of the Scriptures. In contrast to Algiers and Oran, the evening was warm, lively and full of laughter, questions and interest. Brendan found himself getting quite upset as the evening progressed. How easy it was to be a Christian in these circumstances – and how hard in places like Algeria.

Leaving Melilla the following morning was similar to his entry the previous evening – patrol boats, passport checks, then a friendly smile and a wave. He rounded the headland of Bou Mahroud by mid-morning and paddled sedately along the coastline all day, seeing no-one and very few signs of human life. He was reluctant and a bit scared to engage with Moroccans until he got to Tangiers for his speaking engagement there, as Morocco was 31st worst on the Open Doors list, making it not that much better than Algeria.

The following day, he stopped briefly at the Peñon de Velez de La Gomera, a fortress still manned by the Spanish Foreign Legion and, like Melilla, part of Spain. Brendan chatted to a guard whose job was to protect single-handedly the 85m of the isthmus which constituted the shortest land border in the world. He seemed to be fairly laid-back about it, as he didn't seem to be carrying a weapon and was eating a cake while he chatted.

The next day was his last in Morocco – his destination: Tangiers. He paddled northwards up to the headland of Ceuta, another Spanish enclave which had an even worse illegal immigrant problem because it was directly across from Gibraltar, less than 30km away. Brendan gave the headland a wide berth to avoid patrol boats and found himself suddenly battling some strong currents. He got through them but it slowed him considerably on his last four long hours into Tangiers.

But then finally he was there. He paddled in a fairly bedraggled state into the long beach near a hotel which, incredibly, was called the Movenpick Hotel. Brendan didn't want to read anything into this coincidence, and indeed, as he stepped out of the kayak he realised that he'd beached right where there happened to be a kayak-hire shop. The owner came out, expecting Brendan to be returning one of the shop's kayaks, but realised that his craft was a rather superior model to those which he was hiring out.

"Oooh," he said, admiring the Nordkapp. "Good kayak," he said, correctly perceiving that Brendan was English.

"It's a Nordkapp LV," said Brendan, as if he knew about sea kayaks.

"Aaah," said the kayak-man. "I have heard of those but never seen one. May I?" He bent over and examined the inside of the cockpit and murmured approvingly of the various lines and fittings. "Very good kayak."

"Do you want to buy it?" asked Brendan, nonchalantly.

"To buy – me?" said the kayak-man incredulously, as if he'd been offered the chance to buy a ticket for the Miss World Show. "I will not have enough money, I am sure, because it is such a *special* kayak." Brendan wondered whether he'd ever met someone who drove such a hard bargain against himself. This man was the worst haggler in the world.

"I will sell it to you for £1,000," said Brendan, anxious not to exploit the situation or this man's vulnerability or love for this "special" kayak. He could see the man's brain doing the calculation, and then the thrill when he realised that he might have enough to buy it.

"I will have the money tomorrow," said the man. "Please do not sell it to anyone else."

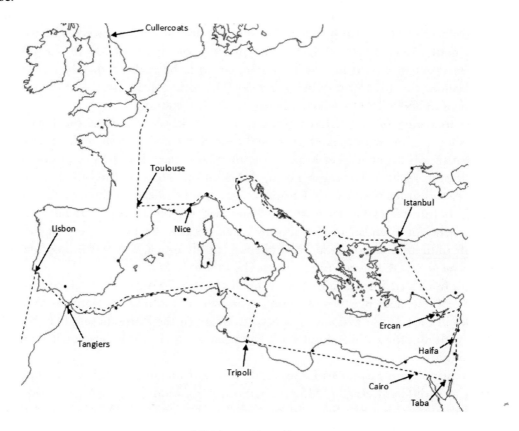

Nations 19 to 47

Brendan reassured him by asking him to look after the Nordkapp overnight. The man's face lit up even more – as if he was being offered a night with Miss World. Brendan unpacked the kayak and reconstructed the GO-kart, which he wheeled up to the hotel, booked a room, dumped his GO-kart, peeled off the rather stinky wet-suit, showered and dressed. He asked the hotel reception to call him a cab, and set off with the Moroccan GNT and the rest of his Arabic "business cards" to St. Andrew's Church – just off the Grand Socco.

Its tall white tower, a bit like a minaret, overlooked the square (and the cemetery on the other side) and such a strategic site was a surprise in a country where Christians were not treated with the most gracious hospitality. The priest-in-charge of the Anglican congregation was pleased to see him, as he'd advertised the meeting as well as he could and was expecting a good crowd that evening – and so it proved. Despite the presence of some surly observers who looked almost as unhappy as their Algerian counterparts, the rest of the audience were well up for it and the evening went really well. They even held a collection, and Brendan was amazed to be told that it had netted over 10,000 dirhans. The priest wrote it as 10,000 MAD – which Brendan thought was an interesting comment, until he realised that MAD was the abbreviation for the Moroccan currency. The priest told him that it was the equivalent of about £800 – which was impressively generous.

The following morning, having completed the kayak sale with the bleary-eyed kayak-shop owner, who looked as if he'd indeed spent the night with Miss World, Brendan set off to the airport in plenty of time and relaxed as the plane took off for the half-hour flight to Lisbon in Portugal, Nation 47. He'd planned to meet another Methodist Minister friend who'd gone straight from College to serve in Papua New Guinea before relocating to Portugal. Peter had set up an early evening speaking engagement for Brendan in the airport hotel, because Brendan's next flight didn't take off until after ten o'clock. He'd checked in his baggage as transit luggage so as long as he got there before 9pm he would be OK to board.

Peter translated for the talk and the small crowd who'd gathered seemed to enjoy it. One of the audience was a young man who'd escaped to Portugal from the troubles in East Timor and was delighted to be given the Portuguese GNT. Brendan talked with him for a while about East Timor, aware that he'd be visiting it himself in a few months' time.

The plane from Lisbon to Cape Verde took off on time at 2215h and landed at 0030h – a different day, a different nation, a different continent, but the same satisfaction at raising another wad of cash for Watoto. Cape Verde was dark and warm, but then Brendan expected that at just after midnight on an island only 1,000 miles from the equator, and was glad to get into the air-conditioned hotel and then into bed.

***

He got chatting after breakfast with the hotel receptionist – who seemed intrigued at Brendan's GO-kart and particularly the writing on the side of it. Brendan explained what his journey was about and the receptionist looked admiringly, adoringly, almost worshipfully at him as if he was some kind of mega-saint. Brendan handed her the GNT, printed in Portuguese – showing her the inscription inside, but then rushed off for the airport before she prostrated herself in front of him or asked him to bless a handkerchief.

His flight to Dakar was leaving at noon, so he was bang on schedule. As the plane took off and levelled out above the Atlantic Ocean, Brendan reflected with satisfaction that the administrative glitches from Detroit seemed to have disappeared, as nothing had really gone wrong since he'd had a word about it in Cairo. The next leg, though, was going to be something different, slightly dangerous, and potentially disastrous.

Day: Date	Itinerary (* indicates TV interview) ([18] indicates new nation)	Bike (km)	Car/ Bus (km)	Train (km)	Kayak/ Sail (km)	Boat (km)	Air (km)
Totals brought forward		3116	1404	0	928	254	3319
39: 23/6/11	At sea					361	
40: 24/6/11	Valetta, Malta[42]						
41: 25/6/11	Tunis[43]					432	
42: 26/6/11	Bizerte				94		
43: 27/6/11	Tabarka				120		
44: 28/6/11	Ain Barber, Algeria[44]				127		
45; 29/6/11	Collo				120		
46: 30/6/11	Taza				118		
47: 1/7/11	Azeffoun				115		
48: 2/7/11	Algiers				128		
49: 3/7/11	Gouraya				123		
50: 4/7/11	Ain Brahim				138		
51: 5/7/11	Oran				133		
52: 6/7/11	Ez Ziatane				131		
53: 7/7/11	Melilla, Spain[45]				121		
54: 8/7/11	Reheha, Morocco[46]				112		
55: 9/7/11	beyond Aarhob				115		
56: 10/7/11	Tangiers				131		
57: 11/7/11	Lisbon, Portugal[47]; Cape Verde[48]						3435
Totals carried forward		3116	1404	0	2754	1047	6754

Chapter 26: Indoctrination

Fahada had been encouraged in Cairo by her father's interest in stopping Brendan, yet scared by his even deeper interest in Esther, and deliberately played down further mention of Esther – talking instead at length with her "controller" Saeed about Brendan's itinerary. Saeed promised that he'd be in touch after he'd consulted "the brothers". Her father told her to await his orders. "I'm going to take charge of everything from now on," he said.

Fahada's earlier excitement now turned to indignation, but she steeled herself not to react outwardly, playing the subservient daughter her father imagined her to be. But behind her hijab she was seething. How dare he take over in such an arrogant way!

For the next fortnight, she dutifully did nothing – ignoring several opportunities to hassle Brendan as he crossed North Africa and even had the gall to speak publicly in strict Muslim countries. What a fool... there was no telling what the religious authorities would do if provoked. As Brendan passed through Libya, Algeria and Morocco, Fahada eagerly listened for news of Brendan being arrested or deported, but nothing awkward happened at all[49]. She read about a Nigerian Christian being expelled from Libya for evangelising, but nothing about Brendan. She read about Christians being blocked from worship in Oran, but nothing about Brendan. One woman was prosecuted for carrying a Bible in her handbag, but Brendan had several Bibles in his GO-kart and got away with it. Christians were imprisoned for illegal meetings, but Brendan seemed to be untouchable. Morocco was experiencing a purge of Christianity, so Fahada had high hopes there, but nothing happened. Well, nothing happened to Brendan anyway. Moroccan security forces arrested 18 at a Bible Study, expelled 20 Christian aid workers from an orphanage and threw out over 70 foreign aid workers – all during the few days Brendan spent in Morocco. Then he turned up bang on time in Tangier enquiring about flight arrangements. He was leading a charmed life.

She continued to hear nothing from Saeed or her father so decided that she would try some small acts of sabotage which didn't point a finger back at her. She would be meeting him again in a fortnight in Guinea, but between then and now Brendan had over two weeks of cycling through very remote areas, where the roads were rough and it was not unknown for people just to disappear and never be seen again. She saw it as a challenge, and an opportunity.

---

[49] The incidents of persecution described are real events, catalogued in Open Doors' accounts of the Persecuted Church in North Africa in the summer of 2010.

Then Fahada received a phone call from Saeed. "Hello, Fahada," he gushed, slimily. "I need to meet up with you again. We have made plans to resolve the Brendan problem once and for all."

She tried to stifle a giggle but couldn't help herself and was chastened when Saeed told her off. "I'm taking this very seriously and perhaps you should wake up to your responsibilities too."

"Sorry," mumbled Fahada, submissively – all the time thinking, "Git."

Saeed then surprised Fahada. "I will see you at 12.30pm tomorrow at the Hard Rock Café downtown."

"What!" she shouted. "You're already here?"

"Oh yes, Fahada. I've been here for over a week – and I have found out some very interesting facts about Esther Blanchett and yourself – some *very* interesting facts. I will see you tomorrow." And he put the phone down.

Fahada paled. What could she do? How had it all gone wrong? Her secret was out – or at least it would be unless she did exactly what Saeed said. But what would the price of his silence be? She shuddered at the thought of all the various possibilities, from the financial to the lewd to the violent. She knew that she could cope with indulging Saeed sexually if that was the blackmail demand he chose, even though he was repulsive – and she could pay him more money than he'd ever imagined if that was what he chose. But if he asked her to do something to Esther she really would be in difficulty. Esther was the goose that kept laying golden eggs for her – and she was rather fond of not only the lifestyle but also the lady who provided it. But Fahada was absolutely sure of one thing – there was no way she would allow Saeed to ruin everything by telling her father about her relationship with Esther. No way.

The following day she dressed quite provocatively, showing more of her bosom than she would normally do. She'd decided to challenge Saeed rather than submit meekly to him. He would see a different side of her from that which she'd shown in Cairo. By 12.30pm she was sat at one of the window tables drinking a coffee, looking out at the river – ignoring the geographical oddity of seeing the *Canadian* town of Windsor on the *southern* bank because her mind was focussed sharply on thwarting Saeed.

She saw him swaggering (or was it waddling?) up the sidewalk and then entering the Café as if he was a regular, affecting a walk that was a cross between John Wayne and Charlie Chaplin. He'd obviously been watching too many films. He looked around, taking his sunglasses off, and then doing a double-take when he saw Fahada and what she was wearing. He came across, failing miserably to keep his eyes off her cleavage.

"Well, Saeed, this is a surprise," said Fahada, taking the initiative as she'd planned.

"It's not the only surprise," said Saeed, recovering. The opening ripostes had been delivered.

"What do you mean?" asked Fahada, still playing the innocent until she knew precisely what Saeed had heard or seen.

"You seem to have done very well for yourself," said Saeed, snidely. "You no longer live in your own apartment, like you used to. Now you live in the big house out of town where they have so many security men with dogs and there are cameras and barbed wire all the way round."

Fahada raised an eyebrow. He'd been out to the house. She must be careful. "Have you been spying on me?" she asked, in an off-hand, joking sort of way.

"Oh *yes*, we have." He was almost drooling.

"And what have you discovered from this little spying trip of yours?" asked Fahada, still clinging to her innocent facade.

"Oh, all kinds of things – none of which would impress your father, should he find out…" Saeed left his sentence dangling in the air like a rollercoaster car at the top of the drop, obviously thinking how clever he was. Then he succumbed to the gravity of his little plot and whispered, "But of course he doesn't have to find out, does he?" And in that one screaming, heart-stopping moment, the blackmail plot hurtled into focus. Fahada was pressed back in her seat, as if on a real rollercoaster. Her thoughts whirled and she felt sick. She'd never liked him. He'd climbed higher than his intelligence could cope with. When he'd emerged from the gene pool there must have been a drought. Now he was playing this pathetic game of blackmail and she could guess from his fascination with her breasts what price he would be asking for first. She sighed nonchalantly and stood up.

"Come on then, Saeed. Let's get it over with. My apartment's three blocks away."

Saeed's mouth dropped open. For a woman to talk like that to a man was shameful, yet he'd expected more resistance. In a funny way he felt cheated. Red-faced, he followed her out and scurried after her as she walked quickly to her apartment.

Fahada took off her jacket as soon as she got in and started to get undressed. "OK, let's get this over with." She revealed the skimpiest bra that Saeed had ever seen and then took that off as well, facing Saeed so that he got the full effect.

Saeed instantly went from gangster to youngster. He went bright red and jumped to his feet. "No, no!" he shouted, and ran off into the bathroom. "Please, get dressed, I beg you!" Fahada smiled at his embarrassment. This might be easier than she'd imagined.

He emerged from the bathroom rather shamefaced but blustering that she'd misunderstood him. He'd not been trying to coerce her or anything because he was a good Muslim. This statement seemed to give him courage and he sat down and turned quietly serious. "You have turned into a harlot, Fahada, an affront to the

Prophet. It is my duty to bring you back into the true religion[50]. If you're willing to submit then there is no reason why your father needs to know about your jaahiliyyah, your time of ignorance away from your Islam." He paused and looked up, and Fahada nodded for him to continue. She might just get away with it after all.

"Praise be to Allah!" continued Saeed, recovering his sense of superiority. Fahada bowed her head as if she were truly penitent and Saeed got all pious. "It will be an honour to bring you back into your Islam. You have obviously been lured by infidel teachings into confusion and apostasy in your heart. I will give you some teachings which will help you overcome any difficulty."

Fahada wondered how long it would take. She was due back at the office in 20 minutes.

"When people promise to follow the true religion, even if they have been living in a state of abomination, it will have a far-reaching effect on their personality and behaviour, and give them a fresh start and a new direction in life, completely different from the way they were during their jaahiliyyah. Their hearts will be purified and filled with a sense of chastity, so that they look with revulsion and disgust both at their own former deeds and at the ignorant world of promiscuity, infidelity, nakedness and utter corruption that exists in the society around them. Are you ready to do that, Fahada?"

She nodded. Yet everything in her revolted against what this patronising toerag was saying.

"Praise be to Allah! You will come back to fitrah, the natural state of wholeness and purity of heart of which Shaytan has robbed you during your days as a sinner. If you take this new direction in life freely, and if it is truly accompanied by total submission to the commands and prohibitions of Allah, who revealed our religion of Islam with all its laws, then you will be counted among the faithful believers once again."

Fahada wondered if that was it, but Saeed hadn't finished yet. She resisted the urge to look at her watch. Saeed pulled a book out of his bag, opened it and began to read a tract that was sellotaped into the front of the book.

"There are two sources of proof to support our belief in the mercy of Allah, one from the sharee'ah and one from history. The shar'i evidence is to be found in numerous places in the Qur'an, for example: "Those who commit illegal sexual intercourse – whoever does this shall receive the punishment. The torment will be

---

[50] The quotations from Islamic authorities and the Qur'an itself, used by Saeed, are accurate. The argument Saeed uses is based on an answer actually given to a worried husband enquiring how best to bring back to faith his lapsed Muslim wife, on the Islamic "agony-aunt" website www.islam.tc/ask-imam.

doubled to him on the Day of Resurrection, and he will abide therein in disgrace, except those who repent and believe, and do righteous deeds. For those, Allah will change their sins into good deeds, and Allah is Oft-Forgiving, Most Merciful." [al-Furqaan 25:68-70]"

Come on, urged Fahada, silently, to herself. It's getting late. I'm going to be in trouble if Esther wants me and I'm not there. But he still hadn't finished.

Saeed read on: "Concerning the phrase "Allah will change their sins into good deeds", Sa'eed ibn Jubayr said: "Allah changed them from worshippers of idols into worshippers of the Most Merciful, and changed them from those who fight the Muslims into those who fight the mushrikeen (polytheists), and from those who marry mushrik women into those who marry believing women." Al-Hasan al-Basri said: "Allah changed them from evil deeds to good deeds, from shirk (polytheism) to ikhlaas (purity of faith), from promiscuity to chastity, from kufr to Islam.""

He drew breath. Fahada began to hope, but immediately her hopes were dashed.

"Concerning the historical evidence, there are a number of stories of Muslims who entered Islam after having been kuffaar (disbelievers), and how they changed and became righteous. Among these stories is the following: "Abd-Allaah ibn Maghfal told of a woman who had been a prostitute during the days of ignorance before Islam. A man passed by her, or she passed by him, and he touched her. She said: "Stop it! Mah! Allah has done away with shirk and has brought Islam." So he left her alone and went away." Saeed shut his book.

"At last!" breathed Fahada. But there was more.

"So, Fahada, if you come back to your true Islam and become a true Muslim once again, adhering to this pure sharee'ah, worshipping Allah as He wants to be worshipped, obeying His commands and heeding His prohibitions, then Insh'Allah you will not encounter or suffer the temptations of which you have been a victim. Moreover, you will have the means of keeping chaste, such as marriage, which will help you to refrain from doing haraam deeds; marriage is enjoined by this sharee'ah. The one who chooses a pure and clean way has no need to enter the mire of illicit relationships. I ask Allah to guide you and keep evil away from you. May Allah bless our Prophet Muhammad."

Saeed paused again, for longer this time, and Fahada dared to look up. Saeed was smiling, not smirking as he had been previously. He obviously believed that he'd achieved something very special and was rather proud of himself. He didn't have the discernment to realise that she'd not only failed to be persuaded, but actually been repelled by his indoctrination attempts. Fahada steeled herself and ingratiatingly thanked him for his wisdom and guidance. "Saeed, I'm ever so sorry but I am afraid that I have to return to work now or I will be in trouble."

Saeed's smile disappeared. "Oh, what a pity - and I return to Egypt tomorrow. But I'll meet you tonight, for dinner, when I'll tell you what your mission will be. I'll stay here while you go back to work, then you can cook dinner for us while we talk business."

Arrogant git, thought Fahada. You can have beans on toast. At least I'll only have to put up with you one more time.

Chapter 27: Nations 49 - 52

Brendan's first action after checking into his Dakar hotel was to take a ferry 3km out to Goree Island, to visit the Maison des Esclaves (House of Slaves). One of his journey's big themes was that restrictions on all freedoms – physical or otherwise – were equally pernicious and soul-destroying. Goree was a symbol pointing to deeper, broader injustices. Brendan expected the island to be drab, befitting its history, but instead it was a shocking riot of colour: pink and purple bougainvilleas draped across Mediterranean-style buildings painted in salmon and orange and accented in aqua. It was a highly emotive place, especially the Door of No Return through which millions of enslaved Africans, it was claimed, left the continent. The tour guide led Brendan through the basement cells, out through the Door of No Return, and held up iron shackles, like those used to bind enslaved Africans.

Brendan spoke that evening in the Catholic Cathedral in Dakar, and gave the Senegalese GNT to a scruffy-looking couple who wandered in halfway through his talk, who turned out (God-incidently) to be the proprietors of The Chain Gang, Dakar's funkiest bike-shop. It was the start of the rainy season, so the following morning a drenched but warm Brendan trundled off on his newly-purchased mountain bike, pulling the GO-kart, along the steaming road east out of the city. In fact the only way out was east because of the long peninsula on which Dakar was situated. Brendan followed the N2 to Thiès, passing through a forest which sluiced water in bucketfuls onto him as he cycled under the canopy of trees, then emerging into endless open savannah. The Sahara was creeping further south year by year, so the wet season was a blessing for the people of northern Senegal who lived on a hand-to-mouth basis and needed the harvest to stave off starvation.

Brendan spent his nights under canvas, cycling ever north-eastwards in the unceasing warm rain on decent roads which appeared to have more pot-holes the further north he went. The countryside seemed to be given over wholly to ground-nut cultivation, and several farmers were out digging and repairing irrigation channels to maximise the crops. They stopped, stared, smiled and waved at the curious sight of Brendan and the GO-kart passing slowly by...

He reached Louga by late afternoon on the second day, and decided to go for the shorter, scenic option through the fertile Lake Guiers valley rather than the longer haul round the coast on the better-surfaced N2. The rain barely made any difference to the cracked earth of the plateau, and when he arrived at the southern end of the lake it was no surprise that the Ferlo valley extending eastwards looked dry too. But the reason was that the flow was held back by hydraulic valves, so those down the valley got the mosquitoes from the stream but not the volume of water which they needed to grow the crops. In contrast, the Lake Guiers valley was thriving: abundant bird life including flamingos, ibises and spoonbills; sugar plantations and plenty of greenery. Water-control was power, it seemed – and the people of the Ferlo valley were obviously powerless. The inequality could be *seen*.

After rejoining the N2 at the Senegal River, he headed east along increasingly dodgy road surfaces, averaging two punctures a day, either on the bike or more frequently on the GO-kart. He could usually avoid pot-holes with the bike, but the GO-kart sometimes had a mind of its own and veered off into a trench or mini-crater.

He camped overnight at Lerabe in the Forêt de N'Dioum Dieri. From the tent he could see rows of mud huts behind a fence and wondered what they were. He found out the following morning, as he struck up a conversation in French with a lady at the entrance to the refugee camp. The camps were set up for black Fula tribesmen and their families fleeing the ethnic cleansing by the Arab-controlled Mauritanian regime in 1989. They hadn't returned, even after the Muslim dictator Taya was toppled in 2005, because they were terrified by the threat of racial injustice and even slavery back in Mauritania, which ingloriously held the world record for the highest proportion of slaves amongst its registered population.

Brendan followed the N2 along the border for the next three days, stopping near various desperately poor townships with buildings which looked as if they would fall down at any moment. He was pleased that it was the rainy season – the heat and humidity were still unbearable even with the rain, but it would have been much worse without. It was like being in a sauna with sprinklers. He eventually reached Bakel, which had a ferry crossing to the Mauritanian town of Gouray on the other bank, so Brendan, having looked at Mauritania for the last five days, finally got to enter it, giving his Mauritanian GNT to the bemused caretaker of the Gouray church, explaining that he was "voyageur d'un long voyage" and wanted to "donner ce livre à quelqu'un dans chaque pays", which he thought was quite fluent but it seemed to spark no reaction. Perhaps he'd chosen the one person in Mauritania who didn't speak French...

Back in Senegal, he cycled the N2 all the way to its terminus at Kidira, where he crossed the border into Mali, only going 200m further before finding and handing over the Malian GNT to a shopkeeper. Brendan tried to explain what it was and why he was giving it – only to meet with the same smiling incomprehension that he'd encountered in Mauritania. He backtracked into Senegal, and camped that night at the meeting-point of the N1 and N2, having travelled over 800km on the same road, along the same river. Tomorrow it's onwards and westwards, he thought, as he settled down for the night at the crossroads.

Unfortunately that point was the exact spot where hippos came ashore to look for grass to eat – or a tent if there happened to be one handy. None of the books he'd read indicated that hippos had a taste for camping, only grass. But Brendan woke in the middle of the night to hear a loud chomping noise extremely close to his head, and grass-ripping noises from both sides of the tent. He leapt out of the tent, making lots of noise but not impressing the huge hippos surrounding him, which continued to graze like cows in the moonlight. One hippo was, indeed, eating the end of his tent, which must have been made of some hitherto-unknown hippo-delicacy, because even when Brendan pulled all his stuff out of the tent and tried to pull the tent away from the hippo, he was unable to, as it was standing on the tent while it munched away at the walls. Brendan scurried round to let the guy ropes down, which disconcerted the hippo a little because its snack crumpled over its face and it backed away with a snuffle and a snort. It kept tight hold, however, of its mouthful of tent, trailing the whole tent behind it, so Brendan was no better off.

Brendan's trivia-stacked memory chose that moment to unearth the fact that the hippopotamus was responsible for more human deaths than any other African animal, but that such deaths were mostly down to the hippo's fear rather than its aggression. These great armoured tanks didn't appear fearful, but if one turned nasty and killed him, it didn't really matter why, did it? So when one comical fatty with its pink undersides and shortsighted Oliver Hardy stare looked up from its midnight feast to find a hairless biped at close quarters, why shouldn't it turn homicidal? In a rush, the hippo stomped forwards across the flattened tent, but Brendan leapt out of the way, onto his bike and set off along the slightly-uphill road as if it were a downhill section of the Tour de France. The hippo got its bearings and charged behind him, bellowing and growling and spraying dung around like a lawn sprinkler. Brendan kept going, head down, pedalling furiously. Fortunately the road *was* downhill after the bend and he managed to pull away. He sensed that the hippo had given up, and when he looked round there was indeed nothing to be seen except a huge shape silhouetted by the moon, like the African equivalent of the Hound of the Baskervilles, bellowing at him from the top of the hill down which he'd just fled. The bellowing went on for some time, before the hippo turned with a snort and a last swish of dung, and stomped off back to the river-bank.

Brendan could *hear* his pulse, but he gradually calmed himself down and took stock of his situation. He had to go back to get his GO-kart and whatever was left of his tent and sleeping-bag, but there was no way he was going back until the hippos had all gone back to the water. He parked his bike against the trunk of a tree, climbed into its branches and tried unsuccessfully to get some sleep.

When the sun eventually came up after several cramped and deeply uncomfortable hours, spent with sharp knobbly tree-branches sticking into unyielding parts of his anatomy, Brendan climbed gingerly down, having checked that the coast was clear. He pushed the bike back up the slope, finally ruling out a hippo ambush only as he approached the remains of his tent. The sleeping bag was intact apart from massive muddy footprints and hippo dung splashes decorating it in an avant-garde Paisley-esque design. The GO-kart was upside-down but intact too. It had similar markings from the dung but importantly it was uncrushed and towable. The tent must have got wrapped around the hippo's leg and was halfway down the river-bank, but the hippos were safely out in the middle of the river, so Brendan scooped it up and climbed back up to the road. When he unravelled the tent, the damage was confined to a huge hole in the end wall, with some wonderful teeth-marks around the ragged edge of the fabric. It would still be serviceable as a tent as long as he didn't mind a window being left open, so he'd probably got off quite lightly. He packed up and set off westwards along the N1 towards Tambakounde, speeding along the road through the rain-splashed but still parched Sahel, camping that night near a village called Bala, but it didn't look anything like the place in Wales.

Tambakounde was a town built around a crossroads and that pretty much said it all. There was a railway station which failed to throb with life of any sort, either mechanical or human. But nearby there was a bar, called Chez Francis, where a friendly Australian called Croc served Brendan a huge, ice-cold bottle of Bière la Gazelle for CFA600 (60p). As he drank by the side of the road, he savoured the taste, the chance to rest, and the lack of hassle, apart from a few beggar boys. Brendan had formed a beggar policy, which was to give something to the first beggar he saw each day, and that was it till the next day, when the first beggar got a few coins again. He reckoned that there were three options: you either gave to nobody, which was between you and your conscience; or you gave to everybody, which was between you and your bank manager; or you gave something to somebody on a pre-determined basis. It wasn't in any way solving the underlying problem, but, as they say, a handout a day keeps the conscience at bay... But was that good enough?

Brendan finished his beer and pedalled off, on the N6 now, towards Manda, a small town touching the border with Gambia. It was a good 50km but the beer must have refreshed him, for it was easy going, even in the warm rain.

The following morning he entered Gambia (in the rain, of course) at the Fatoto border-crossing and turned west. The map showed Gambia like a mangled éclair, with the river as its cream, misshaping the nation as it snaked its way 320km to the Atlantic, making the road a much better transport option. Curiously, there was no ferry service anyway along the river, reputedly because most Gambians couldn't swim and were terrified of water. Brendan could hardly believe this, given the way the river defined the very shape of the country, but perhaps the river's crocodiles, snakes and hippos had something to do with it as well.

He stopped briefly in Basse to change his money, and bought some barbecued goat meat and sweet bananas from a street vendor. At least in Gambia they spoke English, and Brendan could put his pathetic French away for the time being. He was planning to follow the "southern bank road" all the way to the coast, but was told by the vendor that after Georgetown he should revert to the "northern bank road" because the asphalt had just been relaid all the way to the coast. It was a bit longer than the original route, but would be quicker. Brendan's plans were very flexible because he was to meet his son-in-law Paul in a speedboat *somewhere* in Gambia, dependent on where a boat could be purchased. The advantage of Paul and Ruth working for Watoto was that they could both take time out to support Brendan in whatever ways needed, as the money coming in was well worth their wages... Paul had flown in the previous day and was busy looking, but had already drawn a blank at Kafountine, the preferred meeting-point down the coast. They would have to see what came up.

The wind blew Brendan along to Basang where, when he stopped for some water, a small child took one look at him, burst into tears, and ran to her mother. It seemed a bit over-dramatic until Brendan was told by the woman that her child had never seen a white man before. On the outskirts of the town Brendan was stopped at a roadblock where the officials discussed his route with him, recommended the route which the street vendor in Basse had suggested, enquired about his home country (they were very interested), marital status (commiserations were given), job (respect and curiosity), and his impressions of the country so far (they laughed when he asked why it always rained).

The winds were still from the east and it wasn't long before Brendan arrived at the turn-off to the northern bank road just before Georgetown. The town was situated on McCarthy Island in the middle of the river. On the ferry Brendan got talking to a teacher from the local Methodist school, who asked him to drop by the school the following morning. He directed Brendan to a backpackers' hostel on the north bank which was a peaceful, pretty but empty place. There was no electricity, so lighting was supplied by oil lamps and candles. Monkeys ran amok in the trees overhead, reminding Brendan that he'd been too thrifty to get a series of rabies injections before he set off from the UK. The shortage of guests meant that Brendan had no problem buying the use of a bed, which meant a comfy night despite discovering a giant millipede curled round the leg of the bed.

Brendan dutifully went to the Methodist school for the assembly, and was invited to talk to the children. He immediately noticed the paucity of resources compared to British schools, but also the discipline and commitment of staff and pupils to do the best with what was available. Brendan found it all rather humbling. He even had a quick burst of pride at being Methodist, which didn't happen that often. He explained what he was trying to do, which went over the heads of most of the children, who'd never left their river let alone their country. He gave the Gambian GNT to the headteacher to keep for the whole school. He promised to pray for the schoolchildren, and they promised to pray for him.

But Brendan had to press on. He'd phoned a message through to Paul the previous evening via Fahada in Detroit, and they'd agreed that Paul should look for the right boat on the river and the coast around the capital – and Brendan would attempt to make it to Banjul in two long days from Georgetown. The road was perfectly smooth, courtesy apparently of the Taiwanese government (why?). Cows outnumbered cars. Brendan tried to do some calculations as he pedalled along in the incessant rain, but the implications were a bit beyond him. Whatever he did differently from the itinerary would knock one of the percentages under 30%. He decided, over the 11 hours of fairly boring cycling that day to Farafenni, that he would cycle down from the capital Banjul to his original rendezvous point with Paul at Kafountine, which would keep him in balance all round with regard to the quotas. This was communicated to Paul via Fahada in Detroit that evening. The message back was that Paul thought that he'd found a boat suitable for the task, but he didn't want to buy it until Brendan had seen it. It was in Barra, so Paul would arrange a viewing for the following evening once Brendan arrived safely. This was good news, as this boat would be crucial not only for the passage down and round the coast of West Africa, but, would be needed again, after Brendan had explored into the interior by car, from Equatorial Guinea to Angola. So it had to be sturdy and reliable.

He found himself rather excited as he cycled down the still-wonderful road towards the coast, and was overjoyed to meet up with Paul as planned at the Barra ferry terminal, which was little more than a concrete adjunct with a cluster of houses, at the edge of the wide river estuary. There was little to show so far from the recent pledge by the Gambian President to turn the shanty town into a commercial centre for the North Bank Region. President Jammeh had, however, made some progress in empowering women, as was proved by the boatyard to which Paul took Brendan. It was a business set up by the local compin, or feminist co-operative. The women had been able to access interest-free loans to start up businesses and this particular compin had started a boat company. And they had bought cheaply and restored lovingly a most amazing boat.

Day: Date	Itinerary (* indicates TV interview) ([18] indicates new nation)	Bike (km)	Car/ Bus (km)	Train (km)	Kayak/ Sail (km)	Boat (km)	Air (km)
Totals brought forward		3116	1404	0	2754	1047	6754
58: 12/7/11	Dakar, Senegal[49]						629
59: 13/7/11	Mékhé	109					
60: 14/7/11	N'Guermalal	99					
61: 15/7/11	Richard Toll	92					
62: 16/7/11	Lerabe	108					
63: 17/7/11	Pété	97					
64: 18/7/11	Ouro Sagui	94					
65: 19/7/11	Bokiladaji	100					
66: 20/7/11	Kidira, via Mauretania[50] and Mali[51]	106					
67: 21/7/11	Bala	120					
68: 22/7/11	Manda	93					
69: 23/7/11	Georgetown, Gambia[52]	116					
70: 24/7/11	Farafenni	113					
71: 25/7/11	Barra	106					
Totals carried forward		4469	1404	0	2754	1047	7383

Chapter 28: Nations 53 – 54

The boat was, Paul explained, a Birchwood Executive 22, which meant that it was 22 foot long. He showed a rather distracted Brendan the Volvo AQ115A petrol inboard engine, the good-sized saloon with V-berth converting to double bed, plus the four-seater dinette which converted to another double bed, the well-equipped galley and two small toilet cubicles. Brendan was unable to concentrate properly, though, because the boat was a startling shade of pink. And *everything* was pink – paintwork inside and out, flooring, even the lifebelt. The boat was called the Pink Lady, and was on sale for five million CFA, which startled Brendan until he realised it was about £6,000. He took Paul to one side. "Will it do the job?"

"I think so," said Paul. "I'm quite good with engines and this one looks relatively new and sounds pretty good. What do you think?"

"I haven't got a clue," said Brendan. "But I already hate the colour scheme."

"It will certainly get us talked about, two men all alone in a small pink boat!"

"I know," said Brendan with a grin. "I've already been on a love boat in the Adriatic. But will it survive the crossing to São Tomé and back?"

"The women got it from Cape Verde, so it must have survived that sea-crossing. It looks OK to me, and it's pretty fast so it should maintain a decent daily schedule."

"But if anything goes wrong, will you be able to mend it? I'm useless at anything like that."

"I know," said Paul, with a smile. "Ruth told me. But I spent many holidays as a child fishing from my uncle's boat on Lake Albert, so I know about small boats like this. Trust me, Brendan, on this one."

So Brendan arranged to buy the boat the following day as long as their maiden voyage across the mouth of the river went well. Paul had already arranged the provisional transfer of funds from Oracle in Detroit, so he would stay behind to finalise the sale before joining Brendan the following evening in Kafountine. They asked if they could stay on the boat overnight, which delighted the ladies, convinced now that they wanted it as a love-boat.

The voyage across the river went smoothly. They managed quite a decent speed when Paul dared to open up the throttle, creating a wash which annoyed several fishermen. Paul dropped Brendan and his bike at Banjul harbour and turned back to the other side of the river to complete the sale. Brendan set off through the busy city, south to Diouloulou where the coast road split off for the small resort at the end of the road, literally. Brendan was there by late afternoon, but had to wait a few hours before Paul showed up. He'd had to make a few purchases for the boat – bed sheets and quilts, towels, toilet rolls – none of which, thankfully, were pink.

Brendan sold his bike to a British tourist for £50. He hopped on board carrying the GO-kart and they anchored off the coast. The boat had handled well, averaging

15kph without Paul pushing or the boat complaining, but the engine used up virtually all its petrol over the 80km – almost one gallon of petrol for every 3km – so it was a good job that Paul had purchased four spare drums of 30 gallons each.

The Pink Lady performed well over the next two days, chugging uncomplainingly down the coast, past the half-submerged and deserted island of Carabane which appeared to consist solely of mangroves, forests of coconut trees and sandy beaches. Further on, they passed the border with Guinea-Bissau at Cap Skiring, where sea-front hotels lined beautiful sandy beaches, again lined with coconut trees and empty of any sign of human life.

Guinea-Bissau was a low-lying swampy country, with bits and bobs of islands randomly strewn. It had recently suffered great political unrest, with its President killed by the army in 2009, but Brendan and Paul saw only soggy but empty forests and smelly but silent mangroves. They dropped anchor as planned just off the village of Ondame, went ashore and found the villagers gathering around a big fire. After allaying the initial surprise and fear of the villagers, Brendan and Paul were invited to sit with them. The villagers seemed to speak a language all of their own, but when Brendan showed them the Guinea-Bissau GNT, which had been translated into Criolu, a language derived from Portuguese, the elders seemed to understand it. Food was brought out, and bowls of rice given to both of them, with a choice of sauces. Brendan's tasted unsurprisingly of fish, but had onions, tomatoes and other unidentifiable things floating in it, whereas Paul's seemed to be coconut-based with bits of mango. At least, he thought and hoped that it was mango…

The village was very poor. Brendan and Paul wondered whether there was much contact with anyone else, or much possibility for trade or aid. Everyone was thin, and Brendan guessed that the "old men" of the village were probably younger than him. The chief elder was thrilled to be given the GNT, and bowed low before stalking rather pompously back to the largest of the rondavels.

The similar-sounding but different nation of Guinea was at the far side of the Rio Geba. The first 100km of Guinea was the same as Guinea-Bissau – lots of wide estuaries, mangrove forests and smelly vegetation. The incessant rain made the day rather sullen and foreboding, even at its end when they anchored near Kamsar, a dirty harbour for big container ships loaded with bauxite or other mining products. As they continued south, the trees thinned out, interspersed with fields and tiny villages in any clearing or bay. The rain cleared a little in the afternoon, bringing a muggy weight in the air which made Brendan long for more rain. Up ahead they caught sight of the peninsula of Conakry and its offshore islands jutting out into the ocean, and mid-afternoon saw them motoring into the harbour near the tip of the peninsula, carefully steering round the mangroves which surrounded the peninsula like a stockade.

Ruth rushed from the hotel on receipt of Paul's phone-call, and was there jumping up and down as they pulled up outside their hotel for the night, the appropriately named Hotel Petit Bateau, located on a breakwater extending over 500m into the ocean, far from the noise of the city. Nearby was the Port Authority HQ, so Brendan could wander down later and complete the formalities there. Several hugs later, they stepped straight from the boat into the hotel reception. The white-painted balconies and walkways reminded Brendan of the upmarket end of Butlins at Skegness, but the location was rather more exotic, and the sea-views much more spectacular.

Day: Date	Itinerary (* indicates TV interview) ([18] indicates new nation)	Bike (km)	Car/ Bus (km)	Train (km)	Kayak/ Sail (km)	Boat (km)	Air (km)
Totals brought forward		4469	1404	0	2754	1047	7383
72: 26/7/11	Kafountine	85				7	
73: 27/7/11	Ondame, Guinea-Bissau[53]					188	
74: 28/7/11	Kamsar, Guinea[54]					232	
75: 29/7/11	Conakry *					184	
Totals carried forward		4554	1404	0	2754	1658	7383

Chapter 29: Illumination

Jack Turner was agonising over his District's remaining Stationing issues. Two Circuits were hoping – even at this late stage – that he could pull a rabbit out of the hat, so he was on his way to the Methodist Conference in Southport to see if the final Stationing Committee meeting could help. In a few days' time, Conference would ratify all the appointments for the following year and then it would normally be another 12 months before any new appointments could be made. It was a bit like the football transfer window, but it was nearly shut. The difference was that, unlike the frenetic activity as the football deadline approached – everyone available, anyone approachable, rumours whizzing around – Stationing tended to whimper out for lack of available personnel, so no-one really expected anything to happen this late on.

Jack had already confirmed with the Circuit out to the west of the District which had just suffered the sudden death of a Minister, that they would have a year to readjust and make careful plans, rather than make a hasty decision which they might regret. It would also give the widow and her disabled son a whole year to work out where they were going to live.

Which left only Jact, in the North Tyneside Circuit. Caridad, the Cuban Minister, had been getting great results there, but the deal with the Cuban Church was for two years, and it could create an undesirable precedent if he stayed longer. This surfing idea of his was probably a trumped-up scheme to allow him and his family to stay in Britain, where the pay and conditions of ministry were so much better than in Cuba. Jack really needed to find a replacement so that he could insist that Caridad left. The true benefit of Caridad's ministry would be seen, of course, in how things developed at Jact after he'd left.

But who would still be unstationed at this 11th hour (and 59th minute)?

⁎⁎⁎

At the pre-Conference Stationing Committee, there were only three Ministers still available, and 27 Circuits still wanting a Minister. A further 31 other Circuits "left without" during the normal Stationing rounds had decided to go down a different route – employing a layperson to fill the gap and/or re-arranging pastoral oversight between the remaining staff.

The Ministers still available all seemed to Jack to be "damaged goods" and he didn't hold out much hope. It might even be better if the other Circuit Ministers covered Jact between them for a year. The fact, though, that North Tyneside had gone down this way before when Brendan Priest had left (Jack shuddered just thinking about him) meant that another Stationing non-result would go down like leprosy.

The three Ministers were slotted in somewhere or other, when up popped news of another Minister coming on-stream. He'd been a Bible College lecturer in Fiji for the last 28 years but wanted to return to England for his last few years before retirement. He wasn't fussy where he was stationed, as long as it wasn't in London. Aha, thought Jack. This looks more promising...

The man – unfortunately called Cecil (not a popular Geordie name, Jack noted ruefully) – had written many theology books and was an authority on the history of Methodist mission in the Pacific, so Jack hoped that he could transfer some of that missiological expertise to the outreach possibilities in Jact. Jack persuaded the other Chairs and, with only two days before Conference and Cecil still in Fiji, no further testing of the match was possible, so the Stationing Committee went for it – and Conference a few days later ratified it.

***

Each year, Jack looked forward to the ordination services, which always happened on the Sunday afternoon of Conference. The ordinands became Ministers by being "received into Full Connexion" at the Conference morning session, but that was the human bit of sorting out Church business. The ordination service was the real *spiritual* high point. Jack looked forward not just to his batteries being recharged as he listened to the "charge" given to the ordinands by a renowned preacher (their final words of advice before being "sent out"). Nor was it just him feeling part of something important and life-changing, as the question was put at the end of their long period of training and probation: "Do you believe that they are by God's grace worthy to be ordained?" and the whole congregation shouted back, "They are worthy!" The major reason was that Jack caught up there with old friends, who usually gathered at the ordination service linked with their old College.

So Jack was going to Blackburn, where those trained in Manchester were being ordained, including, by happy coincidence, one of the probationers from his own District. He was pleased to see that the preacher was one of his ex-tutors from Manchester, a now-retired ex-President of Conference called Richard, who'd led a Ministers' Study Day on the book of Acts in Jack's own District less than two years ago – not that Jack could remember much about it except that it had trawled through most of the first half of Acts. Richard was a good man and a well-respected Minister, but he was a bit evangelical for Jack's own tastes. Even so, it would be good to chat to him again and the others who would be there from the old College[51].

***

The atmosphere was hot and sweaty despite the airy expanses of Blackburn Cathedral. Methodism a few years ago had taken the wise decision to hold most if not all of its ordination services in large Anglican churches, not because of the Apostolic Succession or anything spiritual, but because they could hold more people. The place was packed, but, looking round, Jack could see several of his cronies from College, and had the chance before the service to have a brief chat with Richard too.

The high drama of the well-scripted and immaculately-choreographed ordination liturgy began – with a few catchy modern songs to appease modernists but with good solid hymns for the true Methodists, Jack noted with approval. Then came the reading from the Bible and the "charge". The reading was announced as being from the book of Acts and Jack groaned inwardly as he thought that the charge would be a re-hashing of the Study Day stuff that he'd already heard. But then he realised that the reading was from later on in Acts. Richard had obviously read the rest of Acts too, so he decided to give his old tutor the benefit of his attention.

"The reading is from Acts chapter 13, verses one to three," said the ex-Vice President given the honour, sounding a bit put-out that he'd only been given three verses to read.

Jack thought the same. "That shouldn't take long," he murmured to the lady sitting next to him, who snorted as if it was the funniest thing she'd ever heard.

"In the church at Antioch there were prophets and teachers: Barnabas, Simeon called Niger..." It was a shame, really, that the ex-Vice President hadn't asked beforehand about Simeon's nickname because he wouldn't then have mispronounced it "nigger". A few people near Jack started laughing and most looked embarrassed. It wasn't the best of starts for poor Richard who had to follow this.

The ex-Vice President continued, oblivious to the effect his reading was having: "...Lucius of Cyrene, Manaen (who had been brought up with Herod the tetrarch) and Saul. While they were worshipping the Lord and fasting, the Holy Spirit said, "Set apart for me Barnabas and Saul for the work to which I have called them." So

---

[51] Richard is loosely based on Revd. Tom Stuckey, one of my own tutors at Hartley Victoria College, Manchester, in the mid-1980s. Tom delivered a Ministers' Study Day on the book of Acts for the Newcastle District in 2008, which sparked ideas and led to me researching Acts and writing "Thule for Christ's Sake" in 2009-2010. I am greatly indebted to Tom in all kinds of ways, and to the congregation at Cullercoats, who endured numerous sermons on Acts whilst my ideas were taking shape. I apologise to Tom if I've put inappropriate words into his/Richard's mouth...

after they had fasted and prayed, they placed their hands on them and sent them off."
And here endeth the lesson," finished the ex-Vice President, rather pompously. Jack
shook his head, amazed that somebody of such questionable calibre should have got
such a high-profile role.

Richard tried to diffuse the embarrassment straightaway. "Once, when I was just a
lad, hundreds of years ago..." (he paused for the polite laughter to subside) "...I was
asked to read a lesson and confidently said that Jesus was going to Kay-per-Norm –
because that's what Capernaum looked like to me, and it was only afterwards that I
was told that my confidence was misplaced." The congregation laughed again, but
unfortunately this attempt by Richard to skirt over the ex-Vice's gaffe only drew
more attention to it. The ex-Vice went bright red – knowing that he'd boobed but
still not understanding precisely how badly.

Richard pressed on. "Did you know that the first church to be called Christian,
was this church at Antioch? It says so in Acts 11:26. What I want to suggest to you
today, whether you're about to be ordained or have a long-standing ministry,
ordained or lay, is that the Antioch church ought to be the model for our modern-
day Methodist Church..."

Richard recapped a bit of the stuff that Jack remembered from the Study Day –
how it was at Antioch that the blessing of God once more became apparent, after
Jerusalem had failed to engage with its full calling: to witness to its own people, but
also to Judea and Samaria and to the ends of the earth. Jack, unhelpfully, thought of
Brendan Priest again. Silly man – to take things ridiculously literally.

Then, to Jack's surprise and annoyance, Richard mentioned Brendan by name: "I
hope that you're all following the adventures of my ex-student, Brendan Priest, who's
travelling around the world to highlight the world's needs and the Church's Great
Omission as it fails to prioritise mission. I hope that you're fired up by his example,
too, because we need to live as if we really believe that our trust in God is all we
need."

"He obviously doesn't know Brendan Priest very well!" objected Jack, under his
breath. The woman sitting next to him snorted again. Perhaps she had a nasal
condition...

Richard carried on. "Antioch had caught God's blessing because it dared to defy
the Jerusalem guidelines, preaching to the Gentiles as well as the Jews, and it was *at
that point* that "The Lord's hand was with them and a great number of people believed
and turned to the Lord." Richard was quoting from Acts 11:24, and Jack remembered
this point from the Study Day. Here we go, Jack thought, settling down in his chair
for Richard to go over the familiar ground. But he didn't.

"So how should we copy what the Antioch church did?" asked Richard. "Well, let
me tell you four things that I think are crucial – for them and for us. Firstly, it is a

matter of being prepared to step outside our comfort zones for the sake of the Gospel – even if Church rules say otherwise."

Jack thought that Richard was wrong to make a point of this, because these young Ministers might spin off in all kinds of weird directions if they weren't mentored properly by experienced Superintendents who knew how things should be done. Richard seemed to anticipate Jack's silent objections, because he told a few funny stories of how he'd messed up along the way but somehow it had all turned out well.

"Secondly, I want you to look at the list of apostles and preachers who gathered with Barnabas and Paul in Antioch. The two of them spent a year or more in Antioch, teaching and mentoring people in the faith, and drew many people from far and wide into the church there – all different sorts, as we have heard. There was Barnabas himself, a man sent from Jerusalem to check out developments in Antioch, who recognised that the Holy Spirit was directing them and gave his approval; then there was a man called Simeon who was probably, as we have heard, black..."

The congregation roared with laughter at this point and the ex-Vice President went red again as he realised finally where he'd gone wrong.

"...then a man from Africa called Lucius of Cyrene, who may well have been an Arab; Manaen, who was one of Herod's old cronies and part of the Jewish establishment, and finally Paul himself, who was still being called Saul at this point. What an odd group of people, and the Church is still full of oddballs, as you ordinands will have already found in the churches you serve. Don't ever try to make them similar to you or even to each other. Enjoy the richness of diversity that they bring. But make sure that you keep and develop a sense of unity too, as these Antiochene Christians did, worshipping and fasting."

Jack reflected on the Ministers and people amongst whom he had responsibility. They were a funny group too. He even started to feel a bit warmer towards the absent Brendan Priest, but then quickly dismissed this as being an absurd and unwarranted over-reaction.

"Thirdly, I want you to notice what the Antioch church leaders did. They were mega-successful, and had built up a powerful congregation with many gifted people to whom they could delegate some of the tasks of ministry. They didn't *need* to worry about themselves. They weren't even under persecution, like many other churches were, across the Mediterranean region. They were sitting pretty. So what did they do? They worshipped and fasted. Worship – fine, of course they would do that. It would boost their profile because the worship would be fantastic. It would draw people in. But they not only worshipped, they fasted. Now, that isn't something that happens very often in our Methodist Church, is it? We fast sometimes when a real crisis comes along, to heighten our sense of calling on God, but usually we rely on easier, less sacrificial forms of prayer. When did you last fast?"

Richard paused at this point, before answering his own question.

'Exactly! But Antioch had church leaders who could have sat back and watched the people and the money roll in – but they didn't. They continued to prostrate themselves before God and seek God's guidance. If it were me, I wouldn't have bothered. I would have assumed that God must be blessing me because it was all going so well. "If it ain't broke, don't fix it!" You've probably already heard someone say that in your churches. But I hope, and pray, that in whatever circumstances you find yourselves over the years of your ministry, you'll keep seeking God and be prepared to do whatever He tells you – like they did in Antioch."

Richard had everyone's attention now. They hadn't noticed or appreciated this point. They also recognised that they were all guilty of sitting back in their comfort zones and weren't very sacrificial about anything. Jack felt a pang, as if God was speaking directly to him. What about you, Jack? What about your comfort zones, Jack? It was disconcerting, but riveting.

"And there's one more point I want to make. It refers to what happened next. A ridiculous command from God: that they should let their best resources go. "Set apart for me Barnabas and Saul for the work to which I have called them." The two people who had been most crucial in the development of the church, who had been the ones to draw in all these people, who were regarded as the ones so tuned in to the will of God that the people would follow them anywhere – *Barnabas and Saul* were the ones whom they had to give up, for the sake of the Gospel. How crazy is that?"

The congregation all shook their heads in bewilderment. It was daft, wasn't it?

"The church at Antioch could so easily have fallen into the trap of thinking that *their* experience was the whole picture, and that *their* bit was the most important bit of all, to which the best resources needed to be devoted. And so many of us fall into that trap today – whether it's *our* Women's Fellowship or *my* Circuit or *my* Stationing. But God had a bigger agenda than just *their* little bit of the world – or *ours* today. God knew that only when the Antioch church was prepared to let these two apostles go would the mission be extended throughout the known world. And it is only when *we* are prepared to let go of what is precious to *us* that God's mission will flourish. And if you remember that, you will have a deeply fruitful and rich ministry!"

Everyone was transfixed. This was revolutionary, turning everything which they usually valued on its head. Jack was speechless – not because he disagreed, but because he'd just heard God speak to him through Richard. This was a Word for him, as well as these ordinands. He realised in a flash that he'd got completely the wrong end of the stick about Fresh Expressions and ventureFX and all the other developments in the Methodist Church, which he'd thought were irrelevant and personnel-draining but which he now saw as being precisely what it was all about.

"So I want you to go away from here remembering Antioch as a clear example of what it means for us to be an apostolic church. Apostle means "sent out" and we have to be a sending Church, or we will die in a slowly-shrinking whirlpool as our beloved church goes down the plug-hole in this modern post-Christian society. So don't give up! Winston Churchill was invited back to his old school to give the valedictory speech to the leavers, and they all gathered in great anticipation as the grand old statesman shuffled up to the podium. "Don't give up," he said, looking around at all the bright, shiny faces. "Don't give up. Don't give up." Then he sat down. I want *you* to keep going too. It will be tough as the Church has to make some tough decisions about where it devotes its precious resources, the most precious of which are you ordinands and your colleagues. Test everything, but test it by the criterion of whether it is prioritising God's mission rather than the Church's comforts. Look at what the Antioch church did when they received this crazy Word from God. "So, after they had fasted and prayed, they placed their hands on them and sent them off." They tested this Word out by further hard prayer and fasting. Then they obeyed. Some of you will be called to live out your calling within the churches of our Connexion, and we send you out, having placed our hands on you in ordination. Some of you will go into Fresh Expressions of Church, or even be sent to the ends of the earth like Brendan Priest. We're all different, and will be called differently. But we're all the same too as we *seek* God's continuing call on our lives, as we *test* God's call and as we *obey* God's call, wherever it takes us. May God bless you on your continuing journey."

Jack couldn't move. It was as if a bomb had gone off in both his head and his heart as he was simultaneously caught up in an explosion of grace. Richard was the catalyst, challenging him at the very core of himself, but it was God who'd turned him around and blown him away. He felt humbled and exhilarated, drained yet energised. It was suddenly a different world.

The presentation of the ordinands culminated in the wonderful question and resounding answer: "They are worthy!" yelled the congregation, as much as Methodists are capable of yelling liturgically. Jack felt a God-surge within him as he remembered how *he'd* felt when they'd been speaking of *him* at Wesley's Chapel in London on June 28th 1988[52]. It had been a Tuesday, he remembered, pointlessly. But the touch of God *now* seemed to confirm the shouts of the congregation 23 years ago in Wesley's Chapel, acclaiming that he, Jack Turner, was worthy too. He knew that he'd fallen short, but also that he'd been made worthy by God's grace to pursue his ministry with new direction and renewed impetus. He *was* worthy! And he would prove it.

The actual ordinations then took place, with each ordinand in turn surrounded by seven or eight representatives of the Church who placed their right hand on the ordinand's head during a special, powerful prayer. Holy Communion was celebrated, which turned into a shambles as people didn't know where to go for bread and wine,

---

[52] The details are of my own ordination.

but somehow that added to Jack's sense of renewed call. An hour ago he might have tut-tutted at the lack of decorum, but it didn't matter now if things weren't quite as ordered as they might be. Communion itself was no longer a routine or ritual for Jack, as it so often had been, but a real point of confirmation in which he sensed that God fully accepted him and was equipping him for his future ministry.

Esther was born in one of the less wealthy suburbs of Detroit, but after having her DNA tested on a PBS programme called "African American Lives", she discovered that her maternal line originated among the Guerze ethnic group in Guinea[53]. She often joked that one day she would "go find her kinfolk" and this was her big chance. Her researchers discovered, not unsurprisingly, that she came from slave stock, with her African ancestor's voyage to America undoubtedly part of the infamous triangular trade whereby American slavers brought cheap goods from America to sell to the European market, then imported cheap European goods to sell on to coastal African chiefs in exchange for people captured in tribal conflicts, whom they took back to America as slaves.

The researchers traced Esther's American ancestors back to a slave-girl called Blanche on the estate of a Samuel B. Fugate in Russell County, Virginia[54]. They found a 1796 tax receipt signed by the county officer, called Isaac Vermillion, which indicated that Fugate paid a $1.50 tax levy for two black slaves bought that year, along with revenue from two other slaves, four horses, some land and a clock. Narrowing down the search, they uncovered a bill of trade dated 16th January 1795 between Fugate and a John Hawkins for a "niger girl of about twenty years" who cost the relatively high price of $300 because she was at the optimum age for breeding. A trawl through shipping records revealed that a John Hawkins had docked in Charleston, South Carolina, with 500 slaves from the Rio Pongo and Rio Nunez areas, having set sail on 15th June 1794 from the "Delos Islands" – now known as the Îles de Los, 4km offshore from Conakry. But there the trail came to an abrupt end, for names were not deemed important for slaves shipped from Africa – they were just cargo.

Esther had come to see the region from which her ancestors were taken, and spent the last two days visiting the Kamsar (Rio Nunez) and Boffa (Rio Pongo) areas further up the coast, which Brendan and Paul had passed on their way down. Meanwhile her techie team had been scouting around for the best backdrop for the interview.

---

[53] This part of Esther's story is based on a TV interview with Oprah Winfrey about her Liberian roots.

[54] The account of the fictional Blanche's journey from Kassa to America is based on research about the real-life Kassa slave factory of Miles Barber. The voyage of John Hawkins is accurate, as is the trade between him and Samuel Fugate, and the records and receipts cited here exist as described in the relevant state archives.

They decided in the end that it would be poignant to film in the most likely place from which the slaves were shipped off to America. The researchers had narrowed this down to Kassa Island in the Îles de Los. All the heavily-forested volcanic islands had been used as anchoring points for ocean-going ships, because the captains were scared both of the diseases prevalent along the coast, and of the poorly-mapped sand-bars and reefs. But Kassa uniquely had a lee shore with beaches where longboats could land cargoes, so it was chosen by Miles Barber as the headquarters of his slaving empire, with such success that Kassa became known as Factory Island. It was at the remains of the wharf that they planned to film, for there also they discovered the remains of two barracoons or holding-pens for marketable slaves.

Esther had scripted the interview carefully to begin with her own travels and reflections, with camera shots of the ruins of the wharf and the barracoons, and then turn the focus onto Brendan. When the time came for the interview itself, at 6pm that evening, Brendan was still only half-sure what was going to be asked, and was surprised when her opening question was about his own reflections on slavery. He recounted his experience of the island off Dakar, with its Door of No Return – and linked it to what he'd learnt about Mauritania with its appalling record of present-day slavery.

Then Esther asked him about his other adventures. He described how difficult it was to speak openly in both Algeria and Morocco in the presence of stony-faced Muslim observers, and how restricted he'd felt travelling through mostly Muslim countries since Cairo. He then lightened the mood with stories about his rainy-season cycling and particularly the mad hippo in Senegal, holding up to the camera the tent with its chew-marks and footprints, at which Esther laughed and then looked theatrically concerned. He mentioned the funny looks he and Paul got from travelling in a bright pink boat – whereupon the camera panned across to the Pink Lady bobbing up and down by the wharf. Esther laughed again.

Ruth was brought into shot, and described how well the fundraising was going – over $200,000 was pledged per country which projected a total of almost $40 million. "But we have a problem," she said. "Watoto needs money *now*, so that it can equip the Gulu Bulrushes properly before it's too late for children still dying unnecessarily in the Gulu area. Because my dad has already visited over 50 countries, we're asking you to send a quarter of the money now, rather than all of it at the end. If you all do that, when we film at Gulu we'll be able to show you the new Bulrushes in action. But you need to do it *now*, this minute, to the phone number shown on your screen." It was powerful stuff, reinforced by Esther's closing plug for the Gulu interview in ten weeks' time, and the one from Luanda in-between.

Back in the hotel, Brendan had the bliss of a lovely room all to himself, with Ruth and Paul next door. He discovered that even though the sailing wasn't physically demanding, he was pretty tired all the same, and he slept like a log.

***

After breakfast and a teary farewell with Ruth, Brendan and Paul chugged away in the Pink Lady – in the rain, of course. The one playing skipper could shelter under the high awning which sheltered the instruments, while the other could rest in the cabin. This is how it was for the next few days. They stopped at Freetown, where Brendan spoke in the St. John's Maroon Church. He'd imagined a purple/red building but it turned out to be a small, white, colonial church – named after runaway slaves called maroons. Sierra Leone was two-thirds Muslim and only a quarter Christian, but Brendan felt more at home here than in any African country so far. The Krio edition of the GNT was given to the Muslim caretaker of the church, who didn't seem to have a conflict-of-interest problem – a job was a job, and a gift was a gift.

The next stops were firstly offshore at Kakhei, and secondly in Monrovia, the capital of Liberia. Both days were very similar but the evening venues very different – the first a quiet, tranquil evening bobbing up and down in the middle of nowhere, the second a bustling port with loud dock-noises continuing through the night. Brendan gave his talk at Monrovia's First United Methodist Church, founded in the 1820s by 88 settlers from Baltimore looking for a home back in Africa for black Americans. Brendan couldn't quite get his head around it. Blanche was being transported across from Africa to America at the end of the 18th century and 20 years later some black Americans were heading back in the opposite direction. The church was full and lively, and Brendan was introduced to a church member called Helen, who mentioned that she happened to be the Speaker of the House of Representatives[55]. Brendan was so surprised and thrilled that he gave her the Liberian GNT. 40% of the population were actively Christian, and Brendan reckoned that, if it wasn't for the rain, he could settle here.

The next two nights were spent in quieter locations, off River Cess Town and then Sasstown. They sounded similar but couldn't have been more different. In the first town there were hundreds of sturdy houses and shops but also simmering discontent, due to the main employers (the logging companies) threatening to pull out because of incessant attacks by rogue elephants. In Sasstown there was much less of everything: no employment other than subsistence farming, and rainforest threatening to encroach and swallow up the township, but everyone smiled and laughed at Brendan as if they thought his skin colour was a novelty trick.

---

[55] Ellen Johnson Sirleaf, a Methodist and the current *President* of Liberia, is a member of this church, but any link or similarity is unintentional.

The coast changed from Liberia to Côte d'Ivoire the following day, but the voyage on the Pink Lady was much the same for the next week: rain; chugging along for hour after hour; a brief respite from the rain in the late afternoon; more rain in the evening. They stopped in two quiet overnight locations, then the big city-port of Abidjan, followed (in Ghana) by Azulewani, Cape Coast and Tema, and ending over the Togo border in the big port of Lomé. There was a rhythm to it all, but it was a sleepy rhythm, and Brendan found himself longing for the overland adventure to come beyond Togo.

Brendan enjoyed his time onboard, shared rather intimately with Paul. He'd not really had the chance to have a good man-to-man conversation with his new son-in-law over Christmas, so the sleepy rainy days of this pink voyage became long conversations about anything and everything. They discovered from their different backgrounds that they believed in the same evangelistic strategy of indigenous independence and freedom, and had chats which extended over several days about such diverse subjects as the role of women, poetry, the struggle of the Church to co-exist peacefully with Islam, diet, how to build the best campfire, how to bring up children – and even football. It was a wonderful time of discovering what made each other tick.

When they reached Lomé, Brendan was sad to leave Paul and the Pink Lady, but looked forward to renewing his acquaintance with both boat and skipper for the last week of this maritime leg. Paul was going to sail the 1,300km coastline of Benin, Nigeria, Cameroon and Equatorial Guinea while Brendan drove inland for 11 days, before they met again like Stanley and Livingstone. At least, that was the plan.

Brendan had given away three more GNTs since Monrovia. The first was at the ultra-modern Cathedral in Abidjan, where an imposing statue outside was meant to portray the cross and two elephant tusks but looked to Brendan like a haphazard bit of scaffolding. The second was at the Methodist Church in Cape Coast, next to the castle which had been the headquarters for the British slave trade on the Gold Coast until the mid-19th century. The third was at the Sainte Anne clinic run by an order of Catholic nuns in Lomé, which Esther had asked Brendan to visit because of her friendship with a venture-capitalist called Alix Marduel, who'd set up the clinic for cataract removal in Togo, as a result of which many lives had been transformed[56].

After parting company with Paul, Brendan arranged the free-hire of a Hertz 4x4 for his adventures into the interior, which would involve some roads impassable in a normal family car. Fortunately Detroit hadn't screwed up the arrangements and he

---

[56] The real-life Sainte Anne Clinic is a 15 bed clinic in the Lom-Nava suburb of Lomé, managed by its visionary founder Sister Delphine Gafan. Pioneering work in cataract-removal is undertaken, with much of the fundraising then and now being raised through Dr. Alix Marduel, a French doctor turned venture-capitalist.

had a bright-red new Dacia Duster waiting for him the next day. Were his frustrations at an end?

Day: Date	Itinerary (* indicates TV interview) ([18] indicates new nation)	Bike (km)	Car/ Bus (km)	Train (km)	Kayak/ Sail (km)	Boat (km)	Air (km)
Totals brought forward		4554	1404	0	2754	1658	7383
76: 30/7/11	Freetown, Sierra Leone[55]					149	
77: 31/7/11	Kakhei					202	
78: 1/8/11	Monrovia, Liberia[56]					196	
79: 2/8/11	River Cess Town					164	
80: 3/8/11	Sasstown					162	
81: 4/8/11	Mani, Côte d'Ivoire[57]					168	
82: 5/8/11	Fresco					172	
83: 6/8/11	Abidjan					179	
84: 7/8/11	Azulewani, Ghana[58]					179	
85: 8/8/11	Cape Coast					152	
86: 9/8/11	Tema					141	
87: 10/8/11	Lomé, Togo[59]					167	
Totals carried forward		4554	1404	0	2754	3689	7383

Chapter 31: Vaccination

After a weekend away with Ben, Louisa arrived back in work on the Tuesday morning to some very bad news: that the staff kitchen was still infested by ants; that her holidays would now be put back from August to October; and, worst of all, that she and Sister Lilian were going to be on duty together every shift.

Louisa's heart sank, her post-weekend buoyancy instantly deflated when she read the memo. Why would Sister Lilian want them to work together when she made Louisa's life so unpleasant? But, even as she said it to herself, Louisa knew why: it was only through making life difficult for her that Sister Lilian derived job-satisfaction and a boost to her own self-esteem. How sad that her only boost came from diminishing others...

The holiday change was a pain too – the advantage was that she should get a better deal, because flights and hotels were cheaper outside school holidays, but did she really want to go on holiday in October? And then she had a brainwave – how about linking up with her Dad? She might even be able to get Ben to come with her if it meant visiting somewhere exotic. She wondered where her Dad would be at that time, and couldn't wait to look it up on the schedule when she got home.

A little happier, she turned back to her duties. She had the staff kitchen to de-ant yet again.

***

When Louisa finally got back home after her long and miserable shift, she almost couldn't be bothered thinking about holidays. She'd been treated like a naughty child by Sister Lilian and publicly shouted at on three occasions – once about the staff kitchen (because, despite Louisa's best efforts, ants had still been seen), once about the cross Louisa was wearing round her neck (which slipped out into view when she bent down to make a bed), and once about a patient's notes (which weren't quite as Sister wanted them). But when she slumped in front of the television, watching some programme without really seeing it, she decided that she must approach her holiday positively. It would be something to set her sights on, and an important respite from Sister Lilian when it finally arrived. So she went to consult her Dad's schedule, blu-tacked to the kitchen cupboard above the kettle. She was thrilled to read that he was due to visit Gulu during the two weeks when she was off. "Yes!" she shouted.

With a frozen pizza cooking in the oven, she thought how wonderful a holiday in Gulu would be. Not only would she catch up with her Dad – and Ruth and Paul, who were bound to be there to visit Paul's family and because of the Esther interview there – she could also explore a country she'd only glimpsed at Ruth's wedding. She wondered if she could persuade Ben to go with her. He was away at his Gran's for tea so she'd have to wait till he got back.

***

"Hi Ben," she muttered as he gave her a kiss and a hug. "I've had a crap day, how was yours?"

"Uh-uh," said Ben, instantly recognising the no-win conversation he was already involved in. He joked sometimes that he could write a book about the ways women opened conversations so that the bloke always came off worst. If he told the truth and said that he'd had a good day, he would then feel guilty that she'd had a bad day. If he lied and said that he'd had a bad day too, she would press him to explain how bad his day had been and then prove that her day had been even worse. He decided that a non-committal answer was probably wisest: "Not too bad, I suppose."

It worked, because Louisa instantly ignored his answer and launched into the familiar diatribe about how awful Sister Lilian had been, capping it with the dreadful news that she would have to endure her *every* shift. Ben was already slipping into "silent listening" mode – it involved making the right grunts in the pauses when Louisa drew breath – but then he noticed something different about Louisa. She'd started to get excited about something. He listened more carefully.

"...so it looks like I'll be able to catch up with Dad and Ruth and have a really good holiday all at the same time – isn't that great?"

"Yeah, that's great – where did you say again?"

"Gulu, you plank. You weren't listening at all, were you?"

"But that's in Uganda," Ben said, suggesting geographical competence but then spoiling it by adding: "That's a long way away, isn't it?"

"Of course it is. It took me and Mum about ten hours from Heathrow to Entebbe and then another hour's flight up to Gulu. But it would be fun, wouldn't it?"

"Sounds good," said Ben. "I wish I could come with you."

"Oh, but I want you to! You will, won't you?"

"What, me – go to Uganda? I've only been abroad once and that was with Mam and Dad to Fuengirola. I couldn't go to Uganda!"

"Why not?"

"Well, I couldn't afford it, for one thing. It must cost over a thousand quid to go on holiday to somewhere like that, and I just haven't got that sort of cash."

"But I have," said Louisa. "I'll pay for you."

Ben spluttered into his coffee. "I couldn't let you do that."

"Why not?"

"Because... Well, because..." Recognising that he'd walked into another no-win conversation, in which he would either be accused of chauvinism or lack of interest, he suddenly had a spark of inspiration. "Because I don't like injections and you're bound to need injections for going to Uganda."

Louisa jumped on top of him, laughing. "You're not scared of needles, are you?" She tickled him. "A big lump like you scared of a tiny scratch from a little needle?" She squealed and tussled with him as he fought her off.

"No, I am. Seriously. I really don't like needles."

Louisa realised that he wasn't making it up. What a wuss! She did injections all the time and never thought about it. She settled down and thought hard. What sort of vaccinations would they need? She went over to the computer and quickly found the answer: hepatitis A and B, typhoid, yellow fever, meningococcus, and a top-up of tetanus/diphtheria if needed. And they would need malaria tablets too, which didn't come cheap.

"Only one or two," she said. "Not a problem. I'll come with you to hold your hand."

***

In actual fact, it turned out to be rather more complicated than "one or two". Poor Ben got dragged off to his doctor's surgery where an initial injection for both hepatitis A and B was followed a week later by yellow fever and typhoid jabs. He'd already had his meningococcus vaccine at school but it was time for the booster, so he had that too. He was OK with tetanus because he'd been given a jab for that a couple of years ago when he got bitten by a neighbour's dog. Louisa had had all of them when she'd gone out to Uganda for Ruth and Paul's wedding. A few weeks before they left, Ben would have to have a second dose of Hep A and B vaccine.

***

Louisa found to her surprise that she was buoyed up and able to smile through all the bad stuff at work, now that she knew that she'd soon be flying off with Ben and enjoying a complete change of perspective. She kept praying for Sister Lilian and her colleagues and the whole unit, and kept smiling – even though (or was it because?) it seemed to make Sister Lilian even angrier...

The next day, Louisa was told that her morning job was to dust the patients' bedside cupboards and the TV/phone monitors, despite the fact that the cleaners were supposed to do that. Instead of getting demoralised about it, though, Louisa decided to do a song and dance as she dusted, a cross between Mary Poppins and Ken Dodd, which made the patients laugh but not the Sister, who glowered in her usual way.

"Less than two months to go. Keep smiling, Louisa," she said to herself, through gritted teeth...

Chapter 32: Nations 60 - 67

Brendan's Duster was a rather smart and shiny compact 4x4 with air-conditioning, lots of space and an engine that sounded more like a contented lion, with a soft growl, than the high-pitched screech of his last Hertz car. It looked chunky and rugged, with its imposing chrome grille and high ground clearance almost begging to be taken over the toughest terrain. It also boasted spare fuel tanks, bolted into the anchor-points in the boot, to safeguard a steady rate of progress without worrying where the next petrol station was.

Brendan left the Sainte Anne Clinic in Lomé, having handed over the Togo GNT to an old lady who told him that after last week's cataract operation she could now read for the first time in ten years. He headed due north up the Eyadéma, the main highway in Togo, named after the ex-ruler who died in 2005 after nearly 40 years in charge. And it wasn't raining! Togo in August was "between rainy seasons", according to the man at Hertz, which sounded like a description of a surprisingly sunny afternoon in Manchester. The terrain alternated between savannah and woodland plateau – pretty boring really, though it was odd to see differently-designed huts from the ones he'd seen in Senegal. Instead of the short fat rondavels, these were taller, narrower huts with big straw-thatched roofs that made each one look like a giant mushroom.

Brendan maintained a cruising speed of 80kph, which meant that it was late afternoon when he reached Kara, where he diverted east to the Benin border. The surface was more uneven, but still there were no significant craters. He slowed down to the border, and was pleased on the other side to be back on a proper road, and only 20km away from the market town of Djougou.

Benin looked on the map like Togo – a small narrow strip of land extending upwards from the sea. In fact, it was twice as big as Togo and seemed more fertile, with green fields planted amidst the thorny yellow savannah, rich dark forests, and long-branched baobabs popping up in the middle of the savannah, odd-looking as if upturned by an angry giant. Djougou was sleepy when Brendan arrived in the late afternoon, and he drove to the Roman Catholic church in the marketplace and went inside to find the priest.

He found himself gatecrashing a meeting between a group of nuns and the Bishop. He apologized in his stumbling French and explained who he was and what he was doing in Benin, and asked if he might stay somewhere for the night.

"You must stay with me!" ordered the Bishop, who was called Paul (pronounced Powell, the French way). "And you must come with me to the Saint Ambrose Centre which I have to visit next." He was very bossy.

One of the Sisters of Saint Augustine, who were staying in the Bishop's House during their week-long meeting about mission, asked Brendan a very hesitant question. "I don't suppose... No, you couldn't be... Or maybe you are... Please, can you tell us... Are you the Minister who appears on "See Esther"?"

Brendan smiled and nodded, at which the whole group of nuns leapt as one from their seats as if on Sister Act. "But we've been praying for you!" squeaked one of them. "The Holy Father told us to pray for you and we've never stopped!" said another, and a third asked Brendan if he would tell them all about last year's journey as well as this one.

"You must speak about your journeys at the Saint Ambrose Centre too," said the Bishop. "That is where the diocese's lay leaders are trained, and they need encouragement for their mission in regions where animism is rife and the Christian Gospel is considered only an add-on or a threat."

So they all drove a few kilometres across to the Centre, and Brendan did a version of his talk while the Centre Director translated the talk into French. The GNT was entrusted to one of the lay leaders to give away on his next foray into the far north.

After a pleasant dinner with the nuns, who asked for more of his stories and then showed a surprising interest in what Esther really looked like and what she wore, Brendan slept well and woke refreshed for the journey north.

The Dacia Duster looked as if it ought to cope well on the more uneven surfaces, but the first time Brendan found a bad pot-hole the crash and subsequent engine clatter did nothing to reassure him. He kept a steady pace of about 50kph in the knowledge that he only had about 300km to travel that day. The road headed north-west, back on a diagonal towards the Togo border but never reaching it. At Porga border post he was only about 3km from Togo, but the country he was entering was Burkina Faso.

The road ran alongside the boundary fence of the Pama Wildlife Reserve. Brendan looked out for signs of life through the fence, but could see nothing except once when a monkey ran across the road in front of him, climbed up the fence, and sat on the top laughing at him. Two hours after the border, he was driving into Fada N'Gourma, which had originally been called Bingo, prompting Brendan to think of his long-dead grandma, who would have been thrilled for him to visit a town named after her favourite pastime.

Unfortunately Brendan's travel deadlines didn't allow a trip to the capital city, Ouagadougou, which was 200km to the west. He didn't know much about it but it had eight vowels and only three consonants, and that alone would make it worth visiting one day. He had to make do with the small town of Fada, whose welcome signs proclaimed that the population was 50% Islam, 50% Christian and 100% animist, before announcing with a big smiley face: "Bienvenue tout le monde." It wasn't that they couldn't do the arithmetic – the signs emphasised their mutual acceptance of other religions. Ancient animist rites were still highly valued, even amongst Muslims and Christians, as shown when the local Catholic priest proudly told Brendan that he'd just been appointed a shaman in his ancestral tribe. Brendan wasn't sure what to do with his GNT, so he gave it to the priest who promised that he'd pass it on to another shaman from his village, whom he kept inviting along to Mass.

After sleeping in the back of the Duster, wedged between the spare fuel tanks and his GO-kart, Brendan set off a bit stiffly east towards the border with Niger. He was not only struggling with muscular trouble after his night in the car, but also with a bad attack of the Number Threes. Paul had introduced him on the Pink Lady to what he called the Poop Scale. When Brendan laughed and asked whether that was about weight or the sound made when it drops into the pan, Paul gave a much more detailed description, which started with the statement that everyone knows the difference between a Number One (pure liquid) and a Number Two (average solid), but that the Scale extended from One to Three. "So if I were to say that I had just had a bad attack of the One Point Fours, you would know that I was referring to a bout of diarrhoea. And if I was to say that I had struggled with a Two Point Three, you would also know what I meant."

"So what's a Number Three?" asked Brendan.

"It's described by a fourteen letter word beginning with N."

"What's that, then?"

"Nnnnnnnnnnnnnnn!" said Paul with a hoot of laughter.

But Brendan was now finding that Number Threes weren't funny at all – in fact his constipation was causing him not just discomfort in the form of belly-ache, but a general feeling of bloatedness and anxiety. It was not dreadfully hot, but he suspected that he wasn't drinking as much water as he should, and wasn't eating much fruit or veg. He decided that he'd buy lots of fruit, hoping that this would sort him out before he became a candidate for the Richter Scale rather than the Poop Scale.

After buying mangoes, bananas and plums at a street stall, Brendan continued beyond Kantchari to the Niger border by midday, where he ate some of the fruit, picking at the plums during the two hours it took to reach Niamey, his evening destination. The capital city was on the east bank of the mighty river Niger, which was very impressive despite having another 2,000km still to go. It had already flowed further than that on its boomerang route from its Guinean source. The Kennedy Bridge was the only way across, with Brendan scanning ahead to spot the Cathedral. He knew from his notes that Niger was 90% Muslim so wasn't surprised to see the Grand Mosque on the Avenue de l'Islam (where else would it be?), but eventually found the Cathedral two blocks north-west of Place Maourey, its architecture and decor a mix of local and European styles, which Brendan found rather attractive.

Brendan had tried to set up a speaking engagement here, but, receiving no reply, assumed that nothing was going to happen. The priest, however, had received not just a letter from his Archbishop, who happened to worship here too, but also one from the Vatican, encouraging him to set up such a meeting. So Brendan found himself spending the evening in front of about 300 people, dressed very expensively as if they were at a wedding, their singing unrestrained like at the end of a wedding reception. They were certainly up for it.

Brendan asked beforehand, "To whom should I give the GNT?"

The priest replied, "Let them fight for it!"

Brendan wasn't sure what he meant. Assuming that there was a translation hiccup, Brendan forgot about it until the priest whispered to him, "Maintenant la guerre!" and proceeded to set up an auction similar to the one in Istanbul. Brendan hadn't heard of such a thing happening in a Cathedral before, but no-one seemed to mind and, in fact, quite a few people started to show signs of over-excitement.

"Regardez!" said the priest, under his breath, to Brendan. It quickly emerged that there were some very rich people there, but Brendan found himself repulsed by the sight of these rich people paying stupid amounts of money for a book, when their country was one of the poorest in the world, had the world's highest infant mortality rate at 25%, and had 8% of its population officially classified as slaves. At the end of the evening, the priest proudly handed Brendan a cheque for eight million CAF francs (about £10,000), but Brendan had lost interest. Frivolously bandying around that sort of money in that sort of country struck him as absurd and obscene.

He left Niamey the following morning with all kinds of questions and doubts. He didn't resolve them on his long drive across the country, but had them highlighted by an awful experience which shocked him to the core. He was approaching a bend, slowing down because he was uncertain what lay beyond, when he saw a lump at the side of the road, with vultures hopping around. He slowed further, expecting some sort of road-kill, but then noticed that their food was wearing a yellow jumper. He stopped, jumped out, shooing the birds away, to find the body of a child, perhaps ten years old, pitifully and appallingly thin, and partially ripped open by the birds. Beside the child were some pitiful little pyramids of mangoes and bananas. The child must have been waiting at the side of the road in a vain attempt to sell the fruit, but had died either of hunger or illness as he sat hunched at the roadside. He must have been there for several hours, because the feast had been going on for some time, judging by the state of the corpse. Brendan wondered how many drivers had passed, either oblivious or indifferent to the dead child.

Brendan got back into his car, wondering what he could and should do. He sat and prayed, and watched the vultures hop back to their feast. He started the engine and slowly drove off. What else could he do? This was the flagship of Niger's road system, the Route Nationale, but a child could just die at the side of this road and no-one seemed to care. Brendan wanted to get away from Niger, as fast as he could. He wasn't planning on going all the way east anyway, because there didn't seem to be a road into Nigeria. He settled in the car again that night, a few kilometres beyond the small town of Madaoua, preferring discomfort to having to talk to anyone, and crossed the border at Maradi halfway through the following morning.

Nigeria and the other countries in the region had the same inequalities as Niger, but Brendan still felt better when he left Niger and cruised down the rather grand road to Katsina – a large city which gave Brendan the chance to stock up on fruit, because he was solidly, *really* solidly still in the Number Three category. He picked up a tourist guide and read that the ruler of Katsina had been called the Sarki, which made him smile. Brendan had been accused of sarcasm constantly by his ex-wife and daughters, so perhaps he should apply for the job. Then he read that if the people thought the Sarki wasn't ruling very well, they would kill him. Maybe not, then.

He pressed on, eating fruit as he drove. No stirrings below yet. If he didn't produce something soon he would have to call in Dyno-Rod. Rain started falling, and the road suddenly became awash, the torrents flushing away the litter on the road. Brendan wished that he could flush some of his internal debris away as easily. He passed through Kano, wishing that something else would pass through. He kept to the main roads because the graded roads were turning into squelchy quagmires in which he might get stuck, which evoked more thoughts about his constipation. He kept going until it got dark, stopping finally at Makarudi having driven 500km on the odometer for the day, then continued the next day, heading for the border with Cameroon 450km to the east. These were long days, but thankfully the road surface stayed solid (like his internal systems, unfortunately) and despite the rain he was making good progress (unlike his internal systems, unfortunately).

The north of Nigeria was predominantly Muslim, and the last decade had seen all kinds of religious tensions and even massacres. Brendan was very wary of how and where he would do his "witnessing" in Nigeria, and was apprehensive about his planned lunchtime visit to the Roman Catholic Cathedral at Maidaguri. This city in north-east Nigeria had seen some of the worst Christian-Muslim violence, especially as a result of an obscure Muslim sect called Boko Haram which had been responsible, amongst other atrocities, for over 2,000 Christian deaths in four days in 2009, when 11 churches had been burnt down. Brendan had arranged to meet the Diocesan Administrator, to whom he handed the GNT, which was printed in Kanuri, the local language – and this went down particularly well, the Administrator appreciating the care taken to target the local people rather than assume that everybody spoke English, the official national language. He said that he would give it to the local Imam as a gesture of good-will and a sign that he wanted them to share their most precious stories. Brendan wondered whether this would be interpreted correctly, or whether it would backfire.

He slept in the car again on the Nigerian side of the border because the barrier was down, but he was the first person through into Cameroon the next day, and got all the way across the northern needle of the country by mid-afternoon, crossing the

Logone River bridge into his 64th official country (Cameroon didn't count yet because he hadn't done his witnessing in it), which made him virtually a third of the way through the whole list. He decided this warranted a celebration, so he stopped off at a supermarket in Bongor, and bought himself a bottle of red wine. He gave the surprised shop-owner the Chad GNT. She looked a bit alarmed, but perked up when he gave her some money too – to pay for the wine, some fruit and a loaf of bread that together would constitute his evening meal.

He drove on down into the southern Chad savannah. The dusty ground was darkening because of the incessant rain, and green was more and more visible in the red and yellow earth the further south he drove. The daylight faded quickly, and, 10km beyond the city of Moundou, he was ready to stop. He was also ready for something else – finally. He didn't know how many countries he'd visited without making his scatological mark on the landscape but it was more than four. Afterwards, he felt a little weak and several kilograms lighter, but now had a double cause for celebration. The wine didn't last too long and he slept very well.

In fact, he slept in, well beyond his usual alarm call, which was when the sun came up. He was adjusting to a more natural day: activity between dawn and dusk, then rest. His watch didn't really tell him much, because he didn't have a clue how many time-zones he'd crossed since leaving Gambia on the Pink Lady. His watch said two o'clock at dusk that day – not that it mattered.

He was determined to keep to his schedule, hoping that Paul's journey in the Pink Lady round the curving coastline was plain-sailing and trouble-free. Their rendezvous was only four days away, but there were three other countries for Brendan between now and then. He crossed into the Central African Republic early the next day at a place called Bang, not that there seemed anything particularly explosive about the sleepy little village. At the small town of Bouar he deposited the CAR GNT with the caretaker of an evangelical church, and kept going until nightfall, only 5km short of the Cameroon border at Gouara Boulai.

His chance to witness in Cameroon came immediately the next day at the border, as the guard pulled out the Cameroon GNT from the GO-kart and asked Brendan what it was. He seemed very pleased with Brendan's explanation and even more delighted when he was offered the book, and waved Brendan through for the long journey south-west.

Brendan still hadn't adjusted to hot rain in the morning. He preferred the cooler rain of the late afternoon – it was more British... Another sudden dusk; another uncomfortable night in the car; another steamy wet morning. He bypassed Yaounde, the capital city – he'd plenty of time to spare but just couldn't be bothered to drive off the main road and navigate his way in and out, contenting himself to see a shimmer of skyscraper beyond the green-fielded outskirts, but then turning his focus back to the road which continued ever south-westwards. He stopped on schedule just outside the little town of Ebolowa, having stocked up on fruit and water at a little shop which seemed to sell everything.

His last day in the Dacia Duster started with its first puncture, but at least it wasn't raining. To his amazement, he managed to work out how to fit the spare, though he had some worrying moments as he heaved on the wheel nuts before they began to turn. Brendan drove off again after only half an hour's delay, hoping that he wouldn't get another puncture, because he really would be stuffed then.

The road led quickly down to the Equatorial Guinea border at Ebebiyin, which was also the border with Gabon, but the road Brendan wanted turned westwards along the Cameroon border and down to the Atlantic at Bata. It was wonderful to see the ocean again after so much land. He'd driven more than 4,000km in 11 days, with 150km still to go. But this was definitely the homeward stretch now, with the Atlantic breeze refreshing him through the open window.

Unfortunately the road now started to fall apart, and his pace slowed dramatically. Fearful of getting another puncture, he gingerly manoeuvred around the holes which appeared every few metres. The jungle encroached on both sides, and his journey suddenly seemed perilous. It took him seven more dreadful hours to reach Acalayong, the last four hours in darkness. Mbini and Bitika came and went, but these towns were of little help to him, though he stopped at Mbini to buy some fruit, and passed on the EG GNT to the teenager shop-owner. He was anxious to press on, and to re-connect with Paul. The hours dragged on and on and he was getting more and more scared until he finally saw lights in the distance, and slid down the hill into the little port of Acalayong at the end of the road. The Muni estuary separated Equatorial Guinea from Gabon, but nothing could separate Brendan from his bed, that rather small, cramped but utterly heavenly bunk in the Pink Lady into which he collapsed after the briefest of hugs and greetings with Paul.

He'd made it, but that last part of the journey had been appalling, even in a 4x4. He hoped as he drifted off to sleep that he'd never have to undergo anything like that ever again. Little did he know how soon that thought would come back to haunt him.

Day: Date	Itinerary (* indicates TV interview) ([18] indicates new nation)	Bike (km)	Car/ Bus (km)	Train (km)	Kayak/ Sail (km)	Boat (km)	Air (km)
Totals brought forward		4554	1404	0	2754	3689	7383
88: 11/8/11	Djougou, Benin[60]		445				
89: 12/8/11	Fada Ngourma, Burkina Faso[61]		306				
90: 13/8/11	Niamey, Niger[62]		279				
91: 14/8/11	Madaoua		445				
92: 15/8/11	Makarudi, Nigeria[63]		484				
93: 16/8/11	Limani on border		442				
94: 17/8/11	Moundou, Chad[64]		413				
95: 18/8/11	Bouar, CAR[65]		402				
96: 19/8/11	Doume, Cameroon[66]		381				
97: 20/8/11	Ebolowa		393				
98: 21/8/11	Acalayong, Equatorial Guinea[67]		407				
Totals carried forward		4554	5801	0	2754	3689	7383

Chapter 33: Ruination

On the very same day that Brendan arrived in Acalayong after the awful journey from Bata, Cecil Grimshaw arrived in Jact after an awful journey from Fiji. He'd quarrelled with passport control in Nadi about him leaving with all his belongings, which they insisted should be shipped back as freight rather than carried as excess baggage in a passenger jet. In addition, they refused to issue him with a through ticket to London, and wouldn't say why. So he had trouble at Los Angeles because he hadn't got a US entry visa but nor was he a transit passenger because he didn't have a through ticket. So he was detained in the "refused entry" holding pen at LAX for 36 hours before he was cleared to fly to Britain.

When he landed at Heathrow he had further trouble because he had no papers to prove that he was employed by the Methodist Church. Ministers bizarrely were not officially classed as employees but "office holders", so Cecil had documentation saying that he was a Minister in Jact but nowhere did it say that he was *employed*. So the passport officers assumed that he was a volunteer, and kept asking him how he would support himself. After a few hours of this, they contacted someone at Methodist Church House in Marylebone Road who confirmed that Cecil was sort-of employed "but the Church doesn't call it that."

Eventually released into the UK, Cecil got on the Piccadilly Line to King's Cross and caught the next train to Newcastle, which happened to be the 6.30pm – and it was so crowded that he had to stand up all the way. It didn't get in until 9.52pm, by which time he was so exhausted that he caught a taxi and finally turned up at the manse at 10.30pm only to find that there was no-one there. He had insufficient cash to pay the taxi and had to phone the Circuit steward to come and pay his fare and let him into a disconcertingly empty house.

Everybody had assumed that they didn't need to worry about furniture, so the steward took Cecil home to their spare room and spent most of the next day scavenging furniture and surplus electrical goods off people in the churches. By the evening, Cecil was back in the manse with a borrowed bed, borrowed sheets, a borrowed wardrobe and chest of drawers, a kitchen with a cooker and units, plus borrowed bits and bobs including a fridge, a table, four chairs and an armchair. And that was it.

He'd learnt how to make do with very little, though, so he didn't really mind living a frugal existence until he sorted himself out. The trouble was that he had his Welcome Service the following evening and would be expected to start work the day after. Worryingly, all that he knew about Jact was that it had enjoyed a brief surge of popularity when its ex-Minister had been lost at sea, and that the Cuban Minister they had had for the last two years had turned things around. And that was it.

He didn't know very much about the area, because he came originally from Sevenoaks. For him, the North of England started at Watford, not even Watford Gap. He had a guide book that he'd bought at Central Station in Newcastle along with an A to Z, and that was it.

In fact, "that was it" was Cecil's problem. He didn't actually know anything and realised that he was completely unprepared for what lay ahead. He hadn't been in a local ministry appointment since the 1970s and he was fairly sure that things would have changed since then, but he didn't know in what ways and by how much.

He got a shock the next day when he visited the church in Jact for the first time and saw the Perspex pulpit and comfy chairs. In Fiji they had wooden benches and a lectern. He met the local church stewards who seemed a friendly bunch, even though they seemed *untraditional*. He was asked whether he would be helping in the Youth Club (Caridad did), whether he wanted to run the Sunday School (Caridad's wife did), how frequently he wanted to go into the schools (as often as Caridad's wife did?), and a million and one other things which Caridad or his wife had done but about which he didn't have a clue. Someone finally mentioned Ben, and he discovered that he had a youth worker – good news, finally!

They said that they wanted him to "do his own thing" and not copy Caridad and his family, but he also got the message loud and clear that he had a hard act to follow. Caridad sounded as if he'd taken the bull by the horns and told people what they should do, and they'd obeyed. So he decided to adopt the same tactic.

"I'll be sticking to the hymn book because I don't like those new choruses."

"I'm hopeless with kids, so I won't be going into any schools to do assemblies."

"I don't want anything to do with Sunday School because I'll be busy with the adults, of course."

"I'll be spending mornings in the study, so if you want me, phone and book an appointment."

"I don't like that Perspex pulpit so I'll be looking for something more suitable for God's Word."

"I'll be conducting a Bible Study on a Friday evening in the church, so the Youth Club will have to meet on a different night."

"I'm not very good at visiting, so I'll expect you laypeople to sort that out and alert me about any emergencies."

"I can't make that Church Council meeting because Tuesday's my day off."

It didn't go down well. In fact, it could only have gone worse if he'd declared that he supported Sunderland, which he didn't do because, when asked what his favourite team was, he replied, "I don't like football" – which was almost as bad.

***

At the Welcome Service a surprisingly more buoyant and smiling Jack Turner than usual was worn down fairly quickly by the concerns and complaints of the church stewards. One even said, "You've sent us a right plonker!" That was perhaps a little unkind, but Cecil certainly seemed to have got off firmly on the wrong foot.

Jack preached what he thought was a rather inspired sermon, using the letters FIJI to list four attributes of the church they were called to be: Frontier-crossers; Inspiration-bearers; Justice-bringers; Incarnation-livers. He wasn't sure about the last one because it sounded like a dish involving offal and condensed milk, but he couldn't think of anything else suitable beginning with I. The congregation didn't really grasp the four points or have a clue what he was on about but they responded to his unexpected enthusiasm. Cecil took notes and kept nodding his head, though Jack wasn't sure whether he was agreeing or just twitching. Jack noted the people's uncertainty about their new Minister, especially their dirty looks when Cecil tut-tutted as several people raised their hands in the air as they sang "And Can It Be". Cecil was dressed in a black 39-button Anglican-style cassock with a black clerical shirt that had one of those all-the-way-round one-and-a-half-inch collars that went out of fashion in Victorian times. "Oo's the penguin?" was what one girl muttered on the way in.

Cecil was introduced afterwards to Ben, who'd chosen to wear his best jeans and least controversial tee-shirt, but this clearly wasn't appreciated by Cecil, who seemed to sneer as they shook hands. Cecil asked where Ben lived, and he replied that he lived in his girlfriend's house in Cullercoats, which left Cecil aghast. They arranged to meet the following morning. Louisa was introduced to Cecil by one of the ladies as Ben's girlfriend, and he looked at her as if she'd just won the Harlot of the Year contest.

***

The following morning, Cecil and Ben met in Cecil's study. After handing Ben a cup of coffee, Cecil began the conversation. "I hope you don't mind me saying so, Ben, but I think that it's inappropriate for you to live with your girlfriend if you are working for the church."

Ben put his coffee down. "Well, Cecil, I hope you don't mind me saying so, but I think that it's inappropriate for you to tell me what to do in my private life."

Cecil looked at him frostily. "And, just so that we don't start off on the wrong foot, I'd like you to dress smartly when you represent the Church at school."

Ben looked at him in bewilderment. "What do you mean?"

"A suit would create the right impression."

"You're having a laugh," said Ben. "And everyone at the school would have a laugh too. No way!"

"What is it you do anyway when you go into school?"

"Well, I do a bit of breakdancing..." (which Cecil had never heard of) "...some djembe-playing..." (which Cecil had never heard of), "...but most of the time I just do beatboxing" (which Cecil had never heard of).

"What does all that mean?" asked Cecil.

Ben showed Cecil a bit of breakdancing, which unfortunately broke a coffee-table. Then he showed him on the broken table-top a percussive beat popular in his djembe workshops, which gave Cecil a headache, and finally showed him what beatboxing was, which made Cecil think that he'd entered a parallel but unrelated universe.

"And what's the point of all that?" asked Cecil, which probably wasn't the most tactful way of expressing his surprise.

"To tell them about the Gospel," said Ben flatly, utterly disillusioned by Cecil's ignorance and disrespect. He was acting more like his old headmaster than a friend and colleague.

"You're kidding!" cried Cecil, "How on earth are they going to come to Church if you do that stuff?"

"But that's what young people are interested in!"

"Not in my church!" said Cecil. And, he thought, that was that.

***

Ben stomped home and thundered into Louisa's kitchen. "That silly bloody man! He'll ruin everything!"

"Yes," said Louisa, who'd just come in from another harrowing day at work. "I rather think he will."

***

Jack Turner was coming to a similar judgement, though he felt that it was too early to write off Cecil completely. He had a chat with the Superintendent Minister and suggested that the Super had a quiet word. Jack wrote himself a memo to check how it was going in a few weeks' time.

***

On his first Sunday, Cecil preached from the opening verse of the opening chapter of Paul's letter to the Romans. "Seeing as only two of you turned up to the Bible Study on Friday evening, I thought I would whet your appetite for next Friday, when I trust many more of you will come to reflect on God's Word."

The congregation looked bemused. Why should anyone want to go to Bible Study on a Friday? Friday nights meant either staying at home for a drink or two with the missus, or going down to the pub quiz with their mates, or clubbing in town if they had any money. Of course some of the older ladies were a bit more sober and upright, but they didn't go out after dark because of other locals who were neither sober nor upright.

Cecil's sermon was a thirty-minute tour-de-force on "Paul, a servant of Christ Jesus", but he only got as far as "Paul", exploring the origins of the name and then discussing the authorship question. He'd put quite a lot of work into it the day before, and felt that he'd given a good account of the leading issues. The congregation, however, seemed to come to a different conclusion.

"Bloody hell!" said one recent convert, who hadn't yet acquired either a more ecclesiastical vocabulary or the ability to keep his voice down during coffee-time. "At this rate it'll take him a couple of years to do the first chapter."

The lady he was talking to was one of the barmaids in the local pub. "Harry won't be pleased if he takes folk away from the pub quiz."

"Absolutely no bloody chance of that," came the instant reply. "I'd rather force chopsticks up my back passage than listen to any more of that tripe!"

One of the older ladies was a little more circumspect. "Oh dear, I do hope that he's going to brighten up a bit. He was, well, a bit *serious*, wasn't he? And where was gorgeous Ben this morning?"

Her friend nodded in agreement. "Yes, it was rather *dull*, wasn't it? And I hope that we'll sing some of the modern songs, those old ones do seem a bit slow, don't they?"

***

Jack Turner got a phone call from the Super the next day. "I think we've got a problem..."

Brendan woke up in a cradle – well, that was what the gentle, soothing, rocking movement felt like – but then he realised that he was back on the Pink Lady. In fact he was 200km out at sea, heading towards São Tomé. Paul, having rested well as he waited, had set off a few hours after Brendan crashed out in the cabin.

Brendan suddenly got a flashback to the previous day, fighting his way through the jungle on a road resembling a 150km trench on the Somme. He shuddered. Then he thought about his Dacia Duster, panicking till he remembered that he needn't worry. There wasn't a Hertz office in Acalayong. In fact, there wasn't a Hertz office in the whole of Equatorial Guinea, but Oracle for once had discovered this well before Brendan set out, and arranged for a cargo ship en route from Douala (Cameroon) to Libreville (Gabon) to stop off in Acalayong to pick up the Dacia Duster and unload it dockside in Libreville, where the Hertz office would be glad to collect it, even though cargo ship was not the usual method for returning their vehicles.

São Tomé eventually came into view in mid-afternoon. Paul's navigation skills had proved sufficient, even though he didn't really have much idea how to navigate at all. He knew what compass bearing he needed from the mouth of the Muni estuary to the very centre of the island of São Tomé, and hoped that any deviation wouldn't prevent him *seeing* the island and heading for it. Good job it wasn't foggy.

He'd also kept track of the distance covered, so that he'd know when to look out for the island. Otherwise he might end up in Brazil, or, rather, drifting without fuel in the mid-Atlantic. But he needn't have worried because the island showed up just when and where it should, and they sailed into Ana Chaves Bay in excellent time for Brendan's 7pm speaking engagement in the old Cathedral.

Padre Zé showed them round, proudly boasting that this was sub-Saharan Africa's oldest Cathedral. Brendan was struck by the simple blue-white azulejo tiles in the frieze and large fresco above the main altar, and the huge statue of Saint Thomas, on whose feast-day Portuguese explorers first landed in the 15th century (hence São Tomé). With modern stained-glass windows, it was all a bit of a hotch-potch, but curiously homely too.

Brendan had time for a quick look round the town before snatching something to eat and going back to the now-full Cathedral. The atmosphere was expectant and interested, which helped him rise to the occasion and the evening went really well. The Portuguese-language GNT was given to the youngest person there, a 14-year-old boy who was clearly thrilled at receiving it, as if he'd never been given anything in his life before this.

After the talk, Brendan and Paul returned to the Pink Lady and they both had a sleep before Paul got up (before the sun did) and started the crossing back to the

African mainland. By mid-afternoon they were nearing the coast, hoping to be somewhere off the jutting point of Gabon's Port Gentil. The last time Brendan had been here, he'd been flying in Esther's Learjet en route to Ruth's wedding, and he was reminiscing about it to Paul when a plane suddenly took off from the airport, helping them to pinpoint Port Gentil precisely in the blur of land ahead. They eased south-eastwards down the coast, stopping eventually in a protected bay at Ozori, 25km south of the airport. As they secured their line against what they thought was a boulder, they realised that it was actually the beached corpse of a huge turtle. Not yet scavenged by birds or insects, it must only just have died, its head wrapped in a plastic bag entwined in the remains of a net.

Brendan went ashore to the village and brought back a local fisherman, who clucked his teeth in annoyance when he saw what they'd found. Despite language difficulties, Brendan and Paul learnt that it was a female leatherback turtle, which must have mistaken the plastic bag for a tasty jellyfish and then had the double misfortune to get caught in the net. The fisherman explained that fishing with surface nets was illegal, because they ensnared too many turtles which needed air to breathe. Once caught, the turtles struggled to escape and often drowned, which is what probably happened to this one if it hadn't suffocated in the bag first. It seemed wrong that humans caused the death of such a monumental creature, over 2m long and weighing more than a ton, its flippers like elephant ears. Brendan was saddened, but the fisherman assembled some friends who dragged it back up to the village, where they set to with knives, butchering the meat and amputating the flesh from the rubbery shell. They offered Brendan and Paul some of the raw meat, but they declined and went back to the boat. Spaghetti hoops on toast seemed morally more acceptable.

Brendan returned to the village the following morning and gave the Gabon GNT to the fisherman as he washed the turtle shell ready for selling to a local trader, even though that was illegal too. Maybe he'd be enlightened when he read the New Testament, if he could read French. He'd *spoken* French to Brendan the day before, so hopefully the Bible Society had got this one right too.

They sailed off down the coast, heading for their overnight destination at the Loango National Park, which they reached by early afternoon and anchored about 100m off the white beach. They had stumbled upon Paradise, and the next few hours were amongst the most magical either of them would ever experience.

It started with a huge whale, either a humpback or a killer whale (they didn't know the difference), leaping completely out of the water about 200m behind them. They both happened to be looking in that direction as they prepared an early dinner, and were spellbound by what they saw. Immediately two more whales leapt out of the water too, and the first one rolled and somersaulted in the water, with its huge trademark tail rising above the water before sinking majestically downwards. The whales sported for several minutes, taking Brendan back to the whale-play he'd witnessed off the coast of South America the previous year – this time even better because it was so close. It was a privilege to be there – such beauty and grace, in such massive creatures.

Breathless, Brendan and Paul sat down, only for Paul to point excitedly towards the beach. It was like a circus show where one act follows another, but this was no forced performance. Two elephants came straight out of the trees opposite the boat and padded down into the water, where they too rolled, paddled and squirted water at each other – anything whales can do, we can do better... A lone buffalo wandered down to the water-line 200m up the beach, but then wandered back as if the water was too cold for him. The elephants too ambled back up onto the beach, rolled around in the sand so that they emerged more yellow than grey, then jogged off into the trees too. But it wasn't over yet.

After their ham curry, they were sitting on deck having a glass of wine when Brendan spotted more movement at the tree-line. Leaves and branches moved, but nothing emerged. Several minutes passed before suddenly a monstrously wide silverback gorilla stomped out of the trees and stalked around, then four female adults, one with babies, appeared. The silverback sat down chewing a ripped-off branch. The babies chased and jumped on each other's backs, whilst the females stood back indifferently. The silverback sat and chewed, imperiously looking around. Too soon, he grunted and moved back into the trees, the females following, cuffing some of the young who seemed reluctant to stop playing. Brendan and Paul couldn't believe what they were seeing. They wondered what would happen next, but that was the end of playtime, it seemed. They watched till darkness fell, hearing some strange noises but seeing nothing more.

At dawn a few deer came down onto the sand but that was all. They waited and waited and, just as they were about to set off, had one last breathtaking experience. Some other deer had wandered down onto the white sand, chewing bits of grass which stuck up at intervals, grazing and enjoying the spray from the rising waves. Then Paul pulled Brendan's arm. "Look!" he whispered, pointing further up the beach. It was a cat, small, probably a leopard (though Brendan thought that leopards were night-creatures), but obviously stalking these deer – tail pointed out, ears stood up like antennae, jumping forwards then freezing only to run head-still once again, edging stealthily forwards. But the deer must have caught wind of it, for they shot off into the forest, with the leopard dashing after them but knowing that it had already lost its chance. Life in Loango was magical but precarious, easily taken. Maybe a microcosm of Africa itself...

Paul reluctantly started the engine and they chugged off southwards, with a relatively short distance to travel that day, and chance to reflect on what they had witnessed of God's amazing creation, some of it "red in tooth and claw" or whatever that poem said which Brendan had learnt at school. In the same spot they'd seen whales, elephants, a buffalo, a family of gorillas, deer and a leopard. It was definitely the place to start a safari company, but presumably somebody had already thought of that. It had been an amazing 24 hours.

Tsagui was their destination, and Brendan noted, as he completed his daily notes and GPS readings, that they were now in the last week of August. If he hadn't been journeying, he'd now be about to start work in his new Circuit appointment. Every Minister in Methodism who moved "station" did so in August, and started work on September 1st. He wondered where he might have been stationed, and knowing that nowhere could come close to Loango, he said a little prayer of thanks – it was a blessing to be here.

From Tsagui they crossed into Congo waters and stayed near a village called Tchissanga. Brendan went ashore and spoke to the villagers, who seemed not to be intimidated by a white man visiting them in a pink boat. He gave the Congolese GNT to the head man of the village because he seemed to expect a gift of some sort from Brendan. The main coastal highway came virtually onto the beach at Tchissanga, so the head man was probably more worldly-wise than he appeared.

They sailed the next day past disputed territory – the Cabinda enclave, officially part of Angola but separated from it by a narrow strip belonging to the Democratic Republic of Congo, and claiming independence from Angola. Brendan remembered that rebels in Cabinda had ambushed and killed some of the Togo football team in the 2010 African Cup of Nations, so he was relieved when they passed into DR Congo waters.

They stopped for the night at Banana, a small and quiet sea-port just north of the Congo River. Brendan gave his GNT to a nun whom he met in a bar. He couldn't quite work out why she was there, but thought that she would pick a more appropriate recipient of it than he could. Back on the Pink Lady, it occurred to him that he'd never seen a nun in a bar before. Perhaps it was a new missionary initiative...

Angola proper was just the other side of the Congo River, and the long straight coastline extended into the horizon. Brendan, now at the end of Day 104, still less than a third of the way through the whole journey, wondered whether he would get through to the finish. So far, so good – but now, approaching Luanda, the Pink Lady story was about to end, the next Esther interview was about to take place, and Brendan's bike ride across Africa was about to begin.

Day: Date	Itinerary (* indicates TV interview) ([18] indicates new nation)	Bike (km)	Car/ Bus (km)	Train (km)	Kayak/ Sail (km)	Boat (km)	Air (km)
Totals brought forward		4554	5801	0	2754	3689	7383
99: 22/8/11	São Tomé[68]					338	
100: 23/8/11	Ozori, Gabon[69]					271	
101: 24/8/11	Loango National Park					166	
102: 25/8/11	Tsagui					165	
103: 26/8/11	Tchissango, Congo[70]					200	
104: 27/8/11	Banana, DR Congo[71]					191	
Totals carried forward		4554	5801	0	2754	5020	7383

Chapter 35: Determination

It was not only Brendan that needed endurance, encouragement and determination for what lay ahead. Louisa too was in an in-between time – awaiting something different whilst steeling herself to continue with the job in hand. She too had the prospect of a change – not from one form of transport to another, but from the utter drudgery of work to the bliss of a fortnight with Ben in Uganda, meeting up with most of her family in Gulu, then spending precious time with Ben seeing the sights and trying to forget completely, for a short while at least, about Sister Lilian.

One lunch-time Louisa was in the canteen queue next to the hospital chaplain, who saw the queue as an opportunity to "network". Normally Louisa would be polite but non-committal, hoping to avoid a conversation which she hadn't chosen, but couldn't help noticing that the chaplain was gazing at her chest. "Hello?" she said, aggressively.

"Hello Louisa." The reply came back immediately. He'd been reading her name-badge.

"Ah, hello, Gareth," she replied, gazing at his chest, with a forced smile, making the point.

"Yes, odd, isn't it? Maybe we should wear name-badges a little higher up... I suppose it must have been a man who decided." They both laughed and Louisa smiled, properly this time. At least he hadn't gone red or changed the subject.

"So, Gareth, how come we don't see so much of you in the Cardiovascular Unit?"

"Aaaaaagh, you're not on there, are you? I would visit but the Sister isn't exactly co-operative. Every time I try she tells me that it's not convenient or she doesn't want me bothering the patients or some other excuse. So it's not for the want of trying!"

"Is she allowed to do that? Aren't you supposed to be part of the team?"

Gareth smiled. "In every ward of the hospital the nurses are happy to see me, except the Cardiovascular Unit. I've even had complaints from church-based Ministers who've tried to visit their members but got sent away. Actually, the chaplaincy team have a name for your Unit: Afghanistan. You don't go there unless you have to, and then you're lucky if you get out alive."

They'd reached the till, and Louisa laughed. "I know exactly what you mean. I have to work there all the time and it's horrible! If I wasn't a Christian, I'd thump her."

Gareth, brightening when she mentioned being a Christian, pointed to the tables, "If you've got the time and energy, tell me about it."

Louisa sat down with him and explained what it was like working in the Unit with Sister Lilian.

He listened carefully, then said, "You know, you really ought to check out your rights with the Union or with senior management. She shouldn't be allowed to get away with that. It's bullying. Do you know why she's like that with you, or does she do it to all of you?"

"She's pretty horrible with everyone, but she particularly picked on me when I started wearing the fish badge." She dug it out of her pocket. "I wear it every day at the start of the shift, and every day she tells me to take it off. No-one else bothers, but she makes a point of dressing me down, and I make a point of wearing it so that she knows I'm not giving in. Even though she tries to humiliate me I just take it on the chin and I've stopped myself getting angry, because if I do she'll try to get rid of me. It all seems to stem from the fish badge, really."

"So it's religious harassment," said Gareth. "That's against the law."

"Oh, she's very careful and crafty. She never quite goes far enough to make it blatantly illegal, and I could never prove it."

"Perhaps I need to try a bit harder to get onto the Unit. If she challenges me, can I say that I have just popped in to have a chat with you?"

Louisa wasn't sure. This could make matters worse for her, yet she knew that Gareth could then insist on being allowed in. "I suppose…"

"Yes, I know what you're thinking. It's a question about trying to be a good Christian witness. I'm employed by the Trust specifically to help people with that and am identifiable by my collar as a clergyman and by my badge as a hospital chaplain, so it's easier for me than you, and it's my job to help you be a good witness too."

"You sound like my Dad," Louisa said, regretting it as soon as the words had left her mouth.

"Oh?"

"He's a Methodist Minister, and he's always banging on about witnessing and about mission. I suppose you lot do it your way, and the rest of us in the Church have to try and do it differently."

"Oh no, I disagree," said Gareth. "It's exactly the same. It's actually much harder for you because people don't expect you to act differently or to *be* different from anyone else. My job's not just about witnessing to patients, but to staff too – and that means helping you, so I'll see you later this afternoon – OK?"

"OK," said Louisa, with a smile. He couldn't make things any worse, surely?

***

She quickly forgot about the conversation when she got back onto the Unit. One of her post-transplant patients had just thrown up all over everywhere and Louisa got the job of tidying her up and calming her down. She spent the best part of half an hour changing Dawn's bed and her clothes, and reassuring her that it wasn't a setback and didn't mean that the anti-rejection drugs weren't working.

Louisa was told by Sister Lilian to stop wasting time and answer a few of the buzzers so that the Sister could get on with her paperwork – so the next hour was spent running around sorting out painkillers, changing beds and helping patients who were struggling post-operatively with the basic functions of life. After her umpteenth bottle and bed-pan, she was about to go to the toilet herself when Gareth appeared in the corridor.

"Hello, Louisa," he said. "Didn't have to gaze at your boobs this time to know who you were."

She laughed. "Good job – they're not that memorable! Anyway, you'd better check in. She's down there at the nurses' station, doing her paperwork while we all run around doing the work."

"Ah, the slaves are revolting, are they?"

"No, but the bed-pans were that I've just had to sort out."

"Lovely. Now, have you got anyone on the Unit whom I can use as an excuse to be here?"

"Well, there's Dawn, over there. She's just been sick and she's worried about whether her body's going to reject her new kidney. She needs quite a lot of reassurance."

"I'm good at reassurance," said Gareth. "I'll see what I can do." He wandered off down the corridor, only to be accosted by Sister Lilian.

"Yes?" she snapped. "What are you here for? I don't remember any of the patients asking to see you."

"Hello, Sister. Actually I've come to see a young lady called Dawn, who I gather is struggling with fear of organ rejection despite the immunosuppressive drugs you have her on, and needs extra reassurance."

Sister Lilian pinched her cheeks in. How did he know about Dawn and what had just happened? She reluctantly put down her pen and told Gareth that she'd see if Dawn wanted a chat. But just then her pager went off, and she got flustered because it told her that she was needed down in Reception. "Oh, just get on with it! But don't bother her for long, or I'll come and throw you out."

Gareth smiled. His friend on Reception had timed the pager just right. "Thank you, Sister," he said, gushingly and probably a bit sarcastically, not that Sister Lilian noticed. If you're determined, he thought to himself, God and a bit of ingenuity will always find a way in.

He went over to Louisa, who was at the other end of the Unit. "That's got rid of her for a few minutes. Now, why don't you show me round and introduce me to the patients?"

Louisa raised an eyebrow. "And just how did you manage that?"

"I got a friend on Reception to page her exactly 3½ minutes after I left there. I timed it just right, and now she's gone off on a false alarm to collect a fictitious package."

Louisa laughed. She liked his style. "Well done – but she'll be furious when she gets back..." They set off across the ward, stopping first at Dawn who was pleased to see them both.

"Hi Dawn, this is my friend Gareth, the hospital chaplain – any time you want to see him or chat to him, just let me know and I'll page him."

"Great!" said Dawn, "But what about the Ayatollah?"

Gareth sniggered. "Don't you worry about her. If you ask for me, she can't easily stop me coming. Tell you what, I'll just go round and say hello to a few others then I'll come back and have a chat with you, OK?"

Dawn smiled. "OK."

So Gareth went round the other bays, and some were surprised to see him. He repeated that he was always happy to come and visit if they wanted a chat – "as long as you don't ask Sister!" He winked, and they laughed knowingly, and winked back. He'd just got back to Dawn's bedside by the time Sister Lilian harrumphed her way back onto the unit, frowning at him as if he was responsible for her wasted journey... "Five minutes!" she barked at him. Gareth ignored her, and winked at Dawn, who laughed but then pretended that she hadn't when the Sister glared at her.

***

After Gareth left, the Sister stomped up to Louisa. "If that was anything to do with you, young lady, you'd better make sure that it doesn't happen again!"

Louisa looked puzzled, and smiled innocently. "What do you mean, Sister?"

Sister Lilian stomped off again down the unit. Louisa laughed to herself, then sighed. It was OK for Gareth to waltz up here and play Sister at her own games, but she had to work with her all the time. Still, maybe if *he* could do it, so could she. Dogged perseverance and determination, with humour and grace – quite a mixture... Quite a witness, too...

Chapter 36: Nations 72 – 78

It was wonderful for Brendan and Paul to see Ruth again in Luanda, but sad to leave the Pink Lady. For all her Barbie colour scheme, she'd served faithfully, and was a real tribute to the Gambian women who'd restored her. Paul set about trying to sell her to someone in Luanda with an eye for a good craft – and colour-blind.

Ruth led Brendan off to Le Presidente Hotel which was a bit dated and past its former glory, but still far more elegant than the cramped cabin of the Pink Lady. Oracle had booked two suites on the 21st floor (one for Brendan and one for Ruth and Paul) and the penthouse suite at the very top for Esther and Fahada, which had been transformed into a studio. The main room had the gallery windows thrown open so that a warm breeze wafted in, and the double bed had been unceremoniously shoved against the bathroom wall so that the cameras and lights could be rigged up facing the elegant windows and the view of the bay outside. Fahada was fussing around with Esther at the desk, but they both broke off when Brendan was shown in, and Esther smiled and gave him a big hug. "Good to see you, Brendan!" she whispered as she squeezed him tightly, "Really good to see you!" Fahada shook hands rather stiffly, and offered a shiny-white smile which didn't reach her eyes. The interview was at 7pm local time to hit the 2pm "siesta" slot in Detroit, so they only had an hour to prepare. Very soon there were only 20 minutes to go, and Esther and Ruth went off to change while Brendan had a quick shave and tried to smooth out the creases in his trousers.

The opening introductions on camera were followed by some humour and facts about the Pink Lady's voyage. They had a good laugh about her but Brendan was quite adamant that she was a fine vessel and made a good sales pitch. Esther then asked Brendan about his car trip, and he spent several minutes describing the Niger paradox of meeting the richest people in the country just before encountering a dead child on the side of the road. "I don't want in any way to belittle the generosity of the people who paid £10,000 for a copy of the New Testament, with all the proceeds going to Watoto and their excellent work, but I can't get my head around how that could happen one day and then the next day in the same country I see a stick-thin corpse of a child being picked over by vultures at the side of the road. Is there not something wrong with a world in which such inequality can exist?"

Esther moved the conversation elegantly over to Watoto and the fundraising. Ruth gave an update of the monies received after her appeal on the last show. "We've received over $5 million in the last three weeks, which is fantastic. It means that all the loans can be settled which Watoto took out on Gulu Bulrushes, and the final installations and equipment can be bought so that it'll be opened next month. In fact, you're all invited to the opening ceremony, because it'll be taking place on our next show when my Dad reaches Gulu. There will already be some children living at

Bulrushes, as the need is already being met even though the building's still unfinished. So, thank you, everyone, but please keep that money coming in so that we can make Gulu Bulrushes the start of something even more special for Watoto and the people of Uganda."

Esther interrupted to say that the money per country was now totalling something in excess of $250,000, projecting a total harvest of $50 million. "Keep going, folks!" she urged every viewer and then "And keep going, Brendan! You're off on a bit of a bike ride now, aren't you?"

"Yes, the next leg is on the bike, all the way across the continent to Maputo on the Indian Ocean, which should take nearly a month. Then I get a car and drive up to Gulu over the next 11 days."

"And have you got your new mountain-bike yet?" asked Esther, coy all of a sudden.

"No, I haven't," Brendan replied, wondering what was going on. Ruth then came into shot, wheeling a very shiny, very sleek but very pink bike, with the GO-kart behind. Brendan fell about laughing. "I love it," he said. "Thank you, Ruth."

The interview ended with them laughing along with Brendan as he came to terms with his Barbie-bike, and Esther turning to the camera for one last farewell before the credits. They all went downstairs to the restaurant and settled in the bar before dinner, with the techies excusing themselves to track down a burger and a less-posh drinking venue. So, once Paul returned, rather forlorn and embarrassed by his failure to secure a buyer for the Pink Lady, the five of them sat down for a leisurely banquet. They all laughed, even Fahada, as Paul imitated some of the looks he'd got at the Club Nautica when he asked, "Is anyone interested in my little pink boat?"

Then Fahada's phone went off, so she went out to answer it. Brendan leaned forwards to Esther, "Is she OK? I rather get the impression that she doesn't like me."

Ruth kicked him under the table. "Ow!" he yelled, looking accusingly at her so that Ruth instantly turned bright red.

Esther laughed, "It's OK, Brendan. I think she's jealous because you get too much of my attention."

Now it was Brendan's turn to go bright red, as he began to understand and put two and two together. "Oh," he said, flustered. "That explains upstairs then..."

"Dad!" yelled Ruth.

"It's OK, Ruth," said Esther, then, turning to Brendan, "Yes, I suppose that does explain upstairs, doesn't it?"

At that point, thankfully, Fahada returned, rather red-faced herself. "You'll never guess! Some woman in Luanda has just seen the show on cable, wants to buy the Pink Lady, and will pay double the price we paid for her in Gambia if she gets to meet us all tomorrow morning!" They all burst out laughing, and agreed that they'd be happy to be blackmailed into a personal appearance for this lady, whoever she was. The atmosphere became lighter and easier as the evening progressed.

Next morning, they and the film crew assembled at the marina and met an exquisitely-dressed and impressive lady, whose chauffeur and bodyguard were standing with her as their own car drew up at the marina. "Good morning," she said, in a rather deep and strong voice. "My name is Sophia Dominica and I'm the Executive Officer of the women's section of the MPLA[57]. I'm a politician, in other words, and a successful one at that!" She gave a big, wide smile and laughed. "And I want to buy your famous little pink boat. Where is she?"

They laughed with her and led her out onto the jetties, and she shrieked with laughter when she saw the Pink Lady at the end, looking like Mr. Bean's car in the reserved car park at Royal Ascot. The shiny bodies and beautiful teak decks of the sleek yachts in the prime moorings seemed to sneer at the ugly pink duckling at the end. "Oh yes! I love her!" she shrieked, clapping her hands together in glee.

They all laughed, and Fahada and Sophia huddled over a cheque-book while the others walked back to the cars. Sophia walked up to Brendan. "I'm impressed by you," she said. "My father was a Methodist pastor, but he was tortured to death by the Portuguese colonial regime, so I never really got the chance to find out what being a Methodist means. If it means bringing the plight of the poor to the attention of the rich, as you're trying to do, then I think I like what you're doing."

"I've got a present for you," said Brendan. He fished around in his coat and brought out the Angolan GNT. "I couldn't think of a better person to give it to. God bless you." The strong demeanour crumpled, and Sophia welled up with tears. "Thank you," she said. "I will treasure it. And I shall read it too."

Back at the hotel, Brendan hugged Ruth, and Paul, and Esther – and even Fahada, though she still held back. Then he was off, on his new, shiny, and very pink, bike.

***

Once out of the city of Luanda, Brendan cycled first the long, straight, new six-lane highway to Viana, then the old road through dusty-brown lowland plains and green terraces and hillocks. He'd no speaking engagements planned for the next three weeks, so his daily schedule was utterly flexible, though he was aiming at 150km or 13 hours per day, depending on the terrain, the weather, his fitness and the absence of disasters. He would be camping each night, so as well as his tent and sleeping bag

---

[57] The real-life Secretary-General of the Organization of Angolan Women is Luzia Inglês, and any similarity is accidental and unintentional, except for the fictional father of Sophia Dominica, inspired by Luzia Inglês's father who was a Methodist Minister, tortured and killed when she was a girl.

he'd three weeks' worth of dried meals and bottled water and would stock up each day with fruit to avert any danger of a Number Three repetition. At least in Angola it was the dry season, so the roads were firm once Brendan got off the asphalt after a few hours. He went down the coastal strip for the first three days, and managed 450km, camping on the outer edges of villages to deter hungry wildlife. He kept his air-horn handy – it'd be useful against small or medium predators. A hungry lion would probably be more enraged than deterred – but in that scenario he wouldn't stand much chance of survival anyway.

From Gumbe on the fourth day, the road continued down the coastal plain, across dry, open scrubby terrain with the road throwing up dust and pebbles which dirtied and sometimes hurt Brendan's ankles. He spent the night by a small forest, during which he was visited by a family of blue duikers – at least that's what he thought they were. He was woken by the sound of something rooting through the twigs and shrubs at the edge of the trees. He looked out warily, expecting something fierce for which he would need the air-horn. Instead, in the moonlight, he saw three small deer with a brown/blueish coat – one with little horns, one without horns, and a little baby – but they seemed oblivious to his presence and harmless even to a coward like Brendan. He watched them for a few minutes then went back inside the tent.

At Caconda he turned onto a dodgy-looking track that cut across southwards. In England it would be called a bridlepath – just wide enough for a vehicle. Its saving grace was that it linked at Matala with the road for which he was aiming. He camped overnight for the first time in the middle of the open savannah, and built a fire to keep away any hungry wildlife. He got up halfway through the night to replenish the fire with twigs and branches from the shrubs around him, but if anything visited during the night he slept through it.

Just beyond Calueque, he came to the start of the great arid expanse which eventually became the Namib Desert to the south-west and the Kalahari Desert to the south-east. He was just cutting across the very top edge of it, though, and was quickly into the bushveld, which would be his terrain for the next four days eastwards. After crossing the border late the following day, he spent his first night in Namibia in the small town of Omafo[58]. For the first time in over a week, he slept in a bed, having turned up unannounced at the church but been welcomed by the priest and invited to dinner.

"I tell you," the priest said, as they started on their dinner, "My whole village is being threatened by the Devil."

Brendan's eyebrows rose. Did he have a zealot on his hands?

---

[58] The campaign in Omafo is factual, and typical of many capital projects in small towns throughout Africa. The entrepreneurs are often dismissive of the communities affected by their "developments".

"The Devil wants to kick us out of our village." He explained that the village was going to court to challenge the legality of the Helao Nafidi Town Council's plans to displace them and build the country's largest casino and entertainment complex on their land. He saw it as a spiritual battle... Brendan gave him the Namibian GNT as a sign of his support.

It took Brendan 3½ days along the Namibian side of the Angolan border to reach the Caprivi Strip. They were hard days: rutted surfaces, boring terrain, little human contact — then, wonderfully a tarred road alongside the broad Okovango River for the last morning to Popa Falls. The kilometre-wide river fell in a series of rapids and cataracts which would have been much more spectacular if it hadn't been the dry season. Just beyond, the road turned southwards towards Botswana, following the course of the river as it split into the swampy channels known as the Okovango Delta. The river, huge as it was, had no outlet to the sea, and ended its 1,600km journey in the alluvial pan in this north-western section of the Kalahari Desert. It was well-known as one of the last completely-unfenced areas of unspoilt, wildlife-rich, natural beauty.

Brendan's road, however, curved round the edge of the Delta, leaving the river at Qurube for the long trek across the Kalahari. There aren't too many people who've ever attempted to cross a desert on a bicycle, but if you were going to do it, the Kalahari would be a good one to choose, because it has a decent road all the way across. Brendan, of course, had already notched up the "deserts that might or might not be deserts" on the south-west coast of South America, and more recently the Negev, so felt that he might be better equipped than most to claim the Kalahari too. Yet his previous experiences made him respectful, not blasé. The very name Kalahari came from the Tswana word "kgala" which means "the great thirst" and Brendan didn't want and couldn't afford to underestimate its dangers. He stocked up on bottled water and fruit at the small town of Nokaneng. The Kalahari didn't look like a desert. The dust was redder, the surface flatter, the acacias and shrubbery sparser, the temperature hotter — but otherwise it wasn't that different from the dusty savannah in southern Angola. The difference was in its sheer size and monotony.

His route seemed to be marked by radio-masts. There was one about two hours out of Nokaneng at the Habu turn-off, and another at Tsau 2½ hours further on. Through the Setata Gate in the Veterinary Fence, Brendan stocked up again on fruit and water at Sehithwa, which had *two* radio-masts, one at either end of the houses. He continued past the end of Lake Ngami without being able to see any water — just a lake-bed with cracked mud. It was a grim reminder of the origin of the name Kalahari. The moon-terrain continued the next day, with Brendan camping just beyond a large settlement called Ghanzi, which made him laugh. "Ganzie" was the Cullercoats word for a fisherman's thick jumper, which was the last thing he needed in the heat of the Kalahari. The town felt as if it had been built somewhere else and dumped in the middle of nowhere. It was full of different sorts of people: little San, formerly nicknamed Bushmen, with their almost oriental appearance; the Tswana group of tribes who could recite their genealogy back to King Mogale in the 14th century; the brightly-clothed Herero from Namibia; and the Afrikaaners, who seemed to believe that they were better than everyone else. Brendan found a church, and gave the Setswana-language GNT to the Herero woman cleaning inside.

Brendan cycled the next day for two hours before the excitement of a road junction. That was the major excitement of the day. There was another road off to the south-west five hours later, but it wasn't anywhere near as thrilling. It was that sort of a day. The next was similar, except that a town appeared halfway through the afternoon. A town! With shops and houses and a radio-mast – and people! It was called Kang which sounded more interesting than it actually was, but after hours of monotony it was great to get off the bike and look around a shop, choose fruit to buy, and talk to someone. He camped outside the little settlement of Morwamosi 50km further on, which he reached as the sun shot down below the horizon in a fantastic red and orange sunset. There was another town and another road junction the next day, the terrain still as boring as ever, but during the next day he sensed that he was coming to the end of the Kalahari, because villages kept popping up more regularly and he even passed through a larger town called Kanye before stopping a few kilometres from the border with South Africa.

It had been an amazingly dull journey, but then what else should he have expected from a desert? The Atacama hadn't been much different last year in Chile, but this was even worse. Was it partly because last year in Chile he'd been coming towards the end of his journey whereas the Kalahari was still only a third of the way through? He'd expected it still to be a bit more exciting, brought up as he was with accounts of intrepid travellers meeting the San, living precariously in extreme conditions, chasing and killing an elusive eland or digging in the sand for underground water. All he'd done was follow a long, unchanging, boring road for over 1,000km. But at least he could tell everyone that he'd cycled across the Kalahari.And not too many people could say that.

Brendan still had a week's cycling to go before he reached Maputo, but it would be over more interesting terrain which had *people* in it, as well as some amazing sights and places. He crossed the border just after dawn, and headed off towards Mahikeng, formerly Mafeking, which conjured up images of Baden Powell but turned out to be a large town with shopping centres and business districts – no Englishmen in knee-length brown shorts singing "Ging gang goolie goolie goolie goolie watcha ging gang goo ging gang goo". Brendan continued south-eastwards, stopping for the night at the Roman Catholic church at Hartbeesfontein, where he gave a talk to about 100 people, and handed the South African GNT to a couple due to get married the following Saturday.

The terrain now reminded him curiously of Yorkshire, but with gold-mines and bougainvillea and exotic place-names: Klerksdorp; Kroonstad and Matlwangtlwang. Two evenings later he was in Lesotho, the encircled nation with conical hats, men on horseback, and amazing mountains. He'd reached his 76th nation – and turned north-east after the border-crossing at Maputsoe, growing ever more excited about his destination. He was visiting the headquarters of Help Lesotho[59], an NGO founded by a Canadian doctor called Peg Herbert, which did work similar to Watoto in Uganda, but without the overt evangelistic sub-theme. Brendan was fascinated to see how they compared.

He was met at the Hlotse HQ by Konesoang Kunene, the CEO in Lesotho – but the charity was essentially run from a bigger office in Ottawa, and unlike Watoto, was still very Canadian, not global. It had only been running for eight years, but Konesoang proudly spoke about all the community projects they were engaged in, mainly up in the mountains: working with the remote Basotho youth to foster leadership, empowerment and gender equity; helping orphans and vulnerable children; helping grandmothers bringing up grandchildren because so many were orphaned by HIV/AIDS; building schools; distributing emergency food supplies to starving children and grandmothers; handing out shoes and school uniforms; running HIV/AIDS awareness and testing clinics, and so much else. It was all excellent work. Brendan handed over the GNT, printed in Sesotho, but wondered if there was anything he could do to spread some of the money he was raising in their direction as well as throughout Uganda. He made a mental note to ask Ruth about this. Even passing through just this tiny corner of Lesotho, Brendan noted the contrast with South Africa – and the poverty in particular.

After bunking down overnight in the HQ, Brendan crossed back into South Africa at Ha Belo, heading north-eastwards up to Bethlehem, which didn't look much like its Middle-Eastern namesake. It looked more like the Bethlehem suburb of Tauranga – the place in New Zealand which he'd visited a few years previously, staying with some friends who'd emigrated there – a small residential area, with its own supermarkets and amenities, but without much character. 3km before Bethlehem, he stopped at a huge roadside cairn, which he'd been told was very significant for the people of Lesotho. On their way to work at the Witwatersrand gold mines, the workers used to drop a stone on the pile to ask their ancestral spirits to protect them from accidents down the mines. On the way back home to Lesotho they dropped another stone on the pile to give thanks for their safe return. Brendan

---

[59] I was very impressed with all that I read about Help Lesotho. Their website www.helplesotho.ca gives details of the projects described here – but my characters (apart from its founder) are fictional.

dropped his own stone on the huge pile, asking God to protect him from accidents, and thanking God for his safe journey so far.

The long cycle ride north-eastwards led from Lesotho towards the similarly small, poor and HIV/AIDS-ravaged nation of Swaziland, which Brendan reached two days later after stops and speaking engagements in Harrismith and Wakkerstroom. The highlight of the second day was passing through the South African city of Newcastle, which was quite unlike the one in Britain. It still had coal-mines; it didn't have a famous football team; it wasn't near the sea and it didn't have any fancy bridges across its river. It did, however, have cold temperatures and rain, so he felt at home.

Brendan entered Swaziland just beyond the town of Piet Retief, named after the Voortrekker leader. He was scheduled to speak and stay in the nation's second-biggest town, Manzini, situated right in the middle of the little country and serving as the nation's commercial and industrial centre, even though the capital Mbabane was only an hour's drive away in the high veld. Manzini had a large Church of the Nazarene next to the secondary school which the denomination ran in the centre of town. Brendan stayed with the Minister who was also the school chaplain, to whom he gave the siSwati version of the GNT to be a gift for the most deserving pupil.

A few kilometres east of Manzini on the Monday morning, Brendan dropped down to the low veld which was much more sparsely populated and presented a typical African bush landscape of thorn trees and grasslands. He was heading for the Mozambique border at Naamacha, eager to reach Maputo as soon as he could, because he was getting fed up of cycling. He passed sugar plantations and fields full of maize and cotton, as well as many ruined bridges, where recent cyclonic flash floods had roared down previously benign channels, twisting and breaking concrete and metal, and causing landslips which carried whole sections of bridge away[60]. Now everything was dry, and the ruined bridges looked silly, as if such weather was impossible.

He had to climb up an escarpment to reach the border but quickly dropped down again through the switchbacks to the coastal plain at Mafuta, and on towards the Indian Ocean which he could smell and see in the distance. He was glad to reach the big white towers of the Cathedral in Maputo, get off his bike, and say to himself that it was another 100 days or more before he had to get on a bike again – and he'd make sure that it wasn't pink.

In fact, the bike had been excellent – a few punctures but no serious mechanical failures. The only problem was its colour, but after a few miles on the roads of Africa

---

[60] There was a similarly devastated Swazi landscape in the summer of 1984, when I spent the summer in Southern Africa as part of my training for the Methodist Ministry. The low veld was very dry, but the ruined bridges and roads testified to the force of a recent cyclone.

it had become a reddish-brown colour and stayed that way till the rain in Newcastle washed it and provoked funny looks again from passers-by. He left it outside the Cathedral, hoping that someone would steal it – and when he looked a few minutes later, it'd gone, and he felt really glad for whoever had taken it. Then he met the Dean of the Cathedral and was re-introduced to the bike, because one of the Dean's colleagues, an East Timorese missionary called Carlos, had taken it inside to make sure that no-one stole it.

"But I don't want it!" Brendan explained, with a laugh. "I left it there on purpose."

"Well then," Carlos said, "Can I have it?"

"Of course!" laughed Brendan. "Do you like pink?"

"Not at all," Carlos replied. "I will paint it the colour of rust."

Brendan had cycled for 26 days non-stop, had clocked up nearly 4,200km, bored for most of the time but sensing that he'd achieved something simply by keeping going. He was looking forward to getting in a comfy car for the next leg.

Day: Date	Itinerary (* indicates TV interview) ([18]indicates new nation)	Bike (km)	Car/ Bus (km)	Train (km)	Kayak/ Sail (km)	Boat (km)	Air (km)
Totals brought forward		4554	5801	0	2754	5020	7383
105: 28/8/11	N'zeto, Angola[72]					164	
106: 29/8/11	Luanda *					203	
107: 30/8/11	Dondo	169					
108: 31/8/11	Quibala	139					
109: 1/9/11	Gumbe	157					
110: 2/9/11	Cuima	166					
111: 3/9/11	Chimbandongo	151					
112: 4/9/11	Mulondo	170					
113: 5/9/11	Calueque	155					
114: 6/9/11	Oumbada, Namibia[73]	143					
115: 7/9/11	Okanyanoma	138					
116: 8/9/11	Kakoro	177					
117: 9/9/11	Katere	183					
118: 10/9/11	Ncasamere, Botswana[74]	165					
119: 11/9/11	Nokaneng	136					
120: 12/9/11	40km after Sehithwa	147					
121: 13/9/11	Ghanzi	149					
122: 14/9/11	40km after junction	158					
123: 15/9/11	Morwamosi	162					
124: 16/9/11	Jwaneng	178					
125: 17/9/11	Pitsane	150					
126: 18/9/11	Hartbeesfontein, South Africa[75]	180					
127: 19/9/11	Matlwangtlwang	181					
128: 20/9/11	Hlotse, Lesotho[76]	164					
129: 21/9/11	Harrismith (SA)	144					
130: 22/9/11	Wakkerstroom	166					
131: 23/9/11	Manzini, Swaziland[77]	172					
132: 24/9/11	Maputo, Mozambique[78]	159					
Totals carried forward		8713	5801	0	2754	5387	7383

Chapter 37: Hallucination

Louisa was getting to know Gareth quite well, for he'd been up to her Unit several times during the last week. Each time he'd been specifically asked for by one of the patients, so Sister Lilian couldn't really object, especially as he timed his visits deliberately not to coincide with either ward rounds or meal-times. He also avoided open visiting times, because he wanted Sister Lilian to acknowledge that he was visiting officially as "one of the team".

Gareth always seemed to find the time to wander up the Unit saying hello to everyone, including the staff – and those like Louisa who felt that they were trudging through a spiritual desert at least felt that there might be an oasis. Louisa rather hoped that the desert had bloomed, like the Isaiah 35 vision which they'd looked at last week in her cell group, and that it would never be desert again. But deserts were also the place for mirages, and the spiritual atmosphere vanished like an apparition one afternoon, when Louisa asked Sister Lilian if she could page Gareth because Dawn was asking to chat with him.

"No, you can't!" she snapped.

"What do you mean?"

"It's very simple, Louisa. You can't page Gareth or any of the other chaplains. I'm not having God-botherers messing with my patients any longer. I've read the rule book and I don't have to admit any of them if it isn't convenient. And it's never convenient for me, so I won't ever allow it! And *that*," she proclaimed rather triumphantly, "is *that!*"

Louisa bit her lip because she sensed a real spiritual tension. This was getting out of hand, but she had to be very sure of her rights and watertight on the rules before she challenged the Sister's edict. So she smiled, turned on her heel and went off to tell Dawn that she'd have to wait for the visit from Gareth. "There seems to be a bit of a disagreement about chaplains' visits," she explained. Dawn smiled, knowingly.

Louisa sought Gareth out in the canteen the following day, and described what had happened. "She can't do that, can she?"

"Unfortunately she can," said Gareth. "Unless it's a life-threatening situation there isn't much that we can do – she's the one who makes the rules on her shift. The other wards accept and welcome chaplains as part of the health care team, but she treats us like we've nothing to offer. And there isn't a thing that we can do about it, I'm afraid."

The oasis was a mirage or hallucination, after all. Nothing could thrive here. The Unit was a desert. Or was it?

Louisa decided that if she wasn't allowed to "bring in" spiritual encouragement from the chaplains, then she'd have to provide it herself for the patients. She decided that she'd ask them all how they were feeling about what was happening to them, and whether they wanted her to pray for them. The patient confidentiality rules didn't apply to her. She could have a look in each patient's notes and see what they'd put for religious affiliation, and this would give her an indicator about anyone who might object to her questions. An increasing number of patients now dared to answer "None" rather than the meaningless default "CofE" of the past, but even as she noticed the "None" answer with some of her patients, she noted too that these very patients had responded most positively to Gareth – and Louisa herself when such conversations arose. Maybe it was stuffy, boring, meaningless religion that they were against, rather than God or faith. Clergy had a lot to answer for, she mused.

Louisa discovered that one of her older patients was down as a Roman Catholic, which was intriguing because there'd never been a Catholic chaplain up to see her. It was unusual even on their Unit for the chaplains not to visit as soon as the patient came back from ICU, and Louisa wondered whether Mary wanted her own priest to visit her, because she seemed quite lonely. She didn't get any visitors except a lady of about the same age, who turned out to be her sister. When Mary was up for a chat, Louisa asked her about her local priest coming in and Mary got a bit embarrassed. "I'm not exactly on speaking terms with Father Gerry after he tried to stop wor Darren going to the Catholic school."

"What do you mean?" asked Louisa.

"Well, wor Darren was baptised in St. Aidan's like we've all been – like you do. But his Mam don't exactly see the point of carrying it on, if you see what I mean. You know, like going to Mass and stuff. So wor Darren's never done his first Communion or nuffin'. So Father Gerry said he couldn't sign his form for Tommy More. So I went in and told him what I thought, didn't I?"

Louisa smiled. "Oh Mary, that's so sad because you seem a bit cut off now, don't you?"

"Yes, I suppose I do, pet. But there's nothing much I can do about it, is there?"

"We'll see," said Louisa. "Leave it with me. But don't you worry, God still loves you!"

Mary smiled. "Thanks, pet."

Louisa had a look in Mary's notes but there was no reference to which parish she was in so she didn't know how to contact Father Gerry about initiating a reconciliation. She meant to find out as soon as she went off duty, but forgot all about it.

***

The next day when Louisa came back on shift, she noticed that someone else was in Mary's bed. "Sister, what's happened to Mary?"

"Who?"

"Mary – you know – that nice old lady who was in bay three."

"Oh yes, I know who you mean. She died last night."

Louisa was dumbstruck. She'd only been chatting to her the day before. Of course, she was familiar by now with the randomness of death and the inability sometimes to predict a patient's outcome, but this really took the wind out of her sails. She had a sudden thought. "What about the Last Rites?"

Sister Lilian looked at her strangely. "What about them?"

"Did Mary get them? The Last Rites?"

"Dunno," said Sister Lilian, off-handedly. "Does it matter?"

"Of course it matters!" cried Louisa. "She was a Catholic! They believe that if you haven't had the Last Rites then you... well, you... well, actually I don't know what they believe but I know they think it's important!"

"Well I don't," snapped Sister. "Anyway, what's it got to do with you? You're not Catholic are you?"

"No, I'm not," said Louisa, "But that's not the point."

But Sister Lilian turned away. She'd had enough of the conversation. "Nothing you can do about it now, is there?" were her parting words.

***

The more Louisa thought about poor Mary, the more upset she got. Mary's sister came into the Unit to pick up her belongings, and Louisa spotted her and went over to express her sorrow at what had happened. Apparently when Mary suddenly got breathing trouble, the Sister on night duty tried to contact the chaplain but he'd already been called out to administer the Last Rites to someone else, and there was no record of Mary's local priest. And she'd died very quickly so it would probably not have been possible anyway.

Louisa felt really guilty. She'd meant to locate and contact Father Gerry, and even though it would have been too late anyway, she still felt awful that she'd forgotten. It was sad that somehow the systems of hospital and Church had failed Mary. If only she'd had that conversation with Mary a bit sooner, and followed it up... Louisa was pretty confident that not getting the Last Rites wouldn't mean that God would slam the Pearly Gates on Mary's fingers and send her down the Warm End – but Mary may have died worrying about that, despite the encouragement with which Louisa was now glad to have left her the previous day.

***

"Not still moping about Bloody Mary, are you?" sneered Sister Lilian towards the end of the shift. And when she saw Louisa fighting back the tears, she laughed and walked away.

The Unit *was* a spiritual desert and it hadn't bloomed. It *had* all been a hallucination, a mirage, an apparition, a figment of her imagination. Sister Lilian transformed the light at the end of the tunnel into the headlight of a train travelling swiftly closer, on a collision course. There was going to be trouble ahead.

Chapter 38: Nations 79 - 84

Trouble was the last thing on Brendan's radar as he drove his shiny red (definitely not pink) Volvo 460 out of Maputo. He'd asked for a 4x4 but Mozambique Hertz didn't have any. He'd never driven a Volvo before, so he was quite excited, especially with the power-steering. Yet despite not looking for it, trouble found Brendan all too soon.

He headed inland for the South African border at Komatipoort, and was there within the hour. A rather pompous official dressed in a blue uniform and a bright orange pullover came across and demanded Brendan's passport and the vehicle documentation, which Brendan found in the glove compartment. "When are you coming back to Mozambique with the vehicle?"

"I'm not," said Brendan. "I'm going to drive it to Mombasa in Kenya and leave it there."

The man's eyebrows shot up. "Kenya?" he cried. "That is too far. You must be lying. No-one drives that far!"

Brendan smiled. "Crazy English people do all kinds of strange things."

The official was not amused. "You will have to pay export duty on the car: 4,000 rand." And he held his hand out, as if he expected Brendan to hand over a wad of cash there and then.

"You must be joking," said Brendan. "It's a hire car. It's not my car and I don't have to pay any export duty. Hertz will bring it back eventually when they have someone wanting to drive a car back to Mozambique."

"Then they pay import duty," said the man. "Another 4,000 rand."

Brendan had never heard anything like it. He'd crossed various frontiers over the last few months and never once had to pay export duty on a hired car. "I want to see your supervisor," he said.

The man bristled. "I am in charge here. I discharge my responsibilities properly and you are disrespecting my authority. Come with me." And he turned round and strutted off to the gate house. Brendan locked the car carefully and followed him into the office. The man sat at a desk and beckoned Brendan forwards. "Now, let's look at this carefully. You obviously do not know the laws of my country and you insist that you are right, even though you are in my country for such a short time, I see." Brendan looked blankly at him. "I also see that you have been visiting many countries over the last few months on this shiny new passport, which is nearly full. I notice too that Israel has made you a persona non grata." He rolled the phrase out on his tongue, relishing it as if showing off that he knew it. "Now you tell me you are on your way to Mombasa. Are you in a hurry?"

Brendan looked blankly at him again. "Yes, I am, really. I'm supposed to be in Makhado tonight."

"Makhado? That is a long way. Many, many hours away. It would be a shame if you were held up here because you didn't understand the border procedures."

Brendan finally realised what was happening. "How much?" he asked.

The man smiled. "Now you understand our border procedures! I would think that 1,000 rand might cover the administration costs involved." He smiled again. Brendan counted out the notes, shaking his head. £100 – just to be allowed through the border! It was shocking. The official counted the notes carefully again and shoved them into his back pocket.

"Can I have a receipt, please?" asked Brendan.

The man smiled. "Unfortunately not, as our receipt machine has broken. We are very poor here in Mozambique, but thank you for spending your money in our country so generously." He laughed and handed Brendan back his passport and vehicle documents. "Have a good day, Mr. Priest, and do come back soon."

Brendan was fuming. It wasn't the money so much as the principle. But he had to pay the bribe because he needed to keep to his schedule. Thankfully the South African border official was not so corrupt, and he emerged into South Africa fuming but thankful that he hadn't been delayed any further.

The South African roads were very good, and he drove at a steady 120kph (though the Volvo could probably have coped with 120mph) for the next hour into Nelspruit, or Mbombela as it was now officially re-named. All the signs still said Nelspruit. Brendan saw in the western suburbs the new football stadium erected for the 2010 World Cup, with its 18 steel towers designed to resemble giraffe necks, but pressed on northwards following signs for the Kruger National Park, not that he would have time to visit.

He did, however, want to visit God's Window, just off-route near Hazyview. Looking down through the gap in the trees to the bottom of the Blyde River Canyon, the third largest in the world, was awesome. The canyon itself was rugged and mighty, but the main reason he wanted to visit was because of the film "The Gods Must Be Crazy". In it, a San from the Kalahari tries to walk to the end of the earth (it rang bells for Brendan) to return to the gods an unwanted gift – a coke bottle dropped from a plane. Xi arrives at God's Window and believes that this must be the end of the world because low cloud obscures the valley floor, so he throws the coke bottle into the void. A big sign prohibited film-buffs from copy-cat littering.

It was a pleasant drive on from God's Window, through Tzaneen to Makhado, but the border incident still rankled. Brendan was not looking forward to crossing the Limpopo into Zimbabwe the following morning.

After a comfy night in a rundown hotel, Brendan set off, with some trepidation because of the political difficulties, to the border at Beitbridge, but he needn't have worried. Everything went smoothly on both sides of the border. The roads were fine, and he whizzed along, marvelling at the kopjes – round granite mountains stuck in the middle of the otherwise flat, mopane-strewn savannah. Yet Mugabe even seemed to be able to cast the country's natural beauty into shadow. At Masvingo, for instance, halfway through the day's journey, Brendan drove through the once-prosperous town, formerly Fort Victoria, a central hub in an area rich with mining and cattle-ranching activity. But now it was derelict and barren. It still had the fine buildings and wide boulevards, but the life seemed to have gone out of it. Even the Great Zimbabwe site, only 20 minutes' drive away from the town, seemed to Brendan to have lost its importance, as if the national spirit had departed.

At Dover, a little town on the main road to Harare, Brendan was glad to stop and reflect on it all. He'd arranged to stay with the Methodist Minister at Dover, because he wanted to visit a local man called Thokozani Tolwani[61]. Brendan had met Thokozani several years ago at a meeting of the Zimbabwe Vigil, a pressure group in Britain to support Zimbabweans in their struggles, and Brendan followed Thokozani's case when he'd nearly been deported from England in 2009 back to Zimbabwe, despite the threats of violence against him for his opposition to the Mugabe regime. Brendan had even written to Phil Woolas, the then Minister of State for Borders and Immigration, to protest against Thokozani's deportation, and had been really pleased when he was released from the Dover Removal Centre in Kent. The irony was that his home town in Zimbabwe was called Dover too, and Thokozani decided to return home voluntarily during 2010 when the Mugabe machine took their foot off the pedal a little at home in an attempt to claw back some international standing.

Brendan was thrilled to meet Thokozani again, and to see that he was in good fettle, though when Thokozani started to tell his story, Brendan realised that nothing in Zimbabwe had changed. Life was still incredibly tough in a country where money had no value and where bartering was the main commercial tool, and where no-one hired anyone else because they had no possibility of paying any wages. Thokozani himself was a farmer, and so could produce food for his family, even though there'd been a bad drought and the harvest last year had been very poor. Human rights violations were still rampant even after the formation of the coalition government; journalists continued to be harassed by the police; dozens were dying every day in state prisons because of preventable and curable diseases like tuberculosis and pellagra; and thousands more were still in jail being denied their right to trial. Property rights weren't guaranteed either and there was the constant threat of farms being invaded and taken over. Corruption was rampant and no-one seemed to have the authority to change that, or be prepared to risk their neck by protesting against it.

---

[61] This fictional character is based on the real-life experiences of Luka Phiri, well-documented in the UK. See www.zimvigil.co.uk/Campaign-News/update-on-luka-phiri.html for further details.

Brendan gave Thokozani the Zimbabwean GNT, and assured him that the rest of the world had not forgotten Zimbabwe, even if the world's media had moved on to more sensationalist locations.

Brendan's route the following day took him to Harare, though he diverted round the city through the suburb of Epworth – because of its famous balancing stones rather than its Methodist name[62]. It was now known unfortunately as the capital's crime centre, which in Harare really did say something, so Brendan looked out of the car window at the columns of stones balancing precariously due to some weird erosion in the long-gone past, but didn't stop. They were also depicted on the Zimbabwean bank-notes, giving an unintended clue (if anyone needed it) about the wobbliness of the currency. Brendan saw a sign too for "God's footprints" which seemed similarly unreliable.

He was glad to get out of the city, and headed eastwards towards his overnight destination, Mwanza in Malawi, knowing that he'd need to re-enter Mozambique to reach southern Malawi. After his experience at Komatipoort, he was reluctant (to say the least) to return to Mozambique, but the only realistic alternative was a 170km extension of his Zimbabwean journey along winding, rough roads in the far north. Because he liked Zimbabwe even less than Mozambique, he decided to brave the customs officials and trust that he'd just chanced upon a rogue rather than that all Mozambique officials were corrupt. In the end, he needn't have worried. The customs posts at Cochemane coming out of Zimbabwe and at Zobue entering Malawi were smooth and trouble-free, which restored Brendan's faith in humankind in general and Mozambique officials in particular. He got to the border just before it shut at 6pm, but hadn't planned it that way because he still didn't have a clue what time zone he was in.

Brendan slept at a small hotel and was off again early the next day. He was eager to explore a country which had fascinated him ever since he'd done a school geography project on it. Since then it had been ravaged by both the iron grip of Hastings Banda and the insidious omnipresence of HIV/AIDS, and this country so rich in natural beauty had become one of the poorest and weakest in the world.

The view from the Mwanza escarpment was wonderful. The road swept down into the Rift Valley, with the city of Blantyre visible through the morning haze 50km away, but Brendan's route swept northwards along the valley until he reached the "Calendar Lake", officially Lake Malawi, but given its nickname because it was 365 miles long and 52 miles wide at its widest point. Its actual name and ownership were still disputed with Tanzania, which naturally preferred both the old Livingstonian

---

[62] John Wesley, regarded as Methodism's founder, was born in Epworth, Lincolnshire.

name of Lake Nyasa and the original boundary which was halfway across rather than the eastern shore-line which Malawi claimed.

No matter to whom it "belonged", it was beautiful. Brendan spent the rest of the day travelling sedately up the lakeside, admiring the blue sheen and gentle sparkle of the water. He stopped frequently, viewing basking hippos or crocodiles or watching fish eagles gliding majestically overhead, one of which dived headfirst into the water at great speed before re-emerging with a flapping fish in its talons. At one viewing point there was a vendor selling barbecued mice, complete with fur, paws, heads and stiffened tails. Brendan bought some fruit instead.

He was sad to leave the lake at Nkhata Bay, yet the short drive into the city of Mzuzu gave him the opportunity to see the other reality of Malawi – urban squalor. It was only the third biggest city, featureless and flat, yet the roadside was teeming with activity and thick with makeshift dwellings – "houses" was too grandiose a word for them. When Brendan finally found the city centre, every other shop was bright pink, and the others filthy, dusty, with cracked or peeling plaster and illegible misspelled signs. Zain, the biggest mobile phone company in Malawi offered some shopkeepers free paint, free labour, a bright pink shop front, a clear new sign and the chance to stand out from the rest and attract more business. For Zain it saved having to pay for billboards, and for a poor shop owner with a bit of nous it was a clear winner, but the effect was to make the whole place look hideous, even if you liked pink – which Brendan, of course, didn't.

The Mwanza Catholic Cathedral was one of the few buildings standing out against the pink tide. The evening's meeting had been planned for weeks, and several hundred people turned up for it, including two Ngoni warriors in full tribal dress who were anxious to have a photo taken with Brendan on the digital camera one of them pulled from his robes. Brendan gave them the Malawi GNT, published in Chitumbuka, but was relieved to be told before his talk that most people understood English, so no translation was required. Afterwards he was wined and dined at the Mzuzu Hotel by Father Andrew, and then shown his sleeping quarters in the accommodation block next to the Cathedral. He shared his room with a small lizard and a small whizzy insect which was attempting the world endurance record for flying round a room without getting killed, so it was some hours before Brendan managed to fall asleep – only for the Cathedral bells to wake him at 6am to announce the new day. Brendan staggered out for the English Mass at 7am, then woke up gradually during breakfast with Father Andrew back at the Mzuzu Hotel.

The car glided along the lakeside, beyond the wonderfully-named towns of Rhumpi and guess-who-it's-named-after Livingstonia, towards the Nyika Plateau – with the ever-present delightful view across the flat, blue water to Tanzania and the peace and grandeur of escarpments on either side. Brendan had a relaxed schedule, so he took some time out to sit and think, and even pray. It was hard to imagine what

David Livingstone must have thought when he "discovered" the lake and encountered the people. Everything had changed so much, but the pioneering missionary "package", however culturally domineering and insensitive, had certainly played its part in introducing people to stories about Jesus. More contentious, of course, was whether it revealed more of the Empire than the Kingdom.

Reluctantly, Brendan drove away from the lake at Karonga, its northern tip, and threaded his way up through the evergreens to the plateau, and on upwards through the undulating hills to the Zambian border at Kanyala, passing signs for the Kayerekera Uranium Mine on the way. The narrow road was surprisingly good, as if it had only just been completed, but perhaps uranium was the reason.

The transition into Zambia was smooth, and 40km later, Brendan reached Nakonde, his evening's destination, and had a quick look round. That was all it took. As a general rule, border towns were pretty lousy places, but he quickly ranked Nakonde among the worst. The frontier between Zambia and Tanzania was open, established decades ago to facilitate trade, so locals and foreigners alike passed freely. There wasn't much on the Tanzanian side either. Back in Zambia, Nakonde was teeming with trade on trucks, bikes and foot, everyone with something to sell – or steal. The local priest pointed out the local ngwangwazi, or hoodlums, milling around near Brendan's car, and beckoned their leader over, pointing to the Volvo and speaking quietly to him. The previously talkative young ngwangwazi suddenly became all bashful, and set up guards front and back. Brendan fished in the back of the Volvo and gave the ngwangwazi the Zambian GNT, much to the young lad's amazement and pleasure. He went over to show his mates.

In Tanzania the following day, Brendan immediately turned off the Tanzam Highway, heading through open terrain to Myunga, the Volvo throwing up an impressive dust-cloud. At Sumbawanga in the early afternoon he joined the major highway, which ran north through the Katavi National Park to Mpanda, where he stopped for the night in a hotel partially burnt down the week before. Apart from the bonfire smell, the room was bearable, even though there were four other people sleeping in it, one of whom kept shouting out as if he was supporting his local football team.

After an uninspiring drive across the open savannah, which had hardly any villages, people, animals or excitement, he was glad to arrive at Lake Tanganyika, the world's longest lake, and Ujiji itself, famous for the "Dr. Livingstone, I presume?" meeting, now just a suburb of Kagoma. Not half as glad, though, as the first missionaries who arrived on 23rd January 1879. The priest at Ujiji showed Brendan extracts from their diary[63]: "We contemplate that shining water with a sense of

---

[63] The quotations come from
www.africamission-mafr.org/CARAVAN_UJIJI_KIGOMA_1879_2009.pdf

expectation, as the Jews from Mount Horeb greeted the Promised Land." The diarist's longing was to "steal them from hell and open for them the door of heaven." The priest at Ujiji also showed Brendan the grave of one of those first missionaries, next to the church, a simple white building which compared favourably for Brendan with the Kagoma Cathedral which he drove past the following day, which was painted maroon and orange and looked like a cinema.

The priest took Brendan up to Mlima Samba, the highest point in the area and formerly the site for animist sacrifices. The priest explained that one of the monks at Ujiji decided to plant a massive cross on the top of the hill to "convert" it for the New Millennium, with two other crosses added in 2004 to stand proudly overlooking a vast area. Brendan approved of this "conversion" of land, as such practices were enshrined in biblical records and had been very much part of the missionary process – adopt and adapt places already associated with religious rites. He gave the Tanzanian GNT to the priest at Ujiji, to be kept in the church which the first missionaries had built, as a sign that the missionary task was still incomplete. Brendan might phrase his own understanding of mission rather differently from their "heaven and hell" language, but the work continued. The main local challenge was the persistent refugee problem, with tens of thousands of Congolese and Burundian refugees still living in camps and special villages in the area.

The small track to the Burundian border the following morning was not even marked on the GPS. Brendan followed a smoke-belching minibus taking an assortment of UNHCR personnel and backpackers to Bujumbura, via the mountains in Burundi. He had to help pull the minibus out once when it ran into a ditch. The landscape was breathtaking, with frequent views over the lake and the Congolese mountains on the other side. The track snaked between villages and clearings in the forest, and Brendan was glad to be following someone who appeared to know where they were going.

Finally they rumbled into the border area. The minibus stopped to let all its passengers out (another awaited them the other side), and Brendan drove on alone to the border near Nyarabanda. There were still all kinds of conflicts and skirmishes between Hutu militias opposing the Tutsi-dominated national army in the south of Burundi. The guards were, therefore, a little suspicious about any vehicle travelling in their area, even one going *into* the "danger zone". They insisted on searching the car, and one guard in particular seemed fascinated by the Burundian GNT. Brendan explained what is what and what it represented, showing him the Kirundi-translated inscription in the front,. When his eyes lit up, Brendan gave him it, and was immediately whisked through the border and waved on his way.

So Nation 83 had been officially "ticked off" but Brendan travelled up the shoreline to the capital Bujumbura at the lake's northern tip. It was a modern city, built around the old colonial town but with its main activity in the market and the docks. There was even a sandy beach, which amazed Brendan because he'd assumed that beaches only happened at the seaside. He drove quickly on around the Kibira National Park to the Rwandan border and on to the capital, Kigali. Brendan had planned for the roads to be rougher and his pace slower, so when he arrived in Kigali it was still only mid-afternoon, giving him lots of time to wander round before his speaking engagement in the Cathedral at 7.30pm.

Since the appalling genocide of 1994, in which over 800,000 were killed, most of them Tutsis murdered by Hutus, Rwanda had made a miraculous recovery, tripling average income and achieving astounding economic growth, with the help of international aid and multinational companies. Kigali itself looked very pleasant, stretched across four ridges and valleys (posher suburbs higher up), and surrounded by higher mountains including Mount Kigali itself.

He was booked into the Faith House accommodation, next door to St. Michael's Cathedral, and his talk that evening went off very smoothly and joyously. Brendan gave his usual patter about the journey but told story after story because the audience seemed to be lapping it up. He realised during it that since leaving the Pink Lady at Luanda he'd actually been quite disheartened, enduring rather than enjoying the journey, and doing it almost as a challenge to his human endurance rather than a response to a divine calling. Now, though, right now, he felt the call once again and felt really good about what he was doing and why he was doing it. He gave the Rwandan GNT to a man with no teeth and only half an arm, who had lost the teeth naturally but had his arms chopped off with a machete in 1994 by Hutus, even though he himself was a Hutu too. A sort of "friendly fire" incident, and one which had transformed his life, not only in terms of disability but also faith, because he'd been cared for in a Christian mission hospital and became a Christian months later, loved into faith by the care given to him.

Brendan felt lighter and happier when he went to bed that night, and this feeling of well-being persisted throughout the next day, as he crossed the Ugandan border and headed north up the western edge of the country. The road wound down from the hills of Kabale to the edge of the Rift Valley, then dropped steeply down near the Kazinga Channel, very near to where Ruth had stayed at Mweya the previous year with some Watoto helpers from Macclesfield. Even from the road, he could see hippos in the channel, and elephants on the southern banks. Africa truly was a remarkable continent.

He stayed his final night before Gulu at Fort Portal, a market town nestling underneath the permanently snow-capped peaks of the Rwenzori mountains, but his thoughts were centred on meeting up once again with Ruth and Paul, and Louisa and Ben, re-visiting Gulu and seeing what Gulu Bulrushes looked like. Oh, and seeing Esther and doing a live interview watched by millions across the globe too, of course.

He couldn't sleep, so set out from his hotel at first light, anxious to do the distance and make the rendezvous as soon as possible. The day whizzed by, and by early afternoon he was approaching Gulu, looking out for the Pink Poodle, the hotel which was now thankfully re-named the Lilian Towers, where the family had stayed for Ruth's wedding last year. He'd flown in and out again the same day by Esther's Learjet, so staying in the hotel was going to be a new experience for him. He turned the corner and there it was – just as he remembered it, as pink as ever. It seemed to be the colour for the journey somehow, but at that very moment he didn't really care.

Day: Date	Itinerary (* indicates TV interview) ([18] indicates new nation)	Bike (km)	Car/ Bus (km)	Train (km)	Kayak/ Sail (km)	Boat (km)	Air (km)
Totals brought forward		8713	5801	0	2754	5387	7383
133: 25/9/11	Makhado (SA)		524				
134: 26/9/11	Dover, Zimbabwe[79]		555				
135: 27/9/11	Mwanza, Malawi[80]		560				
136: 28/9/11	Mzuzu		520				
137: 29/9/11	Nakonde, Zambia[81]		412				
138: 30/9/11	Mpanda, Tanzania[82]		434				
139: 1/10/11	Ujiji		316				
140: 2/10/11	Bujumbura, Burundi[83]		216				
141: 3/10/11	Kigali, Rwanda[84]		266				
142: 4/10/11	Fort Portal, Uganda		350				
143: 5/10/11	Gulu *		386				
Totals carried forward		8713	10340	0	2754	5387	7383

Chapter 39: Indignation

As Louisa looked back, she was amazed that she'd managed to survive the last few weeks. Sister Lilian had been truly obnoxious – rude and aggressive in speech and manner, but still careful not to overstep the legal mark by providing stand-alone evidence of harassment or bullying. Several colleagues were witnesses of the continual grinding-down of Louisa's reserves of patience and good-humour, and of specific incidents when Sister humiliated her and slated her work, but again there was nothing which could be *proved*. Yet somehow she'd endured – with the dangling carrot of the Ugandan holiday and the added fun of Ben's growing excitement about his first big trip abroad – he didn't count Fuengirola because everyone he met there was British.

They'd managed to jump all the logistical hurdles and make their escape – from Newcastle Airport to Schiphol, then Entebbe and the internal flight to Gulu. She thrilled again to the heat and colours of Uganda, and Ben was entranced by the sights Louisa had seen before: women carrying huge bundles on their heads; workers clinging to sacks piled high on a moving truck; the redness of the mud; the crumbling shop-fronts; the contrast between the smart uniforms of the employed and the dowdy rags of those waiting, leaning, watching; a man on a motorbike carrying dozens of live, trussed chickens; massive green clumps of bananas; minibuses displaying religious slogans not destinations; roadside sewerage ditches; long-horned cattle; security guards with guns outside banks; small children playing in the dirt. This was Africa. It had sounds, smells and character all of its own, and Ben (like Louisa) was instantly caught up in it.

Finally, the taxi pulled up outside the Lilian Towers, and they entered a wonderfully cool reception area, grey and silent like a wide stairwell in an office-block. The receptionist whispered, respecting the solemnity of their arrival. They crept upstairs as if they were intruders rather than guests, then flung themselves down in their twin-bedded room and giggled uproariously at the fun of it all, like children suddenly let loose in a dormitory. After a lovely lingering cuddle, Ben sat up against the headboard and stroked her hair. "You know, this is just what I need. Cecil is doing my head in at Jact and I was beginning to lose the plot."

"I know exactly what you mean," said Louisa, stretching, with a long sigh of pleasure. "I feel as if I'm in a different world. Maybe we could stay here forever and never have to worry about any of it again."

Ben laughed. "Yeah," he said, wistfully. "Anyway, your Dad arrives the day after tomorrow so we ought to plan what we're going to do before then and also confirm details of the visit to Murchison Falls for our last four days here."

Louisa sighed. How short a respite they had from the pressures back home... But then she told herself off, determined to make the most of a completely different way of life in a completely different setting.

***

Louisa and Ben spent the next day exploring Gulu, saving Bulrushes for later with the others. Instead they wandered the streets, fascinated by what they saw – a lukeme musician plucking away, utterly focussed, unaware of having no audience; the tired market-women, reflex-swatting flies from their produce; a butcher, hacking away perilously close to his foot pinning the meat; little children standing silent as they broke off from their chase to watch the white people pass; sullen men watching them from street corners; the market with its rushing noisy people, sweet and pungent smells assaulting their senses, shafts of sunlight dazzling through the awnings; a smart new coffee shop right in the centre of town, offering a choice of freshly-brewed coffees and American-style pastries and cookies, six internet stations for laptops, a range of newspapers...

At teatime, they met up with Ruth and Paul, who'd flown in from Nairobi on a connection from New York, and went out to BJ'z for the evening – a local bar and restaurant offering cocktails and a first-class DJ.

***

The four of them were wandering back from lunch in Café Larem (Acholi for "friendship") when the red Volvo drew up outside Reception. Louisa squealed and ran up to her Dad, jumping into his arms as he emerged. Ruth came next, more restrained but still excited, even though it was only five weeks since she'd waved him off at Luanda. Ben and Paul came next, shaking hands and then doing the man-hug-thing rather self-consciously – especially Ben, who hadn't shared weeks with Brendan on a small pink boat like Paul had.

At 5pm they all piled into the Volvo and drove up to the Bulrushes site, which was an old school out to the east of the town. The "See Esther" crew had flown in earlier that morning, and had been filming all day in order to show an edited "guided tour" during the interview, which would be at 9pm because of time-differences.

There were three big rooms, each brightly painted with murals typical of children's wards in any Western hospital: one was a dormitory filled with rows of cots; another an open space with baby-rockers and soft-play mats; the last a medical room with three incubators and three cots, all occupied – presumably other cots could be brought in as needed. They were appalled at the stick-limbs of the babies in the incubators, yet then saw the plumper physiques of those a little older and much

217

healthier. It was a marvellous yet chilling place, because everyone knew that this was but the tip of the iceberg of infant morbidity and neglect in a country where so many parents had been killed by war or HIV-AIDS.

They'd arrived at feeding-time. Bulrushes was already two-thirds full, even though its doors only opened seven weeks ago. Gulu had improved considerably from the previous year, when Ruth and Paul filmed a horrific video of the refugees and camps. Three months ago, the government had officially closed all the camps for Internally Displaced People, telling the 1.6 million people living in them to return to their villages. Over 80% had already left, leaving about 300,000 who were either in the process of leaving or permanently settling in the camps – which should soon become new townships between Gulu and Kitgum. The opening of Bulrushes blessedly coincided with this exodus, for many children – either too frail to travel, or one too many mouth to feed – were abandoned by departing families. Already Bulrushes housed 40 children under three years old, with room for a maximum of 20 more. As soon as they reached the age of three, each child would be transferred into a "family" in the protected environment of the Gulu Watoto village.

Bulrushes looked spruce and colourful, full of laughter as the children played outside after they'd eaten, with a myriad of bright toys like in any Western playgroup. Esther and Fahada were sitting at a picnic table on the grassy area at the rear of the building, away from the children, enjoying a bit of peace at the end of a long afternoon of filming and preparation. Esther stood to welcome them, and the girls caught each other's eye, noticing Fahada bristle when she saw her boss and lover hugging and kissing their Dad.

After sharing their delight at how good Bulrushes looked, Esther said, "We've produced so much good footage that I want to show more of that tonight and spend less time chatting to you, if that's OK, Brendan?"

He didn't feel like he'd got much choice – it was hard to argue with Esther. But he didn't mind anyway, because he didn't really have much to talk about, even though it had been a long five weeks. He was a bit ashamed about his lack of motivation during most of the last month, and worried whether his recent renewal of excitement would last.

Esther started the live show from outside the Bulrushes building, talking in a dramatic whisper as she explained where she was and that it was 9pm so the children were all asleep. They filmed a brief "opening ceremony", with Brendan looking rather self-conscious as the guest of honour. Esther, Brendan and the Bulrushes manager led the camera crew furtively through the building to the open playroom towards the back, where everyone sat in easy chairs ready for the conversation. Esther introduced everyone to camera and then showed the 20-minute presentation they'd prepared earlier. Along with viewers around the world, they watched it avidly, laughing and wiping away a few tears as they watched, hoping that the camera wasn't filming their reactions. The techies had done a brilliant job, showing the brightness and sadness of a place set up to deal with human tragedy on a scale few Westerners could imagine.

When the presentation had finished, Esther immediately asked Ruth about the finances. "It's all paid for!" said Ruth. "Everything you've just seen has been paid for through the sponsorship money which you've sent in over the last two months. Loans have been repaid, and Watoto can now assemble the best personnel and back-up resources. The plan is to make this place a lasting testimony to what human generosity can do in the wake of human cruelty and neglect, and the $8 million you've sent in so far has set Gulu Bulrushes up for the next ten years."

"But there will be lots more to come, so what's the rest of the money going towards?" asked Esther.

"Well, this will be news to Dad because we've kept it a secret until now. Watoto is setting up the "Brendan Priest Trust" to administer the funds which his journey produces. It will be managed by my husband Paul and me from Watoto headquarters here in Uganda but we'll have a continuing role in travelling the world to boost Watoto's work. The model for the education and social development of abandoned and orphan children which Watoto has developed over the years will be offered to other countries in Africa and in Asia too, with China showing great interest in it at the moment. Paul and I are flying out to China next week to see what the possibilities might be."

Esther turned in her seat. "What about you, Brendan? How's all this affecting you?"

"Well, I'm a bit gobsmacked by the Brendan Priest Trust Fund or whatever you called it just now. I haven't done any of this to make a name for myself. But it's great that Ruth and Paul have been given such important roles in Watoto and I'm thrilled for them. I'm especially thrilled to see Bulrushes open for business and already doing so much good. It's wonderful to think that I've helped to make it happen, though the vision and drive for it are largely down to Ruth and Paul."

"And how have the last five weeks gone?"

Brendan paused. "To be honest, I haven't really had a good time. I struggled to keep going, particularly on the long, hard cycle journey across the Kalahari. I'm now one of the few humans on the planet who can say that they have cycled across three deserts, the Atacama in Chile last year, the Negev in Israel and now the Kalahari, but I don't want to do a fourth and will definitely be crossing the Gobi by train."

Esther probed further. "What was the hardest part?"

"I think I lost sight of why I was doing it. I hope I've recaptured that now. The boost came when I gave the Rwandan Bible away to a man whose arms had been hacked off in the genocide of 1994. He'd become a Christian after being cared for by a Christian medical team, who were only out there because they wanted to help those in the greatest need. What I'm doing isn't particularly dangerous or courageous compared to them, and my faith was humbled by that Rwandan, so excited because he could now read the Word of God in his own language. For weeks before that, I was doing it in my own strength, for my own stubborn pride of endurance, and I needed to focus wholly on the mission to which God has called me. For it is *God's* work, righting wrongs, fulfilling omissions, revitalising the Church, supporting those persecuted for their faith, making the world a fairer place. And I am privileged if God keeps letting me play a role in that."

"So what do you want the folk out there to do?"

Brendan thought. The seconds elapsed, precious time going spare... "I want you to pray for me, that I'm kept safe and God-centred. I want you to keep raising money for the amazing work Watoto does. And I want you to transform your neighbourhood. Read Acts 1:8, and think who *your* Judeans and Samaritans are, people living close at hand geographically but in every other way distant from you, and reach out to them in friendship and with the love of God. And think too about your view of the world and the Church you are part of. Do you think of persecuted and martyred Christians as your brothers and sisters? Do you think of the Gulu orphans as your responsibility? *Any* of us can make a difference. What a difference it would make if we *all* decided to live God's way..."

"Well said, Brendan," said Esther as she smiled at the camera. "There's a challenge for you, folks. Next time we see Brendan will be in Iraq in five weeks' time. See you then, my friends, but remember Brendan's challenge. How are *you* making a difference?"

***

They said their farewells at Bulrushes, for Fahada and Esther and the crew were flying out that night. The five of them went back to the hotel, had a final drink in the bar, and went to bed, everyone rather tired after the excitement of the day.

Brendan was off early the next morning for a brief visit to Southern Sudan, but he'd be coming back via Gulu in the late morning, so the others slept in and had a leisurely late breakfast at Café Larem. At 11.30am, they returned to the hotel, and Brendan arrived shortly after for a quick drink together in the bar, before Brendan had to set off for Kumi in the east of Uganda.

***

Louisa was really pleased that she'd met up with her Dad again, but now that he'd gone she felt that the clock was ticking on her impending reunion with Sister Lilian. It wasn't fair that she should intrude even here in Uganda and cast a black cloud over everything. The more Louisa thought about it, the more indignant she became. How dare Sister Lilian hold such power over me? How dare she make my life so miserable? What right does she have to be so nasty?

She was starting to feel that she needed a complete break. Ruth had got herself this amazing and high-powered job within Watoto; her Dad was making high ratings on international television; but all she was doing was surviving a petty personality conflict. Was it worth it?

She'd been torn by Bulrushes. Her heart was moved by the plight of the tiny children and by the obvious benefit of the work, but her head was already calculating whether she could cope with such trauma day after day. It was all a flight of fancy anyway, because she was booked on a plane back to the land of the Dalek in five days' time. And she was determined to enjoy that time with Ben.

***

The five days went too quickly, but they were spectacular. They travelled by train to Pakwatch on the White Nile, and got a taxi for their journey to where Ruth and Paul had spent their honeymoon the previous year. The Paraa Lodge was elevated high above the Murchison Falls, where the already-mighty Nile was forced through a 6m-wide channel before plummeting 40m to a swirling cauldron below, and the luxurious Lodge boasted excellent views of the gorge as well as beautiful grounds in which to relax. They hiked to the falls, took a boat trip out amongst the crocodiles and hippos below the falls, and went on several drives out into the bush, seeing lions, elephants, giraffes, various types of buck and myriad bird species.

They had a wonderful, relaxed time. And on the last evening, as they sat on the balcony of the restaurant, enjoying the noises of the night and the soft clink of glasses and dishes, Ben gave Louisa a little rectangular parcel, all neatly wrapped with a ribbon.

"Ooooh," she said. "I love presents. I haven't a clue what it could be because I haven't seen any shops."

"Just open it," said Ben, serious all of a sudden.

She struggled with the ribbon and paper and unwrapped a cardboard box, which opened to reveal a small blue ring box. Louisa's mouth fell open. "Ben?"

"Just open it," said a now decidedly grim-looking Ben.

Inside was a gold ring with a small diamond, elegant and smart. It was definitely an engagement ring. Louisa looked at Ben, her eyes welling up. "Oh Ben," she said, softly.

"I love you," he said. "Will you marry me?"

"Of course I will." She grabbed his hand. "Oh Ben, I'm so happy. I never expected this. This is... perfect!"

Ben crept round the table and gave her a big hug. "I'm so pleased you said yes. I was more terrified of this than any of those injections which you made me have. I love you so much." They had a long, silent hug. The glasses and dishes still clinked. The night sounds outside still warbled, chirped and coughed. But the world had changed in an instant, and would never be the same again.

***

Ben and Louisa arrived back in Newcastle two days later, after three flights which though long didn't dampen their excitement about being engaged. Not even the thought of Sister Lilian could wreck Louisa's happiness, even though she was due back into work the very next day and wasn't looking forward to it at all.

***

The moment she entered the ward, Louisa could tell that nothing had changed. Some of the patients were different, of course, and some of the familiar patients had undergone a change in their health in the ten days that she'd been away — one had died, but three others were struggling to get their bodies to accept their new organs after transplants, so there was quite a lot of angst around.

Louisa wasn't wearing her ring, because unlike every film where the ring miraculously fits perfectly, hers was too big. She'd taken in it that morning and it wouldn't be ready till the following day. She decided to say nothing until she had the ring on. So she soldiered on, with the usual taunts and grumbles from Sister Lilian. She'd resolved to pray whenever anything nasty happened, and she prayed often during that first day back.

The following day she went in early to the jewellers so that she could wear the ring at work. It was lovely to feel it on her finger and she couldn't understand why people on the Metro and the bus didn't remark on what a lovely ring it was. When she got into work, as usual she was told by Sister Lilian to take her fish badge off.

She smiled, which made the Sister frown. "Ah but, Sister, I've got one other new bit of jewellery to wear today which you can't do anything about." And she held out her hand and showed her the ring.

Sister Lilian scowled. "You? Engaged? Don't make me laugh. What poor idiot has asked you to marry him? He must have been drunk."

"How dare you!" Louisa saw red. "How *dare* you! You have no idea what you're talking about, and you've got no idea what love and generosity are all about. I am so glad I'm not like you, you sour old woman!"

She stormed out of the Unit and went to find Gareth in the chapel, but he was on the wards somewhere so she had him paged from Reception. He appeared a few minutes later, to find Louisa crying her eyes out, black mascara marks down her cheeks, and shaking with fury. "I can't believe that horrible woman!" she shouted, and Gareth led her back down to the chapel and got her to tell him all about it. When she mentioned her engagement, Gareth's face lit up. "Oh, well done! Congratulations! That's wonderful!"

Louisa smiled. If only everyone could be so gracious. She found herself getting more and more indignant at the hold that Sister Lilian seemed to have over her. "Why can't I see her for what she is, and treat her with the contempt she deserves?"

"I wish we could always respond as we should," said Gareth. "But we can't. We're human, after all, and we're a mixed bag of emotions and feelings that don't always come out in a dignified, logical order. At the end of the day, though, we have to be real with others about what we're feeling, and maybe the time has come for you to deal with the truth. I can help set up a meeting with the Union, if you wish, or with the management directly, but it's up to you."

"I'll have a think about it," said Louisa, sniffing at the tissue she'd found in her uniform pocket. "Thanks for listening."

Things were definitely moving toward some sort of confrontation. But who would emerge as victor, or was that the wrong way of looking at it?

Chapter 40: Nations 85 - 93

Uganda and Sudan had recently declared a peace accord to boost cross-border trade. Diplomatic relations had been broken off in the mid-1990s, and agreements had been made and unmade periodically since then, but the latest accord had promised, amongst other things, the upgrading of the road from Gulu north to the border and beyond to Juba[64]. In July 2011, Southern Sudan had become independent – though Esther ruled that Brendan didn't have to visit the rest of Sudan too because it was all one country when he'd started on May 16th. He was one of the first to benefit from the upgrading of the road, as it had only been open for three weeks. The asphalt surface was wonderfully smooth, and his trip to the border took about an hour, rather than the three hours he'd been told to expect for the 120km journey. The old road had been susceptible to flood damage from the Albert branch of the Nile but the new road was constructed on pylons above the worst sections, and Brendan reached and passed the border without any difficulty. His Sudanese journey only extended 3km to the town of Nimule, where he found the small mud-brick Roman Catholic Church in a clearing in the tall grasses to the north of the town, and was welcomed in for a drink of tea. The church seats were white plastic garden chairs very similar to the ones in Brendan's garage back home in Cullercoats, ready for the heat-wave which never materialised. Brendan told the priest what the reason for his visit was.

"But we've been expecting you!" Brendan wasn't sure what he meant. It must have shown on his face, for the priest smiled. "We've been charting your progress because we're big fans of Esther Blanchett. Come, my boy will gather the people." He shouted the boy, and spoke quickly to him. He smiled and ran to spread the news.

So, half an hour later, Brendan was speaking in front of 50 or so Sudanese Christians who sang a song of welcome to him and then listened to a shortened version of his usual talk. The Sudanese GNT was given to the young boy who'd done the running around, whose grin was delightful. Just over an hour later, Brendan was back in Gulu having a drink with his family, and then he bade them farewell too, and set off eastwards to Kumi.

His route took him past several of the outlying IDP camps, now but a shadow of their former selves, but still swarming with people. Brendan couldn't imagine what they'd been like at the height of the crisis. He was soon out into the open land of Northern Uganda, crossing various channels of the huge lake system of Kwania/Kyoga. The new road brought him quickly to Soroti, marvelling at the impressive sugar-loaf mountain which towered over the town, and then on to Kumi

---

[64] At the time of writing, the road from Gulu to Nimule is still as poor as ever, but the new road from Nimule to Juba is under construction.

an hour later, where he'd arranged to stay with a Korean couple who started the African Leaders Training Institute there in the late 1990s. Brendan spoke at what was now the Kumi University Faculty of Divinity and Theology that evening. He had "cards" in various languages, and English ones for the rest. The students were all eager to learn about his views on Christian-Muslim mission, a change from his usual material, so he found the evening both stimulating and exhausting.

It only took him two hours to reach the Kenyan border at Malaba, a bustling and hectic place because the metre-gauge railway crossed there too, and only half an hour to pass successfully into his 86th nation. He reached Kisumu by lunch-time and sat down at Hippo Point for a bite to eat, overlooking the port with its green swathe of water-hyacinth blanketing the water from shore to shore. It spread prolifically every year across the large inlet from Lake Victoria, its long, spongy stalks sticking bulbously above the water before erupting into beautiful lavender/pink flowers, but it clogged up boat access and produced millions of mosquitoes. The hippos didn't seem to mind the deoxygenation of the water, and happily wallowed well away from Brendan, much to his relief.

Brendan drove down Nairobi Road to the small town of Kericho, where a big sign simply said "Maasai Mara" – even though the famous Reserve was 150km away. It was obviously the big tourist draw in the area, and it was where Brendan was heading too. He'd always wanted to visit, and this was his chance. He stopped about an hour short of the Maasai Mara, which meant that he'd a further evening of anticipation.Next morning he was up early, paid his $60, and drove into the Reserve with a whole day of game viewing ahead of him.

Brendan's visit coincided with the return journey of over 1,000,000 wildebeest, 200,000 zebras and 500,000 Thompson's gazelles back to the Serengeti after their migration north for better grazing. Having eaten their fill, they were now returning, huge herds at the Mara river-crossing (especially those killed by crocodiles or lions) providing joy to camera-toting tourists. The northern Reserve, still in Kenya, was now much emptier, with gentle winds rippling through the tall red oat grass, the only signs of life being elephants and giraffes moving slowly across the plain and a lone topi standing on an abandoned termite mound. As Brendan moved into Tanzania, beyond the safari lodge complex of Keekorok, he spotted a pride of lion underneath an acacia tree, and maybe a cheetah stalking a gazelle, but when he stopped and looked back, he could only see the gazelle grazing as if there was no threat whatsoever. The road, snaking round various viewing points, gave Brendan the chance to see wildlife in abundance across open woodland, low hills and bushy savannah. There were hundreds of elephants and giraffes, and an occasional lion lying in the shade of a tree, but most of his sightings were zebra, buffalo and omnipresent small antelopes. As the road swept to the south-east, Brendan overtook an ostrich jogging, head-still, parallel to the road. It must have been going at least 40kph, so either it was escaping from becoming dinner or just out for a jog.

When Brendan crossed the Oldupai Gorge, the site where the Leakeys in 1959 famously discovered "Zinj", the first tool-using humanoid, he knew that he was now approaching the holy of holies, the Ngorongoro – a large, unbroken, unflooded volcanic crater. It formed a natural enclosure for almost every species of animal found in East Africa, including the Big Five – though not, mysteriously, giraffes. He parked at one of the lodges on the rim of the crater, declined to have his photo taken with some Maasai warriors, but managed to get a seat on an afternoon game drive just leaving. The special high-seated jeep edged its way down the 2,000 feet into the bottom of the crater and then slowly worked its way round the popular tracks. It was awesome, but somehow despite seeing all of the Big Five within an hour and a half, it was not as exciting as his Loango experience. Perhaps it was the fact that here it was all set up for him. It wasn't a zoo or safari park where there were walls keeping the animals in, but it felt like that. A black rhino, rarest of beasts and utterly endangered, posed for the cameras as their jeep stopped just 30m away. A leopard draped its front leg sleepily over the branch of the tree it was in, oblivious or uncaring. It was marvellous to see them so close up, but Brendan wasn't as overwhelmed as the other tourists seemed to be, snapping, clicking and whirring as if the recorded mementoes were more important than the experiences themselves.

The jeep party arrived back up at the top at 5pm, dropping Brendan off in the car park. He drove eastwards away from the crater, and out of the Reserve, bunking down in a seedy hotel in Karatu 5km further. As he lay on his bed, reflecting on the day, his thoughts were mostly about freedom. The animals were free, and yet they were confined by human control and their habits and territorial instincts, caught in a raw cycle of random survival, mass migration, prey/predator food chains, drought and external threats from humans – everything well-marketed, predictable, recordable and replayable later by humans in order to impress the neighbours. Brendan wondered whether 21st century human life was any different.

Driving in the heat of the day round the base of Kilimanjaro, he marvelled at the snow on its upper slopes, before continuing eastwards towards the Indian Ocean at Mombasa. It was a long day, but the roads were good and he arrived by late afternoon at the Lotus Hotel, into which he'd been booked by Fahada, just across the road from the white walls and silver dome of Mombasa Memorial Cathedral. It looked like a mosque, as if it wanted to fit in. Inside, though, it had all the arches and paraphernalia of High Anglicanism. Most of the audience seemed to be ex-pats rather than Kenyan, but there were several Arab complexions to be seen too – not unexpectedly, given the history of the city. After his talk, Brendan wandered round the Old Town, a maze of narrow roads slicing between tall white buildings and stunning mosques. While checking out the Swahili architecture and the beautifully-dressed people, he stopped at various street-vendor stalls with their barbecue grills, buying what looked appealing without asking what meat it was.

The following morning, he checked in the Volvo at the Hertz office and got a taxi out to the recently-opened swanky marina at English Point, where he met up with the captain of the super-yacht which would be home for the next week. "The World Is Not Enough", flagship of a group of yachts named after Bond films, looked the sort of fantasy yacht the womanising playboy would relish. It was huge, 140-foot long, with a deep-V hull and sleek white lines. It was incredibly fast, with its bridge windshield so raked that the wipers were redundant at its cruise speed of 40 knots, or 75kph. Brendan was shown quickly round, his mouth gaping at the opulence and space-age design, much to the amusement of the Captain who never failed to smile at visitors' reactions. As they climbed up to the bridge, the engines fired, the mooring lines were thrown back, and the vessel purred out.

The first thing Brendan noticed was the lack of a steering-wheel. Instead, there was a helm out of science fiction: four screens melded into one curved frame; bewildering switches and instruments; three well-padded helm chairs; a joystick control suggesting video-game fantasy-land. Brendan sat in the leather couch extending across the back of the bridge area while the Captain manoeuvred out to sea, and then was given a proper guided tour. The main salon contained thick couches, chairs and ottomans arranged around a chunky cocktail table, but with one finger the Captain lifted the table, then one end of a couch. Everything was designed to look solid, but was actually hollow and weighed very little – which was the secret to the yacht's speed. Everything was lightweight and yet of superb design quality and durability. Multiple cabinets in high-gloss burled walnut were made with the same weight-saving know-how. The Erté marble statues flanking the entrance to the salon looked hernia-popping, but were actually feather-light. Everywhere there were mirrors, making the whole area seem huge. A formal dining room of similar luxury was next-door.

Above was the Skylounge, with its own gaming and cocktail tables and a real ivory bar. Down below, the master suite had its own separate sitting room and bedroom, a king-size island bed surrounded by walnut cabinets and wardrobes, its own refreshment bar, and a deeply-comfortable semi-circular couch facing a 42-inch plasma TV/DVD/CD/stereo. The "head" contained a full set of everything necessary, plus a bidet, a round Jacuzzi set into the wall, and a walk-in wet room with power shower. It was ridiculous. As land receded into the far distance, Brendan tried to get his head around it all – but failed. He decided to accept it and not let it bother him too much.

The speed was deceptive. It didn't look or feel that they were travelling quickly, until Brendan went onto the aft deck and saw the curtain of spray swirling up on either side – and this at only 60% of the maximum speed... The boat didn't bounce much, even though the sea was not smooth. He retreated below to his suite, and pottered about, playing some music, watching part of a DVD before getting bored with it. Halfway through the afternoon, he dozed off and was woken by a steward tugging gently on his arm, summoning him to get ready for dinner. Brendan felt a bit uncomfortable. "Excuse me, but do I need to sort of... dress up for dinner?"

The steward smiled. "No sir. You are the guest, so you set the rules. The captain always wears his dress uniform for dinner, and if you want to dress, you will find various sizes of tuxedo and trousers in one of the wardrobes. But it's up to you."

Brendan decided that he would check it out, and found a white tux and trousers and a dress shirt and bowtie which he thought looked a bit posh for him, but decided to try on anyway. As he finished dressing and was preening himself in the mirror, the steward knocked on the door. "Dinner is served, sir – and, if I may so, you look very elegant."

"Thank you," said Brendan, feeling a bit like James Bond – stirred but not shaken.

***

The yacht eased to a stop as dinner was served. Brendan remarked on it to the Captain. "We've made good progress, and we don't have to rush, so we've dropped our sea-anchor and will only start engines again after breakfast tomorrow. We try to make life on "The World Is Not Enough" relaxed and peaceful, so at night we put the navigational lights on, set proximity alarms through the radar system to alert the night officer on the bridge if any vessel comes too close. The rest of us, hopefully, can have an uninterrupted night's sleep."

***

The bed was a remarkable piece of machinery. A button on the side lowered the mattress onto a water-bed, if the sleeper felt that sleep would be more comfortable not going from side to side with the movement of the boat. Brendan experimented first with his eyes open then with his eyes shut, and decided that both times he felt a bit queasy with the water-bed. Luxury was wasted on him – but he slept like a log.

***

After a leisurely breakfast of fruit juice, kippers, toast and freshly-brewed coffee, the engines fired up and the yacht dipped its bow like a bull preparing to charge, and quickly threw up a curtain of spray. The ocean was deep blue, reflecting the cloudless sky above. Paradise... The Captain took the speed up to 65 knots for a quick burst, and Brendan wondered why it wasn't taking off. It was like being on a huge, luxurious torpedo.

Soon after lunch, land could be seen ahead, and they eased off the speed as they came close, gliding sedately down the western coast of Grande Comore before entering Harbour Bay at Moroni. It looked like a romanticised time-warp of old Arabia, with the bright white colonnades of the "Old Friday" Mosque and narrow streets leading into shadowy passageways round the souk. Brendan stepped ashore from the small landing craft, got waved through the customs post, such as it was – a man sitting in a chair underneath a palm tree – and made for the souk. It ponged a bit, as they didn't seem to believe in either sewers or wheelie bins, but it didn't seem to bother women in colourful wraps chatting on crumbling stone doorsteps, or solemn groups of white-robed men whiling away the hours between prayers playing dominoes on smooth stone benches.

Brendan found the Roman Catholic church wedged between two mosques, as if it was being slowly smothered. Comoros was number 21 on the Open Doors World Watch List of countries where faith costs the most. The priest told Brendan that evangelism was against the law, that Christian converts from Islam were often jailed after being informed against by their relatives, and that most of the 400 known Christians met in homes like the underground church in New Testament times. "Yet we are growing," said the priest proudly. "The church of Jesus always grows the most when it is persecuted." Brendan had heard this many times in different places, but here in Moroni it struck him as a most uplifting and important truth which all Christians should be told over and over again. He remembered his Dad's favourite Bible verse: "Nothing can separate us from the love of God in Christ Jesus" – which Paul wrote to the Christians in Rome suffering persecution. How true – and how *wonderful*.

The priest invited Brendan to a housegroup that evening – the authorities had forbidden the church to open for an extra meeting on top of the permitted daily Mass. As they walked there, Brendan heard more about the Christians' struggles. Muslim extremists were on the increase, goading the easier-going Comoran Sunnis into informing on their neighbours if they showed the slightest interest in Christianity. The house was lit up with fairy lights, in keeping with the report they'd given to the authorities about a welcome party for a British visitor. The whole evening was like Christianity in Nero's Rome: whispering whenever a noise was heard outside, secret-code knocking on the door, drawing the curtains and playing music to obstruct spies. Brendan found it bizarre but utterly humbling. His faith had never really required any great sacrifice or risk, but here Christians were being ostracised, imprisoned and discriminated against quite openly. The house-owner had been "invited" to sell his house to a local Muslim, and was being pressured into moving off the island. Brendan gave the hostess the Comorian GNT, and encouraged the group to read from it each week, remembering him and what he was trying to do to make their plight known, so that they wouldn't feel unsupported or isolated.

As he walked back to the yacht, which sat resplendent and aloof at anchor in the harbour like a spaceship amongst the drab wooden boats, Brendan admired the beauty around him: the orange sunset colours reflected in the coral walls of the mosque; the excited cries of boys jumping off the harbour edge into the water just like they did in Cullercoats; the giant silhouettes of fruit bats fluttering overhead. But he wondered whether tourists caught the oppression and the hatred which hid behind the scenes of what appeared an island paradise.

He dined on board in the sumptuous dining room with the Captain and officers as before. They'd waited for him, and were keen to listen to his reflections. They, of course, didn't have any particular interest in religious persecution, but they listened carefully and told similar stories of their experiences further north – Yemen, Somalia, Eritrea, Oman, the Maldives...

***

It was late afternoon before they docked at Antisiranana Bay on the northern tip of Madagascar, considered one of the finest natural harbours in the world. The city was on the headland, but had very little to offer except for the port. The roads in this part of the island were very bad, so the city lived off the sea and the trade it brought.

Madagascar was not as paranoid against Christianity as the Comoros, but there was considerable opposition nonetheless. Yet the Cathedral and its Immanuel Hall were used extensively and Brendan was introduced to the leader of the Ruth Project, which sought to empower local women – no wonder the local Muslims weren't too keen. At the evening meeting in the new Anglican Cathedral of Saint Matthew, Brendan listened to the testimony of Rasoamanana Tongatsara, a local electrician who'd supervised the electrical installation into the Cathedral and became a Christian at the inauguration service. Now he was training as an evangelist, and Brendan gave him the Malagasy GNT as a reminder of his visit.

***

Another day, another vast distance across a placid ocean, and another island paradise. There wasn't much to the Agalega archipelago, and they didn't get too many casual visitors tying up at St James Anchorage on the island's northern tip. The shallow draft of the yacht meant that it could moor at the pier. There was an airstrip, a police station (not that there was any crime), a doctor's clinic, a Catholic church, a small school and a weather station. About 200 people lived on the island, and it reminded Brendan of Fair Isle in Shetland, but warmer. The village was Vingt-Cinq –

named after the 25 lashes given to runaway slaves. Another question, maybe, for Brendan's impossible pub quiz —was there any other town named after a number? Westbury-on-Severn didn't count, nor Twente in the Netherlands because it was a region. He had a nagging feeling that there might be one in Australia named after the date Captain Cook landed, but wasn't sure[65].

Over 100 people crammed into the little church, not just because there was nothing else to do but because they seemed to have a genuine curiosity about Brendan's global odyssey. The fact that he'd chosen to visit *them* amazed them, and the connection with the outside world was infrequent for most, unwelcome to some, and confusing for Brendan. It was hard to explain the idea of religious persecution, world inequality or other faiths to people so isolated. Yet they warmed to his stories and applauded at the end. Brendan gave the GNT, translated into Creole to the youngest member of the audience, a young girl who hid away under her mother's skirts when Brendan approached her.

***

The finding of Agalega on the map saved Brendan over 1,000km to the main Mauritius islands, but the next voyage was still long – over to Aldabra, by far the westernmost of the Seychelles, yet still over 1,000km away. The Captain warned Brendan that he might be woken by the engines, for they would have to set off around 5am in order to arrive in time at their usual cruising speed.

Aldabra was a group of coral islands around a lagoon, surrounded by a coral reef, described as "one of the wonders of the world" by Sir David Attenborough, as its isolation in this remote area of the Indian Ocean had helped preserve it in a relatively natural state. Landings were restricted to marine biologists, eliminating what UNESCO called "anthropogenic stress" – but fortunately Esther "knew somebody" at UNESCO and managed to secure permission for two hours ashore.

When they arrived within 10km of the atoll in the late afternoon, they had to approach the island at a speed of less than four knots, which meant an extra hour and a half before they were able to drop anchor in the central lagoon and row ashore to the largest of the four islands, Grande Terre. They were met by the lead scientist, who gave them a sheaf of documents explaining the rules, which they were all required to sign. Then he warmed up, introducing himself as Dan, apologising for the bureaucracy but explaining that the Seychelles Government were pretty hot on preserving their natural treasures, and any breach of protocol could jeopardise the whole scientific programme. He showed them round the research station, and pointed out the colonies of giant tortoises in a nearby inlet.

---

[65] Seventeen-seventy, Queensland.

"Aldabra has the largest population in the world of these amazing creatures," he boasted. "Over 150,000, we reckon." Brendan could see nearly 100 black lumps on the rocks opposite, but he wondered how the scientists knew which ones they'd already counted. Brendan was shown some boobies and frigate birds, and another small sharp-beaked bird which Dan said was a white-throated rail, the last of the flightless birds of the Indian Ocean. Brendan looked suitably impressed, but was more amazed at the size of the tortoises.

Dan then asked what Brendan's trip was all about, and got a quick potted version of the usual talk. To Brendan's surprise, Dan listened carefully, then said that he'd been brought up in California in a Christian home. "I'm not really into church and all that," he said. "But I do what I do in order to preserve God's creation." Brendan gave him the Seychelles (English language) GNT, and asked him to keep it on the island. Dan said that there was no problem about them staying in the lagoon overnight, as long as they made sure that there was no pollution from the vessel, and he added, with a smile, "Though I guess a yacht like that would have all those things sorted."

***

They edged out of the lagoon early for their painfully slow exit from the atoll, but it meant that breakfast was quiet and leisurely in the gentle rise and fall of the ocean. Brendan caught up on some emails – and was delighted to read Louisa's news about her engagement. He was selfishly relieved to read later in the email that they were definitely not getting married till he got back – he didn't want to miss it.

Brendan was thrilled to bits with Louisa's news, and decided to celebrate by asking if he could have a go at the yacht's controls. "I can do better than that," said the Captain, with a laugh, and led Brendan out of the bridge to an outdoor helm called the flybridge, positioned directly in front of the windscreen. The wind buffeted what little hair Brendan had as they cruised along at 40 knots, and he asked what it was like travelling even quicker.

"Sit down in Kirk's chair, as we call it. Everything's within reach, just like on the Enterprise. I'll stand behind you and show you what to do." Brendan could just see out over the top of the monitors in front of him, but when he ducked down it was surprisingly calm and unbuffeted. "Clever design, isn't it?" The Captain pointed to the joystick built into the armrest. "That's all you need." He flicked a few switches. "All yours now."

Brendan felt the throb of the engines instantly through the joystick, which jerked in the pull of the cross-waves. It took him some effort to keep everything pointing forwards. But it was amazing to be in charge – sort of.

"Well, you seem to have got the hang of it," said the Captain. "Fancy going a bit quicker?" Brendan nodded with a terrified smile. "Don't worry. It's only like driving a convertible along a bumpy motorway. Here's your speed." He pointed to a dial which was constant at 40. Brendan noted with a frisson of fear that 40 was only halfway round the gauge. "And the button on the top of the joystick increases or decreases your speed by pressing forwards or backwards. Have a go." And he did, nervously. Amazingly the whole yacht slowed or accelerated at his push of a little button. "Beam us up then, Scotty!" yelled the Captain in his ear, so Brendan increased the tempo up to 50, and then 60. It was like sticking your head out of the car window on a motorway, with the wind dragging your cheeks back into a rictus of fear or pleasure.

"Wow, 60mph," said Brendan. "That's fast enough."

"No, 60 knots, which is about 69mph, or 111kph. It is fast, but we can go quicker if you want. The fastest we've ever done is 66 knots, which is still only about 90% of what it's supposed to be capable of."

Brendan cranked it up a bit more, but bottled out at about 65. That was definitely fast enough. His arm was starting to hurt from the grip he had on the joystick, and he was glad when the Captain suggested he eased back down to their cruising speed. He had a flashback to the grainy footage of Donald Campbell's boat doing a somersault, and was glad to hand over to the Captain, who flicked a few switches and sat back. "We're on autopilot again now, so you can relax and take your hand away." Brendan looked down and saw his white knuckles gripping the joystick as if his life depended on it. He relaxed and his whole body sagged, much to the Captain's amusement. "Yes," he said, "It gets everybody like that the first time."

It was mid-evening by the time they got back to Mombasa, but the Captain was happy for Brendan to stay on board till the morning, because their next client wasn't flying in until the afternoon.

"Anybody famous?" asked Brendan.

"I'm not allowed to tell you," said the Captain. But he mouthed "Madonna" and winked.

***

Brendan's flight to Djibouti via Nairobi wasn't due out of Mombasa until early afternoon. He was flying both to avoid Somali pirates who'd been causing havoc in the waters around the horn of Africa, and to cut down on the distances involved. Despite this, the most dangerous section of the whole trip lay in front of him.

***

He collected a 4x4 from the Hertz office at Djibouti Airport, and headed south towards the Ethiopian border. Djibouti seemed to be the usual mixture of rich and poor, with a few entrepreneurs making a killing and most of the people living on very little. The semi-desert landscape meant that most people except nomadic herdsmen and their families gravitated towards the capital city, where unemployment rates were nearly 50%.

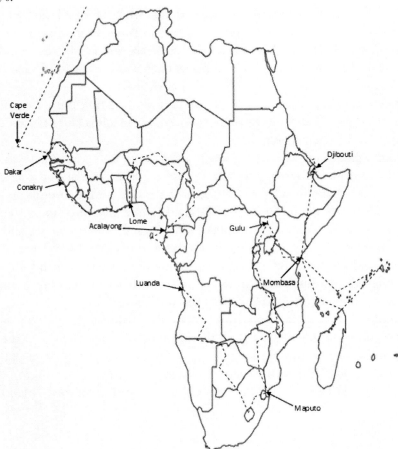

Nations 48 to 91

Once out of the city, the roads emptied, and Brendan's progress was swift and straight, following the railway line at first, then cutting off east for the village of Lasdeit, just over the undefined border in Ethiopia. Brendan got out and tried to converse with the owner of the village shop, but communication was very difficult. Brendan showed him the Ethiopian GNT, and his eyes widened as he read the Amharic inscription in the front. Brendan gave it to him and when the man tried to give it back he gestured that it was a gift. The man bowed, smiled and shook Brendan's hands in his own.

Brendan drove further along the road, which looped northwards. According to his GPS, the road marked the border with Somalia, so anything east of the road should be Somalian territory. The trouble was that the GPS showed no villages whatsoever until the coast, which was bound to be heavily militarised. The road snaked inexplicably round bends even though there was no obstacle in the way, but he saw no-one until finally, about 10km from the sea, over to his right appeared a train of camels making their way slowly north. So he turned sharp right, off the track, bouncing across the hard rock and gravel for about 2km till he got near them. He drove slightly away to the north so that their route would cross his own. He stopped and got out, with the Somali GNT in his hand. Heart in mouth, knowing he was there illegally, he hailed the lead camel-driver, who stopped and waited for Brendan to approach. The GNT was translated into Arabic, so Brendan tried the same greeting which had worked well with the fisherman in Syria. "As-salamu alaykum."

The bespectacled camel-driver bowed his head in greeting, and then said, "English?"

Brendan heaved a sigh of relief. "Yes, English."

"I went to Oxford," the camel-driver said. "Jolly pleased to meet you."

Brendan explained his mission, and his dilemma about the GNT, and the man chuckled. "It does get a bit difficult around here. But you are definitely in Somalia." He pulled a GPS unit out of his pocket to check. "According to this, you are 1.7km into my country. I am an Isaaq, one of the oldest Somali clans, and would be happy to receive your gift for my eldest son who is on the camel behind me. He is only 14, but I am trying to encourage him to think more broadly than some of his school friends."

Brendan handed over the book, and the camel-driver in turn gave Brendan his business card. "Call me if you get stuck. I do have some influence." Brendan looked at the card. The name meant nothing to him: Abdirashid Omaar[66], but underneath it said "politician and tradesman". "You may have seen my little brother Rageh. He works for the BBC." And with that he was gone. It couldn't have gone better.

---

[66] Rageh Omaar, currently an Al Jazeera presenter and previously the BBC world affairs correspondent made famous by his war reports from Iraq, has a brother called Mohamed Abdullahi Omaar, who is a Foreign Minister in the Somali Government. Mohamed wears spectacles and studied at Oxford, but the rest of the story here is pure fiction.

Day: Date	Itinerary (* indicates TV interview) ([18] indicates new nation)	Bike (km)	Car/ Bus (km)	Train (km)	Kayak/ Sail (km)	Boat (km)	Air (km)
Totals brought forward		8713	10340	0	2754	5387	7383
144: 6/10/11	Nimule, Sudan[85]; via Gulu to Kumi (Uganda)		462				
145: 7/10/11	Kaboson, Kenya[86]		389				
146: 8/10/11	Karatu (Tanzania)		331				
147: 9/10/11	Mombasa (Kenya)		490				
148: 10/10/11	at sea						
149: 11/10/11	Comoros[87]					935	
150: 12/10/11	Antisiranana, Madagascar[88]					734	
151: 13/10/11	Agalega, Mauritius[89]					815	
152: 14/10/11	at sea						
153: 15/10/11	Aldabra, Seychelles[90]					1116	
154: 16/10/11	Mombasa (Kenya)					954	
155: 17/10/11	Djibouti[91]						2032
156: 18/10/11	Ladeit, Ethiopia[92]; Somalia[93]; Djibouti		181				
Totals carried forward		8713	12193	0	2754	9941	9415

Chapter 41: Machinations / Nations 94 - 103

Fahada was in turmoil. Her controller, Saeed, returned the evening after the striptease incident and told her what her "mission" was. She was "chosen" to strike a blow at the heart of the Great Satan, America, by helping to assassinate Esther Blanchett. And she was to prepare for it by helping to get rid of Brendan Priest. The trouble was that she didn't really want to do either, and especially not helping to kill Esther. Why kill the goose that kept laying golden eggs? How would that make the world a better place or Islam a better religion? And how was Islam glorified by bumping off Brendan? Even though he was promoting Christianity he wasn't attacking Islam.

Saeed, as imperceptive as ever, assumed that she was back on track as a Holy War warrior. Fahada only had to give him regular updates on Brendan's schedule and itinerary. He hinted that the easiest place to "do the deed" would be in South East Asia – Indonesia, Cambodia maybe. He would let Fahada know in advance so that she could give him precise timings and locations.

She felt awful. She'd initially been jealous of the attention which Brendan was getting from Esther, but that had worn off, only for her brother's killing to re-ignite her desire to lash out. But would Brendan's death bring comfort or satisfaction? And, of course, if it were to emerge that she had a hand in it, she'd lose everything – because if she wasn't in prison she'd certainly be kicked out by Esther.

***

Over the next few weeks, Fahada kept hoping that somehow Brendan would trip up. He survived the rampant hippo and the potential border difficulties and had no problems on the long cycle ride across Southern Africa. She'd been unable to do anything about his steady progress up through Eastern Africa and had to smile at him in Gulu. He'd kept on schedule throughout, and made the start-time for the fancy yacht spot-on. A delay there would have been wonderful. Surely the most fervent Islamic territory on the planet would stop him – maybe? If Brendan were sailing, there'd be a wonderful opportunity to alert some of the piracy gangs terrorising the waters around the Horn – but he wasn't. Maybe she could still arrange something for his voyage up the Yemeni coast...

There was still some uncertainty about how Brendan would "witness" in Somalia and Saudi Arabia. The plan was for him to nip across the border, evading the authorities, and find some stray herdsman. With a bit of luck he might run into a patrol or misjudge where the border was and get himself arrested. Iran too was always a good bet for a bit of anti-western co-operation, so she'd see about disrupting his brief visit there as well, if nothing happened beforehand. And then, of course, there were Afghanistan and Pakistan. Surely *somewhere* she could force Brendan to abandon his journey – and it was all for his own good, because otherwise he'd probably end up dead. And maybe if she *did* manage to mess up Brendan's plans, the Holy War assassins would lose interest in Esther too, or be ordered to stand down because they'd failed with Brendan...

It was rather annoying, therefore, when Fahada received the report of Brendan's successful "witness" in Somalia. She'd have to be more proactive, and not assume that Brendan would trip himself up.

***

Fahada reckoned that her best chance for sabotaging Brendan might well be during his boat journey across the Bab-el-Mandab, the narrowest part of the Gulf of Aden between Djibouti and Yemen. It was only 30km across, but with a steady flow of super-tankers backwards and forwards. The chances of Brendan's little boat getting across safely were decent, but not certain – and he might get attacked, as this was "Pirate Alley". Fahada sent a press release out to Al Jazeera, announcing that Brendan had reached Djibouti and would be setting off across Bab-el-Mandab and up the Yemeni coast during the next week. That should do the trick, she thought.

Oblivious to this, Brendan collected the speedboat arranged for him in Djibouti, and sailed up the coast to a small town just across the Eritrean border called Rahaita, with just one small public building, an Ethiopian Orthodox Tewahdo Church. Brendan wondered if they did martial arts, but the priest told him that "tewahdo" meant "unity". Brendan confessed that he'd assumed that everyone would be Muslim, but the priest was happy to correct him. "Over half Eritrea Christian," he said, beating his chest proudly. "But the rest hate it. They hit us. They lock us up. They force us to be soldiers." Brendan already knew from Open Doors that over 2,000 Christians were thought to be currently in detention – many of them in military camps – across Eritrea, which was number 12 on the Watch List. At least one Christian, Efrem Habtemichel Hagos[67], had been martyred in 2010, dying of malaria and pneumonia because he was refused medical treatment until he renounced his faith. Brendan told the priest that many Christians across the world were praying for his country constantly. He handed over the GNT, translated into Afar, as a sign of their oneness (tewahdo) in Christ.

Next day, Brendan had to cross the Bab, wary of pirates but also of playing chicken with the super-tankers which wouldn't even see him let alone be able to avoid him if he got in their way. He decided to drift gradually into the centre of the

---

[67] Open Doors' records show that Eritrean Christian Efrem Habtemichel Hagos (37) died on March 2nd 2010 while in solitary confinement in Adi-Nefase military camp in Assab.

straits rather than take a perpendicular crossing-route, keeping an eye on the tankers and waiting his chance – then just going for it. With a top speed of 40 knots, he should be able to out-run the big boys, who had to go at a more sedate pace because of the relatively crowded shipping lanes. He aimed for the promontory of Ras Menheli on the Yemeni side. He found himself quickly in the middle of the shipping lanes, with one super-tanker charging up the strait behind him and another crossing in front. More worryingly still, he spotted a medium-size boat heading straight for him right down the middle of the channel. He prepared the flare in case they were pirates, but he was hailed from a distance by a loudspeaker. "Stop your boat immediately!" The order came in a Southern US accent. When he slowed to a halt, as instructed, the voice continued. "Y'all are in the Maritime Security Patrol Area and Ah am required by international law to check your documentation. Ah am coming aboard!"

Brendan cut the engine completely and his speedboat drifted to the side of the patrol boat, and an officer in a crisply-starched naval uniform jumped down onto Brendan's boat and demanded his papers. "What y'all doing?" said the officer, once he'd established that Brendan was British and wasn't a pirate. So Brendan told him, and the officer asked if he was the man who'd been on "See Esther". Brendan nodded. "Well, next time ya see the gal, give her a kiss from me, will ya, bud?" And the officer punched him playfully on the shoulder and said, "Only foolin'. Ah reck'n y'all are doing a good job. Stick close by us, we'll see y'all across."

***

Fahada got a jubilant report that night from Brendan, who'd reached Aden. He was speaking at the historic Christ Church, previously requisitioned by the Communist Government after British withdrawal in 1970, and then re-dedicated as a church in 1997 when the Grand Mufti ordered that freedom of worship should be given to Christians "in the same way as Muslims can worship freely in Britain."

"If only such enlightened views were more prevalent," Brendan mused to Fahada. "I was very impressed by Christ Church. It's a lively multinational congregation of ex-pats, holding numerous health clinics as well as hosting self-help groups for all kinds of people. There was a good crowd there too! I gave away over 200 of my "business cards" and an offering raised over $1,000, for which the chaplain wrote a cheque and gave it to me – he said that carrying lots of American currency wouldn't be a wise move. That's great, isn't it?"

"Yes. Great," said Fahada. Where were the pirates when she needed them?

***

Brendan's boat was a 2004 Regal 2250 powered by a single Volvo 5.0L 270hp petrol engine. It wasn't a smart boat, and had seen better days. Its cockpit had scuffed grey leather seats. The cabin was big enough for a fold-down double bed and two seats at other times, and up top there was a walk-through transom with shower, compass, cockpit sink, CD player, chemical loo, and removable carpets. It handled really well, giving a smooth and soft ride with decent fuel economy. It would, he hoped, do the business. It just looked a bit drab. Brendan's major logistical problem was fuel. The boat drank about 50 litres of petrol for every 100km, so he'd purchased and strapped on two spare tanks – all in addition to the 204 litres in the main tank. He should be able now to go 800km before he needed to refuel, which could be invaluable given the inhospitable coastline ahead. The extra tanks made the boat look less stream-lined, but appearance wasn't really the top priority. His most economical speed, according to the manual, was 27 knots, or about 50kph. He'd probably be bouncing up and down a bit at that speed on the open sea, but he didn't have much choice. It was a heavily-laden speedboat, therefore, that left Aden, and ploughed its way up the Yemeni coast, making the planned overnight stop in Jilah, where Brendan managed to replenish the fuel tank from a petrol pump in the harbour.

Midway through the next morning, he was alarmed to see two speedboats hurtling out from a deserted coastline to intercept him, each carrying three men. As they got closer he saw that they held guns and then heard a shot, so he stopped the boat and waited for them to come alongside. It was his worst nightmare: pirates. They all had scarves across their face, and Brendan was terrified. He'd heard of various kidnappings and murders by pirates, and feared the worst. A British couple had been kidnapped and held hostage for a year recently[68], and the story about their treatment was pretty grim reading. The leader jumped into Brendan's boat and pushed him into the helmsman's chair, shouting words at him which Brendan couldn't understand. Then, "Who... are... you?"

Brendan said his name and added, "British." The pirate nodded.

"Boat old," he said, looking around with the sort of look that Brendan had seen before on a car-salesman. Brendan shrugged. "Money?" said the pirate. Brendan shrugged again, and pointed into the cabin. The pirate's answer was to signal one of the gunmen to jump into the transom and look around. It didn't take long. He emerged holding Brendan's wallet and the Yemeni GNT, which Brendan had got out the night before and hadn't packed away again.

The pirate leader looked through the wallet, took out a wad of American dollars then threw the wallet back into the cabin. He riffled through the notes, turning up his nose at how little there was. Then he shrugged, tucked the money into his pocket,

---

[68] Paul and Rachel Chandler were released on November 14th 2010 after 388 days in captivity.

then grabbed the New Testament and opened it, his eyes widening when he read the inscription. "You, priest?"

Brendan wasn't sure whether it was his surname or his job that was being asked for, so he nodded. The pirate laughed. "Not rich?" he asked.

Brendan shrugged and smiled. "Not rich – especially now that you have my dollars."

The pirate laughed again and said something to his men. They laughed too. Things seemed to be lightening up. "Bad men," he explained pointing to his crew. "Need many prayers." Then he laughed again, jumped back into his own boat, and signalled his men to move away. "Pray for us!" he yelled as they left, and laughed. He really was a very happy pirate. Now he had a New Testament to read as well, because he took that as well as Brendan's money.

Brendan sat back in amazement that he'd survived and got off relatively lightly. At least he was still alive, and was so grateful that as a result of the collection in Aden he had a cheque tucked away in his luggage rather than wads of cash, which might have signalled that he was worth kidnapping. As it was, they'd taken about $300 and even left him his credit card. No worries about giving away the Yemeni GNT either, he thought, with a smile. He suddenly went all shaky and went inside to make a cup of tea. As he waited for the kettle to boil, he sat and prayed for the pirates, and their victims past and future. He drank his tea, which helped calm him down a bit, and said another prayer of thanks. He hadn't had the time or inclination to pray as the pirates attacked, but he was very grateful that God hadn't held that against him.

He set off again, amazed that he could. He was still dazed when he dropped anchor off the town of Sayhut, and phoned up Fahada on the satellite phone to share the news. She sounded very concerned, but relieved that he'd survived the experience. He asked her to try to keep the news quiet because he wanted to tell the girls himself rather than have them worrying about him.

***

Fahada couldn't believe it. The very outcome that she'd been working towards – and then they'd let let him off! She'd never heard of pirates being merciful before, and couldn't work out what had gone wrong. Brendan was definitely leading a charmed life. The only hope now on this "leg" was if he ran out of fuel or the boat had engine trouble, but there was no way that she could influence either of those possibilities. She'd deliberately bought a dilapidated boat hoping that it might not be up to the voyage, but so far it was proving annoyingly reliable. She still had a week to conjure something up for Brendan's short stop in Iran, if he didn't get arrested first trying to land in Saudi Arabia without a visa. All was not lost...

Brendan's journey up the Yemeni and Omani coasts went very smoothly. He was sure that some of his fillings were being shaken loose by the constant bouncing, but otherwise he was bearing up well. His back and arms stiffened from being in the same position for hour after hour, but a bit of stretching and rubbing usually eased the discomfort, and undisturbed nights meant that he was always fresh for the next day. He found places to refuel when he needed to, and the days passed. It was all progress, however slow. Eventually he rounded the peninsula into the Straits of Hormuz, waved at a few more super-tankers, and passed down the southern coastline of the Persian Gulf, marvelling at the decadence and opulence of the emirates' sea-front architecture. Two days later he reached Doha in Qatar for the final refuelling before Iraq.

The GNTs had been given away to random individuals who happened to be on hand at the points where Brendan wanted to offload them. In Salalah it was the harbour petrol-pump attendant; in Fujairah it was the harbour-master; in Doha it was a shopkeeper. At the next evening destination of Galali in Bahrain, it was the harbour-master again. The Saudi Arabian GNT was going to be the difficult one. There were over 300km of Saudi Arabian coastline between Bahrain and the Kuwaiti border – surely there would be someone wandering along who would receive Brendan's gift? He had to be careful, though, because he'd no right even to be in Saudi waters and a patrol boat would be bad news. He decided to sail through the night, at low speed to minimise engine noise and without lights to avoid coastal patrols.

He was soon lost in the darkness once he'd left the neon of the Bahrain waterfront. He extinguished all lights and chugged along at 15 knots to create minimal wash. There was sufficient moonlight to show any islands or other obstructions but Brendan kept his eyes skinned. By 3am he'd reached Al Jubayl Industrial City, which was lit up brighter than Blackpool. Petrochemical plants, gas complexes, refineries, and factories galore flared, shone or flashed, creating light pollution on an unprecedented scale – the largest industrial complex in the world and looking like 40 Middlesbroughs in a row. Brendan gave it a wide berth, because it was also home to a naval base.

By sunrise, he'd increased speed and was only about 80km from the Kuwaiti border. He came into shore at a village called As Saffaniyah, and was relieved to see an old man on an antique bicycle wobbling his way along the coastal road. Brendan chugged past him and waved, and the man waved back. Brendan continued for 200m before letting the boat glide into the stony beach, jumping out as it gently grounded, and splashing his way to land, GNT in hand. He emerged onto the road 30m in front of the wobbly cyclist, who stopped, bewildered by this strange man in western clothes waving a book at him. Brendan approached cautiously, seeing the fear in the man's eyes, holding the book out in front of him, like a store Santa with a nervous child. He hoped that the old man could read and that the Arabic squiggles on the page were the right dialect of squiggle. The man looked at the book without taking it, drew an old pair of spectacles from the top pocket of his thawb, and put them on. They had round frames and springy sides which needed wrapping round his ears, like Mahatma Gandhi's. The old man read the inscription and smiled, took the GNT from Brendan and placed it carefully into another pocket of his long shirt, put his hands together and salaamed to Brendan, before cycling on along the road. Brendan smiled. He hadn't said a word, but a good act of witness had taken place.

The next GNT was given to the senior Catholic priest in Kuwait City, who said that he'd give it to the next person who asked him what Christianity was all about. Brendan had arrived at the Kuwait Yacht Club marina just before midday, absolutely exhausted as he hadn't slept for over 24 hours. He hailed a taxi from the Yacht Club, having paid an extortionate mooring fee, and arrived at the Bishop's Villa in the Cathedral grounds in time to be taken upstairs, shown a room, and encouraged to rest. He was then woken up by a housekeeper telling him that dinner was ready in the dining-room. It was 6.30pm and he'd been sound asleep for over six hours. It was strange to have slept in a normal bed again, but wonderful. The evening went well and he had a good chat with the Bishop and other clergy based at the Cathedral. He asked them what life was like in Kuwait, and listened sympathetically as they explained how hard it was to engage evangelistically with the local people, even though he knew that there was far more freedom in Kuwait than most countries in the Persian Gulf.

***

Fahada had prepared well for Iran. She hadn't held out much hope of sabotage through the emirates, and was frustrated to hear how easily the Saudi Arabia "witness" had happened. Iran, however, was another matter. Brendan was due to cross Kuwait Bay and sail into the Shatt al-Arab waterway – the scene of intense territorial disputes, one of the main reasons for the 1980s war, and where an uneasy "peace" held, based on the thalweg principle of the deepest channel being the border[69]. But there were frequent arrests, raids and seizures too, and Fahada was planning a kidnap attempt to stop Brendan making the Basra interview the next day. Esther would be furious because it'd be too late to make alternative arrangements.

---

[69] The precise drawing of river boundaries has been important throughout history, including the Danube dispute in Central Europe, where the thalweg principle was established: "thal" means "valley", and "weg" means "way".

The easier places for an attack would be away from the larger towns and industrial complexes of Abadan and Korramshahr, and probably at the northern end because the waterway narrowed from 800m at its mouth to 200m at Basra. Fahada had spoken to Saeed about the possibility of arranging a snatch squad in the Shatt al-Arab, and Saeed promised that he would see what he could do. "My worry though, Fahada, is that the Iranians will get the credit for the abduction. How will this help Holy War?"

"I know," Fahada agreed. "But the result will be a significant delay in Brendan's plans. It'll be several days at least before the British can secure his release, and he'll be well behind schedule. So he'll push himself harder, become more tired and less security-conscious, so it should be much easier for Holy War to "do the deed" in South East Asia, as you are planning."

Saeed seemed satisfied with the logic of Fahada's strategy, and went away to make the arrangements. But the day before the proposed abduction, Fahada still hadn't heard back from Saeed, and concluded that he'd boasted more than he could deliver, as always. So she posted another press release on Al Jazeera and hoped that the possibility of him slipping through unnoticed would diminish markedly.

***

When Brendan entered the Shatt al-Arab he was very conscious of his vulnerability. There were numerous boats on the waterway, mostly large freighters bringing goods to or from Basra, but also small boats belonging to the marsh Arabs who lived on both banks. He got frequent stares from their passengers or crew, but kept carefully to the Iraqi side, to avoid any incident. All went well for a couple of hours, and he was planning where to cross for giving away the GNT, when he noticed a small speedboat keeping pace with him on the Iranian side of the waterway. He slowed; it slowed. He increased the speed; so did the other boat. It didn't look good. He didn't fancy his chances of outrunning them, nor of taking them on because the other boat had at least three people onboard. He didn't know what to do.

This went on for some time, and then, as he was drawing level with Abadan, the waterway bent round to the west and a small island came into view in the middle of the water, restricting the waters to a narrow defile, so the Iranian boats were bunching to get round the bend. Up ahead, there were further bends, and a plan formed in Brendan's mind. He waited until a large freighter in Iranian waters blocked off the view of the other speedboat, then roared forwards and round the bend, before breaking quickly across the waterway into a small inlet he'd seen on the Iranian bank. The inlet quickly turned a corner, and Brendan pulled in quickly round the bend and waited to see if he'd been spotted by the other boat, relieved when nothing followed him in. After a minute or two he was convinced that, having fallen for his trick, they must have roared ahead to catch him up.

He was in a steeply-banked tributary snaking through a valley. He pressed on a little further, hoping to find someone, anyone. Coming round the next bend he found himself in a sandy cove with a small tented settlement on its bank. Children were playing in the shallow water, but squealed and ran up the slope when Brendan's boat rushed in and stopped where they'd been playing. They watched warily from the top of the rise, as Brendan got out of the boat with the GNT and placed it open on the sand. He went back into the boat, smiled and beckoned the children to see what he'd given them. The bravest of them edged down, grabbed the book and scuttled back up the slope, where the others huddled round and pointed at the inscription at the open page. Then they looked up, waved and smiled. Brendan waved back as he turned the boat round.

He edged back down towards the main waterway, worried about the other speedboat but also about avoiding ships as he crossed back to Iraq. He decided just to go for it – much to the surprise of a local fisherman puttering past in his small boat. Brendan headed straight across and had timed it just right, because two big freighters heading north were taking up the whole waterway, obscuring the view. One was trying to overtake the other but painfully slowly, like lorries on a motorway. Once across, Brendan slowed to the pace of the leading freighter, keeping parallel with it for the rest of his voyage, making sure that he would be protected from sight and attack. He even waved at the crew as they approached Basra and got some camaraderie going with them in case the Iranians tried one last time.

The British had formally withdrawn from Basra at the end of April 2010, and all American combat troops had left Iraq in the August, but there was still much evidence of a continuing Western influence over the city. The main activity seemed to be in the various markets and bazaars lining the waterway, where Brendan could also see American-type fast-food outlets and high-rise buildings, including the five-storey Basra Sheraton on Corniche Street, newly reconstructed after the damage and looting of the Iraq War. This was where Esther and Fahada, and Ruth, were staying, and where the interview that evening would be filmed. Esther, of course, had booked the penthouse suite on the top floor, giving a panoramic view over the city and the waterway.

Brendan stopped at the hotel moorings, which consisted of a beautifully hand-painted wooden sign above polished decking. A flunky in a uniform helped him tie up, and Brendan gave him a $10 tip which seemed to be acceptable. He would leave Fahada to worry about selling the boat. He was just glad to have got there safely. He ran across the road into the hotel and was very happy to be met by Ruth, Esther and Fahada outside the restaurant on the first floor, where they'd been enjoying a drink and saw him arrive. Fahada, as usual, looked at him strangely (what on earth was going on with her?) but Esther and Ruth rushed up to him at the same time and they had a group hug. It was good to see them again. The setting was very odd, a pockmarked hotel in the middle of what had recently been a war-zone, but at least it wasn't a war-zone any more.

His next country, Afghanistan, however, was.

Day: Date	Itinerary (* indicates TV interview) ([18] indicates new nation)	Bike (km)	Car/ Bus (km)	Train (km)	Kayak/ Sail (km)	Boat (km)	Air (km)
Totals brought forward		8713	12193	0	2754	9941	9415
157: 19/10/11	Rahayta, Eritrea[94]; Aden, Yemen[95]					322	
158: 20/10/11	Jilah					397	
159: 21/10/11	Sayhut					380	
160: 22/10/11	Salalah, Oman[96]					403	
161: 23/10/11	Al Likbi					362	
162: 24/10/11	Shannah					435	
163: 25/10/11	Masqat					423	
164: 26/10/11	Fujairah, UAE[97]					300	
165: 27/10/11	Abu Dhabi					413	
166: 28/10/11	Doha, Qatar[98]					397	
167: 29/10/11	Galali, Bahrain[99]					234	
168: 30/10/11	Manifah, Saudi Arabia[100]; Kuwait City[101]					196	
169: 31/10/11	Khorramshahr, Iran[102]; Basra, Iraq[*103]					167	
Totals carried forward		8713	12193	0	2754	14370	9415

Chapter 42: Domination

Louisa's war-zone was much the same as it had been when she left for Uganda. She was definitely getting obsessional about the Sister, because She was the only thing she could think about – not only when she was at work or thinking about work, but even when she was shopping, cooking or trying to relax. When the phone rang, Louisa would imagine that it was Her. She took to looking out of the upstairs window when the doorbell rang, just to make sure that it wasn't Her. She was very wary when she was out of the house, in case She was just around the corner, waiting for her. She started to have nightmares every night which featured Her – chasing her, trying to kill her, humiliating her, and even chopping her up into little bits with an axe. Louisa dreaded all her shifts and was becoming utterly demoralised. She still kept wearing the fish symbol on her lapel, but was "inspected" by Her at the start of every shift and ordered to remove it, which she did. Sister liked to make a point of dressing Louisa down in front of colleagues and patients.

One young girl called Donna was waiting for a heart transplant. She asked Louisa one day, "Why do you continue to provoke the Sister with your fish badge? I've been here for two months now and the same thing happens every shift."

It was a fair question. Louisa thought hard before she replied. "I don't do it because I think that she will change her mind or that things will get any better. It probably makes her even madder. I wear the fish to remind myself that Jesus put up with far worse." Donna nodded her approval. When Louisa went round the unit saying goodbye to all the patients as she finally went off duty half an hour after the end of her shift, Donna even asked her to pray for her.

The other nurses started to smile at Louisa much more. One of them started asking her questions, whenever they were changing beds together or having a cup of tea during snatched break-time, about what she believed and why. One of the consultants even sidled up to her and asked her how she was getting on, "because I've noticed that Thunder Thighs seems to have it in for you." Louisa laughed at his nickname for Sister but was really pleased that even a doctor had noticed what was happening. Everyone in the hospital seemed to know what this harridan was like so why didn't anyone do anything about it?

At the start of one night-shift, the Sister announced that she was going down to the hospital canteen to have a drink and a sit down because she had a headache, so Louisa would have to take charge temporarily. This was totally against all the guidelines but the Sister had been known to do this sort of thing before and the nurses were expected to cover so that she didn't lose any pay or fall foul of the management. Unfortunately a few minutes later on this particular shift, one of the other three nurses started feeling sick and had to go home. Then another nurse got a phone-call from her teenage daughter to say that she'd just been mugged, so she disappeared too, which left Louisa and Bridget all on their own.

This was now dangerous and ludicrous. The regulations required there to be an absolute minimum of three staff on duty at all times. If there was a fire alarm, there was no way that two nurses could evacuate 24 patients safely. But even if things went smoothly, a night shift always threw up multiple calls for help and it was impossible for two nurses to do it all.

Louisa phoned the Sister's mobile, but when she answered she went ballistic with Louisa for having woken her up. The phone's ring brought the headache straight back, and Louisa copped a pile of verbal abuse and was told to phone up one of the other nurses to come in for an extra shift. "She won't get paid for it, but that's what nursing expects in times of emergency. Sort it out and leave me alone!" Louisa couldn't believe it. She did what Sister said, despite helping with the patients, but couldn't find anyone in. So she gave up and phoned the Sister back. The verbals were even worse this time, though it didn't last as long. The Sister rang off abruptly after warning, "You'd better watch out when I get up there."

Louisa was terrified. What was she to do? But at that moment Donna buzzed her to ask her for some pain-killers, so Louisa forged the Sister's signature on the drug-sheet in the usual way and took the paracetamol in, only for Donna to ask her what was wrong. "You look as white as a sheet." Louisa burst into tears and explained what was happening, but at that point the unit door slammed open and the Sister came through, yelling for Louisa.

When Louisa ran out she collided with the Sister who started shouting at her, calling her an idiot who couldn't take any decisions for herself, needed mollycoddling, and was incompetent and unprofessional. Louisa just stood there and took it. She couldn't think straight. One of the patients buzzed for assistance but Sister told Louisa that Bridget would sort it. "I haven't finished with you yet!"

Another buzzer went. "Will you SHUT UP!" yelled the Sister down the unit.

More buzzers went. "I HATE YOU, YOU... BLOODY CHRISTIAN!" screamed the Sister and slapped Louisa across the face, before rushing off to shout at some of the patients and stomping around making a lot of noise, even though most of the patients were asleep (or had been).

Louisa was shell-shocked. She couldn't move, and must have stayed standing where she was for at least a minute, her mouth opening and closing, her cheek burning and her jaw throbbing. The Sister came back and shouted at her to come into her office. Louisa meekly followed her in and the Sister shut the door.

"Don't you EVER provoke me like that again!" she shouted. "And don't even think of reporting me for hitting you. It'll be my word against yours and I assure you that you won't win."

"Yes, Sister," said Louisa meekly.

"Good," said the Sister. "Now get on with your duties and stop bothering me. You've made my headache even worse. Get out of here!" She slumped in her chair and put her head in her hands. Louisa tiptoed out and quietly shut the door behind her. She felt so small, worthless and pathetic. She burst into tears again and trudged down the corridor, only to find Donna in the doorway of her room, looking at her and crying.

"That was horrible!" Donna wailed. "I saw everything, from when she came in and had a go at you to when she hit you and called you a bloody Christian and then stomped off. I saw it all."

Louisa quickly snapped back into professional mode, wiped her eyes and put her arms round Donna, leading her back to her bed. "Yes, it was," she said. "But it'll be our word against hers and no-one will believe us."

"Oh yes, they will," said Donna. "I videoed it on my phone."

Chapter 43: Nations 104 - 112

The successive days' interviews with Esther at Basra and Kabul featured war and peace issues, and Ruth's perspective on Ugandan post-war rehabilitation helped to make the link with the ongoing work of Watoto. Brendan linked what was presently happening in Afghanistan with his great-uncle Nat at Arras in 1916, but was less sure about how this would come across. The whole of the UK had been involved in the First World War, but most people in the West were untouched by Afghanistan, and didn't understand that it was all to defend them from the threat of terrorism.

Brendan made a further link with Christians persecuted for their faith, called to defend eternal values against those who would attack them and force their submission. He mentioned one particular Open Doors case as an example: Alimjan Yimit[70], whose wife Gulnur he was planning to visit in the remote Chinese town of Kaxgar. Brendan had told Open Doors that he wanted to have a face-to-face encounter with the family of a prominent figure from the Persecuted Church at some point on his journey, and Eric Tate had suggested this family because they lived bang-on Brendan's planned route. Esther, however, seemed to be on a "Salute America's Heroes" trip, so Brendan was happy to let that "fight for liberty" theme take precedence. He did raise a few concerns, eyebrows and laughs, however, with his descriptions of evading the pirates in Yemen and the would-be abductors (if that's what they were) in Iran.

He enjoyed the flight in Esther's Learjet, with Ruth, from Basra to Kabul, even though they had to pursue an indirect route to avoid overflying either Iran or Helmand province. But now, with the interview over and the Farsi-edition GNT given to one of the Afghan lighting technicians, Brendan was off northwards in a black 4x4, hopefully away from trouble rather than towards it, though anti-Christian feeling was high all over the country.

Brendan's first objective was the infamous Salang Tunnel in Parwan Province, 100km north of Kabul and the scene of a deadly fire, years of closure, avalanches – but providing a vital link through the Hindu Kush, saving hundreds of kilometres and many hours of driving over high passes.

Brendan found that the dusty road out of Kabul was fine until there was a need for a bridge. Every bridge seemed to be destroyed either by war or flash flood, so at each there was either a rickety replacement or a well-established diversion. At Jabal os Sarai he entered the mountains, and the road climbed up high-sided gorges towards the tunnel. Progress was painfully slow, with small rocks strewn across the road, and evidence of avalanches and rock-slides eating into the outer edge of the roadway all

---

[70] Alimjan Yimit's case is real and ongoing at the time of writing. Open Doors are protecting his real name, but urging their supporters to campaign for his release.

the way to the tunnel. The cratered highway the other side of the Saleng snaked northwards and downwards, with a convoy of slow-moving trucks dictating everybody else's speed. Mazar-e-Sharif came and went to the sound of grinding gears. After Gur-e Mar, he looked for a safe place to stop for the night. It couldn't be in a town, for there were few Westerners this far north and plenty of Taliban. As dusk fell, he headed off the road towards some small foothills a few kilometres away, and found the perfect spot by a stream behind a small hill, surrounded by nothing but rock and dust. More importantly, he was invisible from the road.

He climbed out and unpacked his gear to prepare his evening meal – a freeze-packed chicken curry which took him mentally back to the Arctic last year. When it was ready, he packed everything away again, filled his flask up with water from the stream, climbed into the car, locked all the doors, turned off the interior light, ate his meal, drank some water and settled down for the night in the driver's seat. He had the key in the ignition ready for a quick get-away, but in the end he got four or five hours' sleep and woke up when the sun rose.

Two hours later he crossed the river Amu Darya by means of the grandly-named Afghanistan-Uzbekistan Friendship Bridge. Across the other side was the ancient city of Termez, burial-place of a renowned Sufi leader, its markets and streets teeming with people going about their daily business, in contrast to the sombre insecurities of Afghanistan – and Brendan felt a sense of release.

Uzbekistan once figured in a pub quiz question as one of the only two doubly-landlocked countries in the world i.e. a country totally surrounded by landlocked countries. It was the geography geek in him, Brendan supposed, but Uzbekistan had remained an *interesting* country for him since then, and he was thrilled that he could now say that he'd been there. The other country sharing the same mark of special-ness was Liechtenstein, where he was due to be interviewed in a few months' time. Perhaps he could slip that bit of trivia into the interview – or perhaps not. He didn't want to come across as weird – well, no weirder than he actually was, anyway.

Brendan had a new tactic for "witnessing". Previously his strategy had been to focus on a particular place and wait until then even if a good opportunity presented itself. This had served him well, but he knew that it was a gamble. So he'd decided from now on to give the GNTs away whenever he found a likely recipient. With this in mind, Brendan jumped out of the car and offered the Uzbek version to a gaggle of chatting housewives on a street corner. They took one look at him and bustled away like geese. Perhaps this new tactic wouldn't be as fruitful as he hoped. The second and third attempts met similar responses, but then he cornered an older man who read the inscription in the book, smiled, put it in his shopping-bag and walked off towards the market.

Brendan swaggered back to the car with renewed confidence, and drove off westwards on a small track, barely discernable, which ran parallel to the border river for a further 50km to the unmanned Turkmenistan border at the wonderfully-named village of Baldy. There was even a sign in English, and Brendan took a photo of himself against it. The first person he saw in Turkmenistan was a man looking after goats near the village of Ak-Tepe, who read the GNT's inscription and packed the book away in a bag full of poppies. He was probably the local drug-smuggler, but shook Brendan's hand and offered him a drink out of an old corked bottle. Brendan declined graciously, turned the car round and headed back across the border into Uzbekistan.

The dust and rock of Afghanistan had given way almost immediately in Uzbekistan to vegetation, trees and farmland, and the same was true of Brendan's exit from Turkmenistan. The ancient Dushanbe road swept northwards between forests and agriculture, and even sugar-plantations and vineyards, all the way along the Sukhandarya valley to his overnight destination of Denau, just before the Tajik border.

Tajikistan was the third of the four countries for which he couldn't secure a visa, but the guard at the border sold him one for $20. Somalia and Saudi Arabia had been ticked off his list already so now only North Korea was left. The only thing he knew about Tajikistan was that it was not a happy nation – it had responded to independence from the Soviet Union by engaging in an orgy of self-destruction, ethnic cleansing and economic devastation.

Brendan had lunch at Dushanbe and gave the GNT to a woman selling herbs outside the Cathedral. The road then snaked up the steep-sided Kofarnihon and Vakhsh valleys, often alongside but sometimes hundreds of metres above the rushing river. It was now well into November, and the roads would only be open for another few weeks due to snow. So far there had only been drizzle, but the clouds were gathering in the high mountains, and the road surface became increasingly churned up. Past the abandoned building site for the Rogun Dam, which (if ever completed) would be the world's tallest dam, Brendan turned off the main road – a laughable idea because it was little less than a track – up an even smaller track, which was officially the A372, running to the Kyrgyz border. The road crept round the buttresses of the cliffs following the river, often virtually impassable because of rockfalls or muddy torrents sluicing across the road and threatening to sweep him over the edge. Progress was steady but slow and needed every bit of Brendan's concentration. He was glad of the power-steering, and engaged the four-wheel drive frequently to get through the worst stretches.

He finally arrived, relieved and exhausted, as darkness fell, at the small village of Damburacha. Brendan slept in the car again that night, because it was very cold outside. It wasn't much warmer inside, so he put on more clothes and snuggled into his sleeping-bag. In the middle of an odd and rather disturbing dream, Brendan was awakened suddenly by a huge bang and his head bounced against the door-handle.

When he looked up he found that his car was now sideways and a huge truck was trundling slowly away up the hill. He jumped out of the car and shouted at the back of the truck, which didn't achieve anything. The car, fortunately, instead of being hit and crushed, had been pushed down and round by the high front bumper of the truck, which was so big and heavy that the collision had probably not even registered with its driver, especially if he was half-asleep.

Brendan tried unsuccessfully to get back to sleep, and set off in the murk of the morning, hoping that he could reach the end of the road before the snow shut everything down. The car seemed to be functioning normally, despite its overnight mishap, as he edged on further up the Vakhsh valley and passed the unmanned Kyrgyz border-post at about 7am. The clouds looked threatening up in the mountains, most of which already had snow on their peaks, but down below the the still snow-free road straightened out as the valley widened. The surface of the road was such that a top speed of about 60kph was all that Brendan would risk.

Sary-Tash looked on the map as if it was an important town but in fact it consisted of a few houses and yurts around a crossroads. The tented yurts were packed tightly shut and no-one was to be seen. Brendan finally came across one man who was busy outside his yurt shaking out dozens of rugs from inside. He didn't notice Brendan coming and jumped in surprise when Brendan spoke to him, holding out the Kyrgyz GNT for him to read the inscription. The man yelled behind him, and a small round woman emerged from the yurt with some antique spectacles. When he'd finished reading he went inside with the book. Thinking that that was that, Brendan began to walk off, but the man shouted to him, offering Brendan a bowl of risotto and brandishing a spoon. Brendan suddenly got a wonderful whiff of spiced meat and rice. He nodded at the man and sat down on a rock at the side of the road to eat this meal. "Plov," said the man, which Brendan took to be the name of the dish.

"Very good plov," said Brendan, nodding between mouthfuls. The man smiled.

The man shouted again for his wife, who came out with a small glass with a yellow liquid in. After a short game of charades and pointing by the man, Brendan gathered it was some form of fermented horse milk. He took a sip to be polite, but discovered that it was surprisingly pleasant. He drained the glass, but then regretted it as he felt the liquid expand and burn inside him. He laughed and coughed, and the man laughed too. They bade each other farewell and the man's wife beamed as well.

Brendan still had a long way to go, and the rough road got rougher as it snaked up away from the now tiny Vakhsh river into the mountains. Still the snow kept off, which was just as well because the road surface got appalling at some points and seemed to disappear entirely, leaving a wide stony plateau for Brendan to guess the route and hope for the best. The distance from Sary-Tash to the Chinese border at the Irkestam Pass was only about 70km but took two hours, and it took a further hour and a half to complete the transition from one country to the next. Kyrgyzstan didn't seem bothered about Brendan leaving, but the officials "welcoming" him into China took great pains to make sure that everything was in order before they would let him through.

There was a three-hour time difference involved too, so it was already 4pm when he set off for Kaxgar which was a further 200km away. The snow started falling immediately and quickly began to settle, making the road surface slippery. But now the road was asphalt, not just dust, and a bit of sliding in the snow was nothing compared to the pebble-dashing and crunching pot-holes of the last three days. But then the snow stopped and the endless plains of the arid Taklamakan Desert opened out in front of him. Another desert! It was rock and dust rather than sand, so the 4x4 had no problem, and just as the sun was setting behind him Brendan arrived in Kaxgar. It took him some time to find anyone who could direct him to the house of Gulnur Yimit, the wife of the so-called dissident whose details he'd been given by Open Doors.

Alimjan Yimit[71] was sentenced in October 2009 to 15 years in prison for "divulging state secrets", a trumped-up charge which hid the fact that he'd been targeted because he'd converted from Islam to Christianity and was the leader of a house church. His story, according to Open Doors, showed many of the classic features of persecution: before his arrest he was regularly interrogated; his house was searched, his computer seized; he'd been physically abused; his complaints were ignored; his food retail business had been shut down on the pretext that it was a cover for evangelism. The UN Working Group on Arbitrary Detention had judged that Alimjan's arrest and detention were arbitrary and illegal, but China didn't care. Alimjan's health was deteriorating. His lawyer had lodged numerous appeals through the Chinese legal system but had got nowhere.

Unsure of whether he was at the right house, Brendan knocked on the door and was surprised when a man opened it rather cautiously. "Yimit?" Brendan asked, feeling that he was in the wrong place and had to be careful what he said.

The man broke into a massive grin as he nodded his head. "Yes," he said in English, tapping his chest, "*Alimjan* Yimit. Welcome!" He stepped out to give Brendan a big hug and beckoned him into his small but sturdy house, revealing first a smilingly tearful wife and then, from behind her, two small sons in their pyjamas, getting ready for bed, who'd been frightened by the knock on the door. Four days previously, Alimjan had been hauled from his cell and told that he was to be released and returned to his family to show the generosity and tolerance of the Chinese authorities, but he was warned not to preach Christianity amongst the predominantly

---

[71] The story and family details are as described in Open Doors publicity. The details of their house are fictional, as is, sadly, Alimjan's release.

Muslim Uyghur people of his home town or he would be re-arrested. It had taken him two days to find his way back from the prison, and he'd only arrived home the evening before, to be told by his wife that a strange man from England, who'd been campaigning for his release, was due to visit.

Brendan explained that he was Minister in a church in England, travelling around the world to highlight the plight of Christians such as Alimjan, and to encourage every Christian to take the call to evangelism seriously. Alimjan understood a little English, and translated for his wife and sons. Brendan gave them the Uyghur-edition Chinese GNT, with its inscription in the front, and told them that many letters and campaigns in support of Alimjan had bombarded the Chinese authorities throughout his detention, and that he'd never been forgotten. Tears rolled down Alimjan's cheeks and he put his hands together, closed his eyes, and said what must have been a prayer of thanks as the tears continued to course down his cheeks. Brendan was deeply moved too, and the whole family shared a teary, laughing group-hug with him at the end of the prayer. Then Gulnur shooed the children off to bed and Brendan and Alimjan sat down to talk more, as best they could, about what Christianity meant to them.

Brendan couldn't understand what it must be like to live in such a hostile environment and to have so much harassment just because of what you believed. England was so fortunate to have freedom of religion and yet virtually everyone took this freedom for granted. As Alimjan told his story – his conversion from Islam and the subsequent years of discrimination and persecution – Brendan shook his head in amazement. This was what being a Christian was all about. This was the spirit which had given energy to the first Christians and also kept the faith alive in China during the long Dark Age of Maoist indoctrination. Brendan felt an enormous bond with Alimjan, even though they had only just met. They were brothers.

Gulnur returned and made up a bed for Brendan in front of the fire. The family all slept in the same back room, which was the only other room of the house. Brendan slept well on a pile of rugs with other rugs on top of him. It wasn't the Ritz, but it was warm and cosy. Then, just as he was stirring in the first few hours of daylight, came a loud knock on the door. Brendan sat up, wondering what was happening. Alimjan emerged from the back room and opened the door, to be confronted with three Chinese policemen who pushed their way in and then ignored Alimjan when they saw Brendan. Their leader stepped forward. "Blonde And Pleased?" he said, which would have been an amusing mispronunciation of his name in any other circumstance. When Brendan showed his passport, they took it and grabbed him too, throwing him and all his stuff off in their police van. Brendan looked forlornly at Alimjan and Gulnur, who gestured that they would pray for him.

At the police station next to a huge statue of Chairman Mao in the centre of town, Brendan was jabbered at by various zealous officials, had something stamped in his passport, then was ushered into a room with an even more important-looking official. "Where you go next?" the man asked.

Brendan started to explain his route down through Xinjiang province to the Kashmir border at Pidakkesh, but when the official heard Kashmir he said, "Ah, south!" and picked up the phone. After several minutes, he finally put the phone down and smiled at Brendan. "Kind China people help you go south," he said, handing Brendan over to the policemen in the outer office, barking orders at them as they stood to attention. Their police van took Brendan off along the streets, and arrived, to Brendan's surprise, at the Kaxgar airport, where he was dumped on a plane which already had its engines going. The officer handed over his passport and belongings in a grey canvas bag with Chinese characters on the side, and stood at the top of the plane's steps while a few other Chinese shuffled onboard, then pointed his stick menacingly at Brendan before strutting down the steps. Brendan wondered whether he was being deported or sent to a Chinese city for further interrogation, so it was with some relief that he caught "Islamabad" on the otherwise unintelligible announcement by the pilot.

When he examined his passport it contained something that looked uncannily similar to the Israeli "persona non grata" stamp, which could cause problems for him later when he had to pass through China again to get to Mongolia. Indeed, the next Esther interview was due to take place in Beijing. He rummaged round in his canvas bag, discovering to his relief that they'd not taken his GNTs away, and realised that the Chinese authorities might well have saved him time, money and distance by deporting him. The only difficulty was the re-entry into China, which he would get Esther to investigate. Surely she could work miracles in China too, couldn't she?

He phoned Fahada as soon as he got off the plane in Islamabad airport, asking her to brief Esther immediately so that she could work her wonders. He also asked her to contact Eric Tate at Open Doors to tell him the good news about Alimjan, but also to enquire whether he'd been re-arrested because of Brendan. Lastly, he asked Fahada to inform Hertz that they had a 4x4 vehicle stuck in a remote part of Western China but that he couldn't go back for it. Fahada sighed. She was still trying to sell the old speedboat in Basra.

Brendan organised his flight to Amritsar, then gave Pakistan's GNT to a woman clearing tables in the restaurant. She said that her brother was a Christian and she would give the GNT to him. Brendan encouraged her to read it too, and she nodded.

Amritsar too had a new airport, as Brendan quickly discovered. The flight to Amritsar was even shorter than the one to Islamabad had been, and he was there by mid-afternoon, able to book into a hotel and visit the Golden Temple before dinner. Ever since he'd seen the film "Gandhi", Brendan had been keen to visit the site of the massacre in the grounds of the Temple, and to see the Temple itself. The memorial in the quiet garden was a simple, stark stone telling the story. He saw the bullet-holes in the walls and the well down which people had jumped in a futile attempt to escape. Britain's history was by no means squeaky-clean, and this was a dark reminder of it.

The Golden Temple, by contrast, was serene and majestic. The whole complex was all very beautiful, peaceful and, indeed, holy. Brendan entered via a huge white entrance at the north end, then walked round the lake to the massive Darshani Deorhi Arch. The walk through it onto the causeway was a pilgrimage not just for the Sikhs around him but for Brendan too. He knew nothing about the stories behind the Temple or the Sikh religion, but he couldn't fail to admire and respect the reverence and awe on the faces of the pilgrims. God was definitely here. The Temple itself had four open entrances, symbolising the importance of acceptance and openness to others, and especially the lack of distinction between the four Hindu castes. The architecture and murals didn't do much for him, but the whole experience was very special.

He gave the Indian GNT to the head waiter in the hotel restaurant, who listened politely when Brendan explained how impressed he'd been by the Golden Temple. "Ah, but we Sikhs are able to worship anywhere. We don't need a beautiful temple, even though we have one here at Amritsar. We believe that there is one universal God who is everywhere and wants the best for everyone, so Sikhs try to do good to everyone in order to serve God well."

"Funny that," said Brendan. "That's pretty much what Christians believe too."

***

Brendan set off from Amritsar in another Hertz vehicle, this time a Honda City. Fahada had passed Brendan's message on to Micky Yehu, thinking that he'd be angry and cancel the deal, but he just laughed and said that he'd see to it himself that Brendan was supplied with a new vehicle immediately. So Brendan coasted down the Grand Trunk Road, watching the high mountains of the western Himalayas getting ever closer as he drove south-east through flat countryside. The monsoon season had finished and the Buddha Nullah stream was high, but filthy and stinky. Brendan was dismayed to see dead animals and sewage polluting the stream, because it irrigated the fields and, horribly, provided drinking water for the impoverished farming settlements dotting the countryside. He was glad that he'd filled his water-bottles up at a cafe in Ludhiana where the owner assured him that the water was clean. "From Himalaya," he said. But where had it been more recently?

The road eventually crossed the Ganges at Haridwar, one of the seven holy cities of Hinduism. Brendan arrived at dusk, and was intrigued by the crowds of pilgrims converging on one area of the riverbank. The signs said that it was Har-Ki-Pauri, the steps of Hara or Shiva, and that visitors were welcome to watch Aarti, the evening worship to Goddess Ganga. Brendan didn't believe that rivers should be worshipped but he parked the car anyway and went to see what it was all about. He joined the crowds lining the water's edge and saw that, even though the water was very cold, hundreds were in the river itself. Several priests appeared holding large fire bowls, the gongs in the temples at the Ghat started bonging and everyone started chanting. Then the pilgrims placed bowls into the river – clay bowls either set alight with oil-drenched cloths or with colourful flowers in them, presumably as a symbol of hope and a vessel for their prayers. It looked spectacular, even though Brendan couldn't cope with worshipping a bit of God's creation rather than the God who created it. The Sikh worship at Amritsar had been easy to "tap into", and Brendan still felt a glow from it, but this seemed alien and wrong.

He went back to his car and drove 30km further, before settling down to sleep in the car just before Najibabad. He slept well, and woke only when the sunlight streamed through the window into his face. He didn't feel too good, however, and kept getting stomach pains, so set off without breakfast. A few kilometres further on he had to stop the car, grab the loo roll and rush to the side of the road, where he just managed to pull his trousers down before the most enormous burst of Number One Point Two erupted out of his backside. He staggered back to the car, feeling weak and rather nauseous.

Fortunately the driving was relatively easy, but he had to stop several times during the morning with either sickness or diarrhoea or both at the same time. He felt wretched, and crossed the Mahakali bridge into Nepal without really registering what he was doing. As he continued eastwards, the road got worse, as did his stomach ache and sickness, and he kept retching and cramping all the way through the afternoon, desperately avoiding pot-holes because external bumps only made things internally worse. Eventually he reached Kohalpur and stopped for the night. The cramps got worse and his sleep was interrupted by more trips outside, even though not much was produced at either end by this point in his illness. He was aiming for Kathmandu, but unless things improved on their own he would need medication there and some time to allow them to kick in. Fortunately the friends with whom Ruth had stayed during her gap year were still in Kathmandu working for the United Mission to Nepal, and had offered him accommodation in their home.

It took him all day to drive the 400km to the capital, due to the poor roads and his inability to concentrate. It took him a further hour to find the missionaries' house in the twisting back streets of Patan, south of the River Bagmati. He staggered inside, explaining his plight, and they took charge. He was packed off to bed, medication was found and administered, and the next two days went by in a blur. He no longer cared about his schedule. He was just glad to be looked after and told to stay in bed.

Day: Date	Itinerary (* indicates TV interview) ([18] indicates new nation)	Bike (km)	Car/ Bus (km)	Train (km)	Kayak / Sail (km)	Boat (km)	Air (km)
Totals brought forward		8713	12193	0	2754	14370	9415
170: 1/11/11	Kabul, Afghanistan[*104]						3046
171: 2/11/11	Gur-e-mar		370				
172: 3/11/11	Denau, Uzbekistan[105] via Ak Tepe, Turkmenistan[106]		382				
173: 4/11/11	Damburacha, Tajikistan[107]		359				
174: 5/11/11	Jash-Tilek, Kyrgyzstan[108]; Kaxgar, China[109]		447				
175: 6/11/11	Islamabad, Pakistan[110]; Amritsar, India[111]						635
176: 7/11/11	Najibabad		436				
177: 8/11/11	Kohalpur, Nepal[112]		399				
178: 9/11/11	Kathmandu		404				
179: 10/11/11	Enforced day's rest due to sickness						
180: 11/11/11	Enforced day's rest due to sickness						
Totals carried forward		8713	14990	0	2754	14370	13096

Chapter 44: Resignation

Back in Jact, things were going from bad to worse.

Ben came back from Uganda fired up and willing to give it another go with Cecil, but during the two weeks that he was away, Cecil had contrived to throw several young people off the premises for making too much noise during his Bible Study on Friday evening, and, when Ben read their comments on Facebook, he knew that they were unlikely to come back. At his weekly "supervision" with Cecil, Ben asked what had happened.

"Tell me, Cecil, why is it that three older people take precedence over thirty young people?"

It didn't go down well. "You know full well that I want the church family to devote Friday evenings to the Bible Study group."

"Yes, I know. But is it worth it? Its numbers seem to have fluctuated from two to four, and settled at three. What's the point?"

But Cecil was adamant that he needed to keep going with it, even though it was unfruitful and everything else was falling apart. Ben bizarrely remembered a story about a hungry monkey which starved to death because it grabbed hold of a potato through the bars of a drain and wouldn't let go of it, even though it couldn't eat it.

Cecil hit back. "I've tried to be reasonable. Because you defied me and sided with the Youth Club in refusing to move away from Fridays, I've had to move the Bible Study from the meeting room to the vestry, where it's a bit cramped but we've just managed to fit in."

Ben chuckled to himself as he looked around at the very room in question. The thought of four of them really struggling to fit themselves in was laughable. Even if they were the fattest people in the world they would still be able to fit eight of them in. Cecil brought him back to earth with a bump with the words, "Can you have a word with them to tell them that they can only come if they are quiet?"

Ben exploded. "Of course I can't! You can't say that to young people, and why should I? They're just as important as the older members of the church, but they don't feel that they belong."

"But they have to respect other people in this church – they can't have it all their own way."

Ben couldn't believe it. "But look at it from their point of view. They're happy here, welcomed by the people in the church, and given the run of the place on a Friday night so that they can chill out, play games, listen to music or do whatever they want. The parents are happy because they're not hanging around on street-corners or going into pubs. I'm here to make sure that they don't destroy the place or do anything that they shouldn't. Then along comes a new Minister who starts a Bible

Study on Youth Club night and tells them they can only continue if they are quiet or change their night. Why should they?"

"Because Bible Study takes precedence over social activities," said Cecil. "They can play their games or their music any time and anywhere, but studying the Bible needs a dedicated time without distractions."

"But Friday night's a ridiculous night for a Bible Study. It's the pub quiz. It's a night for going out with mates. No-one in their right minds will turn up for a boring Bible Study on a Friday night!"

Cecil seized on the pejorative word "boring" and ignored Ben's argument. "How *dare* you say it's boring when you've never even been!" he shouted. "I think you need to come along to see what you're missing. I'll expect you this Friday and at least the next four weeks after that."

And that was the end of the "supervision". Nothing about Ben's job in the schools. Nothing about a youth strategy. Ben went away shaking his head. Cecil really didn't have a clue how to supervise, let alone lead a church in 21st century Tyneside. Ben had had enough.

***

On Friday night, Ben and Louisa had a long chat over an early dinner.

"Do you think I should go to his bloomin' Bible Study or not?"

"Of course you shouldn't," said Louisa. "What good would that do?"

"Well, I need to respect his authority and he told me to go, so I probably should."

"Of course, you shouldn't. He's got no right to tell you what to do if it doesn't have anything to do with your job. Anyway, shouldn't you be at Youth Club?"

"Yes, I should. But if I turn up at the Church, Cecil will expect me to go to his Bible Study."

"Well, just ignore him. Your job's with the young people, if there are any left..."

Ben wished that he was as forthright and clear-thinking as Louisa. He didn't like defying Cecil's authority but he did agree with Louisa, and couldn't see any point in sitting in a Bible Study watching any young people who might turn up drift off because he wasn't there. "I'll see what happens," he decided.

***

When he arrived at Jact Church, there were a few youths hanging around, but only a fraction of those around before Ben went off to Uganda. "Hi," said Ben, "I heard what happened. I'm so glad you haven't left in disgust. I do hope that I can persuade you that you are still welcome here."

At that point, Cecil came out. "Glad to see you here, Ben. We're just about to start."

That decided it for Ben. "I'm sorry, Cecil, but I'm staying out here to chat with the lads. I think that's what I need to do."

Cecil looked at him hard for a few seconds, and then went inside, closing the door behind him.

"Well done!" said the cockiest of the young lads. "He's a right pillock. Why aren't there more Christians like you rather than them all being like him?"

Ben quietly and patiently explained that most Christians were actually really kind and generous but that unfortunately they hadn't had the chance to see that yet in Cecil.

They snorted. "And what sort of a name is Cecil? It's so... gay."

Ben laughed with them. "I know what you mean, but you can't have a go at him because of his name. Anyway you're called Niall, aren't you?"

"So?"

"Well, Niall Quinn played for Sunderland, didn't he?" His mates laughed and Niall coloured.

"I'm not named after *him*. My Uncle Niall died just before I was born, so me mam named me after him."

This time, it was Ben's turn to be embarrassed. "I'm sorry, Niall. I wasn't having a go at you, and I'm sorry that I embarrassed you. Friends?"

"Suppose," said Niall, still on the defensive. Then he brightened up. "Anyway, what we goin' to do, then?"

"What about a game of football, seeing as there's a few of us. Some of us could be Newcastle and some of us could be Sunderland, what do you think?" They all laughed, including Niall. "No, we'll just have a kickaround, shall we, on the grass?"

So they dumped their jackets and kicked the ball around for a few minutes, only for Cecil to come out and complain about the noise. Ben didn't want a confrontation in public so he gently led the lads down to the playing field, resolving to have it out with Cecil at the earliest possible moment, once and for all.

***

Sunday was a bit like a ballet, with Ben and Cecil stepping round one another without getting close. Ben noted that the numbers had dropped even further while he'd been away, the Perspex pulpit had been replaced by a wonky wooden lectern, and there was no-one except him under 70. The sermon was still looking at Romans 1:1, but Cecil had got onto the 13th and 14th words "set apart" and was busy trying to persuade the congregation that their job was to distance themselves from worldly activities and instead concentrate on spiritual matters, like his Friday night Bible

Study. As Ben was leaving, Cecil leaned forwards and snapped, "Tomorrow morning, 8.30 sharp in my vestry." It was like being summoned to the headmaster's study for a caning.

***

The following morning, Ben was already there as Cecil arrived to open up. "I thought I'd come along nice and early, so that we have plenty of time to sort things out."

"It may not take too long," replied Cecil, acidly. "It depends on you."

Ben was puzzled by this, but bit his lip and waited for Cecil to set himself down in the chair behind the desk in the vestry. He wasn't invited to sit, but did so anyway.

"So what have you got to say for yourself?" said Cecil, belligerently.

Ben suddenly knew what to say. "I've come to hand in my resignation."

"I was hoping that you'd say that," Cecil said, with a smile. "It saves me the effort of sacking you."

"I think the law calls this "constructive dismissal"," said Ben. "I'm not going without a fight and I'll bring you down with me, you see if I don't."

And he walked out.

Chapter 45: Nations 113 – 119

Brendan rose from his sickbed after two days of doing nothing, being nothing, feeling nothing and wanting nothing except to lie there and let the world go away. Peter and Sally looked after him really well, letting him sleep and bringing him hot milk and toast on the second evening, and then helping him get up and sit in a chair. He shared dinner with them on his third evening, and declared himself fit to continue.

"Let me drive you," said Peter. "I've got to go to a UMN project in Birtamod, so I can help you on your way tomorrow, then get a lift back in the UMN truck the following day." Birtamod was right at the eastern end of the country, virtually in Sikkim. Brendan was thrilled that he wouldn't have to drive on his first day back on the road, when he was still unsure how he would cope.

It was strange sitting in the passenger seat and being chauffeured, but Peter was an experienced driver on Nepalese roads, and that made things relaxed and easy. He didn't drive as quickly as Brendan, but it did mean that they hit fewer pot-holes. Instead of braving the rough tracks east of Bhaktapur, they took the long half-decent road round to the Mahendra highway at Pathlaiya. The road then extended eastwards for ever, and Brendan fell asleep as Peter drove. He woke up well into the afternoon, just as they were pulling into Birtamod. Brendan couldn't believe that he'd slept for so long, but felt much better as a result. Peter, however, looked absolutely shattered, and admitted that he'd never driven so far in one go before. Brendan suddenly remembered that he still had the Nepalese GNT, but Peter said that he'd give it to someone in Birtamod or, failing that, to his Hindu gardener back in Kathmandu.

Brendan was overwhelmed by their care for him, and shed a little tear as they said their farewells. Then Peter strode away to meet his colleagues and Brendan drove off to the border at Kakarbhitta. Fortunately, the crossing back into India was easy and he drove the 40km up the Hill Cart Road to Darjeeling – arriving in time for the obligatory early evening cup of tea. His hotel overlooked the terminus of the "Toy Train", the narrow-gauge steam railway which climbed over 2,000m from Siliguri to Darjeeling in only 80km. It was like going back in time when the evening train departed – banging, whistling, hooting, chugging, hissing.

Despite his day-time snooze, Brendan slept well again overnight, and, after the obligatory cup of morning tea, drove off down the mountain, before cutting across the contours to link up with the main road east. His next nation was Bhutan, a once-secretive nation which had emerged from isolation only a few decades earlier, and only introduced television for the start of the New Millennium. His route snaked across high plateaus and forests, and ended at the Indian town of Jaigaon. Brendan parked just back from the border, and strolled off with the Bhutanese GNT to the crossing, marked by a long wall and a single Tibetan-style gate, patrolled by

Bhutanese Army guards bemused at a non-Indian entering their country. They didn't get too many tourists.

Across the border, Phuntsholing was much quieter than its Indian neighbour, with communal blocks of housing and businesses rather than the mainly detached buildings of India. Brendan quickly found a woman out shopping, who accepted the proffered book, read the inscription and smiled to indicate that she understood. That was good enough for Brendan, who retreated back over the border, turned the car round, and headed back down into India.

Brendan had wondered a few times about the point and lasting usefulness of this border-hopping Bible-distribution. It was but a token gesture, but the most important aspect was the principle and symbolism of going into each country – which didn't require spending huge amounts of time or energy within each country. He'd no hope of being able to communicate with people wherever he went, and the barriers of language and culture meant that anything other than a cursory contact was unlikely. Yet the particular individual or communities visited might well be affected by his strange, short intervention into their daily routines, and some of the recipients so far had seemed particularly grateful and interested.

Back on the west-east highway across Assam, Brendan passed through the Buxa Wildlife Sanctuary – one of the last places where the Indian tiger could be found in the wild. He kept his eyes open, but didn't see one. He did see an elephant, though – distinctively smaller than the ones he'd seen in Africa and with differently-shaped ears. The road trundled on to the Brahmaputra at the small town of Goalpara, where Brendan found a hotel which seemed to cater for Western tourists. Well, it was ensuite and had a comfy bed, which was more than adequate.

The southern bank of the Brahmaputra led eastwards to the city of Guwahati, before Brendan's route climbed up to the city of Shillong, one of the very few in South-East Asia boasting that it was a Christian city. It was also famous as the rock capital of India (catering for music lovers rather than geologists) and for its golf course, the "Gleneagles of the East", legendary as the world's wettest golf course. It was, indeed, raining as Brendan passed through en route to the Bangladesh border.

Bangladesh was going to be another of those "distribute and disappear" witnessing opportunities, with the road from Shillong to Badarpur passing over the border for only a few kilometres – but this included the village of Baligaon. Brendan got out of the car and gave the GNT to a farmer trying to mend his tractor – which must have been one of the first ever made. Its front-plate said that it was a Massey-Harris 20, which presumably was from before Massey Ferguson's merger and pre-eminence. Quite how it had travelled so far and lasted so long was a mystery. The GNT was in Khasi, which might have been the language in that part of the world but was an unhappy reminder to Brendan of his Nepalese diarrhoea problems.

Back in India yet again, Brendan headed further east along the Sagolband Road to Imphal, where he spent his last night in India. The only tourist attractions seemed to be the Maharaja's old palace, a Hindu Temple and the war cemeteries from the Burma Campaign. It was the end of Day 183 – and Brendan celebrated his halfway point by having a curry and an early night. He had a long drive to come – into Burma, now Myanmar.

The border was at Moreh, across the Indo-Myanmar Friendship Bridge. The border guards on both sides, though, were less than friendly, and Brendan found out later that this was one of the main conduits for drug-smuggling from Myanmar to India, so perhaps each side was flexing its muscles. The road to Mandalay, unlike Kipling's ballad[72], was not full of "elephints a-pilin' teak in the sludgy squidgy creek, where the silence 'ung that 'eavy you was 'arf afraid to speak." It was pretty sludgy and squidgy in places but it was due to big trucks lumbering through the dirt-road. It was also long, tiring – and noisy: the trees alive with wildlife sounds; the road snarled up with traffic belching fumes; and the rain beating upon the car roof. It was warm rain, though, and sticky with humidity.

Across the Chindwin river at Kalewa, Brendan kept eastwards up into the hill forests and down again across the Mu River at a town which reminded him of his childhood. It was called Ye-U, which sounded like the "Yeah, you!" shout that followed his incredulity at being told off by his mother. Wonderfully, the next town was Kin-U, which was the way his mother usually gave him his orders. He looked for an Oy-U, but it never materialised.

The road to Mandalay still had no elephants piling teak, but it did have the old capital Shwebo with its royal pagodas, and strings of paddy-fields. And, finally, the river Ayeyarwady, and Mandalay itself – after 14 hours and 500km, averaging less than 40kph. But at least he'd arrived. After a late dinner in the hotel he crawled into bed, having checked the time of his flight the next day to Hue in Vietnam with the hotel receptionist, whom he rewarded for her research with the Myanmar GNT.

The next morning, Brendan had time to walk round the Mandalay Palace and up the Hill to see the Buddhist shrines and pagodas, before driving his Hertz car to the office at the international airport at Tada-U (the way his mother often said goodbye), 35km south of the city.

There wasn't a flight that day, or any day, from Mandalay to Hue. Oracle had messed up yet again. Even the hotel receptionist had somehow got it wrong – the only flights were to destinations in Myanmar, or to Kunming in China, neither of which were much use to Brendan. The airport Help Desk was no help at all. The best bet seemed to be to fly to Yangon, the capital, and see what flights took off from

---

[72] "Mandalay" is a poem by Rudyard Kipling, first published in the collection "Barrack-Room Ballads, and Other Verses" in 1892.

there. But then, looking out of the large window in the empty terminal, Brendan spotted an arrowed sign for private flights, and went off to investigate. The arrow pointed to an old hanger 400m along the road, looking scruffy alongside the rest of the modern airport. He found a leathery-skinned white man snoozing in a chair with his feet up on a table, hat pulled low over his face.

"Hi there," said Brendan, more confident at being able to talk in English.

"Howdy," said the voice under the hat. And the feet left the table, the hat tipped back, and an old wrinkled boozy face looked out. "And what can I do for you, sport?" said the voice, clearly Australian.

"I want to fly to Vietnam. Do you go that far?"

This was met with the sharp intake of breath perfected by all plumbers, builders and car mechanics. Then, "That's a long way." And, "Cost you a fair bit, that will." A pause, then, "Whereabouts in Vietnam?"

"Hue," said Brendan. "Or anywhere near there."

"What do you mean – anywhere near there? You either want Hue or you don't."

"No, you don't understand. It doesn't really matter where I go as long as I enter Vietnam, Laos, Thailand and Cambodia in the easiest and shortest way, ending in Ho Chi Minh City for a flight to Singapore."

When the pilot raised his eyebrows at this, Brendan explained by describing his mission.

"So, if I've got this right," said the pilot, "We don't need to go to Hue because you're ending up in Vietnam anyway for your flight to Singapore. How about I fly you to Vientiane in Laos which is on the border with Thailand, and you can hop over the border and see someone in Thailand? Then I'll take you straight down to Phnom Penh, drop you there and then I'll come on back here while you drive down to Ho Chi Minh City, which is only 200 clicks from Phnom Penh. Whadya reckon?"

Brendan couldn't believe his good fortune. Through Fahada's mistake, he was going to do less distance overall and save a day from his schedule, which would eliminate one of the wasted days in Kathmandu. "How much is that going to cost?" he asked, warily. He'd have to pay for it out of his own account, but he'd ensure that Oracle reimbursed him. It was their mistake in the first place.

"Well, it's for a good cause, so I don't want to rip you off, but it'll cost me quite a bit in fuel. I usually charge $2,000 a day all-in, but how about if we call it $3,000 for two days, and you pay the hotel bill in Vientiane."

"Done," said Brendan. "Do you take Barclaycard?"

"You name it, I can play it," said the pilot, pulling a state-of-the-art PIN credit terminal out of a drawer. "I'm Doug, by the way."

***

After a four-hour flight over wooded mountains and paddy-fields, Doug's Cessna dropped down to Wattay Airport, virtually in the city centre of Vientiane. For the last half-hour they'd been following the Mekong River, which marked the Thai/Lao border, and the airport was right next to the river. At the delapidated domestic hanger, Doug sorted the refuelling, then they both paid for their visas and booked in at the nearby Seng Tawan Hotel, overlooking the river. The room wasn't up to much, and it cost $180, but Brendan couldn't be bothered to look elsewhere and Doug seemed happy.

Popping over the border proved more difficult. Brendan could see people wandering along the other bank of the Mekong, but there were no bridges or river taxis. The hotel receptionist said that she could arrange a taxi to the Friendship Bridge for $10, and he could cross to Nong Khai in Thailand that way. At the bridge, there was a road-sign with a bendy X symbol. Brendan eventually worked out that traffic on the bridge was driving on the left (the law in Thailand), whereas Lao traffic drove on the right, so the sign marked the transition. He was glad to be on foot, because a few drivers didn't get the hang of it. The other side of the long suspension bridge, he gave the GNT to a woman waiting at a bus-stop just as a bus pulled up, so she tucked the book in her shopping bag and got on, scuppering any chance of further conversation. Job done, Brendan set off back across the bridge, showed his visa at the checkpoint and chose one of the many taxis plying for trade.

He was back in time for dinner, which became a prolonged evening of drinking and conversation in the bar with Doug, who seemed to have a prodigious talent for both, whereas Brendan began to get hazy rather quickly. Not wanting to push things after the Nepali dysentery or whatever it was, he retired to bed and tried to get to sleep. Then Doug appeared, still talkative, and it wasn't till the early hours that sleep finally happened. To cap it all, Doug snored. Olympically.

Bleary-eyed, Brendan crawled down to breakfast to find a cheery Doug already packing away fruit, sausages, toast, yoghurt and everything else on offer. He settled for toast and coffee, but even the coffee tasted sour. Brendan gave the Lao GNT as a tip to the maid cleaning the rooms. She wasn't certain what she'd been given, even when the inscription was shown to her, but she smiled and nodded.

***

The flight out of Vientiane crossed the river and headed due south, across the watery Khorat Plateau for hour after hour, until the green slopes of the Dângrêk hills marked the border with Cambodia. Shortly after midday they landed at Phnom Penh Airport, only a few kilometres outside the city itself. Brendan shook hands with Doug, who wished him all the best. Brendan went straight to the Hertz counter for a vehicle to Ho Chi Minh City, spotting a sign on the way for "Dairy Queen", an

American fast-food outlet he recalled from the year before. So he consumed cheeseburger, fries and a chocolate-cookie-flavoured "Blizzard Treat" milk-shake. There's nothing like a bit of ethnic food, Brendan said to himself, as he imagined all the little cholesterols smacking their hands together in glee as they furred up his arteries. Brendan gave the Cambodian GNT to the young woman who served him. She thanked him with a "Have a good day, now!" which sounded too American to be true.

His little Hyundai Matrix beetled its way down the NH1 as if it knew the way. The highway kept to the banks of the Mekong which had taken a more circuitous route through Thailand. The road beyond the border at Moc Bai was wide and full of traffic, and Brendan was relieved to see signs in English to the ultra-modern airport just north of the city centre, where Brendan handed over the car keys at the Hertz office, and booked in at the airport hotel. After a quick conversation with the hotel receptionist, he rushed out with a tourist map, finding the Notre-Dame Basilica just off Dong Khoi Street, and arrived just in time for the 5pm Mass. He realised that he hadn't been in a church for quite a long time, especially to worship, and he was enthralled by the slow solemnity of the liturgy, even though he couldn't understand a word of it. He went forward at the end to speak with the priest, explaining his globe-trotting mission, and gave him the Vietnamese GNT, to give away as he thought best. Brendan was surprised at how good it was to participate in a church service again, and how wonderful he'd found the incomprehensible, yet strangely comfortable and familiar worship. He now had a renewed sense of God being with him, and felt ready for anything.

It was a good job, considering what awaited him in three days' time...

Day: Date	Itinerary (* indicates TV interview) ([18] indicates new nation)	Bike (km)	Car/ Bus (km)	Train (km)	Kayak / Sail (km)	Boat (km)	Air (km)
Totals brought forward		8713	14990	0	2754	14370	13096
181: 12/11/11	Darjeeling (India)		501				
182: 13/11/11	Goalpara via Bhutan[113]		380				
183: 14/11/11	Imphal via Bangladesh[114]		499				
184: 15/11/11	Mandalay, Myanmar[115]		493				
185: 16/11/11	Vientiane, Laos[116]; Nong Khai, Thailand[117]						815
186: 17/11/11	Phnom Penh, Cambodia[118]; Ho Chi Minh City, Vietnam[119]		230				747
Totals carried forward		8713	17093	0	2754	14370	14658

Chapter 46: Extermination / Nations 120 - 125

Fahada felt increasingly that Brendan must have a guardian angel – not that she believed in them. Islam, of course, didn't have them – only the Kirama Katibin, two angels who sat on either shoulder recording good and bad deeds but not influencing choices or outcomes. But Fahada had once asked a colleague about the signs for Guardian Angels in downtown Detroit, and the answer (a volunteer street patrol) led to the more ethereal topic of celestial vigilantes. At least Fahada now knew the general idea, even if she dismissed it as fairy-tale. Yet after Brendan's run of escapes, contingencies and downright good luck, she was beginning to wonder. Her latest attempt at sabotage – a purler of a plan that involved hacking into the Mandalay Airport main computer to create a fictitious flight to Hue – had duped Brendan right until the time of the non-existent flight. Yet he'd *still* managed to wriggle out of the dilemma and even made up time and decreased his distance – it wasn't fair! Either that or somehow her attempts were *fated* to fail.

So it was now left to Holy War, under the excited supervision of Saeed, to do their worst. Having failed twice with major projects in the past they were now definitely in the Second Division of Islamic terrorist groups, and were anxious not to slip further down the rankings. Saeed had been in Indonesia for the last fortnight, planning Brendan's assassination. Only if Holy War succeeded would they then be given permission to have a crack at Esther, Queen of Television and symbol of America.

Fahada was torn. She didn't particularly want any harm to come to Brendan, but she didn't want him to curry any further favour with Esther either. She definitely didn't want him killed, which would clear the way for her father and the repulsive Saeed to attack Esther. So she now had to tweak Saeed's plans so that they stopped (but didn't kill) Brendan, and not in a way that pointed the finger at her. It was all very complicated.

***

Brendan flew in from Vietnam to Singapore and wandered open-mouthed through the opulence of the airport, with its expensive boutiques and harpist playing in the concourse. He checked in at the Airport Hotel before getting a taxi out to Finger Pier for the Sekupang ferry. It was utter chaos, as several ferry companies left from the same dock. Brendan queued first to get his return ticket validated, then again for immigration, then finally for the ferry. A massive backlog at immigration had many people looking nervous about making the boat, which left suddenly after Brendan boarded at 4.50pm. It took him across to Batam Island, only 20km and 45 minutes away, but part of Indonesia, his 120th nation. Crossing the Singapore Strait was lovely, with Brendan avoiding the over-crowded air-conditioned lower decks and letting the breeze cool him on the top deck as he enjoyed the panoramic view.

From Batam you could get a boat to everywhere else. But Batam was also a tax-exempt multinational industrial estate and colony for ex-pats servicing the industry. The other lure on Batam, if the posters on the sea-front were anything to go by, was the naughty nightlife. Brendan, however, was only interested in handing over the GNT, then returning to Singapore for his evening appointment at the Wesley Methodist Church on Fort Canning Road. He quickly found an Indonesian lady who seemed happy to accept a gift from a strange Westerner. She said, "Dank You" and smiled. It wasn't the most fruitful evangelistic conversation ever, but it would suffice. Brendan hopped onto the same ferry upon which he'd arrived, much to the astonishment of the ticket-inspector.

***

Brendan had got out of the habit of speaking in public. The last "speaking engagement" was in Kuwait and seemed a long time ago even though it was actually less than three weeks. When he arrived at the old English-style church it was buzzing. Singapore was one of those places where mega-churches were the order of the day, and he was told that there were over 3,000 people worshippers across the 12 services they held every Sunday. It was a bit different from Jact.

There were only(!) about 800 people packed in for his talk. The senior pastor apologised that there weren't more, but with the changes in the schedule due to Nepal, they'd only had two days to publicise his arrival and make arrangements. Brendan was buoyed by the crowd and, as ever with a good audience, relished telling the stories of his trip so far. The one that had the most impact was the Somalian pirates, a tale which rang true because of piracy in the straits between Singapore and Sumatra. The audience enjoyed the evening too and gave generously into an offering. Brendan finally managed to shift some of his "business cards" – virtually all the ones he had in English, plus a few in Mandarin Chinese and Filipino.

***

The next morning he caught a bus across the Causeway to Johor Bahru, which was in Malaysia. He went through a similarly truncated "witness opportunity", this time with a shopkeeper, and returned to the Airport Hotel in Singapore in good time for his flight to Brunei.

***

Unsurprisingly for a country with such a wealthy reputation, the Brunei airport was rather swanky, but compared unfavourably without a harpist. Outside the air-conditioned concourse, Brendan immediately started to wilt in the tropical humidity, and dived into the Airport Hotel before he faded away in a puddle of sweat. He wondered how people lived in this sort of sticky climate, especially as he saw people wandering around in suits and ties as well as more sensible casual clothes. The hotel receptionist was charmingly sympathetic, and happy to suggest where he should eat and where the nearest church was.

10% of the population were supposed to be Christian, and Brendan set off with high hopes for the St. Andrew's Anglican Church. He met one of the pastors, who explained that whilst it was technically OK to be Christian, they weren't allowed to evangelise and the importing of Bibles and Christian literature was forbidden. Brendan told him that Brunei scored 29th worst on the Open Doors World Watch List, handed over his illegally-imported GNT and asked him to pass it on to the most suitable recipient. He then invited Brendan to address a housegroup meeting that evening, so Brendan went back to the pastor's house, where 15 people gathered for a meal and prayer. The room was full and happy, with a sort of blitz-mentality "boldness in the face of adversity", similar to Comoros. It all seemed a million miles from Singapore's mega-church brand of Christianity, even though it was only an hour and a half away by plane.

The next morning he caught a ten-minute flight to Kota Kinabalu just up the coast in Malaysia, which cost him 29 ringgit (about £6), and flew on from there to Zamboanga at the southern tip of the Philippines.

***

Fahada received the phone call in her lunch break, direct to her mobile phone. In some ways, it was the call she'd been dreading. Yet she needed to be put out of her growing sense of uncertainty. "Saeed here."

"Hello Saeed, what can I do for you?"

"I want to do some last-minute checks with you about the infidel's schedule." Fahada shook her head in exasperation – why was everything so black and white to some people, especially the fanatics?

"What do you want to know?"

"Tell me the arrangements for the infidel getting to East Timor."

Fahada opened up that document on her laptop. "Tomorrow, November 19th, he flies to Brunei from Singapore on Singapore Airlines 2.50pm direct flight, then on the 20th he flies via Kota Kinabalu to Zamboanga in the Philippines by South East Asian Airways, arriving at 11.50am local time, then flying by private charter to Dili, East Timor."

"So, to confirm," said an excited Saeed. "He takes off from Zamboanga airport in a private chartered plane sometime early afternoon on the 20th, and is due to arrive in Dili that evening. Can you give me details of the charter plane?"

"It's a Let L-410 Turbolet officially retired in 2008 from a charter company called Zest Airways[73], but the Zest boss knows Esther so it's been organised between them."

"And why is he not going on a commercial flight?"

"Because there aren't any to East Timor except by Bali or Darwin, which was too big a detour for him. What are you planning to do?"

Esther never heard a reply, if Saeed ever made one, because the phone went dead.

***

Brendan's trip to Zamboanga City airport, at the tip of Mindanao Island in the Philippines, was brief but effective, because (as planned) he handed the GNT to a Roman Catholic nun waiting there. He needed to press on to East Timor for an evening meeting in Dili with Roman Catholic leaders. East Timor and the Philippines were the only predominantly Christian nations in Asia, but East Timor was struggling to survive after its epic fight for independence from Indonesia, and suffered dire poverty because of trade blockades and transport problems, as well as frequent riots and military uprisings. It wasn't a very safe place.

At Zamboanga, Brendan walked across to the Zest hanger 300m down from the main terminal, and met Barry, a ruddy-faced, pot-bellied American who was the pilot of the turboprop plane, which had 19 seats but only the one passenger for this series of trips. Brendan was going from Zamboanga to Dili, then on to Palau via a refuelling at Sorong in Papua province, and from there to Fukuoka in Japan after refuelling twice: first at Tuguegarao on the northern tip of the Philippines, then Naha on Okinawa. It was the sort of route for which you needed your own plane – so it was a good job that Brendan knew Esther who knew someone who owned a few planes and didn't mind letting him have one for a week.

The flight began with Brendan sitting, by invitation, in the co-pilot's seat. "Don't press anything," said Barry, with a laugh. "But if I keel over, grab the controls and yell "Help" into the radio." With that, he laughed loudly, did his pre-flight checks, taxied round to the runway and took off so smoothly it was like being in a computer game. "It gets a bit boring now until we come in for landing, so why don't you go back and catch some Zs? If you lie across the back seats you can just about lie out

---

[73] Zest Airways, formerly Asian Spirit, is a successful airline based in Pasay City, Philippines. Its last Let L-410 was retired in 2008.

flat. I'll yell if I'm dying." He had a cracking sense of humour, but it didn't really put Brendan at ease. The hum of the engines, though, quickly lulled him off to sleep.

***

Brendan woke up to Barry yelling at him, "Brendan, I'm dying! Grab the controls. Grab the controls. Radio Mayday. Help!" But after an abrupt adrenalin rush, he realised he'd been dreaming. Barry *was* shouting at him, though. "Come on, you sleepy beggar, wake up. We're approaching Dili now, just turning for the approach. Do you want to come up here or stay where you are?" Brendan grunted that he would stay where he was. "Well, put your seat-belt on."

As Brendan sat up and fastened his seat-belt he noticed that they were still over the ocean, but crossing an island just off the East Timor shoreline. He watched as a bright light flashed from behind a truck and a plume of smoke shot up like a flare, but it meant nothing. A fraction of a second later, there was a huge flash in the cockpit and a massive noise that instantly became nothing as his eardrums ruptured, pain instantly searing through his head as he closed his eyes and screamed. The last thing that registered with him was heat and an intense feeling of being squeezed and crushed and the sudden realisation that he couldn't escape. Then everything disappeared and he was somewhere else and he didn't care any more.

Chapter 47: Termination

Fahada heard the news on CNN. A small plane had been blown up as it approached an airport in East Timor. Her heart sank yet raced as she alerted Esther, who rushed down the corridor to Fahada's office. They watched the newsflash again and kept watching as more details came in, confirming their suspicions. Esther phoned the boss of Zest to find out if he knew anything more, and managed to connect even though, understandably, he was a bit busy dealing with the immediate aftermath, confirming that there were only two people on the plane and asking Esther to contact "Mr. Priest's family" while he contacted the pilot's.

Esther phoned the numbers she had for Ruth and Louisa, but could only get through to their voicemails. She didn't want to leave a message except to ask them to contact her as soon as possible. Ruth rang back an hour later from Kampala, and Esther had the dreadful task of explaining what had happened and that they were awaiting further news. Louisa phoned three hours after that, at the end of her shift, and Esther told the story again, with the added detail that they'd found some debris from the plane near the airport at Dili. It had only been a few hundred feet high when the explosion had happened, but there was no news about any survivors. The wreckage was scattered, and they were expecting more news any time soon.

***

The news, when it came from the Zest HQ, was not good. The plane's cockpit had been obliterated by the explosion so there was no chance that the pilot could have survived. The fuselage was dreadfully smashed up and they hadn't found the tail section yet, so there was not a lot of hope for Brendan either. They would phone with any news as soon as they got it. Distraught ever since the first news broke, Esther was now calmer but still dreadfully upset, and Fahada comforted her, wondering how soon Holy War would come after Esther. She busied herself passing the news on to Ruth and Louisa, who were crying on the other end of the phone and obviously didn't know what to do.

***

An hour later came confirmation that the remains of the pilot had been found in the wreckage. He'd been killed instantly as the bomb went off in the cockpit – if a bomb was indeed what had happened. Air-accident investigators were flying in from Darwin to examine the wreckage, but there was no sign of Brendan's body, or the lost tail section.

Esther was inconsolable. "I can't believe it. Poor, poor Brendan. I feel so *responsible!* What on earth can I say to Ruth and Louisa?" Fahada tried to comfort her, but Esther couldn't stop repeating the same phrases, over and over again. Fahada passed the latest message about the pilot to the girls, but nobody knew how to react. There was still no concrete news about Brendan either way. The waiting was awful.

Half an hour later came the news that the tail section had been recovered from a beach, but again there was no sign of Brendan's body. Esther was ashen by this time, and started shaking, and Fahada got worried so called Security to get the Oracle doctor. "And be quick about it!" The doctor arrived, instantly gave Esther some medication to calm her down and told her to rest. It was like telling Dracula to try an apple. Esther was buzzing and fizzing and ranting and pacing and shouting and weeping. She didn't know what to do, but there was no way she was going to rest.

An hour later, finally, came news about Brendan: a section of seats had been discovered in the middle of some rocks on the deserted beach, and Brendan had been found strapped into his seat, *and he was still alive* – conscious, with some bad injuries, but *alive!* There were no further details at that point, but Esther was thrilled, and insisted on phoning the girls herself.

"He's alive! They've found him. He seems to be injured but we don't have any more details. He's conscious though, so hopefully it won't be anything too serious. I'm flying out there and I'll get you out there too as quickly as possible. But it's good news, at last!"

***

Brendan awoke into a blurry world of light and shadow, with figures floating across his vision and a deep, grinding sense of pain somewhere and everywhere. He couldn't feel anything, yet knew that he could move. But when he tried, he felt that nothing connected and things were clicking as if some parts of him weren't as they should be. He could hear a deep silence that was complete but wasn't comforting. He felt something cold on his face, then saw a face mouthing something at him, but it was like TV when the mute was on. Something pulled at him, and he felt a sudden release and unbearable pain in his chest and his arms, and then his legs as he was picked up and bounced. Every movement was agony. Then oblivion. One minute: pain, everywhere; then nothing. The drugs kicked in but he was unaware of anything.

***

"They've got Brendan onto a helicopter en route to a hospital." That was the report which Esther received and passed on to Ruth and Louisa. Then, to Fahada, "How are you getting on with flights for Ruth and Louisa?"

"It's not going to be cheap. Newcastle to Dili is 13,000km; Entebbe to Dili 10,300km; Detroit to Dili for us in the Learjet is 15,300km, so we're talking big distances and two Gulfstreams, which Jet Taxi are offering us for $45,000. Is that OK?" Esther nodded without thinking about it. "They say that they should be able to get Louisa from Newcastle to Dili in 17 hours and Ruth from Kampala in 11 hours. We should get there in 19 hours in the Learjet, factoring in the refuelling stops, so they'll probably get there before us."

"Let's go," said Esther.

Fahada wanted to ask about the re-scheduling of Esther's other commitments – the meetings and shows of "See Esther" over the next few days, and so on. But Esther was now focussed totally on Brendan, and nothing else mattered, including Fahada herself. "This is not going well," Fahada mumbled under her breath. Even so, surely Brendan couldn't keep going after this, could he? She kept her thoughts to herself, of course – she'd have to be very careful how she played this...

***

Louisa got the phone message at the end of the worst shift yet. She was still undecided as to what she should do with the video evidence of Sister Lilian's abuse, but that all disappeared as she phoned the number Esther had given her, fearing the worst and having those fears confirmed. First, "Plane crash". Then, as she stepped into a taxi, "Feared dead". She rushed home, continually monitoring her phone. Later, the message was "No sign of a body". Then, at last, wonderfully, "Found alive but injured". Finally, "Gulfstream for you and Ben at Newcastle Airport".

She phoned Ben at the first alert that the plane had crashed, before she knew any more details, telling him to get home as quickly as possible. They hugged each other through the other messages, then threw some clothes into a bag and grabbed a taxi to the airport.

***

Ruth received the message surprisingly calmly, almost as if she'd been expecting something to happen. She phoned Paul who was up in Gulu, and told him to grab a car and get down to Kampala as fast as he could. It would take him at least seven hours. During that time she sat in the Watoto office in Kampala, dazed, surrounded by people sharing the vigil with her, empathising as bulletins arrived, trying to encourage Ruth but also not set her up for further heartbreak later. Finally, just before Paul came through the door, the phone rang again to say that her Dad had been found alive but injured – and Ruth instantly burst into tears with the receiver still at her ear.

Everyone round her kept a respectful silence, assuming the worst because of the tears, ready to start bereavement support, only for Ruth to put the phone down, pause, then shout, "They've *found* him! He's *alive!*" Everybody cheered wildly, only to hush again as Ruth said that he was being taken to hospital with serious but unknown injuries. Then Paul arrived, and Ruth collapsed into his arms.

Half an hour later, Ruth received the final message about a Gulfstream ready to take them both to East Timor – and she and Paul rushed off to pack some clothes.

***

Back in Dili, Brendan had been taken straight to the General Hospital, run by the International Red Cross. It was only a small 210-bed hospital, but had a small Intensive Care Unit and a dedicated surgical team. Badly-battered but anaesthetised, Brendan was taken straight to the operating theatre, because at the very least he needed the horribly-visible compound fractures in both arms pinned. One leg was broken too, and his shoulders dislocated or broken, as well as several ribs. They were more concerned, though, about internal injuries. More fatalities happened after a bomb through "blast lung" than external injuries from debris or bomb fragments, and they were anxious to check for other internal injuries and brain damage. His eardrums had ruptured, which is why his hearing had gone, but burns up his eyelids indicated that he'd instinctively shut his eyes and probably saved his sight. He was burnt too on his face and arms, but nothing too serious, as the seats in front must have shielded him from most of the heat, pressure wave and flying debris.

The air-accident investigators were already at the wreckage trying to work out what had happened. Fortunately for Brendan, the plane had been very low, so the injuries sustained hadn't been made worse or fatal by the impact on the ground. The seat into which Brendan was strapped had shielded him from penetrating injury on the rocks, and he'd survived principally because the seat "landed" backwards between rocks and slammed to a halt against one particularly huge rock without somersaulting. His limbs had been thrown about, though, which is why he had so many fractures and dislocations.

***

Within 36 hours of the explosion, Brendan was sitting up in bed on the post-operative ward, able to hold a conversation with a mightily-relieved Ruth and Louisa, and Ben and Paul were waiting outside with Esther and Fahada. Brendan had already been interviewed by the Timorese police and the crash investigators, and told them what he'd seen out of the window as they flew over the offshore island. The investigators nodded knowingly, as if what Brendan was describing matched their initial findings. The surgeon also came, and told him that they'd "reduced" his dislocated shoulders and done the pinning of both forearms. His lower leg fracture had not needed pinning, but he had a plaster cast on his leg as well as both lower arms. He had six rib fractures but there was no obvious internal damage, and the way he'd recovered consciousness after the surgery encouraged them to rule out brain injury. His ears would heal but it might take some time.

He'd also been visited the day before by none other than the President of East Timor, José Ramos-Horta[74]. The president suggested that the beach at Dili must have some kind of good-luck charm about it, as he himself survived an assassination attempt in 2008 because he'd been jogging on the same beach when his home was attacked, so he avoided the initial massacre and returned only to get shot "a few times". The president offered his regret for the "incident" and explained that the fight to retain democracy in East Timor was still a struggle. Since he won the Nobel Peace Prize in 1996, the international community initially stirred into action to offer arms-length support, but since independence they'd been left largely to themselves. "It was in partnership with the Church that we won and have kept our independence," he continued. "And that was recognised when Bishop Carlos Belo and I won the Peace Prize together. He's now working in Maputo, the last I heard, as a missionary."

Brendan smiled. It sounded like the Carlos who'd got Brendan's pink bike. It was amazing how God brought different individuals in his story together. He told the story of the pink bike to the President, who laughed. "That sounds like my friend Carlos. He was always keen to get something for nothing!"

When Ruth and Louisa arrived, they had a bit of a cry, which Brendan joined in with and not just out of politeness. The incident had really shaken him, because Barry was dead, and he'd very nearly been killed as well. Then Ruth and Louisa left, and Esther and Fahada came in, and Esther burst into tears so Brendan started crying again. They shared a clumsy "virtual hug" which was awkward because of the casts on Brendan's arms, the gauze on his face protecting the burns, and the fragility of his torso because of the broken ribs. Fahada kept back, but asked if she could take some photos of him, which made him laugh, which hurt, and made him cry again. She snapped away while Brendan chatted with Esther.

---

[74] The President, José Ramos-Horta, survived an assassination attempt on 11th February 2008, in exactly these circumstances. The 1996 Nobel Peace Prize was shared by him and Bishop Belo, for their efforts towards East Timor's peaceful transition to independence. Carlos Belo is, indeed, at the time of writing, a missionary in Maputo. The conversations and depictions of both individuals, however, are entirely fictional.

"Well, Brendan," said Esther. "I guess that puts paid to our project, doesn't it? There's no way we can carry on now."

"What do you mean?" asked Brendan.

"Well, look at you. I can't see you kayaking up South America or biking through Europe after injuries like this."

"Why not?" said Brendan. "The doctor reckons that it'll take about a week or ten days before they're prepared to discharge me, and then I'll have the plaster casts off in another three weeks or so. So there's no reason why I shouldn't continue."

Esther shook her head and smiled. Fahada dropped her pen and stared at him. "I suppose that's good news, Brendan," said Esther. "But you'll be way behind schedule. Let's just wait and see."

***

Two days later, the air accident investigators confirmed that Brendan's plane had been hit by a missile, fragments of which, found in the plane cockpit, had given a very precise identification. It was a 9K38 Igla missile, Russian-built, but one of a batch sold to Egyptian Islamists in 2002. It would have been fired by a single operator from a shoulder-launcher, which is what Brendan must have seen. They'd handed over the case to a specialised CIA unit, because Barry was an American citizen and this was being regarded an act of terrorism.

Fahada's known background as a Muslim and her origins in Egypt meant that her mobile phone and laptop were impounded immediately "just as a precaution", and her filing cabinet back in Detroit was examined too "as a precaution". It was quickly discovered that her immigration papers were false so she was arrested in Dili and escorted on a plane back to America.

Esther was interviewed at length in her hotel in Dili about what she knew of her personal assistant and the Oracle recruiting procedures which had been duped so easily. She was exonerated of any personal accountability but warned that she'd probably be called as a witness in Fahada's trial, though that was a long way off.

***

One thing was sure: Fahada's career as a terrorist had been abruptly terminated.

Chapter 48: Stagnation

There were various theories about the source of the phrase "it all went pear-shaped". Jack Taylor favoured the glass-blowing origin, because it described what was happening at Jact perfectly. If a glass vessel being blown was heated too vigorously, it became too fluid and distorted under gravity as it cooled, resulting in a pear-shaped vessel instead of a sphere. To Jack, Caridad appeared to have warmed things up at Jact rather too quickly, and now that things were cooling down under Cecil, it was all going saggy, blobby and heavy.

After Ben's departure, the youth club didn't come back. Nearly 67% (i.e. two) of the total attendance at the Bible Study reported to Cecil that they'd felt intimidated by the tattooed young men hanging around the church as they went in for their Friday penance of Bible Study with Cecil. Now the doorway was clear, the building was quiet, the Bible Study uninterrupted by any noise except the deafening silence of what was missing. The numbers at the Bible Study dwindled too, because Mrs. Edwards (the other 33.3%) did her back in. Despite the low numbers, Cecil prepared diligently, the two attendees listened dutifully and that was about all anyone could say about it. By mid-December they reached the fourth verse of the opening chapter of Romans but had got a bit bogged down for the last few weeks on "the Spirit of holiness". Cecil was excited that by Easter they would reach the opening greetings in verse seven, where Paul finally says hello.

Sarah Lanleigh abandoned the Bible Study after the first two weeks and got quite cynical after Ben left. She had a theory that Cecil was either paying the two old ladies to keep going, or had offered a prize to the last one remaining. Another theory was that they were only allowed out of the rest home on a Friday night and, having been barred by the pub for shouting out answers in the quiz, went to the only other place that was warm. They didn't come on a Sunday, so nobody except Cecil knew them or ever saw them around and about. Sarah herself kept attending Sunday worship, but the main reason was to chart the downward spiral. She kept a graph at home on which the decline looked like a ladder against a wall.

Methodism had a curious ritual each year called the October Count, in which the church was required to tell headquarters how many were attending worship. In the last year of Brendan's appointment, the numbers had been boosted up to a weekly average of 57, mainly due to the Harvest Festival falling on the first week of October and a baptism boosting the numbers later on. The following October, Caridad and his family boosted the figures up to 65 (even though the Harvest was the last week in September), and then the next year they rose to 111. Cecil's first October managed 108 *in total*, over five Sundays, an average of 22 when it was rounded up. And he'd only arrived in September. By any standard, it was a notable achievement to have ruined everything so quickly.

By mid-December the usual congregation was down to 12, but was slightly higher when it was a preacher from elsewhere in the Circuit. Cecil asked the Superintendent to plan him at Jact as often as was allowed, which made the Super's dilemma worse. Everyone in the Circuit had heard how uninspired and uninspiring Cecil was, so no-one really wanted him to preach at their chapel. What could the Super do? At the following week's Circuit Meeting, with Cecil present, someone commented that Jact seemed to be stagnating, whereupon Sarah Lanleigh stood up and addressed the Superintendent Minister who was chairing the Meeting. "It's not stagnating, it's poisoned. It's got way beyond stagnation. Even algae and lower forms of pond-life couldn't stay alive in the lifeless atmosphere at Jact. You need to act quickly or it'll be gone forever."

The Super went home and phoned the District Chair. Something had to be done.

Chapter 49: Nations 126 - 129

It was now nearly a fortnight since the terrorist attack, and much had happened while Brendan waited for his injuries to heal: Fahada had been arrested and deported back to America where, presumably, she would eventually stand trial; Esther had encamped outside his hospital room during the day and taken up residence in the poshest hotel in Dili at night; Ruth and Paul were in the same hotel, as were Louisa and Ben; and Brendan himself was growing increasingly restless and at the same time increasingly determined. "Don't you see?" he said to Ruth, "This is a very powerful opportunity to witness. I'm a hot news item and this is a real chance to say and do something very powerful for the Kingdom."

"Or is it just pig-headedness on your part – the Priest testosterone having one final fling?"

"Yes," he sighed. "I suppose there is a bit of that as well. But I wasn't just thinking of carrying on, showing true grit and determination and so on. I was thinking about Fahada."

"What do you mean?"

"Forgiving her, and saying so to the media. And...," he paused but then pressed on quickly, before she could interrupt, "...it wouldn't be all show. I really *do* feel sorry for her. It looks as if she's been groomed all her life by these terrorists and didn't have much choice. Then she got confused by her feelings for Esther, and it got twisted and came out wrong. I really don't feel anything but pity for her."

"Oh Dad," said Ruth, placing her hand on top of his. "I think that's lovely. By all means do that – but I'm still not sure that you're fit enough physically or mentally to carry on."

***

Later on that morning, he broached the subject to Louisa, but it was harder work.
"What are you on about, Dad? She tried to *kill* you!"

"I know she did, Louisa, but what good is there in retaliating or ranting about her? I've always preached that when disaster strikes you've got a choice: either to witness to the power of good over evil by showing restraint and forgiveness, or to witness to the power of evil over good by turning vindictive and vengeful. And I think I now know what that means."

"Well, it's OK for you to preach on telly about forgiveness, but what about Barry's family – how are they going to feel?"

"Yes," said Brendan. "That's a good point. I don't know what they're going through. I don't know anything about them. But surely I shouldn't let that affect anything I say. I've got to be true to me and what I believe in."

Louisa sighed. "I know – but it's all so wrong. She may not have killed you, but she's killed off your chances of finishing the journey, so Watoto won't get anywhere near the funds they need."

"But I *am* going to carry on, Louisa. They'll still get their money, and the care they deserve – probably *more* when people hear that I'm carrying on."

"But how *can* you, Dad? How *can* you carry on when you're stuck here like Mister Stiff?" – at which they both burst out laughing. It was so true – he did look rather incapacitated for someone who was supposed to be rushing around the world.

Brendan drew breath. It still hurt when he laughed. "I've been looking at the schedule with Esther. She's going to help – coming with me to Palau and Japan in the Learjet. Then she returns to the States and I'm on public transport for a fortnight, most of it sitting on the Trans-Siberian Railway all the way to St. Petersburg. Then I'm speedboating down to Belgium, hopefully with Paul crewing as my arms and leg will still be in plaster. But then I nip across to London to get the casts off, and I'll be on my way again. My old friend Arnold in Detroit has taken over my schedule and he's pretty confident that with a bit of tweaking we can still complete it all within the year, if we get a few lucky breaks." They both burst out laughing again as they realised what he'd just said.

"I don't know what to say, Dad. I think you're mad, but I do love you." And with that, Louisa wrapped her arms gently around him, and whispered in his ear. "I'm dead proud of you, Dad."

It meant the world to him. His daughters mattered hugely to him – and not just because they were his daughters. He'd come to the conclusion that most of his first journey – and indeed most of this journey so far – was still only witnessing to "Jerusalem". The apostolic commission in Acts 1:8 was to go to Jerusalem – but also to Judea and Samaria and to the ends of the earth, and whilst geographically he'd done that, culturally he hadn't. He was still, largely, talking with people who shared his own faith and cultural outlook. But Ruth and Louisa were Judea and Samaria to him. He realised, as parents often realise only afterwards, that he'd become slowly cut off from them culturally and thus socially. They'd still been polite with their Dad (and he with them) but there'd been no real sharing of moments or stories because they were now moving in different circles. But somehow, accidentally, almost *because of* the journey, they too had got caught up in what it meant to "live as if it were true" (as his old College Principal defined faith) and realised, like their Dad, that mission was what it was all about. Without realising it, he'd been witnessing to them too – his own Judea and Samaria. And taking God's call seriously had borne fruit even in his own family.

Brendan had come to realise, as he journeyed, that there was only so much that he could do. The real work of mission to which he was pointing everyone was not flitting around the world like he was doing. His was a bit of a one-off calling – a sort of globe-trotting symbol of and pointer to *real* mission, which involved knuckling down to live out faith in communities, with others, over years of patient witness and incarnational living – like he'd done in Jact. He also knew instinctively that he was called to be a visitor to foreign cultures rather than a settler within one of them, and that he'd found his "missiological niche". Everyone was different, but this role of globetrotting "advert" was right for him, he felt. Whether some would interpret that harshly was up to them. At least with Ruth and Louisa he seemed to be doing it right.

***

Later that afternoon, Brendan and Esther planned their interview for the following morning, which had to be filmed at 3am to catch the 2pm live slot in Detroit. For the last fortnight Oracle had been showing old footage, recorded for just such an eventuality, but tonight's was going to be a mega-show, already syndicated to be shown simultaneously by many other broadcasters around the world. They would share the live feed at Brendan's hospital bed in East Timor – a nation which few people had heard of before this but now was on everybody's lips. Fahada's snaps of a battered, bruised, bandaged and plastered Brendan, released to whet people's appetites, had appeared on newspaper front pages across the world.

On the stroke of 3am, in the darkened hospital, bright lights shone on Brendan, and Esther theatrically strode in and sat by his bed as the introductory music played. Arnold and the techies had flown in to ensure that the world heard and saw Esther in East Timor – all through a few cameras, cables and satellites. Brendan thought wistfully that if John Wesley had had this sort of technology, the world really would have been his parish. By design, Ruth and Louisa were sitting either side of Brendan, holding his outstretched hand. It was a bit corny, but Esther assured them that America liked corny. It seemed manipulative to the five British people present, but Esther was quite firm. "I know what I'm doing," she announced, in a voice that discouraged opposition.

Esther told the story of what had happened. It wasn't really news to anyone, because the world had been intrigued by the shadowy figure of Fahada, and she'd become a Mata Hari figure as her secret life as a spy within Oracle was embellished beyond recognition. Esther had been ready for the headlines about their relationship, but got embarrassed only when the media hyped up how easily she'd been hoodwinked and manipulated by this exotic Muslim terrorist. Then she turned to Brendan, and the camera panned in on his gauze-protected face. "What do you think about what's happened, Brendan?"

He paused, not just for dramatic effect but to get his thoughts in order. "I feel sorry that my new friend Barry lost his life because of me. I apologise to his family for having unwittingly drawn him into danger and I feel a great weight of responsibility for what has happened, even though I know it wasn't my fault. I also feel sad that someone felt that they wanted to kill me. What I've been saying all along is that the world should pull together to help each other, rather than keep up this relentless and fruitless power-struggle to be top dog. What would be gained by silencing me? I just hope that I can still play my part in making the world a better place. Talking of which, the big news is that I'm going to carry on. My two daughters support me in this, though they took a bit of persuading. I want to complete the task of going to all nations by May 16th next year. I want to continue raising money for Watoto's work amongst the disadvantaged people of Africa, and highlighting the plight of Christians who are persecuted for their faith." He paused. "I suppose I could be counted as one of them now..." He paused again. "So I'm asking for your continuing support, folks. It's not going to be easy, since these plaster casts have to stay on for the next five weeks, but I'm determined to do it."

"Why does it matter so much to you?" asked Esther.

"Because to give in now would send out the message that evil can destroy what's good. I believe that good triumphs over bad if people trust God to help them. I believe that God's love always wins the day, even though it gets knock-backs along the way. Look at history. Have the various empires lasted? They have for a while, but always there's another one waiting to be that bit more powerful or to have bigger weapons. So what *has* lasted? Well, the Gospel has lasted. The Christian Church hasn't been perfect – far from it in some centuries – but the Gospel message of love has prevailed. I want to continue preaching that message wherever I go and even by the very fact that I'm continuing. Maybe my perseverance is a sign of God's love triumphing over terrorism."

"So what do you feel about Fahada?"

Brendan paused. This was not as easy. He felt both girls spontaneously squeeze his hand. "I feel sorry for her – I really do. I don't know much about what's happened to her in the past, but that's not really the point. I want to say in front of everyone – and maybe Fahada herself, if you're able to watch this from whatever prison you are in back in the States – that I *forgive* you, Fahada. Completely, unreservedly. The world only gets more twisted if we harbour grudges or seek revenge – and that has nothing to do with the Gospel."

Esther paused, to let people take in what he'd just said. "So what happens now?"

"Well, apparently I've been here now for 12 days, but I'd caught up a few days so I'm only about a week behind schedule. I'm well in hand with the non-powered travel, keeping it above 30% on water and land, so I can catch up by altering some of the ways in which I'm going to travel to various countries. But the people back in Detroit have got all that in hand and I'll just do as I am told."

***

The rest of the day was spent sleeping and packing. The doctors fussed around, advising against going and suggesting as much rest as possible, particularly to ease discomfort from his broken ribs. His facial burns were now OK without the gauze and ointment but they recommended that he went carefully and avoided bright sunlight. Via Arnold's plane, Esther had brought Brendan a state-of-the-art electric wheelchair, with both steering and movement operated by a remote which Brendan could hold and use despite all the plaster-casts.

***

Everyone left the following day in Esther's Learjet. It was a bit cramped, with Esther, the three film-crew, stiff-limbed Brendan and four family members, but they all crammed in for the 2,000km flight to Palau.

They were taken by taxis from the airport to the Roman Catholic Church in Koror, where Brendan showed off his wheelchair skills in front of a packed church before the serious conversations about the issues raised in the "See Esther" interview, which everyone in Palau seemed to have watched. Brendan spotted some Muslim women standing at the back of the church, and asked them to come forward. They were very reluctant, but Brendan held out his plastered arms to them, begging them to come as a sign of partnership and friendship. He gave them the Palauan GNT, one of several Arnold had brought with him as hastily-reprinted replacement for the ones blown up in the air crash. The whole gathering applauded, and Brendan felt pleased that he'd been able to forge firmer links between Muslims and Christians in Palau. Maybe it was a sign of fruitfulness to come.

***

The next morning they were off in the Learjet again for Japan, which was over 3,000km away. They would need to refuel on Okinawa, before completing the journey to Fukuoka on the southernmost island of "mainland Japan". Okinawa emerged from the endless blue sea as a refuge for their fuel-starved plane. They didn't see much of it, because they landed, taxied to a different stretch of concrete round the corner from the main terminal, refuelled while they stayed on the plane, then taxied out and took off again.

They landed at Fukuoka airport an hour later, and said their farewells. Ruth and Paul helped Brendan off the Learjet and escorted him in his wheelchair into the main terminal. Esther and the Americans were flying on to Tokyo, and would be going from there back to Detroit via Attu in the Aleutians, Anchorage in Alaska, and Seattle – all of which were on American soil. Louisa and Ben were flying with them back to Detroit, and would then catch the earliest flight they could back to Newcastle, for they had their job futures to sort out. Ruth and Paul were staying around with Brendan till they could put him onto the Trans-Mongolian train at Beijing. Ruth had another meeting there before flying back to Uganda, and Paul was flying on to make preparations in St. Petersburg to help Brendan with a further section of the journey.

In the airport, Brendan found it weird seeing no signs in English script and was glad that he was being escorted – because there was no way that he could have found his way on his own. Ruth somehow managed to sort out where they were going and how to get there. They were taxied off first to Nishitetsu Grand Hotel, then to the Daimyomachi Catholic Church for the 4pm Mass and the informal reception arranged for afterwards.

The Japanese Catholic priest spoke excellent English and told Brendan that everyone in the room spoke excellent English too. Brendan was reminded once again how much better than Britain every other country was at speaking several languages. They chatted together about forgiveness, which seemed to be the main topic of conversation. One old man stood up. "Mister Priest, I am 93 years old." Brendan thought that he looked about 60, and smiled in silent respect for his longevity. "I served in the 15th Army during the Second World War and was sent to Burma and Thailand and saw many atrocities. I am ashamed to say that I took part in some awful things and even though I had little choice I am racked with guilt about what happened. I have travelled to Burma and Thailand several times since the end of the war to ask for the people's forgiveness. When I returned back to my home in Nagasaki at the end of the War, I found that my home and my family had disappeared and there was only rubble left of my town. I have met Americans since and I have told them that I forgive them. We Japanese *understand* about giving and receiving forgiveness."

Brendan nodded and bowed in respect. The old man had said it all. Everyone needs both to forgive and be forgiven – it was part of the human condition, across all cultures. Brendan gave the Japanese GNT to the old man, who said that he'd give it to the young couple next door. "They listen to my stories and nod when I tell them about the war, but they don't really understand about forgiveness. Maybe this will help."

***

Brendan, Ruth and Paul got a taxi the next day down to the port and travelled via Beetle to the skyscraper city of Busan in South Korea. The Beetles were a fleet of high-speed hydrofoils owned by JR Kyushu, which shot across the Korea Strait in under three hours, and it was an exhilarating ride. At Busan they caught a KTX train along the Gyeongbu Line to Seoul, which took a further 2½ hours, then took a taxi to the Yoido Full Gospel Church[75] on Yeouido Island, in the heart of the city. This was a visit Brendan had been looking forward to ever since he started planning the journey, for this was the biggest church in the world, with over a million members linked to it. He wanted to see what it was like.

The church headquarters looked from the outside like a football stadium. When he got inside he was handed a brochure and asked if he preferred one of their fleet of mobility scooters during the visit. Brendan's mind went back to the old fold-up wheelchair at Jact that usually sat in the space in the disabled toilet designed for wheelchairs. He hadn't been able to persuade the stewards that this space was for disabled people already in wheelchairs to wheel themselves into, so that they could slide onto the toilet, and not for empty wheelchairs which actually prevented disabled people from accessing the toilet at all. The stewards had nodded in agreement, but the next time he looked the fold-up wheelchair was always back in its usual place.

As well as getting the welcoming right, Yoido seemed to have everything else sorted too. They had a Prayer Mountain for spiritual retreats, their own Hansei University for evangelists, their Elim Welfare Town which was a combination of a job centre and advice centre for the unemployed and homeless. They had 527 pastors and over 100,000 elders and deacons.

Brendan read the story of the church's development, starting with dramatic spiritual healings and powerful preaching from two Korean pastors, Yonggi Cho and Jashil Choi, and from the establishment of cell groups. He went through to the main worship area, which only seated 25,000 at a time, so there were seven services each Sunday, three on Wednesdays, one on Thursdays and Saturdays and a daily all-night prayer vigil and dawn prayer service. And that was just at the headquarters. The church had planted 19 other regional sanctuaries around the country and over 150 "prayer houses" which, along with youth mission projects, employed a further 500 pastors. It all sounded ridiculously successful. Brendan couldn't quite get his head around it all. Was this the ultimate church, or was it something different from a single church? Clearly its strength lay in the cell groups, which functioned as the essential fellowship and missional organism, with over 23,000 of them seeking always to welcome new people and multiply into new cells once their membership reached

---

[75] All details of the church are accurate at the time of writing. Yoido is classed as the biggest church in the world, but it seems actually to operate largely how a denomination operates in most other countries: shared vision, governance, training and resources, with a multiplex approach to how these are delivered simultaneously in many different locations. The individuals are fictional, including the senior pastor – deliberately anonymous and unidentifiable from any of the Yoido leadership or personnel.

double figures. The whole thing was dynamic and expanding rapidly, but what was at its soul?

Brendan asked to see one of the pastors, and was introduced to a smartly-dressed young man who answered Brendan's questions fluently, as if he'd learnt the answers off-by-heart and knew them word-perfect. Was this real? Brendan pressed on beyond the sales-pitch about the senior pastor's vision and dedication to ask what the driving thrust of it all was. Was it a big business? A personal empire? Was it a church or a denomination? What held it together, if anything?

The pastor talked about the cell system, and how it all hinged on that. Obviously it was impossible for a million people to know one another or feel like a family unit, so membership of a cell was crucial. Yoido seemed able to multiply cells (positively) when they were still growing and missional, which contrasted with cell groups in British churches, where the tendency was for someone to force cells to divide (negatively) when they were already too well-established and thus reluctant to sacrifice their togetherness. The Yoido cell system sounded much better to Brendan – the pastor knew what he was talking about and the theology sounded right. The results were pretty spectacular too.

Then the pastor asked about Brendan, and he told him who he was and why he was there. The pastor's eyes immediately lit up and he asked if he could inform the leadership team. Brendan nodded and was then overwhelmed to be presented to none other but the senior pastor himself, who happened to be visiting the church headquarters before going out for the night to Prayer Mountain. He greeted Brendan warmly. "We have heard about you and have prayed for you on Prayer Mountain since the terrorist attack. We keep a constant 24-hour vigil up there and have 45 pastors always in attendance for up to 10,000 people at any one time. We will continue this prayer for you until journey's end – so wherever you are in the world at every moment there will be someone here praying for you."

Brendan was humbled by this, and said so. He asked Ruth to get him the Korean GNT and presented it to the senior pastor, adding, "I know that you don't need a copy of the New Testament for you know it well, but I want to give it to you in recognition that we are partners in mission and seeking to fulfil the Great Commission, albeit in rather different ways."

The pastor was delighted, and thanked Brendan. "I will put it on display in our entrance hall, explaining that even in Britain there are evangelists!" They all laughed.

***

Ruth and Paul went off shopping in Seoul despite the cold and Brendan stayed in the hotel, reflecting on his visit to the church. He didn't think it was better than anywhere else – it was just different. In some ways it was easier here to be a Christian because everything was in place to make it as comfortable and attractive as possible. The following day, however, he was going to the nation where it was hardest of all to be a Christian: North Korea. Was it just coincidence that the easiest country in which to evangelise and the hardest country to just survive in as a Christian shared the same small peninsula?

***

It was only 40km to the border, and every tour company in Seoul seemed to be competing for clientele. Brendan, Ruth and Paul found themselves on a bus with 20 other tourists. Brendan found his thoughts going back to old MASH episodes which were his only real source of knowledge about the Korean War. As they got closer to the Demilitarised Zone (DMZ), the road skirted the edge of the Han River. It could have been any waterway in rural Asia except for the barbed wire punctuated with regular guard towers.

They changed buses and after a cursory passport inspection entered the DMZ at Camp Bonifas. They were taken on an open-top train into the "third infiltration tunnel", one of several shown off as evidence of North Korea's invasion plans, each tunnel designed so that 30,000 troops an hour could pile into South Korea. They then progressed into the Joint Security Area, and were taken into the Peace Pagoda, which seemed a bit of a ridiculous name when everywhere was bristling with the trappings of war and this border was the most heavily armed strip of land on the planet. Perhaps they were heavy on irony, here. Or maybe hope...

They were escorted to the three conference huts which straddled the border, romantically called T1, T2 and T3. Brendan wondered why they needed three of them. Inside were tables with neat lines of microphones on either side of the line marking the border, with both South and North Korean soldiers in intentionally intimidating poses standing guard at either end of the rooms. The guide told them that they were free to walk around the conference room and could cross from South to North if they wished but they shouldn't try to leave by the other exit or try to look at the North Korean guards too closely as eye-to-eye contact was considered intimidatory. Brendan was carrying the second Korean GNT on his lap as he drove his wheelchair round the table but there was no possibility of him handing it over to the guard not just because of his plastered arms but because it would probably cause an international incident and get them all arrested.

Outside the conference huts was the so-called Bridge of No Return, which rang all kinds of bells for Brendan about the slave trade, and particularly the Door of No Return on the island off Dakar. After the Korean War, some POWs were given the choice of which side of the bridge to settle – but once they chose they couldn't change their mind – hence the name. But freedom surely meant offering an *ongoing* freedom to choose, didn't it? Anything else was exploitation of the powerful over the weak, which resulted in slavery of one sort or another.

On the way back Brendan reflected that at least he'd taken the GNT into North Korea. The NK guards would have noticed it and the big cross which Brendan was wearing around his neck, which he'd deliberately pulled out from underneath his clothing. He asked the tour guide whether she had any advice about the GNT, and she suggested as they entered the museum in Camp Bonifas that he leave it there. The manager was very interested and took lots of notes because he wanted to make an exhibit out of the GNT – which made Brendan feel much better. Maybe a North Korean would come here and read what Brendan's trip was all about.

Going back down the eerily-empty 12-lane Freedom Road away from the border – designed for South Korean tanks to rush to the border, but with booby-trapped bridges to stop North Korean tanks advancing smoothly on Seoul – Brendan wondered how it would all end. As a lad he'd thought that the Berlin Wall would never come down, that apartheid would not be dismantled and that the Soviet Union was an undefeatable super-power – all of which proved incorrect in a relatively short time-frame. So why did this relatively parochial conflict drag on? How could it be resolved? Was it up to North Korea to give up its ideology and start spending its money on feeding its people, or should the United Nations step up its attempts to negotiate a peaceful settlement? Brendan was glad that he didn't have to find a solution, but hoped that there was someone working on it. It seemed a bit ridiculous to run tours when the only things to see were propaganda and brinkmanship.

Back in Seoul he went again to the Yoido Full Gospel Church, and spent over an hour in the prayer chapel. It didn't seem much of a contribution to the peace effort, but he didn't know what else to do. He wrote a message and posted it into a box of prayer requests which would be taken up to Prayer Mountain and distributed to the intercessors up there.

***

The next day, Ruth, Paul and Brendan took the train from Seoul to Incheon and caught the 1pm ferry, due in at Tianjin 25 hours later. He slept beautifully – even though the cabin he shared with Ruth and Paul was small and the bunk narrow. He awoke stiff-backed, but well-rested. He'd not realised quite how battered his body and mind were, and how difficult it would be when he was on his own.

***

They disembarked a few minutes early, and queued to get through immigration. This was China, from which Brendan had been expelled just a short while ago. His passport didn't include the deportation notice scrawled by the official at Kaxgar, because that passport had been destroyed, along with the rest of his luggage, in East Timor. He hoped that the immigration officials didn't have computerised lists of undesirables. Despite the huddle of officials, they didn't look particularly organised, and Brendan's passport was stamped without further ado. They seemed more interested in Paul because he was black, and were bemused by the fact that he was married to a white woman. Perhaps Brendan should use them as a distraction in the future if there were any more immigration worries.

They crossed to the train station just 100m away from the ferry terminal, with Paul and Ruth trundling their luggage as Brendan whirred along in his wheelchair. They boarded a waiting train only a few minutes before it left, and it was only an hour and 15 minutes more before it eased into Beijing station.

Day: Date	Itinerary (* indicates TV interview) ([18] indicates new nation)	Bike (km)	Car/ Bus (km)	Train (km)	Kayak/ Sail (km)	Boat (km)	Air (km)
Totals brought forward		8713	17093	0	2754	14370	14658
187: 18/11/11	Singapore[120]; via Karimun Besar, Indonesia[121]					40	1090
188: 19/11/11	Johor Bahru, Malaysia[122]; Brunei[123]		16				1290
189: 20/11/11	Zamboanga, Philippines[124]; Dili, East Timor[125]						2648
190: 21/11/11 until 200: 1/12/11	Hospital						
201: 2/12/11	Hospital *						
202: 3/12/11	Palau[126]						1951
203: 4/12/11	Fukuoka, Japan[127]						3078
204: 5/12/11	Seoul, South Korea[128]			442		218	
205: 6/12/11	North Korea[129] and back						
206: 7/12/11	Incheon – Tianjin ferry			176		807	
207: 8/12/11	Beijing (China)			149			
Totals carried forward		8713	17109	767	2754	15435	24715

Chapter 50: Cross-examination

Any building given the name "The George H. W. Bush Center for Central Intelligence" was always likely to raise both an ironic eyebrow and a cynical quip. The CIA HQ in Langley, 15km west of Washington DC, may well have amused many but it was a dour and chilling place for anyone held prisoner there – such as Fahada.

She was presented with the evidence stacked up against her: transcripts of the phone conversations with Saeed; a document file found in her filing cabinet relating to Brendan's schedules, revealingly marked in red whenever his plans had gone wrong; a "scrapbook" file on her laptop about a known Al-Qaeda terrorist who'd been killed in Afghanistan earlier that year; CCTV evidence of her and Saeed meeting in a well-known restaurant in Detroit. It all stacked up, and Fahada knew it.

She confessed to everything, but said nothing about her father, hoping that they wouldn't make the link.

***

Days later, she was brought out from her cell to face another interview.

They had more evidence to show her: forged passport documentation to get her into the United States, faxed from London with MI5 documents about a terror cell based around a fictitious wholesalers in Finsbury; DNA evidence linking her to Mustafa Abu al-Yazid, the Al-Qaeda terrorist killed in Afghanistan; research about the Cairo origins of Mustafa Abu al-Yazid and Egyptian intelligence reports about Holy War; and, most damning of all, birth records for a Fahada al-Yazid, born in Cairo on April 4th 1982. Unluckily for Fahada, Egypt had been a pioneering nation for birth registry, moving from the traditional Arab optional system of registration by midwife to compulsory registration of all children from 1962, with hefty fines for transgressors. So Mustafa Abu al-Yazid (senior) had dutifully registered his daughter a week after her birth, and this was to prove his (and her) undoing.

Saeed had already been arrested by the Egyptian police and was undergoing interrogation in Cairo without any results yet being disclosed to the CIA. The CIA were aware, though, that Egyptian Intelligence knew their home terrorist groups and networks, and that an Embaba raid had netted Mustafa Abu al-Yazid (senior). Routine DNA tests were carried out on everyone arrested in the purge, speeded up in the wake of American requests relating to the family of Mustafa Abu al-Yazid (junior), and the links in the family dynasty had been joined up.

Fahada wept as she heard this news, passed on by a smug CIA official who seemed impassive to her crying. He then showed her a clip from "See Esther" with Brendan's hospital-bed interview, which produced more tears but also amazement about Brendan's declaration of forgiveness. Fahada was bewildered by what Brendan said. There was no way Islam would countenance that sort of mercy because Muslims were expected to adhere to strict codes of justice. If there was one word that captured the essence of all Islamic laws and teachings, it was Justice. She remembered one particular saying from the Qur'an[76]: "We sent aforetime our messengers with clear Signs and sent down with them the Book and the Balance, that men may stand forth in Justice." It had been drilled into her by her father.

Mercy and forgiveness were alien concepts to her. Her father had taught her that mercy was included in the Qur'an but usually it meant refraining from cruelty, administering a quick death, or giving alms to a beggar. But she also knew that these were internal Muslim-to-Muslim guidelines and certainly didn't include non-Muslims. Her father had always seen Christians as infidels and Crusaders, always and in every generation out to crush the followers of the Prophet. She wanted to find out more about Christianity if it enabled people to be as serene as Brendan. It sounded and appeared much more satisfying and fulfilling than the Islam of her upbringing.

She told the man from the CIA everything she knew about her father, her brother, the men who had come to their house when she was a girl, about the arms stash under the floorboards which she wasn't supposed to know about, and about the plot to insert her as a sleeper in a prominent position in the United States. She went back to her cell feeling light-headed. She sat down on her bed and opened the Bible which she'd previously ignored.

---

[76] Al-Hadeed 57:25

Chapter 51: Nations 130 - 133

Brendan waved a Mister Stiff farewell to Ruth and Paul from the Trans-Mongolian Express after they'd ensured that he understood his travel arrangements through to St. Petersburg. Brendan felt suddenly very isolated and helpless as he sat awkwardly in his seat, about to embark on one of the longest train journeys in the world. He discovered within 20 minutes of setting off that there were various contestants for this title, due to the incessant prattling of a fellow-passenger. The most popular claimant, apparently, was the 9,829km Moscow to Vladivostok "Rossiya" seven-day train and especially its weekly extension to Pyongyang in North Korea, which was even longer at 10,267km and nine days two hours. And not a lot of people knew that. Brendan would have happily stayed ignorant. An American candidate for geek of the year explained to the whole seating car that the current longest scheduled train journey was *actually* a through-train from Donetsk in Ukraine to Vladivostok that was longer still, but Brendan's eyes had already glazed over by then and he didn't catch the details[77]. The train was surprisingly modern and clean. The seats were comfortable and Brendan's fears of hard wooden pews, smelly women snoring on his shoulders and people bringing live chickens on board were all unfounded. He kept spotting Westerners, but they seemed to be further down the train, except that is, for Hank, his roommate. Hank, of course, inevitably, was the anorak.

It had been an early start, for the train left Beijing at 7.45am, so Brendan snoozed for a bit to cut out the background hum of Hank explaining to the poor woman directly opposite that at the Mongolian frontier trains were jacked up to have their bogies changed from standard gauge to Russian gauge. At one point Brendan woke to the sound of Hank's voice... "...the manual bogie exchange is due to be supplemented with the faster and automatic variable gauge axle system of the SUW 2000 type made by ZNTK..." before thankfully he fell asleep again. It could have been, of course, one big nightmare and he might not have awoken at all.

The sturdy woman who presided over Coach 317 delivered trays of hot tea in white porcelain cups. As the engine toiled up steep wooded hills, they all jostled for position for the spectacular views of the Great Wall. Even Hank shut up, for a moment. The Westerners on the train soon became allies in the struggle to survive Hank. They had plenty of time to talk in the corridor and the dining car because the seats on the train's west side became uncomfortably hot in the afternoon sun. They gazed at large sheep herds as the landscape changed from trim green gardens and tidy fields to tawny-brown soilscapes.

---

[77] I have researched this as thoroughly as I can. There do seem to be people who get excited about this sort of information – but nowhere could I find the actual distance covered by the Donetsk-Vladivostok train.

"Lunch open," cried an attendant – oddly in English, and incongruously at 4pm. They drifted up to the dining car and Brendan had a $3 dinner of fried chicken and rice from a menu heavy on pork. The sun, a yellow-pink ball, was already sinking towards the dusty gray horizon. They stopped regularly at provincial stations, which gave the passengers an opportunity to get out of their seats, wander off the train, buy food from the station vendors, go to the station toilet, or just dive for any vacant seat further away from Hank. He got very excited at Datong, because it was apparently the last place in the world which still made steam engines, and he described their "Aiming Higher" class in such detail that they all wished there was a sniper they could hire to aim at Hank.

Then came the Gobi. Brendan was experienced at crossing deserts, but only on bikes. Going across on a train would be a much more relaxed experience. Brendan had awoken again to Hank's annoying commentary and decided to find out what there was at the end of the train. He discovered the caboose, an empty storage car which gave a view back along the railway track just travelled. It was magical, and not just because it was Hank-free. The landscape was bleak: endless stretches of untapped beauty, extreme landscapes and rugged terrain, punctuated by an occasional cluster of humans, dilapidated buildings, livestock or piles of rubbish. The uniqueness of it seemed to be that here in Central Asia the territory appeared undiscovered, the desert plains unmapped, the rivers and lakes undeveloped, the forests uncut, the mountains unmined. What Brendan was seeing was almost certainly how it looked centuries, maybe even millennia, ago. The sheer vastness of it all was quite shocking, yet then he found himself wondering how long it would be before they built shopping centres and parking lots.

There was a latent spirituality about the landscape too, Brendan felt. The rugged terrain seemed to be saying loud and clear that humans *don't* reign supreme over the earth – and that we don't and *can't* control the environment. There was a subliminal message here: that, except for the scattered Mongolians glimpsed occasionally eking out a living in the barren desert and the harsh steppe, most of us would die out here, with or without GPS. Brendan reflected ruefully that this was probably why we build railway tracks across deserts and trains to speed over them, and why people think that it's the height of sophistication to travel in jets high above – because we've duped ourselves that by going around it, through it or over it as fast as possible we've somehow overcome it.

At 20.37 precisely, bang on time, they arrived at the Erlian frontier station. Hank shot off the train to witness the "changeover of bogies" as he described it, which reminded Brendan of a schoolboy dare he'd participated in with Tony Hughes when both of them were sporting bad colds. Everyone else waited patiently in the station waiting-room to try to escape the full impact of the triumphal martial music blaring out of the platform loudspeakers, and revelling in the few moments of Hank-free heaven. Brendan decided to celebrate being in Mongolia by going to bed early. He'd upgraded his ticket from second-class (four berth) to first-class (two berth), which meant that he had only one sleeping companion to annoy every night rather than three. It cost him $225 more, but he thought that the extra cost was justified given his awkwardness at getting ready for bed and his clumsiness if he got up in the night. It was comfortable enough, once Brendan had got over the narrowness of the bunk and the bed-cover which looked, felt and smelled horribly similar to his grandma's purple velvet curtains. He was almost immediately confronted with a Chinese immigration official demanding exit paperwork. Brendan drifted off to sleep while waiting for the train to move, only to be woken up by an unsmiling Mongolian officer, ghostlike in her pale makeup and dark lipstick, for a passport check. Hank had appeared, but Brendan didn't care – he had ear-plugs.

Brendan slept well and woke at 7:30am to the train's rhythmic rocking. Opening the blinds, he saw wide, undulating sands beneath a gray watercolour sky. It was like an ocean. He wheeled himself off to the samovar at the end of the car to make himself a cup of tea, then to the caboose to drink it. A sand-blasted town passed slowly by, an old man standing erect in a bright-yellow vest at a railway crossing, his right hand stretching out to signal "Stop!" – even though there was no vehicle in sight.

The sky turned robin's-egg blue. Powder-puff clouds coasted above infinite grasslands. Horses and goats grazed near their herders' white gers, identical to the Kyrgyz yurts. A Mongolian dining car had replaced the Chinese coach, with a more extensive menu that included tasty cheese omelettes with shredded flecks of tough meat. Mongolia's cuisine, Brendan learnt, bore no resemblance to Mongolian fare back home. He wondered what meat it was, then saw a two-humped camel trotting along at the side of the train, only 20m or so from Brendan's window. As he watched, the camel suddenly started urinating down its back legs as it ran, then shot a sloppy green jet out of its backside which stuck to the moistened fur of its legs. It made the omelette taste all the more succulent. He didn't know whether Mongolians ate camels but he hoped that the meat was mutton.

They stopped mid-morning at a town called Choir and were invited during a 25-minute break to have their photos taken at the statue of Mongolia's first cosmonaut, Jügderdemidiin Gürragchaa. Brendan had to write the name down slowly because there was no way he could remember it if anyone asked. Just after lunch, the train pulled into Ulan Bator, where most of the compounds contained gers as well as wooden houses. Brendan waved goodbye benignly at Hank, who looked up briefly from his train guide as Brendan wandered off into the most northerly and coldest capital city in the world. Despite the cold, there were dozens of children begging in the streets outside the station, but he wheeled his way through them to the taxi rank in bewilderment. Where did they all come from? Where, if anywhere, did they live? How did they survive the cold?

The Mongolian countryside had been vast, beautiful, open and clean, but the capital was the opposite. A huge cloud of smog engulfed the city, the streets were full of rubbish and the chaotic roads were a death-trap. And it was cold. Not Resolute Bay cold, but still cold enough to induce instant teeth-chattering after so many hours on a heated train. Brendan used sign-language to explain to the taxi-driver that he was heading for the Roman Catholic Cathedral, and they drove away through the beggars. The newly-finished Cathedral turned out to be a huge round brick building designed to resemble a ger.

The Bishop introduced himself in very good English as Wince (pronounced Vinchay) and gave Brendan a guided tour. It was all very impressive. The Cathedral ran a playgroup, English classes, a technical school, soup kitchens, two farms, and a care centre for 120 disabled children. There were courses in anger management too, in order to try to reduce Mongolian's most prevalent crime – violence against women. The "Verbist Centre" was home to over 100 street children previously living in the sewers.

Brendan's talk that evening felt rather odd – sat in a chair with his limbs spread-eagled. Wince quickly explained what had happened, but everybody here seemed to be an Esther fan and already knew all about it. The audience oooh'd and aaah'd in all the right places, and were especially interested in Brendan's expulsion from China and his encounter with the Yemeni pirates, despite being over 1,500km from the sea. Brendan produced the GNT to more ooohs, and Wince explained that the first Mongolian version of the Bible had only been printed in 2004 so Bibles were still rare. Brendan asked for the GNT to go to the Verbist Centre to be used by the street children, and there was a great clucking of approval.

The next Trans-Mongolian train didn't leave till lunchtime, so Brendan enjoyed a bit of a lie-in, followed by a relaxed morning at the Verbist Centre, hearing of their work with street children, before being driven back to the station in hopeful anticipation of a Hank-less journey. There was no Hank, but there were plenty of passengers on an overcrowded train. Despite this, he managed to find a reasonably empty seating car.

Quickly the scenery outside the window changed from crumbling buildings and derelict factories to gently-sloping hills, and the sky turned from grey smog to cottony-white cumulus clouds lolling in blue skies. Mongolia was as picturesque as it was empty and bereft of non-essentials. Despite the absence of apparent progress, Brendan found it almost impossible to take his eyes off the prodigious nothingness for fear of missing *something*. Then his companions for the next four days appeared, and he began to miss Hank. Perhaps unsurprisingly, Brendan found himself suddenly surrounded by Mongolians rather than Chinese or Russians as on the earlier train.

These passengers were making the journey not because they were keen to check out Moscow's onion-dome architecture or eat borscht, but to offload shoddy goods to people on the train and at every station at which they stopped. Brendan sat silently as he observed their merchandise, which spilled out from huge square canvas bags. Jeans, shirts, blouses, hoodies, sweatshirts, coats, jackets, suits, hats, skirts and dresses (micro-mini, mini, tea length, ballerina length, full length, midi, maxi, small, medium, large, huge and massive), pants and bras, corsets, underwear and socks, doublets and singlets, everything in all manner of fabrics: denim, wool, chiffon, velvet, satin, silk, cotton and colours galore. All displayed on hundreds of plastic mannequins which lined the narrow passageways and the vestibules connecting the cars. The corridors also contained more square canvas bags overflowing with copies of designer purses, travel bags and luggage. The train had suddenly turned into a church jumble sale.

Their arrival at Sükhbaatar at dinner-time saw the Mongolians jumping out onto the platform with mannequins and bags, performing a spontaneous market-scene for the bewildered citizens, before jumping back on board as the train, without warning, started to pull out of the station. The 20km further to the Russian border saw them frantically filling the washroom with hundreds of mannequins and dozens of the square canvas bags, until the train looked like a train again. The border checks were sketchy but still took hours. Brendan went to his bunk while one Mongolian shut himself in the washroom on top of the bags, so that the border guards couldn't get in. There was much banging, but Brendan had his ear-plugs in. He slept well, even when someone barged in to crash onto the top bunk. Meanwhile rain, sleet and snow pounded the train as they traversed the monochrome greys of the Siberian wilderness. Inside, the temperature rose in the muggy atmosphere of unwashed bodies.

Brendan awoke stiff as a board and not just because of his plastered limbs. He staggered upright to stretch his back and get a cup of tea. He had a sore throat and swollen glands and felt dirty. The seating car was full of sleeping Mongolians – and bags and mannequins. It was like his college changing-rooms – steamy, noxious with strange smells of an animal nature, and clothes everywhere. The only things thankfully missing were naked bodies.

They skirted the scenic south-western shoreline of Lake Baikal, reputed to be the world's oldest and deepest lake and to contain over 20% of the world's freshwater supplies. They crossed over countless bridges and through dozens of tunnels, with the clear waters as an ever-present beautiful back-drop. They stopped for half an hour in Irkutsk but the temperature outside the train was -20° so no-one got out – except the Mongolian traders, of course, but when they realised that there were no potential buyers, they piled back in and shut the door.

There followed three days of monotonous, steamy, stale-sweaty inactivity while the frozen eastern steppes sped by outside. Brendan's glands swelled up more and he felt pretty rough as he looked out at the white and grey of Siberia, but it was as if the outside world had stopped existing. There was only the train. The stops got less regular because of the cold, and even when there was a stop the Mongolians stayed inside – continuing with whatever they were doing, whether it was sleeping, sweating, scratching themselves or swearing their guttural curses at each other. They swept through places with names that Brendan had never heard of, but were obviously major towns and cities – and finally reached Omsk on the Irtysh River. This was Brendan's opportunity to leave his Mongolian companions, for here he diverted onto a two-carriage regional train which re-joined the main route at Yekaterinburg after a detour into Kazakhstan at Petropavl.

***

The train stopped in the station at Petropavl after a protracted stop at the border, and – as Brendan had hoped – he was joined by a local couple who didn't know quite what to make of this European with three plaster casts on his limbs. The man, whether fortuitously or providentially, spoke good English and told Brendan that he was a lecturer at the Petropavl College and was travelling to Kurgan with his wife for their annual week's holiday. Brendan explained who he was and what he was trying to do, and they were thrilled to receive the Kazakhstan GNT. They'd never been to church, but his recently-deceased grandmother had been a Christian and would have been pleased that they'd met Brendan and had the chance now to read a Bible. Brendan hoped that there was something for them to do at Kurgan, but when they got out there a few hours later, the town looked as bleak as every other. It seemed very unfair– why could they only have a holiday when the temperature was -20°?

The outside world was still white and grey, but the steppe was gradually folding away into rolling countryside, then foothills promising greater peaks ahead. Indeed, these were the foot-soldiers to the Urals, the Europe/Asia continental divide, marked just outside Yekaterinburg by a white obelisk at the side of the track. Random clumps of trees became great swathes of majestic forest. Herds of animals scratching for grass through the snow gave way to fields for cultivation once the snow went. Then the wild landscape gave way to buildings of a bygone era: tiny onion-shaped domes or the hulks of long-abandoned nuclear plants. More cities: Perm; Kirov; Gorky (officially now Nizhny Novgorod but still calling itself Gorky on its station signs); Vladimir; then, finally, the Yaroslavsky Terminal in Moscow, after nearly 8,000km of railway. The train arrived at 6.07pm, 11 minutes late.

But that wasn't the end of Brendan's railway experience. He wheeled himself down the ramp to the Metro to Belorusskiy Station, just three stops along the Koltsevaya circle line, where he caught the sleeper train to Cologne. Its first stop would be at Minsk, the capital of Belarus and Brendan's next destination. His first-class ticket cost $150, which gave him a single-berth compartment – an easily-justifiable treat after the experiences of the last week. The train left promptly at 9.09pm, and Brendan fell almost instantly asleep. There were no border stops and Brendan almost missed getting off at Minsk at 7am the next morning. At least he felt a little better. His glands were not as swollen, his throat not as sore. The last week had been bewilderingly tiring because of all his mobility difficulties and his illness – yet at the same time utterly dull, just sitting around with little opportunity to talk because of language difficulties, and with very little of interest to see because of the horrible wintry conditions outside. He had plenty of time to think because of all this, and had come to some interesting conclusions about himself, his journey – and about mission.

He'd felt very little bond, if any, with the surly Mongolian traders, which had shocked him. He'd thought that he'd feel some affinity with everyone – but their hardness, and their desire to make money at all times, had really shocked him. He found them utterly unlikeable. They'd got the entrepreneurial spirit of western capitalism without anything else, as if it was a new religion at which they'd thrown themselves wholeheartedly but unthinkingly. He'd have had nothing to say to them, even if they'd shared a common language. So what did that say about him? And what did it say about God's call to mission? They clearly were very different from him – neither Jerusalem nor Judea/Samaria – but the call was also to go to the ends of the earth...

He'd wrestled with this and come to the conclusion that he was not cut out for evangelising to Mongolian black-marketeers. In a way, he found this comforting, because it didn't mean that there was something wrong with him, rather it was further evidence of his long-held belief that evangelisation was most effective when it came from within a shared culture, like Steve Saint amongst the Waodani with whom he'd chosen to live and work. Missionaries had to spend *time* with people. This challenged the usefulness of him thrusting GNTs into the hands of surprised residents of the various countries he visited, sometimes ridiculously fleetingly. The purpose of this, however, was not to kid himself that he'd played a significant role in bringing the Gospel to these individuals or their countries, but to provide a symbol of the worldwide calling to engage in mission.

Brendan knew himself. At root he was a shy individual who felt out of his depth in unfamiliar surroundings, so it was courageous for him just to dare to enter countries very different from Britain, let alone attempt to engage with individuals there. Brendan felt that he was acting in a representative role, bringing the Church's care into those situations – like in Jact. He was not just himself but represented God's people, and even God. It was an awesome calling, but it actually made it so much easier for clergy than laypeople to go into unfamiliar territory.

Jact had been unfamiliar territory for him at first, even though they sort-of spoke a common language. But he'd settled there, got to know what made people tick, invested his time in their midst and so formed friendships which made evangelism easier. He earned the right because he lived amongst them. What he was now doing was utterly different from that, but it was not a denial of that fundamental principle. Actually he felt *encouraged*, for he was engaging in a symbolic act to indicate what the Church should be doing because it had the evangelism gene in its DNA. The whole Church needed to pull together, reaching across national boundaries to assist its brothers and sisters in all nations to evangelise the people around them.

Nations 92 to 131

That was also why it was so important to get the message about the Persecuted Church across to those who couldn't imagine that such persecution existed. A denial of the very existence and struggles of the Persecuted Church was the opposite of how it should be. If we aren't a *worldwide* family in Christ, we aren't a family at all, Brendan concluded. He still felt guilty about the Mongolian traders, but maybe the quality work that he'd seen in Ulan Bator might raise up evangelists to work amongst Mongolians to challenge their idolatry of self or money.

Refreshed and encouraged, Brendan wheeled himself off to explore Minsk by taxi. The city had suffered under various imported regimes, most recently the Soviet system, which left a black hole when it collapsed in the early 1990s. Brendan could see signs of a resurgent national confidence in the reconstruction of the city centre, but there were still the expected tractor plants and refrigerator works.

He'd arranged a meeting in the Roman Catholic Cathedral which had just celebrated its 300th anniversary since its inception as a Jesuit monastery church – and its 13th anniversary as a renewed Cathedral. It was a large, white, baroque monstrosity, in Brendan's opinion, but the people seemed to love it and what it represented. It was now close to Christmas, and the increased programme of worship at the Cathedral had precluded anything other than an early afternoon meeting. This suited Brendan well, because the Minsk to St. Petersburg sleeper left at 5.40pm. A good crowd had gathered by the 2pm start, and Brendan wheeled himself in to great acclaim, and they listened avidly as he told some of the now all-too-familiar (to him) stories which most of the audience were hearing for the first time. He reflected that the Gospel Good News was like that: almost too familiar to some so that they became blasé about it, yet shockingly life-changing for others. The Belarus GNT was handed to the taxi-driver who took Brendan back to the railway station. He slept well again, despite the gaudy Christmas lights in the train corridor, the inebriated fellow-travellers and the joviality of the attendant, who insisted on singing carols even in the middle of the night. At about 5am, Brendan woke up suddenly, and wheeled himself off to find a cup of tea, encountering the happy attendant in the dining car. Brendan quizzed him about his cheeriness, and the attendant said that it was because he would be seeing his newborn grandson for the very first time. Even though he didn't have any presents for the day-old little one, he felt that he'd received the best Christmas present in the world. Brendan was quite moved by this, and gave the attendant the Russian GNT to pass on to his new grandson. They both burst into tears as the train chugged on through the darkness, finally emerging into St. Petersburg's Vitebsky Station at 8.52am.

Brendan was thrilled to see Ruth and Paul waiting for him as he trundled down the luggage ramp in his wheelchair and broke down as they hugged him – part relief, part gratitude for their commitment to him, part recognition of his loneliness and vulnerability. He still felt ill.

"Thank you, God," he mumbled, through the tears.

Day: Date	Itinerary (* indicates TV interview) ([18] indicates new nation)	Bike (km)	Car/ Bus (km)	Train (km)	Kayak/ Sail (km)	Boat (km)	Air (km)
Totals brought forward		8713	17109	767	2754	15435	24715
208: 9/12/11	Ulan Bator, Mongolia[130]			1167			
209: 10/12/11	en route						
210: 11/12/11	en route						
211: 12/12/11	en route						
212: 13/12/11	en route			2839			
213: 14/12/11	Petropavl, Kazakhstan[131]			272			
214: 15/12/11	en route						
215: 16/12/11	Moscow			2029			
216: 17/12/11	Minsk, Belarus[132]			674			
217: 18/12/11	St. Petersburg, Russia[133]			697			
Totals carried forward		8713	17109	8445	2754	15435	24715

Chapter 52: Contamination

Louisa and Ben had nothing planned for Christmas because the East Timor incident threw everything up in the air (including Brendan – though he landed relatively safely on Dili beach). They knew that Paul would be helping Brendan, so presumably Ruth would be abroad with them for Christmas. They didn't really want to stay at home while Ruth and Paul got to whizz off to exciting places, so they decided to invite themselves along too. It looked like that would mean going to Poland, which would be a new adventure. Louisa had been worried about her Dad traversing Asia in his plastered state, and was relieved when Ruth phoned from St. Petersburg to hear that he'd survived the experience, even though he looked a bit pale and wobbly. She heard how the Mongolians had spoilt his rosy-tinted view of people, but he was now more realistic.

Louisa's outlook was all too realistic. She knew that she had to get away from the Freeman and anywhere would do. It wasn't, of course, the hospital itself, the patients or the role – it was Sister Lilian. She'd spoilt the job for Louisa, and made nursing feel dirty, her whole vocation poisoned. She had video evidence now, courtesy of Donna's phone, but she was unsure what to do with it. She could hand it over to the union officials or to senior management, and presumably Sister Lilian would be disciplined and possibly even sacked. That would be justice, but was that what was best? It would solve the immediate problem, but do nothing to help Sister Lilian become a better person. If anything, it would harden her heart even more against Louisa and the Church.

Sister Lilian, of course, didn't know about the video evidence and was as nasty as ever, having a sarcastic comment about everything that Louisa did. When she got back after shooting off to East Timor, Sister Lilian told her that it would be counted as holiday unless she was prepared to make the time up by taking extra shifts. When Louisa asked if it could be regarded as compassionate leave, the Sister laughed. So she was glad to think about going away, even though she had to be back for the afternoon shift on the 27th or she'd be in more trouble. Then she had a difficult decision to make

***

St. Petersburg was considered one of the most beautiful cities in the world. Looking out of the hotel window, Brendan could see why. Directly ahead was the vast snowed-in lemon-wedge of the neo-classical Mikhailovsky Palace, designed to resemble a Russian country house. To the left were the flamboyant gold and tutti-frutti onion domes of the Church of the Saviour on the Blood. Built as a nationalist rebuke to this elegant Europhile city, the church deliberately copied St. Basil's in

Moscow. To the right, Brendan could just see the golden spire of the Engineers' Castle, a quirky apricot-coloured château built by the rightly paranoid Czar Paul, strangled with his own sash 40 days after moving in. And, finally, in the distance across the Neva River, the festively-lit Soviet-era television tower, erected by a brigade of sturdy female comrades. What a snapshot of Russia: architectural hubris, nationalist reaction, regicide by sash, muscular Socialist women conquering new heights — all out of one window, framed by the bright winter snow.

They went down together to the Central River Yacht Club on Petrovsky Island, to view the boat which Paul had bought for the next "leg". The Club was a grand place with a grand past, established in 1860 and bestowed royal patronage by the tsar on its 50th anniversary. The boat was not so grand but looked just as old. In fact, Mystery was a "gaff-rigged 20-foot sloop", according to the brochure, built by H.R. Stevens in Southampton in 1887 for "harbour and coastal sailing". It detailed other specifications which meant nothing to Brendan. Paul had understood more and been suitably impressed. Brendan was relieved to see that the cabin below had two settee berths and a compact galley with a two-burner calor gas hob and grill. There was a chemical loo and a sink, so all basic needs were met, but it wasn't much like "The World Is Not Enough". There was a gaff sail if they wanted to do proper sailing, but the powerful-looking Evinrude E115FPX outboard motor was supposed to cruise sedately all day at 25 kph and only consume two gallons of petrol per hour.

It would definitely do, especially as it wasn't pink.

Chapter 53: Nations 134 - 144

Relaxing together for the rest of the day meant an early start the next. Ruth and Paul loaded the cabin cupboards with food and other essentials for the magical Mystery tour which lay ahead, everyone made their farewells, Paul sprang (and Brendan clambered stiffly) onboard, and they cast off. They chugged out into Neva Bay and headed out towards the newly-completed St. Petersburg dam – a 40km, 8m-high flood-protection project. Ruth waved them off then headed back into the city for her luggage. She was flying to Newcastle to spend the week with Louisa and Ben.

Mystery chugged out of one of two large openings in the dam into the Gulf of Finland. The shipping into and out of the dam was busy and posed all kinds of potential difficulties, but Paul once again showed that he knew what he was doing. It was a good job too, because Brendan felt pretty useless, his main responsibility being to steer the boat with stiffened arms. If Paul couldn't do everything else, it wouldn't get done. There were only small icebergs to avoid and not too many – sometimes by December the passage to St. Petersburg was already completely blocked by pack ice. The cold caught in Brendan's throat, and he had several painful coughing fits. They spent the afternoon acquainting themselves with the eccentricities of their own boat and the confusing navigation of larger ships. The others seemed to be passing each other in two adjacent oppositely-travelling convoys, which seemed a bit strange until Paul discovered a sea-chart for the Gulf of Finland showing shallows at its eastern end, with a deeper channel dug down the middle for larger vessels. At least they had their own stretch of water to themselves.

By late afternoon, as the sun dipped close to the horizon, they'd passed from Russian to Finnish waters, and could see the small island of Haapasaari up ahead, with its distinctive tower rising up above the trees. It was the easternmost Finnish island with a permanent population, so Brendan had chosen it as his destination. It only had 24 residents, but its impressive wooden church had 240 seats and a big eagle lectern.

"Why do you have such a big church?" Brendan asked the man who showed them round.

"It was here when I was born."

Brendan didn't get the logic. "But why was it built so big, when there were never many people on the island?"

"No-one knows," said the man, as if it was a blessing from God rather than just bad planning.

Brendan gave him the Finnish GNT. "Will you keep it in the church, for visitors as well as the locals?" The man nodded. "Who takes the services?" asked Brendan.

"No-one does. We only open the church in summer, when the visitors come."

Was this a microcosm of European Christianity's problems? Was Church of interest only as a historic curiosity or tourist attraction? The absurd idea of using church buildings for worship seemed counter-cultural. Brendan shuddered. The next five weeks crossing Europe could be hard work.

After a cold night on Mystery, they set off the following day to the southern coast of the Gulf, trying to follow the western (Finnish) side of the invisible Russian border. They were tracked all the way by a Russian patrol boat, which had allowed them out of Russian waters but didn't want to let them back in. Once they got into Estonian waters, having crossed the main east-west shipping channel, the temperature seemed to warm up, the sky and sea lightened from grey to blue, and the seagulls started to caw and glide overhead as they neared land. Tallinn was a curious mixture of old and new: the Silicon Valley of the Baltic alongside medieval fortifications; cobbled alley-ways twisting off modern shopping streets; the 314m bright-white TV tower stretching beyond the 124m dark spire of St. Olaf's Church.

It was not to St. Olaf's that they headed for their evening meeting, but the Methodist Church on Narva Road. On the way, Brendan was intrigued by the gaudy door to the House of the Brotherhood of Blackheads, which was not a support-group for acne-sufferers but a fellowship of medieval German merchants. But the modern angular architecture of the Methodist Church impressed him even more, even if it did look like concrete origami. The acoustics were wonderful and Brendan could easily be heard even from his sitting position. Dozens of students from the Baltic Methodist Theological Seminary were present, one of whom was chosen to receive the Estonian GNT, and the whole evening was a great success. After the evangelistic non-event of Haapasaari, it restored Brendan's hopes for this European leg of his journey.

After another cold night on board, Brendan and Paul sailed south-west along the coast into the Gulf of Riga. They kept along the southern coast of Saaremaa to the small harbour at Kuressaare, where a medieval castle had watched the town yo-yo between Russia, Sweden, Denmark, Estonia, Catholic, Protestant, Communist and just about every other type of ownership imaginable. There was also a small Methodist Church, which was where Methodism in Estonia was established in 1907 through some visiting preachers from St. Petersburg, and where Brendan spoke that evening to a small congregation. He was humbled by the monument to Pastor Martin Prikask, who'd been arrested by Soviet officials in the church before being exiled to Siberia and martyred for his faith in 1942. Estonia today was very different, free to worship how its citizens wished – but it reminded Brendan of the other countries he'd visited where Christian martyrdom still happened.

The next day they sailed down the Torgu peninsula and across the 25km of sea to Latvia. The wind whistled in their faces and hurt Brendan's throat, so they were glad to make the harbour. The priest had cajoled several dozen people in for Brendan's talk, and the Latvian GNT went to an old wrinkled lady who, according to the priest, had kept the church there going throughout the long decades of Soviet oppression.

They continued southwards the next day, crossing the Lithuanian border at about midday – not that there was any obvious sign of the transition. They chugged on southwards to the Curonian Spit, a natural string of land dividing the Baltic Sea from the Curonian Lagoon, which they followed as it stretched thinly south-westwards, forming the final tip of Lithuania and the northernmost tip of the curious Russian enclave of Kaliningrad Oblast. They stayed overnight at the small resort of Neringa, close to the Russian border, where they gave the Lithuanian GNT to the harbour-master because there was no-one else around.

They could see no patrol boats out to stop Mystery from entering Russian waters, but just to be safe they sailed further out into the Baltic Sea. This westernmost part of Russia was heavily militarised and had produced heroes such as Alexei Leonov, the first man to walk in space, long used by Brendan in his sermons as an illustration of commitment and trust. The scientists had done their calculations but no-one actually knew what would happen until Leonov opened the door of Voskhod 2. It was a good parable of what stepping out in faith was all about, even if Leonov was an atheist.

They sailed parallel to the Vistula Spit, a narrow sand-barrier similar to the Curonian Spit to its north, dividing the Baltic from the Vistula Lagoon, the only opening into which was at Baltiysk, giving access to the ice-free naval bases which Russia was so dependent upon for its European operations. They stayed well clear and took a bearing across the open sea towards the Hel Peninsula in Poland. Once they cleared the Russian-Polish border the sun came out as if they were on an old anti-Soviet propaganda film. The sea calmed and the wind died down, granting them a safe passage across the open sea. They saw very few other boats and soon made out the tall red-brick lighthouse in Hel. That night, Brendan wrote in his diary: "Arrived in Hel. Much warmer."

Brendan and Paul were thrilled to see Ruth waiting for them as they stumbled off the boat, and even more excited when Louisa and Ben emerged as well from the harbour-master's office. It was Christmas Eve – and Brendan was surrounded once again by his family. Brendan said to them all, "You know, despite my broken limbs, all is well, for God is with us."

Louisa told him to shut up. "That's enough preaching for today, Dad. Give your sore throat a rest and let your hair down."

Everybody burst out laughing. It was a standing family joke, having a playful dig at their bald father.

"Thank you, God," Bendan mumbled, for the second time in a week, again through tears.

***

It had been a complicated journey for Ruth, Louisa and Ben, setting off from Newcastle on the 23rd at 11am, flying to Dublin, where they connected with a Ryanair flight to Gdansk which landed just after 8pm. They stayed in a hotel overnight, and discovered that every afternoon there was a regular boat trip out to Hel and back – which made them giggle. On arrival they sorted out two nights' accommodation at the local pub, and had just ordered drinks when Ruth caught sight of Mystery approaching the harbour. They rushed down and were there to welcome them.

Everywhere except the pub was shut – including the church, even though it was Christmas Eve. Inside, most of the locals seemed to be warming themselves around the fire, which became another ironic reflection later that evening in Brendan's diary. They'd strung up some Christmas lights, and the inhabitants of Hel seemed rather jolly, and keen both to talk about themselves and listen to Brendan about his journey. He gave the Polish GNT to the landlord.

"I shall keep it right here," the landlord said, pointing to a glass cabinet behind the bar. "There will always be a Bible in Hel." He laughed, though the other drinkers didn't understand his English or the point of the humour. Brendan smiled, secretly proud of bringing the Gospel to what seemed an otherwise God-forsaken spot, and not only in terms of its name. Once they'd returned to Mystery, and he'd been helped onboard, he sent Paul back to spend the night with Ruth, assuring him that he would be all right for one night on his own.

Paul collected him for breakfast at the pub on Christmas morning, but then everybody had to go their separate ways. Ruth, Louisa and Ben were unable to travel anywhere on Christmas Day, so they settled in for the day at the pub before catching the boat back on Boxing Day afternoon, connecting with the evening flight from Gdansk to Dublin, then the following morning flying back from Dublin to Newcastle at 9.30, getting in just in time for Louisa's afternoon shift at the Freeman. Brendan and Paul sailed along the peninsula to the wonderfully-named Wladyslawowo, then along the north coast of Poland to the tiny fishing village of Jaroslawiec, where they anchored off-shore for the night. There were no Christmas lights, no signs of life at all onshore, so they stayed on the boat and cooked their Christmas dinner: dried turkey curry. They went to sleep early because they had a long and difficult day ahead of them: the full-day crossing of the Baltic Sea, via the island of Bornholm, to Ystad in Sweden.

Fortunately the next-day weather was benign, and Mystery negotiated the waves confidently. They stopped for a short break at Rønne harbour on Bornholm, admiring the picturesque cobbled streets and low-timbered houses of the port, but eager to take advantage of the good weather for the shorter journey across to Ystad.

Ystad was the setting for the Inspector Wallander books by Henning Mankell. It had the quaint old houses, medieval churches and winding streets that Brendan imagined, but was even sleepier than he'd thought possible. It was December, and fearfully cold, but Brendan would have expected a little bit of life. The old Klostret Church looked solid, austere and forbidding. It was also frightfully cold, and Brendan wasn't surprised when only about 20 people turned up in layers of thick clothing for his scheduled talk that evening. If he hadn't been giving the talk, he wouldn't have left home either, especially as his throat was once again really sore. He gave the Swedish GNT to a lady whose gloves were so thick that she couldn't wrap her fingers round the edge of the book and had to tuck it under her armpit to carry it home. Brendan had wrapped socks and gloves round his exposed fingers and toes – but he could feel the tingle as the blood struggled to make it round. Ystad was at almost exactly the same latitude as Cullercoats but it seemed much colder. When they got back on board Mystery, they put the heating up to full blast to make sure that nothing anatomically significant dropped off.

Sheltered by the bulk of Denmark looming to the west, they sailed round to the Sound and underneath the massive pylons of the Öresund Bridge which joined Copenhagen with Malmö. The Sound was very busy with vessels of various sizes, even though the temperature was so inhospitable. There was even a wind-surfer, who must have escaped from a lunatic asylum. They anchored off Höganäs for the night, and kept to the Swedish coast the following day as they chugged northwards. The morning after that they finally crossed the Kattegat to the northernmost tip of Denmark at Skagen, then across the Skagerrak to Kristiansand in Norway, but this time the wind and waves were not particularly helpful, and Brendan felt quite sick as they pitched and lurched their way across in the fading light of the late-December afternoon. So it was a great relief when they sighted the Norwegian coastline and crawled into Kristiansand harbour. Brendan felt a bit useless with his stick limbs as Paul did all the work, running backwards and forwards while Brendan sat there immobile apart from a quick dash or two to the side to offload surplus stomach contents, which made his throat even sorer.

Brendan was disconcerted by the knowing winks of the fishermen who heard about his seasickness that evening in the Cathedral, which could seat 1,800, but there was still a good feel even with 200. At least they all sat near the front, rather than spread out like wind turbines, as the Jact congregation used to. The Norwegian GNT was given to the loudest of the laughing fishermen, even though his dire weather predictions left Brendan more worried than ever about the passage back across the Skagerrak the following day. The distance was about 120km to Hanstholm in Denmark, but a storm could make it much more difficult, lengthy and nauseous.

It lived up to all Brendan's worst expectations and fears. Grey was the word for it. Grey sea; grey sky; grey complexion as Brendan fought unsuccessfully to keep his breakfast down. As the percussion section of God's orchestra crashed and flashed, the boat bucked and tossed like the arm of a crazed violinist but Brendan's retches were not particularly musical – they hurt. Mystery, however, kept climbing up from the troughs and breasting the crests with plucky enthusiasm, as if this was the best adventure she'd ever had. Instead of a steady cruising speed of 25kph, they managed only about 12, but used up the same amount of fuel each hour. Paul stoically sat out in his yellow oilskins, hand on the wheel, slumped like an exhausted canary, water pouring off his hood into his lap. Brendan was inside the cabin, separated from the water but not from its effects, watching the contents of the sick bucket slop backwards and forwards, and wishing he was anywhere else.

At last, at long last, Paul banged on the roof of the cabin and pointed ahead. Brendan groggily looked round and saw the whirling light of the lighthouse at Hanstholm, and felt an immediate surge of thanksgiving welling up inside him, not dissimilar from other up-surges over the last ten hours, but with a more pleasing after-effect. He sensed now how Jonah must have felt on the boat in the teeth of the storm and sloshing around in the juices and slop of the fish's gut, and the elation he must have felt when he was vomited onto dry land. He hadn't ever empathised with Jonah before, but now understood how evangelising at Nineveh must have been a piece of cake compared to the first bit of the story.

Thankfully they'd not made any arrangements for speaking engagements over the next few days, so they called it a day, even though the schedule called for another 50km to Thyborøn. Paul and Brendan were both absolutely shattered, for different reasons, and they merely tied up in the harbour and crawled into their bunks with a few biscuits, saying little to each other but each recognising that this had been the hardest day of all for them both.

Over the next four days the rest of the North Sea coast mercifully drifted by without incident or excitement. They passed Thyborøn by mid-morning and made that day's scheduled destination of List in Germany easily. There wasn't much to see at the northernmost village in Germany except lots of sand dunes and flat barren moorland, but there was a pub hosting a New Year's Eve party, which they joined even though they didn't have a clue what most people were saying. Brendan remembered at the pub that he'd forgotten to give the Danish GNT away, so they put in at a small town on the Danish mainland early the next day and found a shopkeeper happy to receive it – along with some money in exchange for bread, fruit and cheese.

The relatively sheltered waters off the German and Dutch coast, protected from the might of the North Sea by offshore islands, led to Den Helder, with its bright red cast-iron lighthouse "Lange Jaap" dominating the skyline. They gave the Dutch GNT to the lighthouse-keeper, who was in the pub along with the rest of the villagers. There seemed to be a pattern to community life – and Church didn't figure in it.

They chugged onwards, ever onwards, on their last day at sea, cruising down the benign Netherlands coastline. At school Brendan had once mistakenly called the country the Neitherlands, and now he realised the accidental accuracy of that description. The landscape was neither one thing nor the other; neither land nor sea; neither clear nor misty; neither pleasant nor unpleasant; neither here nor there. He was glad when they finally arrived at Zeebrugge. By this time, Brendan and Paul had run out of things to say to each other, and kept a companionable silence on the boat like an old married couple in a restaurant.

They laughed about this in the restaurant that evening, both of them giddy at being on solid ground once more, able at last to share how much each had hated the trip down from Norway and longed for its end. They gave the final GNT to the restauranteur, who worked as the waiter while his wife worked as the chef. He seemed curious about them as if he'd never seen a Ugandan or a man with three limbs in plaster before. When they explained what they were doing and where they'd come from, the man whistled and rolled his eyes as if it was the craziest thing. When Brendan told him *why* he was making the trip and about the plane crash in East Timor, the waiter went white, crossed himself and refused to take any money off them for their meal. They returned to their hotel and were reunited with Ruth who'd just flown in from London with Esther, Arnold and the rest of the film crew, ready for the interview scheduled for the next day in London. They'd flown over to Belgium to fly Brendan back with them, while Paul stayed in Belgium to try to sell Mystery. The boat had done them proud, especially in the storms between Norway and Denmark, but they wouldn't be sorry to see the last of her.

The worst leg of the journey so far for Brendan was over. The next day he flew in Esther's jet from Brugge to London to get his plaster casts off, with the film crew taking footage of him climbing stiffly on and off the plane. They filmed the casts being sawn off in the private London hospital which Esther had arranged, then at 9pm filmed a live interview in which Brendan tried to describe how awful the passage through the storm had been and how thankful they were to be on dry land. Ruth reported that the donations received at Watoto had levelled off a bit, but encouraged people to keep getting sponsors to join them in raising even more money as the total number of countries visited by Brendan grew. Esther made much of the "Bible in Hel" joke but also played the emotional card by keeping referring to Brendan's injuries, encouraging him to show the viewers how wasted his arms and legs were after so much inactivity. One leg was twice as big as the other.

"So, Brendan," she concluded, "Where are you off to next? You won't be able to do anything too taxing until your body gets its muscles back, will you?"

"I hope so," Brendan replied. "I'm off to Ukraine on a bike."

Day: Date	Itinerary (* indicates TV interview) ([18] indicates new nation)	Bike (km)	Car/ Bus (km)	Train (km)	Kayak / Sail (km)	Boat (km)	Air (km)
Totals brought forward		8713	17109	8445	2754	15435	24715
218: 19/12/11	Haapasaari, Finland[134]					172	
219: 20/12/11	Tallinn, Estonia[135]					173	
220: 21/12/11	Kuressaare					228	
221: 22/12/11	Júrkalne, Latvia[136]					157	
222: 23/12/11	Neringa, Lithuania[137]					179	
223: 24/12/11	Hel, Poland[138]					183	
224: 25/12/11	Jaroslawiec					173	
225: 26/12/11	Ystad, Sweden[139]					198	
226: 27/12/11	Höganäs					163	
227: 28/12/11	Öckero					193	
228: 29/12/11	Kristiansand, Norway[140]					216	
229: 30/12/11	Hanstholm, Denmark[141]					119	
230: 31/12/11	List, Germany[142]					247	
231: 1/1/12	Schillig					197	
232: 2/1/12	Den Helder, Netherlands[143]					247	
233: 3/1/12	Zeebrugge, Belgium[144]					219	
234: 4/1/12	London hospital *						
Totals carried forward		8713	17109	8445	2754	18499	24715

Chapter 54: Decontamination

At 2pm on December 27th, Louisa arrived for the afternoon shift, resolved for action. When Sister Lilian greeted her with the usual sneer and caustic comment about the fish symbol which Louisa was told to take off, Louisa asked if she could meet with her in private. The response was a raised eyebrow and another put-down, but they arranged to talk midway through the morning, after the doctor's rounds.

"What's all this about, then?" demanded Sister Lilian, when the door was shut.

"I want you to stop treating me so badly and picking on me."

"I don't know what you mean," snapped the Sister. "You get treated the same as everyone else."

"Come off it, Sister," said Louisa, shaking with a sudden burst of adrenalin. "You know what I'm talking about: giving me the worst duties; altering my holiday dates; making nasty comments about my performance in front of the staff and patients; having a go at me about my faith..."

"Ah yes, your so-called faith..." sneered Sister Lilian. "Aren't you supposed to submit to authority and take pleasure in serving others?" She smiled as she leant forwards, aggressively, like a hungry cat to an injured bird.

"Yes it is, in many situations. But not when the authorities concerned misuse their power and become vindictive. Anyway that isn't the point."

"Ah, there you go again. Always taking the moral high ground, but you haven't got a leg to stand on. You get the duties that I assign to you because I'm the Sister and you have to do what you're told. You continue to defy me every shift by wearing that stupid badge and you continue to push your religion on the patients. Well, I won't have it. In future there'll be no more bloody Christianity on this ward and I'll do everything I can to have you thrown out. I can't stand you Christians with your bloody self-righteousness. I've got rid of the chaplains and I'll make sure that I get rid of you too."

"But you can't do that," Louisa complained. "That's religious discrimination."

"Not the way I'll go about it. You've got no proof and it'll be just my word against yours, so either shut up or do us all a favour and just get out."

Louisa couldn't believe the effrontery of the woman. "But don't you remember that time when you screamed at me in the ward and hit me?"

"Of course I do. You provoked me. But I seem to remember warning you not to bring that up. You haven't got a shred of proof."

"Well, that's where you're wrong, actually. One of the patients videoed the whole thing on her phone and I've made copies."

"I don't believe you!" snarled Sister.

"Have a look at this, then," said Louisa, fiddling with her phone. "I think you'll find that it's quite a good recording, and the bit where you hit me is particularly impressive. You can see the expression on your face and hear the slap quite clearly. Let me just find it..." She handed it over to a suddenly silent Sister Lilian, who watched and listened as the damning evidence unfolded. Then an amazing transformation took place. The crusty exterior cracked and a tear rolled down the Sister's face. She folded in on herself and started to sob, her whole body shaking silently. Louisa was appalled, yet bewildered too. What was she supposed to do? "I'm sorry," came a mumble from somewhere inside the quivering mess in front of Louisa. Then more shaking, some audible sobs and gulps. "I'm sorry. I don't know what to say."

Louisa just sat there, unsure what to do next, trying to resist her natural urge to go and put her arm round someone so distressed. It was all so... dirty. Even after this confession, she felt as if there was something really nasty going on, and she felt contaminated by it, as if it was trying to suck her in somehow. She felt a sudden surge of malevolence, threatening her, and it was so powerful that she stood up and backed against the wall[78].

"Help me, Jesus!" Louisa cried, and Sister Lilian crumpled into a heap on the floor. She lay like a corpse across the floor. Louisa couldn't quite take in all that was happening, but she remembered feeling an overwhelming sense of evil and that she'd cried out to Jesus for help, and the Sister had instantly fallen to the floor. Now what was she supposed to do? She stood against the wall, palms and back spread against it as if she wanted to get as far away from Sister Lilian as possible. Time seemed to stand still, but it must only have been a few seconds before the Sister whimpered on the floor and started to "come round". Louisa bent down and helped her up.

"W..w..what happened?" Sister Lilian eventually stuttered.

"I'm not sure," said Louisa. "How do you feel?"

"I feel light." It struck Louisa as an odd thing to say for a woman built like a plinth. Then she noticed Sister Lilian clenching her eyes shut. "Bright light," mumbled the Sister, to clarify that it was not her weight that she was discussing.

---

[78] It is very difficult to describe a religious experience of any kind. The phenomenon described in this chapter is "spiritual warfare", the awareness and experience of an ongoing conflict between good and evil spiritual forces being played out in the physical world. This "warfare" usually manifests itself psychologically or emotionally, but sometimes is expressed outwardly and affects its participants physically and spiritually too. Whatever vocabulary we choose to describe it, it is a reality which affects people at the very core of their being. The spiritual encounter described here makes use of religious vocabulary which may seem archaic, but which often proves effective in "naming and shaming", overturning curses with blessings, and other sub-plots in the complex area of deliverance and healing ministry.

Louisa prayed hard in a split-second. Then she found herself speaking words that didn't come from her brain, that weren't consciously-planned sentences and vocabulary but words that she never imagined she would ever say, let alone in front of Sister Lilian: "We will stand strong against the evil happening here," she declared, with a boldness that wasn't part of her. "We will *not* let the Devil win. I declare God's power over evil and ask Jesus to help me stand firm against any attempt to make me be vindictive, letting Satan win. I *forgive* you, Lilian, in the name of Jesus!"

The Sister cried out as if she'd been struck with a mallet, then lay still, though Louisa could see her chest moving up and down. Louisa could suddenly sense a tingling in her fingers and a shiver ran up her spine. Inexplicably, it was easier to sit down on the floor, her back pushed against a chair, than to remain standing. She found herself looking upwards, neck straining backwards, as if she was looking at something in the corner of the ceiling behind her. And all there was... was light, bright light, pulsating and burning yet neither hot nor warm nor cold, strobing down on her even when she shut her eyelids because it was too bright. But she knew that it was good, and that she was safe. Wonderfully safe.

Time no longer existed.

Then she heard Sister Lilian rousing herself from the floor and Louisa decided that it was time to come back to the present moment. And that was what it was, a decision[79]. She knew that she had complete freedom to do whatever she wanted – to stay in the special moment or to come out of it. More mumbles from Sister Lilian brought Louisa to the reality of the office and the unreality of what had just happened to them both.

"How do you feel?" Louisa asked for the second time.

"I feel lighter," said Sister Lilian, "As if a rucksack's been taken from my shoulders. Like I could float away."

Louisa had a weird image of the still-cubic Sister floating out of the window like an overweight Tinkerbell. But then she focussed on what she thought she'd heard. "Are you saying that something's changed?"

"Yes, I feel different. I feel lighter as if something big has gone away. I feel younger – no, not younger, freer. Oh, I don't know. I'm talking rubbish – but I know that I feel better."

---

[79] It is one of the central tenets of spiritual warfare that, when believers are being blessed with a powerful experience of God's presence and love, they are always in control, and can respond to external stimuli and conversation and choose to get up and walk away. God always gives freedom and choice. This is in sharp contrast to the "possession" of a victim by evil spirits.

"You know what I reckon?" asked Louisa. "I think that God has healed you of something that was eating away at your soul. I felt the power of God in this room and I think that you did too. Am I right?"

"Yes, I think you're right. But I don't know why." And with that, Sister Lilian burst into tears.

***

It seemed as if the whole day had been spent in that office, but when Louisa and the Sister emerged, it was still only 10.30am. Sister Lilian told the rest of the nurses what needed to be done in what order – it was as if nothing had changed, and yet everything was different. Louisa returned to her duties, unsure what to do. Should she let the Sister off, in the light of what God had done in the office? Should she forgive her but still continue with the disciplinary route to ensure that justice was seen to be done? Or would that be unnecessarily vindictive? If God had enabled Louisa to forgive Sister Lilian, should she not forget any thought of discipline? If anything, things were more complicated for her now, because she had a hard moral dilemma to solve.

***

At the end of the shift, Louisa was called into the Sister's office. This was nothing new, of course, so the other nurses just shrugged their shoulders sympathetically at Louisa when they heard the summons. Yet something had definitely changed. "I don't really understand what happened this morning," said the Sister, "But I know that a great load has lifted from me and I'm really grateful to you for that. I feel very different, and very tired – and I'm so sorry that I've been horrible to you for so long." Louisa stood there, not knowing what response to make. Was this contrition, or more manipulation? "I've decided to ask for a transfer to another hospital," said Sister Lilian. "And what I want to ask is: If I go somewhere else, will you give me the chance to prove that I can be a good nurse? If you hand in that film, I'll be sacked, and I won't be able to get another job anywhere. I know it's unfair to ask you this, but I hope that you'll give me another chance."

Louisa stood still, not daring to breathe in case it changed the atmosphere somehow. And yet she had her wits about her too, realising that a transfer could mean that there was no pressure on Sister Lilian to stick with her new-found nicer self. "OK," she said, "I'll do you a deal. If you put in an application now to transfer exactly six months from today, and if you *prove* to me, the other staff, the patients and the hospital in the next six months that you've changed, then I'll delete this evidence.

But you *must change* – it's the only way you're ever going to be a good nurse. Is that a deal?"

"Yes," said Sister Lilian, humbly. "Thank you."

***

The next morning, Sister Lilian breezed into the ward with a big smile on her face. "Hello, everyone," she declared. "I'm sorry that I've been so horrible, but I've changed. Everything's going to be better now."

The nurses looked at one another in astonishment. Had she been drinking? Was it a trick? The patients looked at one another in astonishment too. Donna winked at Louisa, who went bright red. "I don't know how you did it," Donna said, later, "But well done. Hey, I couldn't help but notice, you're wearing your fish badge."

"Yes," said Louisa, with a smile. "But have you noticed that Sister's wearing one too?"

Chapter 55: Nations 145 - 154

Brendan's plaster-less arms and leg were half the size they had been, and he walked lopsidedly because one leg was so much heavier than the other. When he got on his new bike at Brugge, having flown back from London in Esther's Learjet, he was hard-pressed to keep it in a straight line. The arms weren't too much of a problem, but the uneven legs certainly were. His throat still hurt too. It was cold. Somehow the lack of musculature seemed to add to the chill, even though he was wearing leggings rather than shorts. It felt like when he'd wobbled off from the kerb in Cullercoats, 235 days ago.

After 2½ hours of gentle pedalling out of Brugge, he stopped for coffee in a small café in the quiet centre of Ghent. He continued on smaller N roads parallel to the autoroute for the next 4½ hours, all the way to the outskirts of Brussels, where he stopped again – at a public toilet in the Rue de la Victoire. He calculated that he'd already completed 100km, without falling off once, or even feeling too much of a reaction to his previous inactivity – but he still had 50km to go, so he pressed on. The road to Perwez was straightforward too, but when he eventually arrived at just after 6.30pm, his legs were tired and his arms and back stiff. He hadn't really doubted his capability back on a bike, but it was a relief to complete the first full day.

He'd arranged an evening meeting at Perwez, and another for the next night in Luxembourg, so he was pleased to make both distances in decent time, so that he could shower and change in a reasonably relaxed way before the evening. In both places, he found the churches rather austere, the audiences rather unresponsive, and the atmospheres rather flat. Perwez's event was in Saint Trond's church, a plain and cold brick building with poor lighting, hard seats and no amplification. The audience were huddled inside their coats and never really warmed up in any sense. At Luxembourg, Brendan spoke in the Notre-Dame Cathedral, which was brighter and ornate, but the attendance still sparse. Furthermore, both audiences had the Jact disease of sitting at least 3m from each other, as if they were ready in case suddenly they were told to whirl their coats around their heads without hitting anyone. More probably, they were either antisocial or were insuring against catching anything infectious, but unfortunately they didn't seem to have caught the Holy Spirit either. At both churches he gave away GNTs, in Perwez to a wizened old man who could have modelled for a gargoyle and in Luxembourg to a young couple who were the youngest there by about 30 years. Brendan wondered if they'd come by mistake. He gave out some of his "business cards" at each place too, getting rid of all his Flemish cards and a few German ones.

The next day he veered southwards, continuing southwards through France. The only bright spot in an otherwise dull day was a town called Lunéville which summed up what he felt about his own sanity at that point. He'd encountered this sense of boredom and pointlessness before, on the previous cycling journey across Southern Africa. Was it the cycling? At least in a car there were endlessly changing landscapes, but even though he was constantly passing through different towns and villages they all looked much the same. The people too were blurs, indistinct and insignificant. He chided himself for getting too preoccupied by the itinerary and not relishing the journey. The whole point about mission was people, loved by God, and indifference was bad news.

He stayed in a small pension in Azereilles, and contemplated how he could put things right. He had 16 more days of cycling to go before Odessa, and various speaking events planned – one for each nation he'd be passing through. He resolved to make the most of those encounters, but also to take time out along the way to engage with people, not just whizz past them. He started living out his intentions the following morning, smiling at the baker's delivery boy as he set out on his rounds, only to get a rude gesture in return. Undaunted, he carried on smiling at people, getting some generous smiles in return and even having a kiss blown at him by a young lady with bright red lipstick.

He was worried by the Vosges mountains he could see ahead of him, especially the tall, rounded granite mounds of the Hautes Vosges to the south. But the Tunnel Maurice Lemaire avoided the only mountainous part, and he emerged into the Rhine valley at Colmar, the birthplace of Frédéric Bartholdi, the sculptor who designed the Statue of Liberty. The only evidence was the plaque on the Fontaine Schongauer which Bartholdi sculpted in the centre of town. Brendan stopped in a café for a late lunch, enjoying a half-bottle of dry Riesling in the capital of the Alsatian wine region while he chatted with some of the locals, who perked up once they realised that he was drinking some of the local tipple. In fact, the company was so convivial that Brendan realised with a lurch that he was seriously late and needed to press on.

Fortunately, he was now on the level, cycling down the Rhine valley parallel to the river, past Mulhouse, across the Swiss border, and was back on time as he cycled along the Elsässerstrasse into the centre of Basel. He was staying with the Bishop, no less, in a house just opposite the impressive Basel Münster itself. As Brendan cycled into the city in the gathering gloom of a mid-January late afternoon, the red sandstone cathedral suddenly lit up. It looked like a wedding cake – its trademark twin slender towers, colourful diagonal roof-tiles and chunky cross-shaped architecture perched high on its tiny base amidst the high-rise buildings of the city. Brendan was looking forward to Basel Münster, because one of his reformation heroes, Erasmus, was buried there. Erasmus had impressively managed to incur first the admiration and later the displeasure of both Luther and Calvin. He'd impressed them both at first by his scholarship and his dislike of formal empty ritual, but then upset Martin Luther by trying to reform the Roman Catholic Church from *within* rather than leaving it. John Calvin only really started his reforming crusade after

Erasmus' death, but poured scorn on Erasmus for supporting the Catholic doctrine of free will rather than Calvin's own belief in predestination. Erasmus's "middle road" seemed to upset everyone, but he stuck to his guns and Brendan admired him for that. He was a bit disappointed with the tomb, though – just a pillar with an inscription, as if no-one was sure whether to be proud of Erasmus or not.

The Cathedral itself was stark and plain, and again there were hard wooden seats which didn't make for a relaxed atmosphere. Furthermore, Brendan's talk was in the side transept and it all suggested peripheral business tucked away in a corner rather than affirming mission as the Church's central task. After the euphoria of the contacts he'd made during the day, Brendan considered it a let-down, but told himself off over dinner and woke up the next morning determined to keep concentrating on the people along the way as well as the way itself.

A long day followed – across the full width of Switzerland to the tiny principality of Liechtenstein, the other of the doubly-landlocked nations along with Uzbekistan. Brendan smiled at people the whole way, but most people got on with their own business and Brendan only rarely got a friendly response. Surely the little enclave of Liechtenstein, dependent upon tourists to boost their economy, would be a bit friendlier, wouldn't it?

The Cathedral in Vaduz was dedicated to St. Florin, who had nothing to do with coinage but was reputed to be pretty good at changing water into wine, which would have earned a bob or two if traded upon. There wasn't much conviviality kicking around, however, on a dreary January afternoon, and the shops were shut when Brendan finally, wearily, pedalled into town only an hour and a half before the evening meeting. The Cathedral was no bigger than Jact Methodist Church. Actually, Vaduz was no bigger than Jact, but was a capital city. The congregation that evening also reminded Brendan of the Jact he'd known – a spread-out scattering of retired people who didn't get out much. It wasn't very uplifting. The Liechtenstein GNT, published in German, was given to the liveliest-looking person there, who happened to run the Tourist Office. Brendan hoped that it would spur her on to do a bit of witnessing herself "on the job".

The snowy Austrian Alps lay ahead for Brendan, so he slept well, and rose early. Across the border into Austria and the quaint medieval town of Feldkirch, he veered off to the east, running parallel with the E60 autobahn, which curiously ran all the way to Irkeshtam on the Kyrgyzstan-China border, which Brendan had passed through only ten weeks ago. The route kept to the valleys, much to Brendan's relief as cycling in snow would be particularly unpleasant. He stayed that night in the small town of Haiming, spoke to about 40 bored-looking people in the church and felt that Europe really was at the bottom of the league in terms of evangelistic fervour. From what Brendan had observed over the last few days, it wouldn't be long before there was no-one left.

Over the next ten days the same pattern emerged: early start; eastwards pedalling; no smiles from anyone; brief stops in unwelcoming places; arrival at destination; early to bed. At Kaplice in the Czech Republic, Bratislava in Slovakia, Debrecan in Hungary and Piatra Nearnt in Romania he did evening talks – but they were uninspired and uninspiring. His glands swelled up again and he felt pretty ill. He was seriously getting deflated and wondered if he himself was turning into a lukewarm advert for the Christian faith, like his audiences. He gave away his "business cards" and tried his best to make his presentations lively, but found it increasingly difficult to discern any positive response whatsoever. The days were getting tedious; the scenery flat and uninteresting; the wooden expressions on people's faces inviting no contact or communication. To make it even worse, it rained continually for the whole ten days.

Then, with only three days to go before Odessa, the sun came out. Everything had been grey and wet, but as soon as he crossed the border into Moldova, the world became warm and friendly. People smiled; children waved; the scenery became suddenly beautiful; God was not dead after all.

One of the questions he'd been asked in Iceland when he'd given his talk about the journey down the Americas was where God fitted into it. Brendan had thought this a strange and unfair question, because God was the reason for the journey, the Originator of the idea, the One who'd helped him out at frequent points when he needed help and the One to whom the whole journey was dedicated.

"But where was God as you travelled?" the questioner had persisted – a short blonde scruffy-looking journalist from one of the Christian newspapers in Reykjavik.

"He was everywhere," Brendan had answered.

"But you never speak as if you were aware that God was everywhere with you," persisted the Icelander. It was an interesting point, which made Brendan feel a bit unholy, as he realised what the journalist was suggesting. He hadn't taken a Bible with him. He hadn't found himself saying lots of prayers along the way. He'd found that God responded when he cried out for help, and Brendan tried to remember to thank God for this – but often he'd felt as if he was on his own, doing it in his own strength. At first he'd shrugged this off as just his way of doing spirituality, but the Icelander's question had set into motion a whole load of doubts in Brendan's mind about how spiritual he really was, if at all.

The trip across the Kalahari had been mind-boggingly tedious, and Brendan hadn't really thought about God much at all. He probably hadn't prayed for the whole of that part of the trip. He'd sort-of reminded himself continually *why* he was doing the trip, but that was the only bit where God got a look-in. Now, after a similarly unexciting and dispiriting stretch of the journey, the same doubts were rising up and threatening to choke him.

Why couldn't he have an easy, disciplined prayer-life like everyone else seemed to enjoy? Why did he experience such heights of spirituality at times and yet neglect God at others? Here he was, two-thirds of the way through an epic journey, watched by millions of people through "See Esther", so why did he feel such a fraud? Or was it true that God *was* with him, even though he wasn't always aware of God? Maybe his own shortcomings shouldn't call into question the viability and importance of his God-inspired journey? Why now, when the sun came out, did God re-appear? Of course, Brendan knew that God had not disappeared and that the fault was entirely his, but why did it happen like this for him? Perhaps he should move to Moldova, where the sun shone and God was very real.

The sun burst out as soon as Brendan crossed the river Prut at the Sculeni Bridge. The sudden warmth of the sun was like a celestial sign of approval, as if this was a new world with new possibilities. It was already late in the day, and he was pretty exhausted when he arrived at Petresti, the first town in Moldova. The sun, however, had not finished for the day, producing a vivid sunset as its finale.

The people of Petresti were wonderful that evening. They crowded into the church and the priest described how poor they were materially but how rich they were spiritually. Several dentally-challenged old ladies grinned as he spoke to Brendan. The priest explained that neighbouring Romania's entry into the European Union had crippled them financially, because their access to sell their own produce and buy cheap goods in the Romanian markets was cut off at a stroke. They'd have to get a visa now from the capital, Chisinau.

"Yet see how happy they are!" said the priest. And they certainly seemed radiant in their faith, dancing slowly as they sang unaccompanied. The women laughed and the men smiled as if this was the best place in the world, despite the downturn. The priest translated Brendan's talk and the people laughed, sighed, shouted and generally had a wonderful time. They then had a sort of singalong in which Brendan was encouraged to offer a solo, which the crowd applauded even though they didn't have a clue what All Things Bright and Beautiful meant.

The priest took Brendan back to his house and shared two bottles of Moldovan wine with him over dinner. Dinner was some sort of beef stew but the wine was heavenly – orange/brown in colour, but it was the potency and the rich flavour which knocked him away. He wasn't really very good at the wine-tasting game, and usually got the cheapest he could find because he reckoned that anything expensive would be wasted on him. But now he thought that he could taste, at various times in the evening from the same wine, raisins, barley sugar, nuts, apricots and dates. It was very sweet and warming, almost like a glass of port. It burnt the back of his throat but also make him pleasantly drowsy. He was gently wakened by the priest and shown upstairs to his bed.

Eventually by mid-morning, the tympani section in Brendan's head put away their drumsticks, and he realised that he'd managed 20km or more in the first hour and a half, and was on track for Floreni, a small town just past the capital, Chisinau. The day's distance wasn't huge, which was probably a good job in the light of his hangover, but he still needed to concentrate and complete the task, especially as the road had more potholes than proper surface. As the hours slid by, Brendan found himself smiling again at people as he passed, and getting greetings yelled back at him. At least, they sounded like greetings. Moldova continued to wear a smile – even when he reached the capital. Chisinau was a curious mixture: on the one hand it tried to be a modern city, with office-blocks and shopping centres and even out-of-the-ordinary architecture such as Kentford, Sky Tower and the Union Fenosa headquarters. On the other hand, there were old Soviet-style clusters of drab, featureless, rabbit-hutch housing blocks. He passed a courtyard containing several Soviet tanks and even a MIG fighter jet, but he couldn't work out whether it was a museum or a themed bistro.

Half an hour later Brendan reached Floreni, which didn't have a lot going for it and ought not to rely on tourism for its future. It did have a hotel of a sort, but it was a poor sort: the room was tiny, the bed narrow, the bathroom down a dingy corridor, its light going on and off randomly as if it was motion-sensitive (but it wasn't) and the window boarded up. The owner, however, seemed really pleased to have a guest, and invited Brendan to eat dinner with him and his wife. There wasn't much hope of there being anywhere else to eat, so Brendan agreed with some trepidation. The meal, however, was wonderful, and the wine plentiful – different bottles for each course, finishing off with a plum brandy that was so powerful that Brendan could have sworn it hissed when he spilled some on the table. He couldn't see whether it left a mark because he couldn't see at all by then.

Moldovan mornings were, by tradition now, difficult – blurry-mouthed, brain-fuzzed, leg-heavy. But once again, after an hour or two, Brendan emerged into a cheery and pleasant world full of people waving at him as he pedalled by. Curiously, the first big town was Bender, as if to remind him that sobriety was a better option. Brendan continued on towards the Ukrainian border, aware that he was passing through territory disputed between Moldova and the internationally-unrecognised PMR, the Pridnestrovian Moldavian Republic. He passed lorries with EUBAM on the side – the European Union Border Assistance Mission, set up after border rows in 2006 – but had no trouble when he reached the border at Pervomaisc, apart from having to pay a "fine" of €5 to the Ukrainian customs officer because he didn't have a Transnistrian visa.

Three hours later, the remarkably straight road led Brendan right into the centre of Odessa to the top of the famous Potemkin Steps, a long staircase down to the harbour area. It was hard work taking a bike down, especially one with a bouncy GO-kart on the back. Brendan found the white-towered, onion-domed Uspensky Cathedral near the railway station. This was where he was due to give his talk that evening – but it was a massive building which would seat thousands and he wondered if there'd been some mistake. He wandered around until he saw someone who seemed to know where they were, and was pleased to discover that the person spoke English. "I've come to talk here tonight," said Brendan.

"Ah, yes."

"Do you know if the priest is here?"

"Ah, yes."

"Could you take me to him?"

"Ah, yes."

Thankfully the priest came along at that point, and greeted Brendan in perfect English. "I see you've met Piotr," he said. "He's not the brightest of our guides but he does smile at everyone."

Brendan reflected on this, and quickly concluded that a smile was probably the most important qualification for a welcome-desk operator or guide. Too many church doorkeepers looked like undertakers.

"Let me show you our most famous Lady," said the priest, escorting Brendan across to a small brown icon which was apparently the reason why Odessa had not been destroyed in the Crimean War. Brendan couldn't stop himself wondering why its baby Jesus had a well-groomed short-back-and-sides. He wasn't really into icons, but he made respectful sighs of artistic and spiritual appreciation.

The talk that evening was in one of the many side chapels, and the audience of a 150 or so people seemed to enjoy it, even though it needed the priest (who was called Gregori) to translate. Brendan had emptied his GO-kart of all his Ukrainian cards, and managed to get rid of them all. The Ukrainian GNT was given to Piotr, whose face lit up even more. Brendan was whisked off by Gregori to the presbytery, where he left his luggage, and from there to a nearby restaurant for supper. Early on in the meal, after only a couple of glasses of wine, Brendan arranged with Gregori that his bike would be passed on to someone who needed it, and settled back in his chair to enjoy the meal. He discovered that he was very tired. It was almost as if the whole bike-journey had been done on auto-pilot, and only now was his body reacting to the physical test through which it had been put. He didn't remember much about the meal – only that the evening extended smoothly into pleasant oblivion.

Illichivsk, 17km away, was the port for the Black Sea ferry to Poti in Georgia. The taxi dumped Brendan at the entrance, and he walked into a bustling harbour area – with several ships docked at various wharves, lots of people milling around, and the smells of engines, fish and sea competing for his attention. He found the right ferry, bought his ticket, found his cabin, then went out on the side-deck to watch the preparations for departure. It was only when he chatted to a German cyclist that he realised that this ferry was actually yesterday's afternoon ferry which had only just got round to departing – apparently this was not unusual.

As the UKR ferry sailed past the tall red-and-white hooped lighthouse towards the open sea, Brendan breathed in the cold smell of the water, the breeze catching in his throat and making him cough, so he slipped inside to the warmth of the passenger lounge. It was nice to be able to relax – a good bit of the journey was coming up.

Totals brought forward		8713	17109	8445	2754	18469	24715
235: 5/1/12	Perwez	146					
236: 6/1/12	Luxembourg[145]	162					
237: 7/1/12	Azereilles (France)	133					
238: 8/1/12	Basle, Switzerland[146]	140					
239: 9/1/12	Vaduz, Liechtenstein[147]	175					
240: 10/1/12	Haiming, Austria[148]	112					
241: 11/1/12	Kufstein	106					
242: 12/1/12	Lenzing	121					
243: 13/1/12	Kaplice, Czech Republic[149]	126					
244: 14/1/12	Grafenworth (Austria)	110					
245: 15/1/12	Bratislava, Slovakia[150]	123					
246: 16/1/12	Tatbanya, Hungary[151]	128					
247: 17/1/12	Karacsond	120					
248: 18/1/12	Debrecan	142					
249: 19/1/12	Ciucea, Romania[152]	144					
250: 20/1/12	Targu Mures	148					
251: 21/1/12	Piatra Nearnt	158					
252: 22/1/12	Petresti, Moldova[153]	148					
253: 23/1/12	Floreni	120					
254: 24/1/12	Odessa, Ukraine[154]	149					
Totals carried forward		11424	17109	8445	2754	18469	24715

Chapter 56: Recrimination

Back in Jact, the situation was going not from bad to worse but from appalling to catastrophic. It was now nearly the end of January, and Cecil had been in charge for five months. Ben had been out of a job for 11 weeks, and had complained to the District Chair about "constructive dismissal". Unfortunately Caridad had never got round to such formalities as a contract, so a solicitor friend had told Ben that legally he didn't have a leg to stand on. Jack Turner felt a huge burden of guilt about Ben's departure, because it was Jack who'd brought Cecil to Jact. It had seemed sensible at the time, but was beginning to look as good a decision as King Priam of Troy saying to his mates, "That looks like a nice wooden horse, let's bring it into the city."

The Superintendent Minister went to see Jack in the run-up to Christmas and advised that something should be done about Cecil before he turned everybody away. The Circuit Stewards had also gone to see Jack to complain that Cecil was hopeless and was ruining all the good work that Caridad had done. A week ago, Jack had visited Cecil and asked him how things were going.

"It was a bit tricky at first," admitted Cecil. "But now that we've sorted out a few issues, we can start to build things up."

"And how are the church folk?" asked Jack.

"Pretty good, I think. We've got quite a few strong Christian people here who are really applying themselves."

"How many?"

"Oh, well, maybe a dozen or so..."

"And what happened to all the people who were here when Caridad was here?"

"Oh, they were never really *committed*, you know. It was a bit of a personality thing, centred around Caridad himself. They never really got involved, it was all a bit... well, showy."

Jack raised an eyebrow. "What about that young man who used to work here?"

"Oh, you mean Ben? He didn't stick either. No commitment or loyalty – you know what these young people are like!"

"So what's happened to the young people's work?"

"It never really got properly established, so I'm afraid it dwindled away."

"What about the work with the families?"

"I decided to concentrate on the faithful ones who've earned my time and attention by their perseverence and prayer-support. Then we can build up all these other projects from a firm foundation. I likened it in our Bible Study last week to the idea of the Remnant."

Jack didn't really want a theological argument, but he knew darned well that the Remnant was what was left of a community after it had undergone a catastrophe. Yet Cecil seemed to think that the disasters happening all around him were all part of

God's plan, and none of them was his fault. Cecil was dangerously close to the heresy that urged the Church to concentrate its efforts not on mission but on shedding peripheral hangers-on who might divert the saved away from The Only True Way. In other words, Jack thought that Cecil was an idiot. And he resolved to get rid of him.

***

Ben, meanwhile, was half-heartedly applying for jobs, but the churches were not taking on too many beatboxers or street-dancers, and certainly not in the North-East. It had to be a local job, because Ben and Louisa were now so close, and were talking quite seriously now about when they should get married – and where. They'd assumed that it would be at Jact, but now that was out of the picture. Maybe they both ought to look for jobs in another part of the country, but Louisa was very reluctant to be forced out of her job and her lovely new house in Cullercoats just because of some daft git of a Minister.

***

The trouble for Jack was that Cecil technically had not done anything wrong. He hadn't broken any Standing Orders or committed any disciplinary offences. The "constructive dismissal" of Ben was nasty and unpleasant, but because Cecil had inherited an employment situation where there was no contract, no District approval, no centralised stipend and no job description, he'd not blotted his official copy-book. Nor had he preached anything contrary to Methodist doctrine, though his views on the Remnant were coming dangerously close. In the Methodist Church it was very difficult to be removed just because you were inept and drove everyone away. There was a popular saying that a good Minister couldn't build up a church on his own but a bad Minister could destroy one very quickly without anybody's help. Cecil seemed to be trying his best to prove it.

Jack met with the Super and the Circuit Stewards and suggested that they consider a curtailment, which would remove Cecil at the end of July but there would be no replacement for at least a year because the Stationing process worked a year in advance. "Frankly," he said, "It's better to go without for a year than to have a complete wally, but don't quote me on that." They all smiled. At least they were all singing from the same hymn-sheet, and it was refreshing to hear the Chair admit that he'd made a colossal mistake.

"But what do we do in the meantime?" the Super asked. "It's all falling apart so quickly that there may be nothing left by the summer!"

"Leave it with me," said Jack. He'd had an idea. There was a little-known Standing Order[80] relating to suspension. S.O. 013(3)*a)* stated that "If the responsible officer believes on reasonable grounds that an office-holder is incapable through mental illness or otherwise of duly exercising office... or that for the preservation of good order in the Church the office-holder should on some other ground be suspended under this Standing Order and if the office-holder does not resign, then the responsible officer may suspend that office-holder from the exercise of any or every office in the Church..." Jack had never encountered, let alone administered a suspension. He knew that others had, and phoned up one particular Chair who'd talked at Stationing Committee a few weeks earlier about imposing a suspension. It was not something that any Chair wanted to do, but, in an emergency, Ministers sometimes needed to be taken out of a situation for their own good as well as their churches' good, and the Standing Order was there for that very reason.

"The key phrase in the Standing Order," said the Chair, "is "for the preservation of good order in the Church". This can mean that he's making a pig's ear of it. Tell him also that he can appeal to a specially-convened Pastoral Committee because, if you don't, you might get into trouble yourself. But you can suggest to him also that his ministry there would be extremely difficult to take up again whether he won the appeal or not. It sounds a bit cruel and manipulative, but we have a responsibility sometimes to take hard decisions and see them through."

Jack phoned Cecil and made an appointment to go round to see him the very next morning.

"It's about a serious matter and I shall be bringing the Superintendent and the Circuit Stewards with me. Please invite someone to support you in the meeting if you wish, and may I suggest that you cancel all appointments and meetings for the rest of the day."

"That's OK," said Cecil. "I don't need anyone to hold my hand and I am perfectly capable of deciding after the meeting what I shall do for the rest of the day, thank you very much."

***

The following morning, Jack arrived at Cecil's manse shortly before 8.30am, to find that the Circuit Stewards were already there, had rung the doorbell but got no reply. They kept ringing, but continued to get no reply – and started to get worried. "What if he's, you know...?" said the Super, pulling his head to the side in a grotesque parody of a hanging.

---

[80] That is exactly what it says. How it is best interpreted and administered is more debatable.

"Don't be daft," said Jack, who'd been fearing the very same outcome. "He must have overslept." But Jack didn't really believe it, and he rather suspected that no-one else believed it either. "Anyone got a key?" No-one had, but one of the Circuit Stewards remembered that he probably did have a key back home, left over from the time when they'd been doing some hurried decorating before Cecil arrived. He went off to search for it.

"What do you think?" The Super had sidled up to Jack and whispered in his ear. "He won't have... will he?"

"Don't ask me," said Jack. "I suppose he may well have been upset about the meeting, even though he didn't know what it was about. He'll have had his suspicions, though..."

At that point the Circuit Steward re-appeared, brandishing a key. "I think this is the one. Who's going to do the honours?"

Everyone looked down at their feet as if their shoes had just become fascinating. "Give it here," said Jack, pushing forwards, grabbing the key and turning to the door. He was worried too about what they might find. The key turned and Jack entered warily. "Hello? Cecil?" The others crept in behind him, looking furtively around as if they expected to see feet dangling from the upstairs banister, and sniffing to detect any smell of gas.

The house was empty. No Cecil. None of Cecil's meagre possessions either. Nothing except the furniture and fittings, which they themselves had supplied from the local charity shops and from their lofts. On the mantelpiece, however, was an envelope bearing Jack's name. He opened the envelope, slipped the note out, unfolded it and read it silently to himself.

The others waited.

Time stood still.

Jack cleared his throat and announced that he would read it out.

In a precise and clear voice he read: "I never liked it here. It's too cold. I'm going back to Fiji."

Chapter 57: Nations 155 - 163

Brendan's arrival in the port of Poti, Georgia marked his 155th nation, which meant that there were only 39 left. He still had over 100 days to go and was on schedule despite the unplanned fortnight's stay in East Timor. The ferry had taken a blissfully relaxed 45 hours to cross the Black Sea, docking just as the sun was coming up through the rusty lattice of a huge crane.

He only had to get to Tbilisi that day, a journey of just over 300km, so he wandered over to the railway station, bought a ticket, and went off to get some breakfast before the train's scheduled departure at 9.30am. He boarded the train at 9.10am and sat there for the next 2½ hours before the carriage lurched as the engine finally announced its arrival. A further 90 minutes ensued before it lurched again and they eventually groaned out of the station and crawled eastwards across the flattest and dullest terrain Brendan had seen since, well, the last bit of boring terrain – was it Hungary? Belgium? Russia?

Brendan had assumed that he would be fascinated by the rolling kilometres of landscape, but the truth was that most of it looked identical. The people looked different, of course, but then in a way they looked identical too, for they were merely the background scenery for his journey. This all brought him back to the symbolism and purpose of his trip (which remained laudable and godly) and the reality and fatigue of it all (which didn't help him to be terribly spiritual most of the time). He tried to smile at people, but often they looked at him woodenly and he made no impact whatsoever on their lives. It disappointed him in a way that he'd finally come to this realisation, but in another way it strengthened his belief in an "incarnational" model of mission, which required a would-be evangelist to settle into a community in order to share its story and add his or her own. He'd been greatly impressed at Ministerial Training College by Vincent Donovan's book "Christianity Rediscovered"[81], in which the author described his own experience of living with the Masai in Kenya, and how he'd learnt so much from the Masai. He'd assumed that he would be bringing the Gospel to them, but the reality was that, as they shared stories and life together in Kenya, they discovered the Gospel together and found signs pointing to Jesus, without importing ideas from anywhere else.

The slow train rumbled, huffed and lurched its way across the featureless Georgian countryside, then through valleys between rollercoaster forests to the capital itself. Brendan noticed the high stands of the Dinamo Tbilisi football stadium out of the window as they came through the suburbs. He remembered that the first

---

[81] A classic, still available: DONOVAN, Vincent, "Christianity Rediscovered: An Epistle from the Masai", Orbis Books, Second Edition, 1982.

football match he'd ever seen on a colour television was Liverpool losing here in the European Cup, sometime in the late 1970s[82]. Of course it was then the USSR, and everything was very different now, as he discovered when he walked from the station to Freedom Square. The square had once been Lenin Square and boasted a huge statue of him, which was torn down in 1991 and replaced with one of St. George slaying the dragon.

Brendan strolled along the grandeur of Rustaveli Avenue and soon reached his destination for the evening, the Kashveti Orthodox Church of St. George – presumably the whole country was named after him. There was a sign outside which announced that the church was "ქაშვეთის წმინდა გიორგის სახელობის ტაძარი" which didn't mean much to Brendan, but the building looked just like the photo he'd been given by Fahada long ago, so he knew that it was the right place. It looked rather grand, both outside and inside, with frescoes lining the walls. Brendan was greeted by the priest, whom he'd emailed earlier in the day from an internet café in Poti. Lado thankfully spoke English really well. Brendan had been called "Laddo" a few times in his youth, but Lado explained that his was a very distinguished Georgian name. He backed it up by showing Brendan the frescoes in the church which were the work of the country's most famous artist, Lado Gudiashvili. Brendan thought the frescoes a bit basic, but they were beautifully coloured and made the whole place very picturesque.

"Kashveti is a word meaning "giving birth to a stone"," Lado volunteered, as if he were the tour-guide. When Brendan looked puzzled, Lado laughed. "It was a scandal at the time. David of Gareja, one of the famous Assyrian Fathers, was accused of getting a local Tbilisi nun pregnant, and prophesied that she would give birth to a stone, which, of course, she did!" Hmmm, Brendan thought. That was some miracle, and highly convenient...

They imported some chairs for the evening, as the Georgians usually worshipped standing up, and the audience poured in, over 200 of them, who, with the help of Lado's translating, seemed to lap up Brendan's presentation. The Georgian GNT went to a bent old lady whom Lado pointed out to Brendan. "She is over 100 years old, and has prayed here every morning, when she hasn't been ill, since the start of the war with Germany, when her fiancé went off with his army brigade and never came back. The Russians were frightened of her and used to let her into the church even when they kept everyone else out." When Brendan gave her the GNT, she turned to Lado and spoke for a good minute or so. "She says that she doesn't want to keep this for herself, but that this must be kept on a chain outside the main door of the church so that everyone can come and read it." Brendan smiled and nodded, and the old lady smiled and nodded too. It was a beautiful idea.

---

[82] Dinamo Tbilisi 3, Liverpool 0 (European Cup, October 3rd 1979)

The next day, Lado directed Brendan to the Hertz office on Leselidze Street, and Brendan drove the two of them 60km south-east to the David Gareja monastery sitting astride the Georgia-Azerbaijani border. Brendan was amazed at the scale of the monastery complex, which stretched across the whole side of the mountain, and included hundreds of cells, churches, chapels, refectories and living quarters hollowed out of the rock face. He'd never seen anything quite like it.

They continued down into Azerbaijan proper, and stopped for lunch at a small town called Qazax, which would be a purler of a word to get at Scrabble, thought Brendan – if you were allowed place-names... There was a small church there, and Lado found a nervous-looking old man to whom Brendan gave the Azerbaijani GNT. Lado explained what it was, and who Brendan was, and the man nodded as if he understood, but regarded Brendan like an alien just emerged from a spaceship.

Next stop was Azatamut, a village just over the border in Armenia, and an almost identical conversation took place with an almost identical old man from an almost identical church. Then they retraced their steps, arriving back in Tbilisi at 5pm, and took the car back. It had been a productive day for Brendan, ticking two more nations off his list.

"Tonight I treat you," said Lado.

They walked through to the Old City, a different world from the grand avenues and modern blocks of the Tbilisi Brendan had seen up to that point. Instead: Tennessee Williams-style old balconies, ancient churches, winding streets and charming shops. There was so much to see: a curiously abandoned street-car, the art galleries of Chardini Street, stunning tableaux of modern art lining Sioni Street, old sulphur bath-houses and tantalising views of the Narikala Fortress. "Here we are," announced Lado, and a jaw-dropping Brendan followed him into Café Casablanca[83], complete with its own white piano, Humphrey Bogart quotations on the menu and enormous film posters on the walls. "This is my favourite place in the whole world," Lado boasted, which seemed a bit hyperbolic after their visit to the monastery in the cliff – but it was still pretty amazing.

The food was a combination of American steak-house and Moroccan bazaar-café, but the cocktails were distinctly American and priced accordingly. There was light jazz music playing, and halfway through the evening, a black pianist in a white jacket started to play "As Time Goes By", and everyone joined in the singing. It was a great evening and Lado was great company. He seemed to want to explain the plot and even recite the script to Brendan, but Brendan assured Lado that he'd seen and enjoyed the film.

***

---

[83] It really does exist, in the heart of Old Tbilisi.

Brendan caught the train out to Tbilisi airport, and by mid-morning was en route to Colombo in Sri Lanka. It was a bit of a mystery why there was a direct flight between the two countries, but it served Brendan's purposes well. He relaxed into his seat and looked forward to the next nine days of non-stop air travel and frantic island-hops, taking him 40,000km across to the other side of the world. It would be exhausting, but at least it wouldn't be physically demanding – all that he had to do was sit in a seat, jump out for "appearances", give a few talks, and enjoy the experience. It was going to take him to some of the most remote, exotic but least-visited places on the planet and to some of the most modern and cosmopolitan cities. This was the part of the trip to which he'd been most looking forward.

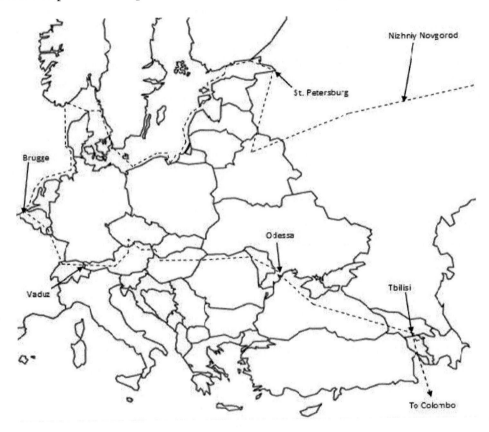

Nations 132 to 158

***

The plane landed at Colombo's Bandaranaike Airport, where, by prior arrangement, Brendan met a Catholic nun called Conceptua from the nearby

Katuwapitiya parish, who told him about their efforts to evangelise amongst a mostly Buddhist community centred round the famous Agurukaramulla Pansala temple. "It's all very friendly," she said. "But they talk about us as "Little Rome" and look down on us as a foreign religion – imported and therefore less authentic." Brendan gave her the Sri Lankan GNT and encouraged her to use it to show the Catholic people in Negombo that they were not the only ones intent on fulfilling the Great Commission.

He then walked across to the Sri Lankan Airways desk to check in for the flight to Malé, the capital of the Maldives, and patiently waited to board. He was surprised to see a whole pack of nuns holding a prayer meeting in the boarding area, centred round a young woman waiting to board the same flight as Brendan. He went across to them, introduced himself and joined in the circle of prayer. "What are we praying for?" he asked.

"We are from the St. Lucia Cathedral in Colombo," one of them told him. "Our sister Margarita is going to the Maldives to try to evangelise there, but it is illegal so we are praying for spiritual armour to protect her."

"How about I sit with her on the flight and continue the prayers as we fly in?" Brendan offered, and they smiled and clapped with excitement that their prayers were already being answered. "You can help her," they said.

"But I'm only there for one evening," said Brendan. "I'm speaking at a hotel about my trip round the world, encouraging people to take mission seriously."

"Even better!" their spokeswoman said, jumping up and down with glee, as if Brendan was the secret ingredient which would make their project a success. "You can be the one to smuggle the Bibles in!"

Brendan was taken aback, but didn't like to refuse straightaway. "What do you mean?"

"We've just received 20 copies of Luke's Gospel translated into the Dhivehi language, so we want to make sure that they get through to the people of the Maldives safely. But if Margarita gets caught smuggling them in, they'll throw her into prison and our plans will be ruined. We've been praying about this for six months, and now we *know* that we are doing the right thing."

Brendan wasn't too sure. What if *he* were caught smuggling and thrown into prison? What about *his* plans? "But I've got the whole New Testament translated into Dhivehi. Look, I'll show you." And he ferreted around in his hand luggage and pulled out the GNT. They were all amazed because they didn't think that anyone had translated further than just the one Gospel. "It's a sign!" they cried. "Praise God!"

Brendan wasn't sure about all of this, but felt a real burst of warmth at their exuberance and its effect on him. He shook his head in amazement and said, "OK – let's go for it!"

***

Brendan discovered on the plane that Margarita was originally called Jessi Est and came from Arras, France, until she'd "taken the veil" and been given the name Margarita by her order. As it was a missionary order, she'd served in various places around the world, and had been in Colombo for the last five years. Brendan told her about his visit to the Arras Memorial. She laughed, saying in broken English that she used to live just across the road from the cemetery gates. They got on well together on the short flight across the Indian Ocean, and chatted about their vocations as well as their family backgrounds. Margarita said that she was the daughter of a French count and an Italian waitress, which sounded so far-fetched that Brendan burst out laughing. "Where did they meet?" he asked.

"He went on holiday to Capri and she served at his table in the hotel." It sounded wonderfully romantic, and Margarita's laugh was enchanting. When they landed at Malé Airport, Brendan and Margarita acted as a married couple, chatting and laughing with one another to hide their fear as they approached the customs desk. To their horror, they were beckoned over by one of the officials.

"Passports," he ordered.

They handed them over. He raised an eyebrow when he saw that they were from different countries. "You married?" he asked.

"Yes," said Brendan, as if it were the most ridiculous question he'd ever been asked.

The customs officer then compared their passports. Their hearts were beating furiously, but nothing could alter the fact that their surnames were not the same. He looked at their names and shrugged his shoulders. "Welcome to the Maldives," he said, and smiled, handing the two passports back. They somehow managed to muster a smile back and passed through, deafened by their heartbeats which seemed loud enough for everybody to hear.

"Sacre Dieu," whispered Margarita.

"I don't believe it," muttered Brendan. "How on earth...?"

When they got out of the airport, they were at a ferry terminal. Hullule Island had nothing except the airport on it – the main island of Malé was ten minutes away across the ocean. Surrounded by excited tourist passengers and huge piles of suitcases, they didn't dare speak about what had happened back at the airport. It was the same when they got to the other island – everybody crammed into taxis according to their hotel, and the two of them found themselves squashed into a taxi with a rather large and loud Texan couple. Eventually they reached the Central Hotel where Brendan was due to speak and Margarita had a room booked. She'd been booked into a twin room, much to the horror of the receptionist. "We change it," he promised. "No, no, that's OK – really it's fine," said Brendan, much to the other man's bewilderment. He couldn't understand why this couple didn't want a double bed. They got upstairs and collapsed onto the beds, shrieking with laughter and relief.

"I don't understand," said Brendan. "They didn't even look at my bag or anything. How did we get away with our names being different?" He flipped open the two passports, both of which the customs man had handed back to him. In such a heavily Islamic country the woman was not expected to be able to take responsibility for anything serious, even her own passport. Then Brendan laughed and laughed, until Margarita came across to have a look. "Incredible," said Brendan, tears of laughter running down his face.

"What is it?" said Margarita. "What's so amusing?"

"Your name!" shouted Brendan. "Jessi Capri Est."

"What's so funny about that? I can't help it if they gave me a silly middle name because that's where they met. It is very romantic, I think."

"But look how they've written it, in capital letters, with no real space between the three names! Look! It says: JESSICAPRIEST. It looks like Jessica Priest!" Margarita didn't understand what Brendan was on about.

"Look!" said Brendan. "Look at my passport. Look at my name – Brendan Priest. It's... wonderful!"

Margarita, who had had no idea what Brendan's last name was, cottoned on, and shrieked with laughter too. "God is good," she said, when she'd regained the ability to speak. "It's a miracle, yes?"

"Yes," said Brendan. "I rather think it is."

***

After a peculiar evening meeting in the lounge of the hotel, speaking to mostly European and American tourists, with not a single Maldivian in sight except behind the non-alcoholic bar, Brendan and Margarita went upstairs to their room, and had a brief conversation before Brendan had to leave for the airport. Margarita told him her plans. She was going to try to get a job in a local bar or hotel and befriend some of the locals, hoping to discern the right time to speak about her faith. The Maldives may be Paradise according to the tourist brochures, but it was the sixth-worst nation in the world for the persecution of Christians, according to Open Doors. It was illegal to be anything other than a Muslim, and any converts to Christianity could be sentenced to death by the Islamic courts. There wasn't a single church building throughout the nation, and no Bible in the Dhivehi language. But there was, now, a copy of the New Testament. Brendan got it out and handed it to Margarita, who said that she would treasure it. "I shall use the copies of Luke's Gospel to win 20 people to Christ," she said. "Then I shall give them this as the Bible for their church."

***

Brendan left Malé on the 10.45pm Malaysia Airlines flight to Kuala Lumpur, which connected with a 13-hour flight to Sydney, leaving at 9am. It had been a remarkable 24 hours.

***

Australia was another whistle-stop visit. The briefest of conversations in the airport chapel; the handing-over of the Australian GNT – "I'll keep it open in the chapel, for everyone to use when they pass through here," said the chaplain; then a flight out just after midnight to Auckland.

The mighty Pacific Ocean awaited Brendan. Within a week he would be across the other side of it – 12,000km as the crow flies (though it would be pretty exhausted if it tried), but over 25,000km on the route Brendan was taking. It was going to be quite a week.

***

The Pacific was so big that all the land-mass of the Earth, plus another Africa, could be squeezed into it and there would still be sea-room to spare. It had been named by Magellan who encountered calm weather and gentle waves all the way across on his global circumnavigation in 1521. It wasn't like that for Brendan. The flight from Sydney to Auckland started with thunder and lightning and continued in a storm of epic strength. The plane bounced up and down and side to side and Brendan felt as sick as a dog throughout. No-one tried to sleep even though it was the middle of the night. The pilot kept giving interesting facts about the weather conditions but Brendan only listened with half his attention, his antennae scanning the announcements for phrases such as "Mayday!", "Emergency!" and "We're all going to die!" The pilot scoffed at one point: "Some people mistakenly call these mini-tornadoes, but these ones are only registering F2 on the Fujita Scale[84] so they're

---

[84] Devised by Tetsuya Fujita in 1971, this 13-level scale (F0–F12) was designed to connect the Beaufort scale and the Mach number scale. F1 corresponds to the 12th level of the Beaufort scale, and F12 to the impossible wind-speed of Mach 1.0. F0 was placed at a position specifying no damage (approximately the 8th level of the Beaufort scale). Fujita intended that only F0-F5 be used in practice, as this covered all possible levels of damage to homes as well as the expected limits of wind speeds. F2 describes wind-speeds between 181kph and 253kph, and is officially designated a "strong tornado".

just a wall of wind, really. Nothing to worry about!" Brendan had never heard of the Fujita Scale but he didn't like the sound of F2. It sounded mid-scale, which, as it was measuring tornadoes, was a bit scary.

The battering of the wind was in totally the wrong direction, so the ordinarily 3½ hour flight actually took over five hours. It was utterly miserable, and Brendan was drained by the time they wobbled into land. He hadn't actually been sick, but sort-of wished that he had been. He couldn't have felt worse. It was a huge relief to get out of the plane and stagger his way into the airport, and a tired joy to see some familiar faces. The family who'd emigrated to New Zealand some years before, and whom he'd visited on his last sabbatical, had driven up from Tauranga to meet him. It was great to see them, even though he only had a few hours with them before he had to be back at the airport for the flight to Fiji. They gave him a lift out to Mount Eden, a suburb south of the city, where they drove up the extinct volcano to view the city below them. A meeting had been arranged with ecumenical church leaders at the small white clapboard Methodist Church just below the volcano, and Brendan's friends sat patiently listening to him speak about the primacy of mission. At the end of the meeting, he gave the Maori GNT to the only Maori present, who happened to be the cleaner/caretaker of the church who was waiting to lock up after them. They went next-door to the Simla Indian Café, and spent the next hour reminiscing about old times over the "ten-dollar dinner".

The flight to Nadi in Fiji was mercifully much more pacific, and they landed on time at 10.30pm local time. A plane from Los Angeles had just landed, by coincidence carrying another Methodist Minister, called Cecil. Without realising it, the two ex-Ministers of Jact were waiting at adjacent carousels for their luggage. Brendan was relieved to see his name on a board being held by someone waiting for him – the biggest man Brendan had ever seen. Wesley squeezed himself into the driver's seat of a minibus but overlapped across the handbrake onto the passenger seat as well. "In you get," said Wesley, displaying a smile just as wide as his frame, "Plenty of room for a kaivalagi like you!" Brendan wasn't sure whether this was a polite term or whether he was being patronised or insulted. "It means foreigner," explained Wesley, reading his thoughts. "But because most foreigners are a lot thinner than a kaiviti or indigenous Fijian, it has come to mean "thin". Not all Fijians are as well-shaped as me, but most are bigger than you little tourists." And he laughed, looking across to check that Brendan was smiling too.

Wesley explained that he was the church steward of Nadi Methodist Church and was giving Brendan hospitality overnight before his breakfast meeting with the Methodist leadership. They drove for about ten minutes in the dark without Brendan seeing any lights or buildings, but then Wesley turned off and stopped at one of the dark houses. As Brendan staggered out of the minibus, and was greeted by Wesley's similarly well-proportioned wife, he realised how tired he was and, after a few minutes' polite conversation, was glad to retreat to a bedroom and collapse.

***

The Fijian Methodist Church[85] was the majority Christian denomination, and had been put under increasing pressure from the country's government, which had forced the Church to cancel its annual Conference and choir festivals for the next five years. The Districts and Circuits were also having their activities restricted, with administrative meetings banned. Wesley explained the situation as they drove to the meeting at the Hard Rock Café in Port Denarau Marina: "In the UK, I suppose it's easy to take religious freedom for granted. The Methodist Church in Fiji simply wants to worship God and serve the people of Fiji with their ministry, but the government's unreasonable restrictions are making the Church's daily life almost impossible."

Who would have thought that such a Paradise would have such repressive practices? When Brendan arrived at the Marina complex, he was amazed once again at the luxury items in the shopping plaza and the super-yachts bobbing around in the marina itself. Tourists were flocking off buses to the various ferries for the offshore islands, and Brendan remembered well when he'd been here before and spent a few days on Bounty Island, a paradise escape-from-it-all in the Mamanucas.

In the Café, he was introduced to various Methodist leaders whose names he instantly forgot, for the names all included lots of syllables with multiple use of the letters "u", "j", "k" and "l". All of them had been charged with "attending an unauthorized meeting" (church) a few years ago, been held for questioning by the police, accused of spying on the government, and banned from holding any services or meetings. The dispute had continued despite attempts by the Church in Fiji and in Britain to find a way forward.

"We are a people who believe in knocking," said one Minister. "Even till midnight!" Everybody laughed.

"Knock, knock!" shouted another Minister – but it wasn't a joke...

"What do you do about the ban?" asked Brendan.

"Oh, we get round it by meeting "accidentally" in cafés and bars, or on boats," said one of them.

"And I'm a chaplain to the police," said another. "And Tuikilakila over there is a chaplain in the military – and we keep leading worship in police-stations and army-barracks. It's only public worship that we can't do."

"But what about the ordinary people?" asked Brendan.

---

[85] This dispute with the Government is still on-going at the time of writing. The ban is currently until 2014.

"It's amazing how little groups just happen to meet under a tree or in a field or on a beach, and somehow a Minister is there too," said another Minister, laughing. "The Church is growing, not disappearing!"

Brendan was pleased to meet them, and promised to promote their struggle when he returned to the UK. He gave the President of the Fijian Conference his Fijian GNT and the President promised that he would keep it as a reminder that Christians should continue the mission of the Church – no matter what. Brendan enjoyed his breakfast and the prayers which followed, but had to leave early because he was due to meet a certain lady back at the airport. Wesley had packed away the equivalent of four breakfasts, but his stomach still rumbled as he eased himself like a human water-bed into the driver's seat.

***

Esther and her pilot and film-crew were waiting in the executive lounge at the airport – which wasn't up to *her* executive standard. "Look at these seats!" she exclaimed in disgust. "They're *vinyl*!" But then she recovered her usual charm and greeted Brendan. "Hi Brendan, how are you doing? How's that throat? We flew in last night from Detroit but haven't really slept much, because we had to refuel several times on the way here. We even had to make use of old George Washington, didn't we, boys?"

They nodded. Brendan looked blank. Esther laughed.

"USS George Washington, to be precise. I just happen to know the man who's in charge of it."

Brendan spluttered. "You mean you set your plane down on an aircraft-carrier on the strength of knowing the captain?" Even Esther didn't have the ability to pull strings at that level, had she[86]?

"No, silly. Not the captain. It's the Admiral of the Pacific Fleet whom I know. He arranged it with the captain as a booster for his people. All I had to do was wave at the folks and they even topped up the tanks for free!"

Brendan shook his head at the lady's pizzazz. He looked across at the pilot. "And how was landing on an aircraft-carrier?"

The pilot grinned. "An interesting experience. Had to change my pants afterwards. And taking off wasn't much different." They all laughed.

"The trouble is that the Pacific is so big!" complained Esther. "It took us four stops in all from Detroit: Phoenix, George W, then Kiribati and American Samoa and

---

[86] I imagine that no civilian has the power to manipulate the U.S. Navy, so this is pure "imaginative licence".

here. We didn't get here till gone midnight, so I'm looking forward to a good night's sleep tonight. Where are we going to be?"

"The Solomon Islands," said Brendan. "But we have to go via Vanuatu."

"Whatever..." said Esther as she walked off out of the Executive Lounge, with everyone else scurrying off after her. "We'd better get on with it, then!"

Day: Date	Itinerary (* indicates TV interview) ([18] indicates new nation)	Bike (km)	Car/ Bus (km)	Train (km)	Kayak /Sail (km)	Boat (km)	Air (km)
Totals brought forward		11424	17109	8445	2754	18469	24715
255: 25/1/12	Ilichevsk – Poti ferry		17				
256: 26/1/12	Ilichevsk – Poti ferry					990	
257: 27/1/12	Tbilisi, Georgia[155]			251			
258: 28/1/12	Qazax, Azerbaijan[156]; Achajar, Armenia[157]		164				
259: 29/1/12	Tbilisi; Colombo, Sri Lanka[158]; Malé, Maldives[159]			16			5959
260: 30/1/12	Sydney, Australia[160]						9522
261: 31/1/12	Auckland, New Zealand[161]; Nadi, Fiji[162]						4289
Totals carried forward		11424	17290	8712	2754	19459	44485

Chapter 58: Nations 164 to 173

The flight to Vanuatu took little over an hour. Brendan, Esther and the film-crew were whisked off in a black limousine to the Parliament Building, where Brendan and Esther were filmed being greeted by a choir of school girls singing the Vanuatu national anthem, "Yumi, yumi, yumi," which had Brendan and Esther stifling giggles. They were greeted by the President himself. "Welcome to my country!" he cried, expansively. He wasn't as big as Fijian Wesley but he certainly wasn't malnourished, and he had a similarly massive smile.

"Thank you, Mister President," mumbled Brendan, bowing his head a little in respect.

"Oh, don't worry about all that," said the President. "Just call me Iaru[87]." He planted a big kiss on Esther's cheek and then did it on the other cheek too.

"Pleased to meet you," said Esther, somewhat taken aback. She could land on aircraft-carriers but kissing a President still took her breath away.

They were shown round by Iaru – not that there was a lot to see. The Parliament chamber, like the rest of the building, was modern, with what looked like a despatch box at one end of a long wooden table. It all looked a bit Westminster-ish to Brendan, who remarked on this to the President. "Deliberately so," he replied. "We are very proud of our Westminster model, but have added a few refinements, which we stole from the French." He roared with laughter. "That's why I'm the President rather than anything else. I don't think I would make a very good queen!" He guffawed again. Quite a hoot, old Iaru. He led them through to his private chambers, and ordered drinks for them all, then asked Brendan questions about his journey and its aims. Brendan answered them as best he could, but then asked Iaru what the main issues were for his Government and people.

"The same as any other little country: poverty and cultural independence. Vanuatu is one of the poorest countries in the world and yet was top in a recent survey of the happiest countries. We get the best out of the rich world without damaging our own way of life. So we've become a tax haven and international finance centre for offshore funds, but also people can pay their bills in sea-shells and pig tusks." He laughed loudly again.

Brendan gave him the GNT, translated into the Bislama language. "Please keep it here in the Parliament Building, so that the Gospel is at the centre of your nation." Iaru nodded and smiled. "Oh, and one more thing," said Brendan. "What does "Yumi, yumi, yumi" mean?"

---

[87] At the time of writing, the first name of the President of Vanuatu is Iolu, but there any similarity or link ends. Vanuatu's National Anthem, economy and Parliament building are as described. But the rest is fiction.

Iaru laughed and started to sing:

> "Yumi, Yumi, yumi i glat long talem se, Yumi, yumi, yumi i man blong Vanuatu
> God i givim ples ia long yumi, Yumi glat tumas long hem,
> Yumi strong mo yumi fri long hem, Yumi brata evriwan!"

And then he sang it again, this time in English.

> "We, we, we are happy to proclaim, We, we, we are the people of Vanuatu
> God has given us this land, We have great cause for rejoicing
> We are strong and we are free in this land, We are all brothers."

"Good, isn't it?" he asked.
They nodded. Yes, it was good.

***

By the time they got back to the airport, it was early afternoon, but they were under no time pressures, because they only had a further 1,300km (and an hour and a half) to go to Honiara International Airport, which turned out to be a small ex-military airfield 10km east of the capital of the Solomon Islands.

Honiara was on the island of Guadalcanal, which Brendan had heard about as a battle in the Second World War but knew precious little else. The airfield, then known as Henderson Field, had been a major focus for fighting between Allied and Japanese forces, due to its strategic position for the protection of American convoys to Australia and New Zealand. Brendan learnt all this from a big sign in the airport terminal, and their limousine-driver told them his version of the Guadalcanal campaign, despite the fact that he was only about 16 years old.

They arrived at the Heritage Park Hotel on the sea-front after a peculiarly slaloming journey along the dramatically-straight Kukum Highway. The driver must either have been avoiding livestock or potholes or imaginary strafe-bombers – or been drunk. On the way they'd passed a burnt-down Chinatown and some pretty grubby buildings. Honiara didn't offer a tourist much choice: either scuba-dive Japanese shipwrecks or visit the American war memorial. The town had escaped devastation from an earthquake-triggered tsunami in 2007, but looked ravaged anyway.

Brendan was to speak at the white-spired Wesley United Church, and arrived with the film-crew half an hour before the meeting was due to start, to find people packing out the building, eager to catch sight of... Esther. When they realised that she wasn't with them (she'd stayed at the hotel to get an early night), there was uproar, and one of the film-crew was sent back to fetch her. The audience didn't seem to take much interest in Brendan, but they sat through his talk patiently while they waited for Esther to arrive. Brendan saw her taxi arrive through the window of the church, and hastily gave away the GNT before the hubbub and excitement of her entry, after which the whole meeting disintegrated into chaos. It probably would look good (or make Esther look good) when it was broadcast, but it didn't do much for Brendan's confidence.

***

A rejuvenated Esther breezed into breakfast eager to start the next part of the journey, which would take them to the easternmost part of Papua New Guinea, Bougainville. In fact, they were going to Buka, an island just to the north of the main island, which is where the airport was. Bougainville and Buka were part of the Solomon Islands archipelago in every way except politically, and less than an hour later they landed just north of the Buka Passage. As they alighted from the plane, they were met by a greeting party of schoolchildren and parents, who unfurled a big banner declaring "We ♥ Esther". Brendan didn't particularly want to be a celebrity, but it was beginning to needle him that no-one seemed to think that what he was doing was important.

Esther waved to the crowd and Brendan waved too, rather sheepishly. The crowd fell back respectfully as a man strode forward to greet them. He stopped a few metres away and bowed. "Name belong me Emmy Money Hill. Good fellow long bung him you." Or, at least, that's what it sounded like. They were all bemused. Had he really said that his name was Emmy Money Hill? They were relieved when he stepped forwards towards them and said, in perfect English, "That's the formal greeting over, let's go and have a drink, shall we?" As they walked across to what may be a town hall, just 100m from the entrance to the airstrip, he explained further. "The greeting is a traditional one in our official language which is called Tok Pisin. Everyone speaks it even though there are three other tribal languages. It means, "My title is munihil or chief of chiefs. You are welcome here. How are you?" You've probably heard of Pidgin English – well, this is our variation on it."

Brendan plucked up his courage and asked, "Munihil sounds very powerful – are you like a king?"

The munihil laughed. "No, we're ruled by the government in Port Moresby. On the island, though, we have clan chiefs called tsunonos, and they appoint one tsunono to be the munihil. I became a tsunono when my father died, even though I was studying at Otago University at the time, and I've been munihil for three years nearly."

"How did you become munihil?" asked Esther.

"I killed a lot of pigs." He replied, and laughed. "The one who has the most pigs to kill for the feast is usually regarded as the most powerful, and deemed to be the favourite of our ancient ancestors whose spirits must approve of the tsunonos' choice."

"So your religion's based on shamanism and ancestor-worship, is it?" asked Brendan.

"Sort of," said the munihil. "But most of us are Christians really. As for me, I'm a Methodist."

As Brendan and the munihil, whose real name was Terence, got talking, Brendan realised that Christianity had to sit alongside traditional beliefs as a sort of "translation" and not try to suppress them. Terence talked of God as Sunahan and Jesus as the son of Sunahan. Mary, mother of Jesus, was a teitahol or woman chief. When Brendan gave Terence the GNT, Terence turned to the end of John's Gospel, and showed Brendan the words of Jesus on the cross to Mary his mother, referring to one of Jesus' disciples[88]. Instead of "Woman, here is your son," the Tok Pisin version read, "Teitahol, here tsunono be you." It left Brendan more amazed than ever at the skill of the translators. They'd got it exactly right.

***

After a further wave to the crowd, they took off for their overnight destination, the small settlement of Tafunsak on the island of Kosrae, the nearest bit of the massively-spread nation of Micronesia. It was still only a two hour flight, and they landed on the tiny off-shore airstrip in mid-afternoon, leaving them the rest of the afternoon to sightsee while the film-crew scurried off to prepare for the evening meeting. Brendan had spent the flight reading about Micronesia. It covered an area of over 2,600,000km^2, and consisted of over 600 islands, but all the land in total only took up a measly 700km^2. There was, in other words, a lot of water. Kosrae was at the easternmost end of the nation, nearly 3,000km away from its westernmost point.

At the airport, Brendan and Esther separated. She went to check out the hotel, and Brendan stayed chatting to the lady behind the tourist desk. Trying to show off his newly-revised knowledge, Brendan asked her about the American missionaries who had "discovered" the island in Victorian times.

"Oh, we go a lot further back than that!" said the lady, whose name-badge identified her as Angie. "There have been people here since the Polynesian seafarers arrived about 2,000 years ago, and when the Americans came they discovered advanced fishing and agricultural communities."

---

[88] John 19: 26

"Oh," said Brendan, feeling that he'd committed the unforgivable sin of being a patronising Brit. "Sorry!"

"Don't worry about it," said Angie. "The Americans also discovered that the communities here were being destroyed by disease and alcohol."

"Where had that come from?"

"France originally, then disenchanted British whaling crews who decided to settle in what seemed an island paradise. They were known as beachcombers."

"Oh dear," said Brendan. "Sorry, again. We haven't done you any favours, have we?"

"The American missionaries did a lot of good here when they arrived, even though they made everyone wear different clothes. They built schools, discouraged drinking and made the beachcombers feel so uncomfortable that they left."

"And what's Kosrae like now?" Brendan asked.

"It's Paradise," she said, with a big grin. "We have a wonderful climate, with plenty of showers at this time of year to water the crops and make the air nice and fresh. Kosrae has mountains, jungle, white sandy beaches, and is known as the Jewel of Micronesia. I hope you enjoy your stay here!"

"So what do you suggest I do if I only have a couple of hours to spare?"

Angie thought hard. "You haven't enough time to visit the Neolithic ruins on Lelu or Menke or the marine park at Utwe-Walung, but you could go to the Wiya Cave."

"What's that?" asked Brendan.

"It's where we learnt to count," Angie said with an enigmatic smile. "I'll get you a lift." She picked up the phone and had a quick conversation. "Philip will take you there. Have a good time!" She pointed to the door and a black taxi pulled up outside. "My son will take good care of you!" Angie shouted after Brendan.

The taxi only travelled about 3km before turning off into a quarry. Philip explained as they walked to the huge cave opening that it was home to thousands of Island Swifts. The cave went back only about 20m; the floor was slippery with bird droppings so walking inside was pointless, but Brendan could see that the whole vast ceiling was covered in clumps of birds, like grapes on a vine. A sign at the side of the cave told the story: the cave was believed to have once cut through the island, and giants living there taught Kosraeans how to count. As they walked back through the trees, Brendan was buzzed by a huge orange bird. "What was that?" he cried.

Philip laughed. "That was a flying fox. It's a bat, really, and I don't know why it's called a flying fox. A fox is like a dog, isn't it?" Brendan nodded, and Philip continued. "I suppose they are big. Their span is wider than a man's reach. Their bodies are actually quite puny but all you see is their big orange wings." He turned to Brendan and smiled. "You can probably have it for dinner tonight at the hotel. It's supposed to be good if you're asthmatic."

***

Brendan was disappointed to scan the hotel menu and find no flying fox. He plumped for pork fahfah, which turned out to be soft taro, cuts of pork in lime sauce, and described on the menu as "food for chiefs". He was offered kava, but decided that he'd better stick to fruit juice, because he still had to speak at the evening meeting.

It was held at the white-steepled church on the edge of the trees. The atmosphere inside was dark and sweaty, with over 200 people packed in and the film-crew desperately trying to rig up some lighting. The evening began with a dramatic entrance by the church choir, who marched in carrying ornate five-pointed stars on sticks called teforah. First the women, singing and dancing as they came, then the men, swaying rhythmically with their stars. When a bell sounded they raised their teforah overhead, corkscrewed their bodies and whooped in a rather odd but synchronised chorus, stabbing down rather aggressively with their teforah at the end, to great applause.

"Follow that," Brendan thought, ruefully. But he did, and they seemed to enjoy his stories and sighed and clapped at the right points. Brendan usually used the GNT to mark the end of the talk, and when he showed it they all aaah'd with anticipation. When Brendan gave it to a young lady in the choir with a beautiful smile, they all clapped enthusiastically and the young lady shyly gave Brendan a kiss and linked arms with him. He hoped that he hadn't accidentally become engaged to her without realising it.

***

The next three days passed in what became a predictable pattern: one stop at lunch-time, meeting local dignitaries or crowds more interested in seeing Esther than Brendan; then an afternoon flight to their evening destination; speaker meetings in small churches; wonderful food and beautiful beaches everywhere; bright-blue water and sky for most of the day, but usually a swift shower in the afternoon.

Their hairiest landing was on the narrow horseshoe of Ebon Atoll in the Marshall Islands the following lunchtime, as the narrow strip of land between lagoon on the one side and ocean on the other was only as wide as the runway. To make it worse, the wind was blowing sideways. The evening landing at Nauru wasn't much better, coming in over the roofs of the government building and school, with the runway finishing out at sea on a pontoon specially built for jets. They stopped just in time before the railing.

Banaba Island in Kiribati was only half an hour's flight-time from Nauru and shared with it the dubious blessing of being rich in phosphate. The questions after the evening meeting in Tuvalu later that same day also became a discussion about climate change, as Tuvalu's highest point was only 4.5m above sea-level. Brendan told them that he'd recently been to the Maldives, whose highest point was only 2.3 m above sea-level, and where the government had recently televised an underwater cabinet meeting to publicise their vulnerability to global warming. This amused the Tuvaluans no end.

The third day out of Kosrae brought Brendan across the international date line to Apia in Western Samoa so after starting out on today he embraced tomorrow before then going back over the date line in the afternoon (which afternoon?) to yesterday which was still today on his original reckoning. Then he slept overnight in Neiafu, Tonga to wake up in his original tomorrow before crossing the date line again to enter tomorrow's tomorrow, but by then he'd spent a day doing it so he was thoroughly lost and didn't know what day it was. He found a map of the Pacific on the plane and drew a line from Fiji to all ten countries he'd visited in the last five days, amusing himself when he realised that he'd drawn a perfect horse's head. It reminded him of the Godfather film[89] and, in turn, his recent brush with would-be assassins – which didn't seem a good omen...

***

The flight to Tahiti the next morning took four hours and a full tank of fuel. It meant 2,600km flying into a headwind, but landing at the only international airport with a triple AAA, not for its quality but its name: Faaa Airport at Papeete. Disappointingly it was sometimes spelled Faa'a, but having the same three letters in a row was much more fun, and gave Brendan one more question for his ongoing impossible pub quiz.

Tahiti had a reputation for being exotic and peaceful, but Brendan's brief sortie during refuelling gave him a different impression: expensive and awful. Yes, it had palm trees. Yes, it had plenty of its famous black pearls for sale (at ludicrous prices). Yes, it had beautiful clear blue-water lagoons and ever-available $15 cocktails – but it clearly over-traded on the "paradise" label and didn't actually feel like a real place. It was full of honeymooners and French people, not that Brendan had anything particularly against either category – but it also had dirty streets, traffic jams, and all the paraphernalia of a place which took your money but gave you little for it. He wandered into a Gaugin museum but incredibly it didn't have a single painting by Gaugin in it. Because Tahiti was technically part of France, Brendan felt that, other

---

[89] In Coppola's "The Godfather", film producer Jack Woltz upsets Don Corleone. The next morning, Woltz wakes up next to the severed head of his favourite prized horse – a sign that they can get to him any time...

than the refuelling, the whole 90 minutes he'd spent there had been a waste of time. Perhaps Papeete and Faaa were not typical of Tahiti – certainly Bora Bora and Raiatea had better reviews – so maybe he shouldn't judge the whole of French Polynesia so hastily...

Two hours later they landed at Reao airstrip. The tiny atoll was a long thin island with only 350 inhabitants – according to Junior, the man who helped them refuel. They'd only used up half their fuel since Tahiti, but there was no land now for nearly 3,000km and that was the fullest extent of their fuel capacity, including the safety reserve that they were not supposed to add into the calculations. They needed every litre they could get into the tanks, and would have to fly carefully and hope for a favourable wind to ensure a safe landing on Easter Island.

Over the last three or four days Esther had become much more withdrawn and detached, spending hours just reading and sleeping during the day, and not entering greatly into the conversations over dinner. Brendan sidled up to her one evening. "Are you OK?"

She sighed. "Yes, dear. To be honest, I'm getting bored, just stuck in the plane for days on end. How you keep travelling for a whole year just amazes me! I'm not used to such inactivity and I'm having a struggle being cut off from the rest of the world. Sad, really, isn't it?"

Brendan smiled. "We're all different, and you can't be what you're not cut out to be. But maybe you need a bit of time to stop and think *why* you do what you do..."

"Hmmm," said Esther, clearly not convinced. "I tell you what, though, I'm really looking forward to Easter Island – I've always wanted to go there."

"Me too," said Brendan, hoping Easter Island wouldn't be a let-down, like Tahiti. But they had to get there first.

Brendan couldn't quite adjust to the sheer emptiness and vastness of the Pacific. The idea that Easter Island was at the extreme range of their Learjet and that their next stop, Robinson Crusoe Island, was even further away, over 3,000km from Easter Island, scared him silly – not just because of the risk that they may not have enough fuel, but also that vast distances between tiny dots of land didn't seem possible on a supposedly crowded planet.

They arrived at Easter Island just as the sun was setting, with the fuel gauge firmly on zero and red lights flashing. Just as they came into land, a buzzer went off in the cockpit to indicate that they only had ten minutes' flying time left, according to the pilot. "No problem!" he said, but Brendan could see the sweat patches under his arms and the relief on his face.

They happened to arrive in the middle of the annual Tapati festival, offering Polynesian dancing and music that featured wooden pipes and tambourines. Their hotel in Hanga Roa had a disco with a different style of music reverberating, so they didn't get much sleep, especially as they'd arranged with their guide to be taken out to see the dawn at Ahu Tongariki. The 15 huge moai statues there all faced the sunset, so dawn was a brilliant time for photos, looking straight at the sun and silhouetting the faces of the statues, some of which were 9m high. The guide told Brendan that the biggest one weighed 82 tons, but that no-one knew why they'd been made or how they'd been brought to their positions. Each one would have taken a team of six men a whole year to make, and over 200 men to pull on wooden sledges, if that was how it was done.

It was an effort to get up after only a few hours' sleep, but well worth it. There was something very powerful about the sheer effort and dedication that had gone into the moai, and something very moving about watching the dawn break behind the ancient sentinels. Brendan and Esther just sat, not speaking, as the film-crew took their footage. Brendan remembered a book called "The Idea of the Holy" by a German called Rudolf Otto[90], who coined the word "numinous" to describe an "experience of a mystical reality outside of oneself". This dawn was numinous. But with a long day ahead of them and a deadline to meet, they were in the air again by 6.30am.

Their next stop, Robinson Crusoe Island, was part of Chile too, but 3,005km to the east and thus even scarier to reach in a plane with a technical range of only 2,700km. Fortunately the winds were favourable, giving maximum fuel economy, so they had only red lights and no buzzer as they landed five hours after take-off. Alexander Selkirk had been voluntarily marooned here in 1704 and lived in solitude for over four years, inspiring Daniel Defoe's Robinson Crusoe. The Chilean Government decided to rename the island in 1966 to drum up tourism revenues, but Brendan had had enough of it after half an hour. Esther didn't even get off the plane.

Only an hour after take-off they crossed the Chilean coastline near Santiago. Brendan was in South America again, with many memories, especially when they crossed the Andes and flew over Argentinian farmland before landing at Mercedes in Uruguay. They landed at 2.15pm, leaving them only 45 minutes to set up for a live broadcast in the plane at 3pm to synchronise with the 2pm start of "See Esther" back in Detroit. It was a tight schedule, but they made it. Ruth and Paul had flown in via Buenos Aires, and it was great to see them again, but they didn't really have time to do much catching-up before they were all needed back at the plane. The film-crew rushed around setting up satellite dishes and microphones before the start of the programme – but they deliberately left it all a bit untidy so that the viewers got a true sense of their recent arrival and tiredness. From that point of view, it worked, but Esther was surprisingly downbeat too. It was good to see some of the footage that

---

[90] OTTO, Rudolf, "Das Heilige...", English translation by J. W. Harvey, "The Idea of the Holy, An Inquiry into the Non-rational Factor of the Divine and its Relation to the Rational", O.U.P., 1923.

the film-crew had been editing over the last day or so, and it meant that there was less time for the interview, which was rather dry and lacklustre.

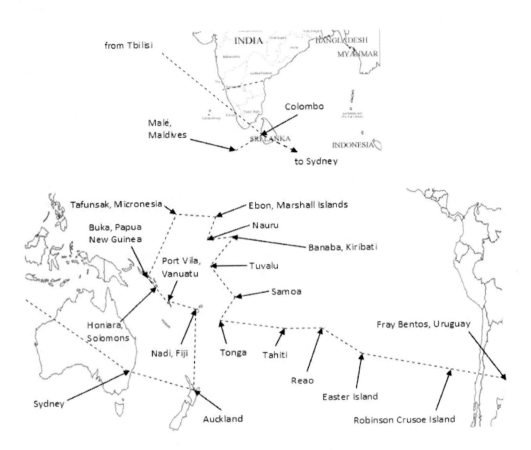

Nations 159 to 183

Afterwards, Esther said her farewells to Brendan. She was staying overnight in a hotel in Mercedes, but Brendan was going in the opposite direction, to a town with a famous name from which the most arduous leg of his whole journey would begin the next day. Fray Bentos reminded him of the beef dinners in a tin which he had in his digs at University, but the town itself, 40km from Mercedes on the banks of the Uruguay River, was devoid of the meat-processing which made it famous. The old factory was now a Museum of Meat Extraction. Even though there probably weren't many such museums in the world, Brendan decided to give it a miss.

Paul had arranged with the only hotel in town for them to stay there overnight, and for a two-man kayak to be brought to the hotel by special charter from Buenos

Aires. Ruth, Paul and Brendan shared a pleasant dinner together, looking out over the placid river, but they soon retired early to bed. The next day was the start of the longest kayak journey anyone had ever taken on the planet, as far as they knew – breaking all kinds of records, but more importantly, if all went smoothly, Brendan and Paul would spend the next three months in each other's company until the completion of Brendan's epic journey. If all went smoothly...

Day: Date	Itinerary (* indicates TV interview) ([18]indicates new nation)	Bike (km)	Car/ Bus (km)	Train (km)	Kayak/ Sail (km)	Boat (km)	Air (km)
Totals brought forward		11424	17290	8712	2754	19459	44485
262: 1/2/12	Port Vila, Vanuatu[163]; Honiara, Solomons[164]						2248
263: 2/2/12	Buka, PNG[165]; Tafunsak (Kosrae), Micronesia[166]						2122
264: 3/2/12	Ebon, Marshalls[167]; Nauru[168]						1246
265: 4/2/12	Banaba, Kiribati[169]; Tuvalu[170]						1635
266: 5/2/12	Apia, Samoa[171]; Neiafu, Tonga[172]						1758
267: 6/2/12	Tahiti; Reao; Easter Island						6899
268: 7/2/12	Robinson Crusoe Island; Fray Bentos, Uruguay[173] *		40				4908
Totals carried forward		11424	17330	8712	2754	19459	65301

Chapter 59: Imagination

Back in Jact, things were going anything but smoothly. Cecil's sudden departure was greeted with relief all round, but it left a gap. At least Cecil had been steering the ship, even though it was towards the rocks, but now Jact began to experience RSS: the rudderless-ship syndrome. They needed someone to be the focal point, someone whom people would respect, follow and support. But who was there who ticked all those boxes? In Methodism everything usually started and finished in August/September. A ministerial appointment, though, would take a further 18 months because it was now early February and they'd missed the Stationing deadline for the coming September. They could try to get someone from overseas – or a Minister who suddenly became available, but that was how they'd got Cecil, so the Circuit were understandably not keen. Jack Turner wondered about asking a Supernumerary (retired) Minister to help out, but the chances of someone being willing to return to full-time work having retired were pretty slim, and Jack wanted to resurrect the work with children, young people and families which Caridad had spearheaded and Cecil had destroyed, and a retired person might not have the street cred to deliver that. It needed a more imaginative approach...

***

Louisa and Ben were still uncertain about what the future held, but pressed on with their wedding plans anyway. They didn't really need to worry about money, but nor did they want a no-expense-spared wedding which spoke more of the strength of their finances than the strength of their relationship. They wanted to wait until Brendan finished his epic trip, and give enough time for Ruth and Paul and Louisa's Mum to ensure that their diaries were clear. So it would be summer, at the earliest. They pencilled in August 4th as a likely date, and set about the preliminaries. They went to see the Super about the logistics of getting married at Jact now that Cecil had gone. It would be great to get married in a church building that meant something special to both of them. They rather hoped that Brendan would feel able to do as much of the service as was allowed, though they knew that they needed an "authorised" Minister there for the legal necessities. August 4th was available, so they inked it in, and started to tell the people who mattered most. They didn't want a conventional wedding because they weren't that sort of people. Ben was into beatboxing, street-dance and percussion. Louisa was into, well, anything that wasn't what had put her off Church in the first place. Together they tolerated traditional worship but yearned for something a bit zingier and a bit more contemporary culture-wise. They'd have to use their imagination...

***

Jack organised a meeting with the stewards at Jact to discuss the church's short-term future. He outlined the logistical difficulties which went with the usual types of ministry and invited people to join in an open discussion. He threw in some of the possibilities; the meeting threw them around a bit, then threw them all out. There was a silence. "What about Ben?" asked Sarah Lanleigh. The others murmured their approval.

Jack managed to nod and furrow his brow at the same time. "Well, Ben is obviously a thoroughly nice and talented young man who's got a lot to offer, but he hasn't had any formal training for ministry as far as I know. How do you think he could provide what we need?"

The Super stepped in at that point. Up till then he'd kept quiet. "If we're serious about reviving the link with the families and young people, then we have to think outside the box. The fact that Ben has shown that he can get alongside people whom we usually struggle to reach is far more important than whether or not he's got the right paper qualifications. Surely we can work something out, and cover the ministerial stuff amongst the rest of us?"

Jack nodded thoughtfully. No furrowed brow now. "I'm not sure how we'd categorise his appointment, but it sounds like a good temporary measure at the very least. How about we get Ben in and chat with him about it? All agreed?"

***

Ben and Louisa were relaxing in Louisa's flat at Beverley Terrace watching TV, when the phone went. Louisa answered it and handed it over to Ben. "It's Jack Turner, the District Chair!" she whispered, then raised her eyebrows and shrugged her shoulders as if to say, "What on earth does *he* want?" Louisa found it hard to follow the conversation. Sometimes Ben seemed pleased, and said comments like "Yes, of course, I would" and "That sounds really good" and "I'd love to". At other times he frowned and said, "I'm not sure", "That wouldn't be my first choice" and "Not really". The conversation ended with Ben scribbling something on a scrap of paper by the phone and saying, "OK, I'll see you then. Thanks!" He turned to Louisa and said, "I'm not sure exactly what he's offering, but I've got an interview on Thursday afternoon."

Louisa fired off a volley of questions: "Where? What does he want you to do? Will we have to move house?"

"No, we won't," said Ben, pausing as if he was still working it out. "Don't laugh, but I think he wants me to be the new Minister at Jact." They were *both* silent after that. Then they tried to work out what on earth this could mean. Was this the product of a fertile imagination, or was it fantasy-land? And, most importantly, was God in it?

***

Jack went back home to read up about the various forms of new ministry opportunities and schemes emerging from Methodist HQ, to see if any of them fitted the situation at Jact. Unfortunately none of them did. The ventureFX pioneer ministry programme sought to set up fresh expressions of church amongst young people, which wasn't quite what was envisaged at this stage at Jact. Or was it? Maybe that was something for the future, but the problem was that it was geared to work *outside* existing church structures rather than within them, so Jact didn't quite seem to fit the criteria.

Seeing that there wasn't an easy way to slip Ben's appointment into an existing scheme, Jack decided he'd have to use his imagination. He knew that the Church required pastoral accountability to be in the hands of a Minister – though in some cases on paper only if the actual care was delegated to laypeople. So Jack set about creating a job description for Ben which gave him the pastoral care of the people in Jact (under the nominal supervision of the Super) without the Sunday duties of leading worship. Ben, of course, would have to be specifically trained for that. The job description also included responsibilities for shaping church policy and practice around priorities, and community involvement, for all of which Ben had already shown great promise.

The Superintendent seemed happy to fill the preaching slots with lay preachers, and planned more regular visits from himself to lead Holy Communion. Jack Turner also offered his help when he wasn't involved anywhere else, which meant at least once a quarter on the preaching plan at Jact. The Super, as required by Standing Orders, would lead the Church Council meetings, but every other meeting would be chaired either by Ben or one of the church stewards. Ben would be specifically encouraged to take up his former responsibilities as a Schools Worker, but this would be extended, if he was willing, to the two Jact primary schools as well as the secondary schools. He'd be encouraged also to re-establish meetings for the local young people on the Methodist premises at Jact. The bonus was that Jack offered District funding for Ben's appointment for three years, so that the North Tyneside Circuit would be able to concentrate on recruiting part-time workers to supplement the areas of work which, assuming Ben's efforts bore fruit, showed most promise.

***

At Thursday's Church Council, Ben sought assurances from the church stewards that they were fully behind him coming back. They promised him that he'd be given a substantial budget to invest in the work amongst the local youth, that they wouldn't expect him to visit all of *them* but to spend his time with those in the community who had had some contact with the Church in Caridad's time, but who hadn't been seen since. They also begged him to re-introduce his skills to Sunday morning worship. "I still can't get over you spinning on your head!" said one of the ladies. "It wasn't so much that I was impressed (though I was), it was just so wonderful to see the young people open-mouthed and excited."

Ben signed up straightaway. Then he told them that he and Louisa wanted to get married there in August and they all gave him a kiss. Except the Superintendent, that is – but he seemed jolly pleased.

Chapter 60: Nations 174 - 176

Paul had spent many childhood afternoons in a pirogue, his uncle's boat made from a hollowed-out tree-trunk. He'd sailed his uncle's small sailboat too, and learnt all about engines from its outboard motor – but he'd never been in a kayak. Now he was going to spend the next two months in one. The plan was for him and Brendan to paddle 1,300km up the Paraná River to its confluence with the Paraguay River, then up the entire length of the Paraguay (2,600km) to its headwaters just south of Diamantino in Brazil. They'd then get their kayak overland to the head-waters, just *north* of Diamantino, of the Tapajós River, which flowed northwards for 1,900km till its confluence with the Amazon, and paddle down to its mouth (660km). Their route continued up the coast for a further 1,950km from the Amazon delta to Port of Spain on Trinidad. It would amount to about 8,500km, which was a ridiculous distance to attempt in a kayak – especially if you'd never been in one before.

All the records were for solo kayakists – and Brendan himself held quite a few of them from his Arctic exploits of 2010 – but he was confident that no other pair of idiots would have attempted anything like this. Ruth thought that they were both mad, but she was family so didn't count. She waved them off from the jetty in Fray Bentos and watched them wobble their way downstream, with Paul nearly toppling over in the back of the kayak and banging himself and Brendan on the head with his paddle. It wasn't an auspicious start.

The kayak was a two-cockpit whitewater version which towed a gear-toting raft. It was made of polyethylene and designed to bounce off rocks rather than crumple on impact. Paddling downstream for this first stretch proved a good training exercise, because the frequency of stroke didn't matter – they were merely adding a little extra propulsion to an already steady current. It did, however, train Paul to synchronise his own paddle-strokes with Brendan's in order to prevent corkscrewing. Within a few minutes, however, they found a decent rhythm, and upped the pace. Both Paul and Brendan found their shoulders tightening and their arms dropping as the day wore on, but they kept going, encouraged by the speed at which the banks of the wide river sped past. It took them six hours to reach the narrows at Nueva Palmira, just before the main channel of the Paraná delta, 90km from Fray Bentos. Their pace had been pretty impressive, so they decided to celebrate with a late lunch of bread and fruit. The real test was to come, as they well knew. The next four weeks would mean paddling upstream with their speed considerably slower.

It was a shock when they caught the adverse current of the river, and they seemed to be going nowhere, but they soon found that it was much easier near the bank, and started to make progress. Fortunately they only needed to go a further 47km to their overnight destination, but it took them the best part of six more hours. The scenery was spectacular: low overhanging branches containing brightly-coloured birds, even fluorescent kingfishers and an owl which was spooked when Paul inadvertently banged his paddle against its branch. The kayak dodged through the water-lilies, some of which were in full bloom. But they were too exhausted and sore to appreciate their surroundings, and collapsed in a heap when they finally reached the R12 roadbridge which marked the end of their day. After they wearily set up camp underneath the roadbridge and ate a quick-and-easy dried curry meal, they lay down in their tent and reflected on their first day.

"8kph is not going to be fast enough," declared Brendan. "It'll take us three months at this rate, not two." Paul sighed. "Presumably as our fitness levels increase, we will be able to increase our speed." Paul grunted. "I wonder whether we'll struggle when we meet the other channels of the river and the flow is stronger." Paul started to snore. He was already asleep. Brendan smiled and got into his sleeping-bag too. His throat was sore again – it must be the exercise, he thought.

***

The next few days saw their pace quicken, despite the force of the concentrated current which hit them once they got beyond the delta, which happened after only a few hours on the very next day. There were still loops off around islands, but all the channels returned to one. They maintained daily distances averaging 130km, but this varied considerably depending on where the small riverbank settlements were for overnight stops. They needed to be near other humans in order to buy drinking water, even though they carried several large bottles in reserve on their storage raft. Brendan had nightmares about the raft not being there when they finished the day's paddling, so they attached four separate ropes to it, snatching glances behind them, when they remembered, to check that everything was still connected.

One other anxiety was about the wildlife. The official mouth of the Paraná was called Tigre, after the jaguars once hunted in the forest there. Brendan frequently heard crashing in the undergrowth and imagined all kinds of hungry beasts weighing up how many mouthfuls it would take to eat him. They'd seen a few otters, and a deer of some sort, but nothing bigger than that – so far.

Towards the end of the second afternoon, Paul suddenly shouted and held aloft an impressively large fish with sharp-looking teeth. He'd dangled an improvised fishing line and caught a whopper. Brendan wasn't too thrilled when Paul gutted the fish that evening and spilt some of the innards on Brendan's sleeping-bag, but the dinner afterwards was superb, even though the smell lingered for nearly a fortnight. Paul caught a few other fish during the first week, but nothing like that first one.

***

The river snaked its way past fields, forests and then, increasingly, towns and industrial areas as they progressed northwards, with Brendan and Paul paddling upstream in what was usually (and comfortably) a narrow lake giving hardly any sign of a current. They passed small settlements with waving children and bored women, larger towns with roads, quaysides and workmen unloading goods from big boats, and even larger towns and cities such as Ramallo, San Nicolás de los Arroyos and eventually Rosario, the third biggest city in Argentina. Much of the scenery from Ramallo onwards was built-up, with more industry than agriculture, until the day after Rosario, when monotonous countryside prevailed for a week – except for the city of Esquina.

On the third day after Esquina, however, they had a memorable day. They'd camped at a small place called Empedrado, reputedly the Pearl of the Paraná, not that they noticed any particular charms or difference. Within ten minutes of setting off, Brendan's paddle got hooked up on a small bloated dead dog in mid-channel, but that wasn't the headline of the day. Brendan noticed that he hadn't coughed for a few days and his throat felt a little better. But that wasn't the headline. They came to the city of Corrientes, and paddled underneath the impressive General Belgrano Suspension Bridge – but that wasn't the headline of the day either.

An hour after the city, they arrived at Paso de la Patria, a small headland at the confluence of two rivers which was the first part of the next nation, Paraguay, and turned left up the Paraguay River. This was the headline. It marked the first real achievement of their epic kayak journey, apart from keeping going – which was an achievement in itself, especially for Paul. They'd completed 1,300km of the Paraná, and were starting what could well be the first ever upstream navigation of the entire length of the Paraguay. According to the itinerary, it would be another 19 days before they pulled the kayak out of the river at its source.

They stopped for lunch in Paso a couple of kilometres upstream. The town was very small, but it did have a bank at which Brendan acquired some Paraguayan currency, called Guarani, which took Brendan away on a memory trip, re-visiting one of his favourite films. Brendan was once asked by schoolchildren in Jact what his favourite film was. He'd come up with the answer "The Mission"[91] – which meant absolutely nothing to them. Roland Joffé's 1986 film told the story of a Jesuit mission to the Guarani tribespeople above the Iguazu Falls, 300km east of the Paraguay River. The Guarani territory, however, extended across to the Paraguay, and Brendan

---

[91] The film portrays the contrast between the "pure" motivations of some of the Jesuits (who sought acceptance by the Guarani so that they could introduce them to Jesus) and the political power-games of other Church officials (who considered the Guerani as pawns who could be sacrificed to win their own battles). It touches on themes still relevant both missiologically and politically.

was looking forward to encountering some of the indigenous people. It was a far cry now from the mid-18th century when the Guarani were under attack from slave-traders. It was good to see that the Guarani were honoured by the name of the national currency, but also that the Guarani language, alongside Spanish, was the official language. His GNT was in Guarani, and he looked forward to handing it over.

The chance came later that day, when they stopped just past the old colonial town of Humaitá. Beyond the old fortress, Brendan and Paul noticed a small settlement on the eastern bank, and decided to see if they could camp there. Wonderfully, they'd chanced upon one of the few remaining traditional Guarani villages that far west. The villagers were Christians, and went to Mass in Humaitá each morning, before the men fished or tended their cattle and crops, and the women made traditional handicrafts for a craft-shop in town. They lived in traditional longhouses, and invited Brendan and Paul to eat with them and sleep in the guest section of the longhouse. The space was segregated into family "apartments", with huge rugs hanging down from beams as decorative dividers. It was warm and muggy, with smoke from the open fire drifting along the length of the building. The guest section was at the very end, with a couple of bunks set against the wall and a rudimentary sink and toilet.

"This is an amazing place to live," said Brendan to the headman, who was called Juan.

"Is different from your house, no?" replied Juan, in broken English.

"Yes," said Brendan.

"No," said Paul.

They all looked at each other, and laughed. Paul explained. "My family in Africa used to live in a village like you have here, fishing, raising cattle and planting crops, with the women making traditional handicrafts like you do here. We lived in separate family huts, close together, each with their own fire. But we didn't have toilets!"

Everyone laughed. "Are there many Guarani like you, still living the traditional way?" asked Brendan.

"No, no," said Juan. "Most not Christian, not Guarani spirit-gods, not nothing except money, money, no?" He rubbed his fingers together in the worldwide sign for cash deals or corruption. "They work tourist guides, boats, camioneros, anything that pay money, no? Old ways die."

Brendan handed over the GNT. "Aaah," said Juan, fingering it lovingly, reading the inscription. "For me?"

"For all of you, and the Guarani who have forgotten Jesus."

"Yes," said Juan. "I take it and tell them of Jesus. Very good, no?"

***

They stopped the next day for lunch at Pilar, a well-kept yet strangely archaic city, with cars and lorries alongside horse-drawn carts on the streets. There were exotically-coloured sculptures of parrots in some of the trees, a reminder of what had once been, as if the whole town was now a museum. The Cathedral was ridiculously grandiose for its setting amongst rundown properties, and merely emphasised the absurdity of the town. There were several banks, but all were shut for some unknown reason – had they arrived on a bank holiday? There were parks but they were empty. One hot-dog stand lurched drunkenly and seemingly abandoned in one of the squares, but as they approached, a young man unfolded himself from underneath a tree, and served them.

The Catholic influence showed in the place-names they passed, such as San Fernando, Tres Marias, and the Argentine city of Formosa. According to Brendan's guidebook, the city curiously was the exact antipodes of the island of Taiwan, formerly known as Formosa.

Then, alarmingly, they encountered the river's more dangerous fauna. First, a shoal of piranha fish, foot-long, bug-eyed and hungry, if the snapping razor-teethed surface-display was anything to go by. Paul had never encountered anything quite like it, and was terrified. Brendan had seen various films where piranha stripped the flesh off a human in a few seconds, but he knew that the reality was much less ferocious. Next they encountered an alligator, log-like and inactive as they cruised past, only realising what it was after they'd passed it. Finally, spectacularly, in one deserted stretch of greenery, they came across the scene of a kill. The grey-brown corpse, the head of which they couldn't identify, was huge – legs stiff and splayed, upper torso ripped empty, head crushed and ripped. As they drifted warily alongside, but kept a safe distance from shore, they saw its snout and recognised it as a tapir. It hadn't been killed in the last few minutes, because the blood was dried and the body partially eaten. Then, as if from nowhere, an enormous jaguar was suddenly standing snarling on top of the carcass, baring its teeth at them, legs locked, ears cocked and tail curling aggressively. Slowly, without a word, as if they'd practiced the synchronised manoeuvre for hours, they drew their paddles into the water to turn the kayak away, staring in case the jaguar jumped in after them and they needed to paddle for their lives. It was a majestic sight, but they realised only after half a minute that they were both still holding their breath.

The river was still over a kilometre across most of the time, sometimes forming a miniature lake. Channels kept spurring off, like railway tracks in a shunting yard, joining and parting constantly. The banks of the river were getting emptier, with occasional glimpses of a road running parallel to the river, until the Paraguayan riverbank grew villages and industry as Asunción drew near.

They decided to indulge themselves and headed for Hotel Guarani, for sentimental reasons. It was only 300m back from the river, but they still felt ridiculous carrying their kayak and raft through the streets. The hotel itself was a triangular skyscraper in the centre of the city, close to the pink-tinted Cathedral and the night-clubs, as they found to their cost later on. The city was gloriously neon after dark, but the night's humidity demanded open windows, though there was little breeze to make sleeping easier and plenty of noise to make it harder. The days now were becoming unpleasantly hot too, and frequently populated by flies, ants and mosquitoes. They'd both dosed up on anti-malaria drugs in preparation for this, but it was pretty dismal whenever they passed through a swarm. Thankfully the insects seemed territorial and didn't travel with them, and their usual remedy was to splash water up into the air to disperse the pesky critters and provide an instant cooling-down.

The wide river no longer marked the Argentina-Paraguay border, but snaked relentlessly northwards to the Brazil-Paraguay border 520km away as the kayak glides, but only 350km as the crow flies. But they weren't crows and so it would take five days to meander to this next milestone. Brendan and Paul found that most of the time they shared a contented and companionable silence, but at points through each day one of them would spark up a conversation. They sorted out most of the world problems including global trade issues, climate change and why footballers are paid so much. They told stories about their upbringing, giving insights into their very different lives and experiences. They talked about liberation theology, compared the poems of Uganda and Wordsworth, discussed gender justice and tested each other with general knowledge questions. They sang sometimes, which must have scared the wildlife away because they saw very few mammals or reptiles, only insects. Brendan told Paul about Ruth as a small girl. Paul talked about some of the experiences they'd shared in Gulu. They discovered a common interest in ornithology, and tried to be the first to see a species of bird. Paul was first to see a toucan, nestling on a branch overhanging the river. Brendan saw a huge snake a little further upriver, hanging down from another overhanging branch. They thought that it was probably a boa-constrictor, but, whatever it was, they kept a little further out from the bank afterwards.

The days rolled by, not boring by any means, but forming a pattern into which they slipped comfortably. They stopped near various estancias and puertos each night, which varied from small deserted bays to the quayside of a tourist resort with well-heeled people strolling along riverside walks, playing golf or riding horses.

On the first day out of Asunción, they passed Puerto Antequera, the operational base for a boat ministry called the Angel Del Rio (River Angel), a floating Christian medical and dental surgery for the riverside communities. On the third day they passed the city port of Concepcion, which had sawmills, flour mills, cotton gins, sugar and castor-oil refineries, tanneries – and a dreadful smell... On the fifth day, they reached San Lazaro, at the confluence of the Paraguay and Apa Rivers. They were now in limestone country, with several caves and lumpy mountains as well as the green, flat plains which they'd traversed for the last few days. They continued up the same Paraguay River, now forming the border with Brazil until the Bolivian border 360km north, both as the kayak glides and the crow flies, for the river's course was now pretty straight.

They saw more wildlife now too, but nothing too exotic: capybara (metre-long guinea pigs), similar-sized wild boar, a fox, a pair of anteaters and a live tapir. There were plenty of deer too, and wild dogs, some almost wolf-like in size and bearing. They saw parrots as well as toucans, raptors which looked like eagles, herons, storks and even a flamingo. The landscape was uniformly flat with occasional forested patches, with Brazilian hills visible on the north-east horizon and nothing but undulating Paraguayan plains to the west. The river wandered a bit, occasionally doubling back on itself for no obvious reason, narrowing ever so slightly now – 1,000km from its outflow into the Paraná, and 2,300km from the Atlantic.

They finally reached the bottom end of the curious wedge in the extreme east of Bolivia known as the Dionisio Foianini Triangle. The Paraguay River turned north-eastwards along the Bolivia-Brazil border, and Brendan and Paul stopped near the end of the Triangle at Puerto Busch. It was not a town, or even a port, but swampland from which the Bolivians were hoping to create a major port so that their ships could reach the Atlantic without having to go into Brazil. It was named after the Nazi/Fascist President of Bolivia who'd seized power in a coup in 1937 and shot himself in 1939. Dionisio Foianini was the Minister of Mines and Petroleum in Busch's Cabinet, but the pathetically little wedge of land named after him revealed his lack of real influence in Bolivia's destiny. Busch only got a marsh named after him, though, so perhaps old Foianini did OK for himself after all.

Puerto Busch had nothing but a few Bolivian national guardsmen protecting a building site – though it was unclear who'd want to attack it. Brendan and Paul got out of the kayak, explained who they were and what they were doing, asked if they could camp there (the answer was No) but handed over the Bolivian GNT to the captain of the guard anyway, asking him to put it away safe for when the port was built. At this, the captain crossed himself and asked Brendan to bless the port and the guardsmen, which Brendan didn't baulk at, as he'd frequently blessed patients in hospitals who hadn't realised that Methodist clergy didn't really do that sort of thing. He reckoned that he'd as much right as a Catholic priest to say "God Bless You". The guardsmen still wouldn't let them camp, so they crossed back over the river and spent their first night in Brazil, which was to be their home for the next 32 days, the longest stay in one country during the whole of Brendan's journey. The next longest, not counting the 13 days laid up in East Timor, was the measly nine days he'd spent crossing Angola by bike.

They pressed on, the river narrowing all the time. After Corumbá, it meandered round the western edge of the Pantanal, a huge wetlands area of cattle ranches interspersed with tropical forests which flooded even in the dry season. They lost count of the different species: capybara, fish, caiman, Jaibaru storks, kingfishers, macaws, giant otters, deer, parrots, howler monkeys, coatimundis (racoon-like creatures), herons, humming-birds and many more. They saw fish jumping out of a shallow mud-pool for oxygen, and ants running up and down a tree trunk, one of which bit Paul quite painfully. The guidebook identified the ant, warning that 40 bites were enough to kill a man, and that the indigenous people long ago tied their enemies to tree trunks and watched them die in agony.

The river split into various tributaries and it became tricky to decide which to take. Brendan found their GPS invaluable in both providing a map and plotting their course. On more than one occasion the wider tributary proved to be an off-shoot rather than the main channel, and they'd have been fooled without the GPS. They reached Cáceres, the "Porta do Pantanal" on their seventh day in Brazil. They were now only three days from the source of the river, and were getting increasingly excited. They stayed in a campsite opposite the Cathedral, but Brendan didn't spend long inside except for a quick look and prayer because they were saving their Brazilian GNT and "witnessing" until Diamantino. They dined out at a small restaurant called Gulla's which had the odd custom of weighing the food they chose from the buffet and charging them per kilogram[92].

The river's meanderings got worse, backwards and forwards so their progress seemed dreadfully slow, but it meant that they were drawing ever closer to their destination. At midday on the third day, they reached Alto Paraguai, a village whose name hinted that they were at the source, but the stream ran on through the town, still just about navigable though their paddles kept hitting the bottom and sides. They were on a tight schedule, due to arrive at Diamantino before 2pm when the next live interview was supposed to take place. A few laboured kilometres and 30 minutes further on, they gave up, attaching a rope to the front of the kayak and pulling it along till they reached a small sign, pitifully insignificant, marking the point where the stream disappeared into a wall, but it proclaimed "fonte do rio" – and that was it. The end, or rather the source, of the fifth longest river in South America, but with no fanfare of trumpets, no welcoming committee, and nothing to do except pick up the kayak and raft, and carry them down the dirt road 2km further into Diamantino. They arrived at 1.40pm, hot and sweaty.

But there they found not just a fanfare of trumpets but a stage full of amplifiers blaring loud music, not a welcoming committee but a whole town in fiesta mood.

---

[92] Gulla's restaurant in Cáceres really does operate this rather idiosyncratic pricing structure.

Not for them, of course. Esther had come to town. And the show was about to begin.

Day: Date	Itinerary (* indicates TV interview) ([18] indicates new nation)	Bike (km)	Car/ Bus (km)	Train (km)	Kayak / Sail (km)	Boat (km)	Air (km)
Totals brought forward		11424	17330	8712	2754	19459	65301
269: 8/2/12	End of road nearest to Parana mouth (Argentina)				160		
270: 9/2/12	Obligado				145		
271: 10/2/12	Rosario				117		
272: 11/2/12	Parana				145		
273: 12/2/12	Santa Elena				119		
274: 13/2/12	Esquina				116		
275: 14/2/12	Puerto Lavalie				132		
276: 15/2/12	Empedrado				140		
277: 16/2/12	Humaita				131		
278: 17/2/12	Formosa, Paraguay[174]				137		
279: 18/2/12	Asuncion				147		
280: 19/2/12	Estancia Lomas				118		
281: 20/2/12	Puerto Tacuro Pyta				137		
282: 21/2/12	Puarto Cooper				122		
283: 22/2/12	Puerto la Victoria				119		
284: 23/2/12	Puerto Gaurani				133		
285: 24/2/12	Estancia Riacho Alegre				131		
286: 25/2/12	near Puerto Busch, Bolivia[175]				97		
287: 26/2/12	MS228 bridge, Brazil[176]				132		
288: 27/2/12	east of Tres Bocas				136		

289: 28/2/12	east of Lagoa Mandore				128		
290: 1/3/12	Lagoa Uberaba 1/3				95		
291: 2/3/12	at end of road 17.12S, 57.36W				126		
292: 3/3/12	at end of road 16.71S, 57.76W				119		
293: 4/3/12	Caceres				135		
294: 5/3/12	Porto Estrela				130		
295: 6/3/12	west of MT160/MT409 junction				134		
296: 7/3/12	Diamantino *	2			83		
Totals carried forward		11426	17330	8712	6318	19459	65301

Chapter 61: Nomination

Louisa was thrilled. Everything seemed to be coming good for them: Ben had the prospect of a new job, which would stretch him but also throw up exciting possibilities for working with all ages in Fresh Expressions; their marriage plans were steaming ahead, though they still had to work out how to get Jools and his Full Voice Orchestra[93] into the wedding liturgy (beatboxing still hadn't found its way into the Methodist Worship Book); it looked, on the strength of Ben's job, as if they could now stay in Beverley Terrace and make a top-floor married home in what had been Louisa's private space; even work at the Freeman was better than it had been for ages.

Sister Lilian had retained her transformed personality. She wore the fish badge on her uniform every day, smiled at Louisa and the other nurses, allowed Gareth and the other chaplains onto the Unit whenever they wanted, and even paged them herself. She even smiled at the patients and started being a nurse not just a manager.

***

Gareth sought Louisa out the first time that he'd been welcomed onto the Unit. "What on earth's happened to the Ayatollah?"

Louisa smiled. "God happened." She explained how things had come to a head when Sister Lilian hit her and she had video evidence of it.

"Make sure you keep hold of that," Gareth said. "But why has that made such a difference and where was God in it?"

"I confronted her with the evidence and she fell to pieces, but then I got this immediate sense of evil and cried out to God for help and suddenly she fell to the floor. I was really scared and yet curiously calm as well. When she came round I spoke some strange words about forgiveness which didn't really seem to be from me – and she fell to the floor again, and so did I. I don't remember too much about it but we both felt the powerful presence of God."

"Blimey. That's amazing," said Gareth. "Wonderful. And you're sure it's not an act?"

"No. I would've seen through it. And the proof is in its lasting effect – real fruit of the Spirit stuff."

"Well, that's the true test. Keep prompting her to stay with God and keep wearing her fish badge. Pray for her and encourage her to pray for her own protection, because the devil's obviously going to be miffed that he's lost her for now – and he'll

---

[93] This is the fictional beatbox group of which Ben was a member when Louisa first met him at Greenbelt in "Thule for Christ's Sake".

try to get her back. Remember how, immediately after Jesus' baptism, he was immediately under attack by the Devil in the wilderness? It's always like that – we're most vulnerable to attack after a big spiritual high."

"So what do you think I should do?" asked Louisa.

"Tell her that she's got to prove herself over time."

"That's exactly what I said," said Louisa, relieved that she'd not been too hard on Sister Lilian. She'd been having second thoughts about their "deal". "I told her that I'd only destroy the evidence if she kept going for six months as a changed woman, and then transferred out of our Unit."

***

Two months after the God-incident, Sister Lilian was persisting on her new path, and ensuring that Louisa knew that she was *enjoying* the spiritual journey which God had kick-started. Every Monday shift she told Louisa about the Sunday worship she'd been at. She'd also started an Alpha Course on Tuesdays at Heaton Baptist Church, so every Wednesday Louisa got an account of what she'd learnt. It was pretty impressive – and it really didn't seem like an act.

Louisa decided to speed things along. She asked if she could have a word with her at the end of a shift. "I've changed my mind about our deal," she said.

Sister Lilian's face fell. "Oh no! *Please* don't tell the Nursing Manager. I'm trying my hardest, *really* I am."

"It's not that," said Louisa. "I've decided to hand over that video evidence for you to deal with however you want, but I think you should keep it safe somewhere and even play it back from time to time to remind yourself how far you've come from those bad old days. What do you think?"

"I don't know. I'm thrilled in a way, but I'm worried that if I don't have the threat hanging over me I might not be so motivated to keep going."

"But you don't want to return to your old ways, do you?" asked Louisa gently.

"Of course not!" Sister replied. She thought for a moment. "I know. I'll take it off you but put it in this glass cabinet in my office. So you can see if it's still there, and I'll see it and remember what God's done for me. How does that sound?"

"Sounds good to me," said Louisa, smiling. "Here it is." She handed over the memory card from the phone. "There are no copies."

"Thank you," said Sister Lilian, even coming round the desk and giving Louisa a hug. It was like being embraced by a soft-fronted pillar-box.

***

373

A few days later, Louisa looked into Sister's office at the start of a shift. The memory card was still there in the glass cabinet.

"I've got a letter from management for you," said Sister Lilian with a grin, handing over a large white envelope. "Go on. Open it!"

Louisa couldn't think what this could be about. Nervously she wondered whether it had all been a trick, the memory card was now wiped, and this letter meant that she was getting the sack. But then she pulled out the posh invitation card inside and read it, instantly regretting her doubts. She couldn't believe her eyes.

> *The Royal College of Nursing are pleased to invite*
> ### *Louisa Priest*
> *to their Annual Congress*
> *at the ACC Liverpool*
> *from 2ⁿᵈ to 6ᵗʰ April*
> *in recognition of her nomination for this year's RCN Award of Merit.*
> *RSVP to Room 210, 20 Cavendish Square, London WC1X 8HL by*
> *March 24ᵗʰ.*

"What's all this about?" asked Louisa, dumbfounded. She'd never been nominated for anything in her life.

"Six weeks ago, I contacted the North of Tyne branch of the RCN and told them I wanted to nominate you for an award, and told them what you'd done to support me – without going into all the details, of course. They sent me to the Northern Regional Committee and I repeated my presentation and handed in a reasoned statement supporting the nomination, along with three other statements of commendation I got from other people in the hospital. Then I heard that RCN England had received your nomination and were putting you on a short-list of six for their annual Award of Merit[94]. And here's the proof! I'm so thrilled I could burst!"

Louisa was astonished. All this had happened long before the new "deal" had been struck. Here was proof that Sister Lilian really *had* changed. It was worth another hug, even though Sister Lilian's hugs were breath-taking. Literally.

---

[94] The RCN do give an annual Award of Merit each year at their Annual Congress, which is held at Easter. The process of nomination is as described here. The Award of Merit is almost always given, though, for services to the RCN itself, rather than to nursing.

Chapter 62: Nations 176 - 178

Gold-diggers accidentally discovered diamonds at Diamantino in 1746. The projected amount of diamonds was greatly overestimated, however, and many people in the expanding town were disappointed, and dribbled away to seek their fortune elsewhere, leaving a shrinking town with a name which mocked their dashed hopes. It'd been like that ever since. Diamantino was virtually at the South American Pole of Inaccessibility, which meant that there was nowhere else on the continent further away from the sea. It was about as remote as it could be. Nobody really came to Diamantino – until now.

Esther had come, with two helicopters, a film-crew, satellite dishes, a staging system, cables and, most excitingly, global exposure – which to the middle-of-nowhere inhabitants was like discovering the biggest diamond in the world, bringing the possibility of new life, new people, and an unknown future different from their humdrum inevitabilities. And now two bedraggled adventurers had come too, looking like they'd been beamed down from another time and place. One was white and coughed a lot, the other black; both were wet and smelled like they'd emerged from a swamp. They were carrying a kayak, and when they appeared in the town square suddenly people were squealing and running and embracing, which bemused the locals and sent the technicians scurrying away to finalise their systems and check that everything worked. Game on, as it were.

It was Ruth who'd done most of the squealing and running, delighted and relieved to see both her husband and Dad arrive on cue, just as she was starting to worry that they'd miss the "See Esther" window of opportunity and have to hang around for another day. They were so near to showtime that the film-crew suggested that Brendan and Paul go back round the corner to be filmed live coming into the square, re-enacting the squealing, then proceeding straight into the interview. Arnold agreed and approached Esther with the change of plan. She agreed that it'd look good on TV and lead well into the rest of the programme. The re-enactment was a bit odd, but they managed it without it being too false, and Brendan and Paul settled down on the stage on two plastic chairs, with their once bright-yellow, now mid-brown kayak in front of them. They looked exhausted, and this came across on camera as they shared the conversation and described some of the highlights of their 4,000km journey up-river to the most remote place in South America.

Brendan gave good descriptions of the evening with Juan and the Guarani, and the encounter with the jaguar. Paul spoke about the piranha shoal and his subsequent fear of capsizing. Ruth spoke about developments in Watoto, the continuing increase in sponsorship pledges, and the plans they were making about setting up Watoto-style villages for AIDS orphans in other parts of Africa, notably Swaziland, Mozambique, Malawi and Tanzania. She urged people to continue raising money, before Esther returned to Brendan. "You appear to be still *just about* on schedule for completing the journey in the year, despite the enforced hospital stay in East Timor. Do you think you can still do it?"

"I don't see why not, if we continue as we are," Brendan replied. "I've had a bad throat for a few weeks now, but hopefully it won't get any worse. I'm not sure about the percentages, though. To complete the challenge I must keep above 30% on both land and water without engine-power, and under 50% by air. We've found an itinerary that "worked", so I hope that it's working out right on the actual journey."

"Well, we're monitoring every kilometre you do, as you know, but the folks at home probably don't." Esther turned to the camera. "Brendan's got a GPS which charts his progress, so we calculate the distances covered and what forms of transport he uses." She turned back. "And have you come to any big conclusions, Brendan?"

Brendan paused. "I've not really achieved what I hoped I would. I wanted to be an advert about the importance of mission, but I'm not sure that wandering around the world was the right way to do it, because mission has to be done by living *amongst* people, not popping in then waving goodbye. So my biggest conclusion is that Christians have to knuckle down to doing everything in a mission-minded way *where they are*. A few people are called to move and settle amongst different people and encourage mission to happen there, but most of us have to do it at work, in our friendships, down the pub, on the golf-course or wherever we meet people." He drew breath, and then continued. "I'm also sorry that I've not done more for the Persecuted Church. I should have spent longer in some places, exposing the difficulties faced by the Christians there, so that the rest of the Church would wake up to the plight of their brothers and sisters in Christ. But I'm thrilled that something is happening for Watoto. It is great to know that their work will grow and flourish in other nations as well as Uganda because of what I'm doing. Maybe something good will come of all this," he finished, humbly.

"Well, Brendan, to cheer you on your way, I've got two bits of exciting news to share with you. Your other daughter, Louisa, has emailed a message for me to share with you that she's been nominated for a Royal College of Nursing Award of Merit, which is a national honour, so well done, Louisa!" She clapped to the camera and Brendan's face lit up with a big, proud grin. "But there's more! It's just been announced that you're amongst those who've been nominated for this year's Nobel Peace Prize! What about that?"

Brendan was amazed. "Crikey. I don't understand that. What have I done for world peace? Who on earth would nominate me?"

"Apparently, the nominations are made by previous Nobel laureates. And you've been nominated by two people from East Timor – whom I believe you've met, Brendan – who jointly won the Peace Prize in 1996. I should add that there are 93 other nominations, but it's still a huge honour." Everyone clapped, and Esther turned to the camera and finished the show with a flourish.

***

The film-crew packed everything away while Esther, Arnold, Ruth, Brendan and Paul sat in the town's only hostelry and enjoyed dinner. Next was a meeting hastily arranged by the local Catholic priest back in the town square at which the whole of Diamantino were hoping to see Esther again – and Brendan too if they must. What happened was that Esther merely waved and smiled and it was Brendan who stole the show – telling them captivating stories about his journey and why he was doing it, explaining about the need to be mission-minded and Jesus-centred. He waved the Brazilian GNT at them, spoke about its significance, read the inscription in his faltering Portuguese, and asked them who should receive it on behalf of them all.

"Juanita," someone shouted. "Enfermeira!" other voices cried. "Sim!" "Concordo!"

Brendan turned to the priest for help. The priest smiled. "It's OK," he said, "They're all saying the same thing. Juanita is the district nurse or enfermeira, and visits all the people who are sick, for we don't have a doctor. She knows everyone and everyone loves her. She's a good Christian and prays with them too. "Sim" means "Yes" and "Concordo" means "I agree".

"So where is Juanita?"

"She's out visiting an elderly lady up on the plateau, miles away. But I'll give the Bible to her when she returns tomorrow."

So Brendan handed over the book, shook the priest's hand, and walked off the square, back to the pub where they were all staying for the night: Esther in one guest room, Ruth and Paul in the other, and everyone else in sleeping bags on the floor. The helicopters, with everyone except Brendan and Paul packed in, were leaving at first light.

The two travellers said a teary farewell to Ruth, had a hug each from Esther, shook hands with Arnold and the techies, then got themselves ready for the next huge leg of the longest kayak trip ever. The preparations involved shopping for supplies to last them at least a fortnight, and trying to locate where to start.

***

From Diamantino it was now all downhill. Literally so, as 1,837ft above sea-level meant that the source of the river Tapajós, just north of Diamantino, was sufficiently high to enable it to run its course over 2,600km, via the Amazon, to the Atlantic Ocean. The problem was going to be identifying the right stream to start down, but the priest came in handy again. "We know where the best stream is. Many streams flow from here down towards the Arinos, but some are too narrow or shallow or go over waterfalls, which is no good for you. I take you."

The stream was only 3km out of town, and they walked it. The priest helpfully carried the raft, and led them north-west. He stopped, and showed them a lone tree across a field. "Over there!" he pointed. They trudged across the grass and came across a narrow stream gushing out from a spring underneath the tree. Within 20m it was fairly wide but shallow, and after a further 50m it was joined by another stream, and together the streams dug a deeper course now navigable by kayak, even though they had to be careful with their paddles. The priest had probably saved them hours of walking and carrying. They shook hands and stepped gingerly into the kayak.

It was great immediately to feel the current going with them not battling against them, and they were quite cheery as they bumped along, scrunching the bottom of the kayak along rocks, dodging bushes which threatened to snag them or having to push off from soil bars which temporarily grounded them. The stream wandered, because the gradient was very minimal and the water wasn't going anywhere very quickly. They were joined almost every kilometre by another stream, adding to the flow, and making progress gradually easier. It still took them four energy-sapping days to reach a point on the GPS where they could identify that they were on the right river, during which they'd only covered 200km as the crow flies, but actually kayaked nearly 500km. Their arms, shoulders and backs were now very sore again, because their pushing, pulling and steering with paddles made them use different muscles from usual. On two of the evenings, Brendan, charting their course on the GPS, discovered to his dismay that they'd travelled less than 40km in a straight line, but had actually done over 100km. It didn't seem fair, but at least it was progress. These were hard kilometres, but necessary ones.

They were passing through the Cerrado – one moment, extensive savannah; the next, clumps of buriti palm trees randomly strewn across undulating pasture-land – but all interspersed with river valleys trying, like them, to escape the Mato Grosso plateau. The cerrado trees had twisted trunks covered by a thick bark, and broad stiff leaves, as if they had been in a fire – which they probably had, as most years the Cerrado experienced fires which swept vast areas and left little in their wake. Somehow the roots went deep and sustained the charcoal remains to provide new growth and life after death. Life provided many parables...

The Cerrado gave way to swathes of Amazonian rain-forest – not the half-hearted stuff they'd encountered in patches already, but the real thing. Long, steep, downhill stretches of wet forest full of hoots, growls, shrieks, buzzing and drips – as they finally left the plateau in spectacular white-water rapids. Odd furtive movements in the forest on both sides of the river, a leaf moving here, a crack of branches higher up, a cry, a squawk, a silence. It was amazing to glide through it, as if they shouldn't really be there. At the end of Day 303, after seven days' wearisome kayaking from Diamantino – which now seemed like another century, another world – they camped at the confluence of the two rivers Arinos and Juruena. They celebrated with a fish supper, provided by a huge specimen that happened to land on the top of the kayak as they were white-watering down the last kilometres of the Arinos. Presumably the fish had been minding its own business swimming upstream and had an unlucky break. When Paul hit it with the stubby end of his paddle it had an even unluckier break. As they sat by the fire, watching the fish cook and the sun go down over the far bank of the Juruena, they suddenly both caught a sense that all was well with the world. They tried to put their contentment into words but then sat in silence, watching the waters rush, join and flow on together, a parable telling the travellers' story more eloquently than words.

The next morning Brendan and Paul launched into the conjoined river, the Alto Tapajós, hardly needing to paddle except to steer, marvelling at the speed they achieved with so little effort – continually in white-water. They covered the scheduled distance by mid-afternoon and debated whether to press on further, but decided that a longer rest would be preferable. They camped near the small town of Jacareacanga, and walked into town and stocked up. They even bought a fish – but it didn't taste half as nice as the one they'd "caught" themselves.

Two days of long distances followed, with the scenery alternating between rain-forest and open plain, and the river dropped its Alto and became the Tapajós. They camped near Itaituba that night, and bought a piranha fish to cook for dinner. When they examined it, they not only discovered how sharp and tightly-packed its teeth were, but how the triangular teeth interlocked to maximise the effect of their bite. There was another powerful set of rapids and cataracts two days later, the Maranhão Grande, but they managed the ride without too much trouble. Either they were becoming accomplished at kayaking, or they were getting luckier in their choice of entry-point. Below these rapids, they started to encounter big boats, because the river was now navigable all the way to the sea. The river-banks consequently filled with little settlements and quays and even an American town.

Brendan had heard of Fordlandia before, and was looking forward to seeing it. In the late 1920s, Henry Ford bought a large tract of land on the Tapajós River to cultivate rubber for his famous Model T car. It was just one example of how American companies (and governments) exploited South American resources for their own benefit, but Ford uniquely tried to import a mid-western American town, complete with picket fences, fire hydrants, and a golf course. Workers were made to work American hours (meaning that they worked through the heat of the afternoon), eat American food, and live in American-style houses, not suited for the Amazon. Needless to say, the workers resented the imposed lifestyle, the rubber trees failed, and the invention of synthetic rubber led the company to abandon the project altogether. The ghost-town was absurd, yet a powerful and tacky testament to American arrogance.

Past Aveiro, the Tapajós became a 10km-wide channel. They camped 40km further on, just as the rain-forest started again, and sat talking in a riverside café with the owner, who was a rubber-tapper, with the scarred rubber trees visible behind the café. Paul bought Ruth a gift, a multi-coloured rubber ball made from the local trees. When Brendan queried the purchase, an embarrassed Paul admitted that he and Ruth had a private joke going about a song called "Rubber Ball"[95] which had the lyric "Rubber ball, you keep bouncing back to me". Brendan thought that it was sweet, and said so, but that just made Paul's embarrassment worse.

They heard snapping and splashing noises at one point, and the café owner told them that it was only the crocs. He also cautioned them against urinating in the Tapajós. In 1997 a man had done just that in the shallows, only to be attacked by a shoal of small candiru or toothpick fish, which jumped up out of the water at him, one of which managed to lodge in his urethra and necessitate its surgical removal (the fish, not the urethra – or any other body part)[96]. Brendan and Paul took careful note.

At the confluence up ahead, the river swept alongside and tried to join the mighty Amazon. The milky-white Amazon was colder due to the Andes far upstream, the Tapajós deep-blue and warmer. The rivers could be differentiated even when they'd technically joined together, blue and white eddies of water tumbling into each other. At dinner, the menu, printed in Portuguese and English, listed two dishes that whetted their appetite and their curiosity. One dish was "bolinho de pirarucu", which the menu translated as "sheep turds", and the other "isca de pirarucu" or "dog turds". Fortunately the dishes were listed in the fish section of the menu so, when they got fish balls and fish portions, they weren't surprised – but it was almost an anti-climax.

Four days on the Amazon swept them downstream in a flurry of huge cargo ships, slow ferries and sail-boats, stopping near the small towns of Prainha and Vitoria, then the larger port of Macapá, bringing them almost to the end of this second stage of their great kayak journey. The Marco Zero sculpture in Macapá marked their farewell to the southern hemisphere, and Brendan's nineteenth and last crossing of the Equator. For Paul, it was more of a big deal, because, even though Uganda straddled the Equator, he'd lived in the north of the country and had never crossed the Equator till he flew to East Timor.. Finally they reached the end of the Amazon delta, and camped on the beach below a sharp cliff which pointed northwards up the

---

[95] Bobby Vee, 1961.

[96] The fish is also known as the Vampire Fish.

coastline, towards the third and final stage of their journey. They'd now kayaked for 6,500km, but they still had a further 2,000km to go.

***

After the forward surge given by the strong Tapajós and Amazon currents, the transition to side-impact waves and tidal tows was unwelcome and strange, especially for Paul, who had never previously encountered the sea in a kayak. The Amazon turned the ocean to freshwater for several kilometres along the coast, and as they edged northwards through their first morning at sea, the coastline complexity of beach and swamp produced a life-fertilising mixture of salt and fresh water perfect for wildlife. This was the northernmost and most unspoilt state in Brazil. The deforestation rampant across the rest of the Amazonian rain-forest had not yet hit Amapá, and tourism was put off by almost 600km of undeveloped coastline with only three beaches.

By mid-afternoon, as they approached the Araguari River, they were startled by several horizontal surfers doggy-paddling their boards out to sea, which seemed strange because the sea was pretty flat. After a dozen or more had passed in front or behind the kayak, Brendan asked one what is was all about.

"It's the Pororoca, man! It's coming!"

They weren't sure whether it was some sort of monster inland from which they were escaping, or a monster out at sea to which they were sacrificing themselves. They suspected, though, that it was a big wave, and that they'd better scarper. "How long before it comes?" yelled Brendan, hurting his throat.

"Can't you hear it? It's a-coming!"

And it came. Brendan instinctively turned the kayak into the path of the Big Wave, even though he knew that they would get submerged or swept up by it. Their best chance was to get *under* it. Paul understood what was happening, and, as the roar gathered and grew, they drove their paddles hard – right into the approaching wave. They were about 200m off-shore, and had arrived at exactly the wrong time. The wave was about 2m high, but several surfers were riding it and coming straight for them. As the wave hit, the kayak was instantly plucked and thrown backwards, but the force of the wave passed around them and they were submerged for only seconds, though it seemed much longer. They lurched to the surface and looked behind them, seeing the wave funnel into the wide river mouth, then grow in height as it was channelled into a smaller space, surfers whooping, flying and crashing as it swept them upstream and disappeared from view. They were relieved to see that the raft was still attached, but only one rope held it – the other three were trailing in the water, ends snapped like string.

They camped in a sheltered cove – a beautiful spot, with soft evening breezes blowing away the heat of the sun. The days now were dreadfully hot, but at least the cool of the water and the absence of insects 100m offshore made the heat bearable. They'd been very careful to cover up carefully, and the only sunburn suffered was on the backs of their hands. Their dry-suits had done the trick all the way from Uruguay, not only in keeping sea-water out and eradicating sweat, but also minimising chafing in sensitive areas. They were lean and fit and were growing impressive chest and arm muscles, and Brendan almost detected the early signs of a six-pack in a flight of testosterone-induced fancy.

They swung round the headland of Cape Norte towards the island of Maracá and the second of Amapá's three beaches – the attractively-named Boca do Inferno or Mouth of Hell. Back from the narrow beach, the island consisted of permanently wet fields of grasses and clumps of trees on the higher ground. It was probably teeming with wildlife but all they saw was a pair of parrots, and herons and egrets on the swampy shoreline.

The third and final beach was at Calçoene, the wettest place in Brazil (though it stayed dry for them), but more famously the site of the "Amazonian Stonehenge". Brendan and Paul climbed up to see it, but weren't very impressed. The circle of granite monoliths was pretty spectacular on the hilltop, but they weren't convinced by its claim to be an ancient astronomical observatory. The beach was more of an attraction for them, and seeing as they were ahead on their schedule for the day, they indulged in half an hour of swimming and sunbathing.

They finally came to the top of the peninsula which heralded their last night in Brazil, then eased along the marshy coast to Cape Orange, the northernmost point on the Brazilian coastline, separated from French Guiana by the estuary of the Oyapock River. A magnificent lone flamingo, precarious on its pink stick-legs, raised its too-heavy bill and honked a mournful farewell at them.

Guyane, as it was officially known, retained the alternative name of French Guiana because of its position as the easternmost of three ex-colonies: British Guiana, now Guyana; Dutch Guiana, now Suriname; and French Guiana. The armed guards in the patrol boat which stopped them in the middle of the estuary were particularly keen to examine Paul's passport. They explained, once satisfied that they were tourists passing through, that Guyane was suffering an influx of illegal immigrants and clandestine gold-prospectors from Brazil and Suriname, who thus gained entry to the European Union.

They continued north-west to the city of Cayenne, situated on the banks of its namesake river. It looked crowded, poor and dreadfully humid. They could see naked infants wandering aimlessly, and lumpy mothers wafting insects with makeshift fans, and workmen in vests whose arms glistened in the sun. They pressed on up the coast to Kourou, which contrastingly bristled with new wealth.

A quarter of the whole GDP of Guyane came from the Space Centre at Kourou, which Brendan and Paul could see from their campsite that evening. It had been built here by the French because it was only 500km north of the equator, at which latitude the Earth's rotation gave a velocity-boost of approximately 1,800kph when the launch trajectory headed eastwards out to sea. The tall launch-pads and Ariane assembly plants stood out from the flat terrain, and further north they could see more launch-pads and buildings with a huge Russian flag on the side – presumably Soyuz were launching spacecraft from there too.

Brendan and Paul continued up the coast, passing the Îles du Salut, 10km out to sea. They could just make out the northernmost island, Devil's Island, home to the penal colony made famous in Henri Charriere's "Papillon", based on his nine years' incarceration there. The coastline passed back into deserted marshy coastland and eventually into Brendan's 177th nation, Suriname, the smallest sovereign state in South America. Some of the greatest football players to represent the Netherlands were of Surinamese descent – and almost as soon as they left the Wia Wia Reserve, Brendan and Paul saw their first football pitch, and children kicking a ball around. It continued into and beyond the capital, until nightfall in the unpopulated Coppename Reserve.

There were very few settlements along the coast, and Brendan started to worry about offloading the Suriname Dutch GNT, especially as their only other night was to be in another Nature Reserve boasting pre-Columbian ruins but no people. So they stopped mid-afternoon at the village of Totness. It reminded Brendan of Totnes in Devon, where he'd once spent a damp caravan holiday as a child. It was raining in Totness too – the start of the rainy season, one local told him with a smile. He gave the old man the GNT, explaining why he was journeying round the world, and the man tapped his temple as if to say, "Too much sun, young man..."

On April 2nd, Brendan and Paul progressed from an ex-Dutch colony to Guyana, an ex-British colony, and their first evening destination in Nation 178 was called New Amsterdam. Life was full of surprises, and it was going to be (though Brendan had no idea of this at the time) a day for surprises...

Day: Date	Itinerary (* indicates TV interview) ([18] indicates new nation)	Bike (km)	Car/ Bus (km)	Train (km)	Kayak / Sail (km)	Boat (km)	Air (km)
Totals brought forward		11426	17330	8712	6318	19459	65301
297: 8/3/12	13.39S, 56.82W	3			121		
298: 9/3/12	12.47S, 56.71W				109		

299: 10/3/12	11.61S, 56.98W				104		
300: 11/3/12	10.62S, 57.12W				126		
301: 12/3/12	9.72S, 57.52W				153		
302: 13/3/12	8.74S, 57.59W				146		
303: 14/3/12	river junction 7.34S, 58.14W				183		
304: 15/3/12	Jacareacanga				174		
305: 16/3/12	5.20S, 56.91W				169		
306: 17/3/12	Itaituba				168		
307: 18/3/12	40km beyond Aveiro				150		
308: 19/3/12	Santarem				129		
309: 20/3/12	Prainha				164		
310: 21/3/12	river fork 1.41S, 51.98W				170		
311: 22/3/12	Macapa				192		
312: 23/3/12	end of delta				138		
313: 24/3/12	small cove 1.68N, 49.92W				117		
314: 25/3/12	far side of Amata bay				111		
315: 26/3/12	3.00N, 50.97W				100		
316: 27/3/12	top of peninsula				101		
317: 28/3/12	island 4.45N, 51.74W				105		
318: 29/3/12	Kourou				131		
319: 30/3/12	Organabo				106		
320: 31/3/12	Coppename, Suriname[177]				107		
321: 1/4/12	Hertennits				104		
322: 2/4/12	New Amsterdam, Guyana[178]				132		
Totals carried forward		11429	17330	8712	9828	19459	65301

Chapter 63: Carnations

April 2nd was the day of the RCN Awards Dinner. Louisa had decided to go, even though she wasn't expecting to win the Award for which she'd been nominated. She liked the chance to dress up in a posh frock and have a slap-up meal without having to pay for it. The first surprise of the day was seeing Sister Lilian sitting next to her in the conference hall. "What are you doing here?" Louisa asked.

"Thought you'd be surprised!" said Sister Lilian. "I've been involved in the College for ages, and membership secretary in the North of Tyne branch for over ten years. I come here every three years or so, and it's fallen really well this year because I'll get to see you collect your award."

"Huh, we'll see about that," said Louisa. "I've never won anything in my life except the egg and spoon race at Nursery and I cheated at that, so I wouldn't hold your hopes up."

"What do you mean? You've already won it, you noodle!"

"Me?" squawked Louisa. "How do you know?" A woman in front turned round and shushed them.

"It says in the programme. They can give out as many Annual Awards of Merit as they wish – and they've given the 2011 Award to all six of you on the short list. Look!" Sister Lilian handed over the programme, putting her finger on the relevant section. And there it was: her name. RCN Award of Merit. Wow.

She turned the page, and read the short tribute to each winner. Starting with her own, of course:

> "Louisa Priest is an experienced nurse in the Cardiovascular Unit of the world-renowned Freeman Hospital in Newcastle. Over the last year she has been responsible for the implementation of a co-ordinated partnership with the hospital chaplaincy to provide holistic patient care which includes not only the physical and emotional, but also the spiritual. She has exemplified this partnership by single-handedly spearheading a change of approach in her own Unit, bringing the senior nursing staff onboard after protracted negotiation and against initial opposition, which required much energy and foresight. This is only the third time in the history of the RCN Award of Merit that it has been awarded to a nursing practitioner below G grade, thus encouraging all our younger nurses to set themselves the highest standards and help the NHS to develop its policies and practices in the most fruitful way."

Double wow. Then she read the other winners' tributes, and was embarrassed. They were all senior nurses or directors of nursing who had published profession-changing research or been involved in the RCN all their working life. She stuck out like a sore thumb, but she texted Ben and got a quick reply, full of smileys and exclamation marks.

The Awards Dinner was really posh, with circular tables so that they could chat to their regional colleagues and representatives. Louisa sat next to Sister Lilian because she didn't know anyone else and felt out of her depth. Everyone else was well into their fifties and looked like it, whereas she had her best short frock on, showing off her legs and not being too shy when it came to cleavage either. One woman had a fur round her neck, and one of the blokes wore a bow-tie. Sister Lilian wore a grey maxi-dress that made her look like a boulder. The other winners of the Award of Merit were unsurprisingly of a similar age and fashion-ineptitude to the people round Louisa's table. They had official photographs taken, and settled down for all the other awards and fellowships and speeches – and then sloped off to the bar. When she finally staggered back to her hotel room, there was a massive bunch of red carnations against the door, with a card saying, "Power to the people! Love you, Ben xxx"

***

Ben would have loved to be there, but his new job demanded that he attended Jact every Sunday morning, to greet people as they came in, introduce the service, talk about the new people whom he'd met that week, and lead the first section of worship aimed at younger families and children. He'd been in his new job for nearly two months now, and loved it. He'd spent hours talking with the young people, pleading with them to give the Church another chance, and winning them back. He built bridges in the Jact community too, visiting all the schools, doing some of his more spectacular street-dance and beatboxing performances and inviting them to come along to Jact and re-discover how the Church was trying to provide something for all ages and this meant that *their* views mattered. It was a powerful marketing campaign, enhanced by his genuine enthusiasm and passion. He also went round the pubs and clubs, talking about the Church's exciting new start and inviting people to give it a go.

Attendances were up on Cecil's time, not that that was saying much. But they were also up on Caridad's time, and that was something unexpected and deeply encouraging. The Superintendent planned himself there quite often, and he and Ben had a good understanding and "feel" for the new people coming in. Worship was light and fun, but the Super would always slip in something powerful, challenging and reflective in the midst of the stories, interviews and activity. The "sermon" on those Sundays was usually a dialogue between Ben and the Super, with some big topics being tackled which made people sit up and even join in.

April 1st, while Louisa was travelling to the RCN Congress, was Palm Sunday, and Ben recruited a real donkey. It was an impressive opening to the service, especially when the eight-year-old riding it nearly fell off – and even more when the donkey deposited something lumpy on the red carpet. Everyone fell about laughing, and Ben handed the donkey reins over to Sarah Lanleigh, who led it outside and tied it to a tree, then cleared up the poo during the song "Come and see[97]", hoping that people wouldn't. Ben explained the Messianic significance of the entry on a donkey to the children, who were spellbound. He talked about Jesus turning everything upside-down, not just the tables of the money-changers but the whole Temple system and the people's expectations of how God's power would be revealed – it wouldn't be with force, arrogance and domination but through love, humility and vulnerability. Ben got them all to shut their eyes, then beatboxed Jesus going to the cross, including the sound of the nails thumping into his hands, and everyone in Jact Methodist Church was transfixed too.

The Super developed the theme in the sermon, talking about the Carnation Revolution in Lisbon in 1974, so named because the authoritarian regime was overturned not by armed revolutionaries, but by ordinary people taking to the streets handing out big bunches of red carnations, inviting everyone to join them dancing in the streets. Red was a colour rich in meaning, signifying socialism and democracy, but also the blood of Christ on the Cross. The regime had caved in under this massive show of people-power, whereupon the Portuguese Empire imploded, its colonies were granted independence, political prisoners were released, censorship banned, and a new democratic constitution approved. Then he and Ben spoke in quick-fire dialogue.

"Ben and I want to make sure that you make the links."

"You see," said Ben, "What Jesus did, was mirrored by what the people of Lisbon did. And we here in Jact are beginning to reflect this too."

"Both the Christian Church and the Carnation Revolution were led by ordinary people, against an old system that no longer spoke for the people, and both were characterised by an outpouring of happiness. And that's what we're about too."

"Both the Christian Church and the Carnation Revolution brought a sense of freedom of expression, a new start, and people being given the opportunity to forge their own destiny. That's what we're about too. Will you join us?"

"Sometimes the Christian Church messed it up," said the Super. "So did post-revolutionary Portugal. So will we, I'm sure. But if we all get involved, maybe we can build something very special here. Will you join us?"

The people stood and applauded. When a prayer and dedication time was called for, people came to the front in their dozens to sign their names on a big chart headed, "I want to be a follower of the revolutionary Jesus." At the end of the

---

[97] Graham Kendrick's 1989 Passion song "Come and see"

service, 153 people[98] had signed their names. Ben gave all 153 a red carnation to take home. He'd done a deal with the florist. It was a huge "catch", but it was only the beginning of the fishing story...

---

[98] 153 was the number of fish caught in the miracle described in John's Gospel, chapter 21.

Chapter 64: Nations 179 - 181

Fishing was the last thing on Brendan's mind as he and Paul progressed westwards along the marshy flatlands of the Guyana coastline. They spent a pleasant if unspectacular night in New Amsterdam, whose claim to fame was having been the first city in the world to regulate where householders could build their privies (not next to a public path). It wasn't one of the world's best-known "firsts". Brendan was more interested in the Mission Chapel, rebuilt by a visitor called Rev. Wray, who'd been horrified at the plight of Guyanan slaves, and stayed 24 years to help them. That's proper mission, thought Brendan – seeing a need and staying to help put it right.

Brendan spoke to a large crowd that evening in the capital Georgetown's Cathedral, the largest wooden church in the world, and gave the Guyana GNT randomly to an up-and-coming cricketer, over whom several young ladies present kept drooling.

***

Brendan and Paul paddled along the coast for three more days without encountering much more of the country or its inhabitants. They passed beaches with interesting names: Father's, Pawpaw, Iron-Punt, Foxes, Turtle, Shell, Luri, Almond – but the whole seaboard was one long beach full of basking turtles, which just sat there, oblivious and seemingly content with life. Humans, however, did not have the same skills at contentment. Guyana and Venezuela had been in territorial disputes for well over a century, and there didn't seem much hope of a resolution. Venezuela claimed most of Guyana whereas Guyana still referred to their western border as the Orinoco River, as designated in 1835 by a German who'd been bribed by the British.

Brendan and Paul came upon the Orinoco Delta midway through their first day in Venezuela, and crossed the mouths of hundreds of streams and rivers over the next day and a half. Some were wide channels; others narrow rivulets. Some, heavy with sediments, were brown; others black with tannic acids. Many were carpeted with vast floating meadows of water hyacinths and grasses, slowly drifting along then sinking under the incoming waves. They camped overnight on the swampy island of Jotajana, but, wary of the tides, stayed close to the kayak in case their island disappeared during the night. The next day brought more of the same, culminating in a firmer campsite at Soburojo in the National Park, where they met a young Venezuelan couple to whom Brendan gave the GNT.

The island of Trinidad was now just 15km offshore, but they only crossed the Columbus Channel when they got to the western end of the National Park, thus completing their journey through South America as they were now heading into the

Caribbean. Trinidad was named by Columbus in honour of the Trinity, one of only two countries which mentioned God in its name (the other being El Salvador) – another question in Brendan's impossible pub quiz. They camped on the beach before paddling off on their final kayaking day through the Serpent's Mouth, which separates the island from Venezuela, and up the coconut-grove coast of the Cedros Peninsula. They saw (but weren't stopped by) gunships in the Serpent's Mouth, presumably stopping drug cartels from South America bringing their produce through Trinidad into the Caribbean markets.

The sheltered waters of the Gulf of Paria were a throwback to the smooth kayaking on their very first day, down from Fray Bentos to the mouth of the Piraná. The Gulf's northern outlet was only a thin channel between the Paria peninsula of Venezuela and the Chaguaramas peninsula of north-west Trinidad, so the gulf's waters were almost always calm and created one of the best natural harbours on the Atlantic coast of the Americas. Beaches, industrial complexes, mangroves and the capital Port-of-Spain all breezed by until finally they reached the marina in Chaguaramas Bay – journey's end. They'd kayaked a total of 8,410km from Fray Bentos. Their route had taken them up the Paraná and Paraguay, down the Tapajós and Amazon, and finally along the Atlantic coastline – an epic, unprecedented journey, smashing the world record for the longest continuous kayak journey. Their little kayak had done them proud, but now they had to swap it for a speedboat, better suited for the journey through the rest of the Caribbean to Belize. The marina was crowded with boats of every shape and size, squeezed in like a nautical game of sardines. "Why is it so busy?" Brendan asked the boatyard manager.

"It's all because of a clause in the insurance policies," explained the manager, grinning as he surveyed his empire. "Caribbean yachts have to berth in a port south of 12°N during the hurricane season. And even though we're nowhere near the hurricane season, many owners don't bother moving their yachts anywhere else." He graciously offered them $500 in part-exchange against an ocean-going speedboat. They explained where they'd come from in it, and the manager was pretty impressed. "If I take your picture with the kayak, and you let me write a piece for the newspaper, I'll knock another $1,000 off the price." The photo was taken, the contract of sale signed, handshakes were exchanged, and Brendan gave him the Trinidad and Tobago GNT too. The manager was thrilled to be associated with Brendan's journey, wished him every blessing, and knocked him another $1,000 off. The rest of the Wharram Tangaroa still cost Brendan $32,500, but, thanks to Barclaycard, he was soon officially the new owner of the Caribbean Queen. It was an over-egged title for a plain but cosy boat, 30 years old but in decent condition, and the manager promised that she would be eminently sellable anywhere in the Caribbean. He would say that, though, wouldn't he?

She was a four-berth 34-footer catamaran, with a full inventory. Brendan and Paul didn't have much idea what some of the listed items meant or what they were supposed to do with them, but they didn't have a lot of choice or time to shop around, so they completed the purchase and walked 50m to book in at the nearest hotel. They dined in the excellent yacht-view restaurant then retired to their twin-bedded room. A faint breeze from the bay wafted the thin curtains as they lay on their beds and contemplated the last leg of this nautical adventure. They still had 34 days, 13 nations, and 5,500km to go, but it seemed to Brendan that they were nearly there.

Nations 174 to 181

The next morning, Brendan was awoken by the clatter of his travel washing line falling off the balcony rails onto the floor. It was one of those cheap travel-kit items "sold at all good stores" – an elasticated, tightly twisted peg-less rope into which newly-washed clothes slotted to dry overnight. The ends of the rope attached to walls, doors or balcony rails, and never came loose unless tugged – on this occasion by a monkey now involuntarily imprisoned inside the shirt Brendan had washed the evening before. Brendan leapt out of bed and grabbed the shirt before it disappeared. The orange-furred monkey looked both aggressive and sad at the same time, stuck its lower jaw out at him and emitted the most *amazing* noise – a deep guttural growl louder than anything Brendan had ever heard. It was like an alarm going off, but several octaves below the usual pitch. Paul, a heavy sleeper, leapt out of bed and cowered against the wall. The monkey jumped off the balcony and swung down to the pool area, where several of its fellows were prowling around, long tails raised like dodgem poles.

Having checked out all the essentials about the Caribbean Queen with the boatyard manager the night before, they set off soon after daybreak, skirting the docks daubed pink from bauxite dust. They chugged between the end of the peninsula and the island of Monos (Spanish for "monkeys"), named after the Red Howlers, one of which Brendan and Paul had already encountered, and out into the open sea. The Caribbean Queen's twin hulls provided a buoyancy which enabled them to feel safe wandering around without holding on. The small waves hardly splashed over the hulls. They swept across to Grenada at a relaxed 30kph though the engine-noise hinted at greater speeds if needed. Fuel economy wasn't a big issue because they had a huge tank and an extra 50-litre auxiliary tank – and when they got to Grenada they still had over a quarter of the main tank left. It took five hours, and they were there in good time for the next "See Esther" episode.

They were now in the same time-zone as Detroit, so the show was due to start at 2pm. Esther, Ruth and the techie entourage met them at the harbour in St. George's, the capital of Grenada and the centre of its water-sports tourism. Esther decided that because the setting was so gorgeous she would conduct the interview outdoors, but the sun was so bright that they retreated indoors to the top-floor suite of her hotel, so that they didn't have to squint or wear sunglasses.

"Well, Brendan," said Esther after the opening titles and introductions, "I can't quite believe that we've come to the last-but-one interview. You started 11 months ago on that foggy Tyneside day, and you're still going, still on track and on the last lap of your journey. Are you surprised?"

"Surprised? No, not really. There's a stubborn streak in me that never wants to give up, and all the difficulties have merely served as extra incentives for me to persevere."

"But Brendan, you've been plotted against, bombed out of the sky, held up by pirates, been given up for dead. Is this normal for you?"

Brendan laughed, coughed, but then got serious. "You'll have to ask Paul if I'm a dangerous person to be with, because he's shared the last few months with me. He must bring me a blessing, though, because nothing much has happened to me since he came onboard, apart from this sore throat. Maybe I wasn't supposed to do it on my own." He tailed off, reflectively. Perhaps mission projects of any kind were not meant to be solitary tasks.

Esther moved on. "My researchers tell me that you're basically on schedule except in one area. You're absolutely on the limit as far as the non-powered sections on land and sea are concerned. We can't easily cope with *any* fluctuations in the distances you do. For instance, you are projected to do a total of 35,500km on the water, of which you have to do at least 30%, or 10,650km, unpowered. Your projected final tally is only *3km* over that, which doesn't leave much margin, so we'll monitor the last few days very carefully to make sure that you don't break the rules."

Brendan shrugged. He didn't really understand any of this. "So what's the problem?"

"The problem is time. We reckon that you're one day behind, and we have to catch that up somewhere. It'll probably mean a spot of night-sailing somewhere along the way."

"Ah well, I suppose I'll just have to do whatever it takes. I'm too far into this journey to give up on it now."

Esther turned to Ruth. "And is it good to have your record-breaking kayaking husband back for an evening?"

Ruth laughed, a bit embarrassed but quickly turning it into a joke. "I don't think he'd ever been in a kayak before, so it's a bit odd having him described as a record-breaker. You'd better ask him what he thinks of it all."

Paul sniggered. "I didn't know how easy it was to break a world record. Brendan doesn't know it, but all I did was sit behind him pretending to paddle from time to time. It was him who did all the work." And Paul broke out into a loud Ugandan laugh that made everybody smile. "Only joking!" he whispered loudly to Brendan whose eyebrows had arched. Everybody laughed again.

Esther turned back to Ruth. "What about the fund-raising?"

Ruth picked up her clipboard and read out some of the figures. "We've had contact from over 700,000 sponsors around the world, ranging from millionaires pledging tens of thousands of dollars to schoolchildren sending us their pocket-money. Some of the letters have been deeply moving, and I want to thank everybody on behalf of Watoto, and the Brendan Priest Trust in particular. So far we've received over $25 million, and are expecting something like $150 million in all, with (we hope) an extra $30 million if my Dad finishes on time and within all the rules. Over 50,000 people have promised to double their sponsorship if it's completed on schedule – so it's worth catching up that extra day, Dad!"

"Well, Brendan," said Esther. "You'll have learnt a lot about yourself, the world, and Life on your travels. But what's been the most *surprising* thing that you've learnt?"

Brendan thought hard. What had he learnt? Plenty about his own resilience, his faith. Plenty about God's care. Plenty about mission requiring long-term commitment. None of these were big surprises, though – more like confirmations of what he already knew. "I think the most surprising lesson is not that God tells us to relax and trust that He wants the best for us, whatever happens. I *knew* that, in my head. The biggest surprise is that I now believe it in my *heart* and that I've been able to give it a go. I was all caught up in trying to *make* the best thing happen, without realising that it was far more important that I trust that *whatever* happens can be the best thing, if I trust God to do his best with it and with me."

Esther gawped at him. Brendan was beginning to get to her.

Day: Date	Itinerary (* indicates TV interview) ([18] indicates new nation)	Bike (km)	Car/ Bus (km)	Train (km)	Kayak / Sail (km)	Boat (km)	Air (km)
Totals brought forward		11429	17330	8712	9828	19459	65301
323: 3/4/12	Georgetown				107		
324: 4/4/12	state line 7.70N, 58.81W				129		
325: 5/4/12	top of Waini peninsula				132		
326: 6/4/12	Jotajana, Venezuela[179]				120		
327: 7/4/12	Soburojo				100		
328: 8/4/12	San Francique, Trinidad and Tobago[180]				97		
329: 9/4/12	Port of Spain				140		
330: 10/4/12	St. George's, Grenada *[181]					167	
Totals carried forward		11429	17330	8712	10653	19626	65301

Chapter 65: Nations 182 - 189

St. Vincent and the Grenadines sounded like a pop group to Brendan, but it was the next nation on his journey, and they reached it easily the next day, with a following wind providing a boost to their speed and fuel economy. They aimed first of all for the conical peak of the active volcano named on Brendan's GPS as Kick 'Em Jenny. It rose 1,300m straight up from the sea, but it was not "kicking", thankfully. They passed from island to island in the Grenadine archipelago, waving at happy children in each one they passed. It was a gorgeous part of the world, with some strange names: Prune Island; Engagement Umbrella[99]; as well as some familiar ones, like Mustique, where they stopped for the night in a hotel called the Firefly[100]. The proprietors, who introduced themselves as Steve and Linda, showed them the visitors' book containing several famous names, including Bill Gates, Shania Twain and Jeremy Clarkson, and they added their own. Stan explained that the royals stayed at Princess Margaret's old estate, Les Jolies Eaux, which was now let out on a weekly basis. "Better to stay here," said Linda. "It's about $25,000 cheaper per week."

The coral reef just offshore looked a funny colour. Steve explained that it was all down to global warming. "The warm water is very pleasant for humans but increasingly unpleasant for the coral reefs, because it kills off the zooxanthellae which provide food for the coral polyps, bleaching and killing large areas of reef." He obviously loved saying the word "zooxanthellae" because he repeated it. "They're like algae." He started to explain about photosynthesis and inorganic molecules but by the time that he got onto "dinoflagellate protozoa and golden-brown intracellular endosymbionts", Brendan and Paul had already tuned out. They could see the effects, however, even from where they were: white bone-like clumps which should have been rainbow-coloured. Climate change was like the Holy Spirit, thought Brendan. You didn't have to understand it, and couldn't pin it down, as long as you could see the results of its activity, and amend your ways in the light of what you saw.

Brendan could see why Mustique had a certain mystique and reputation as a glamour-filled paradise for the rich and famous. But that wasn't really what he was interested in, and they were glad to depart, having given the GNT to Linda, to be kept in the lounge for their visitors. The natural route was north-westwards,

---

[99] A tiny island, officially called Mopion, which has one beach umbrella on it all year round – and no inhabitants. It's ringed by treacherous reefs and thus gets very few visitors to sit under its umbrella.

[100] Steve and Linda are fictional characters, but the Firefly is a real hotel on Mustique, run by Stan and Liz. Les Jolies Eaux is as described, though the rent details are fictional but not necessarily unrealistic.

following the curving archipelago of islands round to Hispaniola and Cuba, but they struck out eastwards instead to take in Barbados. It was a long way, but they arrived in good spirits and able to appreciate the waterfront and ambience of the capital, Bridgetown. They'd heard that Barbados was the richest and most developed of the island nations, and they saw plenty of evidence for this. They sailed into Carlisle Bay and then right into the heart of the capital via the Careenage Canal, which sliced Bridgetown into two and provided a channel into the inner basin where the Parliament buildings and flamboyant apartments stood tall at the water's edge. They also noticed, however, the grubby kids squatting on the corners of some of the minor streets, which got visibly poorer within metres of the main thoroughfares. There was wealth, but it was showy wealth which didn't seem to penetrate much further than the historic and tourist areas.

Brendan was booked to speak at the bright-white, pillared Methodist Church in James Street, and the Minister told him that the earliest Methodists had arrived in Barbados in 1789, intent on Christianising the slaves, but the plantation owners began a campaign of attrition and persecution against them. Methodist meeting houses were pelted with stones and their meetings often interrupted, until in 1823 an angry mob tore down the original chapel in James Street and made several unsuccessful attempts to outlaw Methodism in Barbados. "I think that the burning of the James Street Church was the turning point," said the Minister, smiling. "It seems that when the Church is attacked, it grows!" Brendan smiled and nodded. Here it was again – the reason why the work of Open Doors was so important: the struggling but faithful Christians in the Persecuted Church produced phenomenal fruit. "By 1848 their congregation had grown to over 5,000 and there were eight chapels and four other meeting places!" the Minister proudly declared.

"And what is it like now?" asked Brendan.

"It's still good, but along with wealth we've acquired worldliness. There's a dreadful problem with alcohol and drugs, which we try to combat as best we can and help its victims. We have Alcoholics Anonymous meetings here and clinics for drug addicts. We do our best."

Brendan was encouraged by what he saw as he was shown round. They really were trying their best, and there were hundreds packed into the pews for his talk, listening intently as he got back into the flow of describing his journey's purpose and some of the many adventures he'd had. He handed out "business cards" at the end and a collection was taken up for Watoto, which was supported generously by the people. It seemed very "nice" and "British middle-class", even though everyone was black. Paul remarked later that he felt much less "on show" and more able to be himself, now that he was amongst black people.

***

From Barbados, they sailed west again, to pick up the chain of islands at St. Lucia, at the rate of an island a day: the three island nations of Dominica, Antigua, and St. Kitts and Nevis; then the two non-nations of the Virgin Islands and Puerto Rico. The independence issues had been decided haphazardly throughout the Caribbean – some had been granted it; others had been refused it; some had never asked for it. Everywhere there were warm welcomes, wide smiles and children playing cricket. Every island on which they overnighted had a Methodist church happy to host a meeting at which Brendan could speak – even though his throat was struggling to cope.

There were special memories from each island: St. Lucia's craggy Pitons and a trip to a drive-in volcano; a meal of "mountain chicken" on Dominica which turned out to be frog; getting caught up in the regatta at the beginning of Antigua Sailing Week; staying in St. Kitts in what must be the smallest Methodist manse in the world; the conch-shell markers in the graveyard next to the old Methodist Church at Spanish Town in the British Virgin Islands; the Primera Iglesia Metodista at Fajardo on Puerto Rico at which the Spanish interpreter wore what looked like a bullfighter's outfit.

To catch up a day, they sailed overnight, after the evening meeting at Fajardo, along the northern coast of Puerto Rico to Isabella, then sailed during the next day across to the nearest point of the Dominican Republic, Boca de Yuma. They slept well onboard that night, anchored in the centre of the bay, bobbing gently as the little waves ran round them.

The island of Hispaniola contained Dominican Republic in the east and Haiti in the west. It was only the 22nd biggest island in the world in area, but the tenth biggest in population. The overcrowding was all too evident as they sailed along the southern coast, reaching Santo Domingo, the most populated city in the Caribbean at 3.8 million (second was the capital of Haiti, Port au Prince, with 3.5 million). Santo Domingo was steeped in history, from the 16th century fortress guarding the entrance to the harbour, to the Cathedral of Santa María la Menor, where Brendan was due to speak – the oldest cathedral in the Americas, having been completed in 1540. But it also had the peculiar Columbus Lighthouse – an 800m cross-shaped monument to the Christianisation of America, constructed for the 500th anniversary of Columbus's landing in 1492. Aesthetically, to Brendan, it was horrible – all exaggerated, geometric and dull concrete. Theologically, it also seemed wrong – a cross-shaped monument to a colonist very unpopular at the time in Hispaniola, whom modern scholarship has criticised as the pioneer for the conquistadors who brought disease, murder or slavery to the original Taino tribes of Hispaniola, and took away all their gold and natural resources.

Brendan much preferred the Cathedral. It had a beautiful coral-limestone facade, a long nave and high-vaulted ceiling in a very traditional European style. He felt at home.

***

The coastline (with one brief interlude) was crowded for the next two days with villages, clusters of tiny homes, towns big and small – including Bajos de Haina which had the dubious privilege of being one of the world's ten most polluted towns. It was all densely populated, picturesque but desperately poor. The Jaragua Park was utterly different – no people but kilometres of unspoilt mangroves and forests, with bursts of flamingos and a colony of rhinosaurus iguanas, some over a metre in length, which looked askance as the Caribbean Queen passed the sandbank on which they were sunbathing.

They swept up past the small town of Pedernales to Anse-à-Pitre across the Haitian border. And it was like entering a different world. The town was utterly cramped; life stripped down to mere existence, disease-ridden, abjectly poor. This was post-earthquake, post-refugee, post-cholera, post-civilisation Haiti. It was, in some respects, as if the devastation had happened only yesterday. Brendan and Paul couldn't believe their eyes. It was a post-Armageddon wasteland, full of bewildered no-hopers.

Day: Date	Itinerary (* indicates TV interview) ([18] indicates new nation)	Bike (km)	Car/ Bus (km)	Train (km)	Kayak / Sail (km)	Boat (km)	Air (km)
Totals brought forward		11429	17330	8712	10653	19626	65301
331: 11/4/12	Mustique, St. Vincent and the Grenadines[182]					112	
332: 12/4/12	Bridgetown, Barbados[183]					170	
333: 13/4/12	Hellene, St. Lucia[184]					159	
334: 14/4/12	Roseau, Dominica[185]					188	
335: 15/4/12	St. John's, Antigua[186]					193	

336: 16/4/12	Sandy Point, St. Kitts and Nevis[187]					123	
337: 17/4/12	Spanish Town, Virgin Islands					197	
338: 18/4/12	Fajardo, Puerto Rico, then overnight to Isabella					128 +166	
339: 19/4/12	Boca de Yuma, Dominican Republic[188]					182	
340: 20/4/12	Santa Domingo					163	
341: 21/4/12	Barahona					136	
342: 22/4/12	Anse-à-Pitre, Haiti[189]					149	
Totals carried forward		11429	17330	8712	10653	21622	65301

Chapter 66: Abomination

The border town of Anse-à-Pitre was suffering beneath the radar of the international community. Business was anything but booming and, to make matters worse, pre-existing aid and resources had been diverted to address post-quake needs elsewhere. It was now well over two years since the earthquake altered Haiti forever. Like the capital's overcrowded settlements for displaced people, the modest homes of host families in this rural region were under increasing duress. Daily life in the close quarters of a tent or one-room house had taken away any semblance of privacy. At nightfall, poorly-located latrines – or the complete lack thereof – required women and children to steal away to unlit areas. Few people felt safe. Violence against women had spiralled. The police and the justice system did their best but the rule of law had disappeared and was disregarded by many of the young males who paraded their arrogance. Brendan and Paul stayed with the local Catholic priest, who showed them round what was essentially a refugee camp. Mission involved the simple comforting of the distressed, the reciting of a prayer, the gift of food, offering an unopened bottle of water. Brendan and Paul felt like voyeurs.

It got much worse when they came to Jacmel, a large city on the south coast, just 30km from the epicentre – closer to it than the capital Port au Prince. No-one met them as they stepped ashore, but as they made their way into town, the calmness of the docks gave way to a chaotic, buzzing city where chickens played chicken with the speeding cars and motorbikes shared the streets with goats, dogs and the occasional pig plundering the gutter. They wandered through Jacmel's confusing streets, taking in the long line-ups outside empty-shelved shops, and the haphazard clusters of red and grey Coleman tents. Donated after the earthquake, the tents had become home for many families still afraid to sleep inside their buildings for fear of another earthquake. Brendan and Paul found their way to the ruins of the City Hall, where they'd agreed to meet the Mayor. The building had survived but was branded with a large red, encircled dot, which meant that it was condemned as unsafe.

Bang on time for the meeting, they found the Mayor, sweating in the heat of the day, talking to a man outside the Coleman tents packed shoulder-to-shoulder in the town square. "Hello," the Mayor said, in excellent but accented English, "Welcome to Paradise." He introduced himself as Edwin, and led them to the library across the square, which was the temporary government office. Upstairs, they looked out over the square and the streets leading off it, seeing a crowded market nearby. "It's not as busy now," said Edwin. "Mainly because there isn't any produce and no-one has any money to buy anything anyway." It looked packed to Brendan, all the same. Perhaps they were scavenging. "Where are you staying?" asked Edwin.

"Probably on the boat. It doesn't look like there's much accommodation available here."

"You'll be safer there. It gets a bit hairy at night in town," said Edwin, shaking his head. "You know the harbour, where your boat is? That emptied completely four times on E-Day, as a series of tsunamis swept the sea in and out, leaving fish high and dry on the exposed sand of the sea-floor way out beyond the harbour, only for the water to rush back in and flood the town." They walked out along a rubble-strewn road, buildings crumbling either side. "See those people?" said Edwin. "They're walking quietly and seem to be listening. Do you know why?" They shook their heads. "They're listening for the voices of those who lie dead beneath the rubble. We are hard to die here, so people walk quietly." Brendan wasn't sure whether this was a reference to Haitian voodoo or zombie cults, or whether the people were simply respecting a place where bodies still had to be recovered.

"Why have the buildings not been cleared?" Brendan asked.

Edwin smiled and shrugged. "With what? At night people still sleep there, to be near their loved ones underneath." They came to another square, in which there were a few bare market stalls, but fewer people. Brendan looked more closely, and the only things for sale were used flip-flops, sacks of charcoal and expired cold-medicine. He looked round the square and shook his head – this was all wrong. Jacmel was still a beautiful place, the turquoise ocean still curving around steep green mountains, palm fronds arching over colourful houses and bright flowers spilling over walls. It was just that the colourful houses were ruins and the walls were piles of bricks. Edwin showed them another neighbourhood in which every house was painted with a red dot. Some were flattened, as if the Monty Python foot had squidged them from above, seven floors concertinaed into two metres of compressed death. Others listed far to one side as though taking a rest. Some were torn open, revealing iron bed-frames or women cooking yams. There was still the faint sweet tang of death, two years on.

Edwin left them when they circled back to the library, and they picked their way back down to the harbour. It was now mid-evening, and people were coming out to get ready for bed. Women were washing themselves or their laundry in plastic buckets or settling little ones on blankets in the street, men were brushing their teeth or standing and drinking, and watching. Brendan and Paul felt uncomfortable as they walked briskly past, feeling the eyes on their backs. They were glad to get back to the boat.

***

The next morning, Brendan's voice had almost gone but they set off again on foot, watching as queues formed, presumably for food. Chunks of cinderblock and pastel-painted plaster lay among twisted wrought-iron railings as if New Orleans had crashed out of the sky. They passed the rubble of what had been the Fosaj Art

School, a bold community art project – and then the equally devastated ruins of the Cine Institute, a world-famous film school. Maybe art died on E-Day too, but then Brendan and Paul turned a corner and saw a square full of artists plying their trade: painting; carving intricate wooden boats; sculpting junk into art. No-one was buying, of course, but they were expressing their souls: ars gratia artis.

They'd arranged to meet the Jacmel Methodist Minister, called Pierre. He stretched his arms wide as if proudly showing off his "patch". And he *was* proud. "There's a Creole word for when you have to make do: degaje. In my opinion the ability to degaje is what gives this culture the spirit of resiliency that I so admire." He chatted to people as they walked along the streets. They arrived at a school playing field. "After the earthquake, we had a tent city with 6,000 homeless people on this football pitch. People ate only once a day, crime was rampant and a prostitution ring sprang up within a week. But then they realised that camps were not the answer, and started a programme to construct shelters. A Swiss NGO called Medair built metal-framed tent-like structures that were designed to evolve from temporary shelters into permanent homes as families accumulated the means – wood, corrugated tin and plastic sheets – to build onto them. And that's what's happened." They came to one such home. It had bricks inexpertly laid in a wall along one side of the shelter, a corrugated iron sheet for the roof, but still a tarpaulin for one of its walls. "This man is lucky," said Pierre. He owned the land before his home fell down, so he can rebuild. Those only renting have nowhere and must stay in the camps."

Brendan couldn't believe the devastation. "What happened to the relief agencies?" he croaked. "Did they not come here?"

"Oh yes," said Pierre. "But they have all gone. Canada in particular was very good because the family of their Governor General, Michaelle Jean, live here, and she stayed here often as a child. The Canadian DART team were excellent." Brendan pictured some beer-bellied pub team helping out, but Pierre, seeing his bewilderment, explained that DART stood for Disaster Assistance Response Team. "They built a field hospital and a water-purification system. They cleared rubble and unloaded aid supplies from sea-barges with their heavy lifting gear, but then after two months they left, taking all their equipment with them. And we've received little help since."

"What about the government – are they not interested in helping?"

"They said that their priority was to protect people from the hurricanes, so all their efforts had to go into that. But they concentrated on Port-au-Prince, and forgot Jacmel after the Canadians came. When the Canadians left, they still forgot us. There are mountains between here and the capital and they can't see us, so we do not exist."

They turned a corner to find a brand-new, thriving school building which looked like it had been beamed in by a spaceship. It stuck out not like a sore thumb but like an unhurt thumb on a mangled hand. "This doesn't look like degaje," rasped Brendan, hoping that he'd got the word right.

"Certainly not," laughed Pierre. "This is our brand new school, the École Nationale Jacob Martin Henriquez, which serves about 600 students, from kindergarten through to Grade Seven. It was sponsored by the American Honeywell Corporation," Pierre said. "It has a modern computer lab, a library, and five classrooms!"

"For 600 children?" asked Brendan.

"We are used to big class sizes in Haiti." Pierre laughed again. "More important still are the training workshops for our builders which are held here. The Americans teach what they call "sustainable building methods" so our new buildings should withstand future earthquakes and hurricanes."

"But what about the rest of Jacmel?" asked Brendan.

"They still have very little. But even so they have more than the people in the camps. I'll take you to see for yourself tomorrow, if you like." That created a bit of a dilemma for Brendan and Paul. They'd already lost the day they'd made up, and would have to do another night-sail if they missed another day. But Brendan didn't feel that he could leave without seeing everything.

Pierre took them on one last bit of sight-seeing – to Jacmel's premier hotel. Leading the way down some empty, rubble-strewn streets, he stopped outside high wrought-iron gates, fastened with a heavy padlock. They bore the hotel's name: The Jacmelienne Beach Hotel. "Don't worry about the gates," Pierre shouted, stepping through a massive gap in the wall. The once-plush hotel now had its shutters firmly and probably permanently closed. "It must have been very nice, but since the earthquake the only thing that has changed is the colour of the water in the pool, which has gone from brown to yellow and now, as you see, to a delicate shade of green." It seemed to sum up what was happening to the whole country. But what would tomorrow be like?

Chapter 67: Rejuvenation

Pierre picked them up in his battered Citroen. "Hurricane Tomas destroyed some of the camp I am taking you to," said Pierre. "Then, because they had no proper water supplies, an outbreak of cholera spread very quickly."

He turned onto a mud-track, which led up to what looked at first like a Japanese prisoner-of-war camp during the Second World War. Wooden poles held up rickety wire fences, with people pacing aimlessly up and down looking at the ground. All it needed was Lieutenant Sato and a few bayonets and it was Tenko all over again.

It was huge. Thousands of shelters, draped with polythene or corrugated metal to keep the rains out, with the middle of the alleys channelled for both drainage and sewerage. Everyone looked downcast and despairing. It was heart-breaking. Pierre took them up one of the alleys and stopped at a flimsy shelter, tapping on the corrugated roof. A man emerged, dressed in trousers and a dirty vest. He smiled at Pierre, but frowned when he saw Brendan and Paul. "This is Henri," said Pierre. "My church steward from Jacmel. But of course he can no longer serve because he lives here. His house was flattened and his family were all killed. Only Henri survived."

Henri invited them in, and they ducked their heads and entered a square room about two metres across. There were no seats, only a makeshift bed against one loose-planked wall, The three of them sat on the bed and Henri squatted in the dirt. "You are very welcome in my home," Henri said. "But I am sad that I cannot offer you a drink or some refreshment because I have no food. We eat once a day at the central food hall. God is good to me because I have a roof which doesn't leak and walls which only let a little of the wind through, but I wish He would give me more to eat."

Brendan was choked. He'd never encountered anything like this before. Earthquakes and hurricanes were awful tragedies, but this was an abomination. Why had nothing happened to re-settle these people? How could people be left to live like this? Paul sat, silent too. The only thing Brendan could think of was to pray, which he did out loud in his now perpetually raspy voice. "God, thank you for the faithful witness of Henri and thousands like him who are strong in faith despite their awful circumstances. Please help them to find food for their bellies, good homes again in the towns, and a new life."

Pierre looked across at Brendan and Paul and saw the tears coursing down their cheeks. Pierre too was crying. "I thank you, my brothers," Henri said. "Please remember me when you go back to your home." Brendan gave him the Haitian GNT, which promptly made Henri cry too.

Pierre led the two of them back to his car, and they drove in silence back to Jacmel, and their boat – which seemed suddenly much more comfortable yet uncomfortably so. They thanked Pierre, and promised that they would try to publicise the plight of his people, and especially Henri. Pierre nodded, and drove away. They'd seen enough – too much, maybe. They certainly would never forget what they had seen.

***

They sailed late the following morning with a heavy heart. They wanted to stay but they needed to go. They needed to stay but they wanted to go. It was appalling that there could still be, in this supposedly-civilised world, people living in such abject poverty. Paul, however, had seen plenty of hardship in the camps in Northern Uganda after the civil war, and was not as shocked as Brendan. "Yet that was after a war," Paul reflected out loud. "This is after a natural disaster. Does that make it different? Whatever the cause, in both places thousands of people are displaced and frightened. Did you notice, that except for Henri everybody else seemed to have a glazed look, desperate and yet beyond desperation? People in camps always wear that expression."

Brendan nodded. "They looked to me as if every bit of life and hope had been sucked out of them..."

They sailed on through the afternoon, quietened, reflecting. The sun sank lower until only orange, red and dark blue could be seen. It was beautiful. Maybe, Brendan thought, God was sending them this sunset to assure them that He was still there, that hope often sank but would inevitably rise again renewed, rejuvenated, reinvigorated in a daily bulletin of Good News. That was what they needed too: reinvigoration; rejuvenation; something to cheer them and renew their faith. It appeared soon afterwards, in a rather peculiar form.

They passed numerous small villages lit up along the southern coast of Haiti, and breezed between Île à Vache (Cow Island) and the main coastline. The island was where Henry Morgan, a Welsh pirate, kept his base for Caribbean privateering. They saw no pirates, but they did encounter something which in its way was just as weird – a tiny, pure-white sandbank, several kilometres from any other land, on which a couple were sitting at a table eating a sumptuous candlelit dinner, complete with silverware and crystal glasses for the wine. There was no boat, no sign to explain what they were doing there, and the couple themselves just waved and resumed their dinner, in the middle of the sea. It was bizarre. A kilometre or so towards the main island, they passed a launch chugging slowly towards the sandbank bearing an advertising placard on its side for "Honeymoon dinners on the Isle of Love". Perhaps he was bringing dessert.

With a smile on their faces again, they sailed near to land, anchored for the night, and slept long and late, recapturing some of their drained energies. They sailed slowly up the long western finger of Haiti pointing towards Cuba, and reached Careasse at about 4pm. They anchored in the little harbour there, and crashed out again early, but at ease with the world despite its injustices. The whole Haitian experience had bolstered their resolve.

Day: Date	Itinerary (* indicates TV interview) (^{18} indicates new nation)	Bike (km)	Car/ Bus (km)	Train (km)	Kayak/ Sail (km)	Boat (km)	Air (km)
Totals brought forward		11429	17330	8712	10653	21622	65301
343: 23/4/12	Jacmel					95	
344: 24/4/12	Jacmel						
345: 25/4/12	Jacmel						
346: 26/4/12	Careasse					241	
Totals carried forward		11429	17330	8712	10653	21958	65301

Chapter 68: Nations 190 - 193

There was no easy or quick way to visit Jamaica, Cuba and the Bahamas by boat, because Jamaica and the Bahamas were like two tennis players either side of a net (Cuba). The shortest route for Brendan and Paul was to sail across to Jamaica, then virtually circumnavigate Cuba anti-clockwise (with a short dash to the Bahamas). Brendan had an idea how to catch up another day: instead of the projected two-days-there-and-back crossing to the Bahamas from mid-Cuba, he'd found a Bahamian island down near the eastern tip of Cuba which could be visited in one very long day.

They breezed across the Jamaica Channel with a following wind which sped them along to Port Antonio's sparkling new marina, landscaped with gazebos and a beautiful wooden promenade containing boutiques, souvenir shops, a restaurant and bar. They headed up Fort George Street, passing old wooden houses with delicate fretwork and charming balconies, reflecting architecture of a bygone era. Halfway up they passed the Demontevin Lodge – where they were staying that night. They went in to register and dump their bags, had a quick cup of tea, then went back down to Harbour Street and the beautiful Methodist Church building, built nearly two centuries ago by Dutch Naval Officers. Brendan's voice was a bit better and the evening talk went well, with the small church packed. The Minister assured Brendan that his fame had spread throughout the Caribbean, because everyone watched "See Esther", had followed his journey avidly and were thrilled that he was visiting their town. The next morning there were crowds on the marina to wave them off towards Cuba, which would take 12 days to circumnavigate, before the final push down to Belize.

Brendan wasn't sure what to expect of Cuba. He knew that it was still on the Open Doors Watch List, but also was experiencing church growth on an unprecedented scale. His own Newcastle Methodist District had a link with the Methodist Church in Cuba, and he'd been updated regularly with the amazing stories emerging from post-Castro Cuba. In just the last few years over 500 new churches had been planted across the nation and would-be Methodist Ministers were only allowed to proceed if they'd already proved their worth by planting several new congregations. Brendan was glad that they hadn't brought that in in England or there would be very few Ministers around. His successor at Jact, Caridad Diego, was from Cuba and had achieved great results at Jact in a very short time – after Brendan had slogged away for years without much visible fruitfulness at all.

It was a full day's sail from Port Antonio to Santiago de Cuba, home to 500,000 people, the nearest point on Cuba's south coast, and its second city. It was from the balcony of the city hall there that Castro proclaimed the victory of the Cuban Revolution in January 1959, but Brendan and Paul concentrated on locating the Methodist Church. They were tired after their long sea-journey, and weren't in the mood for sight-seeing. They found the church up one of the main streets – a big old building that had obviously survived the "dark ages" and emerged into the light again over the last few years. Inside, it was throbbing – lots of people milling around; office staff busy at computers or photocopiers; prayer huddles in the corridors. Brendan and Paul got caught up in its intensity, even though they were tired, and the evening was a spectacular worship event, not just a talk. Brendan spoke about his journey of faith as a Methodist Minister in the UK, then his journeys round the world after taking seriously his call from God, about God's protection on both journeys and his views on mission and the Persecuted Church. The congregation lapped it up, and the prayers and praise went on and on, long after Brendan had hoped to be tucked up in bed. They were exhilarated but exhausted when they finally crawled in.

Pedro, the Minister, was up at 6.30am for a prayer meeting, but they were still out for the count until he returned for breakfast at 8.30am. He looked a bit disappointed, and they asked why. "Only 200 at prayers today. Usually 350, 400." It was no wonder that the churches were experiencing revival and expansion – they were devoted to their faith in a way that British Methodism rarely saw. It was a similar sense of spiritual excitement which had seen the rise of Methodism in the first place, and it was amazing to see people so fired up about their faith. Pedro explained that people got up to pray before going to work, did their job, returned home to eat and pray with the family, then the father would usually come along to daily evening worship at the church, which usually lasted two or three hours and involved preaching and times of ministry and prayer. "The Holy Spirit *always* come," he said, in his clipped Cuban English. "*Always* come. So we wait on God and see what happens."

"Do you think God is doing something special here in Cuba?" asked Brendan.

"1960s and 1970s very hard for us," said Pedro. "Only five out of 140 Ministers left at end of 20 years of Castro. In 1980s we start to awake and find refuge in God. We pray and fast and Holy Spirit come. No clever stuff – just waiting on God." Brendan nodded. Christianity was quite simple really. It was the Church which usually complicated things. Pedro continued: "God gave us evangelists from amongst those converted. Then he gave us Evangebicys[101] for them." Brendan and Paul laughed at the strange word. "We call bicycles "bicy" so when Florida churches send 500 for our 500 evangelists, we call them Evangebicys. Then God gave 500 new churches through work of evangelists. Simple, really."

"And are you one of those 500?" asked Paul.

"No, no," laughed Pedro. "I am too old. I am one of five Ministers from old times. Only two of us left now. Most Ministers under 30 years old and only been Christian two or three years."

---

[101] All the detail about Cuba's Methodist Church is accurate, including the Evangebicys.

It was very different from Britain.

***

They sailed eastwards, briefly detouring several kilometres out to sea to give a wide berth to Guantánamo Bay – the largest harbour on the south side of the island. When the George Bush Administration set up the Detention Camp there in 2002 to hold detainees from Afghanistan and Iraq, it became notorious for waterboarding and other torture, and one of President Obama's first edicts was that it should be closed. But there were still some detainees held there, and Brendan and Paul had no wish to provoke a meeting with American military patrols.

They rounded the easternmost tip of Cuba at cactus-lined Cape Maisí and stopped at the tropical garden town of Baracoa, where they were greeted by a man washing his piglets in the sea. The town looked quaint in an old, dilapidated sort of way, surrounded by a beautiful landscape of banana trees and coffee plantations and a table-topped mountain called El Yunque prominent on the skyline. Its cobblestone streets were lined with one-storey buildings whose peeling, carnival-coloured paint jobs and weathered tile roofs added, rather than detracted, from their charm. The locals watched Brendan and Paul curiously from wide verandahs. Some approached to sell them sweets – especially the local delicacies: white chocolate in round, flat cakes encased in palm bark or a sweet drink called cucurucho, which left an odd burning sensation in the back of Brendan's throat. The Methodist Church here was a much more ramshackle building than in Santiago de Cuba, but it was just as intense and bustling – for the entire time between late afternoon and 11pm.

The following morning, walking back to the Caribbean Queen, they passed a park dedicated to Christopher Columbus. His statue, hand-hewn out of a giant tree stump, stared inland with a stern expression, as if he didn't like what he saw. Brendan rather liked it – the view, that is, not the statue, which he thought looked like one of his old Sunday School teachers. There was a plaque there, informing them that Baracoa was once Cuba's capital, yet this was not a town trumpeting faded colonial grandeur; rather it was a huge village in disrepair, with its colonnaded colonial shacks in tumbledown rows beyond the Cathedral ruins, where cockerels, piglets and stray dogs mingled with grubby children, everything cloyed with the sickly-sweet smell of Cuba's only chocolate factory. The heavy, purple clouds didn't help lift the gloom.

This was the day for Brendan to visit his 192nd nation, after which there would be just two to go. The people at Oracle had approved his suggestion of crossing the sea here. The Bahamas was an island nation – actually, 29 islands, 661 cays and 2,387 islets. He wasn't sure what differentiated one category from the others. The nearest point to Cuba was the one they were now aiming for: Matthew Town on the island of Great Inagua, with a population of about 1,000. The clouds mercifully saved their ammunition and, by the time they were well into the rougher waters of the Caribbean, the sky cleared, the winds died and the passage was relatively pleasant. The Caribbean Queen still rocked a little from side to side, but the twin hulls helped to keep Brendan from feeling too queasy. Paul was a natural sailor and kept a quiet, smiling calm about him at all times – except once when they saw large shark fins close to the boat.

Matthew Town was a one-industry town, like the colliery villages in the North-East of England which died when the coal ran out. On Great Inagua, it was salt. Brendan didn't know anything about salt, so the manager of the salt farm showed them round. It turned out to be a relatively simple operation: salt-water was pumped through canals to salt pans, where the wind and sun evaporated the water, leaving a salt layer over a permanent floor of highly-compressed salt. Massive harvesters raked through the salt once the salt pan had been drained, and their conveyor-belts deposited it into giant dump trucks that carried it to the factory to be rinsed (with concentrated brine) and stored in massive stockpile "salt mountains" for export to all points on the compass. It was efficient environmentally too. They stocked the salt pans with brine shrimp, a favourite food of the tens of thousands of flamingos living there (the largest flock in the Western Hemisphere). The flamingos got their distinctive pink colour from the shrimp. Their droppings added nutrients to the water, which in turn bred an excess of algae, turning the water dark and thus accelerating the evaporation process by absorbing additional solar energy, which increased salt production. The shrimp thrived on the algae-rich environment, and reproduced, providing more food for the flamingos. Everybody was catered for. Brendan felt like an expert. He gave the Bahamian GNT to the manager, explaining that Jesus encouraged Christians to be salt, giving enhanced flavour to the world.

They set off back to Baracoa, knowing that it would be well after dark before they arrived. Conditions now were much worse, and Brendan threw up several times as they crossed the 100km Old Bahama Channel, hurting his throat again. Somehow it felt even worse in the pitch black of the night. Paul was very sympathetic but also faintly amused that someone like Brendan who had done so many thousands of kilometres at sea could still produce such an impressive display of sea-sickness. At least it didn't rain.

The following morning, after a slow and still delicate getting-up, they continued up the Cuban coastline in the middle of a storm. They hunched in the cabin and watched the coastal landscape blur by in clouds of spray and rain lit by lightning. Water gushed down from the hills, turning the rivers a strange burgundy and the sea an apocalyptic brown. They drew closer to the beaches, with a thousand tides-worth of coconut husks and driftwood strewn beneath towering royal palms. Further on, the Toa, a dark emerald green, swirled moodily into the sea. The rain ceased, leaving an ammonia tang, which hurt Brendan's throat again. Three people fished quietly; a clutch of girls washed clothes; two lovers mysteriously embraced in the shallows. Then no-one else, until they arrived at El Ramon in the late-afternoon, a small town nestled into the corner of Nipe Bay.

There was, as yet, no Methodist Church at El Ramon, so Brendan and Paul enjoyed a leisurely evening meal in the town's only restaurant, which had only two dishes to choose from: pargo relleno (described as "fish") and lechón a la criolla ("meat"). They decided to try both dishes and share them. The pargo turned out to be red snapper stuffed with shrimps, lobster and ham, served with onion rings and peppers on a bed of rice – and they both agreed that it was exquisite. When the lechón arrived, they asked what meat it was, and the waiter said "little pig", which reminded them of the man washing his piglets in the sea at Baracoa. The dish itself, though, was very tasty – roast pork in an orange sauce – and they were OK as long as they didn't think about it...

Halfway through the following day, they passed the popular seaside resort of Guardalavaca, with its pristine white sands and grubby-looking once-white concrete hotels. The beaches and coves of the northern coastline alternated with rocky crags and multi-coloured forests, but then gave way eventually to the 20km Santa Lucia beach, an international diving Mecca for its long coral reef, only 200m offshore, and the many shipwrecks it'd caused over the centuries. Not wanting to add to the list, Brendan and Paul sailed very carefully parallel to the beautiful white beach and edged gently into Nuevitas Bay, and the picturesque fishing village of La Boca just inside its entrance. Once again they enjoyed a relaxing evening – no Methodist Church, no feverish praying, no earnestness or exhorting – just a quiet, simple dinner. Maybe, Brendan thought, he was better suited to a slower pace of spirituality. It meant he could rest his voice too.

They kept on the outside of the coral reef all the way west to Cayo Coco, but kept close. The water got a bit rough out in the so-called "Blue River" of the Gulf Stream, where Hemingway once reckoned the best and most abundant fish in the world were to be found. They were now into the Jardines del Rey – an archipelago of islands where the deep green of natural forest contrasted vividly with the white coral beaches and the occasional colony of bright-pink flamingos. The water was crystal-clear, tranquil and various shades of blue. It was obvious why these shores were popular with divers, and also with ornithologists, because the islands were full of birds of all shapes, sizes and colours, especially the white ibis, locally known as the coconut bird, after which Cayo Coco was named. They stayed on the boat that night, anxious to avoid the loud, bright all-inclusive resorts.

After a middling day of average distance, fair weather and companionable silence, they reached the unspoilt beaches and sand dunes of Cayo Fragoso, where they saw a herd of enormous guinea-pigs, each about half a metre long. Brendan wondered if he'd discovered some kind of freak island where guinea-pigs had evolved into monsters, but was told by a man on a boat anchored just offshore that they were called hutia. "There's millions of 'em, mate!" said the blond, sun-tanned Australian, sitting on deck with a Fosters in his hand as if auditioning for Crocodile Dundee IV. All he needed was a hat with bobbing corks and he'd be the complete stereotype.

The next day was very sunny, for a change, though as the sun got up they began to wish for cooler temperatures and greater cloud-cover. They reached Hicacos Point, the northernmost point of Cuba, at about 4pm, but sailed on to the bright lights of Varadero, the most popular resort on Cuba which even once attracted Al Capone for his summer holidays. They kidded themselves that it was just to give them a head-start on the following day's journey. They couldn't find a Methodist Church in Varadero, but then again, they didn't look. They did find several clubs, hundreds of restaurants, and thousands of young people ready to spend the weekend celebrating something or other. They quickly ducked into a restaurant, enjoyed a leisurely dinner, and crept back to the boat as if they'd been playing truant.

The following day was Brendan's 356th, meaning that there were only 10 days to go. He couldn't quite believe it. He was nearly there...

They arrived in Havana by mid-afternoon, after an unremarkable but productive run down Cuba's north-west coast. They'd seen very little of Cuba, really – but now they saw the distinctive Havana version of it – with traffic, lots of it. Pickups, taxis, pedestrians trying to cross roads, horse-drawn carts, buses, cars, bicycles and scooters, and even traffic lights. Most of the cars were big, chunky, pre-1959 American gas-guzzlers and it was, in that respect, like walking into a film set. They found their way to Vedado, and to the William Carey Methodist Church on J Street. "Vedado" meant "game reserve", but the only animals visible were the bouncers outside the La Rampa clubs, on duty even though it was only late afternoon. Broken noses and bow-ties were a combination that always unsettled Brendan and made him feel rather puny, and these particular specimens looked like they'd spent their childhoods pulling the wings off insects and crudely dissecting dead animals, and progressed in adulthood to pulling the wings off pelicans and crudely dissecting live humans. The Methodist Church, just down the street, seemed altogether more welcoming.

William Carey had never been to Cuba, and wasn't a Methodist, so it was a puzzle why the main Methodist Church in Havana was named after him – it must be because he was regarded as the "father of modern missions". At the end of the 18th century, Carey had fired up the British Churches about mission. He lived it out too, taking his family to India and enduring many troubles as he lived out his famous dictum: "Expect great things from God; attempt great things for God." Perhaps it was a good name for any church, Brendan decided, and a worthy one for him to visit as part of his epic journey, following in Carey's missionary footsteps. Inside, another hubbub of activity: people milling around; secretaries busy typing; meetings happening in offices; printers chattering; singing from a chapel somewhere in the complex; phones ringing. Brendan and Paul introduced themselves, and were whisked through to see one of the Ministers. "Welcome, welcome. We are delighted to see you, and we have everyone very excited about you worshipping with us tonight. We begin with prayer at six till seven, then worship from seven till nine, then you will speak and we will pray some more."

There didn't seem much else to say. It was going to be another busy, *long* evening.

***

The following morning, Brendan and Paul wandered sleepily through the Old Town back to the harbour where the Caribbean Queen was moored. The Cathedral stood out like St. Paul's in pre-skyscraper London, towering high above a maze of narrow streets. Round every corner was another historic building, courtyard, piece of city wall, ornate gateway or archway. There was no time to explore, but it was definitely a place to re-visit.

Having stocked up on fuel, aware that there was little hope of refuelling until they reached Mexico, they sailed out past the La Cabaña fortress into the Caribbean once again. Two hours later, 64km west of Havana, they officially entered the Gulf of Mexico, which began at the 83°W meridian. There were no signposts to mark the transition. The engine coughed and wheezed a bit (sounding a bit like Brendan, actually), but they chugged on till it got dark, reaching a little island shaped exactly like a dinosaur, and woke up at dawn to press onwards, finally at dusk reaching the western tip of Cuba, Cape San Antonio, just as the Roncali Lighthouse began its double flash, every ten seconds, all night.

It quickly became clear that the thin curtains couldn't keep the light out, and that it would drive them both crazy, like a luminous version of the Chinese water torture. Brendan's evening was suddenly dominated by the need to predict the end of the ten-second gap. After an hour, they up-anchored and moved the boat under an overhanging mangrove thicket which finally stopped their discomfort. At least there wasn't a foghorn.

The following morning, they set off bright and early for what they assumed would be a straightforward crossing of the Yucatán Strait to Cancún on the Mexican coast. Things, however, were to turn out rather differently. It was rather choppy out in the waters swirling round the Guanacahabibes Peninsula, and the engine "pinked" a little, not quite catching but then surging forwards as if it had just realised what it was supposed to do. Then the waves and currents settled as they got out into the open sea. The trouble really hit in the early afternoon, when they switched from the main tank to the auxiliary tanks which they'd filled in Havana. Straightaway, the engine started backfiring and coughing, and, within a few minutes, had died altogether. They were in the middle of the sea, with no radio, only the satellite phone. Brendan phoned Detroit, and was patched through to Arnold.

"Houston, we have a problem," said Brendan, in a light-hearted manner.

"You have many problems, for which you can get counselling," quipped Arnold back. "How can I help?"

"We appear to be stranded in the middle of the sea with a dead engine – about 120km from Mexico."

"Ah. In that case you really *do* have a problem. My immediate reaction is that we can't help you. But you do have a bit of leeway. You're a day up now, so hopefully time will not be a factor. If Paul can't fix it, you'll probably have to sail her in."

"But we've never really done any sailing and we don't know what to do!"

"Now's the time to learn," said Arnold with a chortle. "Can you see anything at all except ocean?"

"Nope."

"You should be able to avoid colliding with anything, then." And, with that, the phone went dead.

***

Paul spent half an hour checking fuel-leads from the auxiliary tanks to the engine, but they were clear. His conclusion was that they'd been sold dodgy fuel. "Remember how the engine coughed and spluttered on the way down from Havana? Well, that was when the new fuel was mixed in with the old fuel, and there must have been enough good fuel left for the engine still to function, albeit wheezily. When we shifted purely to the new fuel in the auxiliary tank, it immediately fouled the engine and everything cut out. There's nothing we can do until we get to Cancún." So they got the sail out of the locker under the wheel, and tried to work out what to do. It wasn't straightforward, by any means, but at least the conditions were calm, which would help them sort out the sail, but would also now mean inertia. They didn't have to choose which sail – there was only one – but they still had to work out how to attach it to the mast and hoist it. Once it was up, they would have to work out how to point it in the right direction to catch the breeze, assuming and hoping that there might be one by then.

Paul remembered a little about sailing from his childhood, and they managed to rig up the right toggles to the right loops, and within 20 minutes had the sail aloft, and had worked out how to swing the boom using the ropes attached to it. Then the wind, conveniently, arrived. Inconveniently, it was blowing across them. They pulled the wheel round from one extreme to the other, and pushed and pulled the sail from side to side, but all that they succeeded in doing was to turn round and drift off to the side. After a few more circumnavigations of the same spot, Brendan finally got the hang of it and managed to keep the boat stationary, using sail and wheel to keep the boat head-on to the wind. Then, as Paul pushed the boom away and Brendan turned the wheel away, the Caribbean Queen gently started sailing. Backwards. They tried again, reversing their actions, and the Queen, slowly, almost majestically, turned in the right direction and nudged forwards. The sail began to crack and blow but filled when Paul got the angles just right, and they pulled forwards more quickly. Brendan adjusted the wheel to get them pointing roughly in the right direction, and they breathed a sigh of relief.

The only drawback was that they were heading south, rather than south-west. They had to find out how to work *with* the wind even though it wasn't really doing them any favours. Brendan turned the wheel as far as he could but they still weren't quite on the correct heading. They yelled, pointed and gesticulated at each other, and then attempted to turn the boom round using the ropes and releasing the sail. Immediately the boom swung round violently, dragging Paul half-overboard as he clung onto the ropes, and nearly taking Brendan's head off. Paul adjusted the angle of the sail, which filled up once again on its new setting, and when Brendan turned the wheel the boat sped forwards, cutting across the wind in the right direction. The sail and wheel together pulled them round onto the correct course. Goodness knows what manoeuvre they'd just completed, but it seemed to have worked. Perhaps now that they'd done it once, they could repeat it with a bit more elegance. They jerked their way drunkenly further across the Yucatán Strait, before the wind died completely, and they could do nothing but take in the sail, rest and check their position with Brendan's GPS. In four hours' sailing, they'd managed about 25km in the right direction. Whether this was down to luck, skill or current, they'd at least made *some* progress.

The wind got up in the night, but they decided to do nothing, and lay down in their bunks to harness their energy for the morning. They slept a little, but the waves were crashing in from the side and sleep wasn't easy for Brendan. Paul slept on, of course, oblivious. In the morning, they found that the wind had turned, mercifully in the right direction. According to Brendan's GPS they still had 95km to go before Cancún, and they also had to work out how, when they reached land, to steer and stop the boat when and where they wanted. Paul had a theory about that. "We ought to seal off the auxiliary tank, clean all the tubes and leads, and see how much proper fuel we still have left in the main tank. We did the switch before we had to, and we should still have at least a few litres in the bottom. When we get near, we'll see if we can get the engine started. Otherwise we'll just have to drift in slowly until we hit something." He did the required cleaning and sluicing, the sail tied in place for long periods as the wind propelled them forwards. In mid-afternoon they sighted the Cape Catoche lighthouse on the northernmost point on the Yucatán Peninsula, but managed to swing away on course for Cancún, 50km down the eastern coast.

As they neared Cancún, still driven by the wonderfully accurate breeze (well done, God!), they saw that there was a small island in their way. They were heading for the brand-new bright-white towers of Puerto Cancún, a state-of-the-art resort development located on the last stretch of beach in Cancún's famous hotel zone. The development included a golf course, five-star hotels and apartments, a resort village, commercial areas, a business park, and, most importantly, a marina. But they had to get there, and Isla Mujeres was in the way. They steered round the island's edge, as close as they dared, then cut the sail and allowed the boat to drift as they approached the entrance to the marina. Saying a little prayer, Brendan pushed the ignition button for the engine, and waited while it whirred and coughed, and died. He tried again, and again, as he watched the boat slewing round toward the concrete pillars guarding the marina entrance. And wonderfully, just as the boat was sailing sidewards within 20m of the pillar, the engine caught, and surged, and steadied.

Saying another, better prayer, Brendan hauled the wheel round, the boat turned easily away and they chugged into the marina as if there was nothing wrong. They found an empty slip and tied up next to a yacht that dwarfed the Caribbean Queen. A white-uniformed officer from high up on deck sneered at them, reminding Brendan of the way in which the bodybuilders looked at him long ago in the Wallsend gym. He waved cheerily, and the officer spat over the side and withdrew. Charming, thought Brendan.

He and Paul wandered off to the marina office and arranged for a sample of the dodgy fuel in the auxiliary tank to be tested, the tank to be drained, the fuel leads checked, and both tanks to be re-filled. They strolled into the complex, and ended up at the clubhouse of the golf course, for dinner and drinks. The golf course was not yet completed, but neither Brendan nor Paul were there for the golf. They booked in for dinner – and overnight. They felt that they deserved it, and after a drink or several they'd probably have fallen in as they tried to transition from slip to boat. Perhaps drunken sailors were the reason it was called a slip.

Mexico didn't count as one of his nations because Brendan had already passed through on his first journey down the Americas, so they'd nothing else to do the following (late) morning except wander slowly back to the marina and check in at the office to see whether the work on the boat had been completed.

"You got bad fuel," said the man in the office. "Where you get it?"

"Havana," Brendan said.

"Pah!" spat the man. "Is mostly dirty water. Them ladrones they rip you off!" And, proud of his grasp of English idiom, he roared with laughter. "Is good, no?" They nodded. Great, that's what it was. He continued: "We do good fuel, no dirty water fuel here. This Mexico, good place. Cuba bad. We no rip you off." Then he proceeded to name a sum in American dollars that called his previous statement into question. But Brendan was past caring by this time and handed over his credit card.

***

They chugged out of the marina and headed south, round the luxury hotels built on the Nichupte Lagoon, and thrilled at the engine noise. Engines *were* rather useful, especially now that they'd experienced what it was like without one. They glided between the beautiful beaches and Isla Cozumel, and continued southwards along the Riviera Maya, which stretched along the east coast of the peninsula and was visited by millions of tourists every year. They eventually stopped as darkness fell, in a small bay called Puerto Madero, all too aware that they needed to make use of every bit of daylight so they could reach Belize City the following evening. It was 439km from Cancún to Belize City, and they'd completed over half already – but there was still a long day ahead.

It was a bit poignant to wake up and start the engine on the final day at sea. Brendan and Paul had been together far longer than most fathers-in-law and sons-in-law share in a whole lifetime – and Paul and Ruth had only been married for 18 months. They chugged steadily down the Mexican coast – the only excitement being a chance encounter with a huge manatee, which swam under the boat and then did a sort of somersault on the surface, as if showing off. Eventually they reached the end of the Mexican mainland, and crossed over into Belizean waters as they passed a long island with endless beaches and very few humans, then across Chetumal Bay to the jutting peninsula of Belize City. They sailed past the entrance to the main port, and on to Cucumber Beach Marina, 5km further south, breezing jauntily through the channel between the long breakwaters, and mooring at one of the spacious timbered-deck docks.

They'd done it! Now all that they had to do was to sell the boat, make the evening meeting at the Cathedral, check the flight times the following day and hope that nothing went wrong at this late stage. As if...

Day: Date	Itinerary (* indicates TV interview) ([18] indicates new nation)	Bike (km)	Car/ Bus (km)	Train (km)	Kayak / Sail (km)	Boat (km)	Air (km)
Totals brought forward		11429	17330	8712	10653	21958	65301
347: 27/4/12	Port Antonio, Jamaica[190]					211	
348: 28/4/12	Santiago de Cuba, Cuba[191]					214	
349: 29/4/12	Baracoa					207	
350: 30/4/12	Matthew Town, Bahamas[192] and back					212	
351: 1/5/12	El Ramon (Cuba)					147	
352: 2/5/12	La Boca					198	
353: 3/5/12	Cayo Coco					168	
354: 4/5/12	Cayo Fragoso					136	
355: 5/5/12	Varadero					131	
356: 6/5/12	Havana					150	
357: 7/5/12	Playa de Surines					146	
358: 8/5/12	western tip of Cuba					163	
359: 9/5/12	21.59N, 86.04W				25	88	
360: 10/5/12	Cancún, Mexico				95		
361: 11/5/12	Puerto Madero					239	
362: 12/5/12	Belize City[193]					217	
Totals carried forward		11429	17330	8712	10773	24585	65301

Chapter 69: Fascination

It was now three months since Ben had started work again in Jact, and everything had been going really well. Jack Turner, the District Chair had shared worship with Ben on two occasions since his appointment – the initial Sunday of re-introduction, explanation and commissioning; and the Sunday just gone, when Jack had noticed the change in the Jact congregation over those three months, and commended them all for it – and especially one radical idea of Ben's. They'd agreed, back at the Church Council which endorsed the Circuit decision, to go with Ben's startling suggestion that they bring the time of the worship forwards by 22 minutes[102]. Everyone had looked at him in amazement when he suggested it. "What's the point of that?"

"Church always starts at boring times like 11 or 10.30. Why don't we signal to the people of Jact that our church is going to be different? And I can say to the kids I see at school that "we start 10.08 – don't be late!" It's quite catchy, isn't it?

"But won't people just come at 10.30 and miss the first 20 minutes?"

"I don't think they will. Are you willing to give it a go? And if, after a couple of months, it isn't working, we'll go back to the usual time."

They gave it a go – and it worked splendidly. They put a big sign outside: "We are the 10.08 church – come and see what you're missing!" There was a small bright piece of paper underneath, which described the new arrangements and announced Ben as the new Minister. The fact that it wasn't explained *why*, made people ask questions. The next Sunday, lots of people came at 10.00 (assuming a misprint), and were greeted with tea, coffee and cake, and then at precisely 10.08 the worship began with three songs, during which people finished their coffee and gradually joined in. The following week it worked a treat: people coming earlier still because they liked a relaxed start and the opportunity for a snack beforehand. Ben's crazy idea had worked.

Ben led the first part of the worship every Sunday, aiming it especially at children and young people, leaving the appointed preacher to cater for the needs of the older folk later on after the Young Church (not Sunday School because "we're not a flippin' school") decamped to the hall. Word had quickly spread that Cecil had left and that Ben was back – and it was like the days of Caridad all over again. The people flocked back. So worship quickly became vibrant, well-populated and a focal point for Ben's links with the community.

His involvement in the local secondary school picked up from where he'd left it, and flourished as he now felt that the whole church endorsed what he was doing. He organised an after-school drop-in "Chill" every Monday and Wednesday, when the

---

[102] The idea for 10.08 came from the real-life 3.08 Nailsea – a short-lived Fresh Expression meeting at 3.08pm every Sunday in Nailsea, Hampshire.

young people could chat, do homework or listen to music. The school gave them 15 laptops when they got upgrades, and set them up in one of the church rooms with wifi access to the church's new internet connection. The Church Council agreed to purchase special memory-sticks as gifts from the church for every child who attended, so that they could take their homework round with them. The memory-sticks had a big cross emblazoned on them, and became quite a witness around the school. An ICT technician at the school came down and organised parental controls on the church network, and the response from parents was very positive. Ben often had 30 or 40 young people milling around the premises, and prioritised this as one of the most important events of his week. Every Chill included at least one significant spiritual conversation.

He was also well received into the two Jact primary schools. Julia Diego had established some really positive and fruitful links with them both (as well as other schools in the Circuit), and it was easy for him to get in, introduce himself and become involved in Collective Worship once a fortnight at each school. Because he offered skills that other clergy didn't possess, namely drumming, breakdancing and beatboxing, he went down a treat with both children and staff. Children told their parents that they wanted to go along on Sunday to Church, and a surprising number of the parents wanted to come along too. Within a month of Ben's return, there were over 100 people in worship and there was even talk of having to hold two services on a Sunday morning to fit everyone in.

The church people came up trumps as well, taking on board pastoral duties normally expected of a Minister. "Don't worry about us," Sarah Lanleigh said to Ben at the Church Council. "We'll look after one another and free you up to do the really important work." Ben popped in to pray with anyone who was ill, and scored lots of points whenever he did that. He visited new families who'd started coming on Sundays, and made initial plans to hold two Alpha courses after the summer holidays: one during the day for elderly people and unemployed parents only available when their kids were at school; and one in the evening for those in daytime work. Some had already been to an Alpha Course run by Julia Diego, but wanted to "come along and see if it was different this time." Ben drafted in some of the people who'd been most moved by Alpha last time to train as helpers.

***

Jack was amazed how well it was going. The twice-weekly Chill, he thought, was a master-stroke, and the Mondays and the Wednesdays led naturally into the Friday night Youth Club, where sometimes up to 100 young people packed into the premises, with some playing football on the playing field just down the road under Ben's supervision, and others lounging around at church under the eyes of a few parents and a couple of Christian teachers from the secondary school. Three or four old ladies from the Church came along every Friday too: making drinks in the kitchen and having a good natter with one another and the young people. This was a prime example of the sort of ministry that the Methodist Church was seeking to stimulate, whether they called it Fresh Expressions or ventureFX or whatever. It was exciting!

***

The previous week, Jack had attended a conference in Leeds sponsored by the World Council of Churches uninspiringly titled "Ecclesiology and the Social Reality of the Church", but it turned out to be really helpful and challenging. Speakers from across Britain told their stories about how they were engaging with people completely "unchurched", but most of the talk was about the "mixed economy" Church. It seemed to mean traditional church co-existing with but continuing separately from Fresh Expressions. What seemed to be happening at Jact, however, was a genuine new start for an already-established church as it tried new possibilities even if it turned everything upside-down. This seemed to Jack to be the best model of all, because it made the church premises not the stereotypical "place where we don't go" but a vibrant place at the heart of the community, which people visited for different things at different times. The young people of Jact didn't seem to have inherited the traditional scepticism about church premises, and were happy to come into a place where they'd be warm, able to chill with their mates without getting hassled, and where they could get free drinks. Some even enjoyed talking about God.

***

Jack wrote down some of his reflections and sent them off to various people: the District Evangelism Enabler, the Connexional Fresh Expressions Co-ordinator and the organiser of the conference he'd attended, who was the head of the Ecclesiological Investigations Department (EID) of the World Council of Churches. Jack chuckled at the department's title – had the WCC not realised that its initials spelt out a major Muslim festival?

He was surprised to get a swift response from Dr. Helmut Schweisser, the EID chairman, inviting him to bring the leader of the Jact project over with him to Bossey, in Switzerland, for an International Conference on Mixed Economy Church, all expenses paid. Helmut wanted a video presentation on what they were doing at Jact – he was fascinated in this second-wave of Fresh Expressions work, which made use of Church premises rather than spurning them for secular buildings. The Connexional Fresh Expressions Co-ordinator also replied quickly, offering the use of a film crew to produce a professional-looking short film. Jack promised to hand this on to Ben, and see whether they could co-ordinate everything in readiness for the WCC Conference in July. Sadly for Jack, this clashed with the Methodist Conference, which he had to attend, so he got in touch with Dr. Schweisser and asked if his invitation could be passed over to one of the new young Christians from Jact.

It seemed that as news about Jact's 10.08 church spread, not only the local community but the international Church found it fascinating...

Chapter 70: Nation 194

Paul managed to sell the Caribbean Queen within an hour of trying. He was referred by the manager of the marina to "one of my friends" who was willing to pay $30,000 as long as the deal was completed that day, which, of course, suited Brendan and Paul fine. They met at the marina and a long, black limo pulled up, out of which jumped two Honey Monsters dressed in suits. But whereas the Sugar Puffs giant was friendly and played with children, this pair looked as if they ate children. Then, as if in a Bugsy Malone re-take, a man stepped out wearing a posh suit and carrying a briefcase. He looked round, as if checking that his security was guaranteed, then walked over to the office and looked at the rough-planked wall with distaste. He sat down in the manager's chair, having taken a folded handkerchief from his pocket to cover the seat of the chair. "Sit," he ordered.

The transaction took all of two minutes. They handed over the catamaran's papers in exchange for the briefcase – inside which were neatly tied bundles of new bank-notes. There were 15 bundles, and each paper strip had $2,000 printed neatly on it. Brendan blinked, wondering whether he'd stumbled into a gangster film, but it really was happening. "I'd hoped that you would write me a cheque," Brendan said. "Tomorrow I have to take this lot with me on a plane, or try to bank it here."

The man sneered. "I don't do cheques." He reached into his pocket and drew out another bundle and tossed it to the marina manager. "Pleasant to do business with you." And with that rather unfortunate slip, betraying his lack of finesse with the English language, he was gone. His exit marked the end of one problem, but the start of another: banking funny money laundered from some drug-baron's nefarious activities.

***

Belize's Cathedral was in the grip of its bicentenary celebrations, having been the first new building in British Honduras. The interior was all mahogany and sapodilla, and looked very English-Anglican. The Dean bustled out and greeted Brendan, explaining that everything was set up for their 8pm gathering. "The local press are here, setting up alongside the BBC lot." This was news to Brendan. He'd washed his hands of the BBC after they'd shown so little interest in him earlier. But here they were once again, turning up at the end of his journey, wanting to cash in on his hard work. Brendan wandered in, determined to tell them what he thought. But then he recognised Tarquin, who'd been sent by the BBC to interview Brendan at Puerto Toro, the southernmost village in the world, as he reached the end of his first journey. And here he was again – a small wiry skinhead with a tattoo of a Frankenstein bolt on his neck, greeting Brendan with a very deep voice in a strong

Liverpudlian accent."Alright, Wacker?" Paul looked doubtfully at both Tarquin and Brendan. It all sounded like gibberish. "Oos ar kid?" Tarquin continued, pointing to Paul.

"Ah, yes," said Brendan, feeling posh even as he said it. "This is my son-in-law Paul."

"Dat's de ticket," said Tarquin, and got back to his task with the techies. Then he mopped his brow and exclaimed, "Ot enuf to crack de flags in dis gaff!"

Paul drew Brendan to one side. "What was all that about?"

Brendan smiled. "Tarquin is from Liverpool and I think he said "How are you, my old friend?", then "Who are you with?", then "Good", then "It's hot enough in this place to crack the flagstones"." Paul couldn't understand how someone who didn't speak English could work for the BBC, but when it came to the interviews after Brendan's talk, Tarquin kept the Liverpudlian accent but dropped the Scouse vocabulary.

***

They slept in the Dean's spare bedrooms, having checked with the airport that their seats on the following day's flight to Miami were booked and that if they were off by 8.30am they'd have plenty of time to check in, and bank the money. And everything the following morning, remarkably, went smoothly. Over an early breakfast, the Dean brought up the subject of the money. "What are you planning on doing, because the banks here don't open on a Sunday?"

Brendan's jaw dropped. He hadn't realised that it was Sunday. Throughout his journey, one day blended into another, and Sundays had to be travel-days too, even though he was fully aware that Sabbath principles of rest and relaxation were highly sensible in a world that so often demanded high-energy living. "I don't know what to do," he admitted. "I hadn't realised that it was a Sunday."

"I thought as much," smiled the Dean. "So I've come up with a solution. You give me the money. I give you a cheque, which I guarantee will not bounce. My father died last month and left me with plenty of money, so my balance is very robust at the moment."

"But will the bank not worry about you depositing the money?" asked Brendan.

"Oh, don't worry about that. The manager of the bank comes to our Cathedral every morning before he goes to work. I'll explain the situation to him and everything will be fine."

The Dean then excused himself. He had to get ready for the first service of the day, but one of the Cathedral staff would drive them out to the Philip Goldson International Airport, about half an hour away in Ladyville, next to the BATSUB base. It sounded like the latest underwater crime-fighting scheme in Gotham City, but it actually meant the British Army Training Support Unit, Belize, stationed at Price Barracks. Everything went smoothly. Brendan and Paul caught their flight which left on time at 11.30am and relaxed into the comfortable seats of the American Airlines Boeing 737 for the four-hour flight. As they levelled off at 30,000ft, Brendan started to relax – only 72 hours to go.

***

It was at Miami that the hassles began.

They landed at 5.30pm after circling above the thunder-clouds at Miami International Airport for over an hour before the captain was given permission to drop down into the murk to land. They'd already by this time missed their connection through to New York, and were comforted that, despite only having 66 hours to go, they still had a little breathing-space. They realised as soon as they disembarked that they'd landed at the worst possible time. The E Terminal was packed, and presumably designed by someone who liked mazes. Both international-arriving and transit passengers had to claim their luggage before clearing U.S. Customs. It didn't seem logical to have to queue with those going to stay in the USA but, because their Shannon flight was via JFK Airport in New York, they were treated the same. And the treatment was appalling.

It took two hours for American Airlines to get their luggage off the plane and into the baggage claim area. Most people's luggage seemed to have been damaged: suitcase handles broken; puncture holes in the canvas sides of large bags. Brendan and Paul didn't have very much – just an overnight bag each, but they had to wait with everyone else. Finally, just as they were giving up hope, their two bags appeared on the conveyor belt, looking crumpled but intact. There were now 64 hours to go.

The next challenge was the U.S. Immigrations and Customs area on level 1 of their Terminal. At least they didn't have to walk very far – only about 10 minutes' stroll, which was much less than everyone else, judging by how drained they looked. There were no travelators, and piles of people and luggage everywhere, so their progress involved more twists and turns than the slalom at the Winter Olympics. When they arrived at the queue, there was only about 100m of humanity in front of them.

An hour and a half later, they'd progressed about 50m.

An hour after that, they were nearly there.

As they got closer, they began to realise why it was taking so long. There were only three "desks" occupied, and each person was taking at least 10 minutes to progress through. When they finally got there, there were 61 hours to go. Brendan approached the lady on the desk, handing over his immigration card.

"Revés," she barked.

"Pardon?"

"Revés!" It was shouted even louder this time.

"What?"

Brendan was then given a torrent of Spanish which didn't sound particularly welcoming. And this little woman, as wide as she was tall, was glaring at him and telling him off. She snatched the immigration card off him and turned it round in her hand. "Revés?" She said, the Queen of Sarcasm.

"Why are you speaking Spanish at me?" asked Brendan, unable to stop himself. "This is America, isn't it? Has the plane been diverted? Am I back in Cuba?" He could do sarcasm too.

The woman clearly wasn't impressed. She shouted to her left and two beefy customs officers appeared, with guns at the ready. "Le fuera," she snapped. They grabbed Brendan and hauled him off into their office, feet dragging along the floor as if they'd already broken his legs. He yelled that he was a British citizen, and shouted to Paul to contact the embassy, but the door slammed shut. He was thrown into a room, separated from his bag, and had the door locked so he was imprisoned.

Paul, meanwhile, was asked politely for his immigration card and passport. "What about my friend?" he asked, pointing to the door Brendan had been dragged through.

"¿Es usted con él" spat the woman. "Oy, Juan! Chico! Le fuera también!" So Juan and Chico came out and hauled Paul off into another room, down the corridor.

***

Two hours later, there were 59 hours to go, and Brendan had seen no-one, nor heard anything except the buzz of the air-conditioning. He'd given up all hope of leaving Miami that night, but didn't know what would happen about his bag, Paul, his connection or his future.

Then a man appeared. "So, Meester Priest, you think you clever, eh? Clever remark to Major in Immigration Control not good, Meester Priest. Where you wish to go, Meester Priest – back to Ireland in preety green and white plane or off to Krome Detention Centre in preety green and white van, eh? Miami International Airport called MIA, also known as Missing in Action. You want to be MIA, Meester Priest?"

Brendan gulped. "To Ireland, please, in a plane. As soon as possible."

"Ah, you in hurry, eh, Meester Priest?"

"Yes, I am, actually. And I don't appreciate being kept here. Can I now leave, please?"

The officer looked at him. "Yes, you go now, Meester Priest." He walked to the door and held it open. Brendan had to shrug past him to exit.

"What about my bag?" he asked.

The man smiled. "Ah, sorry, Meester Priest. Your bag is MIA. So sorry!" Brendan couldn't believe it! They'd hassled him, imprisoned him, stole his bag, and had the cheek to laugh about it! "Welcome to America, Meester Priest... Have a good day!" shouted the official after him, laughing as Brendan left the corridor and found himself back in the Terminal concourse, to be greeted by a distraught Paul.

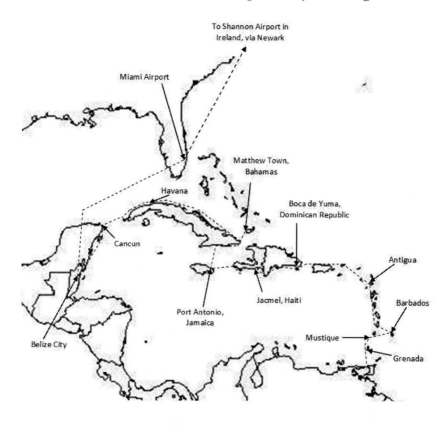

Nations 182 to 194

"Brendan, thank goodness you're OK. What on earth happened to you?"

"Oh, I'm OK, I suppose, but they nicked my bag and left me to stew for a bit before some Hitler came in and tried to put the frighteners on me."

"Did it work?" asked Paul.

"Yes, it did," said Brendan, weakly. "What about you?"

"They had me in too, but let me go after about half an hour's questioning about who we were, what we were doing, why we were here etc. I think they just wanted to throw their weight around."

"Yes," said Brendan. "But what do we do now?"

Paul smiled. "Don't worry. We'll have to stay here tonight, then catch the midday flight out to Newark Airport in New York. Then we can fly direct to Shannon, getting in at 6.45am the day after tomorrow. We'll still be on time – but if anything goes wrong after that, you could be in trouble."

Brendan forced out a laugh. "I'd better not be cheeky to any more officials then, had I?"

After a sleepless night, stretched out across hard, plastic seats in Miami Airport, Brendan was in no mood for anything the following morning. He must have fallen asleep at one point because he woke with a start when a cleaner banged her trolley into his foot. He had no clothes other than those he was wearing, and no sense of humour after the appalling way in which he'd been treated. There were 49 hours to go.

They made their way across to the check-in desks, following the coloured dots on the floor until they led straight to a brick wall, and then guessing. He kept a surly silence as they were processed through the check-in – even when the official asked, "No luggage, Mister Priest?" Paul's baggage was weighed and labelled with a Shannon Airport label, which reassured them that they would be treated as transit passengers at Newark. They sat down in the departure lounge, watching the big display which gave details of all the flights. The board stated that the Newark flight was delayed by an hour so they settled in for another long, uncomfortable wait. When it got near to their scheduled departure time, Paul went for a little stroll, but came running back through the lounge to drag Brendan off to the boarding gate, which was just about to close.

"What's happening?" shouted Brendan breathlessly, his throat on fire as Paul hauled him through the gate.

"The gate shows different information from the big screen. Apparently it's the gate you have to look at, because the airline updates that info, whereas the big screen only shows the info which the FAA has. The FAA monitors every flight but gets its information a bit late sometimes." They made it – just. There were 47 hours to go.

***

They took off on time, and arrived on time at Newark, at 4.33pm. When they got off the plane and into the transit lounge, there were 43 hours to go. They'd nearly three hours to wait for their overnight flight to Shannon, but the atmosphere at Newark was much more relaxed and friendly than at Miami. They left Newark at 8pm, only half an hour late. There were 40 hours to go.

They slept. Wonderfully. Peacefully. Refreshingly. After the dreadful night in Miami, they probably could have slept upside-down, but the Continental Airlines 752 was extremely comfortable and warm. They arrived ahead of time, at about 6am on a murky and blustery Irish morning, with lots of weather being carried in off the Atlantic by the same winds that had carried them so quickly across the pond. There were now 30 hours to go.

Brendan was, at long last, in Ireland, his 194th and final nation. Once he linked up with Ruth at Brandon Bay, received from her the Irish (Gaelic) GNT and gave it away, his task was complete, though he still had to get back to Cullercoats by noon on the 366th day to complete the challenge that Esther had set him. He'd taken a while to work out why his deadline was Day *366*, but at noon on the second day he'd only completed one full day, so it *did* make sense.

***

When Brendan and Paul emerged out of the Arrivals Hall at 6.30am, they were met by a whooping Ruth, who'd flown from Kampala to Heathrow two days earlier, then flown straight across to Shannon thinking that she'd just catch her Dad and husband as they flew in from JFK. She hadn't been feeling very well for a few days now, so at least the delay meant that she'd more time to hire a car, sort out a hotel on the Dingle peninsula, and meet Esther's plane when it arrived with the film crew, ready for the final interview. Esther had not been best pleased by the delay as it meant rescheduling the "See Esther" line-up again, but they showed another of their "reserve shows" and raised everyone's expectations about the following day's climactic interview. Ruth had been following Brendan and Paul's progress on her laptop, and, despite feeling pretty sick first thing that morning, was now ready to whisk them straight off to Brandon Bay, only 90 minutes away by road. There were 29 hours to go, but the interview couldn't take place until 7pm, to link with the 2pm time-slot in Detroit, so Brendan had plenty of time to kill.

They arrived in the tiny village of Cloghane just before 9am. It was still a bit early in the year for tourists, so they went straight to the hotel. The O'Connor's Guesthouse[103] was a wonderful traditional Irish pub with its outside walls painted orange and light blue, and an old pub sign hanging outside the low front door. They were immediately offered breakfast and invited to settle in for the rest of the day. Brendan, however, decided that his journey would be incomplete if he didn't climb up his namesake's mountain, which towered over Cloghane. He set off late morning, and Ruth went with him, having perked up a bit as the morning progressed. As they climbed, Ruth asked him about the journey. "Do you feel that you've achieved what you set out to achieve?"

---

[103] O'Connor's is the name of the pub in Cloghane, as described, but the rest is fictional.

Brendan thought for a few seconds. "I'm not sure that I knew what I was hoping to achieve. In one sense, I was just trying to be obedient, but I knew too that I didn't want to go straight back into Circuit, so I was happy to grasp any opportunity to avoid that, if I'm honest."

"But you must have had some big dreams, some hopes...?"

"I suppose I wanted to raise enough money to get Bulrushes built in Gulu, and we achieved that pretty quickly. After that, though, I suppose my only other hope was that people would follow my progress and it'd make a difference to how the world viewed the Church and the Church viewed the world."

"Well, you certainly grabbed everybody's attention when you got blown out of the sky in East Timor. How are you, by the way? Does it still hurt at all?"

"Not really. I've had a dreadful sore throat for a while now and swollen glands – but I don't think that's anything to do with East Timor. Emotionally, though, it hurts. Do you know what's happened to Fahada?"

Ruth shook her head. She hadn't heard any updates either. "I didn't think that I'd made much of an impact on the world stage either, but I suppose being nominated for the Nobel Prize meant that somebody noticed."

"Don't hold your breath, though, Dad. I heard a few days ago that you haven't made the shortlist of 20 names for the final decision in September. Sorry."

Brendan laughed. "I thought it was a bit strange that I'd even been nominated, but I did meet both the winners from East Timor and I suppose it was down to them."

Now it was Ruth's turn to laugh. "You're too modest, Dad. You've had an amazing impact on lots of people, including Paul and me. And Louisa. And even, so I hear, Jack Turner."

"Really?" Brendan couldn't believe it. Old Tina, who'd had no time at all for Brendan before he left? Now, that *was* an achievement. Ruth told him what she'd picked up from Louisa and Ben about the ups and downs of life at Jact, and of Jack Turner's apparent conversion to trying unconventional methods to achieve evangelistic targets. Brendan couldn't understand how it'd happened but he was glad that it had.

"And what about all those people who've been influenced around the world? Plenty of people have been in touch with us through the website to speak about the impact you've had on them. Don't underestimate the effect of what you've done, Dad."

At the top there was a large metal cross by the remains of Brendan's Oratory, a small stone building believed to have been used by Saint Brendan. He'd prayed on the mountain with his friends before setting off in a small boat across the Atlantic, defying scoffers who said that such absurd trust in God would lead to certain death. Brendan Priest had taken his namesake saint as a prime example of what can happen when Christians take God at His word. Just as Saint Brendan returned, much later, to prove that his trust in God was well-placed and his calling genuine, so latter-day Brendan had completed his epic and ridiculous journey, and felt humbled, thrilled, relieved and thankful to God.

The summit was windswept and cold, but Brendan and Ruth stood quietly for several minutes. Brendan picked up a stone from the summit and took it down with him, as a memento. The journey was now complete, even though he still had to return to Cullercoats within the allotted time and rules in order to complete the "See Esther" challenge.

Chapter 71: Destination

"Well, Brendan," said Esther, at the start of the interview. "Here you are, in the west of Ireland, your final nation, and you've done it! Well done!" She started clapping and so did the many people gathered in the lounge of O'Connor's Guesthouse. Cloghane didn't see many celebrities, so the villagers were determined to make the most of it. The camera panned round the small room, as Esther continued her introduction. Paul seemed to have a silly grin on his face. "But we're still not quite there yet, are we, Brendan?"

"No, the challenge that you set me, 15 months or so ago, was to visit every other nation in the world which I didn't cover on my previous journey, and to return home within a calendar year. And at the moment, I've got 17 hours left to get back to Cullercoats in the North East of England. I'll be getting myself to Dublin overnight, then flying at 9.30am tomorrow morning to Newcastle, then back to the coast before midday. I should do it, if nothing goes wrong."

"So those folk out there who've pledged to double their sponsorship if you complete the challenge will be anxious to see how tomorrow goes, won't they, Brendan?"

"Ah but it's not just completing it within the time, but also within the set parameters for distance travelled and percentages without powered transport. I haven't a clue where we are up to on that score..."

"We're *just* OK, I think, Brendan. We've put every kilometre which you've travelled into the computer, and projected forwards to your destination in North East England. The grand total comes to 146,804km, which is well under the 150,000 we set as the maximum. You folks at home should see the figures appearing on your screens right now. Brendan will have completed 73,400km by air, which is only 2km under 50% of the total – but that's all we need. In fact, Brendan, that's the reason you have to go overland to Dublin tonight, because we have to make sure that you keep under that 50% limit." Brendan smiled inanely. All these figures were going over his head.

"You've done about 35,400km on water, which is over the minimum limit of 35,000, so that's OK. And 10,773 of those kilometres have been done without engines, which is 30.5% of the total distance on water, which is nicely over the 30% limit!" Brendan kept grinning. It was beyond him.

"Which only leaves us two more rules: we have to make sure that you go over 35,000km on land – which we've also achieved, with over 38,000km; and we have to make sure that you are over 30% on non-motorised land transport – and that's where it's even closer than the air distance. According to our calculations, when we land in Newcastle, you'll still have to do 7km on your bike, which will make you over the 30% by *less than half a kilometre*. So make sure tonight as you drive across Ireland that you stick to the route, otherwise you'll have to do even more tomorrow on your bike!" Brendan grinned, though he wasn't really following. As long as he was going to be OK, that was all he needed to know. He wasn't relishing doing any more cycling, though.

"Tell us about the sponsorship, Ruth. Where are we up to?"

"Well, Esther, if everything goes well tomorrow, we'll not only be due the $165 million – yes, one hundred and sixty-five million dollars – which has been pledged and is *now due* since Dad's completed the full list of nations. We'll also receive a further $35 million from those who pledged to double their sponsorship. Altogether that will make a whopping $200 million for the Brendan Priest Trust, serving Watoto in their work with the most vulnerable people in Africa. So let's hope that everything goes smoothly tonight and tomorrow."

"And we'll be there, folks," announced Esther. "Tune in at the same time tomorrow to see recorded highlights of Brendan's arrival home. Now, Brendan, tell me about the highlights of the trip from your point of view..."

And so the questioning continued until just a minute or so before the scheduled end of the interview. Brendan braced himself for the final question. "Now, Brendan, I want to take you back to the little Brazilian village of Diamantino, in the middle of nowhere. Ruth and I met you there when you completed your trip up-river, and before you started your trip down-river to the Amazon and the Atlantic. Can you remember what you and Paul did after the interview?"

Brendan was confused. "Not really. I think we just had something to eat and went to our beds. I'm pretty sure that we were exhausted and had an early start the next day."

"But that's not all that happened, as Ruth will now enlighten us."

Brendan looked at Ruth, who'd gone bright red, and Paul, now beside her, whose skin colour didn't permit him to turn red, but who still wore that silly grin. "Brendan Priest," said Ruth quietly, but the microphone picked it up very clearly. "You're going to be a Grandad!"

The final credits rolled as the lounge of the O'Connor Guesthouse erupted in a spontaneous explosion of shouting, applause and laughter. There was a final, beautiful camera shot of Brendan in the middle of the hubbub, with his mouth open and his eyes filling up with tears.

***

Afterwards, Brendan ran through a printout of Oracle's calculations. It was a real pain to have to do some more cycling – and it would be a race to get back to Cullercoats before the deadline. He should still be OK though, as long as everything went smoothly.

But it didn't.

They started well, with a jubilant Ruth and Paul driving Brendan across to Dublin Airport, setting off at 2am, after about four hours' sleep. Brendan left the final GNT with the landlord, who promised to keep it in the lounge as a reminder of Cloghane's night of fame. The roads were empty, and they sustained an excellent speed across Ireland, arriving at the airport shortly after 6am. Ruth, suffering from morning-sickness, went off to hand in the keys of the hire-car, as she didn't want to watch Brendan and Paul tucking into a fried breakfast. They all then checked in for their Ryanair flight, and took off on time. There were 2½ hours to go.

The flight itself was OK – a bit basic, but on time, which was what mattered. The problem came when they were approaching Newcastle. "There's a bit of fog," announced the captain, cheerily, "So we'll just go round a few times until it clears." They were due in at 10.35am, and it was only a short delay, but it was 11.09 when Brendan tumbled off the plane – and 11.25 before they cleared the airport. 35 minutes to go.

None of them had any baggage – Brendan because MIA had rendered his MIA, the others because, thinking ahead, they'd entrusted their stuff to Esther, whose Learjet had flown in earlier direct from Shannon so that the film-crew could set up for Brendan's arrival. Louisa was waiting for them in Esther's hire-car, and roared off towards Newcastle. She screeched round the roundabouts leading to the Inner Ring Road, and swerved round the bend at Jesmond onto the Coast Road. Mercifully, the traffic was clear, the lights turned to green as she approached and they arrived at Battle Hill 15 minutes after setting off from the airport. Ben was waiting with Brendan's training bike at the top of the slip-road – which was exactly 7km from their house in Cullercoats. There were 20 minutes to go.

Brendan didn't really have the right kit on for cycling. Only 7km to go, but this meant maintaining an average speed of 21kph, which was quite a speed on a bike when you were wearing an old pair of trainers, long trousers and a sweatshirt – and when you'd just travelled round the world. At least it wasn't raining.

He avoided the downs and ups of the underpasses by shooting along the slip roads, maintaining a good pace – but was it good enough? Ruth, Paul and Louisa kept alongside him, shouting out his speed, and that kept him pushing along, though his thigh muscles complained as he tackled the long pull up to Tyne Met College. Then he was speeding past Silverlink and piling on the speed down from Tynemouth Pool to the Broadway roundabout, in a mad dash for the line. It was still only 11.56 as he came to the roundabout, with only just over a kilometre to go.

"Come on, Brendan," he urged himself onwards. "You can do it." And then, as he slowed for the roundabout, the car in front suddenly smacked its brakes on. Brendan swerved as he braked but crashed straight into the back of the car and was thrown sideways, head-over-heels into the lamppost at the side of the road. He wasn't badly hurt – just a few scratches and scrapes, but the bike's front wheel was bent and useless. Without thinking, he yelled for Louisa and the other two to sort out the aftermath of the accident, and ran off downhill towards the Park Hotel, round the corner and downhill again, past the aquarium and the parking places, towards St. George's and Beverley Terrace.

He ran as hard as he could, aware of the crowd up ahead, the TV lights and people gathered on the grass across from his house, the flags strewn across the road, the cones narrowing to a funnel like at the end of the Great North Run. But he was also painfully aware that he *must* have missed the deadline. He passed the first of the people clapping him on, then more people cheering as he saw the tape wittily stretched across the finishing-line. He kept going, absolutely exhausted, his throat burning, his knee hurting where he'd skinned it, and cramped by an awful stitch. He lurched through the line, wrapping the tape around him (it was cheap string, actually), collapsed in a heap right in front of a beaming Esther, and looked at his watch, a string of spit dangling inelegantly from his top lip. It was 12.03.

He'd failed by a measly three minutes. $35 million lost because some silly whatsit braked at the Broadway roundabout... But everybody was cheering, as if he'd completed it all in time. Brendan felt really annoyed at the fuss they were making of him, and started to protest.

"I failed!" he croaked. "I *failed*..." And he slumped to the ground.

Chapter 72: Culmination

Brendan lay there on the pavement, with people jumping up and down around him, high-fiving and shouting triumphantly.

"I failed," he whispered. His throat was really hurting. So was his pride.

"No, you didn't," shouted Dwight and Esther in unison. Dwight was there as part of the camera crew – the same guy who'd been there at the start of it all.

Brendan looked puzzled, so Dwight explained. "Don't you remember what happened when you began your journey a year ago? Just as you were setting off on the stroke of noon, the foghorn went off and I called you back? It was 12.04 when you started for real, so you finished with a minute to go!"

Ruth and Paul, Ben and Louisa pulled up in the hire-car. They rushed at Brendan. "Did you do it, Dad? Did you do it?"

The final leg (of this journey)

Brendan looked up from the floor. "Yes," he said quietly. "One minute to spare, apparently. Yes, I did it!"

And they all clapped, shrieked, jumped and high-fived. Dwight approved. Esther continued to beam. It made for good TV.

Brendan sat back on the grass, surrounded by noise, lights and people, looking at his house across the road. It stood strong and tall, bunting across the doorway, inviting, welcoming him back.

Wor Brendan's come home, he thought.

And yet he knew, even as he thought it, that the journeying wasn't over...

Day: Date	Itinerary (* indicates TV interview) ([18] indicates new nation)	Bike (km)	Car/ Bus (km)	Train (km)	Kayak/ Sail (km)	Boat (km)	Air (km)
Totals brought forward		11429	17330	8712	10773	24585	65301
363: 13/5/12	Miami (USA)						1231
364: 14/5/12	Shannon, Ireland[194]						6522
365: 15/5/12	Brandon Bay *		524				
366: 16/5/12	via Dublin to Newcastle, then Cullercoats	7	16				346
totals		11436	17870	8712	10773	24585	73400
Percentages and overall totals		30.00% of 38118		All land 38118	30.47% of 35358	All water 35358	49.99% of 146804

Postscript

I hope you've liked this book. I've tried to incorporate comments and questions, complaints about unfinished business, and novel-writing know-how from those who've been good enough to contact me after reading "Thule for Christ's Sake". I've enjoyed writing it, though I am aware that not *all* the unfinished business is yet complete. Please send any feedback to me at s.earl@hotmail.co.uk.

Brendan's next journey will be a rather different one.

Chapter headings

Yes, I know it's a bit bizarre to have these at the end rather than the beginning, but these, along with the actual itinerary included in the text, will enable you to locate at what stage in the journey Brendan visits each nation. They will also indicate which " -nations" are visited along the way.

"Go to all nations, therefore, discipling them..." (Matthew 28: 19)

1. germination
2. explanation
3. insubordination
4. examination
5. elimination
6. combination
7. coronation
8. co-ordination
9. detonation
10. denomination
11. divination
12. incarnation
13. Nations 19-20
14. assassination
15. Nations 21-24
16. discrimination
17. Nations 25-28
18. consternation
19. Nations 29-34
20. impersonation
21. Nations 35-38
22. assignation
23. Nations 39-41
24. alienation
25. Nations 42-48
26. indoctrination
27. Nations 49-52
28. Nations 53-54
29. illumination
30. Nations 55-59
31. vaccination
32. Nations 60-67
33. ruination
34. Nations 68-71

35. determination
36. Nations 72-78
37. hallucination
38. Nations 79-84
39. indignation
40. Nations 85-93
41. machinations + Nations 94-103
42. domination
43. Nations 104-112
44. resignation
45. Nations 113-119
46. extermination + Nations 113-125
47. termination
48. stagnation
49. Nations 126-129
50. cross-examination
51. Nations 130-133
52. contamination
53. Nations 134-144
54. decontamination

55. Nations 145-154
56. recrimination
57. Nations 155-163
58. Nations 164-173
59. imagination
60. Nations 174-176
61. Nations 155-163
62. nomination
63. Nations 176(still)-178
64. carnations
65. Nations 179-181
66. Nations 182-189
67. abomination
68. rejuvenation
69. Nations 190-193
70. fascination
71. Nation 194
72. destination
73. culmination

"The Lord appointed seventy-two, and sent them out ahead of him to every place and town with these instructions... "The harvest is plentiful, but the workers are few... Go!" " (Luke 10:1-3)

Lightning Source UK Ltd.
Milton Keynes UK
173428UK00001B/63/P